Thomas Bond

A digest of foreign exchanges

Thomas Bond

A digest of foreign exchanges

ISBN/EAN: 9783337115296

Printed in Europe, USA, Canada, Australia, Japan

Cover: Foto ©Andreas Hilbeck / pixelio.de

More available books at **www.hansebooks.com**

A

DIGEST

OF

Foreign Exchanges

CONTAINING AN

ABSTRACT

OF THE

Exiſting Laws and Cuſtom of Merchants

RELATIVE TO

BILLS AND NOTES.

A SHORT

METHOD OF CALCULATION,

WITH CORRECT

TABLES OF EXCHANGE

OF THE

MONIES, WEIGHTS AND MEASURES
Of Foreign Nations compared with ours.

OF

INTEREST AT ONE PER CENT.

AND OF THE

VALUE OF GOODS, FROM ONE TO TEN-THOUSAND
Pounds, Gallons, Yards, Ells, &c.

Being an Epitome of all that is uſeful in every ſimilar Pub-
lication.

By Sir THOMAS BOND, Bart.

DUBLIN:
Printed by ALEX. STEWART, No. 86, *Bride-ſtreet.* M,DCC,XCV.

To the Right Honorable

DAVID LATOUCHE, and *Co.*

GENTLEMEN,

To addrefs you in the common Language of Dedications, would neither become Me, as the Author, nor You, as the Patrons of this Work.

It muft be evident to every one, that I place it under the Protection of your Name, as its beft and fureft Recommendation to Public Favor :

Becaufe an Houfe, which, for fo many Years, and in fo many Inftances, has been the Stay and Support both of public and private Credit, muft certainly be the beft Judge of the Utility of fuch Performance.

And I flatter Myfelf, that it will be pleafing to my Fellow-Citizens, that I embrace this Opportunity of expreffing my Gratitude to an Houfe, that has honor'd Me with fo many kind Notices, and has at all Times favor'd me with fuch particular Friendfhip, as obliges Me to be,

Gentlemen,

Not only Your very refpectful,

But ever grateful,

And obedient Servant,

THOMAS BOND

PREFACE.

IT is with much pleasure that Sir Thomas Bond embraces this opportunity of expressing, his most sincere gratitude to the many Noblemen and Gentlemen who have honor'd this Work with their Names.

When such a list of subscribers appears in the front of a book, where almost every letter of the alphabet begins with so many RIGHT REV. and RIGHT HON. signatures, it is almost needless to say any thing in recommendation of such a work, which together with its author has been so highly honor'd.

He only presumes to say, that it is an epitome of all that could be found useful in every similar production; excluding every unnecessary page. That the value of the books so epitomized, would together amount to a much larger sum, than the price of this small volume. Not to say any thing of the trouble saved to the Reader, by presenting him in one point of view, with a quantity of information, which otherwise would be difficult and tedious to collect.

He hopes he has said as much on the *American Exchanges* as may be necessary for business. He admits he has been shorter on that head than any other: because, tho' we have acknowledged the independance of their States, we don't seem to have acknowledged their Monies; Exchanges being still rated on Pounds, Shillings and Pence.

He is persuaded the *comparative view* of the Monies, Weights and Measures of Foreign Nations, will be found remarkably useful, even to Gentlemen not in Trade, as it may frequently help to render a News-paper intelligible.

TABLE OF CONTENTS.

	Page
Exchanges with England	1
——— with France	24
——— with Holland and Flanders	58
——— with Denmark	88
——— with Banco and Current Money	98
——— with Spain	101
——— with Portugal	141
——— with Venice	124
——— with Genoa and Leghorn	130
——— with Germany	140
——— with America	142
Value of the Current Monies of Turkey, Asia and Africa; — Alſo the antient Monies of the Jews, Greeks & Romans	14[illegible]
Comparative View of the Weights and Meaſures of Foreign Nations	146
A Table of Simple Intereſt	[illegible]
A Table of the Value of Goods	[illegible]

SUBSCRIBERS NAMES.

A

HIS Grace William Lord Archbiſhop of Armagh, Primate of all Ireland, 3 Books
Rt.Hon.Ld. Viſc. Allen
Hon. Rich. Anneſley
Rob. Alexander, Eſq;
Aldm. Tho. Andrews
Hen. Alexander, Eſq;
John Allen, Eſq;
Rev. Gilbert Auſtin
Philip Abbot, Eſq;
Geo. Armſtrong, Eſq; 2 Copies
Atkinſon & Woodward
Joſeph Andrews, Eſq;
Allan and Son, Eſqrs.
Edw. Andrews, Eſq;
James Anderſon, Eſq;
John Aubry, Eſq;
Arth. Anneſley, Eſq;
Valen. Atkinſon, Eſq;
Tho. Archdeakon, Eſq;
John Ardell, Eſq;
James Abbot, Eſq;
Tho. Ray. Alſop, Eſq;
Rob. Acheſon, Eſq;
Samuel Adams, Eſq;
Rob. Alliſon, Eſq;
Mr. Geo. Armſtrong
Mr. John Alexander
Mr. Mich. Allen
Mr. W. Allen, 2 Books
Mr. Samuel Adams
Mr. Chr. Antiſell
Mr. Wm. Atkinſon
Meſſrs. W. & J. Alder
Mr. Wm. Abbot
Mr. Garret Andrews
Mr. Tho. Atkinſon
Mr. Chr. Allen
Mr. Tho. Abbot
Mr. Wm. J. Aldridge
Mr. Patrick Aylward
Mr. John Ayres
Mr. W. H. Archer
Mr. Tho. Armitage
Mr. Wm. Anderſon
Mr. Tho. Angier
Mr. John Adair
Mr. Wm. Adrien
Mr. Tho. Adams

B.

Rt. Hn. Earl of Bective
R. H. Earl of Belvidere
Rt. Hon. Jn. Beresford
Hn.&Rev.C. Broderick
Sir James Bond, Bart.
J. C. Beresford, & Co.
Col. James Blaquiere
Lt. Col. Wm. Baillie
Maj. Brown, 83d Reg.
Rev. Dean Blundell
Rev. John Barker
Cap. P.R. Bermingham
Rev. Richard Bourne
William Burton, Eſq;
Hugh Bowen, Eſq;
Ber..fd. Burſton, Eſq;
Henry Brabazon, Eſq;
Rd. Paul Bonham, Eſq;
John Bradſhaw, Eſq;
J. Bloſſet, Eſq;
James Bradiſh, Eſq;
Edward Bulkeley, Eſq;
Andrew Bell, Eſq;
William Ball, Eſq;
An. Blackburne, Eſq;
Ulick Burke, Eſq;
Patrick Bride, Eſq;
Edward Bell, Eſq;
Hen. Gonne Bell, Eſq;
John Ball, Eſq;
Tho. Broughall, Eſq;
Thomas Bond, Eſq;
John Barber, Eſq;
Charles Bury, Eſq;
Chriſtop. Bellew, Eſq;
Wm. Beaufort, Eſq;
All. Bellingham, Eſq;
Robert Birch, Eſq;
John Ball, Eſq;
Thomas Boys, Eſq;
Edward Byrne, Eſq;
Oliver Bond, Eſq;
Edmund Beaſley, Eſq;
Richard Brown, Eſq;
William Blair, Eſq;
David Boſquet, Eſq;
John Browrigg, Eſq;
John Beeby, Eſq;
Rich. Broughton, Eſq;
Wm. Burrows, Eſq;
Thomas Black, Eſq;
William Bayly, Eſq;
Roger Barrett, Eſq;
John Bourne, Eſq;
Robert Bellew, Eſq;
Chas. Blakeney, Eſq;
Walter Bourne, Eſq;
Jn. Blennerhaſſet, Eſq;
William Boys, Eſq;
Tho.Ann. Brown, Eſq;
Peter Baker, Eſq;
D. Babington, Eſq;
Dominick Blake, Eſq;
Richard Bayly, Eſq;
Alexan. Boſwell, Eſq;
Peter Bayly, Eſq;
Milo Bagot, Eſq;
Thomas Blood, Eſq;
Francis Bennett, Eſq;
Mathew Blair, Eſq;
John Boyce, Eſq;
Wm. Beauman, Eſq;
Henry Burke, Eſq;

John Rose Baker, Esq;
Bell & Blacker, Esqrs
John Bury, Esq;
Thomas Brown, Esq;
Samuel Belson, Esq;
John Bell, Esq;
Daniel Bennison, Esq;
Henry Barge, Esq;
William Bates, Esq;
Francis Blake, Esq;
Abraham Boyd, Esq;
W. S. A. Bird, Esq;
Robert Burton, Esq;
George Burdett, Esq;
John Bouliote, Esq;
Capt. John Bunker
Mess. Burns&Whithead
Messieurs Beauman and Masterson
Mr. Richard Brown
Mr. John Busby
Mr. Alexander Bell
Mr. Charles Bourns
Mrs. Sarah Bell
Mr. Wm. Kt. Berry
Mr. Richard Basteville
Mr. John Bird
Mr. Thomas Bible jun
Mr. Charles Brown
Mr. Charles Betagh
Mr. Thomas Barnet
Mr. Michael Boylan
Mr. William Bennet
Mr. Thomas Barker
Mr. Thomas Butler
Mr. John Bennis
Mr. Robert Breading
Mr. Thomas Bennet
Mr. Adam Boyd
Mr. Edward Bennett
Mr. John Beavy
Mr. Michael Butler
Mr. William Boyd
Mr. Edward Butler
Mr. Fred. Pr. Bolton
Mr. Thomas Barnes
Mr. T. Barrington, jun
Mr. James Beggs
Mr. Theoph. Bolton
Mr. John Brett
Mr. Robert Brunton
Mr. Robert Burnet
Mr. Theobald Billing

Mr. William Bunn
Mr. Edward Bray
Mr. Thomas Brown
Mr. Joseph Byrne
Mrs. Magdalene Byrne
Mr. James Ball
Mr. Francis Barber
Mr. Ambrose Binns
Mr. John Boake
Mr. James Balantine
Mr. Thomas Badge
Mr. William Begg
Mr. Richard Black
Mr. Patrick Brophy
Mr. James Baird
Mr. Peter Brodie
Mr. Frederick Byrne
Mrs. Margaret Bourke
Mr. Peter Browne
Mr. Edwin Browne
Mr. William Bell
Mr. William Barber
Mr. P. Byrne, Booksr.
Mr. C. Browne, Booksr.
Mr. M. Butler, Booksr.
Mr. David Bates
Mr. William Bradshaw
Mr. William Bell
Mr. James Bowden
Mr. James Bennet
Mr. John Boyce
Mr. Thomas Butler
Mr. Arthur Battersby
Mr. Patrick Bardon
Mr. Felix Byrne
Mr. Thomas Beahan
Mr. Edmund Bamford
Mr. John Barrington
Mr. George Burnet
Mr. Robert Byrne
Mr. Francis Barker
Mr. William Bowls
Mr. Wm. Brownlow
Mr. Tho. E. Butler
Mr. Samuel Blood
Mr. Andrew Bouk
Mr. Benjamin Byrne
Mr. James Blacker
Mr. George Banish
Mr. John Burrowes
Mr. John Brenan
Mr. John Barker
Mr. Lawrence Beahan

Mr. William Bardin
Mr. Michael Brien

C

His Grace Abp. Cashel
Rt. Rev. Bp. of Cloyne
Rt. Hon. Earl Carrick
Rt. Hon. Earl Clonmell
Rt. Hon. Lord Caledon
Rt. Hon. Lord Cahier
Sir Hen. Cavendish, Bt.
Sir Malby Crofton, Bt.
Sir Jas. Campbell, Bt.
Rev. Dean Coote
Rev. Tho. Cradock
Lieut. Col. Cradock
Wm. Christmas, Esq;
Maur. Coppinger, Esq;
Josiah Crampton, Esq;
Richard Creagh, Esq;
James Crawford, Esq;
Andrew Caldwell, Esq;
Alexander Carrol, Esq;
Jn. Davs. Coates, Esq;
Rob. Cornwall, Esq;
Tho. Croker, Esq;
David Courtney, Esq;
John Cash, Esq;
Wm. Colville, Esq;
Wm. Cope, Esq;
Henry Cope, Esq;
Wm. Caldbeck, Esq;
Lel. Crosthwait, Esq;
David Courtney, Esq;
George Campbell, Esq;
Rich. Cudmore, Esq;
Ambrose Cox, Esq;
J. Chamley, Esq;
Dav. Fred. Clark, Esq;
Joshua Clibborn, Esq;
Cha. Carrothers, Esq;
Rob. Carrol, Esq;
John Chambers, Esq;
Alexander Carr, Esq;
And. Carmichael, Esq;
Luke Cassin, Esq;
George Cullen, Esq;
Overstreet Carson, Esq;
Rich. Cave, Esq;
Rich. Coob. Carr, Esq;
Tho. Cahill, Esq;
William Curtis, Esq;
John Cuthbert, Esq;

John Campbell, Esq;
Alexander Castell, Esq;
Th Carter & Co. Esqrs.
William Crosbie, Esq;
Joseph Cahill, Esq;
Cooper Crawford, Esq;
Patrick Cruise, Esq;
Tho. Carey, Esq;
Tho. Church, Esq;
Bryan Conolly, Esq;
Willo. H. Carter, Esq;
James Cowley, Esq;
Tho. Caffe, Esq;
Edmund Costello, Esq;
William Corbet, Esq;
Will. Crawford, Esq;
Patrick Clancy, Esq;
James Crawford, Esq;
Joseph Carter, Esq;
Edw. Constable, Esq;
Math. Connally, Esq;
James Conolly, Esq;
William Cooke, Esq;
Duke Cooper, Esq;
Nicholas Corith, Esq;
Henry Conroy, Esq;
Rich. Collis, Esq;
Ch. Todd & Co. Esqrs.
Anthony Carroll, Esq;
John Clarke, Esq;
John Conroy, Esq;
Mr. William Crosby
Mr. John Cox
Mr. James Caffray
Mr. William Crombie
Mr. John Collins
Mr. John Costly
Mr. Samuel Collins
Mr. John Christie
Mr. Daniel Crosby
Mr. Francis Coleman
Mr. William Clark
Mr. John Crosthwait
Mr. William Collier
Mr. William Coulson
Mr. Dennis Cronin
Mr. John Clinton
Mr. John Clinton
Mr. Philip Costello
Mr. Alexander Clark
Mr. Bernard Cummons
Mr. John Copeland
Mr. William Conlan

Mr. David Clark
Mr. Henry Clements
Messrs. Cooper & Orr
Mr. Joseph Clare
Mr. James Carroll
Mr. Tho. Collis
Mr. Francis Codd
Mr. Luke Cuffe
Mr. Barth. Coley
Mr. Christoph. Cullen
Mr. John Creighton
Mr. Alex. Campbell
Mr. Wm. H. Cullimore
Mr. Richard Cranfield
Mr. Joshua Conally
Mr. Lawrence Crow
Mr. Richard Campbell
Mr. Nathan. Callwell
Mr. George Cook
Mr. John Connally
Mr. Nicholas Clark
Mr. Lawrence Cruise
Mr. James Cruise
Mr. Peter Crawford
Mr. Walter Caffray
Mr. Joseph Cahill
Mr. Dougl. Campbell
Mr. Tho. Conroy
Mr. Hugh Cuming
Mr. Henry Carroll
Mr. Patrick Connor
Mr. Edw. Clark
Mr. Hugh Carroll
Mr. Peter R. Courtney
Mr. Charles Curtis
Mr. John Clark
Mr. John Clark
Mr. Tho. Cardiff
Mr. Patrick Cruise
Mr. Luke Connor
Mr. William Cadge
Mr. Tho. Corker
Mr. Anthony Carey
Mr. William Campbell
Mr. Edw. Cope
Mr. Barth. Cooke
Messrs. J. & J. Carrick
Mr. Hugh Craig
Mr. George Creighton
Mr. John Chambers
Mr. John Charrurier
Mr. M. Chamberlaine
Mr. Rich. Cross

Mr. William Corbet
Mr. Patrick Crow
Mr. Joseph Caffin
Mr. Mathew Crosbie
Mr. St. Geo. Campbell
Mrs. Ann Cahill
Mr. John Chandler
Mr. Patrick Carroll
Mr. Charles Colgan
Mr. William Cody
Mr. Edw. Calder
Mr. Tho. Colclough
Mr. Charles Carr
Mr. W. P. Carey
Mr. Henry Crosbie
Mr. William Collins
Mr. Nathaniel Creed
Mr. John Collier
Mr. H. H. Caddell
Mr. Abr. Creighton
Mrs. Harriet Colbert
Mr. Michael Corkran
Mr Hugh Carroll
Mr. Belfield R. Cane
Mr. William Connell

D

Most Noble Marquis of Drogheda
Rt. Hon. Lord Dillon
Lord Bp. of Dromore
Lord Visc. De Vesci
Rt. Hon. Ld. Dunboyne
Chevalier Destours
Rev. Dean Digby
Lieut. Col. Dunne
Capt. D Dalton
Arthur Dawson, Esq;
John Dunn, Esq;
Arthur Dunn, Esq;
Philip Doyne, Esq;
Robert Donovan, Esq;
S. J. Dowell, Esq;
John D'Arcy, Esq;
William Disney, Esq;
Pat. Dease, Esq;
Jn. Dease & Co. Esqrs.
Rich. Dodd, Esq;
T. D'Arcy, Esq; 2 Books
John Duffy, Esq;
Jeremiah Dwyer, Esq;
William Dodd, Esq;
John Draper, Esq;

William Duncan, Esq;
Frederick Darley, Esq;
Samuel Darling, Esq;
Wemys Disney, Esq;
Peter Dillon, Esq;
Tho. Dwyer, Esq;
Edm. Doran, Esq;
John Dwyer, Esq;
Stephen Dixon, Esq;
John Domville, Esq;
Josias Dunn, Esq;
Robert Donovan, Esq;
James Dance, Esq:
Timothy Driscoll, Esq;
William Davis, Esq;
Robert Deey, Esq;
James Davis, Esq;
Math. Donnelan, Esq;
Valentine Dunn, Esq;
John Dillon, Esq;
Whitmore Davis, Esq;
Emanuel D'Arcy, Esq;
John Darby, Esq;
Charles Duffin, Esq;
Tho. Dunn, Esq;
Arthur Dunn, Esq;
James Dixon, Esq;
Patrick Daly, Esq;
William Dawson, Esq;
George Digby, Esq;
Bernard Dolan, Esq;
Mathew Dowdal, Esq;
Stephen Darley, Esq;
John Duncan, Esq;
William Drury, Esq;
Mr. Samuel Dudgeon
Mr. John Davis
Mr. Dennis Doyle
Mr. James Davock
Mr. Hill Darley
Mr. Isaac Dejoncourt
Mr. Michael Dalton
Mr. Charles Dubois
Mr. Arthur Darley
Mr James Day
Mr. George Drew
Mr. Luke Duff
Mr. William Davis
Mr. William Dalton
Messrs. J. & B. Doyle
Mr. James Dixon
Mr. Barn. Delahoyde
Mr. Alexander Durdin
Mr. Tho. Dawes
Mr. Joseph Dixon
Mr. Patrick Dowdall
Mr. Tho. Doran
Mr. Theophilus Dixon
Mr. Michael Dillon
Mr. John Debenham
Mr. William Dykes
Mr. Joseph Dowling
Mr. James Dillon
Mr. Joseph Dunn
Mr. James Donovan
Mr. John Duigenan
Mr. James Dawson
Mr. James Daniel
Mr. Richard Dunckley
Mr. James Dodd
Mr. John Derham
Mr. Lawrence Darby
Mr. B. Dugdale Bookslr.
Mr. V. Dowling Bookslr.
Mr. Bernard Dowling, Bookseller, 4 Books
Mr. Gilmor Dames
Mr. Samuel Dooley
Mr. Benjamin Doxey
Messrs. Dowling & Co.
Mr. John Dodd
Mr. Edw. Doyle
Mr. Rich. Duff
Mr. Pat. Donegan
Mr. Ellis M. Draffen
Mr. Rob. Philis Davis
Mr. J. Duff
Mr. Francis Dempsy
Mr. John Dunn
Mr. Daniel Doyle
Mr. Wm. H. Dawson
Mr. Edw. Daly
Mr. William Dalton
Mr. Edw. Dunn
Mr. John Davis
Mr. John Dumas
Mr. James Doyle

E

Hon. John Evans
Robert Eustace, Esq;
Usher Edgworth, Esq;
Cha. Echlin, Esq;
John Evans, Esq;
Cha. Este, Esq;
John Evat, Esq;
James Edwards Esq;
Gaspar Erck, Esq;
George Eskildson, Esq;
John Edwards, Esq;
Richard Eustace, Esq;
Mr. Pat. Early
Mr. Pat. Edgar
Mr. Rob. Edmonson
Mr. William Esdall
Mr. John Edwards
Mr. Rowland Eustace
Mr. Edw. Egerton
Mr. Cha. Elton
Mr. Constantine Egan
Mr. Christopher Eades
Mr. William Evans
Mr. Daniel Esperiatt
Mr. Henry M. Egglesfo
Mr. Benj. Eaton

F

Rt. Hon. Earl Farnham
Rt. Hon. Earl Fingall
Sir John Freke, Bart.
Rt. Hon. J. Fitzgerald
Lieut. Col. Wm. Fitch
Steph. Fitzgerald, Esq;
Alderm. Tho. Fleming
Patrick French, Esq;
Warden Flood, Esq;
John Forde, Esq;
David Freeman, Esq;
Roger Ford, Esq;
Anthony Ferguson, Esq;
William Fletcher, Esq;
Frazer, Reed & Sons, Esq
Cha. Frizell, Esq;
H. Loftus Frizell, Esq;
Peter Fox, Esq;
Luke Fox, Esq;
Forbes, Hog, Paxton & Co. Esqrs.
Lundy Foot, jun. Esq;
William Furlong, Esq;
Charles Farren, Esq;
Tho. Faris, Esq;
James Fyffe, Esq;
John Fullerton, Esq;
James Farrel, Esq;
John Ferns, Esq;
Hen. Farrell, Esq;

James Farrell, Esq;
Anth. Fox, Esq;
John Farrell, Esq;
James Fitzsimons, Esq;
William Fay, Esq;
Edward Fisher, Esq;
Sam. Fitzpatrick, Esq;
John Ferguson, Esq;
Rob. Fitzgerald, Esq;
James Farquhar, Esq;
Wm. Ferguson, Esq;
David Fitzgerald, Esq;
Charles S. Foster, Esq;
Jn. B. Fitzsimons, Esq;
Rob. Hen. French, Esq;
Fred. Falkiner, Esq;
Peter French, Esq;
William Freeman, Esq;
Samuel Foster, Esq;
Pat. Fitzsimons, Esq;
Mr. Andrew Finley
Mr. John Fuller
Mr. John Farrell
Mr. William Forbes
Mr. James Fletcher
Mr. Robert Foot
Mr. William Finn
Mess. Frenches & Eyatt
Mess. French & Baillie
Mr. Patrick Flood
Mr. Pat. Fitzpatrick
Messrs. P. & J. Foley
Mr. Patrick Flinn
Mr. Christ. Fitzsimons
Mr. Pat. Jos. Flinn
Mr. Tho. Fullam
Mr. Patrick Foley
Mr. Wm. Fitzgerald
Mr. Rob. Fyan
Mr. Rich. Fox
Mr. Rob. Fannin
Mr. James Fegan
Mr. John Fogarty
Mr. Rob. Fletcher
Mr. Wm. Facon
Mr. Wm. Faulkner
Mr. Edw. Fitzgerald
Mr. Cha. Farrell
Mr. G Folingsby, Books.
Mr. William Fry
Mr. Michael Farrell
Mr. Rich. Freeman
Mr. Martin Fitzgerald
Mr. Tho. Finn
Mr. John Fitzpatrick
Mr. Lawrence Flynn
Mr. Patrick Farrell
Mr. Tho. Fagan
Mr. Peter Farrell
Mr. Lawrence Fox
Mr. Francis Farrell
Mr. William Fenner
Mr. Hugh Fitzpatrick, Bookseller
Mr. John Fitzpatrick
Mr. Luke Finnagan
Mr. Joseph Figsbee
Mr. John Field
Mr. Robert Fletcher
Mr. David Fletcher
Mr. Tho. Farrell

G

Rt. Hon. Earl Granard
Rt. Hon. Visc. Gosford
Hon. Denis George, a Baron of the Excheq.
Rev. Ar. Grueber, D.D.
George Gun, Esq;
John Gayer, Esq;
J. Geoghegan, Esq;
Rich. Grace, Esq;
Tho. Goold, Esq;
Daniel Geale, Esq;
Wm. Glascock, Esq;
James Glascock, Esq;
Tho. Garde, Esq;
Henry Gonne, Esq;
Wm. G. Galway, Esq;
John Galloway, Esq;
Benjamin Gault, Esq;
Fortesc. Gorman, Esq;
Peter Grehan, Esq;
Humphry Gonne, Esq;
John Giffard, Esq;
Robert Gray, Esq;
Rich. Guinness, Esq;
Henry Green, Esq;
James Gregg, Esq;
Coane Gaven, Esq;
John Glew, Esq;
Waterh. S. Green, Esq;
Alex. Gordon, Esq;
Joseph Griffith, Esq;
W. P. Gilborne, Esq;
Francis Gregory, Esq;
Marmad. Grace, Esq;
Hen. J. Gower, Esq;
Joseph Glenny, Esq;
John Glynn, Esq;
Wm. Glascott, Esq;
Arthur Guinness, Esq;
Capt. Adam Gilles
Mr. John Grierson
Mr. Josh. Geoghegan
Mr. Benjamin Glorney
Mr. Barth. Gannon
Mr. James Gaven
Mr. James Gaynor
Mr. Cornelius Gautier
Mr. Tho. Guinan
Mr. John Gibson
Mr. John Gray
Mr. John Gill
Mr. Tho. Glynn
Mr. John Gale
Mr. W. Gilbert, Books.
Mr. John Gasson
Mr. Cornelius Gannon
Mr. Stanhope Gresham
Mr. William Geraghty
Mr. Frederick Gibson
Mr. Robert Gibson
Mr. Tho. Gibson
Mr. John Gardner
Mr. William Gibson
Mr. Michael Gernon
Mr. William Gorman
Mr. Richard Gibbons
Mrs. Sarah Gibson
Mr. George Goff
Mr. Bernard Graham
Mr. Christ. Griffith
Mr. James Grace
Mr. James Geoghegan

H

Rt. Hon. Lord Visc. Harberton
Rt. Hon. Ld. Headfort
Rev. Dr. Hamilton, Dean of Armagh
Hon. Wm. Henn
Alex. Hamilton, Esq;
Hugh Hill, Esq;
John Hatch, Esq;
Sackv. Hamilton, Esq;

Peter Holmes, Esq;
Alex. Holmes, Esq;
William Henn, Esq;
Thomas Hackett, Esq;
Hugh Hamilton, Esq;
Hans Hamilton, Esq;
Hen. C. Holland, Esq;
Patrick Halpin, Esq;
Alderm. Js. Hamilton
Tho. Hendrick, Esq;
Philip Henry, Esq;
Rob. Howard, Esq;
Isaac Homan, Esq;
James Hartley, Esq;
John Hendrick, Esq;
John Harford, Esq;
Abr. V. Horton, Esq;
John Hunt, Esq;
John Hart, Esq;
James Hodgson, Esq;
John L. Hume, Esq;
John Hines, Esq;
John Hughes, Esq;
James Haire, Esq;
Cha. N. Hoffman, Esq;
Edward Hill, Esq;
Eph. Hutchinson, Esq;
Wm. Humphrys, Esq;
Humphrys & Son, Esqs
Andrew Hamilton, Esq;
Henry Hutton, Esq;
John Hague, Esq;
Wm. Holtship, Esq;
Patrick Henegan, Esq;
Charles Haskins, Esq;
Michael Harris, Esq;
Hartley Hodson, Esq;
John Harrison, Esq;
Robert Hamilton, Esq;
A. Hawksworth, Esq;
Tho. P. Hewitt, Esq;
Wm. L. Hobart, Esq;
Stephen Hanley, Esq;
William Harvey, Esq;
John Perc. Hunt, Esq;
Pat. Halfpenny, Esq;
Joseph Hamilton, Esq;
Nathaniel Hone, Esq;
Paul Houston, Esq;
Robert Hart, Esq;
John Hawkins, Esq;
Pat. Hogan, Esq;
Tho. Howard, Esq;

John Harden, Esq;
Nicholas Halyday, Esq;
Skeff. Hamilton, Esq;
Edw. Hamerton, Esq;
Hawksley & Rutherford, Esqrs.
John Hill, Esq;
John Healy, Esq;
James Heavisid, Esq;
Henry Hewitt, Esq;
Edw. Hudson, Esq; M.D.
Hen. Harrington, Esq;
Benjam. Higgins, Esq;
John Hill, Esq;
John Hewson, Esq;
Rowley Hyland, Esq;
Hugh Holmes, Esq;
Mr. Mich. Hutchison
Mr. William Hughson
Mr. Charles Hunt
Mr. Samuel Hardy
Mr. Charles Harricks
Messrs. Hunt & Kearney
Mr. William Hunter
Mr. Thomas Howie
Mr. Silvester Harney
Mrs. Mary Ann Hevey
Mr. William Henigan
Mr. William Hoey
Mr. Denis Hyland
Mr. Thomas Hannan
Mr. John Hutton
Mr. Nicholas Hart
Mr. Robert Hunter
Mr. Michael Hughs
Mr. William Hendy
Mr. John Hewetson
Mr. James Hamilton
Mr. James Heiton
Mr. Joseph Handley
Mr. James Hilles
Mr. Thomas Heath
Mr. William Harris
Mr. Patrick Hannan
Mr. Jervis Harrison
Mr. Robert Hall
Mr. William Howard
Mr. Patrick Hughs
Mr. Robert Henderson
Mr. Daniel Hutton
Mr. Edward Hearn
Mr. William Houston
Mr. George Homan

Mr. Christ. Humphrys
Mr. Wm. Higginson
Mr. James Hewitt
Mr. William Hearn
Mr. Tho. Huddleston
Mr. Edw. Hudson, jun.
Mr. William Holmes
Mr. T. Harding, M.R.I.A.
Mr. Patrick Hynes
Mr. Edward Hamilton
Mr. Peter Hoey, Bookseller, 6 Books
Mr. William Holmes
Mr. John Halpin
Mr. John Higgins
Mr. James Harrington
Mrs. Sarah Hargrate
Mr. Thomas Hodgens
Mr. John Howard
Mr. Robert Hudson
Mr. Edm. Hammond
Mr. Wm. Hamilton
Mr. Andrew Hanly
Mr. Christ. Humphrys
Mr. Peter Halpin
Mr. Thomas Hatton
Mr. John Hoey
Mr. Barth. Hackett
Mr. John Harpur
Mr. Abraham Y. Hill
Mr. Tho. Edw. Hay
Mr. James Howlin

Rt. Hon. Lord Jocelyn
Sir Allen Johnson, Bt
John J. W. Jervis, Esq;
Eyles Irwin, Esq;
Fred. Edw. Jones, Esq;
Richard Jebb, Esq;
Rev. Thomas Jones
Alderm. Wm. James
John Johnston, Esq;
Jaffray & Hautenville, Esqrs.
T. Johnston, Esq; M.D.
Meredyth Jenkin, Esq;
Henry Jackson, Esq;
James Johnston, Esq;
Peter Jackson, Esq;
John Jones, Esq;
George Jennings, Esq;

Wm. Ph. Irwin, Eſq;
Alex. Jordan, Eſq;
Thomas Irwin, Eſq;
William Jolly, Eſq;
T. Johnſon, Eſq; M.D.
Mr. William Jolly
Mr. Thomas Jordan
Mr. Thomas Johnſton
Mr. T. J. Jones
Mr. James Jackſon
Mr. Samuel Jeſſop
Mr. James Jones
Mr. John Jones
Mr. F. Joville
Mr. James Johnſton
Mr. Wm. Jenkinſon
Mr. Mathew Johnſon
Mr. Richard Jackſon
Mr. W. Jones, Bookſ.
Mr. Jn. Jones, Bookſ.
Mr. Robert Jeſſon
Mr. John Jackſon
Mr. William Jones
Mr. Thomas Jones
Mr. George Jones
Mr. William Jewſter
Mr. George Johnſon
Mr. John S. Johnſton
Mrs. Ann Johnſton
Mrs. Mary Inns
Mr. Thomas Jones

K

Rt. Hon. Earl Kilkenny
Rt. Hon. Lord Kilmaine
Rt. Rev. John Lord Biſhop of Killala
Rt. Rev. George Lord Biſhop of Kildare
Rt. Rev. Thomas Lord Biſhop of Killaloe
Rt. Rev. William Lord Biſhop of Kilmore
Rt. Hon. Lord Kinmar
Rev. Dean Keatinge
Francis Knox, Eſq;
John Kirwan, Eſq;
William Kilbee, Eſq;
Thomas Kemmis, Eſq;
William Keon, Eſq;
Charles King, Eſq;
Anthony King, Eſq;
John Kells, Eſq;
Michael Kelly, Eſq;
John Kelly, Eſq;
Arthur Keene, Eſq;
Francis Kiernan, Eſq;
Benjam. Kearney, Eſq;
Patrick Kernan, Eſq;
William Knott, Eſq;
William King, Eſq;
Lawrence Kenny, Eſq;
Gilbert Kilbee, Eſq;
Burrows Kelly, Eſq;
William Kenny, Eſq;
Thomas Kirwan, Eſq;
Edward Keane, Eſq;
Thomas Kelly, Eſq;
Samuel Kathrens, Eſq;
Edward King, Eſq;
Thomas Keck, Eſq;
Patrick Kelly, Eſq;
Patrick Kavenagh, Eſq;
Mr. Michael Kearney
Mr. Robert Keeling
Mr. Thomas Kinſela
Mr. Thomas Kindre
Mr. Roger Keane
Mr. Denis Killikelly
Mr. John Killikelly
Mr. James King
Mr. John Kearns
Mr. Hall Kirchoffer
Mr. Daniel Kinahan
Mr. James Kavenagh
Mr. Robert Kelſall
Mr. Andrew Kennedy
Mr. William Keating
Mr. Henry Keegan
Mr. Nich. Kildahl
Mr. William Keene
Mr. Thomas Keogh
Mr. James King
Mr. Daniel Kochler
Mr. Chriſt. Kelly
Mr. Barnaby Kelly
Mr. Thomas Kenuan
Mr. Patrick Keating
Mr. Joſ. A. Kavenagh
Mr. Robert King
Mr. Frederick Kinnier
Mr. G. Sim. Kirchner
Mr. Nicholas Kelly
Mr. Pat. Kavenagh
Mr. Patrick Kane
Mr. George Kidd
Mr. Michael Keating
Mr. Thomas Keary
Mr. Neh. Donn. Kelly
Mr. Law. Kennedy

L

His Grace William Duke of Leinſter
Rt. Hon. Viſc. Leitrim
Rt. Hon. Lord Liſmore
Rt. Hon. Sir Hercules Langriſhe, Bart.
Rt. Hon. D. La Touche
Major Gen. Lyon
Lieut. Col. Loftus
Peter La Touche, Eſq;
P. D. La Touche, Eſq;
Aldm. Joſ. Lynam
Aldm. W. Lightburne
Rev. John Lord
Rich. R. Lyſter, Eſq;
Rev. Jn. Leahy, M.A.
Rev. Edward Ledwich
Joſhua Leathley, Eſq;
John Leeſon, Eſq;
Peter Lock, Eſq;
John Leech, Eſq;
George Lunell, Eſq;
Nich. Le Favre, Eſq;
Paul Le Bas, Eſq;
Philip Lawleſs, Eſq;
Robert Lloyd, Eſq;
William Little, Eſq;
Jonathan Lynch, Eſq;
John Lloyd, Eſq;
Lewis Laurent, Eſq;
Robert Lyons, Eſq;
John Levinge, Eſq;
Ambroſe Lane, Eſq;
Thomas Leland, Eſq;
James Law, Eſq;
George Ledſam, Eſq;
Simon Langly, Eſq;
Rev. John Lyſter
Peter Legh, Eſq;
William Large, Eſq;
Thomas Lee, Eſq;
Edward Lyſaght, Eſq;
John Lloyd, Eſq;
Tho. L'Eſtrange, Eſq;
Thomas Lloyd, Eſq;

John Lawder, Esq;
Richard Lawless, Esq;
James Ledwith, Esq;
John Leigh, Esq;
William Lecky, Esq;
Alexander Lynar, Esq;
Mr. Michael Lacy
Mr. Patrick Long
Mrs. Isabella Lynch
Mr. Lewis Lyons
Mr. John Langston
Mess. G. Lanauz & co.
Mr. William Lindsay
Mr. Thomas Leech
Mr. Cook Lucas
Mr. Thomas Lanigan
Mr. David Lunt
Mr. A. Lambermont
Mr James Lambert
Mr. George Laing
Mr. William Langford
Mr. Patrick Lawless
Mr. Richard Lambert
Mr. Arthur Law
Messrs. Lynch & Young
Mr. Richard Longford
Mr. Samuel Lawrence
Mr. Patrick Lambert
Mr. Barth. Lambert
Messrs. Lyons & Boyle
Mr. John Lyons
Mr. Thomas Le Favre
Mr. Joseph Langstaff
Mr. John Lett
Mr. John Lumly
Mr. Edward Lamprey
Mr. James Linam
Mr. Ambrose Ledwich
Mr. Edmund Lynch

M

Rt. Hon. Ld. Mountjoy
Rev. Richard Murray, Provost of T.C.D.
Rt. Hon. the Ld. Mayor
Rt. Hon. Jn. M. Mason
V. Montgomery, Esq;
Hon. Baron Metge
John Metge, Esq;
John Macartney, Esq;
W. Montgomery, Esq;
A. C. Macartney, Esq;
Bar. C. Meredith, Esq;
Major Minchin
Bla. O. Mitchell, Esq;
Edward Mayne, Esq;
Hen. G. Moloney, Esq;
John F. Malpas, Esq;
G. & J. L. Maquay, Esqs
John E. Madden, Esq;
Rand. M'Donnell, Esq;
Wm. Molesworth, Esq;
George Moore, Esq;
Leon. Mac Nally, Esq;
Joshua Minnitt, Esq;
Moller, Dixon & Sneyd, Esqrs.
Michael Mills, Esq;
Robert Mercer, Esq;
R. Melville Esq; A.M.
Sam. Middleton, Esq;
William Moore, Esq;
Whit. Mackean, Esq;
Robert Magee, Esq;
J. D. Martini, Esq;
John M'Laughlin, Esq;
Richard Maxwell, Esq;
John Medlicott, Esq;
Geo. P. Maquay, Esq;
Denis Moore, Esq;
Maguire & Keightly, Esq
Philip Molloy, Esq;
Nicholas Mahon, Esq;
Mark M'Mahon, Esq;
John Mason, Esq;
Ross Maguire, Esq;
Michael M'Carty, Esq;
Samuel Madder, Esq;
Thomas Mangan, Esq;
Hugh Mulhollan, Esq;
Joseph Mayne, Esq;
John Moore, Esq;
Arthur Maxwell, Esq;
John Fin. Moore, Esq;
Richard Mangan, Esq;
John M'Clean, Esq;
Henry Morley, Esq;
John M'Kenly, Esq;
M'Laughlin & Co. Esqs
John Medcalf, Esq;
Richard Morrin, Esq;
Ross M'Can, Esq;
John Mulock, Esq;
William Mulay, Esq;
Robert Mayne, Esq;
Maxwell & Mee, Esqs.
Folliot Magrath, Esq;
Richard M'Nab, Esq;
Wm. Mathews, Esq;
Allan Maclean, Esq;
Merv. Mathews, Esq;
Stephen Miller, Esq;
John Mosse, Esq;
Henry Maryon, Esq;
Jos. Meredith, Esq;
Wm. Maturin, Esq;
Daniel M'Gutty, Esq;
Cha. H. Meares, Esq;
James M'Clatchy, Esq;
William M'Kay, Esq;
John Murphy, Esq;
Geo. Mauleverer, Esq;
Simon Maddock, Esq;
Hugh Molloy, Esq;
Mich. Magrane, Esq;
Al. Montgomery, Esq;
Mr. John Millikin
Mr. John Merrit
Mr. Patrick M'Dermot
Mrs. Margaret Moore
Mr. Wm. M'Cready
Mr. Barth. Mons
Mr. Daniel M'Clean
Mr. James Moore
Mr. Thomas M'Bride
Mr. John Mack
Mr. Mich. Murphy
Mr. James M'Allister
Mr. Barnaby Murray
Mr. Rich. M'Donnell
Mr. Thomas Morgan
Mr. Joseph Maddock
M. James M'Anally
Mr. James Mullay
Mr. Nicholas Murphy
Mr. Hugh Murphy
Mr. Mathew M'Cabe
Mr. Robert Morgan
Mr. Pat. M'Loughlin
Mr. Bernard Murray
Mr. James Marsh
Mr. Michael M'Cann
Mr. Maurice Malone
Mr. John M'Evoy
Mr. George Magrane
Mr. George Molloy
Mr. James M'Cabe
Mr. William Mossop

Mr. John Monks
Mr. Tho. M'Nemara
Mr. Wm. M'Connell
Mr. Thomas Mooney
Mr. William Mooney
Mr. And. Maiben, jun.
Mr. Rob. M'Gowen
Mr. Thomas Murphy
Mr. George Moran
Mr. Lawrence Malone
Mr. Samuel Middleton
Mr. Edward Madden
Mr. Peter Martin
Mr. Robert Mallet
Mr. Timothy M'Evoy
Mr. Michael M'Evoy
Mr. Timothy Mahony
Mr. Wm. Montgomery
Mr. Thomas Meyler
Mr. Thomas M'Calley
Mr. Ja. M'Connochiey
Meſſrs. Mercier & Co. Bookſellers
Mr. Charles Moore
Mr. Wm. M'Kenzie
Mr. James Miffett
Mr. William Murray
Mr. Richard Magee
Mr. Joſhua Maſon
Mr. Samuel Maſon
Mr. Edward Murphy
Mrs. Jane Morgan
Mr. Peter Martin
Mr. Dennis Madden
Mr. R. Morphet
Mr. Owen Mullanphy
Mr. Andrew Murphy
Mr. Hugh M'Gedy
Mr. John Millea
Mr. Seacombe Maſon
Mr. Thomas Mackay
Mr. John Moffitt
Mr. John M'Nemara
Mr. Joſhua Martin
Mr. James Mehain
Mr. Patrick Melly

N

Newport & Sons, Eſqrs
Col. Nugent
Edward Nugent, Eſq;
Hill Netterville, Eſq;
James Norton, Eſq,
James Nugent, Eſq;
Thomas Neville, Eſq;
George Nowlan, Eſq;
Math. Newport, Eſq;
John Naſh, Eſq;
Daniel Nihill, Eſq;
Joſhua Nunn, Eſq;
Arth. R. Neville, Eſq;
Adam Nixon, Eſq;
William Norris, Eſq;
Roger North, Eſq;
Thomas Nuttall, Eſq;
Mr. Richard Nun
Mr. John Norton
Mr. George Newton
Mr. James Nicholas
Mr. Mead Neſbit
Mr. Edward Nicholſon
Mr. William Nugent
Mr. John Nicholſon
Mr. Mark Nugent
Mr. Wm. Nicholſon
Meſſrs. Neilſon, Bayne & Co.
Mr. Edmond Nugent
Mr. John Newman
Mr. Timothy Nowland
Mr. George Norman
Mr. Ambroſe Nicklin
Mr. William Nunn
Mr. Benjamin Newitt
Mr. Andrew Nicoll

O

R. Hn. Ld. Oxmantown
Rt. Rev. Lord Biſhop of Offory
Sir Edw. O'Brien, Bt.
Capt. Lewis O'Donel
O'Brien & Comerford, Eſqrs.
Henry Ottiwell, Eſq;
John B. O'Ferrall, Eſq;
William Ottiwell, Eſq;
James Ormſby, Eſq;
John O'Connor, Eſq;
Denis O'Brien, Eſq;
John Orr, Eſq;
John O'Donnell, Eſq;
William Oſbrey, Eſq;
Samuel O'Neill, Eſq;
Timothy O'Brien, Eſq;
Pat. L. O'Reilly, Eſq;
John Orr, Eſq;
George Overend, Eſq;
John O'Reilly, Eſq;
John Ormſton, Eſq;
Mr. Michael O'Brien
Mr. Thomas O'Connor
Mr. Andrew O'Connor
Mr. Thomas O'Neill
Mr. Patrick O'Neill
Mr. John O'Gara
Mr. Mich. D. O'Reilly
Mr. James O'Leary
Mr. John O'Neill
Mr. Henry O'Hara
Mr. Charles O'Neill
Mr. William Oſborne
Mr. Daniel O'Hara
Mr. Thomas Oldham
Mr. William Oſborne
Mr. Dom. O'Connor
Mr. Lewis O'Neill
Mr. Michael O'Brien
Mr. Jas. O'Flagherty
Mr. Mich. O'Hennefy
Mr. James G. O'Brien
Mr. Andrew O'Brien
Mr. John O'Donnell
Mr. James O'Brien

P

Sir Law. Parſons, Bart.
Rev. Archdeac. Palmer
George Putland, Eſq;
George Punſonby, Eſq;
George Powell, Eſq;
Tho. Prendergaſt, Eſq;
Pat. O. Plunkett, Eſq;
William Preſton, Eſq;
Vaughan Pendred, Eſq;
Francis Patterſon, Eſq;
J. Pollock, Eſq;
Ro. Powell, Eſq, High Sheriff of the City
Tho. Prendergaſt, Eſq;
Simon Purdon, Eſq;
Joſhua Pim, Eſq;
John Parkinſon, Eſq;
Foden Perrin, Eſq;
James Purcell, Eſq;
Henry Pettigrew, Eſq;

Philip Pendleton, Esq;
Richard Plunket, Esq;
George Pentland, Esq;
Wm. Pilkington, Esq;
Joshua Pounden, Esq;
John S. Peach, Esq;
Daniel Pineau, Esq;
We. & Jn. Phelps, Esqs
Mr. William Potter
Mr. James Porter
Mr. William Pike
Mr. Jonas Pasley
Mr. George Parvisol
Mr. William Parker
Mr. Edward Parke
Mr. William Peck
Mr. William Pike, jun.
Mr. Thomas Palmer
Mr. David Pickering
Mr. Thomas Parr
Mr. Thomas Parsons
Mr. John Parr
Mrs. Jane Phelan
Mr. Richard Passmore
Mr. Richard Pearson
Mr. Mathew Perry
Mr. James Palmer
Mr. Mathew Parker
Mr. Thomas Perry
Mr. G. Perrin, Booksr.
Mr. W. Porter, Booksr.
Mr. J. Potts, jun. Booksr.
Mr. George Payne
Mr. John Proudfoot
Mr. Edward H. Percy
Mr. William Phipps
Mr. Christ. Phillips
Mr. Robert Patterson
Mr. Francis Potter
Mr. — Parker
Mr. Andrew Patterson

Q

Mr Terence Quinn
Mr. Edmond Quinan
Mr. Pat. Quinn
Mr. John Quinn

R

Rt. Hon. H. L. Rowley
Robert Ross, Esq;
Rev. Archd. Robinson
Rev. Dudl. Ch. Ryder
Col. Jas. F. Rolleston
Alderm. John Rose
Alderm. Samuel Reed
John Ray, Esq;
John Ratcliffe, Esq;
John N. Richards, Esq;
William Rawlins, Esq;
Edward Reynolds, Esq;
Walter Redmond, Esq;
Thomas Rickard, Esq;
Charles Reily, Esq;
John Roche, Esq;
Jos. M. Rainsford, Esq;
Steph. Hen. Rice, Esq;
John C. Rogers, Esq;
Adam Rutherford, Esq;
Joseph Rolleston, Esq;
Allen Ruxton, Esq;
Capt. Richard Roberts
Mr. Ben. Rivet
Mr. John Rainsford
Mr. John Robinson
Mr. William Robinson
Mr. Patrick Ryan
Mr. Nugent Reilly
Mr. David Roch
Mr. Michael Roth
Mr. Alex. Robinson
Mr. Patrick Ryan
Mr. Wm. Rathborne
Mr. Nicholas Roe
Mr. John Robinson
Mr. Richard Robinson
Mrs. Eliz. Rhames
Mr. Richard Roe
Mr. Edm. Rouarke
Mr. Peter Roe
Mr. John Reeves
Mrs. Eliz. Russell
Mr. William Rogers
Mr. James Reaf
Mr. John Renshaw
Mr. Thomas Rork
Mess. Roberts & Cunliff
Mr. John B. Reeves
Mr. Cornelius Reilly
Mr. Charles Robertson
Mr. George Raymond
Mr. James John Ryan
Mr. William Risk
Mr. Thomas Rogers
Mr. Jn. Rice, Booksr.
Mr. Philip Reilly
Mr. John Rice
Mr. Edward Reilly
Mr. James Rooney
Mr. Lawrence Roth
Mr. Robert Reeves
Mr. Dominick Rooney
Mr. Alexander Robe
Mr. Thomas Reynolds
Mr. John Rea
Mr. Terence Reilly
Mr. Edward Ryan
Mr. William Ross
Mr. Pat. Reilly
Mr. William Reynolds
Mr. Christ. Rigney

S

Rt. Hon. Earl Shannon
Rt. Hon. Ld. Sunderlin
Hon. Col. Southwell
Hon. Bowen Southwell
Hon. Baron Smith
Sir Ann. Stewart, Bt.
Sir Walter Synnot, Bt.
Sir George Shee, Bt.
Aldm. Hen. G. Sankey
Rev. James Strong
Major Dan. H. Shaw
Rev. John Subremont
Rev. Joseph Stopford
James Stewart, Esq;
John Stewart, Esq;
Nathaniel Sneyd, Esq;
William Smith, Esq;
Henry Shears, Esq;
Henry Stewart, Esq;
John Swan, Esq;
John Sankey, Esq;
Edward Smith, Esq;
Henry Standish, Esq;
John Smyth, Esq;
Eustace Stawell, Esq;
Jones Stevelly, Esq;
Ralph Smyth, Esq;
Robert Shaw, Esq;
Hugh Strahan, Esq;
Smith & Prentice, Esqs.
Wm. Sweetman, Esq;
Sims, Patterson & Sims, Esqrs.

Patrick Sweetman, Esq;
Gregory Scurlog, Esq;
Geo. Sutherland, Esq;
Stukey Simon, Esq;
Edward Stephens, Esq;
Jonas Stott, Esq;
William Stephens, Esq;
Thomas Segrave, Esq;
H. A. & J. Skeys, Esqs
John Still, Esq;
Luke Stritch, Esq;
John Saunders, Esq;
David Sherlock, Esq;
Henry Cha. Sirr, Esq;
Richard Swift, Esq;
George Shaw, Esq;
Thomas Stoney, Esq;
James Somerville, Esq;
James K. Sherry, Esq;
Robert Smith, Esq;
John Steele, Esq;
John Spiller, Esq;
John Sheridan, Esq;
James Symes, Esq;
Walter Sweetman, Esq;
Scott & Berry, Esqrs.
Alexander Stillas, Esq;
Robert Sutter, Esq;
James Stables, Esq;
Richard Stafford, Esq;
John Semple, Esq;
John Stafford, Esq;
Ben. N. Stephens, Esq;
Richard Sankey, Esq;
Bryan Stapleton, Esq;
R. A. Fl. Sharp, Esq;
Henry Stamer, Esq;
George Shannon, Esq;
Smith & Skerman, Esq
John Scott, Esq;
Andrew Savage, Esq;
Wm. B. Swan, Esq;
Thomas Savage, Esq;
R[illegible] Sin[illegible]
Lorenzo Sensi, Esq;
R. Sandys, Esq;
Rich. F. Sharkey, Esq;
Patrick Smyth, Esq;
Rev. Andrew Staunton
Mr. Jeremiah Sullivan
Mr. George Strong
Mr. William Simmons
Mr. George Shee

Mr. Stephen Slator
Mr. Daniel Sullivan
Mr. John Stinson.
Mr. Richard Smith
Mr. John Sceales
Mr. J. T. Sinnett
Mr. Nicholas Sherlock
Mr. John Sweeny
Mr. Valentine Sharkey
Mr. Thomas Sherrard
Mr. James Sinclare
Mr. Thomas Segrave
Mr. John Stroker
Mr. Mathew Shannon
Mr. Philip Sullivan
Mr. William Sinnett
Mr. Patrick Sullivan
Mr. Richard Skellern
Mr. Francis Smith
Mrs. Alice Savage
Mr. Charles Smyth
Mr. Edward Shannon
Mr. Alfred Smyth
Mr. William Shannon
Mr. William Scott
Mr. Jonathan Sisson
Mr. William Stirling
Mr. John Shaw
Mr. Thomas Smithson
Mr. Brabazon Supple
Mr. Geo. Stephenson
Mr. John Stephenson
Mr. Richard Strong
Mr. William Salmon
Mr. Patrick Sandford
Mr. John Shene
Mr. George Smitten
Mr. Richard Spear
Mr. W. Sleater, Books.
Mr. Rob. Jos. Shuter
Mrs. Susan. Singleton
Mr. Patrick Savage
Mr. John Silly
Mr. Roger Sweeny
Mr. Thomas Smyth
Mr. James Sinnott
Mr. Owen Sexton
Mr. Thomas Saunders
Mr. Peter Smyth

T

His Grace William Ld. Abp. of Tuam

J. Toler, Esq; Sol. Gen.
Francis Talbot, Esq;
William Tighe, Esq;
Richard Thwaites, Esq;
Thomas Twigg, Esq;
Alderm. Th. Truelock
George Thomas, Esq;
Fred. Thompson, Esq;
William Tennant, Esq;
Benjam. Thomas, Esq;
William Tisdall, Esq;
George Tharp, Esq;
Eman. Thomasyn, Esq;
Samuel Tyndall, Esq;
William Taylor, Esq;
James Tandy, Esq;
John Tate, Esq;
John Tubos, Esq;
Benjamin Tydd, Esq;
Daniel Tracy, Esq;
James Thomas, Esq;
Wm. Thwaites, Esq;
Arthur Thomas, Esq;
Marmad. Taylor, Esq;
Lewis Thomas, Esq;
Hugh Trevor, Esq;
H. & J. Thompson, Esqs
Mr. James Tredenick
Mr. Peter Tourell
Mr. M. A. Tindall
Mr. Andrew Turnbull
Mr. Michael Tigh
Mr. Walter Troy
Mr. Wm. N. Thomas
Mr. Lawrence Tigh
Mr. T. Trueman, sen.
Mr. George Tinkler
Mr. Richard Toucher
Messrs. G. & A. Tickell
Mr. John Teeling
Mr. John Talbot
Mr. James Tomlinson
Mr. Jervis Taylor
Mr. Michael Ternan
Mr. George Teeling
Mr. George Trench
Mr. Francis Thome
Mr. Philip Tracy
Mr. Edward Tretham
Mr. John Todd
Mr. Thomas Tracy
Mr. Nicholas Tallan
Mr. John Tookey

Mr. Robert Thompson
Mr. John Taylor
Mr. Anth. Thompson

V

Rev. James Verschoyle, Dean of St. Patrick's
John Verschoyle, Esq;
Henry Upton, Esq;
Henry Upton, Esq;
George Vicars, Esq;
Richard Vidler, Esq;
William Vavasor, Esq;
Ch. Hall Vernon, Esq;
Thomas Vincent, Esq;
Th. B. Vandelure, Esq;
Mr. Peter Venables
Mr. Nicholas Vickers
Mr. Robert Verner

W

The Most Noble the Marq. of Waterford
Rt. Hon. the Earl of Westmeath
Rev. Dean Warburton
Sir Henry Wilkinson
William Walker, Esq; Recorder of Dublin
Aldm. W. Worthington
Rev. Hen. L. Walsh
Rev. Rich. Woodward
Rev. James Whitelaw
Owen Wynne, Esq;
Robert Wybrants, Esq;
Peter Wybrants, Esq;
Richard Waller, Esq;
George Waller, Esq;
Joshua Wilson, Esq;
Thomas Walker, Esq;
W. Whitingham, Esq;
Charles Ward, Esq;
Robert Weir, Esq;
Joseph White, Esq;
Tho. Waite, Esq; M.D.
Joseph Watson, Esq;
Hen. W. White, Esq;
Ignatius Weldon, Esq;
Peter Warren, Esq;
John White, Esq;
John Weekes, Esq;
Richard Walker, Esq;
Barth. Wallis, Esq;
Richard Waddy, Esq;
Add. Willcocks, Esq;
Chr. S. Williams, Esq;
Robert Warren, Esq;
Wm. Williamson, Esq;
Thomas White, Esq;
William Walker, Esq;
Henry Wheeler, Esq;
Thomas Webb, Esq;
John Webb, Esq;
Tho. J. White, Esq;
John Wetherall, Esq;
Wm. L. Walker, Esq.
Wm. Leef. Wall, Esq;
May. C. Walker, Esq;
George White, Esq;
James Warren, Esq;
Tobias Wade, Esq;
Rich. Willcocks, Esq;
Mess. W. & R. Williams
Mr. Richard Walsh
Mr. Richard Williams
Mr. Thomas Wade
Mr. John Williams
Mr. Thomas Watson
Mr. Joseph Wright
Mr. Thomas White
Mr. William Walsh
Mr. Thomas Whelan
Mr. John White
Mr. Benjamin Wright
Mr. John Walsh
Mr. Barth. Ward
Mr. Richard White
Mr. Jacob Willan
Mr. Thomas Wolfe
Mr. Griffith Williams
Mr. John Walsh
Mr. Charles White
Mr. Thomas Walker
Mr. John Watson
Messieurs Weldon and Murphy
Mr. Henry Walker
Mr. John Wilkinson
Mr. Oliver Walsh
Mr. Joseph Wesman
Mr. Jos. Williamson
Mr. Wm. Wainright
Mr. Joseph Wade
Mr. Fran. Rob West
Mr. Samuel Whyte
Mr. Pat. Wogan, Books.
Mr. Patrick Walsh
Mr. John Wyles
Mr. Joseph Walker
Mr. Nicholas Wade
Mr. Thomas Wickins
Mr. Francis White
Mr. William Williams
Mr. John West
Mr. John West
Mr. Richard Wade
Mr. Rowland Walsh
Mr. Barth. Ward
Mr. William Warren
Mr. T. Watts, Booksr.
Mr. Henry Walker
Mr. W. Wilson, Books.
Mr. Thomas Whitby
Mr. John Waddeck
Mr. James Walker
Mr. Thomas Ward
Mr. G. M. Warner

Y

Rt. Hon. Lord Chief Baron Yelverton
George Young, Esq;
Robert Yeates, Esq;
John Young, Esq;
Mr. George Young
Mr. John Yeates
Mr. Samuel Yeates
Mr. John Yoakley

Z

Richard Zouch, Esq;

EXCHANGES

BETWEEN

England *and* Ireland.

The following are Decimal Multipliers fitted to every Rate of Exchange; by which, if any Sum of Money be multiplied, the Product will be the Money into which it was intended to be exchanged: of which Examples will be given.

ENGLISH into IRISH.				IRISH into ENGLISH.			
RATE.8th	Multpr.	RATE.8th	Multpr.	RATE.8th	Mulpr.	RATE 8	Mulpr.
6 per Ct.	1.06	10 per Ct.	1.1	6 per Ct.	.9434	10p.Ct.	.909
1	1.06125	1	1.10125	1	.94228	1	.908
2	1.0625	2	1.1025	2	.94117	2	.9072
3	1.06375	3	1.10375	3	.94	3	.906
4	1.065	4	1.105	4	.93896	4	.905
5	1.06625	5	1.10625	5	.93786	5	.9039
6	1.0675	6	1.1075	6	.93676	6	.9029
7	1.06875	7	1.10875	7	.93567	7	.9019
7 per Ct.	1.07	11 per Ct.	1.11	7 per Ct	.93458	11p.Ct.	.9009
1	1.07125	1	1.11125	1	.93348	1	.8998
2	1.0725	2	1.1125	2	.9324	2	.8988
3	1.07375	3	1.11375	3	.9313	3	.8978
4	1.075	4	1.115	4	.93023	4	.8968
5	1.07625	5	1.11625	5	.92915	5	.8958
6	1.0775	6	1.1175	6	.92807	6	.8948
7	1.07875	7	1.11875	7	.927	7	.8938
8 per Ct.	1.08	12 per Ct.	1.12 25	8 per Ct.	.926	12p.Ct.	.8928
1	1.08125	1	1.1215	1	.9248	1	.8918
2	1.0825	2	1.12275	2	.92378	2	.8908
At PAR	1.08333	3	1.123	3	.92308	3	.8897
3	1.08375	4	1.12525	4	.9216	4	.8888
4	1.085	5	1.1265	5	.92059	5	.8879
5	1.08625	6	1.12775	6	.9195	6	.8869
6	1.0875	7	1.128	7	.91848	7	.8859
7	1.08875						
9 per Ct.	1.09			9 per Ct	.9174		
1	1.09125			1	.9163		
2	1.0925			2	.9153		
3	1.09375			3	.91428		
4	1.095			4	.91324		
5	1.09625			5	.9122		
6	1.0975			6	.91116		
7	1.09875			7	.91		

A Scale for Decimals of one Pound Sterling.

Shillings		Shillings		Pence		Pence	
1 Shilling is	.05	11 Shillings is	.55	1 Penny	.004	11 Pence is	.046
2 ———	.1	12 ———	.6	2 ——	.008		
3 ———	.15	13 ———	.65	3 ——	.012		
4 ———	.2	14 ———	.7	4 ——	.016	———	
5 ———	.25	15 ———	.75	5 ——	.02		
6 ———	.3	16 ———	.8	6 ——	.025		
7 ———	.35	17 ———	.85	7 ——	.029	1 Farth.	.001
8 ———	.4	18 ———	.9	8 ——	.034	2 ——	.002
9 ———	.45	19 ———	.95	9 ——	.038	3 ——	.003
10 ———	.5	———		10 ——	.042		

Use of the foregoing Tables.

What is the value of 100*l.* English at par, in Irish money; and of 108*l.* 6*s.* 8*d.* Irish, in English money?

	*l.*100 English		108*l.* 6*s.* 8*d.* is *l.*108 .333
Multiplier at Par	1 .08333	Multiplier at Par	92 .308
product	108 .333	product	*l.*100 English
equal to	108 6 8 Irish		

Any sum at any rate of Exchange, will be found to answer if multiplied by the tabular number annexed to the Rate, and the shillings and pence (if any) thrown into the form of a Decimal Fraction, by the Table at the head of this page.

But to accomodate such Gentlemen as would not wish to use Decimals, I subjoin an Operation, and a set of Tables, calculated in the usual way.

What will be the value of 360*l.* English in Irish Money, at 10¾ per Cent.

As 100 is to 110¾ so is *l.*360 to *l.*398 14

110

39600

for the ¾ { ½ of 360 — 180
{ ½ of 180 — 90

divided by 100)39870

Quotient *l* 398 14

By the following Tables *l.*300 at 10¾ is *l.*332 5

60 is 66 9

*l.*398 14

Exchange *l.* 398 14 English into Irish, at 10¾ per Cent.?

As 110¾ is to 100 so is *l.* 398 14 to *l.* 360

```
  4              100
 ---           -----
 443           39870
                   4
              ------
divided by  443)159480
              ------
Quotient      l.360  English
```

By the following Tables

300	at 10¾	*l.* 270	17	7½
90		81	5	3⅞
8		7	4	5⅛
	14		12	7¼
		l. 360		

LONDON

LONDON ON DUBLIN

Eng.	At 6			At 6⅛			At 6¼			At 6⅜			At 6½		
£.	£.	s.	d.	£.	s.	d.	£.	s.	d.	£.	s.	d.	£.	s.	d.
1000	1060	0	0	1061	5	0	1062	10	0	1063	15	0	1065	0	0
900	954	—	—	955	2	6	956	5	0	957	7	6	958	10	0
800	848	—	—	849	0	0	850	—	0	851	—	0	852	—	0
700	742	—	—	742	17	6	743	15	0	744	12	6	745	10	0
600	636	—	—	636	15	0	637	10	0	638	5	0	639	—	0
500	530	—	—	530	12	6	531	5	0	531	17	6	532	10	0
400	424	—	—	424	10	0	425	—	0	425	10	0	426	—	0
300	318	—	—	318	7	6	318	15	0	319	12	6	319	10	0
200	212	—	—	212	5	0	212	10	0	212	15	0	213	—	0
100	106	—	—	106	2	6	106	5	0	106	7	6	106	10	0
90	95	8	—	95	10	3	95	12	6	95	14	9	95	17	0
80	84	16	—	84	18	0	85	—	0	85	2	0	85	4	0
70	74	4	—	74	5	9	74	7	6	74	9	3	74	11	0
60	63	12	—	63	13	6	63	15	0	63	16	6	63	18	0
50	53	—	—	53	1	3	53	2	6	53	3	9	53	5	0
40	42	8	—	42	9	0	42	10	0	42	11	0	42	12	0
30	31	16	—	31	16	9	31	17	6	31	18	3	31	19	0
20	21	4	—	21	4	6	21	5	0	21	5	6	21	6	0
10	10	12	—	10	12	3	10	12	6	10	12	9	10	13	0
9	9	10	9	9	11	0	9	11	3	9	11	5	9	11	8
8	8	9	7	8	9	9	8	10	0	8	10	2	8	10	4
7	7	8	4	7	8	7	7	8	9	7	8	11	7	9	1
6	6	7	2	6	7	4	6	7	6	6	7	7	6	7	9
5	5	6	—	5	6	1	5	6	3	5	6	4	5	6	6
4	4	4	9	4	4	10	4	5	—	4	5	1	4	5	2
3	3	3	7	3	3	8	3	3	9	3	3	9	3	3	10
2	2	2	4	2	2	5	2	2	6	2	2	6	2	2	7
1	1	1	2	1	1	2	1	1	3	1	1	3	1	1	3
S. 10	0	10	7	0	10	7	0	10	7	0	10	7	0	10	7
9	0	9	6	0	9	6	0	9	6	0	9	6	0	9	7
8	0	8	5	0	8	5	0	8	6	0	8	6	0	8	6
7	0	7	5	0	7	5	0	7	5	0	7	5	0	7	5
6	0	6	4	0	6	4	0	6	4	0	6	4	0	6	4
5	0	5	3	0	5	3	0	5	3	0	5	3	0	5	3
4	0	4	2	0	4	3	0	4	3	0	4	3	0	4	3
3	0	3	2	0	3	2	0	3	2	0	3	2	0	3	2
2	0	2	1	0	2	1	0	2	1	0	2	1	0	2	1
1	0	1	0	0	1	—	0	1	0	0	1	—	0	1	—
D. 6	0	0	6	0	—	6	0	—	6	0	—	6	0	—	6
5	0	0	5	0	—	5	0	—	5	0	—	5	0	—	5
4	0	—	4	0	—	4	0	—	4	0	—	4	0	—	4
3	0	—	3	0	—	3	0	—	3	0	—	3	0	—	3
2	0	—	2	0	—	2	0	—	2	0	—	2	0	—	2
1	0	—	1	0	—	1	0	—	1	0	—	1	0	—	1

Irish	At 6			At 6⅛			At 6¼			At 6⅜			At 6½		
£.	£.	s.	d.	£.	s.	d.	£.	s.	d.	£.	s.	d.	£.	s.	d.
1000	942	5	8	941	3	6	941	3	6	940	1	4	938	19	4
900	848	1	1	847	1	2	847	1	2	846	1	3	845	1	4
800	753	16	6	752	18	9	752	18	9	752	1	11	751	3	5
700	659	11	11	658	16	5	658	16	5	658	—	1	657	5	6
600	565	7	5	564	14	1	564	14	1	564	—	10	563	7	7
500	471	2	10	470	11	9	470	11	9	470	—	8	469	9	8
400	376	18	3	376	9	4	376	9	4	376	—	6	375	11	8
300	282	13	8	282	7	2	282	7	2	282	—	5	281	13	9
200	188	9	1	188	4	8	188	4	8	188	—	3	187	15	10
100	94	4	6	94	2	4	94	2	4	94	—	1	93	17	11
90	84	16	1	84	14	1	84	14	1	84	12	1	84	10	1
80	75	7	7	75	5	10	75	5	10	75	4	1	75	2	4
70	65	19	2	65	17	7	65	17	7	65	16	1	65	14	6
60	56	10	8	56	9	4	56	9	4	56	8	1	56	6	9
50	47	2	3	47	1	2	47	1	2	47	—	—	46	18	11
40	37	13	9	37	12	11	37	12	11	37	12	—	37	11	2
30	28	5	4	28	4	8	28	4	8	28	4	—	28	3	4
20	18	16	11	18	16	5	18	16	5	18	16	—	18	15	7
10	9	8	5	9	8	2	9	8	2	9	8	—	9	7	9
9	8	9	7	8	9	5	8	9	5	8	9	2	8	9	—
8	7	10	9	7	10	7	7	10	7	7	10	4	7	10	2
7	6	11	11	6	11	9	6	11	9	6	11	7	6	11	5
6	5	13	—	5	12	11	5	12	11	5	12	9	5	12	8
5	4	14	2	4	14	1	4	14	1	4	14	—	4	13	10
4	3	15	4	3	15	3	3	15	3	3	15	2	3	15	1
3	2	16	6	2	16	5	2	16	5	2	16	4	2	16	4
2	1	17	8	1	17	7	1	17	7	1	17	7	1	17	6
1	—	18	10	—	18	9	—	18	9	—	18	9	—	18	9
S. 10	—	9	5	—	9	5	—	9	5	—	9	4	—	9	4
9	—	8	5	—	8	5	—	8	5	—	8	5	—	8	5
8	—	7	6	—	7	6	—	7	6	—	7	6	—	7	6
7	—	6	7	—	6	7	—	6	7	—	6	7	—	6	6
6	—	5	7	—	5	7	—	5	7	—	5	7	—	5	7
5	—	4	8	—	4	8	—	4	8	—	4	8	—	4	8
4	—	3	9	—	3	9	—	3	9	—	3	9	—	3	9
3	—	2	9	—	2	9	—	2	9	—	2	9	—	2	9
2	—	1	10	—	1	10	—	1	10	—	1	10	—	1	10
1	—	—	11	—	—	11	—	—	11	—	—	11	—	—	11
D. 6	—	—	5	—	—	5	—	—	5	—	—	5	—	—	5
5	—	—	4	—	—	4	—	—	4	—	—	4	—	—	4
4	—	—	3	—	—	3	—	—	3	—	—	3	—	—	3
3	—	—	2	—	—	2	—	—	2	—	—	2	—	—	2
2	—	—	1	—	—	1	—	—	1	—	—	1	—	—	1
1	—	—	1	—	—	1	—	—	1	—	—	1	—	—	1

Eng.	At 6⅝			At 6¾			At 6⅞			At 7			At 7⅛		
£.	£.	s.	d.	£.	s.	d.	£.	s.	d.	£.	s.	d.	£.	s.	d.
1000	1066	5	—	1067	10	—	1068	15	—	1070	—	—	1071	5	—
900	959	12	6	960	15	—	961	17	6	963	—	—	964	2	6
800	853	—	—	854	—	—	855	—	—	856	—	—	857	—	—
700	746	7	6	747	5	—	748	2	6	749	—	—	749	17	6
600	639	15	—	640	10	—	641	5	—	642	—	—	642	15	—
500	533	2	6	533	15	—	534	7	6	535	—	—	535	12	6
400	426	10	—	427	—	—	427	10	—	428	—	—	428	10	—
300	319	17	6	320	5	—	320	12	6	321	—	—	321	7	6
200	213	5	—	213	10	—	213	15	—	214	—	—	214	5	
100	106	12	6	106	15	—	106	17	6	107	—	—	107	2	6
90	95	19	3	96	1	6	96	3	9	96	6	—	96	8	3
80	85	6	—	85	8	—	85	10	—	85	12	—	85	14	—
70	74	12	9	74	14	6	74	16	3	74	18	—	74	19	9
60	63	19	6	64	1	—	64	2	6	64	4	—	64	5	6
50	53	6	3	53	7	6	53	8	9	53	10	—	53	11	3
40	42	13	—	42	14	—	42	15	—	42	16	—	42	17	—
30	31	19	9	32	—	6	32	1	3	32	2	—	32	2	9
20	21	6	6	21	7	—	21	7	6	21	8	—	21	8	6
10	10	13	3	10	13	6	10	13	9	10	14	—	10	14	3
9	9	11	11	9	12	1	9	12	4	9	12	7	9	12	9
8	8	10	7	8	10	9	8	11	—	8	11	2	8	11	4
7	7	9	3	7	9	5	7	9	7	7	9	9	7	9	11
6	6	7	11	6	8	1	6	8	3	6	8	4	6	8	6
5	5	6	7	5	6	9	5	6	10	5	7	—	5	7	1
4	4	5	3	4	5	4	4	5	6	4	5	7	4	5	8
3	3	3	11	3	4	—	3	4	1	3	4	2	3	4	3
2	2	2	7	2	2	8	2	2	9	2	2	9	2	2	10
1	1	1	3	1	1	4	1	1	4	1	1	4	1	1	5
S. 10	0	10	8	0	10	8	0	10	8	0	10	8	0	10	8
9	0	9	7	0	9	7	0	9	7	0	9	7	0	9	7
8	0	8	6	0	8	6	0	8	6	0	8	6	0	8	6
7	0	7	5	0	7	5	0	7	5	0	7	5	0	7	6
6	0	6	4	0	6	4	0	6	5	0	6	5	0	6	5
5	0	5	4	0	5	4	0	5	4	0	5	4	0	5	4
4	0	4	3	0	4	3	0	4	3	0	4	3	0	4	3
3	0	3	2	0	3	2	0	3	2	0	3	2	0	3	2
2	0	2	1	0	2	1	0	2	1	0	2	1	0	2	1
1	0	1	—	0	1	—	0	1	—	0	1	—	0	1	—
D. 6	0	—	6	0	—	6	0	—	6	0	—	6	0	—	6
5	0	—	5	0	—	5	0	—	5	0	—	5	0	—	5
4	0	—	4	0	—	4	0	—	4	0	—	4	0	—	4
3	0	—	3	0	—	3	0	—	3	0	—	3	0	—	3
2	0	—	2	0	—	2	0	—	2	0	—	2	0	—	2
1	0	—	1	0	—	1	0	—	1	0	—	1	0	—	1

Irish	At 6⅝			At 6¾			At 6⅞			At 7			At 7⅛		
£.	£.	d.	s.	£.	s.	d.	£.	s.	d.	£.	s.	d.	J.	s.	d.
1000	937	17	3	936	15	4	935	13	5	934	11	7	933	9	9
900	844	1	7	843	1	9	842	2	1	841	2	5	840	2	9
800	750	5	10	749	8	3	748	10	9	747	13	3	746	15	9
700	656	10	1	655	14	9	654	19	4	654	4	1	653	8	10
600	562	14	4	562	1	2	561	8	—	560	14	11	560	1	10
500	468	18	7	468	7	8	467	16	8	467	5	9	466	14	10
400	375	2	11	347	14	1	374	5	4	373	16	7	373	7	10
300	281	7	2	281	—	7	280	14	—	280	7	5	280	—	11
200	187	11	5	187	7	—	187	2	8	186	18	3	186	13	11
100	93	15	8	93	13	6	93	11	4	93	9	1	93	6	11
90	84	8	1	84	6	2	84	4	2	84	2	2	84	—	3
80	75	—	7	74	18	9	74	17	—	74	15	3	74	13	7
70	65	13	0	65	11	5	65	9	11	65	8	4	65	6	10
60	56	5	5	56	4	1	56	2	9	56	1	5	56	—	2
50	46	17	10	46	16	9	46	15	8	46	14	7	46	13	5
40	37	10	3	37	9	5	37	8	6	37	7	8	37	6	9
30	28	2	8	28	2	—	28	1	4	28	—	9	28	—	1
20	18	15	1	18	14	8	18	14	3	18	13	10	18	13	4
10	9	7	6	9	7	4	9	7	1	9	6	11	9	6	8
9	8	8	9	8	8	7	8	8	5	8	8	2	8	8	—
8	7	10	—	7	9	10	7	9	8	7	9	6	7	9	4
7	6	11	3	6	11	1	6	10	11	6	10	10	6	10	8
6	5	12	6	5	12	5	5	12	3	5	12	1	5	12	—
5	4	13	9	4	13	8	4	13	6	4	13	5	4	13	4
4	3	15	—	3	14	11	3	14	10	3	14	9	3	14	8
3	2	16	3	2	16	2	2	16	1	2	16	—	2	16	—
2	1	17	6	1	17	5	1	17	5	1	17	4	1	17	4
1	0	18	9	0	18	8	0	18	8	0	18	8	0	18	8
S 10	0	9	4	0	9	4	0	9	4	0	9	4	0	9	4
9	0	8	5	0	8	5	0	8	5	0	8	4	0	8	4
8	0	7	6	0	7	5	0	7	5	0	7	5	0	7	5
7	0	6	6	0	6	6	0	6	6	0	6	6	0	6	6
6	0	5	7	0	5	7	0	5	7	0	5	7	0	5	7
5	0	4	8	0	4	8	0	4	8	0	4	8	0	4	8
4	0	3	9	0	3	9	0	3	8	0	3	8	0	3	8
3	0	2	9	0	2	9	0	2	9	0	2	9	0	2	9
2	0	1	10	0	1	10	0	1	10	0	1	10	0	1	10
1	0	0	11	0	0	11	0	0	11	0	0	11	0	0	11
D. 6	0	0	5	0	0	5	0	0	5	0	0	5	0	0	5
5	0	0	4	0	0	4	0	0	4	0	0	4	0	0	4
4	0	0	3	0	0	3	0	0	3	0	0	3	0	0	3
3	0	0	2	0	0	2	0	0	2	0	0	2	0	0	2
2	0	0	1	0	0	1	0	0	1	0	0	1	0	0	1
1	0	0	1	0	0	1	0	0	1	0	0	1	0	0	1

Eng.	At 7¼			At 7⅜			At 7½			At 7⅝			At 7¾		
£.	£.	s.	d.	£.	s.	d.	£.	s.	d.	£.	s.	d.	£.	s.	d.
1000	1072	10	—	1073	15	—	1075	—	0	1076	5	0	1077	10	0
900	965	0	0	966	7	6	967	10	0	968	12	6	969	15	0
800	858	—	—	859	—	—	860	—	0	861	0	0	862	—	0
700	750	15	6	751	12	6	752	10	0	753	7	6	754	5	0
600	643	10	—	644	5	—	645	—	0	645	15	0	646	10	0
500	536	5	—	536	17	6	537	10	0	538	2	6	538	15	0
400	429	—	—	429	10	—	430	—	0	430	10	0	431	—	0
300	321	15	—	322	2	6	322	10	0	322	17	6	323	5	0
200	214	10	—	214	15	—	215	—	0	215	5	0	215	10	0
100	107	5	—	107	7	6	107	10	0	107	12	6	107	15	0
90	96	10	6	96	12	9	96	15	0	96	17	3	96	19	6
80	85	16	—	85	18	—	86	—	0	86	2	0	86	4	0
70	75	1	6	75	3	3	75	5	0	75	6	9	75	8	6
60	64	7	—	64	8	6	64	10	0	64	11	6	64	13	0
50	53	12	6	53	13	9	53	15	0	53	16	3	53	17	6
40	42	18	—	42	19	—	43	—	0	43	1	0	43	2	0
30	32	3	6	32	4	3	32	5	0	32	5	9	32	6	6
20	21	9	—	21	9	6	21	10	0	21	10	6	21	11	0
10	10	14	6	10	14	9	10	15	0	10	15	3	10	15	6
9	9	13	2	9	13	3	9	13	6	9	13	8	9	13	11
8	8	11	7	8	11	9	8	12	0	8	12	2	8	12	4
7	7	10	1	7	10	3	7	10	6	7	10	8	7	10	10
6	6	8	8	6	8	10	6	9	0	6	9	1	6	9	3
5	5	7	3	5	7	4	5	7	6	5	7	7	5	7	9
4	4	5	9	4	5	10	4	6	0	4	6	1	4	6	2
3	3	4	4	3	4	5	3	4	6	3	4	6	3	4	7
2	2	2	10	2	2	11	2	3	0	2	3	—	2	3	1
1	1	1	5	1	1	5	1	1	6	1	1	6	1	1	6
S. 10	0	10	8	0	10	8	0	10	9	0	10	9	0	10	9
9	0	9	7	0	9	8	0	9	8	0	9	8	0	9	8
8	0	8	7	0	8	7	0	8	7	0	8	7	0	8	7
7	0	7	6	0	7	6	0	7	6	0	7	6	0	7	6
6	0	6	5	0	6	5	0	6	5	0	6	5	0	6	5
5	0	5	4	0	5	4	0	5	4	0	5	4	0	5	4
4	0	4	3	0	4	3	0	4	3	0	4	3	0	4	3
3	0	3	2	0	3	2	0	3	2	0	3	2	0	3	2
2	0	2	1	0	2	1	0	2	1	0	2	1	0	2	1
1	0	1	—	0	1	—	0	1	—	0	1	—	0	1	—
D. 6	0	0	6	0	0	6	0	0	6	0	0	6	0	0	6
5	0	0	5	0	0	5	0	0	5	0	0	5	0	0	5
4	0	0	4	0	0	4	0	0	4	0	0	4	0	0	4
3	0	0	3	0	0	3	0	0	3	0	0	3	0	0	3
2	0	0	2	0	0	2	0	0	2	0	0	2	0	0	2
1	0	0	1	0	0	1	0	0	1	0	0	1	0	0	

Irish	At 7¼			At 7⅜			At 7½			At 7⅝			At 7¾		
£.	£.	s.	d.	£.	s.	d.	£.	s.	d.	£.	s.	d.	£.	s.	d.
1000	932	8	—	931	6	3	930	4	7	929	3	0	928	1	5
900	839	3	2	838	3	8	837	4	2	836	4	8	835	5	4
800	745	18	4	745	1	—	744	3	8	743	6	5	742	9	2
700	652	13	7	651	18	5	651	3	3	650	8	1	649	13	0
600	559	8	9	558	15	9	558	2	9	557	9	9	556	16	10
500	466	4	—	465	13	1	465	2	3	464	11	6	464	9	8
400	372	19	2	372	10	6	372	1	10	371	13	2	371	4	7
300	279	14	4	279	7	10	279	1	4	278	14	10	278	8	5
200	186	9	7	186	5	3	186	0	11	185	16	7	185	12	3
100	93	4	9	93	2	7	93	0	5	92	18	3	92	16	1
90	83	18	3	83	16	4	83	14	5	83	12	5	83	10	6
80	74	11	10	74	10	1	74	8	4	74	6	7	74	4	11
70	65	5	4	65	3	10	65	2	3	65	—	9	64	19	3
60	55	18	10	55	17	6	55	16	3	55	14	11	55	13	8
50	46	12	4	46	11	3	46	10	2	46	9	1	46	8	0
40	37	5	11	37	5	—	37	4	2	37	3	3	37	2	5
30	27	19	5	27	18	9	27	18	1	27	17	5	27	16	10
20	18	12	11	18	12	6	18	12	1	18	11	7	18	11	2
10	9	6	5	9	6	3	9	6	2	9	5	10	9	5	7
9	8	7	10	8	7	7	8	7	5	8	7	3	8	7	0
8	7	9	2	7	9	0	7	8	10	7	8	8	7	8	5
7	6	10	6	6	10	4	6	10	2	6	10	1	6	9	11
6	5	11	10	5	11	9	5	11	7	5	11	6	5	11	4
5	4	13	2	4	13	1	4	13	—	4	12	11	4	12	9
4	3	14	7	3	14	6	3	14	5	3	14	4	3	14	3
3	2	15	11	2	15	10	2	15	9	2	15	9	2	15	8
2	1	17	3	1	17	3	1	17	2	1	17	2	1	17	1
1	0	18	7	0	18	7	0	18	7	0	18	7	0	18	6
S. 10	0	9	3	0	9	3	0	9	3	0	9	3	0	9	3
9	0	8	4	0	8	4	0	8	4	0	8	4	0	8	4
8	0	7	5	0	7	5	0	7	5	0	7	5	0	7	5
7	0	6	6	0	6	6	0	6	6	0	6	6	0	6	6
6	0	5	7	0	5	7	0	5	7	0	5	6	0	5	6
5	0	4	8	0	4	7	0	4	7	0	4	7	0	4	7
4	0	3	8	0	3	8	0	3	8	0	3	8	0	3	8
3	0	2	9	0	2	9	0	2	9	0	2	9	0	2	9
2	0	1	10	0	1	10	0	1	10	0	1	10	0	1	10
1	0	0	11	0	0	11	0	0	11	0	0	11	0	0	11
D. 6	0	0	5	0	0	5	0	0	5	0	0	5	0	0	5
5	0	0	4	0	0	4	0	0	4	0	0	4	0	0	4
4	0	0	3	0	0	3	0	0	3	0	0	3	0	0	3
3	0	0	2	0	0	2	0	0	2	0	0	2	0	0	2
2	0	0	1	0	0	1	0	0	1	0	0	1	0	0	1
1	0	0	1	0	0	1	0	0	1	0	0	1	0	0	1

Eng.	At 7⅞			At 8			At 8⅛			At 8¼			At 8⅜		
l.	£.	s.	d.	£.	s.	d.	£.	s.	d.	£.	s.	d.	£.	s.	d.
1000	1078	15	0	1080	0	0	1081	5	0	1082	10	0	1083	15	0
900	970	17	6	972	0	0	973	2	6	974	5	0	975	7	6
800	863	0	0	864	0	0	865	0	0	866	0	0	867	0	0
700	755	2	6	756	0	0	756	17	6	757	15	0	758	12	6
600	647	5	0	648	0	0	648	15	0	649	10	0	650	5	0
500	539	7	6	540	0	0	540	12	6	541	5	0	541	17	6
400	431	10	0	432	0	0	432	10	0	433	0	0	433	10	0
300	323	12	6	324	0	0	324	7	6	324	15	0	325	2	6
200	215	15	0	216	0	0	216	5	0	216	10	0	216	15	0
100	107	17	6	108	0	0	108	2	6	108	[illegible]	0	108	7	6
90	97	1	9	97	4	0	97	6	3	97	8	6	97	10	9
80	86	6	0	86	8	0	86	10	0	86	12	0	86	14	0
70	75	10	3	75	12	0	75	13	9	75	15	6	75	17	3
60	64	14	6	64	16	0	64	17	6	64	19	0	65	0	0
50	53	18	9	54	0	0	54	1	3	54	2	6	54	3	9
40	43	3	0	43	4	0	43	5	0	43	6	0	43	7	0
30	32	7	3	32	8	0	32	8	9	32	9	6	32	10	3
20	21	11	6	21	12	0	21	12	6	21	13	0	21	13	6
10	10	15	9	10	16	0	10	16	3	10	16	6	10	16	9
9	9	14	2	9	14	4	9	14	7	9	14	10	9	15	0
8	8	12	7	8	12	9	8	13	0	8	13	2	8	13	4
7	7	11	0	7	11	2	7	11	4	7	11	6	7	11	8
6	6	9	5	6	9	7	6	9	9	6	9	10	6	10	0
5	5	7	10	5	8	0	5	8	1	5	8	3	5	8	4
4	4	6	3	4	6	4	4	6	6	4	6	7	4	6	8
3	3	4	8	3	4	9	3	4	10	3	4	11	3	5	0
2	2	3	1	2	3	2	2	3	3	2	3	3	2	3	4
1	1	1	6	1	1	7	1	1	7	1	1	7	1	1	8
S. 10	0	10	9	0	10	9	0	10	9	0	10	9	0	10	10
9	0	9	8	0	9	8	0	9	8	0	9	8	0	9	9
8	0	8	7	0	8	7	0	8	7	0	8	7	0	8	8
7	0	7	6	0	7	6	0	7	6	0	7	6	0	7	7
6	0	6	5	0	6	5	0	6	5	0	6	6	0	6	6
5	0	5	4	0	5	4	0	5	4	0	5	5	0	5	5
4	0	4	3	0	4	3	0	4	3	0	4	4	0	4	4
3	0	3	2	0	3	2	0	3	2	0	3	3	0	3	3
2	0	2	1	0	2	2	0	2	2	0	2	2	0	2	2
1	0	1	1	0	1	1	0	1	1	0	1	1	0	1	1
D. 6	0	0	6	0	0	6	0	0	6	0	0	6	0	0	6
5	0	0	5	0	0	5	0	0	5	0	0	5	0	0	5
4	0	0	4	0	0	4	0	0	4	0	0	4	0	0	4
3	0	0	3	0	0	3	0	0	3	0	0	3	0	0	3
2	0	0	2	0	0	2	0	0	2	0	0	2	0	0	2
1	0	0	1	0	0	1	0	0	1	0	0	1	0	0	1

Irish	At 7⅞			At 8			At 8⅛			At 8¼			At 8⅜		
l.	£.	s.	d.	£.	s.	d.	£.	s.	d.	£.	s.	d.	£.	s.	d.
1000	926	19	11	925	18	6	924	17	1	923	15	9	922	14	5
900	834	5	11	833	6	8	832	7	4	831	8	2	830	8	11
800	741	11	11	740	14	9	739	17	8	739	0	7	738	3	6
700	648	17	11	648	2	11	647	7	11	646	13	0	645	18	1
600	556	3	11	555	11	1	554	18	3	554	5	5	553	12	7
500	463	9	11	462	19	3	462	8	6	461	17	10	461	7	2
400	370	15	11	370	7	4	369	18	10	369	10	3	369	1	9
300	278	1	11	277	15	6	277	9	1	277	2	8	276	16	3
200	185	7	11	185	3	8	184	19	5	184	15	1	184	10	10
100	92	14	0	92	11	10	92	9	8	92	7	6	92	5	5
90	83	8	7	83	6	8	83	4	8	83	2	9	83	0	10
80	74	3	2	74	1	5	73	19	9	73	18	0	73	16	4
70	64	17	9	64	16	3	64	14	9	64	13	3	64	11	9
60	55	12	4	55	11	1	55	9	9	55	8	6	55	7	3
50	46	7	0	46	5	11	46	4	10	46	3	9	46	2	8
40	37	1	7	37	0	8	36	19	10	36	19	0	36	18	2
30	27	16	2	27	15	6	27	14	11	27	14	3	27	13	7
20	18	10	9	18	10	4	18	9	11	18	9	6	18	9	1
10	9	5	4	9	5	2	9	4	11	9	4	9	9	4	6
9	8	6	10	8	6	8	8	6	5	8	6	3	8	6	1
8	7	8	3	7	8	1	7	7	11	7	7	9	7	7	7
7	6	9	9	6	9	7	6	9	5	6	9	4	6	9	2
6	5	11	2	5	11	1	5	10	11	5	10	10	5	10	8
5	4	12	8	4	12	7	4	12	5	4	12	4	4	12	3
4	3	14	1	3	14	0	3	13	11	3	13	10	3	13	9
3	2	15	7	2	15	6	2	15	5	2	15	5	2	15	4
2	1	17	1	1	17	0	1	17	0	1	16	11	1	16	10
1	0	18	6	0	18	6	0	18	6	0	18	5	0	18	5
S. 10	0	9	3	0	9	3	0	9	3	0	9	2	0	9	2
9	0	8	4	0	8	4	0	8	3	0	8	3	0	8	3
8	0	7	5	0	7	4	0	7	4	0	7	4	0	7	4
7	0	6	5	0	6	5	0	6	5	0	6	5	0	6	5
6	0	5	6	0	5	6	0	5	6	0	5	6	0	5	6
5	0	4	7	0	4	7	0	4	7	0	4	7	0	4	7
4	0	3	8	0	3	8	0	3	8	0	3	8	0	3	8
3	0	2	9	0	2	9	0	2	9	0	2	9	0	2	9
2	0	1	10	0	1	10	0	1	10	0	1	10	0	1	10
1	0	0	11	0	0	11	0	0	11	0	0	11	0	0	11
D. 6	0	0	5	0	0	5	0	0	5	0	0	5	0	0	5
5	0	0	4	0	0	4	0	0	4	0	0	4	0	0	4
4	0	0	3	0	0	3	0	0	3	0	0	3	0	0	3
3	0	0	2	0	0	2	0	0	2	0	0	2	0	0	2
2	0	0	1	0	0	1	0	0	1	0	0	1	0	0	1
1	0	0	1	0	0	1	0	0	1	0	0	1	0	0	1

Sterling.	At Par			At 8½			At 8⅝			At 8¾			At 8⅞		
£.	£.	s.	d.	£.	s.	d.	£.	s.	d.	£.	s.	d.	£.	s.	d.
1000	1083	6	8	1085	0	0	1086	5	0	1087	10	0	1088	15	0
900	975	0	0	976	10	0	977	12	6	978	15	0	979	17	6
800	866	13	4	868	0	0	869	0	0	870	0	0	871	0	0
700	758	6	8	759	10	0	760	7	6	761	5	0	762	2	6
600	650	0	0	651	0	0	651	15	0	652	10	0	653	5	0
500	541	13	4	542	10	0	543	2	6	543	15	0	544	7	6
400	433	6	8	434	0	0	434	10	0	435	0	0	435	10	0
300	325	0	0	325	10	0	325	17	6	326	5	0	326	12	6
200	216	13	4	217	0	0	217	5	0	217	10	0	217	15	0
100	108	6	8	108	10	0	108	12	6	108	15	0	108	17	6
90	97	10	0	97	13	0	97	15	3	97	17	6	97	19	9
80	86	13	4	86	16	0	86	18	0	87	0	0	87	2	0
70	75	16	8	75	19	0	76	0	9	76	2	6	76	4	3
60	65	0	0	65	2	0	65	3	6	65	5	0	65	6	6
50	54	3	4	54	5	0	54	6	3	54	7	6	54	8	9
40	43	6	8	43	8	0	43	9	0	43	10	0	43	11	0
30	32	10	0	32	11	0	32	11	9	32	12	6	32	13	3
20	21	13	4	21	14	0	21	14	6	21	15	0	21	15	6
10	10	16	8	10	17	0	10	17	3	10	17	6	10	17	9
9	9	15	0	9	15	3	9	15	6	9	15	9	9	15	11
8	8	13	4	8	13	7	8	13	9	8	14	0	8	14	2
7	7	11	8	7	11	10	7	12	0	7	12	3	7	12	5
6	6	10	0	6	10	2	6	10	4	6	10	6	6	10	7
5	5	8	4	5	8	6	5	8	7	5	8	9	5	8	10
4	4	6	8	4	6	9	4	6	10	4	7	0	4	7	1
3	3	5	0	3	5	1	3	5	2	3	5	3	3	5	3
2	2	3	4	2	3	4	2	3	5	2	3	6	2	3	6
1	1	1	8	1	8	1	1	1	8	1	1	9	1	1	9
S. 10	0	10	10	0	10	10	0	10	10	0	10	10	0	10	10
9	0	9	9	0	9	9	0	9	9	0	9	9	0	9	9
8	0	8	8	0	8	8	0	8	8	0	8	8	0	8	8
7	0	7	7	0	7	7	0	7	7	0	7	7	0	7	7
6	0	6	6	0	6	6	0	6	6	0	6	6	0	6	6
5	0	5	5	0	5	5	0	5	5	0	5	5	0	5	5
4	0	4	4	0	4	4	0	4	4	0	4	4	0	4	4
3	0	3	3	0	3	3	0	3	3	0	3	3	0	3	3
2	0	2	2	0	2	2	0	2	2	0	2	2	0	2	2
1	0	1	1	0	1	1	0	1	1	0	1	1	0	1	1
D. 6	0	0	6	0	0	6	0	0	6	0	0	6	0	0	6
5	0	0	5	0	0	5	0	0	5	0	0	5	0	0	5
4	0	0	4	0	0	4	0	0	4	0	0	4	0	0	4
3	0	0	3	0	0	3	0	0	3	0	0	3	0	0	3
2	0	0	2	0	0	2	0	0	2	0	0	2	0	0	2
1	0	0	1	0	0	1	0	0	1	0	0	1	0	0	1

Irish	At Par			At 8½			At 8⅝			At 8¾			At 8⅞		
£.	£.	s.	d.	£.	s.	d.	£.	s.	d.	£.	s.	d.	£.	s.	d.
1000	923	1	6	921	13	2	920	11	11	919	10	9	918	9	8
900	830	15	4	829	9	10	828	10	9	827	11	8	826	12	8
800	738	9	2	737	6	6	736	9	6	735	12	7	734	15	9
700	646	3	1	645	3	2	644	8	4	643	13	6	642	18	9
600	553	16	11	552	19	10	552	7	2	551	14	5	551	1	9
500	461	10	9	460	16	7	460	5	11	459	15	4	459	4	10
400	369	4	7	368	13	3	368	4	9	367	16	3	367	7	10
300	276	18	5	276	9	11	276	3	7	275	17	2	275	10	10
200	184	12	3	184	6	7	184	2	4	183	18	1	183	13	11
100	92	6	1	92	3	3	92	1	2	91	19	1	91	16	11
90	83	1	6	82	18	11	82	17	0	82	15	2	82	13	3
80	73	16	11	73	14	7	73	12	11	73	11	3	73	9	6
70	64	12	3	64	10	3	64	8	10	64	7	4	64	5	10
60	55	7	8	55	5	11	55	4	8	55	3	5	55	2	2
50	46	3	1	46	1	7	46	0	7	45	19	6	45	18	5
40	36	18	5	36	17	3	36	16	5	36	15	7	36	14	9
30	27	13	10	27	12	11	27	12	4	27	11	8	27	11	1
20	18	9	2	18	8	8	18	8	2	18	7	9	18	7	4
10	9	4	7	9	4	4	9	4	1	9	3	10	9	3	8
9	8	6	1	8	5	10	8	5	8	8	5	6	8	5	3
8	7	7	8	7	7	5	7	7	3	7	7	1	7	6	11
7	6	9	2	6	9	0	6	8	10	6	8	8	6	8	7
6	5	10	9	5	10	7	5	10	5	5	10	4	5	10	2
5	4	12	3	4	12	2	4	12	0	4	11	11	4	11	10
4	3	13	10	3	13	8	3	13	7	3	13	6	3	13	5
3	2	15	4	2	15	3	2	15	2	2	15	2	2	15	1
2	1	16	11	1	16	10	1	16	9	1	16	9	1	16	8
1	—	18	5	—	18	5	—	18	5	—	18	4	—	18	4
S. 10	—	9	2	—	9	2	—	9	2	—	9	2	—	9	2
9	—	8	3	—	8	3	—	8	3	—	8	3	—	8	3
8	—	7	4	—	7	4	—	7	4	—	7	4	—	7	4
7	—	6	5	—	6	5	—	6	5	—	6	5	—	6	5
6	—	5	6	—	5	6	—	5	6	—	5	6	—	5	6
5	—	4	7	—	4	7	—	4	7	—	4	7	—	4	7
4	—	3	8	—	3	8	—	3	8	—	3	8	—	3	8
3	—	2	9	—	2	9	—	2	9	—	2	9	—	2	9
2	—	1	10	—	1	10	—	1	10	—	1	10	—	1	10
1	—	—	11	—	—	11	—	—	11	—	—	11	—	—	11
D. 6	—	—	5	—	—	5	—	—	5	—	—	5	—	—	5
5	—	—	4	—	—	4	—	—	4	—	—	4	—	—	4
4	—	—	3	—	—	3	—	—	3	—	—	3	—	—	3
3	—	—	2	—	—	2	—	—	2	—	—	2	—	—	2
2	—	—	2	—	—	2	—	—	2	—	—	2	—	—	2
1	—	—	1	—	—	1	—	—	1	—	—	1	—	—	1

Eng.	At 9			At 9⅛			At 9¼			At 9⅜			At 9½		
£.	£.	s.	d.	£.	s.	d.	£.	s.	d.	£.	s.	d.	£.	s.	d.
1000	1090	0	0	1091	5	0	1092	10	0	1093	15	0	1095	0	0
900	981	0	0	982	2	6	983	5	0	984	7	6	985	10	—
800	872	—	0	873	—	0	874	—	0	875	0	0	876	—	—
700	763	0	0	763	17	6	764	15	0	765	12	6	776	10	—
600	654	—	0	654	15	0	655	10	0	656	5	0	657	—	—
500	545	0	0	545	12	6	546	5	0	546	17	6	547	10	—
400	436	—	0	436	10	0	437	—	0	437	10	0	438	—	—
300	327	0	0	327	7	6	327	15	0	328	2	6	328	10	—
200	218	—	0	218	5	0	218	10	0	218	15	0	219	—	—
100	109	0	0	109	2	6	109	5	0	109	7	6	109	10	—
90	98	2	0	98	4	3	98	6	6	98	8	9	98	11	—
80	87	4	0	87	6	0	87	8	0	87	10	0	87	12	—
70	76	6	0	76	7	9	76	9	6	76	11	3	76	13	—
60	65	8	0	65	9	6	65	11	0	65	12	6	65	14	—
50	54	10	0	54	11	3	54	12	6	54	13	9	54	15	—
40	43	12	0	43	13	0	43	14	0	43	15	0	43	16	—
30	32	14	0	32	14	9	32	15	6	32	16	3	32	17	—
20	21	16	0	21	16	6	21	17	0	21	17	6	21	18	—
10	10	18	0	10	18	3	10	18	6	10	18	9	10	19	—
9	9	16	2	9	16	5	9	16	7	9	16	10	9	17	1
8	8	14	4	8	14	7	8	14	9	8	15	0	8	15	2
7	7	12	7	7	12	9	7	12	11	7	13	1	7	13	3
6	6	10	9	6	10	11	6	11	1	6	11	3	6	11	4
5	5	9	0	5	9	1	5	9	3	5	9	4	5	9	6
4	4	7	2	4	7	3	4	7	4	4	7	6	4	7	7
3	3	5	4	3	5	5	3	5	6	3	5	7	3	5	8
2	2	3	7	2	3	7	2	3	8	2	3	9	2	3	9
1	1	1	9	1	1	9	1	1	10	1	1	10	1	1	10
S. 10	0	10	10	0	10	11	0	10	11	0	10	11	0	10	11
9	0	9	9	0	9	9	0	9	10	0	9	10	0	9	10
8	0	8	8	0	8	6	0	8	8	0	8	9	0	8	9
7	0	7	7	0	7	7	0	7	7	0	7	7	0	7	8
6	0	6	6	0	6	6	0	6	6	0	6	6	0	6	6
5	0	5	5	0	5	5	0	5	5	0	5	5	0	5	5
4	0	4	4	0	4	4	0	4	4	0	4	4	0	4	4
3	0	3	3	0	3	3	0	3	3	0	3	3	0	3	3
2	0	2	2	0	2	2	0	2	2	0	2	2	0	2	2
1	0	1	1	0	1	1	0	1	1	0	1	1	0	1	1
D. 6	0	—	6	0	—	6	0	—	6	0	—	6	0	0	6
5	0	—	5	0	—	5	0	—	5	0	—	5	0	0	5
4	0	—	4	0	—	4	0	—	4	0	—	4	0	—	4
3	0	—	3	0	—	3	0	—	3	0	—	3	0	—	3
2	0	—	2	0	—	2	0	—	2	0	—	2	0	—	2
1	0	—	1	0	—	1	0	—	1	0	—	1	0	—	1

Irish	*At* 9			*At* 9⅛			*At* 9¼			*At* 9⅜			*At* 9½		
£.	£.	s.	d.	£.	s.	d.	£.	s.	d.	£.	s.	d.	£.	s.	d.
1000	917	8	7	916	7	7	915	6	7	914	5	8	913	4	10
900	825	13	9	824	14	10	823	15	11	822	17	1	821	18	4
800	733	18	10	733	2	1	732	5	3	731	8	6	730	11	10
700	642	4	0	641	9	3	640	14	7	640	0	0	639	5	4
600	550	9	2	549	16	6	549	3	11	548	11	5	547	18	10
500	458	14	3	458	3	9	457	13	3	457	2	10	456	12	5
400	366	19	5	366	11	0	366	2	7	365	14	3	365	5	11
300	275	4	7	274	18	3	274	11	11	274	5	8	273	19	5
200	183	9	8	183	5	6	183	1	3	182	17	1	182	12	11
100	91	14	10	91	12	9	91	10	8	91	8	6	91	6	5
90	82	11	4	82	9	5	82	7	7	82	5	8	82	3	10
80	73	7	10	73	6	2	73	4	6	73	2	10	73	1	2
70	64	4	4	64	2	11	64	1	5	64	0	0	63	18	6
60	55	0	11	54	19	7	54	18	4	54	17	1	54	15	10
50	45	17	5	45	16	4	45	15	4	45	14	3	45	13	2
40	36	13	11	36	13	1	36	12	3	36	11	5	36	10	7
30	27	10	5	27	9	9	27	9	2	27	8	6	27	7	11
20	18	6	11	18	6	6	18	6	1	18	5	8	18	5	3
10	9	3	5	9	3	3	9	3	0	9	2	10	9	2	7
9	8	5	1	8	4	11	8	4	9	8	4	6	8	4	4
8	7	6	9	7	6	7	7	6	5	7	6	3	7	6	1
7	6	8	5	6	8	3	6	8	1	6	8	0	6	7	10
6	5	10	1	5	9	11	5	9	10	5	9	8	5	9	5
5	4	11	8	4	11	7	4	11	6	4	11	5	4	11	3
4	3	13	4	3	13	3	3	13	2	3	13	1	3	13	—
3	2	15	0	2	14	11	2	14	11	2	14	10	2	14	9
2	1	16	8	1	16	7	1	16	7	1	16	6	1	16	6
1	0	18	4	0	18	3	0	18	3	0	18	3	0	18	3
S 10	0	9	2	0	9	2	0	9	1	0	9	1	0	9	1
9	0	8	3	0	8	3	0	8	2	0	8	2	0	8	2
8	0	7	4	0	7	4	0	7	3	0	7	3	0	7	3
7	0	6	5	0	6	5	0	6	4	0	6	4	0	6	4
6	0	5	6	0	5	6	0	5	5	0	5	5	0	5	5
5	0	4	7	0	4	7	0	4	6	0	4	6	0	4	6
4	0	3	8	0	3	8	0	3	7	0	3	7	0	3	7
3	0	2	9	0	2	9	0	2	9	0	2	8	0	2	8
2	0	1	10	0	1	10	0	1	10	0	1	10	0	1	9
1	0	0	11	0	0	11	0	0	11	0	0	11	0	0	11
D. 6	0	0	5	0	0	5	0	0	5	0	0	5	0	0	5
5	0	0	4	0	0	4	0	0	4	0	0	4	0	0	4
4	0	0	3	0	0	3	0	0	3	0	0	3	0	0	3
3	0	0	2	0	0	2	0	0	2	0	0	2	0	0	2
2	0	0	1	0	0	1	0	0	1	0	0	1	0	0	1
1	0	0	1	0	0	1	0	0	1	0	0	1	0	0	1

Eng.	At 9⅝			At 9¾			At 9⅞			At 10			At 10⅛		
£.	£.	s.	d.	£.	s.	d.	£.	s.	d.	£.	s.	d.	£.	s.	d.
1000	1096	5	—	1097	10	—	1098	15	—	1100	—	—	1101	5	—
900	986	12	6	987	15	—	988	17	6	990	—	—	991	2	6
800	877	—	—	878	—	—	879	—	—	880	—	—	881	—	—
700	767	7	6	768	5	—	769	2	6	770	—	—	770	17	6
600	657	15	—	658	10	—	659	5	—	660	—	—	660	15	—
500	548	2	6	548	15	—	549	7	6	550	—	—	550	12	6
400	438	10	—	439	—	—	439	10	—	440	—	—	440	10	—
300	328	17	6	329	5	—	329	12	6	330	—	—	330	7	6
200	219	5	0	219	10	—	219	15	—	220	—	—	220	5	—
100	109	12	6	109	15	—	109	17	6	110	—	—	110	2	6
90	98	13	3	98	15	6	98	17	9	99	—	—	99	2	3
80	87	14	—	87	16	—	87	18	—	88	—	—	88	2	—
70	76	14	9	76	16	6	76	18	3	77	—	—	77	1	9
60	65	15	6	65	17	—	65	18	6	66	—	—	66	1	6
50	54	16	3	54	17	6	54	18	9	55	—	—	55	1	3
40	43	17	—	43	18	—	43	19	—	44	—	—	44	1	—
30	32	17	9	32	18	6	32	19	3	33	—	—	33	0	9
20	21	18	6	21	19	—	21	19	6	22	—	—	22	0	6
10	10	19	3	10	19	6	10	19	9	11	—	—	11	0	3
9	9	17	3	9	17	6	9	17	9	9	18	—	9	18	2
8	8	15	4	8	15	7	8	15	9	8	16	—	8	16	2
7	7	13	5	7	13	7	7	13	9	7	14	—	7	14	2
6	6	11	6	6	11	8	6	11	10	6	12	—	6	12	1
5	5	9	7	5	9	9	5	9	10	5	10	—	5	10	1
4	4	7	8	4	7	9	4	7	10	4	8	—	4	8	1
3	3	5	9	3	5	10	3	5	11	3	6	—	3	6	0
2	2	3	10	2	3	10	2	3	11	2	4	—	2	4	0
1	1	1	11	1	1	11	1	1	11	1	2	—	1	2	0
S. 10	0	10	11	0	10	11	0	10	11	0	11	—	0	11	0
9	0	9	10	0	9	10	0	9	10	0	9	10	0	9	10
8	0	8	9	0	8	9	0	8	9	0	8	9	0	8	9
7	0	7	8	0	7	8	0	7	8	0	7	8	0	7	8
6	0	6	6	0	6	7	0	6	7	0	6	7	0	6	7
5	0	5	5	0	5	5	0	5	5	0	5	6	0	5	6
4	0	4	4	0	4	4	0	4	4	0	4	4	0	4	4
3	0	3	3	0	3	3	0	3	3	0	3	3	0	3	3
2	0	2	2	0	2	2	0	2	2	0	2	2	0	2	2
1	0	1	1	0	1	1	0	1	1	0	1	1	0	1	1
D. 6	0	—	6	0	—	6	0	—	6	0	—	6	0	—	6
5	0	—	5	0	—	5	0	—	5	0	—	5	0	—	5
4	0	—	4	0	—	4	0	—	4	0	—	4	0	—	4
3	0	—	3	0	—	3	0	—	3	0	—	3	0	—	3
2	0	—	2	0	—	2	0	—	2	0	—	2	0	—	2
1	0	—	1	0	—	1	0	—	1	0	—	1	0	—	1

Irish	At 9⅝			At 9¾			At 9⅞			At 10			At 10⅛		
£.	£.	s.	d.	£.	s.	d.	£.	s.	d.	£.	s.	d.	£.	s.	d.
1000	912	4	—	911	3	2	910	2	6	909	1	9	908	1	2
900	820	19	7	820	0	10	819	2	3	818	3	7	817	5	0
800	729	15	2	728	18	7	728	2	0	727	5	5	726	8	11
700	638	10	9	637	16	3	637	1	9	636	7	3	635	12	9
600	547	6	4	546	13	11	546	1	6	545	9	1	544	16	8
500	456	2	—	455	11	7	455	1	3	454	10	10	454	0	7
400	364	17	7	364	9	3	364	1	0	363	12	8	363	4	5
300	273	13	2	273	6	11	273	0	9	272	14	6	272	8	4
200	182	8	9	182	4	7	182	0	6	181	16	4	181	12	2
100	91	4	4	91	2	3	91	0	3	90	18	2	90	16	1
90	82	1	11	82	0	1	81	18	2	81	16	4	81	14	6
80	72	19	6	72	17	10	72	16	2	72	14	6	72	12	10
70	63	17	1	63	15	7	63	14	2	63	12	8	63	11	3
60	54	14	7	54	13	4	54	12	1	54	10	10	54	9	8
50	45	12	2	45	11	1	45	10	1	45	9	1	45	8	0
40	36	9	9	36	8	11	36	8	1	36	7	3	36	6	5
30	27	7	3	27	6	8	27	6	1	27	5	5	27	4	10
20	18	4	10	18	4	5	18	4	0	18	3	7	18	3	2
10	9	2	5	9	2	2	9	2	0	9	1	9	9	1	7
9	8	4	2	8	4	0	8	3	9	8	3	7	8	3	5
8	7	5	11	7	5	9	7	5	7	7	5	5	7	5	3
7	6	7	8	6	7	6	6	7	5	6	7	3	6	7	1
6	5	9	5	5	9	4	5	9	2	5	9	1	5	8	11
5	4	11	2	4	11	1	4	11	0	4	10	10	4	10	9
4	3	12	11	3	12	10	3	12	9	3	12	8	3	12	7
3	2	14	8	2	14	8	2	14	7	2	14	6	2	14	5
2	1	16	5	1	16	5	1	16	4	1	16	4	1	16	3
1	0	18	2	0	18	2	0	18	2	0	18	2	0	18	1
S. 10	0	9	1	0	9	1	0	9	1	0	9	1	0	9	1
9	0	8	2	0	8	2	0	8	2	0	8	2	0	8	2
8	0	7	3	0	7	3	0	7	3	0	7	3	0	7	3
7	0	6	4	0	6	4	0	6	4	0	6	4	0	6	4
6	0	5	5	0	5	5	0	5	5	0	5	5	0	5	5
5	0	4	6	0	4	6	0	4	6	0	4	6	0	4	6
4	0	3	7	0	3	7	0	3	7	0	3	7	0	3	7
3	0	2	8	0	2	8	0	2	8	0	2	8	0	2	8
2	0	1	9	0	1	9	0	1	9	0	1	9	0	1	9
1	0	0	11	0	0	10	0	0	10	0	0	10	0	0	10
D. 6	0	0	5	0	0	5	0	0	5	0	0	5	0	0	5
5	0	0	4	0	0	4	0	0	4	0	0	4	0	0	4
4	0	0	3	0	0	3	0	0	3	0	0	3	0	0	3
3	0	0	2	0	0	2	0	0	2	0	0	2	0	0	2
2	0	0	1	0	0	1	0	0	1	0	0	1	0	0	1
1	0	0	1	0	0	1	0	0	1	0	0	1	0	0	1

Eng.	At 10¼			At 10⅜			At 10½			At 10⅝			At 10¾		
£.	£.	s.	d.	£.	s.	d.	£.	s.	d.	£.	s.	d.	£.	s.	d.
1000	1102	10	—	1103	15	—	1105	—	—	1106	5	—	1107	10	—
900	992	5	—	993	7	6	994	10	0	995	12	6	996	15	—
800	882	—	—	883	—	—	884	—	—	885	—	—	886	—	—
700	771	15	—	772	12	6	773	10	0	774	7	6	775	5	—
600	661	10	—	662	5	—	663	—	—	663	15	—	664	10	—
500	551	5	—	551	17	6	552	10	—	553	2	6	553	15	—
400	441	—	—	441	10	—	442	—	—	442	10	—	443	—	—
300	330	15	—	331	2	6	331	10	—	331	17	6	332	5	—
200	220	10	—	220	15	—	221	—	—	221	5	—	221	10	—
100	110	5	—	110	7	6	110	10	—	110	12	6	110	15	—
90	99	4	6	99	6	9	99	9	0	99	11	3	99	13	6
80	88	4	—	88	6	—	88	8	—	88	10	—	88	12	—
70	77	3	6	77	5	3	77	7	—	77	8	9	77	10	6
60	66	3	—	66	4	6	66	6	—	66	7	6	66	9	—
50	55	2	6	55	3	9	55	5	0	55	6	3	55	7	6
40	44	2	—	44	3	—	44	4	0	44	5	—	44	6	—
30	31	3	6	33	2	3	33	3	0	33	3	9	33	4	6
20	22	1	—	22	1	6	22	2	0	22	2	6	22	3	0
10	11	0	6	11	0	9	11	1	0	11	1	3	11	1	6
9	9	18	5	9	18	8	9	18	10	9	19	1	9	19	4
8	8	16	4	8	16	7	8	16	9	8	17	—	8	17	2
7	7	14	4	7	14	6	7	14	8	7	14	10	7	15	0
6	6	12	3	6	12	5	6	12	7	6	12	9	6	12	10
5	5	10	3	5	10	4	5	10	6	5	10	7	5	10	9
4	4	8	2	4	8	3	4	8	4	4	8	6	4	8	7
3	3	6	1	3	6	2	3	6	3	3	6	4	3	6	5
2	2	4	1	2	4	1	2	4	2	2	4	3	2	4	3
1	1	2	0	1	2	0	1	2	1	1	2	1	1	2	1
S. 10	0	11	0	0	11	0	0	11	0	0	11	—	0	11	0
9	0	9	11	0	9	11	0	9	11	0	9	11	0	9	11
8	0	8	9	0	8	10	0	8	10	0	8	10	0	8	10
7	0	7	8	0	7	8	0	7	8	0	7	8	0	7	9
6	0	6	7	0	6	7	0	6	7	0	6	7	0	6	7
5	0	5	6	0	5	6	0	5	6	0	5	6	0	5	6
4	0	4	4	0	4	5	0	4	5	0	4	5	0	4	5
3	0	3	3	0	3	3	0	3	3	0	3	3	0	3	3
2	0	2	2	0	2	2	0	2	2	0	2	2	0	2	2
1	0	1	1	0	1	1	0	1	1	0	1	1	0	1	1
D. 6	0	—	6	0	—	6	0	—	6	0	—	6	0	—	6
5	0	—	5	0	—	5	0	—	5	0	—	5	0	—	5
4	0	—	4	0	—	4	0	—	4	0	—	4	0	—	4
3	0	—	3	0	—	3	0	—	3	0	—	3	0	—	3
2	0	—	2	0	—	2	0	—	2	0	—	2	0	—	2
1	0	—	1	0	—	1	0	—	1	0	—	1	0	—	1

Irish	At 10¼			At 10⅜			At 10½			At 10⅝			At 10¾		
£.	£.	s.	d.	£.	s.	d.	£.	s.	d.	£.	s.	d.	£.	s.	d.
1000	907	0	7	906	—	—	904	19	6	903	19	1	902	18	8
900	816	6	6	815	8	—	814	9	7	813	11	2	812	12	9
800	725	12	5	724	16	—	723	19	7	723	3	3	722	6	11
700	634	18	4	634	4	—	633	9	8	632	15	4	632	1	1
600	544	4	4	543	12	—	542	19	8	542	7	5	541	15	2
500	453	10	3	453	—	—	452	9	9	451	19	6	451	9	4
400	362	16	2	362	8	—	361	19	9	361	11	7	361	3	5
300	272	2	2	271	16	—	271	9	10	271	3	8	270	17	7
200	181	8	1	181	4	—	180	19	10	180	15	9	180	11	8
100	90	14	0	90	12	—	90	9	11	90	7	10	90	5	10
90	81	12	7	81	10	9	81	8	11	81	7	1	81	5	3
80	72	11	3	72	9	7	72	7	11	72	6	3	72	4	8
70	63	9	10	63	8	4	63	6	11	63	5	6	63	4	1
60	54	8	5	54	7	2	54	5	11	54	4	8	54	3	6
50	45	7	0	45	6	0	45	4	11	45	3	11	45	2	11
40	36	5	7	36	4	9	36	3	11	36	3	2	36	2	4
30	27	4	2	27	3	7	27	2	11	27	2	4	27	1	9
20	18	2	9	18	2	4	18	1	11	18	1	7	18	1	2
10	9	1	4	9	1	2	9	1	0	9	0	9	9	0	7
9	8	3	3	8	3	1	8	2	10	8	2	8	8	2	6
8	7	5	1	7	4	11	7	4	9	7	4	7	7	4	5
7	6	6	11	6	6	10	6	6	8	6	6	6	6	6	4
6	5	8	10	5	8	8	5	8	7	5	8	5	5	8	4
5	4	10	8	4	10	7	4	10	6	4	10	4	4	10	3
4	3	12	6	3	12	5	3	12	4	3	12	3	3	12	2
3	2	14	5	2	14	4	2	14	3	2	14	2	2	14	2
2	1	16	3	1	16	2	1	16	2	1	16	1	1	16	1
1	0	18	1	0	18	1	0	18	1	0	18	1	0	18	0
S. 10	0	9	0	0	9	0	0	9	0	0	9	0	0	9	0
9	0	8	2	0	8	1	0	8	1	0	8	1	0	8	1
8	0	7	3	0	7	3	0	7	2	0	7	2	0	7	2
7	0	6	4	0	6	4	0	6	4	0	6	3	0	6	3
6	0	5	5	0	5	5	0	5	5	0	5	5	0	5	5
5	0	4	6	0	4	6	0	4	6	0	4	6	0	4	6
4	0	3	7	0	3	7	0	3	7	0	3	7	0	3	7
3	0	2	8	0	2	8	0	2	8	0	2	8	0	2	8
2	0	1	9	0	1	9	0	1	9	0	1	9	0	1	9
1	0	0	10	0	0	10	0	0	10	0	0	10	0	0	10
D. 6	0	0	5	0	0	5	0	0	5	0	0	5	0	0	5
5	0	0	4	0	0	4	0	0	4	0	0	4	0	0	4
4	0	0	3	0	0	3	0	0	3	0	0	3	0	0	3
3	0	0	2	0	0	2	0	0	2	0	0	2	0	0	2
2	0	0	1	0	0	1	0	0	1	0	0	1	0	0	1
1	0	0	1	0	0	1	0	0	1	0	0	1	0	0	1

Eng.	At 10⅞			At 11			At 11⅛			At 11¼			At 11⅜		
£.	£.	s.	d.	£.	s.	d.	£.	s.	d.	£.	s.	d.	£.	s.	d.
1000	1108	15	—	1110	—	—	1111	5	0	1112	10	0	1113	15	0
900	997	17	6	999	—	—	1000	2	6	1001	5	0	1002	7	6
800	887	—	—	888	—	—	889	0	0	890	0	0	891	0	0
700	776	2	6	777	—	—	777	17	6	778	15	0	779	12	6
600	665	5	—	666	—	—	666	15	0	667	10	0	668	5	0
500	554	7	6	555	—	—	555	12	6	556	5	0	556	17	6
400	443	10	—	444	—	—	444	10	0	445	0	0	445	10	0
300	332	12	6	333	—	—	333	7	6	333	15	0	334	2	6
200	221	15	0	222	—	—	222	5	0	222	10	0	222	15	0
100	110	17	6	111	—	—	111	2	6	111	5	0	111	7	6
90	99	15	9	99	18	—	100	0	3	100	2	6	100	4	9
80	88	14	0	88	16	—	88	18	0	89	0	0	89	2	0
70	77	12	3	77	14	—	77	15	9	77	17	6	77	19	3
60	66	10	6	66	12	—	66	13	6	66	15	0	66	16	6
50	55	8	9	55	10	—	55	11	3	55	12	6	55	13	9
40	44	7	0	44	8	—	44	9	0	44	10	0	44	11	0
30	33	5	3	33	6	—	33	6	9	33	7	6	33	8	3
20	22	3	6	22	4	—	22	4	6	22	5	0	22	5	6
10	11	1	9	11	2	—	11	2	3	11	2	6	11	2	9
9	9	19	6	9	19	9	10	0	0	10	0	0	10	0	5
8	8	17	4	8	17	7	8	17	9	8	18	0	8	18	2
7	7	15	2	7	15	4	7	15	6	7	15	9	7	15	11
6	6	13	0	6	13	2	6	13	4	6	13	6	6	13	7
5	5	10	10	5	11	0	5	11	1	5	11	3	5	11	4
4	4	8	8	4	8	9	4	8	10	4	9	0	4	9	1
3	3	6	6	3	6	7	3	6	8	3	6	9	3	6	9
2	2	4	4	2	4	4	2	4	5	2	4	6	2	4	6
1	1	2	2	1	2	2	1	2	2	1	2	3	1	2	3
S. 10	0	11	1	0	11	1	0	11	1	0	11	1	0	11	1
9	0	9	11	0	9	11	0	10	0	0	10	0	0	10	0
8	0	8	10	0	8	10	0	8	10	0	8	10	0	8	10
7	0	7	9	0	7	9	0	7	9	0	7	9	0	7	9
6	0	6	7	0	6	7	0	6	8	0	6	8	0	6	8
5	0	5	6	0	5	6	0	5	6	0	5	6	0	5	6
4	0	4	5	0	4	5	0	4	5	0	4	5	0	4	5
3	0	3	3	0	3	4	0	3	4	0	3	4	0	3	4
2	0	2	2	0	2	2	0	2	2	0	2	2	0	2	2
1	0	1	1	0	1	1	0	1	1	0	1	1	0	1	1
D. 6	0	0	6	0	0	6	0	0	6	0	0	6	0	0	6
5	0	0	5	0	0	5	0	0	5	0	0	5	0	0	5
4	0	0	4	0	0	4	0	0	4	0	0	4	0	0	4
3	0	0	3	0	0	3	0	0	3	0	0	3	0	0	3
2	0	0	2	0	0	2	0	0	2	0	0	2	0	0	2
1	0	0	1	0	0	1	0	0	1	0	0	1	0	0	1

Irish	At 10⅞			At 11			At 11⅛			At 11¼			At 11⅜		
£.	£.	s.	d.	£.	s.	d.	£.	s.	d.	£.	s.	d.	£.	s.	d.
1000	901	18	3	900	18	0	899	17	9	898	17	6	897	17	4
900	811	14	5	810	16	2	809	17	11	808	19	9	808	1	7
800	721	10	7	720	14	4	719	8	2	719	2	0	718	5	10
700	631	6	9	630	12	7	629	18	5	629	4	3	628	10	1
600	541	2	11	540	10	9	539	18	7	539	6	6	538	14	4
500	450	19	1	450	9	0	449	18	10	449	8	9	448	18	8
400	360	15	3	360	7	2	359	19	1	359	11	0	359	2	11
300	270	11	5	270	5	4	269	19	3	269	13	3	269	7	2
200	180	7	7	180	3	7	179	19	6	179	15	6	179	11	5
100	90	3	10	90	1	9	89	19	9	89	17	9	89	15	8
90	81	3	5	81	1	7	80	19	9	80	17	11	80	16	1
80	72	3	0	72	1	5	71	19	9	71	18	2	71	16	7
70	63	2	8	63	1	3	62	19	10	62	18	5	62	17	0
60	54	2	3	54	1	1	53	19	10	53	18	7	53	17	5
50	45	1	11	45	0	10	44	19	10	44	18	10	44	17	10
40	36	1	6	36	0	8	35	19	10	35	19	1	35	18	3
30	27	1	1	27	0	6	26	19	11	26	19	3	26	18	8
20	18	0	9	18	0	4	17	19	11	17	19	6	17	19	1
10	9	0	4	9	0	2	8	19	11	8	19	9	8	19	6
9	8	2	4	8	2	2	8	1	11	8	1	9	8	1	7
8	7	4	3	7	4	1	7	3	11	7	3	9	7	3	7
7	6	6	3	6	6	1	6	5	11	6	5	10	6	5	8
6	5	8	2	5	8	1	5	7	11	5	7	10	5	7	8
5	4	10	2	4	10	1	4	9	11	4	9	10	4	9	9
4	3	12	1	3	12	0	3	11	11	3	11	10	3	11	10
3	2	14	1	2	14	0	2	13	11	2	13	11	2	13	10
2	1	16	0	1	16	0	1	16	0	1	15	11	1	15	11
1	0	18	0	0	18	0	0	18	0	0	17	11	0	17	11
S. 10	0	9	0	0	9	0	0	9	0	0	8	11	0	8	11
9	0	8	1	0	8	1	0	8	1	0	8	1	0	8	1
8	0	7	2	0	7	2	0	7	2	0	7	2	0	7	2
7	0	6	3	0	6	3	0	6	3	0	6	3	0	6	3
6	0	5	4	0	5	4	0	5	4	0	5	4	0	5	4
5	0	4	6	0	4	6	0	4	6	0	4	5	0	4	5
4	0	3	7	0	3	7	0	3	7	0	3	7	0	3	7
3	0	2	8	0	2	8	0	2	8	0	2	8	0	2	8
2	0	1	9	0	1	9	0	1	9	0	1	9	0	1	9
1	0	0	10	0	0	10	0	0	10	0	0	10	0	0	10
D. 6	0	0	5	0	0	5	0	0	5	0	0	5	0	0	5
5	0	0	4	0	0	4	0	0	4	0	0	4	0	0	4
4	0	0	3	0	0	3	0	0	3	0	0	3	0	0	3
3	0	0	2	0	0	2	0	0	2	0	0	2	0	0	2
2	0	0	1	0	0	1	0	0	1	0	0	1	0	0	1
1	0	0	1	0	0	1	0	0	1	0	0	1	0	0	1

Eng.	At 11½			At 11⅝			At 11¾			At 11⅞			At 12		
l.	£.	s.	d.	£.	s.	d.	£.	s.	d.	£.	s.	d.	£.	s.	d.
1000	1115	0	0	1116	5	0	1117	10	0	1118	15	0	1120	0	0
900	1103	10	0	1004	12	6	1005	15	0	1006	17	6	1008	0	0
800	892	0	0	893	0	0	894	0	0	895	10	0	896	0	0
700	780	10	0	781	7	6	782	5	0	783	2	6	784	0	0
600	669	0	0	669	15	0	670	10	0	671	5	0	672	0	0
500	557	10	0	558	2	6	558	15	0	559	7	6	560	0	0
400	446	0	0	446	10	0	447	0	0	447	10	0	448	0	0
300	334	10	0	334	17	6	335	5	0	335	12	6	336	0	0
200	223	0	0	223	5	0	223	10	0	223	15	0	224	0	0
100	111	10	0	111	12	6	111	15	0	111	17	6	112	0	0
90	100	7	0	100	9	3	100	11	6	100	13	9	100	16	0
80	89	4	0	89	6	0	89	8	0	89	10	0	89	12	0
70	78	1	0	78	2	9	78	4	6	78	6	3	78	8	0
60	66	18	0	66	19	6	67	1	0	67	2	6	67	4	0
50	55	15	0	55	16	3	55	17	6	55	18	9	56	0	0
40	44	12	0	44	13	0	44	14	0	44	15	0	44	16	0
30	33	9	0	33	9	9	33	10	6	33	11	3	33	12	0
20	22	6	0	22	6	6	22	7	0	22	7	6	22	8	0
10	11	3	0	11	3	3	11	3	6	11	3	9	11	4	0
9	10	0	8	10	0	11	10	1	1	10	1	4	10	1	7
8	8	18	4	8	18	7	8	18	9	8	19	0	8	19	2
7	7	16	1	7	16	3	7	16	5	7	16	7	7	16	9
6	6	13	9	6	13	11	6	14	1	6	14	3	6	14	4
5	5	11	6	5	11	7	5	11	9	5	11	10	5	12	0
4	4	9	2	4	9	3	4	9	4	4	9	6	4	9	7
3	3	6	10	3	6	11	3	7	0	3	7	1	3	7	2
2	2	4	7	2	4	7	2	4	8	2	4	9	2	4	9
1	1	2	3	1	2	3	1	2	4	1	2	4	1	2	4
S. 10	0	11	1	0	11	2	0	11	2	0	11	2	0	11	2
9	0	10	0	0	10	0	0	10	0	0	10	0	0	10	1
8	0	8	11	0	8	11	0	8	11	0	8	11	0	8	11
7	0	7	9	0	7	9	0	7	9	0	7	10	0	7	10
6	0	6	8	0	6	8	0	6	8	0	6	8	0	6	8
5	0	5	6	0	5	7	0	5	7	0	5	7	0	5	7
4	0	4	5	0	4	5	0	4	5	0	4	5	0	4	5
3	0	3	4	0	3	4	0	3	4	0	3	4	0	3	4
2	0	2	2	0	2	2	0	2	2	0	2	2	0	2	2
1	0	1	1	0	1	1	0	1	1	0	1	1	0	1	1
D. 6	0	0	6	0	0	6	0	0	6	0	0	6	0	0	6
5	0	0	5	0	0	5	0	0	5	0	0	5	0	0	5
4	0	0	4	0	0	4	0	0	4	0	0	4	0	0	4
3	0	0	3	0	0	3	0	0	3	0	0	3	0	0	3
2	0	0	2	0	0	2	0	0	2	0	0	2	0	0	2
1	0	0	1	0	0	1	0	0	1	0	0	1	0	0	1

Irish	At $11\frac{1}{2}$			At $11\frac{5}{8}$			At $11\frac{3}{4}$			At $11\frac{7}{8}$			At 12		
£.	£.	s.	d.	£	s.	d.	£.	s.	d.	£.	s.	d.	£.	s.	d.
1000	896	17	2	895	17	1	894	17	1	893	17	1	892	17	1
900	807	3	5	806	5	5	805	7	4	804	9	4	803	11	5
800	717	9	9	716	13	8	715	17	8	715	1	8	714	5	8
700	627	16	0	627	1	11	626	7	11	625	13	11	625	0	0
600	538	2	3	537	10	3	536	18	3	536	6	3	535	14	3
500	448	8	7	447	18	6	447	8	6	446	18	6	446	8	6
400	358	14	10	358	6	10	357	18	10	357	10	10	357	2	10
300	269	1	1	268	15	1	268	9	1	268	3	1	267	17	1
200	179	7	5	179	3	5	178	19	5	178	15	5	178	11	5
100	89	13	8	89	11	8	89	9	8	89	7	8	89	5	8
90	80	14	4	80	12	6	80	10	8	80	8	11	80	7	1
80	71	14	11	71	13	4	71	11	9	71	10	2	71	8	6
70	62	15	7	62	14	2	62	12	9	62	11	4	62	10	0
60	53	16	2	53	15	0	53	13	9	53	12	7	53	11	5
50	44	16	10	44	15	10	44	14	10	44	13	10	44	12	10
40	35	17	5	35	16	8	35	15	10	35	15	1	35	14	3
30	26	18	1	26	17	6	26	16	11	26	16	3	26	15	8
20	17	18	8	17	18	4	17	17	11	17	17	6	17	7	1
10	8	19	4	8	19	2	8	18	11	8	18	9	8	18	6
9	8	1	5	8	1	3	8	1	0	8	0	10	8	0	8
8	7	3	6	7	3	4	7	3	2	7	3	0	7	2	10
7	6	5	6	6	5	5	6	5	3	6	5	1	6	5	0
6	5	7	7	5	7	6	5	7	4	5	7	3	5	7	1
5	4	9	8	4	9	7	4	9	5	4	9	4	4	9	3
4	3	11	9	3	11	8	3	11	7	3	11	6	3	11	5
3	2	13	9	2	13	9	2	13	8	2	13	7	2	13	6
2	1	15	10	1	15	10	1	15	9	1	15	9	1	15	8
1	0	17	11	0	17	11	0	17	10	0	17	10	0	17	10
S. 10	0	8	11	0	8	11	0	8	11	0	8	11	0	8	11
9	0	8	0	0	8	0	0	8	0	0	8	0	0	8	0
8	0	7	2	0	7	2	0	7	1	0	7	1	0	7	1
7	0	6	3	0	6	3	0	6	3	0	6	3	0	6	3
6	0	5	4	0	5	4	0	5	4	0	5	4	0	5	4
5	0	4	5	0	4	5	0	4	5	0	4	5	0	4	5
4	0	3	7	0	3	7	0	3	7	0	3	6	0	3	6
3	0	2	8	0	2	8	0	2	8	0	2	8	0	2	8
2	0	1	9	0	1	9	0	1	9	0	1	9	0	1	9
1	0	0	10	0	0	10	0	0	10	0	0	10	0	0	10
D. 6	0	0	5	0	0	5	0	0	5	0	0	5	0	0	5
5	0	0	4	0	0	4	0	0	4	0	0	4	0	0	4
4	0	0	3	0	0	3	0	0	3	0	0	3	0	0	3
3	0	0	2	0	0	2	0	0	2	0	0	2	0	0	2
2	0	0	1	0	0	1	0	0	1	0	0	1	0	0	1
1	0	0	1	0	0	1	0	0	1	0	0	1	0	0	1

The following Decimal Multipliers are fitted to the Rates of Exchange between England and France, by which if any Sum be multiplied, the Product will be the Money into which it was intended to be exchanged: attending only to the following Rule.

ENGLISH into FRENCH.				FRENCH into ENGLISH.			
RATE.8th	Multpr.	Rate	Multpr.	Rate	Mulpr	Rate	Mulpr
30d.—	24.	35—	20.5712	30—	.04166	35—	.04861
1	23.9004	1	20.4984	1	.04184	1	.04878
2	23.8008	2	20.4254	2	.04201	2	.04896
3	23.7038	3	20.3534	3	.04218	3	.04913
4	23.6066	4	20.2816	4	.04236	4	.04930
5	23.5054	5	20.2104	5	.04253	5	.04948
6	23.4146	6	20.1398	6	.04271	6	.04965
7	23.32	7	20.0696	7	.04288	7	.04982
31—	23.2258	36—	20.	31—	.04306	36—	.05
1	23.1325	1	19.9307	1	.04322	1	.05017
2	23.04	2	19.8620	2	.0434	2	.05034
3	22.9484	3	19.7938	3	.04357	3	.05052
4	22.857	4	19.7260	4	.04375	4	.05069
5	22.7166	5	19.6587	5	.04392	5	.05087
6	22.677	6	19.5918	6	.04401	6	.05104
7	22.5884	7	19.5254	7	.04427	7	.05121
32—	22.5	37—	19.4596	32—	.04444	37—	.05139
1	22.4125	1	19.3939	1	.04462	1	.05156
2	22.3254	2	19.3288	2	.04479	2	.05173
3	22.2396	3	19.2642	3	.04496	3	.05191
4	22.1538	4	19.2	4	.04514	4	.05208
5	22.0692	5	19.1362	5	.04531	5	.05226
6	21.9846	6	19.0728	6	.04541	6	.05243
7	21.9012	7	19.0099	7	.04566	7	.0526
33—	21.8184	38—	18.9475	33—	.04583	38—	.05278
1	21.7358	1	18.8852	1	.04601	1	.05295
2	21.6542	2	18.8235	2	.04618	2	.05312
3	21.5729	3	18.7622	3	.04635	3	.05329
4	21.4925	4	18.7011	4	.04653	4	.05347
5	21.4125	5	18.6407	5	.04670	5	.05364
6	21.3334	6	18.5806	6	.04687	6	.05382
7	21.2546	7	18.5209	7	.04705	7	.05399
34—	21.1758	39—	18.4616	34—	.04722	39—	.05417
1	21.0988	1	18.4025	1	.0474	1	.05434
2	21.022	2	18.3439	2	.04757	2	.05451
3	20.9454	3	18.2857	3	.04774	3	.05469
4	20.8706	4	18.2278	4	.04792	4	.05486
5	20.7942	5	18.1703	5	.04809	5	.05503
6	20.7196	6	18.1132	6	.04826	6	.05521
7	20.645	7	18.0564	7	.04844	7	.05538

EXCHANGE *between* England *and* France.

At Par

1 Ecu or Crown	3 Livres	2s.	5d.	365	parts pence
1 Livre	20 Sous	0	9	788	Do. Do.
1 Sou	12 Deniers	0	0	488	Do. Do.
1 Denier		0	0	041	Do. Do.

What will be the value of *l*.450 in French Money at 32½ per Ecu?

Common operation.

As 32½ pence is to 1 Ecu, so is *l*.450 to 9969 *Livs.* 4 *Sous* 7 *Dens.*

What will be the value of 9969 *Livs.* 4 *Sous* 7 *Dens.* in English Money at 32½ per Ecu?

As 1 Ecu is to 32½ pence, so is 9969 *Livs* 4 *Sous* 7 *Dens.* to *l*.450. Engl.

As Livres, Sous and Deniers, and Pounds Shillings and Pence bear the same proportions one to another, the following Table of parts will answer for both.

For Sous or Shillings the Livre or Pound being the Integer.				For Deniers or pence. the same Integer.	
1	.05	13	.65	1	.004
2	.1	14	.7	2	.008
3	.15	15	.75	3	.012
4	.2	16	.8	4	.016
5	.25	17	.85	5	.02
6	.3	18	.9	6	.025
7	.35	19	.95	7	.029
8	.4	20	1.	8	.034
9	.45			9	.038
10	.5			10	.042
11	.55			11	.046
12	.6			12	.05

Use of the foregoing Table.

Let the Shillings and Pence or Livres and Deniers be reduced into Decimal parts of a Pound or Livre by the Table of Parts, and then let the Money to be exchanged be multiplied by the Tabular Number opposite to the given Rate. I have chosen the easiest Examples, because the most obvious to the reader.

Examples.

What will be the value of *l*.450 10s. English in French Money at 36 pence per Ecu.

English Money	*l*.450 5
Tabu. Numb. at 36 per	20
product by Multipl.	9010 livres

By the common Tables at 36 pEcu

l.400	is	8000
50	is	1000
10s.	is	10
		9010 livres

What will be the value of 9010 Liv. in Eng. Money, at 36 pr. Ecu.

9010 French Money	
.05	Tabular number at 36
450.50	Equal to 450*l*. 10s.

By the common Tables at 36

5000 Livres	is	*l*.250
4000	is	200
10	is	10
		450*l*. 10s.

Eng.	At 30 d.			$30\frac{1}{8}$ d.			$30\frac{1}{4}$ d.			$30\frac{1}{8}$ d.			$30\frac{1}{2}$ d.		
£.	L.	s.	d.	L.	s.	d.	L.	s.	d.	L.	s.	d.	L.	s.	d.
1000	24000			23900	8	4	23801	13	1	23703	14	1	23606	11	2
900	21600			21510	7	6	21421	9	9	21333	6	8	21245	18	0
800	19200			19120	6	8	19041	6	5	18962	19	3	18885	4	11
700	16800			16730	5	10	16661	3	2	16592	11	10	16524	11	10
600	14400			14340	5	0	14280	19	10	14222	4	5	14163	18	8
500	12000			11950	4	2	11900	16	6	11851	17	0	11803	5	7
400	9600			9560	3	4	9520	13	3	9481	9	8	9442	12	6
300	7200			7170	2	6	7140	9	11	7111	2	3	7081	19	4
200	4800			4780	1	8	4760	6	7	4740	14	10	4721	6	3
100	2400			2390	0	10	2380	3	4	2370	7	5	2360	13	1
90	2160			2151	0	9	2142	3	0	2133	6	8	2124	11	10
80	1920			1912	0	8	1904	2	8	1896	5	11	1888	10	6
70	1680			1673	0	7	1666	2	4	1659	5	2	1652	9	2
60	1440			1434	0	6	1428	2	0	1422	4	5	1416	7	10
50	1200			1195	0	5	1190	1	8	1185	3	8	1180	6	7
40	960			956	0	4	952	1	4	948	3	0	944	5	3
30	720			717	0	3	714	1	0	711	2	3	708	3	11
20	480			478	0	2	476	0	8	474	1	6	472	2	8
10	240			239	0	1	238	0	4	237	0	9	236	1	4
9	216			215	2	1	214	4	4	213	6	8	212	9	2
8	192			191	4	1	190	8	3	189	12	7	188	17	1
7	168			167		1	166	12	3	165	18	6	165	4	11
6	144			143	8	1	142	16	2	142	4	5	141	12	9
5	120			119	10	1	119	0	2	118	10	4	118	0	8
4	96			95	12	0	95	4	2	94	16	4	94	8	6
3	72			71	14	0	71	8	1	71	2	3	70	16	5
2	48			47	16	0	47	12	1	47	8	2	47	4	3
1	24			23	18	0	23	16	0	23	14	1	23	12	2
S. 10	12			11	19	0	11	18	0	11	17	0	11	16	1
9	10	16		10	15	0	10	14	3	10	13	4	10	12	6
8	9	12		9	11	2	9	10	5	9	9	8	9	8	10
7	8	8		8	7	4	8	6	7	8	5	11	8	5	3
6	7	4		7	3	5	7	2	10	7	2	3	7	1	8
5	6	0		5	19	6	5	19	0	5	18	6	5	18	0
4	4	16		4	15	7	4	15	3	4	14	10	4	14	5
3	3	12		3	11	8	3	11	5	3	11	1	3	10	10
2	2	8		2	7	10	2	7	7	2	7	5	2	7	3
1	1	4		1	3	11	1	3	10	1	3	8	1	3	7
D. 6	0	12		0	11	11	0	11	11	0	11	10	0	11	10
5	0	10		0	10	0	0	9	11	0	9	11	0	9	10
4	0	8		0	8	0	0	7	11	0	7	11	0	7	10
3	0	6		0	6	0	0	5	11	0	5	11	0	5	11
2	0	4		0	4	0	0	4	0	0	3	11	0	3	11
1	0	2		0	2	0	0	2	0	0	2	0	0	2	0

French	30 d.			30⅛ d.			30¼ d.			30⅜ d.			30½ d.		
Livres	£.	s.	d.	£.	s.	d.	£.	s.	d.	£.	s.	d.	£.	s.	d.
10000	416	13	0	418	8	0	420	2	9	421	17	6	423	12	2
5000	208	6	6	209	4	0	210	1	4	210	18	9	211	16	1
4000	166	13	2	167	7	2	168	1	1	168	15	0	169	8	10
3000	124	19	10	125	10	5	126	0	10	126	11	3	127	1	8
2000	83	6	7	83	13	7	84	0	6	84	7	6	84	14	5
1000	41	13	3	41	16	9	42	0	3	42	3	9	42	7	2
900	37	10	0	37	13	1	37	16	3	37	19	4	38	2	6
800	33	6	8	33	9	5	33	12	2	33	15	0	33	17	9
700	29	3	4	29	5	9	29	8	2	29	10	7	29	13	0
600	25	0	0	25	2	1	25	4	2	25	6	3	25	8	4
500	20	16	7	20	18	4	21	0	1	21	1	10	21	3	7
400	16	13	4	16	14	8	16	16	1	16	17	6	16	18	10
300	12	10	0	12	11	0	12	12	1	12	13	1	12	14	2
200	8	6	8	8	7	4	8	8	0	8	8	9	8	9	5
100	4	3	4	4	3	8	4	4	0	4	4	4	4	4	8
90	3	15	0	3	15	3	3	15	7	3	15	11	3	16	3
80	3	6	8	3	6	11	3	7	2	3	7	6	3	7	9
70	2	18	4	2	18	6	2	18	9	2	19	0	2	19	3
60	2	10	0	2	10	2	2	10	5	2	10	7	2	10	10
50	2	1	8	2	1	10	2	2	0	2	2	2	2	2	4
40	1	13	4	1	13	5	1	13	7	1	13	9	1	13	10
30	1	5	0	1	5	1	1	5	2	1	5	3	1	5	5
20	0	16	8	0	16	8	0	16	9	0	16	10	0	16	11
10	0	8	4	0	8	4	0	8	4	0	8	5	0	8	5
9	0	7	6	0	7	6	0	7	6	0	7	7	0	7	7
8	0	6	8	0	6	8	0	6	8	0	6	9	0	6	9
7	0	5	10	0	5	10	0	5	10	0	5	10	0	5	11
6	0	5	0	0	5	0	0	5	0	0	5	0	0	5	1
5	0	4	2	0	4	2	0	4	2	0	4	2	0	4	2
4	0	3	4	0	3	4	0	3	4	0	3	4	0	3	4
3	0	2	6	0	2	6	0	2	6	0	2	6	0	2	6
2	0	1	8	0	1	8	0	1	8	0	1	8	0	1	8
1	0	0	10	0	0	10	0	0	10	0	0	10	0	0	10
Sou 10	0	0	5	0	0	5	0	0	5	0	0	5	0	0	5
9	0	0	4	0	0	4	0	0	4	0	0	4	0	0	4
8	0	0	4	0	0	4	0	0	4	0	0	4	0	0	4
7	0	0	3	0	0	3	0	0	3	0	0	3	0	0	3
6	0	0	3	0	0	3	0	0	3	0	0	3	0	0	3
5	0	0	2	0	0	2	0	0	2	0	0	2	0	0	2
4	0	0	2	0	0	2	0	0	2	0	0	2	0	0	2
3	0	0	1	0	0	1	0	0	1	0	0	1	0	0	1
2	0	0	1	0	0	1	0	0	1	0	0	1	0	0	1
1	0	0	0	0	0	0	0	0	0	0	0	0	0	0	0
Den. 6	0	0	0	0	0	0	0	0	0	0	0	0	0	0	0

Eng.	At 30⅝ d.			At 30¾ d.			At 30⅞ d.			At 31 d.			At 31⅛ d.		
£.	L.	s.	d.	L.	s.	d.	L.	s.	d.	L.	s.	d.	L.	s.	d.
1000	23510	4	1	23414	12	3	23319	16	9	23225	16	2	23132	10	7
900	21159	3	8	21073	3	5	20987	17	1	20903	4	6	20819	[illegible]	7
800	18808	3	3	18731	14	2	18655	17	5	18580	12	11	18506	[illegible]	6
700	16457	2	10	16390	4	11	16323	17	9	16258	1	3	16192	15	5
600	14106	2	5	14048	15	7	13991	18	1	13935	9	8	13870	10	4
500	11755	2	0	11707	6	4	11659	18	5	11612	18	1	11566	5	4
400	9404	1	8	9365	17	1	9327	18	8	9290	6	5	9253	0	3
300	7053	1	3	7024	7	10	6995	19	0	6967	14	10	6939	15	2
200	4702	0	10	4682	18	6	4663	19	4	4645	3	3	4626	10	1
100	2351	0	5	2341	9	3	2331	19	8	2322	11	7	2313	5	1
90	2115	18	4	2107	6	4	2098	15	9	2090	6	5	2081	8	7
80	1880	16	4	1873	3	5	1865	11	9	1858	1	4	1850	12	1
70	1645	14	3	1639	0	6	1632	7	9	1625	16	2	1619	5	7
60	1410	12	3	1404	17	7	1399	3	10	1393	11	0	1387	19	0
50	1175	10	2	1170	14	8	1165	19	10	1161	5	10	1156	12	6
40	940	8	2	936	11	9	932	15	10	929	0	8	925	6	0
30	705	6	2	702	8	9	699	11	11	696	15	6	693	19	6
20	470	4	1	468	5	10	466	7	11	464	10	4	462	13	0
10	235	2	1	234	2	11	233	4	0	232	5	2	231	6	6
9	211	11	10	210	14	8	209	17	7	209	0	8	208	3	10
8	188	1	8	187	6	4	186	11	2	185	16	2	185	1	3
7	164	11	5	163	18	1	163	4	9	162	11	7	161	18	7
6	141	1	3	140	9	9	139	18	5	139	7	[illegible]	138	5	11
5	117	11	0	117	1	6	116	12	0	116	2	7	115	13	3
4	94	0	10	93	13	2	93	5	7	92	18	1	92	10	7
3	70	10	7	70	4	11	69	19	2	69	13	7	69	7	11
2	47	0	5	46	16	7	46	12	10	46	9	[illegible]	46	5	4
1	23	10	3	23	8	4	23	6	5	23	4	6	23	2	8
S. 10	11	15	1	11	14	2	11	13	2	11	12	3	11	11	4
9	10	11	7	10	10	9	10	9	11	10	9	0	10	8	2
8	9	8	1	9	7	4	9	6	7	9	5	10	9	5	1
7	8	4	7	8	3	11	8	3	3	8	2	7	8	1	11
6	7	1	1	7	0	6	6	19	11	6	19	4	6	18	10
5	5	17	7	5	17	1	5	16	7	5	16	2	5	15	8
4	4	14	1	4	13	8	4	13	3	4	12	11	4	12	6
3	3	10	6	3	10	3	3	10	0	3	9	8	3	9	5
2	2	7	0	2	6	10	2	6	8	2	6	5	2	6	3
1	1	3	6	1	3	5	1	3	4	1	3	3	1	3	2
D. 6	0	11	9	0	11	9	0	11	8	0	11	7	0	11	7
5	0	9	10	0	9	9	0	9	9	0	9	8	0	9	8
4	0	7	10	0	7	10	0	7	9	0	7	9	0	7	9
3	0	5	11	0	5	10	0	5	10	0	5	10	0	5	9
2	0	3	11	0	3	10	0	3	10	0	3	10	0	3	10
1	0	2	0	0	1	11	0	1	11	0	1	11	0	1	11

French	$30\frac{5}{8}$ d.			$30\frac{3}{4}$ d.			$30\frac{7}{8}$ d.			31 d.			$31\frac{1}{8}$ d.		
Livres	£.	s.	d.	£.	s.	d.	£.	s.	d.	£.	s.	d.	£.	s.	d.
10000	425	6	11	427	1	8	428	16	4	430	11	1	432	5	10
5000	212	13	5	213	10	10	214	8	2	215	5	6	216	2	11
4000	170	2	9	170	16	8	171	10	6	172	4	5	172	18	4
3000	127	12	1	128	2	6	128	12	11	129	3	4	129	13	9
2000	85	1	4	85	8	4	85	15	3	86	2	2	86	9	2
1000	42	10	8	42	14	2	42	17	7	43	1	1	43	4	7
900	38	5	7	38	8	9	38	11	10	38	15	0	38	18	1
800	34	0	6	34	3	4	34	6	1	34	8	10	34	11	8
700	29	15	5	29	17	11	30	0	4	30	2	9	30	5	2
600	25	10	5	25	12	6	25	14	7	25	16	8	25	18	9
500	21	5	4	21	7	1	21	8	9	21	10	6	21	12	3
400	17	0	3	17	1	8	17	3	0	17	4	5	17	5	10
300	12	15	2	12	16	3	12	17	3	12	18	4	12	19	4
200	8	10	1	8	10	10	8	11	6	8	12	2	8	12	11
100	4	5	0	4	5	5	4	5	9	4	6	1	4	6	5
90	3	16	6	3	16	10	3	17	2	3	17	6	3	17	9
80	3	8	0	3	8	4	3	8	7	3	8	10	3	9	2
70	2	19	6	2	19	9	3	0	0	3	0	3	3	0	6
60	2	11	0	2	11	3	2	11	5	2	11	8	2	11	10
50	2	2	6	2	2	8	2	2	10	2	3	0	2	3	2
40	1	14	0	1	14	2	1	14	3	1	14	5	1	14	7
30	1	5	6	1	5	7	1	5	8	1	5	10	1	5	11
20	0	17	0	0	17	1	0	17	1	0	17	2	0	17	3
10	0	8	6	0	8	6	0	8	6	0	8	7	0	8	7
9	0	7	7	0	7	8	0	7	8	0	7	9	0	7	9
8	0	6	9	0	6	10	0	6	10	0	6	10	0	6	11
7	0	5	11	0	5	11	0	6	0	0	6	0	0	6	0
6	0	5	1	0	5	1	0	5	1	0	5	2	0	5	2
5	0	4	3	0	4	3	0	4	3	0	4	3	0	4	3
4	0	3	4	0	3	5	0	3	5	0	3	5	0	3	5
3	0	2	6	0	2	6	0	2	6	0	2	7	0	2	7
2	0	1	8	0	1	8	0	1	8	0	1	8	0	1	8
1	0	0	10	0	0	10	0	0	10	0	0	10	0	0	10
Sou 10	0	0	5	0	0	5	0	0	5	0	0	5	0	0	5
9	0	0	4	0	0	4	0	0	4	0	0	4	0	0	4
8	0	0	4	0	0	4	0	0	4	0	0	4	0	0	4
7	0	0	3	0	0	3	0	0	3	0	0	3	0	0	3
6	0	0	3	0	0	3	0	0	3	0	0	3	0	0	3
5	0	0	2	0	0	2	0	0	2	0	0	2	0	0	2
4	0	0	2	0	0	2	0	0	2	0	0	2	0	0	2
3	0	0	1	0	0	1	0	0	1	0	0	1	0	0	1
2	0	0	1	0	0	1	0	0	1	0	0	1	0	0	1
1	0	0	0	0	0	0	0	0	0	0	0	0	0	0	0
Den. 6	0	0	0	0	0	0	0	0	0	0	0	0	0	0	0

Eng.	31¼ d.			31⅜ d.			31½ d.			31⅝ d.			31¾ d.		
£.	L.	s.	d.	L.	s.	d.	L.	s.	d.	L.	s.	d.	L.	s.	d.
1000	23040			22948	4	2	22857	2	10	22766	16	0	22677	3	4
900	20736			20653	7	9	20571	8	7	20490	2	4	20409	9	0
800	18432			18358	11	4	18285	14	3	18213	8	9	18141	14	8
700	16128			16063	14	11	16000	0	0	15936	15	2	15874	0	4
600	13824			13768	18	6	13741	5	9	13660	1	7	13606	6	0
500	11520			11474	2	1	11428	11	5	11383	8	0	11338	11	8
400	9216			9179	5	8	9142	17	2	9106	14	5	9070	17	4
300	6912			6884	9	3	6857	2	10	6830	0	9	6803	3	0
200	4608			4589	12	10	4571	8	7	4553	7	2	4535	8	8
100	2304			2294	16	5	2285	14	3	2276	13	7	2267	14	4
90	2073	12		2065	6	9	2057	2	10	2049	0	3	2040	18	11
80	1843	4		1835	17	2	1828	11	5	1821	6	11	1814	3	6
70	1612	16		1606	7	6	1600	0	0	1593	13	6	1587	8	0
60	1382	8		1376	17	10	1371	8	7	1366	0	2	1360	12	7
50	1152	0		1147	8	3	1142	17	2	1138	6	10	1133	17	2
40	921	12		917	18	7	914	5	9	910	13	5	907	1	9
30	691	4		688	8	11	685	14	3	683	0	1	680	6	4
20	460	16		458	19	3	457	2	10	455	6	9	453	10	10
10	230	8		229	9	8	228	11	5	227	3	4	226	15	5
9	207	7	2	206	10	8	205	14	3	204	18	0	204	1	11
8	184	6	5	183	11	9	182	17	2	182	2	8	181	8	4
7	161	5	7	160	12	9	160	0	0	159	7	4	158	14	10
6	138	4	10	137	13	9	137	2	10	136	12	0	136	1	3
5	115	4	0	114	14	10	114	5	9	113	16	8	113	7	9
4	92	3	2	91	15	10	91	8	7	91	1	4	90	14	2
3	69	2	5	68	16	11	68	11	5	68	6	0	68	0	8
2	46	1	7	45	17	11	45	14	3	45	10	8	45	7	1
1	23	0	10	22	19	0	22	17	2	22	15	4	22	13	7
S. 10	11	10	5	11	9	6	11	8	7	11	7	8	11	6	9
9	10	7	4	10	6	6	10	5	9	10	4	11	10	4	1
8	9	4	4	9	3	7	9	2	10	9	2	2	9	1	5
7	8	1	3	8	0	8	8	0	0	7	19	4	7	18	9
6	6	18	3	6	17	8	6	17	2	6	16	4	6	16	1
5	5	15	2	5	14	9	5	14	3	5	13	10	5	13	5
4	4	12	2	4	11	10	4	11	5	4	11	1	4	10	9
3	3	9	1	3	8	10	3	8	7	3	8	4	3	8	0
2	2	6	1	2	5	11	2	5	9	2	5	6	2	5	4
1	1	3	1	1	2	11	1	2	10	1	2	9	1	2	8
D. 6	0	11	6	0	11	6	0	11	5	0	11	5	0	11	4
5	0	9	7	0	9	7	0	9	6	0	9	6	0	9	5
4	0	7	8	0	7	8	0	7	7	0	7	7	0	7	7
3	0	5	9	0	5	9	0	5	9	0	5	8	0	5	8
2	0	3	10	0	3	10	0	3	10	0	3	10	0	3	9
1	0	1	11	0	1	11	0	1	11	0	1	11	0	1	11

French	31¼ d.			31⅜ d.			31½ d.			31⅝ d.			31¾ d.		
Livres	£.	s.	d.	£.	s.	d.	£.	s.	d.	£.	s.	d.	£.	s.	d.
10000	434	0	6	435	15	3	437	10	0	439	4	8	440	19	5
5000	217	0	3	217	17	7	218	15	0	219	12	4	220	9	8
4000	173	12	2	174	6	1	175	0	0	175	13	10	176	7	9
3000	130	4	2	130	14	7	131	5	0	131	15	5	132	5	10
2000	86	16	1	87	3	0	87	10	0	87	16	11	83	3	10
1000	43	8	0	43	11	6	43	15	0	43	18	5	44	1	11
900	39	1	3	39	4	4	39	7	6	39	10	7	39	13	9
800	34	14	5	34	17	2	35	0	0	35	2	9	35	5	6
700	30	7	7	30	10	0	30	12	6	30	14	11	30	17	4
600	29	0	10	26	2	11	26	5	0	26	7	1	26	9	2
500	21	14	0	21	15	9	21	17	6	21	19	2	22	0	11
400	17	7	2	17	8	7	17	10	0	17	11	4	17	12	9
300	13	0	5	13	1	5	13	2	6	13	3	6	13	4	7
200	8	13	7	8	14	3	8	15	0	8	15	8	8	16	4
100	4	6	9	4	7	1	4	7	6	4	7	10	4	8	2
90	3	18	1	3	18	5	3	18	9	3	19	0	3	19	4
80	3	9	5	3	9	8	3	10	0	3	10	3	3	10	6
70	3	0	9	3	1	0	3	1	3	3	1	5	3	1	8
60	2	12	1	2	12	3	2	12	6	2	12	8	2	12	11
50	2	3	4	2	3	6	2	3	9	2	3	11	2	4	1
40	1	14	8	1	14	10	1	15	0	1	15	1	1	15	3
30	1	6	0	1	6	1	1	6	3	1	6	4	1	6	5
20	0	17	4	0	17	5	0	17	6	0	17	6	0	17	7
10	0	8	8	0	8	8	0	8	9	0	8	9	0	8	9
9	0	7	9	0	7	10	0	7	10	0	7	10	0	7	11
8	0	6	11	0	6	11	0	7	0	0	7	0	0	7	0
7	0	6	0	0	6	1	0	6	1	0	6	1	0	6	2
6	0	5	2	0	5	2	0	5	3	0	5	3	0	5	3
5	0	4	4	0	4	4	0	4	4	0	4	4	0	4	4
4	0	3	5	0	3	5	0	3	6	0	3	6	0	3	6
3	0	2	7	0	2	7	0	2	7	0	2	7	0	2	7
2	0	1	8	0	1	8	0	1	9	0	1	9	0	1	9
1	0	0	10	0	0	10	0	0	10	0	0	10	0	0	10
Scu 10	0	0	5	0	0	5	0	0	5	0	0	5	0	0	5
9	0	0	4	0	0	4	0	0	4	0	0	4	0	0	4
8	0	0	4	0	0	4	0	0	4	0	0	4	0	0	4
7	0	0	3	0	0	3	0	0	3	0	0	3	0	0	3
6	0	0	3	0	0	3	0	0	3	0	0	3	0	0	3
5	0	0	2	0	0	2	0	0	2	0	0	2	0	0	2
4	0	0	2	0	0	2	0	0	2	0	0	2	0	0	2
3	0	0	1	0	0	1	0	0	1	0	0	1	0	0	1
2	0	0	1	0	0	1	0	0	1	0	0	1	0	0	1
1	0	0	0	0	0	0	0	0	0	0	0	0	0	0	0
Den. 6	0	0	0	0	0	0	0	0	0	0	0	0	0	0	0

Eng.	31⅞ d.			32 d.			32⅛ d.			32¼ d.			32⅜ d.		
£.	L.	s.	d.	L.	s.	d.	L.	s.	d.	L.	s.	d.	L.	s.	d.
1000	22588	4	8	22500			22412	9	0	22325	11	8	22239	7	8
900	20329	8	3	20250			20171	4	1	20093	0	6	20015	8	11
800	18070	11	9	18000			17929	19	3	17860	9	4	17791	10	1
700	15811	15	4	15750			15688	14	4	15627	18	2	15567	11	4
600	13552	18	10	13500			13447	9	5	13395	7	0	13343	12	7
500	11294	2	4	11250			11206	4	6	11162	15	10	11119	13	10
400	9035	5	11	9000			8964	19	7	8930	4	8	8895	15	1
300	6776	9	5	6750			6723	14	8	6697	13	6	6671	16	4
200	4517	12	11	4500			4482	9	10	4465	2	4	4447	17	6
100	2258	16	6	2250			2241	4	11	2232	11	2	2223	18	9
90	2032	18	10	2025			2071	2	5	2009	6	1	2001	10	11
80	1807	1	2	1800			1792	19	11	1786	0	11	1779	3	0
70	1581	3	6	1575			1568	17	5	1562	15	10	1556	15	2
60	1355	5	11	1350			1344	14	11	1339	10	8	1334	7	3
50	1129	8	3	1125			1120	12	5	1116	5	7	1111	19	5
40	903	10	7	900			896	10	0	893	0	6	889	11	6
30	677	12	11	675			672	7	6	669	15	4	667	3	8
20	451	15	4	450			448	5	0	446	10	3	444	15	9
10	225	17	8	225			224	2	6	223	5	1	222	7	11
9	203	5	11	202	10		201	14	3	200	18	7	200	3	1
8	180	14	1	180			179	6	0	178	13	2	177	18	4
7	158	2	4	157	10		156	17	9	156	5	7	155	13	6
6	135	10	7	135			134	9	6	133	19	1	133	8	9
5	112	18	10	112	10		112	1	3	111	12	7	111	3	11
4	90	7	1	90	0		89	13	0	89	6	1	88	19	2
3	67	15	4	67	10		67	4	9	66	19	6	66	14	4
2	45	3	6	45	0		44	16	6	44	13	0	44	9	7
1	22	11	9	22	10		22	8	3	22	6	6	22	4	10
S. 10	11	5	11	11	5		11	4	2	11	3	3	11	2	5
9	10	3	8	10	2	6	10	1	9	10	0	11	10	0	2
8	9	0	8	9	0	0	8	19	4	8	18	7	8	17	11
7	7	18	1	7	17	6	7	16	11	7	16	3	7	15	8
6	6	15	6	6	15	0	6	14	6	6	13	11	6	13	5
5	5	12	11	5	12	6	5	12	1	5	11	8	5	11	2
4	4	10	4	4	10	0	4	9	8	4	9	4	4	9	0
3	3	7	9	3	7	6	3	7	3	3	7	0	3	6	9
2	2	5	2	2	5	0	2	4	10	2	4	8	2	4	6
1	1	2	7	1	2	6	1	2	5	1	2	4	1	2	3
D. 6	0	11	4	0	11	3	0	11	3	0	11	2	0	11	1
5	0	9	5	0	9	5	0	9	4	0	9	4	0	9	3
4	0	7	6	0	7	6	0	7	6	0	7	5	0	7	5
3	0	5	8	0	5	8	0	5	7	0	5	7	0	5	7
2	0	3	9	0	3	9	0	3	9	0	3	9	0	3	9
1	0	1	11	0	1	11	0	1	10	0	1	10	0	1	10

French	31⅞ d.			32 d.			32⅛ d.			32¼ d.			32⅜ d.		
Livres	£.	s.	d.	£.	s.	d.	£.	s.	d.	£.	s.	d.	£.	s.	d.
10000	442	14	2	444	8	10	446	3	7	447	18	4	449	13	0
5000	221	7	1	222	4	5	223	1	9	223	19	2	224	16	6
4000	177	1	8	177	15	6	178	9	5	179	3	4	179	17	2
3000	132	16	3	133	16	8	133	17	1	134	7	6	143	17	11
2000	88	10	10	88	17	9	89	4	8	89	11	8	89	18	7
1000	44	5	5	44	8	10	44	12	4	44	15	10	44	19	3
900	39	16	10	40	0	0	40	3	1	40	6	3	40	9	4
800	35	8	4	35	11	1	35	13	10	35	16	8	35	19	5
700	30	19	9	31	2	2	31	4	7	31	7	1	31	9	6
600	26	11	3	26	13	4	26	15	5	26	17	6	26	19	7
500	22	2	8	22	4	5	22	6	2	22	7	11	22	9	7
400	17	14	2	17	15	6	17	16	11	17	18	4	17	19	8
300	13	5	7	13	6	8	13	7	8	13	8	9	13	9	9
200	8	17	1	8	17	9	8	18	5	8	19	2	8	19	10
100	4	8	6	4	8	10	4	9	2	4	9	7	4	9	11
90	3	19	8	4	0	0	4	0	3	4	0	7	4	0	11
80	3	10	10	3	11	1	3	11	4	3	11	8	3	11	11
70	3	1	11	3	2	2	3	2	5	3	2	8	3	2	11
60	2	13	1	2	13	4	2	13	6	2	13	9	2	13	11
50	2	4	3	2	4	5	2	4	7	2	4	9	2	4	11
40	1	15	5	1	15	6	1	15	8	1	15	10	1	15	11
30	1	6	6	1	6	8	1	6	9	1	6	10	1	6	11
20	0	17	8	0	17	9	0	17	10	0	17	11	0	17	11
10	0	8	10	0	8	10	0	8	11	0	8	11	0	8	11
9	0	7	11	0	8	0	0	8	0	0	8	0	0	8	1
8	0	7	1	0	7	1	0	7	1	0	7	2	0	7	2
7	0	6	2	0	6	2	0	6	3	0	6	3	0	6	3
6	0	5	3	0	5	4	0	5	4	0	5	4	0	5	4
5	0	4	5	0	4	5	0	4	5	0	4	5	0	4	6
4	0	3	6	0	3	6	0	3	6	0	3	7	0	3	7
3	0	2	7	0	2	8	0	2	8	0	2	8	0	2	8
2	0	1	9	0	1	9	0	1	9	0	1	9	0	1	9
1	0	0	10	0	0	10	0	0	10	0	0	10	0	0	10
Sou. 10	0	0	5	0	0	5	0	0	5	0	0	5	0	0	5
9	0	0	4	0	0	4	0	0	4	0	0	4	0	0	4
8	0	0	4	0	0	4	0	0	4	0	0	4	0	0	4
7	0	0	3	0	0	3	0	0	3	0	0	3	0	0	3
6	0	0	3	0	0	3	0	0	3	0	0	3	0	0	3
5	0	0	2	0	0	2	0	0	2	0	0	2	0	0	2
4	0	0	2	0	0	2	0	0	2	0	0	2	0	0	2
3	0	0	1	0	0	1	0	0	1	0	0	1	0	0	1
2	0	0	1	0	0	1	0	0	1	0	0	1	0	0	1
1	0	0	0	0	0	0	0	0	0	0	0	0	0	0	0
Den. 6	0	0	0	0	0	0	0	0	0	0	0	0	0	0	0

Eng.	$32\frac{1}{2}$ d.			$32\frac{5}{8}$ d.			$32\frac{3}{4}$ d.			$32\frac{7}{8}$ d.			33 d.		
£.	L.	s.	d.	L.	s.	d.	L.	s.	d.	L.	s.	d.	L.	s.	d.
1000	22153	16	11	22068	19	4	21984	14	8	21901	2	10	21818	3	8
900	19938	9	3	19862	1	5	19786	5	2	19711	0	6	19636	7	3
800	17723	1	6	17655	3	5	17587	15	9	17520	18	3	17454	10	10
700	15507	13	10	15448	5	6	15389	6	3	15330	16	0	15272	14	7
600	13292	6	2	13241	7	7	13190	16	10	13140	13	8	13090	18	2
500	11076	18	6	11034	9	8	10992	7	4	20950	11	5	10909	1	10
400	8861	10	9	8827	11	9	8793	17	10	8760	9	2	8727	5	5
300	6646	3	1	6620	13	10	6595	8	5	6570	6	10	6545	9	1
200	4430	15	5	4413	15	10	4396	18	11	4380	4	7	4363	12	9
100	2215	7	8	2206	17	11	2198	9	6	2190	2	3	2181	16	4
90	1993	16	11	1986	4	2	1978	12	6	1971	2	1	1963	12	9
80	1772	6	2	1765	10	4	1758	15	7	1752	1	10	1745	9	1
70	1550	15	5	1544	16	7	1538	18	8	1533	1	7	1527	5	6
60	1329	4	7	1324	2	9	1319	1	8	1314	1	4	1309	1	10
50	1107	13	10	1103	9	0	1099	4	9	1095	1	2	1090	18	2
40	886	3	1	882	15	2	879	7	9	876	0	11	872	14	7
30	664	12	4	662	1	5	659	10	10	657	0	8	654	10	11
20	443	1	7	441	7	7	439	13	11	438	0	6	436	7	3
10	221	10	9	220	13	10	219	16	11	219	0	3	218	3	8
9	199	7	8	198	12	5	197	17	3	197	2	3	196	7	3
8	177	4	7	176	11	0	175	17	7	175	4	2	174	10	11
7	155	1	7	154	9	8	153	17	10	153	6	2	152	14	7
6	132	18	6	132	18	3	131	18	2	131	8	2	132	18	2
5	110	15	5	110	6	11	109	18	6	109	10	1	109	1	10
4	88	12	4	88	5	6	87	18	9	87	12	1	87	5	6
3	66	9	3	66	4	2	65	19	1	65	14	1	65	9	1
2	44	6	2	44	2	9	43	19	5	43	16	1	43	12	9
1	22	3	1	22	1	5	21	19	8	21	18	0	21	16	4
S. 10	11	1	6	11	0	8	10	19	10	10	19	0	10	18	2
9	9	19	5	9	18	7	9	17	10	9	17	1	9	16	4
8	8	17	3	8	16	7	8	15	11	8	15	3	8	14	7
7	7	15	1	7	14	6	7	13	11	7	13	7	7	12	9
6	6	12	11	6	12	5	6	11	11	6	11	5	6	10	11
5	5	10	9	5	10	4	5	9	11	5	9	6	5	9	1
4	4	8	7	4	8	3	4	7	11	4	7	7	4	7	3
3	3	6	6	3	6	3	3	5	11	3	5	8	3	5	5
2	2	4	4	2	4	2	2	4	0	2	3	10	2	3	8
1	1	2	2	1	2	1	1	2	0	1	1	11	1	1	10
D. 6	0	11	1	0	11	0	0	11	0	0	10	11	0	10	11
5	0	9	3	0	9	2	0	9	2	0	9	2	0	9	1
4	0	7	5	0	7	4	0	7	4	0	7	4	0	7	3
3	0	5	7	0	5	6	0	5	6	0	5	6	0	5	5
2	0	3	8	0	3	8	0	3	8	0	3	8	0	3	8
1	0	1	10	0	1	10	0	1	10	0	1	10	0	1	10

French	32½ d.			32⅝ d.			32¾ d.			32⅞ d.			33 d.		
Livres	£.	s.	d.	£.	s.	d.	£.	s.	d.	£.	s.	d.	£.	s.	d.
10000	451	7	9	453	2	6	454	17	2	456	11	11	458	6	8
5000	225	13	10	226	11	3	227	8	7	228	5	11	229	3	4
4000	180	11	1	181	5	0	181	18	10	182	12	9	83	6	8
3000	135	8	4	135	18	9	136	9	2	136	19	7	137	10	0
2000	90	5	6	90	12	6	90	19	5	91	6	4	91	13	4
1000	45	2	9	45	6	3	45	9	8	45	13	2	45	16	8
900	40	12	6	40	15	7	40	18	9	41	1	10	41	5	0
800	36	2	2	36	5	0	36	7	9	36	10	6	36	13	4
700	31	11	11	31	14	4	31	16	9	31	19	2	32	1	8
600	27	1	8	27	3	9	27	5	10	27	7	11	27	10	0
500	22	11	4	22	13	1	22	14	10	22	16	7	22	18	4
400	18	1	1	18	2	6	18	3	10	18	5	3	18	6	8
300	13	10	10	13	11	10	13	12	11	13	13	11	13	15	0
200	9	0	6	9	1	3	9	1	11	9	2	7	9	3	4
100	4	10	3	4	10	7	4	10	11	4	11	3	4	11	8
90	4	1	3	4	1	6	4	1	10	4	2	2	4	2	6
80	3	12	2	3	12	6	3	12	9	3	13	0	3	13	4
70	3	3	2	3	3	5	3	3	8	3	3	11	3	4	2
60	2	14	2	2	14	4	2	14	7	2	14	9	2	15	0
50	2	5	1	2	5	3	2	5	5	2	5	7	2	5	10
40	1	16	1	1	16	3	1	16	4	1	16	6	1	16	8
30	1	7	1	1	7	2	1	7	3	1	7	4	1	7	6
20	0	18	0	0	18	1	0	18	2	0	18	3	0	18	4
10	0	9	0	0	9	0	0	9	1	0	9	1	0	9	2
9	0	8	1	0	8	1	0	8	2	0	8	2	0	8	3
8	0	7	2	0	7	3	0	7	3	0	7	3	0	7	4
7	0	6	3	0	6	4	0	6	4	0	6	4	0	6	5
6	0	5	5	0	5	5	0	5	5	0	5	5	0	5	6
5	0	4	6	0	4	6	0	4	6	0	4	6	0	4	[illegible]
4	0	3	7	0	3	7	0	3	7	0	3	7	0	3	8
3	0	2	8	0	2	8	0	2	8	0	2	8	0	2	9
2	0	1	9	0	1	9	0	1	9	0	1	9	0	1	10
1	0	0	10	0	0	10	0	0	10	0	0	11	0	0	11
Sou. 10	0	0	5	0	0	5	0	0	5	0	0	5	0	0	5
9	0	0	4	0	0	4	0	0	4	0	0	4	0	0	5
8	0	0	4	0	0	4	0	0	4	0	0	4	0	0	4
7	0	0	3	0	0	3	0	0	3	0	0	3	0	0	3
6	0	0	3	0	0	3	0	0	3	0	0	3	0	0	3
5	0	0	2	0	0	2	0	0	2	0	0	2	0	0	2
4	0	0	2	0	0	2	0	0	2	0	0	2	0	0	2
3	0	0	1	0	0	1	0	0	1	0	0	1	0	0	1
2	0	0	1	0	0	1	0	0	1	0	0	1	0	0	1
1	0	0	[illegible]	0	0	0	0	0	0	0	0	0	0	0	0
Den. 6	0	0	0	0	0	0	0	0	0	0	0	0	0	0	0

Eng.	33⅛ d.			33¼ d.			33⅜ d.			33½ d.			33⅝ d.		
£.	L.	s.	d.	L.	s.	d.	L.	s.	d.	L.	s.	d.	L.	s.	d.
1000	21735	17	6	21654	2	9	21573	0	8	21492	10	9	21412	12	9
900	19562	5	3	19488	14	5	19415	14	7	19343	5	8	19271	7	6
800	17388	13	7	17323	6	2	17258	8	6	17194	0	7	17130	2	2
700	15215	1	11	15157	17	11	15101	2	6	15044	15	6	14988	16	11
600	13041	10	2	12992	9	7	12943	16	5	12895	10	5	12847	11	8
500	10867	18	6	10827	1	4	10786	10	4	10746	5	4	10706	6	5
400	8694	6	10	8661	13	1	8629	4	3	8597	0	4	8565	1	1
300	6520	15	1	6496	4	10	6471	18	2	6447	15	3	6423	15	10
200	4347	3	5	4330	16	6	4314	12	2	4298	10	2	4282	10	7
100	2173	11	8	2165	8	3	2157	6	1	2149	5	1	2141	5	3
90	1956	4	6	1948	17	5	1941	11	6	1934	6	7	1927	2	9
80	1738	17	4	1732	6	7	1725	16	10	1719	8	1	1713	0	3
70	1521	10	2	1515	15	10	1510	2	3	1504	9	7	1498	17	8
60	1304	3	0	1299	5	0	1294	7	8	1289	11	1	1284	15	2
50	1086	15	10	1082	14	2	1078	13	0	1074	12	6	1070	12	8
40	869	8	8	866	3	4	862	18	5	859	14	0	856	10	1
30	652	1	6	649	12	6	647	3	10	644	15	6	642	7	7
20	434	14	4	433	1	8	431	9	3	429	17	0	428	5	1
10	217	7	2	216	10	10	215	14	7	214	18	6	214	2	6
9	195	12	5	194	17	9	194	3	2	193	8	8	192	14	3
8	173	17	9	173	4	8	172	11	8	171	18	10	171	6	0
7	152	3	0	151	11	7	151	0	3	150	9	0	149	17	9
6	130	8	4	129	18	6	129	8	9	128	19	1	128	9	6
5	108	13	7	108	5	5	107	17	4	107	9	3	107	1	3
4	86	18	10	86	12	4	86	5	10	85	19	5	85	13	0
3	65	4	2	64	19	3	64	14	5	64	9	7	64	4	9
2	43	9	5	43	6	2	43	2	11	42	19	8	42	16	6
1	21	14	9	21	13	1	21	11	6	21	9	10	21	8	3
S. 10	10	17	4	10	16	7	10	15	9	10	14	11	10	14	2
9	9	15	7	9	14	11	9	14	2	9	13	5	9	12	9
8	8	13	11	8	13	3	8	12	7	8	11	11	8	11	4
7	7	12	2	7	11	7	7	11	0	7	10	5	7	9	11
6	6	10	5	6	9	11	6	9	5	6	8	11	6	8	6
5	5	8	8	5	8	3	5	7	10	5	7	6	5	7	1
4	4	6	11	4	6	7	4	6	4	4	6	0	4	5	8
3	3	5	3	3	5	0	3	4	9	3	4	6	3	4	3
2	2	3	6	2	3	4	2	3	2	2	3	0	2	2	10
1	1	1	9	1	1		1	1	7	1	1	6	1	1	5
D. 6	0	10	10	0	10	10	0	10	9	0	10	9	0	10	9
5	0	9	1	0	9	0	0	9	0	0	9	0	0	8	11
4	0	7	3	0	7		0	7	2	0	7	2	0	7	2
3	0	5	5	0	5	5	0	5	5	0	5	5	0	5	4
2	0	3	7	0	3	7	0	3	7	0	3	7	0	3	7
1	0	1	10	0	1	10	0	1	10	0	1	10	0	1	9

French	33⅛ d.			33¼ d.			33⅜ d.			33½ d.			33⅝ d.		
Livres	£.	s.	d.	£.	s.	d.	£.	s.	d.	£.	s.	d.	£.	s.	d.
10000	460	1	4	461	16	1	463	10	10	465	5	6	467	0	3
5000	230	0	8	230	18	0	231	15	5	232	12	9	233	10	1
4000	184	0	6	184	14	5	185	8	4	186	2	2	186	16	1
3000	138	0	5	138	10	10	139	1	3	139	11	8	140	2	1
2000	92	0	3	92	7	2	92	14	2	93	1	1	93	8	2
1000	46	0	1	46	3	7	46	7	1	46	10	6	46	14	0
900	41	8	1	41	11	3	41	14	4	41	17	6	42	0	7
800	36	16	1	36	18	10	37	1	8	37	4	5	37	7	2
700	32	4	1	32	6	6	32	8	11	32	11	4	32	13	9
600	27	12	1	27	14	2	27	16	3	27	18	4	28	0	5
500	23	0	0	23	1	9	23	3	6	23	5	3	23	7	0
400	18	8	0	18	9	5	18	10	10	18	12	2	18	13	7
300	13	16	0	13	17	1	13	18	1	13	19	2	14	0	2
200	9	4	0	9	4	8	9	5	5	9	6	1	9	6	9
100	4	12	0	4	12	4	4	12	8	4	13	0	4	13	4
90	4	2	9	4	3	1	4	3	5	4	3	9	4	4	0
80	3	13	7	3	13	10	3	14	2	3	14	5	3	14	8
70	3	4	4	3	4	7	3	4	10	3	5	1	3	5	4
60	2	15	2	2	15	5	2	15	7	2	15	10	2	16	0
50	2	6	0	2	6	2	2	6	4	2	6	6	2	6	8
40	1	16	9	1	16	11	1	17	1	1	17	2	1	17	4
30	1	7	7	1	7	8	1	7	3	1	7	11	1	8	0
20	0	18	4	0	18	5	0	18	6	0	18	7	0	18	8
10	0	9	2	0	9	2	0	9	3	0	9	3	0	9	4
9	0	8	3	0	8	3	0	8	4	0	8	4	0	8	4
8	0	7	4	0	7	4	0	7	5	0	7	5	0	7	5
7	0	6	5	0	6	5	0	6	5	0	6	6	0	6	6
6	0	5	6	0	5	6	0	5	6	0	5	7	0	5	7
5	0	4	7	0	4	7	0	4	7	0	4	7	0	4	8
4	0	3	8	0	3	8	0	3	8	0	3	8	0	3	8
3	0	2	9	0	2	9	0	2	9	0	2	9	0	2	9
2	0	1	10	0	1	10	0	1	10	0	1	10	0	1	10
1	0	0	11	0	0	11	0	0	11	0	0	11	0	0	11
Sou 10	0	0	5	0	0	5	0	0	5	0	0	5	0	0	5
9	0	0	5	0	0	5	0	0	5	0	0	5	0	0	5
8	0	0	4	0	0	4	0	0	4	0	0	4	0	0	4
7	0	0	3	0	0	3	0	0	3	0	0	3	0	0	3
6	0	0	3	0	0	3	0	0	3	0	0	3	0	0	3
5	0	0	2	0	0	2	0	0	2	0	0	2	0	0	2
4	0	0	2	0	0	2	0	0	2	0	0	2	0	0	2
3	0	0	1	0	0	1	0	0	1	0	0	1	0	0	1
2	0	0	1	0	0	1	0	0	1	0	0	1	0	0	1
1	0	0	0	0	0	0	0	0	0	0	0	0	0	0	0
Den. 6	0	0	0	0	0	0	0	0	0	0	0	0	0	0	0

Eng.	At 33¾ d.			30⅞ d.			34 d.			34⅛ d.			34¼ d.		
£.	L.	s.	d.	L.	s.	d.	L.	s.	d.	L.	s.	d.	L.	s.	d.
1000	21333	6	8	21254	12	3	21176	9	5	21098	18	0	21021	17	11
900	19200	0	0	19129	3	0	19058	16	6	18989	0	3	18919	14	2
800	17066	13	4	17003	13	10	16941	3	6	16879	2	5	16817	10	4
700	14933	6	8	14878	4	7	14823	10	7	14769	4	7	14715	6	7
600	12800	0	0	12725	15	3	12705	17	8	12659	6	10	12613	2	9
500	10666	13	4	10627	6	2	10588	4	9	10549	9	0	10510	19	0
400	8533	6	8	8501	16	11	8470	11	9	8439	11	3	8408	15	2
300	6400	0	0	6376	7	8	6352	18	10	6329	13	5	6306	11	5
200	4266	13	4	4250	18	5	4235	5	11	4219	15	7	4204	7	7
100	2133	6	8	2125	9	3	2117	12	11	2109	17	10	2102	3	10
90	1920	0	0	1912	18	4	1905	17	8	1898	18	0	1891	19	5
80	1706	13	4	1700	7	5	1694	2	4	1687	18	3	1681	15	0
70	1493	6	8	1487	16	6	1482	7	1	1476	18	6	1471	10	8
60	1280	0	0	1275	5	6	1270	11	9	1265	18	8	1261	6	3
50	1066	13	4	1062	14	7	1058	16	6	1054	18	11	1051	1	11
40	853	6	8	850	3	8	847	1	2	843	19	2	840	17	6
30	640	0	0	637	12	9	635	5	11	632	19	4	630	13	2
20	426	13	4	425	1	10	423	10	7	421	19	7	420	8	9
10	213	6	8	212	10	11	211	15	4	210	19	9	210	4	5
9	192	0	0	191	5	10	190	11	9	189	17	10	189	3	11
8	170	13	4	170	0	9	169	8	3	168	15	10	168	3	6
7	149	6	8	148	15	8	148	4	9	147	13	10	147	3	1
6	128	0	0	127	10	7	127	1	2	126	11	10	126	2	8
5	106	13	4	106	5	6	105	17	8	105	9	11	105	2	2
4	85	6	8	85	0	4	84	14	1	84	7	11	84	1	9
3	64	0	0	63	15	3	63	10	7	63	5	11	63	1	4
2	42	13	4	42	10	2	42	7	1	42	4	0	42	0	11
1	21	6	8	21	5	1	21	3	6	21	2	0	21	0	5
S. 10	10	13	4	10	12	7	10	11	9	10	11	0	10	10	3
9	9	12	0	9	11	4	9	10	7	9	9	11	9	9	2
8	8	10	8	8	10	0	8	9	5	8	8	10	8	8	2
7	7	9	4	7	8	9	7	8	3	7	7	8	7	7	2
6	6	8	0	6	7	6	6	7	1	6	6	7	6	6	2
5	5	6	8	5	6	3	5	5	11	5	5	6	5	5	1
4	4	5	4	4	5	0	4	4	8	4	4	5	4	4	1
3	3	4	0	3	3	9	3	3	6	3	3	4	3	3	1
2	2	2	8	2	2	6	2	2	4	2	2	2	2	2	1
1	1	1	4	1	1	3	1	1	2	1	1	1	1	1	0
D. 6	0	10	8	0	10	8	0	10	7	0	10	7	0	10	6
5	0	8	11	0	8	10	0	8	10	0	8	10	0	8	9
4	0	7	1	0	7	1	0	7	1	0	7	0	0	7	0
3	0	5	4	0	5	4	0	5	4	0	5	[illegible]	0	5	3
2	0	3	7	0	3	7	0	3	6	0	3	6	0	3	6
1	0	1	0	0	1	9	0	1	0	0	1	0	0	1	9

French	33¾ d.			30⅞ d.			34 d.			34⅛ d.			34¼ d.		
Livres	£.	s.	d.	£	s.	d.	£.	s.	d.	£.	s.	d.	£.	s.	d.
10000	468	15	0	470	9	8	472	4	5	473	19	2	475	13	10
5000	234	7	6	235	4	10	236	2	2	236	19	7	237	16	11
4000	187	10	0	188	3	10	188	17	9	189	11	8	190	5	6
3000	140	12	6	141	2	11	141	13	4	142	3	9	142	14	2
2000	93	15	0	94	1	11	94	8	10	94	15	10	95	2	9
1000	46	17	6	47	0	11	47	4	5	47	7	11	47	11	4
900	42	3	9	42	6	10	42	10	0	42	13	1	42	16	3
800	37	10	0	37	12	9	37	15	6	37	18	4	38	1	1
700	32	16	3	32	18	8	33	1	1	33	3	6	33	5	11
600	28	2	6	28	4	7	28	6	8	28	8	9	28	10	10
500	23	8	9	23	10	5	23	12	2	23	13	11	23	15	8
400	18	15	0	18	16	4	18	17	9	18	19	2	19	0	6
300	14	1	3	14	2	3	14	3	4	14	4	4	14	5	5
200	9	7	6	9	8	2	9	8	10	9	9	7	9	10	3
100	4	13	9	4	14	1	4	14	5	4	14	9	4	15	1
90	4	4	4	4	4	8	4	5	0	4	5	3	4	5	7
80	3	15	0	3	15	3	3	15	6	3	15	10	3	16	1
70	3	5	7	3	5	10	3	6	1	3	6	4	3	6	7
60	2	16	3	2	16	5	2	16	8	2	16	10	2	17	1
50	2	6	10	2	7	0	2	7	2	2	7	4	2	7	6
40	1	17	6	1	17	7	1	17	9	1	17	11	1	18	0
30	1	8	1	1	8	2	1	8	4	1	8	5	1	8	6
20	0	18	9	0	18	9	0	18	10	0	18	11	0	19	0
10	0	9	4	0	9	4	0	9	5	0	9	5	0	9	6
9	0	8	5	0	8	5	0	8	6	0	8	6	0	8	6
8	0	7	6	0	7	6	0	7	6	0	7	7	0	7	7
7	0	6	6	0	6	7	0	6	7	0	6	7	0	6	7
6	0	5	7	0	5	7	0	5	8	0	5	8	0	5	8
5	0	4	8	0	4	8	0	4	8	0	4	8	0	4	9
4	0	3	9	0	3	9	0	3	9	0	3	0	0	3	9
3	0	2	9	0	2	9	0	2	10	0	2	10	0	2	10
2	0	1	10	0	1	10	0	1	10	0	1	10	0	1	10
1	0	0	11	0	0	11	0	0	11	0	0	11	0	0	11
Sou 10	0	0	5	0	0	5	0	0	5	0	0	5	0	0	5
9	0	0	5	0	0	5	0	0	5	0	0	5	0	0	5
8	0	0	4	0	0	4	0	0	4	0	0	4	0	0	4
7	0	0	4	0	0	4	0	0	4	0	0	4	0	0	4
6	0	0	3	0	0	3	0	0	3	0	0	3	0	0	3
5	0	0	2	0	0	2	0	0	2	0	0	2	0	0	2
4	0	0	2	0	0	2	0	0	2	0	0	2	0	0	2
3	0	0	1	0	0	1	0	0	1	0	0	1	0	0	1
2	0	0	1	0	0	1	0	0	1	0	0	1	0	0	1
1	0	0	0	0	0	0	0	0	0	0	0	0	0	0	0
Den. 6	0	0	0	0	0	0	0	0	0	0	0	0	0	0	0

Eng.	34⅜ d.			34½ d.			34⅝ d.			34¾ d.			34⅞ d.		
£.	L.	s.	d.	L.	s.	d.	L.	s.	d.	L.	s.	d.	L.	s.	d.
1000	20945	9	1	20869	11	4	20794	4	6	20719	8	6	20645	3	3
900	18850	18	2	18782	12	2	18714	16	0	18647	9	8	18580	12	11
800	16756	7	3	16695	13	1	16635	7	7	16575	10	9	16516	2	7
700	14661	16	4	14608	13	1	14555	19	2	14503	11	11	14451	12	3
600	12567	5	5	12521	14	9	12476	10	8	12431	13	1	12387	1	11
500	10472	14	7	10434	15	8	10397	2	3	10359	14	3	10322	11	7
400	8378	3	8	8347	16	6	8317	13	9	8287	15	5	8258	1	3
300	6283	12	9	6260	17	5	6238	5	4	6215	16	7	6193	11	0
200	4189	1	10	4173	18	3	4158	16	11	4143	17	8	4129	0	8
100	2094	10	11	2086	19	2	2079	8	5	2071	18	10	2064	10	4
90	1885	1	10	1878	5	3	1871	9	7	1864	15	0	1858	1	4
80	1675	12	9	1669	11	4	1663	10	9	1657	11	1	1651	12	3
70	1466	3	8	1460	17	5	1455	11	11	1450	7	2	1445	3	3
60	1256	14	7	1252	3	6	1247	13	1	1243	3	4	1238	14	2
50	1047	5	6	1043	9	7	1039	14	3	1035	19	5	1032	5	2
40	837	16	4	834	15	8	831	15	5	828	15	7	825	16	2
30	628	7	3	626	1	9	623	16	6	621	11	8	619	7	1
20	418	18	2	417	7	10	415	17	8	414	7	9	412	18	1
10	209	9	1	208	13	11	207	18	10	207	3	11	206	9	0
9	188	10	2	187	16	6	187	3	0	186	9	6	185	16	2
8	167	11	3	166	19	2	166	7	1	165	15	1	165	3	3
7	146	12	4	146	1	9	145	11	2	145	0	9	144	10	4
6	125	13	6	125	4	4	124	15	5	124	6	4	123	17	5
5	104	14	7	104	0	7	103	19	5	103	11	11	103	4	6
4	83	15	8	83	9	7	83	3	7	82	17	7	82	11	7
3	62	16	9	62	12	2	62	7	8	62	3	2	61	18	9
2	41	17	10	41	14	9	41	11	9	41	8	9	41	5	10
1	20	18	11	20	17	5	20	15	11	20	14	5	20	12	11
S. 10	10	9	5	10	8	8	10	7	11	10	7	2	10	6	5
9	9	8	6	9	7	10	9	7	2	9	6	6	9	5	10
8	8	7	7	8	7	0	8	6	4	8	5	9	8	5	2
7	7	6	7	7	6	1	7	5	7	7	5	0	7	4	6
6	6	5	8	6	5	3	6	4	9	6	4	4	6	3	10
5	5	4	9	5	4	4	5	4	0	5	3	7	5	3	3
4	4	3	9	4	3	6	4	3	2	4	2	11	4	2	7
3	3	2	10	3	2	7	3	2	5	3	2	2	3	1	11
2	2	1	11	2	1	9	2	1	7	2	1	5	2	1	4
1	1	0	11	1	0	10	1	0	10	1	0	9	1	0	8
D. 6	0	10	6	0	10	5	0	10	5	0	10	4	0	10	4
5	0	8	9	0	8	8	0	8	8	0	8	8	0	8	7
4	0	7	0	0	7	0	0	6	11	0	6	11	0	6	11
3	0	5	3	0	5	3	0	5	3	0	5	2	0	5	2
2	0	3	6	0	3	6	0	3	6	0	3	5	0	3	5
1	0	1	9	0	1	9	0	1	9	0	1	9	0	1	9

French	34 3/8 d.			34 1/2 d.			34 5/8 d.			34 3/4 d.			34 7/8 d.		
Livres	£.	s.	d.	£.	s.	d.	£.	s.	d.	£.	s.	d.	£.	s.	d.
10000	477	8	7	479	3	4	480	18	0	482	12	9	484	7	6
5000	238	14	3	239	11	8	240	9	0	241	6	4	242	3	9
4000	190	19	5	191	13	4	192	7	2	193	1	1	193	15	0
3000	143	4	7	143	15	0	144	5	5	144	15	10	145	6	3
2000	95	9	8	95	16	8	96	3	7	96	10	6	96	17	6
1000	47	14	10	47	18	4	48	1	9	48	5	3	48	8	9
900	42	19	4	43	2	6	43	5	7	43	8	9	43	11	10
800	38	3	10	38	6	8	38	9	5	38	12	2	38	15	0
700	33	8	4	33	10	10	33	13	3	33	15	8	33	18	1
600	28	12	11	28	15	0	28	17	1	28	19	2	29	1	3
500	23	17	5	23	19	2	24	0	10	24	2	7	24	4	4
400	19	1	11	19	3	4	19	4	8	19	6	1	19	7	6
300	14	6	5	14	7	6	14	8	6	14	9	7	14	10	7
200	9	10	11	9	11	8	9	12	4	9	13	0	9	13	9
100	4	15	5	4	15	10	4	16	2	4	16	6	4	16	10
90	4	5	11	4	6	3	4	6	6	4	6	10	4	7	2
80	3	16	4	3	16	8	3	16	11	3	17	2	3	17	6
70	3	6	10	3	7	1	3	7	3	3	7	6	3	7	9
60	2	17	3	2	17	6	2	17	8	2	17	11	2	18	1
50	2	7	8	2	7	11	2	8	1	2	8	3	2	8	5
40	1	18	2	1	18	4	1	18	5	1	18	7	1	18	9
30	1	8	7	1	8	9	1	8	10	1	8	11	1	9	0
20	0	19	1	0	19	2	0	19	2	0	19	3	0	19	4
10	0	9	6	0	9	7	0	9	7	0	9	7	0	9	8
9	0	8	7	0	8	7	0	8	7	0	8	8	0	8	8
8	0	7	7	0	7	8	0	7	8	0	7	8	0	7	9
7	0	6	8	0	6	8	0	6	8	0	6	9	0	6	9
6	0	5	8	0	5	9	0	5	9	0	5	9	0	5	9
5	0	4	9	0	4	9	0	4	9	0	4	9	0	4	10
4	0	3	9	0	3	10	0	3	10	0	3	10	0	3	10
3	0	2	10	0	2	10	0	2	10	0	2	10	0	2	10
2	0	1	10	0	1	11	0	1	11	0	1	11	0	1	11
1	0	0	11	0	0	11	0	0	11	0	0	11	0	0	11
Sous 10	0	0	5	0	0	5	0	0	5	0	0	5	0	0	5
9	0	0	5	0	0	5	0	0	5	0	0	5	0	0	5
8	0	0	4	0	0	4	0	0	4	0	0	4	0	0	4
7	0	0	4	0	0	4	0	0	4	0	0	4	0	0	4
6	0	0	3	0	0	3	0	0	3	0	0	3	0	0	3
5	0	0	2	0	0	2	0	0	2	0	0	2	0	0	2
4	0	0	2	0	0	2	0	0	2	0	0	2	0	0	2
3	0	0	1	0	0	1	0	0	1	0	0	1	0	0	1
2	0	0	1	0	0	1	0	0	1	0	0	1	0	0	1
1	0	0	0	0	0	0	0	0	0	0	0	0	0	0	0
3 *Den.*	0	0	0	0	0	0	0	0	0	0	0	0	0	0	0

Eng.	At 35 d.			35⅛ d.			35¼ d.			35⅜ d.			35½ d.		
£.	L.	s.	d.	L.	s.	d.	L.	s.	d.	L.	s.	d.	L.	s.	d.
1000	20571	8	7	20498	4	5	20425	10	8	20353	7	2	20281	13	10
900	18514	5	9	18448	8	0	18382	19	7	18318	0	5	18253	10	5
800	16457	2	10	16398	11	6	16340	8	6	16282	13	9	16225	7	1
700	14400	0	0	14348	15	1	14297	17	5	14247	7	0	14197	3	8
600	12342	17	2	12298	18	8	12255	6	5	12212	0	3	12169	0	3
500	10285	14	3	10249	2	2	10212	15	4	10176	13	7	10140	16	11
400	8228	11	5	8199	5	9	8140	4	3	8141	6	10	8112	13	6
300	6171	8	7	6149	9	4	6127	13	2	6106	0	2	6084	10	2
200	4114	5	9	4099	12	11	4085	2	2	4070	13	5	4056	6	9
100	2057	2	10	2049	16	5	2042	11	1	2035	6	9	2028	3	5
90	1851	8	7	1844	16	10	1838	6	0	1831	16	1	1825	7	1
80	1645	14	3	1639	17	2	1634	0	10	1628	5	5	1622	10	9
70	1440	0	0	1434	17	6	1429	15	9	1424	14	8	1419	14	4
60	1234	5	9	1229	17	10	1225	10	8	1221	4	0	1216	18	0
50	1028	11	5	1024	18	3	1021	5	6	1017	13	4	1014	[illegible]	8
40	822	17	2	819	18	7	817	0	5	814	2	8	811	5	4
30	617	2	10	614	18	11	612	15	4	610	12	0	608	9	0
20	411	8	7	409	19	4	408	10	3	407	1	4	405	12	8
10	205	14	3	204	19	8	204	5	1	203	10	8	202	16	8
9	185	2	10	184	9	8	183	16	7	183	3	7	182	10	9
8	164	11	5	163	19	9	163	8	1	162	16	7	162	5	1
7	144	0	0	143	9	9	142	19	7	142	9	6	141	19	5
6	123	8	7	122	19	9	122	11	1	122	2	5	121	13	10
5	102	17	2	102	9	10	102	2	7	101	15	4	101	8	2
4	82	5	9	81	19	10	81	14	1	81	8	3	81	2	6
3	61	14	3	61	9	11	61	5	6	61	1	2	60	16	11
2	42	2	10	40	19	11	40	17	0	40	14	2	40	11	3
1	20	11	5	20	10	0	20	8	6	20	7	1	20	5	8
S. 10	10	5	9	10	5	0	10	4	3	10	3	6	10	2	10
9	9	5	2	9	4	6	9	3	10	9	3	2	9	2	6
8	8	4	7	8	4	0	8	3	5	8	2	10	8	2	3
7	7	4	0	7	3	6	7	3	0	7	2	6	7	2	0
6	6	3	5	6	3	0	6	2	7	6	2	1	6	1	8
5	5	2	10	5	2	6	5	2	2	5	1	9	5	1	5
4	4	2	3	4	2	0	4	1	8	4	1	5	4	1	2
3	3	1	9	3	1	6	3	1	3	3	1	1	3	0	10
2	2	1	2	2	1	0	2	0	10	2	0	9	2	0	7
1	1	0	7	1	0	6	1	0	5	1	0	4	1	0	3
D. 6	0	10	3	0	10	3	0	10	3	0	10	2	0	10	2
5	0	8	7	0	8	7	0	8	6	0	8	6	0	8	5
4	0	6	10	0	6	10	0	6	10	0	6	9	0	6	9
3	0	5	2	0	5	2	0	5	1	0	5	1	0	5	1
2	0	3	5	0	3	5	0	3	5	0	3	5	0	3	5
1	0	1	9	0	1	9	0	1	8	0	1	8	0	1	8

French	35 d.			35⅛ d.			35¼ d.			35⅜ d.			35½ d.		
Livres	£	s.	d.	£.	s.	d.	£.	s.	d.	£.	s.	d.	£.	s.	d.
10000	486	2	2	487	16	11	489	11	8	491	6	4	493	1	1
5000	243	1	1	243	18	5	244	15	10	245	13	2	246	10	6
4000	194	8	10	195	2	9	195	16	8	196	10	6	197	4	5
3000	145	16	8	146	7	1	146	27	6	147	7	11	147	18	4
2000	97	4	5	97	11	4	97	18	4	98	5	3	98	12	2
1000	48	12	2	48	15	8	48	19	2	49	2	7	49	6	1
900	43	15	0	43	18	1	44	1	3	44	4	4	44	7	6
800	38	17	9	39	0	6	39	3	4	39	6	1	39	8	10
700	34	0	6	34	2	11	34	5	5	34	7	10	34	10	3
600	29	3	4	29	5	5	29	7	6	29	9	7	29	11	8
500	24	6	1	24	7	10	24	9	7	24	11	3	24	13	0
400	19	8	10	19	10	3	19	11	8	19	13	0	19	14	5
300	14	11	8	14	12	8	14	13	9	14	14	9	14	15	10
200	9	14	5	9	15	1	9	15	10	9	16	6	9	17	2
100	4	17	2	4	17	6	4	17	11	4	18	3	4	18	7
90	4	7	6	4	7	9	4	8	1	4	8	5	4	8	9
80	3	17	9	3	18	0	3	18	4	3	18	7	3	18	10
70	3	8	0	3	8	3	3	8	6	3	8	9	3	9	0
60	2	18	4	2	18	6	2	18	9	2	18	11	2	19	2
50	2	8	7	2	8	9	2	8	1	2	9	1	2	9	3
40	1	18	10	1	19	0	1	19	2	1	19	3	1	19	5
30	1	9	2	1	9	3	1	9	4	1	9	5	1	9	7
20	0	19	5	0	19	9	0	19	7	0	19	7	0	19	8
10	0	9	8	0	9	9	0	9	9	0	9	9	0	9	10
9	0	8	9	0	8	9	0	8	9	0	8	10	0	8	10
8	0	7	9	0	7	9	0	7	10	0	7	10	0	7	10
7	0	6	9	0	6	10	0	6	10	0	6	10	0	6	10
6	0	5	10	0	5	10	0	5	10	0	5	10	0	5	11
5	0	4	10	0	4	10	0	4	10	0	4	11	0	4	11
4	0	3	10	0	3	10	0	3	11	0	3	11	0	3	11
3	0	2	11	0	2	11	0	2	11	0	2	11	0	2	11
2	0	1	11	0	1	11	0	1	11	0	1	11	0	1	11
1	0	0	11	0	0	11	0	0	11	0	0	11	0	0	11
*Sou.*10	0	0	5	0	0	5	0	0	5	0	0	5	0	0	5
9	0	0	5	0	0	5	0	0	5	0	0	5	0	0	5
8	0	0	4	0	0	4	0	0	4	0	0	4	0	0	4
7	0	0	4	0	0	4	0	0	4	0	0	4	0	0	4
6	0	0	3	0	0	3	0	0	3	0	0	3	0	0	3
5	0	0	2	0	0	2	0	0	3	0	0	3	0	0	3
4	0	0	2	0	0	2	0	0	2	0	0	2	0	0	2
3	0	0	1	0	0	1	0	0	1	0	0	1	0	0	1
2	0	0	1	0	0	1	0	0	1	0	0	1	0	0	1
1	0	0	0	0	0	0	0	0	0	0	0	0	0	0	0
*Den.*6	0	0	0	0	0	0	0	0	0	0	0	0	0	0	0

Eng.	At $35\frac{5}{8}$ d.			$35\frac{3}{4}$ d.			$35\frac{7}{8}$ d.			36 d.			$36\frac{1}{8}$ d.		
£.	L.	s.	d.	L.	s.	d.	L.	s.	d.	L.	s.	d.	L.	s.	d.
1000	20210	10	6	20139	17	2	20069	13	9	20000			19930	15	11
900	18189	9	6	18125	17	6	18062	14	4	18000			17937	14	4
800	16168	8	5	16111	17	9	16055	15	0	16000			15944	12	9
700	14147	7	4	14097	18	1	14048	15	7	14000			13951	11	2
600	12126	6	4	12083	18	4	12041	16	3	12000			11958	9	7
500	10105	5	3	10069	18	7	10034	16	10	10000			9965	8	0
400	8084	4	3	8055	18	11	8027	17	6	8000			797[illegible]	6	4
300	6063	3	2	6041	19	2	6020	18	2	6000			5979	4	9
200	4042	2	1	4027	19	5	4013	18	9	4000			3986	3	2
100	2021	1	1	2013	19	9	2006	19	5	2000			1993	1	7
90	1818	18	11	1812	11	9	1806	5	5	1800			1793	15	5
80	1616	16	10	1611	3	9	1605	11	6	1600			1594	9	3
70	1414	14	9	1409	15	10	1404	17	7	1400			1395	3	1
60	1212	12	8	1208	7	10	1204	3	8	1200			1195	17	0
50	1010	10	6	1006	19	10	1003	9	8	1000			996	10	10
40	808	8	5	805	11	11	802	15	9	800			797	4	8
30	606	6	4	604	3	11	602	1	10	600			597	18	6
20	404	4	3	402	15	11	401	7	11	400			398	12	4
10	202	2	1	201	8	0	200	13	11	200			199	6	2
9	181	17	11	181	5	2	180	12	7	180			179	7	7
8	161	13	8	161	2	5	160	11	2	160			159	8	11
7	141	9	6	140	19	7	140	9	9	140			139	10	4
6	121	5	3	120	16	9	120	8	4	120			119	11	8
5	101	1	1	100	14	0	100	7	0	100			99	13	1
4	80	16	10	80	11	2	80	5	7	80			79	14	9
3	60	12	8	60	8	5	60	4	2	60			59	15	10
2	40	8	5	40	5	7	40	2	10	40			39	17	3
1	20	4	3	20	2	10	20	1	5	20			19	18	7
S. 10	10	2	1	10	1	5	10	0	8	10			9	19	4
9	9	1	11	9	1	3	9	0	8	9			8	19	7
8	8	1	8	8	1	1	8	0	7	8			7	19	5
7	7	1	6	7	1	0	7	0	6	7			6	19	6
6	6	1	3	6	0	10	6	0	5	6			5	19	7
5	5	1	1	5	0	8	5	0	4	5			4	19	8
4	4	0	10	4	0	7	4	0	3	4			3	19	9
3	3	0	8	3	0	5	3	0	3	3			2	19	10
2	2	0	5	2	0	3	2	0	2	2			1	19	10
1	1	0	2	1	0	2	1	0	1	1			0	19	11
D. 6	0	10	1	0	10	1	0	10	0	0	10	0	0	10	0
5	0	8	5	0	8	5	0	8	4	0	8	4	0	8	4
4	0	6	9	0	6	9	0	6	8	0	6	8	0	6	8
3	0	5	1	0	5	0	0	5	0	0	5	0	0	5	0
2	0	3	4	0	3	4	0	3	4	0	3	4	0	3	4
1	0	1	8	0	1	8	0	1	8	0	1	8	0	1	8

French	At 35⅝ d.			35¾ d.			35⅞ d.			36 d.			36⅛ d.		
Livres	£.	s.	d.	£.	s.	d.	£.	s.	d.	£.	s.	d	£.	s.	d.
10000	494	15	10	496	10	6	498	5	3	500			501	14	8
5000	247	7	11	248	5	3	249	2	7	250			250	17	4
4000	197	18	4	198	12	2	199	6	1	200			200	13	10
3000	148	8	9	148	19	2	149	9	7	150			150	10	5
2000	98	19	2	99	6	1	99	13	0	100			100	6	11
1000	49	9	11	49	13	0	49	16	6	50			50	3	5
900	44	10	7	44	13	9	44	16	10	45			45	3	1
800	39	11	8	39	14	5	39	17	2	40			40	2	9
700	34	12	8	34	15	1	34	17	6	35			35	2	5
600	29	13	9	29	15	10	29	17	11	30			30	2	1
500	24	14	9	24	16	6	24	18	3	25			25	1	8
400	19	15	10	19	17	2	19	18	7	20			20	1	4
300	14	16	10	14	17	11	14	18	11	15			15	1	0
200	9	17	11	9	18	7	9	19	3	10			10	0	8
100	4	18	11	4	19	3	4	19	7	5			5	0	4
90	4	9	0	4	9	4	4	9	8	4	10		4	10	3
80	3	19	2	3	19	5	3	19	8	4	0		4	0	3
70	3	9	3	3	9	6	3	9	9	3	10		3	10	2
60	2	19	4	2	19	7	2	19	9	3	0		3	0	2
50	2	9	5	2	9	7	2	9	9	2	10		2	10	2
40	1	19	7	1	19	8	1	19	10	2	0		2	0	1
30	1	9	8	1	9	9	1	9	10	1	10		1	10	1
20	0	19	9	0	19	10	0	19	11	1	0		1	0	0
10	0	9	10	0	9	11	0	9	11	0	10		0	10	0
9	0	8	10	0	8	11	0	8	11	0	9		0	9	0
8	0	7	11	0	7	11	0	7	11	0	8		0	8	0
7	0	6	11	0	6	11	0	6	11	0	7		0	7	0
6	0	5	11	0	5	11	0	5	11	0	6		0	6	0
5	0	4	11	0	4	11	0	4	11	0	5		0	5	0
4	0	3	11	0	3	11	0	3	11	0	4		0	4	0
3	0	2	11	0	2	11	0	2	11	0	3		0	3	0
2	0	1	11	0	1	11	0	1	11	0	2		0	2	0
1	0	0	11	0	0	11	0	1	0	0	1		0	1	0
Sous 10	0	0	6	0	0	6	0	0	6	0	0	6	0	0	6
9	0	0	5	0	0	5	0	0	5	0	0	5	0	0	5
8	0	0	4	0	0	4	0	0	4	0	0	4	0	0	4
7	0	0	4	0	0	4	0	0	4	0	0	4	0	0	4
6	0	0	3	0	0	3	0	0	3	0	0	3	0	0	3
5	0	0	3	0	0	3	0	0	3	0	0	3	0	0	3
4	0	0	2	0	0	2	0	0	2	0	0	2	0	0	2
3	0	0	1	0	0	1	0	0	1	0	0	1	0	0	1
2	0	0	1	0	0	1	0	0	1	0	0	1	0	0	1
1	0	0	0	0	0	0	0	0	0	0	0	0	0	0	0
Den. 6	0	0	0	0	0	0	0	0	0	0	0	0	0	0	0

Eng.	$36\frac{1}{4}$ d.			$36\frac{3}{8}$ d.			$36\frac{1}{2}$ d.			$36\frac{5}{8}$ d.			$36\frac{3}{4}$ d.		
£.	L.	s.	d.	L.	s.	d.	L.	s.	d.	L.	s.	d.	L.	s.	d.
1000	19862	1	5	19793	16	3	19726	0	7	19658	14	1	19591	16	9
900	17875	17	3	17814	8	8	17753	8	6	17692	16	8	17632	13	1
800	15889	13	1	15835	1	0	15780	16	5	15726	19	3	15673	9	5
700	13903	9	0	13855	13	5	13808	4	5	13761	1	10	13714	5	9
600	11917	4	10	11876	5	9	11835	12	4	11795	4	5	11755	2	0
500	9931	0	8	9896	18	2	9863	0	3	9829	7	0	9795	18	4
400	7944	16	7	7917	10	6	7890	8	3	7863	9	7	7836	14	8
300	5958	12	5	5938	2	11	5917	16	2	5897	12	3	5877	11	0
200	3972	8	3	3958	15	3	3945	4	1	3931	14	10	3918	7	4
100	1986	4	2	1979	7	8	1972	12	1	1965	17	5	1959	3	8
90	1787	11	9	1781	8	10	1775	6	10	1769	5	8	1763	5	4
80	1588	19	4	1583	10	1	1578	1	8	1572	13	11	1567	6	11
70	1390	6	11	1385	11	4	1380	16	5	1376	2	2	1371	8	7
60	1191	14	6	1187	12	7	1183	11	3	1179	10	5	1175	10	2
50	993	2	1	989	13	10	986	6	0	982	18	8	979	11	10
40	794	9	8	791	15	1	789	0	10	786	7	0	783	13	6
30	595	17	3	593	16	4	591	15	7	589	15	3	587	15	1
20	397	4	10	395	17	6	394	10	5	393	3	6	391	16	9
10	198	12	5	197	18	9	197	5	3	196	11	9	195	18	4
9	178	15	5	178	2	11	177	10	8	176	18	7	176	6	6
8	158	17	11	158	7	0	157	16	2	157	5	5	156	14	8
7	139	0	8	138	11	2	138	1	8	127	12	3	137	2	10
6	119	3	5	118	15	3	118	7	2	117	19	1	117	11	0
5	99	6	3	98	19	5	98	12	7	98	5	10	97	19	2
4	79	9	0	79	3	6	78	18	2	78	12	8	78	7	4
3	59	11	9	59	7	8	59	3	7	58	19	6	58	15	6
2	39	14	6	39	11	9	39	9	1	39	6	4	39	3	8
1	19	17	3	19	15	11	19	14	6	19	13	2	19	11	10
S. 10	9	18	7	9	17	11	9	17	3	9	16	7	9	15	11
9	8	18	9	8	18	2	8	17	6	8	16	11	8	16	4
8	7	18	11	7	18	4	7	17	10	7	17	3	7	16	9
7	6	19	0	6	18	7	6	18	1	6	17	7	6	17	2
6	5	19	2	5	18	9	5	18	4	5	17	11	5	17	7
5	4	19	4	4	19	0	4	18	8	4	18	4	4	18	0
4	3	19	5	3	19	2	3	18	11	3	18	8	3	18	4
3	2	19	7	2	19	5	2	19	2	2	19	0	2	18	9
2	1	19	9	1	19	7	1	19	5	1	19	4	1	19	2
1	0	19	10	0	19	10	0	19	9	0	19	8	0	19	7
D. 6	0	9	11	0	9	11	0	9	10	0	9	10	0	9	10
5	0	8	3	0	8	3	0	8	3	0	8	2	0	8	2
4	0	6	7	0	6	7	0	6	7	0	6	7	0	6	6
3	0	5	0	0	4	11	0	4	11	0	4	11	0	4	11
2	0	3	4	0	3	4	0	3	3	0	3	3	0	3	3
1	0	1	8	0	1	8	0	1	8	0	1	8	0	1	8

French	36¼ d.			36⅜ d.			36½ d.			36⅝ d.			36¾ d.		
Livres	£.	s.	d.	£.	s.	d.	£.	s.	d.	£.	s.	d.	£.	s.	d.
10000	503	9	5	505	4	2	506	18	10	508	13	7	510	8	4
5000	251	14	8	252	12	1	253	9	5	254	6	9	255	4	2
4000	201	7	9	202	1	8	202	15	6	203	9	5	204	3	4
3000	151	10	0	151	11	3	152	1	8	152	12	1	153	2	6
2000	100	13	10	101	0	10	101	7	9	101	14	8	102	1	8
1000	50	6	11	50	10	5	50	13	10	50	17	4	51	0	10
900	45	6	3	45	9	4	45	12	6	45	15	7	45	18	9
800	40	5	6	40	8	4	40	11	1	40	13	10	40	16	8
700	35	4	10	35	7	3	35	9	8	35	12	1	35	14	7
600	30	4	2	30	6	3	30	8	4	30	10	5	30	12	6
500	25	3	5	25	5	2	25	6	11	25	8	8	25	10	5
400	20	2	9	20	4	2	20	5	6	20	6	11	20	8	4
300	15	2	1	15	3	1	15	4	2	15	5	2	15	6	3
200	10	1	4	10	2	1	10	2	9	10	3	5	10	4	2
100	5	0	8	5	1	0	5	1	4	5	1	8	5	2	1
90	4	10	7	4	10	11	4	11	3	4	11	6	4	11	10
80	4	0	6	4	0	10	4	1	1	4	1	4	4	1	8
70	3	10	5	3	10	8	3	10	11	3	11	2	3	11	5
60	3	0	5	3	0	7	3	0	10	3	1	0	3	1	3
50	2	10	4	2	10	6	2	10	8	2	10	10	2	11	2
40	2	0	3	2	0	5	2	0	6	2	0	8	2	0	10
30	1	10	2	1	10	3	1	10	5	1	10	6	1	10	7
20	1	0	1	1	0	2	1	0	3	1	0	4	1	0	5
10	0	10	0	0	10	1	0	10	1	0	10	2	0	10	2
9	0	9	0	0	9	1	0	9	1	0	9	1	0	9	2
8	0	8	0	0	8	1	0	8	1	0	8	1	0	8	2
7	0	7	0	0	7	0	0	7	1	0	7	1	0	7	1
6	0	6	0	0	6	0	0	6	1	0	6	1	0	6	1
5	0	5	0	0	5	0	0	5	0	0	5	1	0	5	1
4	0	4	0	0	4	0	0	4	0	0	4	0	0	4	1
3	0	3	0	0	3	0	0	3	0	0	3	0	0	3	0
2	0	2	0	0	2	0	0	2	0	0	2	0	0	2	0
1	0	1	0	0	1	0	0	1	0	0	1	0	0	1	0
Sous 10	0	0	6	0	0	6	0	0	6	0	0	6	0	0	6
9	0	0	5	0	0	5	0	0	5	0	0	5	0	0	5
8	0	0	4	0	0	4	0	0	4	0	0	4	0	0	4
7	0	0	4	0	0	4	0	0	4	0	0	4	0	0	4
6	0	0	3	0	0	3	0	0	3	0	0	3	0	0	3
5	0	0	3	0	0	3	0	0	3	0	0	3	0	0	3
4	0	0	2	0	0	2	0	0	2	0	0	2	0	0	2
3	0	0	1	0	0	1	0	0	1	0	0	1	0	0	1
2	0	0	1	0	0	1	0	0	1	0	0	1	0	0	1
1	0	0	0	0	0	0	0	0	0	0	0	0	0	0	0
Den. 6	0	0	0	0	0	0	0	0	0	0	0	0	0	0	0

Eng.	36⅞ d.			37 d.			37⅛ d.			37¼ d.			37⅜ d.		
£.	L.	s.	d.	L.	s.	d.	L.	s.	d.	L.	s.	d.	L.	s.	d.
1000	19525	8	6	19459	9	2	19393	18	9	19328	17	2	19264	4	3
900	17572	17	8	17513	10	3	17454	10	11	17395	19	6	17337	15	10
800	15620	6	9	15567	11	4	15515	3	0	15463	1	9	15411	7	5
700	13667	15	11	13621	12	5	13575	15	2	13530	4	0	13484	19	0
600	11715	5	1	11675	13	6	11636	7	3	11597	6	4	11558	10	7
500	9762	14	3	9729	14	7	9696	19	2	9664	8	7	9632	2	2
400	7810	3	5	7783	15	8	7757	11	6	7731	10	10	7705	13	8
300	5857	12	7	5837	16	9	5818	3	8	5798	13	2	5779	5	3
200	3905	1	8	3891	17	10	3878	15	9	3865	15	5	3852	16	10
100	1952	10	10	1945	18	11	1939	17	11	1932	17	9	1926	8	5
90	1757	5	9	1751	7	0	1745	9	1	1739	11	11	1733	15	7
80	1562	0	8	1556	15	2	1551	10	4	1546	6	2	1541	2	9
70	1366	15	7	1362	3	3	1357	11	6	1353	0	5	1348	9	11
60	1171	10	6	1167	11	4	1163	12	9	1159	14	8	1155	17	1
50	976	5	5	972	19	6	969	13	11	966	8	10	963	4	3
40	781	0	4	778	7	7	775	15	2	773	3	1	770	11	4
30	585	15	3	583	15	8	581	16	4	579	17	4	577	18	6
20	390	10	2	389	3	9	387	17	7	386	11	7	385	5	8
10	195	5	1	194	11	11	193	18	10	193	5	9	192	12	10
9	175	14	7	175	2	8	174	10	11	173	19	2	173	7	7
8	156	4	1	155	13	6	155	3	0	154	12	7	154	2	3
7	136	13	7	136	4	4	135	15	2	135	6	1	134	17	0
6	117	3	1	116	15	2	116	7	3	115	19	6	115	11	9
5	97	12	7	97	5	11	96	19	5	96	12	1	96	6	5
4	78	2	0	77	16	9	77	11	6	77	6	4	77	1	2
3	58	11	6	58	7	7	58	3	8	57	19	9	57	15	10
2	39	1	0	38	18	5	38	15	9	38	13	2	38	10	7
1	19	10	6	19	9	2	19	7	11	19	6	7	19	5	3
S. 10	9	15	3	9	14	7	9	13	11	9	13	3	9	12	8
9	8	15	9	8	15	2	8	14	7	8	14	0	8	13	5
8	7	16	2	7	15	8	7	15	2	7	14	8	7	14	1
7	6	16	8	6	16	3	6	15	9	6	15	4	6	14	10
6	5	17	2	5	16	9	5	16	4	5	16	0	5	15	7
5	4	17	8	4	17	4	4	17	0	4	16	8	4	16	4
4	3	18	1	3	17	10	3	17	7	3	17	4	3	17	1
3	2	18	7	2	18	5	2	18	2	2	18	0	2	17	10
2	1	19	1	1	18	11	1	18	9	1	18	8	1	18	6
1	0	19	6	0	19	6	0	19	5	0	19	4	0	19	3
D. 6	0	9	9	0	9	9	0	9	8	0	9	8	0	9	8
5	0	8	2	0	8	1	0	8	1	0	8	1	0	8	0
4	0	6	6	0	6	6	0	6	6	0	6	5	0	6	5
3	0	4	11	0	4	11	0	4	10	0	4	10	0	4	10
2	0	3	3	0	3	3	0	3	3	0	3	3	0	3	3
1	0	1	8	0	1	8	0	1	7	0	1	7	0	1	7

French	36⅞ d.			37 d.			37⅛ d.			37¼ d.			37⅜ d.		
Livres	£.	s.	d.	£.	s.	d.	£.	s.	d.	£.	s.	d.	£.	s.	d.
10000	512	3	0	513	17	9	515	12	6	517	7	2	519	1	11
5000	256	1	6	256	18	10	257	16	3	258	13	7	250	10	11
4000	204	17	2	205	11	1	206	5	0	206	18	10	207	12	9
3000	153	12	11	154	3	4	154	13	9	155	4	2	155	14	7
2000	102	8	7	102	15	6	103	2	6	103	9	5	103	16	4
1000	51	4	3	51	7	9	51	11	3	51	14	8	51	18	2
900	46	1	10	46	5	0	46	8	1	46	11	3	46	14	4
800	40	19	5	41	2	2	41	5	0	41	7	9	41	10	6
700	35	17	0	35	19	5	36	1	10	36	4	3	36	6	8
600	30	14	7	30	16	8	30	18	9	31	0	10	31	2	11
500	25	12	1	25	13	10	25	15	7	25	17	4	25	19	1
400	20	9	8	20	11	1	20	12	6	20	13	10	20	15	3
300	15	7	3	15	8	4	15	9	4	15	10	5	15	11	5
200	10	4	10	10	5	6	10	6	3	10	6	11	10	7	7
100	5	2	5	5	2	9	5	3	1	5	3	5	5	3	9
90	4	12	2	4	12	6	4	12	9	4	13	1	4	13	5
80	4	1	11	4	2	2	4	2	6	4	2	9	4	3	0
70	3	11	8	3	11	11	3	12	2	3	12	5	3	12	8
60	3	1	5	3	1	8	3	1	10	3	2	1	3	2	3
50	2	11	2	2	11	4	2	11	6	2	11	8	2	11	10
40	2	0	11	2	1	1	2	1	3	2	1	4	2	1	6
30	1	10	8	1	10	10	1	10	11	1	11	0	1	11	1
20	1	0	5	1	0	6	1	0	7	1	0	8	1	0	9
10	0	10	2	0	10	3	0	10	3	0	10	4	0	10	4
9	0	9	2	0	9	3	0	9	3	0	9	3	0	9	4
8	0	8	2	0	8	2	0	8	3	0	8	3	0	8	3
7	0	7	2	0	7	2	0	7	2	0	7	2	0	7	3
6	0	6	1	0	6	2	0	6	2	0	6	2	0	6	2
5	0	5	1	0	5	1	0	5	1	0	5	2	0	5	2
4	0	4	1	0	4	1	0	4	1	0	4	1	0	4	1
3	0	3	0	0	3	1	0	3	1	0	3	1	0	3	1
2	0	2	0	0	2	0	0	2	0	0	2	0	0	2	0
1	0	1	0	0	1	0	0	1	0	0	1	0	0	1	0
Sou.10	0	0	6	0	0	6	0	0	6	0	0	6	0	0	6
9	0	0	5	0	0	5	0	0	5	0	0	5	0	0	5
8	0	0	4	0	0	4	0	0	5	0	0	5	0	0	5
7	0	0	4	0	0	4	0	0	4	0	0	4	0	0	4
6	0	0	3	0	0	3	0	0	3	0	0	3	0	0	3
5	0	0	3	0	0	3	0	0	3	0	0	3	0	0	3
4	0	0	2	0	0	2	0	0	2	0	0	2	0	0	2
3	0	0	1	0	0	1	0	0	1	0	0	1	0	0	1
2	0	0	1	0	0	1	0	0	1	0	0	1	0	0	1
1	0	0	0	0	0	0	0	0	0	0	0	0	0	0	0
Den.6	0	0	0	0	0	0	0	0	0	0	0	0	0	0	0

Eng	At 37½ d.			37⅝ d.			37¾ d.			37⅞ d.			38 d.		
£.	L.	s.	d.	L.	s.	d.	L.	s.	d.	L.	s.	d.	L.	s.	d.
1000	19200			19136	4	3	19072	16	11	19009	18	0	18947	7	4
900	17280			17222	11	10	7165	11	3	17108	18	3	17052	12	8
800	15360			15328	19	5	15258	5	7	15207	18	5	15157	17	11
700	13440			13395	7	6	13350	19	10	13306	18	7	13263	3	2
600	11520			11481	14	7	11443	14	2	11405	18	10	11368	8	5
500	9600			9568	2	2	9536	8	6	9504	19	0	9473	13	8
400	7680			7654	9	8	7629	2	9	7603	19	2	7578	18	11
300	5760			5740	17	3	5721	17	1	5702	19	5	5684	4	3
200	3840			3827	4	10	3814	11	5	3801	19	7	3789	9	5
100	1920			1913	12	5	1907	5	8	1900	19	10	1894	14	9
90	1728			1722	5	2	1716	11	2	1710	17	10	1705	5	3
80	1536			1530	17	11	1525	16	7	1520	15	10	1515	15	10
70	1344			1339	10	8	1335	2	0	1330	13	10	1326	6	4
60	1152			1148	3	6	1144	7	5	1140	11	11	1136	16	10
50	960			956	16	5	953	12	10	952	9	11	947	7	4
40	768			765	9	0	762	18	3	760	7	11	757	17	11
30	576			574	1	9	572	3	9	570	5	11	568	8	5
20	384			382	14	6	381	9	2	380	4	0	378	18	11
10	192			191	7	3	190	14	7	190	2	0	189	9	6
9	172	16		172	4	6	171	13	1	171	1	9	170	10	6
8	153	12		153	1	10	152	11	[illegible]	152	1	7	151	11	7
7	134	8		133	19	1	133	10	2	133	1	5	132	12	8
6	115	4		114	16	4	114	8	0	114	1	2	113	13	8
5	96	0		95	13	8	95	7	3	95	1	0	94	14	9
4	76	16		76	10	11	76	5	10	76	0	10	75	15	10
3	57	12		57	8	2	57	4	5	57	0	5	56	16	10
2	38	8		38	5	5	38	2	11	38	0	5	37	17	11
1	19	4		19	2	9	19	1	6	19	0	2	18	18	11
S. 10	9	12	0	9	11	4	9	10	9	9	10	1	9	9	6
9	8	12	10	8	12	3	8	11	8	8	11	1	8	10	6
8	7	13	7	7	13	1	7	12	7	7	12	1	7	11	7
7	6	14	5	6	13	11	6	13	6	6	13	1	6	12	8
6	5	15	2	5	14	10	5	14	5	5	14	1	5	13	8
5	4	16	0	4	15	8	4	15	4	4	15	1	4	14	9
4	3	16	10	3	16	7	3	16	3	3	16	1	3	15	10
3	2	17	7	2	17	5	2	17	3	2	17	0	2	16	10
2	1	18	5	1	18	3	1	18	2	1	18	0	1	17	11
1	0	19	2	0	19	2	0	19	1	0	19	0	0	18	11
D. 6	0	9	7	0	9	7	0	9	6	0	9	6	0	9	6
5	0	8	0	0	8	0	0	7	11	0	7	11	0	7	11
4	0	6	5	0	6	5	0	6	4	0	6	4	0	6	4
3	0	4	10	0	4	10	0	4	9	0	4	9	0	4	9
2	0	3	2	0	3	2	0	3	2	0	3	2	0	3	2
1	0	1	7	0	1	7	0	1	7	0	1	7	0	1	7

French	37½ d.			37⅝ d.			37¾ d.			37⅞ d.			38 d.		
Livres	£.	s.	d.	£.	s.	d.	£.	s.	d.	£.	s.	d.	£.	s.	d.
10000	520	16	8	522	11	4	524	6	1	526	0	10	527	15	6
5000	260	8	4	261	5	8	262	3	0	263	0	5	263	17	9
4000	208	6	8	209	0	6	209	14	5	210	8	4	211	2	2
3000	156	5	0	156	15	5	157	5	10	157	16	3	158	6	8
2000	104	3	4	104	0	3	104	17	2	105	4	2	105	11	1
1000	52	1	8	52	5	1	52	8	7	52	12	1	52	15	6
900	46	17	6	47	0	7	47	3	9	47	6	10	47	10	0
800	41	13	4	41	16	1	41	18	10	42	1	8	42	4	5
700	36	9	2	36	12	7	36	14	0	36	16	5	36	18	10
600	31	5	0	31	7	1	31	9	2	31	11	3	31	13	4
500	26	0	10	26	2	6	26	4	3	26	6	0	26	7	9
400	20	16	8	20	18	0	20	19	5	21	0	10	21	2	2
300	15	12	6	15	13	6	15	14	7	15	15	7	15	16	8
200	10	8	4	10	9	0	10	9	8	10	10	5	10	11	1
100	5	4	2	5	4	6	5	4	10	5	5	2	5	5	6
90	4	13	9	4	14	0	4	14	4	4	14	8	4	15	0
80	4	3	4	4	3	7	4	3	10	4	4	2	4	4	5
70	3	12	11	3	13	1	3	13	4	3	13	7	3	13	10
60	3	2	6	3	2	8	3	2	11	3	3	1	3	3	4
50	2	12	1	2	12	3	2	12	5	2	12	7	2	12	9
40	2	1	8	2	1	9	2	1	11	2	2	1	2	2	2
30	1	11	3	1	11	4	1	11	5	1	11	6	1	11	8
20	1	0	10	1	0	10	1	0	11	1	1	0	1	1	1
10	0	10	5	0	10	5	0	10	5	0	10	6	0	10	6
9	0	9	4	0	9	4	0	9	5	0	9	5	0	9	6
8	0	8	4	0	8	4	0	8	4	0	8	5	0	8	5
7	0	7	3	0	7	3	0	7	4	0	7	4	0	7	4
6	0	6	3	0	6	3	0	6	3	0	6	3	0	6	4
5	0	5	2	0	5	2	0	5	2	0	5	3	0	5	3
4	0	4	2	0	4	2	0	4	2	0	4	2	0	4	2
3	0	3	1	0	3	1	0	3	1	0	3	1	0	3	2
2	0	2	1	0	2	1	0	2	1	0	2	1	0	2	1
1	0	1	0	0	1	0	0	1	0	0	1	0	0	1	0
Sou 10	0	0	6	0	0	6	0	0	6	0	0	6	0	0	6
9	0	0	5	0	0	5	0	0	5	0	0	5	0	0	5
8	0	0	5	0	0	5	0	0	5	0	0	5	0	0	5
7	0	0	4	0	0	4	0	0	4	0	0	4	0	0	4
6	0	0	3	0	0	3	0	0	3	0	0	3	0	0	3
5	0	0	3	0	0	3	0	0	3	0	0	3	0	0	3
4	0	0	2	0	0	2	0	0	2	0	0	2	0	0	2
3	0	0	1	0	0	1	0	0	1	0	0	1	0	0	1
2	0	0	1	0	0	1	0	0	1	0	0	1	0	0	1
1	0	0	0	0	0	0	0	0	0	0	0	0	0	0	0
Den. 6	0	0	0	0	0	0	0	0	0	0	0	0	0	0	0

Eng	$38\frac{1}{8}$ d.			$38\frac{1}{4}$ d.			$38\frac{3}{8}$ d.			$38\frac{1}{2}$ d.			$38\frac{5}{8}$ d.		
£.	L.	s.	d.	L.	s.	d.	L.	s.	d.	L.	s.	d.	L.	s.	d.
1000	18885	4	11	18823	10	7	18762	4	4	18701	6	0	18640	15	6
900	16996	14	5	16941	3	6	16885	19	10	16831	3	5	16776	14	0
800	15108	3	11	15058	16	6	15009	15	5	14961	0	9	14912	12	5
700	13219	13	5	13176	9	5	13133	11	0	13090	18	2	13048	10	10
600	11331	2	11	11294	2	4	11257	6	7	11220	15	7	11184	9	4
500	9442	12	[illegible]	9411	15	4	9381	2	2	9350	13	0	9320	7	9
400	7554	2	0	7529	8	3	7504	17	8	7480	10	5	7456	6	3
300	5665	11	6	5647	1	2	5628	13	3	5610	7	10	5592	4	8
200	3777	1	0	3764	14	2	3752	8	10	3740	5	2	3728	3	1
100	1888	10	6	1882	7	1	1876	4	5	1870	2	7	1864	1	7
90	1699	13	5	1694	2	4	1688	12	0	1683	2	4	1677	13	5
80	1510	16	5	1505	17	8	1500	19	7	1496	2	1	1491	5	3
70	1321	19	4	1317	12	11	1313	7	2	1309	1	10	1304	17	1
60	1133	2	4	1129	8	3	1125	14	8	1122	1	7	1118	8	11
50	944	5	3	941	3	6	938	2	2	935	1	4	932	0	9
40	755	8	2	752	18	10	750	9	9	748	1	1	745	12	8
30	566	11	2	564	14	1	562	17	4	561	0	9	559	4	6
20	377	14	1	376	9	5	375	4	11	374	0	6	372	16	4
10	188	17	1	188	4	9	187	12	5	187	0	3	186	8	2
9	169	19	4	169	8	3	168	17	2	168	6	3	167	15	4
8	151	1	8	150	11	9	150	2	0	149	12	3	149	2	6
7	132	3	11	131	15	4	131	6	9	130	18	2	130	9	9
6	113	6	3	112	18	10	112	11	6	112	4	2	111	16	11
5	94	8	6	94	2	4	93	16	3	93	10	2	93	4	1
4	75	10	10	75	5	11	75	1	0	74	16	1	74	11	3
3	56	13	1	56	9	5	56	5	0	56	2	1	55	18	5
2	37	15	5	37	12	11	37	10	6	37	8	1	37	5	8
1	18	17	9	18	16	6	18	15	3	18	14	0	18	12	10
S. 10	9	8	10	9	8	3	9	7	7	9	7	0	9	6	5
9	8	10	0	8	9	5	8	8	10	8	8	4	8	7	9
8	7	11	1	7	10	7	7	10	1	7	9	7	7	9	2
7	6	12	2	6	11	9	6	11	4	6	10	11	6	10	6
6	5	13	4	5	12	11	5	12	7	5	12	3	5	11	10
5	4	14	5	4	14	1	4	13	10	4	13	6	4	13	2
4	3	15	7	3	15	4	3	15	1	3	14	10	3	14	7
3	2	16	8	2	16	6	2	16	3	2	16	1	2	15	11
2	1	17	9	1	17	8	1	17	6	1	17	5	1	17	3
1	0	18	11	0	18	10	0	18	9	0	18	8	0	18	8
D. 6	0	9	5	0	9	5	0	9	5	0	9	4	0	9	4
5	0	7	10	0	7	10	0	7	10	0	7	10	0	7	9
4	0	6	4	0	6	3	0	6	3	0	6	3	0	6	3
3	0	4	9	0	4	9	0	4	8	0	4	8	0	4	8
2	0	3	2	0	3	2	0	3	2	0	3	1	0	3	1
1	0	1	7	0	1	7	0	1	7	0	1	7	0	1	7

French	38⅛ d.			38¼ d.			38⅜ d.			38½ d.			38⅝ d.		
Livres	£.	s.	d.	£.	s.	d.	£.	s.	d.	£.	s.	d.	£.	s.	d.
10000	529	10	3	531	5	0	532	19	8	534	14	5	536	9	2
5000	264	15	1	265	12	6	266	9	10	267	7	2	268	4	7
4000	211	16	1	212	10	0	213	3	10	213	17	9	214	11	8
3000	158	17	1	159	7	6	159	17	11	160	8	4	160	18	9
2000	105	18	0	106	5	0	106	11	11	106	18	10	107	5	10
1000	52	19	0	53	2	6	53	5	11	53	9	5	53	12	11
900	47	13	1	47	16	3	47	19	4	48	2	6	48	5	7
800	42	7	2	42	10	0	42	12	9	42	15	6	42	18	4
700	37	1	3	37	3	9	37	6	2	37	8	7	37	11	0
600	31	15	5	31	17	6	31	19	7	32	1	8	32	3	9
500	26	9	6	26	11	3	26	12	11	26	14	8	26	16	5
400	21	3	7	21	5	0	21	6	4	21	7	9	21	9	2
300	15	17	8	15	18	9	15	19	9	16	0	10	16	1	10
200	10	11	9	10	12	6	10	13	2	10	13	10	10	14	7
100	5	5	10	5	6	3	5	6	7	5	6	11	5	7	3
90	4	15	3	4	15	7	4	15	11	4	16	3	4	16	6
80	4	4	8	4	5	0	4	5	3	4	5	6	4	5	10
70	3	14	1	3	14	4	3	14	7	3	14	10	3	15	1
60	3	3	6	3	3	9	3	3	11	3	4	2	3	4	4
50	2	12	11	2	13	1	2	13	3	2	13	5	2	13	7
40	2	2	4	2	2	6	2	2	7	2	2	9	2	2	11
30	1	11	9	1	11	10	1	11	11	1	12	1	1	12	2
20	1	1	2	1	1	3	1	1	3	1	1	4	1	1	5
10	0	10	7	0	10	7	0	10	7	0	10	8	0	10	8
9	0	9	6	0	9	6	0	9	7	0	9	7	0	9	7
8	0	8	5	0	8	6	0	8	6	0	8	6	0	8	7
7	0	7	5	0	7	5	0	7	5	0	7	5	0	7	6
6	0	6	4	0	6	4	0	6	4	0	6	5	0	6	5
5	0	5	3	0	5	3	0	5	4	0	5	4	0	5	4
4	0	4	2	0	4	3	0	4	3	0	4	3	0	4	3
3	0	3	2	0	3	2	0	3	2	0	3	2	0	3	2
2	0	2	1	0	2	1	0	2	1	0	2	1	0	2	1
1	0	1	0	0	1	0	0	1	0	0	1	0	0	1	0
Sou. 10	0	0	6	0	0	6	0	0	6	0	0	6	0	0	6
9	0	0	5	0	0	5	0	0	5	0	0	5	0	0	5
8	0	0	5	0	0	5	0	0	5	0	0	5	0	0	5
7	0	0	4	0	0	4	0	0	4	0	0	4	0	0	4
6	0	0	3	0	0	3	0	0	3	0	0	3	0	0	3
5	0	0	3	0	0	3	0	0	3	0	0	3	0	0	3
4	0	0	2	0	0	2	0	0	2	0	0	2	0	0	2
3	0	0	1	0	0	1	0	0	1	0	0	1	0	0	1
2	0	0	1	0	0	1	0	0	1	0	0	1	0	0	1
1	0	0	0	0	0	0	0	0	0	0	0	0	0	0	0
Den. 6	0	0	0	0	0	0	0	0	0	0	0	0	0	0	0

Eng.	At 38¾ d.			38⅞ d.			39 d.			39⅛ d.			39¼ d.		
£.	L.	s.	d.	L.	s.	d.	L.	s.	d.	L.	s.	d.	L.	s.	d.
1000	18580	12	11	18520	18	0	18461	10	9	18402	11	1	18343	19	0
900	16722	11	7	16668	16	2	16615	7	8	16562	6	0	16509	11	1
800	14864	10	4	14816	14	5	14769	4	7	14722	0	11	14675	3	2
700	13006	9	0	12964	12	7	12923	1	6	12881	15	9	12840	15	3
600	11148	7	9	11112	10	10	11076	18	6	11041	10	8	11006	7	5
500	9290	6	5	9260	9	0	9230	15	5	9201	5	7	9171	19	6
400	7432	5	2	7408	7	2	7384	12	4	7361	0	5	7337	11	7
300	5574	3	10	5556	5	5	5538	9	3	5520	15	4	5503	5	8
200	3716	2	7	3704	3	7	3692	6	2	3680	10	3	3668	15	10
100	1858	1	4	1852	1	10	1846	3	1	1840	5	1	1834	7	11
90	1672	5	2	1666	17	7	1661	10	9	1656	4	7	1650	19	1
80	1486	9	0	1481	13	5	1476	18	6	1472	4	1	1467	10	4
70	1300	12	11	1296	9	3	1292	6	2	1288	3	7	1284	1	6
60	1114	16	9	1111	5	1	1107	13	10	1104	3	1	1100	12	9
50	929	0	8	926	0	11	923	1	7	920	2	7	917	3	11
40	743	4	6	740	16	9	738	9	3	736	2	1	733	15	2
30	557	8	5	555	12	7	553	16	11	552	1	6	550	6	4
20	371	12	3	370	8	4	369	4	7	368	1	0	366	17	7
10	185	16	2	185	4	2	184	12	4	184	0	6	183	8	10
9	167	4	6	166	13	9	166	3	1	165	12	6	165	1	11
8	148	12	11	148	3	4	147	13	10	147	4	5	146	15	0
7	130	1	4	129	12	11	129	4	7	128	16	4	128	8	2
6	111	9	8	111	2	6	110	15	5	110	8	4	110	1	3
5	92	18	1	92	12	1	92	6	2	92	0	3	91	14	5
4	74	6	5	74	1	8	73	16	11	73	12	3	73	7	6
3	55	14	10	55	11	3	55	7	8	55	4	2	55	0	8
2	37	3	3	37	0	10	36	18	6	36	16	1	36	13	9
1	18	11	7	18	10	5	18	9	3	18	8	1	18	6	11
S. 10	9	5	10	9	5	3	9	4	7	9	4	0	9	3	5
9	8	7	3	8	6	8	8	6	2	8	5	8	8	5	1
8	7	8	8	7	8	2	7	7	8	7	7	3	7	6	9
7	6	10	1	6	9	8	6	9	3	6	8	10	6	8	5
6	5	11	6	5	11	2	5	10	9	5	10	5	5	10	1
5	4	12	11	4	12	7	4	12	4	4	12	0	4	11	9
4	3	14	4	3	14	1	3	13	10	3	13	7	3	13	5
3	2	15	9	2	15	7	2	15	5	2	15	3	2	15	0
2	1	17	2	1	17	1	1	16	11	1	16	10	1	16	8
1	0	18	7	0	18	6	0	18	6	0	18	5	0	18	4
D. 6	0	9	4	0	9	3	0	9	3	0	9	2	0	9	2
5	0	7	9	0	7	9	0	7	8	0	7	8	0	7	8
4	0	6	2	0	6	2	0	6	2	0	6	2	0	6	1
3	0	4	8	0	4	8	0	4	7	0	4	7	0	4	7
2	0	3	1	0	3	1	0	3	1	0	3	1	0	3	1
1	0	1	7	0	1	7	0	1	7	0	1	6	0	1	6

French	38¾ d.			38⅞ d.			39 d.			39⅛ d.			39¼ d.		
Livres	£.	s.	d.	£.	s.	d.	£.	s.	d.	£.	s.	d.	£.	s.	d.
10000	538	3	10	539	18	7	541	13	4	543	8	0	545	2	9
5000	269	1	11	269	19	3	270	16	8	271	14	0	272	11	4
4000	215	5	6	215	19	5	216	13	4	217	7	2	218	1	1
3000	161	9	2	161	19	7	162	10	0	163	0	5	163	10	10
2000	107	12	9	107	19	8	108	6	8	108	13	7	109	0	6
1000	53	16	4	53	19	10	54	3	4	54	6	9	54	10	3
900	48	8	9	48	11	10	48	15	0	48	18	1	49	1	3
800	43	1	1	43	3	10	43	6	8	43	9	5	43	12	2
700	37	13	5	37	15	10	37	18	4	38	9	0	38	3	2
600	32	5	10	32	7	11	32	10	0	32	12	1	32	14	2
500	26	18	2	26	19	11	27	1	8	27	3	4	27	5	1
400	21	10	6	21	11	11	21	13	2	21	14	8	21	16	1
300	16	2	11	16	3	11	16	5	0	16	6	0	16	7	1
200	10	15	3	10	15	11	10	16	8	10	17	4	10	18	0
100	5	7	7	5	7	11	5	8	4	5	8	8	5	9	0
90	4	16	10	4	17	2	4	17	6	4	17	9	4	18	1
80	4	6	1	4	6	4	4	6	8	4	6	11	4	7	2
70	3	15	4	3	15	7	3	15	10	3	16	0	3	16	3
60	3	4	7	3	4	9	3	5	0	3	5	2	3	5	5
50	2	13	9	2	13	11	2	14	2	2	14	4	2	14	6
40	2	3	2	2	3	2	2	3	4	2	3	5	2	3	7
30	1	12	3	1	12	4	1	12	6	1	12	7	1	12	8
20	1	1	6	1	1	7	1	1	8	1	1	8	1	1	9
10	0	10	9	0	10	9	0	10	10	0	10	10	0	10	10
9	0	9	8	0	9	8	0	9	9	0	9	9	0	9	9
8	0	8	7	0	8	7	0	8	8	0	8	8	0	8	8
7	0	7	6	0	7	6	0	7	7	0	7	7	0	7	7
6	0	6	5	0	6	5	0	6	6	0	6	6	0	6	6
5	0	5	4	0	5	4	0	5	5	0	5	5	0	5	5
4	0	4	3	0	4	3	0	4	4	0	4	4	0	4	4
3	0	3	2	0	3	2	0	3	3	0	3	3	0	3	3
2	0	2	1	0	2	1	0	2	2	0	2	2	0	2	2
1	0	1	0	0	1	1	0	1	1	0	1	1	0	1	1
Sou 10	0	0	6	0	0	6	0	0	6	0	0	6	0	0	6
9	0	0	5	0	0	5	0	0	5	0	0	5	0	0	5
8	0	0	5	0	0	5	0	0	5	0	0	5	0	0	5
7	0	0	4	0	0	4	0	0	4	0	0	4	0	0	4
6	0	0	3	0	0	3	0	0	3	0	0	3	0	0	3
5	0	0	3	0	0	3	0	0	3	0	0	3	0	0	3
4	0	0	2	0	0	2	0	0	2	0	0	2	0	0	2
3	0	0	2	0	0	2	0	0	2	0	0	2	0	0	2
2	0	0	1	0	0	1	0	0	1	0	0	1	0	0	1
1	0	0	0	0	0	0	0	0	0	0	0	0	0	0	0
Den. 6	0	0	0	0	0	0	0	0	0	0	0	0	0	0	0

Eng.	39⅜ d.			39½ d.			39⅝ d.			39¾ d.			39⅞ d.		
£.	L.	s.	d.	L.	s.	d.	L.	s.	d.	L.	s.	d.	L.	s.	d.
1000	18285	14	4	18227	17	0	18170	6	11	18113	4	2	18056	8	6
900	16457	2	10	16405	1	3	16353	6	3	16301	17	9	16250	16	8
800	14628	11	5	14582	5	7	14536	5	7	14490	11	4	14445	2	10
700	12800	0	0	12759	9	10	12719	4	9	12679	4	11	12639	10	0
600	10971	8	7	10936	14	2	10902	4	2	10867	18	6	10833	17	1
500	9142	17	2	9113	18	6	9089	3	6	9056	12	2	9028	4	3
400	7314	5	9	7291	2	9	7268	2	9	7245	5	8	7222	11	5
300	5485	14	4	5468	7	1	5451	2	1	5433	19	3	5416	18	7
200	3657	2	10	3645	11	5	3634	1	5	3622	12	10	3611	5	8
100	1828	11	5	1822	15	8	1817	0	8	1811	6	5	1805	12	10
90	1645	14	3	1640	10	2	1636	6	8	1640	3	9	1625	1	7
80	1462	17	2	1458	4	7	1453	12	7	1449	1	2	1444	10	3
70	1280	0	0	1275	19	0	1271	18	6	1267	18	6	1263	19	0
60	1097	2	10	1093	13	5	1090	4	5	1086	15	10	1083	7	9
50	914	5	9	911	7	10	908	10	4	905	13	3	902	16	5
40	731	8	7	729	2	3	726	16	3	724	10	7	722	5	2
30	548	11	5	546	16	9	545	2	3	543	7	11	541	13	10
20	365	14	3	364	11	2	363	8	2	362	5	3	361	2	7
10	182	17	2	181	5	7	181	14	1	181	2	8	180	11	3
9	164	11	5	164	1	0	163	10	8	163	0	5	162	10	2
8	146	5	9	145	16	6	145	7	3	144	18	1	144	9	0
7	128	0	0	127	11	11	127	3	10	126	15	10	126	7	11
6	109	14	3	109	7	4	109	0	5	108	13	7	108	6	9
5	91	8	7	91	2	9	90	17	0	90	11	4	90	5	8
4	73	2	10	72	18	3	72	13	8	72	9	1	72	4	6
3	54	17	2	54	13	8	54	10	3	54	6	10	54	3	5
2	36	11	5	36	9	1	36	6	10	36	4	6	36	2	3
1	18	5	9	18	4	7	18	3	5	18	2	3	18	1	2
S. 10	9	2	10	9	2	3	9	1	8	9	1	2	9	0	7
9	8	4	7	8	4	1	8	3	6	8	3	0	8	2	6
8	7	6	3	7	5	10	7	5	4	7	4	11	7	4	5
7	6	8	0	6	7	7	6	7	2	6	6	10	6	6	5
6	5	9	9	5	9	4	5	9	0	5	8	8	5	8	4
5	4	11	5	4	11	2	4	10	10	4	10	7	4	10	3
4	3	13	2	3	12	11	3	12	8	3	12	5	3	12	3
3	2	15	10	2	14	8	2	14	6	2	14	4	2	4	2
2	1	16	7	1	16	5	1	16	4	1	16	3	1	16	1
1	0	18	3	0	18	3	0	18	2	0	18	1	0	18	1
D. 6	0	9	2	0	9	1	0	9	1	0	9	1	0	9	0
5	0	7	7	0	7	7	0	7	7	0	7	7	0	7	6
4	0	6	1	0	6	1	0	6	1	0	6	0	0	6	0
3	0	4	7	0	4	7	0	4	7	0	4	6	0	4	6
2	0	3	1	0	3	0	0	3	0	0	3	0	0	3	0
1	0	1	6	0	1	6	0	1	6	0	1	6	0	1	6

French	At 39⅜ d.			39½ d.			39⅝ d.			39¾ d.			39⅞ d.		
Livres	£.	s.	d.	£.	s.	d.	£.	s.	d.	£.	s.	d.	£.	s.	d.
10000	546	17	6	548	12	2	550	6	11	552	1	8	553	16	4
5000	273	8	9	274	6	1	275	3	5	276	0	10	276	18	2
4000	218	15	0	219	8	10	220	2	9	220	16	8	221	10	6
3000	164	1	3	164	11	8	165	2	1	165	12	6	166	2	11
2000	109	7	6	109	15	5	110	1	4	110	8	4	110	15	3
1000	54	13	9	54	17	2	55	0	8	55	4	2	55	7	7
900	49	4	4	49	7	6	49	10	7	49	13	9	49	16	10
800	43	15	0	43	17	9	44	0	6	44	3	4	44	6	1
700	38	5	7	38	8	0	38	10	5	38	12	11	38	15	4
600	32	16	3	32	18	4	33	0	5	33	2	6	33	4	7
500	27	6	10	27	8	7	27	10	4	27	12	1	27	13	9
400	21	17	6	21	18	10	22	0	3	22	1	8	22	3	0
300	16	8	1	16	9	2	16	10	2	16	11	3	16	12	3
200	10	18	9	10	19	5	11	0	1	11	0	10	11	1	6
100	5	9	4	5	9	8	5	10	0	5	10	5	5	10	9
90	4	18	5	4	18	9	4	19	0	4	19	4	4	19	8
80	4	7	6	4	7	9	4	8	0	4	8	4	4	8	7
70	3	16	6	3	16	9	3	17	0	3	17	3	3	17	6
60	3	5	7	3	5	10	3	6	0	3	6	3	3	6	5
50	2	14	8	2	14	10	2	15	0	2	15	2	2	15	4
40	2	3	9	2	3	10	2	4	0	2	4	2	2	4	3
30	1	12	9	1	12	11	1	13	0	1	13	1	1	13	2
20	1	1	10	1	1	11	1	2	0	1	2	1	1	2	1
10	0	10	11	0	10	11	0	11	0	0	11	0	0	11	0
9	0	9	10	0	9	10	0	9	10	0	9	11	0	9	11
8	0	8	9	0	8	9	0	8	9	0	8	10	0	8	10
7	0	7	7	0	7	8	0	7	8	0	7	8	0	7	9
6	0	6	6	0	6	7	0	6	7	0	6	7	0	6	7
5	0	5	5	0	5	5	0	5	6	0	5	6	0	5	6
4	0	4	4	0	4	4	0	4	4	0	4	5	0	4	5
3	0	3	3	0	3	3	0	3	3	0	3	3	0	3	3
2	0	2	2	0	2	2	0	2	2	0	2	2	0	2	2
1	0	1	1	0	1	1	0	1	1	0	1	1	0	1	1
Sou.10	0	0	6	0	0	6	0	0	6	0	0	6	0	0	6
9	0	0	5	0	0	5	0	0	5	0	0	6	0	0	6
8	0	0	5	0	0	5	0	0	5	0	0	5	0	0	5
7	0	0	4	0	0	4	0	0	4	0	0	4	0	0	4
6	0	0	4	0	0	4	0	0	4	0	0	4	0	0	4
5	0	0	3	0	0	3	0	0	3	0	0	3	0	0	3
4	0	0	2	0	0	2	0	0	2	0	0	2	0	0	2
3	0	0	2	0	0	2	0	0	2	0	0	2	0	0	2
2	0	0	1	0	0	1	0	0	1	0	0	1	0	0	1
1	0	0	0	0	0	0	0	0	0	0	0	0	0	0	0
Den.6	0	0	0	0	0	0	0	0	0	0	0	0	0	0	0

EXCHANGE *between* England, Holland, Brabant, Flanders, &c.

The Par is about 36 Schillings, 7 Groots, or Deniers Flemish, to the Pound Sterling.

The course of Exchange is from 33 Sch. 8½ Grs. to 37 Sch. Flemish, to the Pound Sterling.

Dutch Money compared with English, at Par.

			s.	d.		
8 Pennings — is —	1 Groot or Penny —		0	0	54	Sterl.
2 Groots or 16 Pennings — is —	1 Stiver ——		0	1	09	Do.
6 Stivers or 12 Pence — is —	1 Schilling ——		0	6	56	Do.
20 Schillings — is —	1 Pound Flemish —		10	11	.8	Do.
20 Stivers or 40 Pence — is —	1 Guilder or Florin —		1	9	86	Do.
6 Guilders or Florins — is —	1 Pound Flemish —		10	11	18	Do.
2½ Guilders — is —	1 Rix-dollar ——		4	6	66	Do.

The common method of Calculation is by a Statement of the Rule of Three, reducing the Rate of Exchange, and the Dutch Money to be exchanged into Penningens, if there be any.

Examples.

What will be the value of 678*l.* 9*s.* 10*d.* English, in Dutch Money, at 35 Schils. 3½ Groots Flemish,———say,

As 1*l.* Engl. is to 35 Schs. 3½ Grs.—so is 678*l.* 9s. 10*d.*
6

———

211¾ Stuyvers
16

———

3388 Penningens

The answer will be 2298730 Penningens or 7183 Guis. 10 Stuys. 10 Penn.

Proved,

What will be the value of 7183 Guilds. 10 Stuys. 10 Penn. in English Money, at 35 Schs. 3½ Grs. Flemish, the Pound Sterling? —— say,

As 35 Schs. 3½ Grs. is to 1*l.* so is 7183 Gus. 10 Sts 10 Ps.
6   20

———

211¾ Stuyvers   143670 Stuyvers
16   16

———

3388 Penningens Divide by 3388) 2298730 Penningens

The answer will be, *l.* 678 9 10

I ſhall now (in the next following Table) conſider Schillings and Groots, Stuyvers and Penningens, in their relative proportions decimally, one Guilder being the Integer. In the mean time obſerving that 1 Guilder is equal to 3 Schills. 4 Groots, which at the Par of Exchange, is 1s. 9¾ Engliſh, and that one pound Flemiſh is equal to 6 Guilders, which, at par, is 10s. 11½d. Engliſh.

A Decimal TABLE of *Schillings*, *Groots*, *Stuyvers* and *Penningen*, 1 Guilder being the Integer.

Schillings		Schillings		Groots		Groots		Stuyvers	
1	.3	21	6.3	1h	.0375	11h	.2875	18	.9
2	.6	22	6.6	2	.05	12	.3	19	.9.
3	.9	23	6.9	2h	.0625	**Stuyvers**		**Penningen**	
4	1.2	24	7.2	3	.075	1	.05	1	.003125
5	1.5	25	7.5	3h	.0875	2	.1	2	.00625
6	1.8	26	7.8	4	.1	3	.15	3	.009375
7	2.1	27	8.1	4h	.1125	4	.2	4	.0125
8	2.4	28	8.4	5	.125	5	.25	5	.015625
9	2.7	29	8.7	5h	.1375	6	.3	6	.01875
10	3.0	30	9.0	6	.15	7	.35	7	.021875
11	3.3	31	9.3	6h	.1625	8	.4	8	.025
12	3.6	32	9.6	7	.175	9	.45	9	.028125
13	3.9	33	9.9	7h	.1875	10	.5	10	.03125
14	4.2	34	10.2	8	.2	11	.55	11	.034375
15	4.5	35	10.5	8h	.2125	12	.6	12	.0375
16	4.8	36	10.8	9	.225	13	.65	13	.040625
17	5.1	37	11.1	9h	.2375	14	.7	14	.04375
18	5.4	**Groots**		10	.25	15	.75	15	.046875
19	5.7	½	0125	10h	.2625	16	.8	16	.5
20	6.0	1.	025	11	.275	17	.85		

A TABLE

A TABLE of Decimal Multipliers, for *Dutch* and *English* MONEY, at the feveral Rates of Exchange.

ENGLISH into DUTCH.				DUTCH into ENGLISH.			
RATE	Multpr.	RATE	Multpr.	RATE	Mulp.	RATE	Mulp.
33. 8½	10.1125	35. 2½	10.5625	33. 8½	.09889	35. 2h	.09467
33. 9	10.125	35. 3	10.575	33. 9	.09876	35. 3	.09456
33. 9h	10.1375	35. 3h	10.5875	33. 9h	.09864	35. 3h	.09445
33.10	10.15	35. 4	10.6	33.10	.09852	35. 4	.09435
33.10h	10.1625	35. 4h	10.6125	33.10h	.09839	35. 4h	.09423
33.11	10.175	35. 5	10.625	33.11	.09828	35. 5	.09412
33.11h	10.1875	35. 5h	10.6375	33.11h	.09815	35. 5h	094
34. 0	10.2	35. 6	10.65	34. 0	.09804	55. 6	.0939
34. 0h	10.2125	35. 6h	10.6625	34. 0h	.09792	35. 6h	.09378
34. 1	10.225	35. 7	10.675	34 1	.0978	35. 7	09367
34. 1h	10.2375	35. 7h	10.6875	34. 1h	.09768	35. 7h	.09356
34. 2	10.25	35. 8	10.7	34. 2	.09756	35. 8	.09346
34. 2h	10.2625	35. 8h	10 71.25	34. 2h	.09744	35. 8h	.09335
34. 3	10.275	35. 9	10.725	34. 3	.09732	35. 9	.09323
34. 3h	10.2875	35. 9h	10.7375	34. 3h	.0972	35. 9h	.09313
34. 4	10.3	35.10	10.75	34. 4	.09708	35.10	09302
34. 4h	10.3125	35.10h	10.7625	34. 4h	.09697	35.10h	.09212
34. 5	10.325	35.11	10.775	34. 5	.09686	35.11	.0928
34. 5h	10.3375	35.11h	10.7875	34. 5h	.09672	35.11h	.0927
34. 6	10.35	36. 0	.0 8	34. 6	.09661	36. 0	.09259
34. 6h	10.3625	36. 0h	10.8125	34. 6h	.0965	36. 0h	.09249
34. 7	10.375	36. 1	10.825	34. 7	.09639	36. 1	.09238
34. 7h	10.3875	36. 1h	10.8375	34. 7h	.09627	36. 1h	.09227
34. 8	10.4	36. 2	10.85	34. 8	.09615	36. 2	.09216
34. 8h	10.4125	36. 2h	10.8625	34. 8h	.09604	36. 2h	.09206
34. 9	10.425	36. 3	10.875	34. 9	.09593	36. 3	.09196
34. 9h	10.4375	36. 3h	10.8875	34. 9h	.09581	36. 3h	.09185
34.10	10.45	36. 4	10.9	34.10	.09569	36. 4	.09174
34.10h	10.4625	36. 5	10.925	34.10h	.09558	36. 5	.09153
34.11	10.46	36. 6	10.95	34.11	.09547	36. 6	.0913
34.11h	10.4875	36. 7	10 975	34.11h	.09536	36. 7	.09111
35. 0	10.5	36. 8	11.	35. 0	.09523	36. 8	.09091
35. 0h	10.5125	36. 9	11.025	35. 0h	.09512	36. 9	.0907
35. 1	10.525	36.10	11.05	35. 1	.09501	36.10	.0905
35. 1h	10.5375	36.11	11.075	35. 1h	.0949	36.11	.09029
35. 2	10.55	37.	11.1	35. 2	.09478	37.	.09009

The

The use of the foregoing Tables are the same as in the former Exchanges; that is, if English Money is to be exchanged into Dutch, multiply it by the Tabular Number opposite the Rate in the Dutch column; and for Dutch into English, multiply by the number in the English column, remembring always to express the Shillings and Pence as Decimal Parts of a Pound Sterling, and the Stuyvers and Penningen as Decimal Parts of a Guilder.

Example.

What will be the value of 120*l.* 15 6. English, in Dutch Money, at 35 Guilds. 4 Gr. to the pound Sterling?

Operation.

120*l.* 15 6 is 120.775 Parts
Multiplied by 10.6 Tabular Number

Product in Guilders and Parts 1280.2150, equal to 1280G. 4S. 5P.

Again.

What will be the value of 1280 Guilds 4 Stuys. and 5 Penn. at 35 Guilds. 4 Gr. to the Pound Sterling?

Operation.

1280 Gu. 4 St. 5 Pe. is 128.0215 Parts
Multiplied by .09434 Tabular Number

Product *l.*120.77500310 eq. to 120*l* 15 6

Proved by the common Tables at 35 Sts. 4 Grs.

100*l.*			is	1060g.	St.	P.	
20				212			
0	10			5	6		
0	5			2	13		
0	0	6		0	5	5	
120*l.*	15	6		1280g.	4	5	
G.1000			is	94	6	9½	
200				18	17	4½	
80				7	10	11½	
0	4			0	0	4½	
0	0	5		0	0	½	
G.1280	4	5		120*l.*	15	6	

Exchanges

EXCHANGE *between* England, Holland, Brabant, Flanders, &c.

From 38 Stu. 8½ Groots to 37 Schills. to the pound Sterling, in the Rate of Exchange at the head of each column.

For 34 S. 3½ G. Read 34 Schilling 3½ Groot, and so of all the rest.

In the following Table, from 35 Schills. 5 Gr. to 37 Schillings, the half Groots are omitted; but if in the course of business an half Groot should occur, let the English Money in the column which is an half Groot more than the given rate be subtracted from that which is an half Groot less, and half the remainder subtracted from the latter, will be the answer.

Example for English Money.

What will be the value of 1000 Guilds. at 35 Sch. 6½ Gr.

At 35 S. 6 G.	is	93*l.*	17	11¼
35 7	is	93	13	6½
Remainder		0	4	4¾
Half remainder Subtracted from 93*l.* 17 11¼		0	2	2⅜
Answer at 35 S. 6½ G.		93	15	9

For

For Dutch Money let the ſum in the column which is an half Groot leſs be ſubtracted from the ſum in the column which is an half Groot more, and half the remainder added to the former will be the anſwer.

What will be the value of 100*l.* in Dutch Money, at 35 S. 6½ Gr.

At 35 S. 7 G.	is	1067.10
At 35 6	is	1065.
Remainder		2,10
Half remainder added to 1065,		1.5
Anſwer at 35 S. 6½ G.		1066.5

Exchanges

Eng.	33 *s.* 8½ *g.*			33 *s.* 9 *g.*			33 *s.* 9½ *g.*			33 *s.* 10 *g.*			33 *s.* 10½ *g.*		
£.	G.	s.	p.	G.	s.	p.	G.	s.	p.	G.	s.	p.	G.	s.	p.
1000	10112	10		10125	0		10137	10		10150			10162	10	
900	9101	5		9112	10		9123	15		9135			9146	5	
800	8090	0		8100	0		8110	0		8120			8130	0	
700	7078	15		7087	10		7096	5		7105			7113	15	
600	6067	10		6075	0		6082	10		6090			6097	10	
500	5056	5		5062	10		5068	15		5075			5081	5	
400	4045	0		4050	0		4055	0		4060			4065	0	
300	3033	15		3037	10		3041	5		3045			3048	15	
200	2022	10		2025	0		2027	10		2030			2032	10	
100	1011	5		1012	10		1013	15		1015			1016	5	
90	910	2	8	911	5		912	7	8	913	10		914	12	8
80	809	0	0	810	0		811	0	0	812	0		813	0	0
70	707	17	8	708	15		709	12	8	710	10		711	7	8
60	606	15	0	607	10		608	5	0	609	0		609	15	0
50	505	12	8	506	5		506	17	8	507	10		508	2	8
40	404	10	0	405	0		405	10	0	406	0		406	10	0
30	303	7	8	303	15		304	2	8	304	10		304	17	8
20	202	5	0	202	10		202	15	0	203	0		203	5	0
10	101	2	6	101	5		101	7	8	101	10		101	12	8
9	91	0	4	91	2	8	91	4	12	91	7		91	9	4
8	80	18	0	81	0	0	81	2	0	81	4		81	6	0
7	70	15	12	70	17	8	70	19	4	71	1		71	2	12
6	60	13	8	60	15	0	60	16	8	60	18		60	19	8
5	50	11	4	50	12	8	50	13	12	50	15		50	16	4
4	40	9	0	40	10	0	40	11	0	40	12		40	13	0
3	30	6	12	30	7	8	30	8	4	30	9		30	9	12
2	20	4	8	20	5	0	20	5	8	20	6		20	6	8
1	10	2	4	10	2	8	10	2	12	10	3		10	3	4
S. 10	5	1	2	5	1	4	5	1	6	5	1	8	5	1	10
9	4	11	0	4	11	2	4	11	4	4	11	6	4	11	7
8	4	0	14	4	1	0	4	1	2	4	1	3	4	1	4
7	3	10	13	3	10	14	3	10	15	3	11	1	3	11	2
6	3	0	11	3	0	12	3	0	13	3	0	14	3	1	0
5	2	10	9	2	10	10	2	10	11	2	10	12	2	10	13
4	2	0	7	2	0	8	2	0	9	2	0	9	2	0	10
3	1	10	5	1	10	6	1	10	7	1	10	7	1	10	8
2	1	0	4	1	0	4	1	0	4	1	0	5	1	0	5
1	0	10	2	0	10	2	0	10	2	0	10	2	0	10	3
D. 6	0	5	1	0	5	1	0	5	1	0	5	1	0	5	1
5	0	4	3	0	4	3	0	4	4	0	4	4	0	4	4
4	0	3	6	0	3	6	0	3	6	0	3	6	0	3	6
3	0	2	8	0	2	8	0	2	8	0	2	9	0	2	9
2	0	1	11	0	1	11	0	1	11	0	1	11	0	1	11
1	0	0	13	0	0	13	0	0	13	0	0	13	0	0	13

Dutch	33 s. 8½ g.			33 s. 9 g.			33 s. 9½ g.			33 s. 10 g.			33 s. 10½ g.		
Guild.	£.	s.	d.	£.	s.	d.	£.	s.	d.	£.	s.	d.	£.	s.	d.
10000	988	17	6	987	13	1	986	8	8	985	4	5	984	0	2
5000	494	8	9	493	16	6	493	4	4	492	12	2	492	0	1
4000	395	11	0	395	1	2	394	11	6	394	1	9	393	12	1
3000	296	13	3	296	5	11	295	18	7	295	11	4	295	4	0
2000	197	15	6	197	10	7	197	5	9	197	0	10	196	16	0
1000	98	17	9	98	15	3	98	12	10	98	10	5	98	8	1
900	88	19	11	88	17	9	88	15	7	88	13	4	88	11	2
800	79	2	2	79	0	3	78	18	3	78	16	4	78	14	5
700	69	4	5	69	2	8	69	1	0	63	19	3	68	17	7
600	59	6	7	59	5	2	59	3	8	59	2	3	59	0	9
500	49	8	10	49	7	7	49	6	5	49	5	2	49	4	0
400	39	11	1	39	10	1	39	9	1	39	8	2	39	7	2
300	29	13	4	29	12	7	29	11	10	29	11	1	29	10	4
200	19	15	6	19	15	0	19	14	7	19	14	1	19	13	7
100	9	17	9	9	17	6	9	17	3	9	17	0	9	16	9
90	8	18	0	8	17	9	8	17	6	8	17	4	8	17	1
80	7	18	2	7	18	0	7	17	10	7	17	7	7	17	5
70	6	18	5	6	18	3	6	18	1	6	17	11	6	17	9
60	5	18	8	5	18	6	5	18	4	6	18	2	5	18	1
50	4	18	10	4	18	9	4	18	7	4	18	6	4	18	4
40	3	19	1	3	19	0	3	18	11	3	18	9	3	18	8
30	2	19	4	2	19	3	2	19	2	2	19	1	2	19	0
20	1	19	6	1	19	6	1	19	5	1	19	5	1	19	4
10	0	19	9	0	19	9	0	19	8	0	19	8	0	19	8
9	0	17	9	0	17	9	0	17	9	0	17	8	0	17	8
8	0	15	9	0	15	9	0	15	9	0	15	9	0	15	9
7	0	13	10	0	13	10	0	13	9	0	13	9	0	13	9
6	0	11	10	0	11	10	0	11	10	0	11	9	0	11	9
5	0	9	10	0	9	10	0	9	10	0	9	10	0	9	10
4	0	7	11	0	7	10	0	7	10	0	7	10	0	7	10
3	0	5	11	0	5	11	0	5	11	0	5	11	0	5	10
2	0	3	11	0	3	11	0	3	11	0	3	11	0	3	11
1	0	1	11	0	1	11	0	1	11	0	1	11	0	1	11
Stu 10	0	0	11	0	0	11	0	0	11	0	0	11	0	0	11
9	0	0	10	0	0	10	0	0	10	0	0	10	0	0	10
8	0	0	9	0	0	9	0	0	9	0	0	9	0	0	9
7	0	0	8	0	0	8	0	0	8	0	0	8	0	0	8
6	0	0	7	0	0	7	0	0	7	0	0	7	0	0	7
5	0	0	6	0	0	6	0	0	6	0	0	6	0	0	6
4	0	0	4	0	0	4	0	0	4	0	0	4	0	0	4
3	0	0	3	0	0	3	0	0	3	0	0	3	0	0	3
2	0	0	2	0	0	2	0	0	2	0	0	2	0	0	2
1	0	0	1	0	0	1	0	0	1	0	0	1	0	0	1
Pen 12	0	0	1	0	0	1	0	0	1	0	0	1	0	0	1
8	0	0	0	0	0	0	0	0	0	0	0	0	0	0	0

Eng.	33 s. 11. g.			33 s. 11½ g.			34 s.			34 s. ½ g.			34 s. 1 g.		
£.	G.	s.	p.	G.	s.	p.	G.	s.	p.	G.	s.	p.	G.	s.	p.
1000	10175	0		10187	10		10200			10212	10		10225	0	
900	9157	10		9168	15		9180			9191	5		9202	10	
800	8140	0		8150	0		8160			8170	0		8180	0	
700	7122	10		7137	0		7140			7148	0		7157	10	
600	6105	0		6112	10		6120			6127	10		6135	0	
500	5087	10		5093	15		5100			5106	5		5112	10	
400	4070	0		4075	6		4080.			4085	0		4090	0	
300	3052	10		3056	5		3060			3063	15		3067	10	
200	2035	0		2037	10		2040			2042	10		2045	0	
100	1017	10		1018	15		1020			1021	5		1022	10	
90	915	15		916	17	8	918			919	2	8	920	5	
80	814	0		815	0	0	816			817	0	0	818	0	
70	712	5		713	2	8	714			714	17	8	715	15	
60	610	10		611	5	0	612			612	15	0	613	10	
50	508	15		509	7	8	510			510	12	8	511	5	
40	407	0		407	10	0	408			408	10	0	409	0	
30	305	5		305	12	8	306			306	7	8	306	15	
20	203	10		203	15	0	204			204	5	[illegible]	204	10	
10	101	15		101	17	8	102			102	2	8	102	5	
9	91	11	8	91	13	2	91	16		91	18	4	92	0	8
8	81	8	0	81	10	0	81	12		81	14	0	81	16	0
7	71	4	8	71	6	4	71	8		71	9	12	71	11	8
6	61	1	0	61	2	8	61	4		61	5	8	61	7	0
5	50	17	8	50	18	2	51	0		51	1	4	51	2	8
4	40	14	0	40	15	0	40	16		40	17	0	40	18	0
3	30	10	8	30	11	4	30	12		30	12	12	30	13	8
2	20	7	0	20	7	8	20	8		20	8	8	20	9	0
1	10	3	8	10	3	12	10	4		10	4	4	10	4	8
S. 10	5	1	12	5	1	14	5	2		5	2	2	5	2	4
9	4	11	9	4	11	11	4	11	13	4	11	15	4	12	0
8	4	1	6	4	1	8	4	1	10	4	1	11	4	1	13
7	3	11	4	3	11	5	3	11	6	3	11	8	3	11	9
6	3	1	1	3	1	2	3	1	3	3	1	4	3	1	6
5	2	10	14	2	10	15	2	11	0	2	11	1	2	11	2
4	2	0	11	2	0	12	2	0	13	2	0	14	2	0	14
3	1	10	8	1	10	9	1	10	10	1	10	10	1	10	10
2	1	0	6	1	0	6	1	0	6	1	0	7	1	0	7
1	0	10	3	0	10	3	0	10	3	0	10	3	0	10	4
D. 6	0	5	1	0	5	1	0	5	1	0	5	2	0	5	2
5	0	4	4	0	4	4	0	4	4	0	4	4	0	4	4
4	0	3	6	0	3	6	0	3	6	0	3	6	0	3	6
3	0	2	9	0	2	9	0	2	9	0	2	9	0	2	9
2	0	1	11	0	1	11	0	1	11	0	1	11	0	1	11
1	0	0	13	0	0	13	0	0	13	0	0	14	0	0	14

Dutch.	33 s. 11 g.			33s. 11½ g.			34 s.			34 s. ½ g.			34 s. 1 g.		
Guild.	£.	s.	d.	£.	s.	d.	£.	s.	d.	£.	s.	d.	£.	s.	d.
10000	982	16	0	981	11	10	980	7	10	979	3	10	977	19	10
5000	491	8	0	490	15	11	490	3	11	489	11	11	488	19	11
4000	393	2	5	392	12	9	392	3	1	391	13	6	391	3	11
3000	294	16	9	294	9	6	294	2	4	293	15	1	293	7	11
2000	196	11	2	196	6	4	196	1	6	195	16	9	195	11	11
1000	98	5	7	98	3	2	98	0	9	97	18	4	97	15	11
900	88	9	0	88	6	0	88	4	8	88	2	6	88	0	4
800	78	12	5	78	10	6	78	8	7	78	8	6	78	4	9
700	68	15	11	68	14	2	68	12	6	68	10	10	68	9	2
600	58	19	4	58	17	11	58	16	5	58	15	0	58	13	7
500	49	2	9	49	1	7	49	0	4	48	19	2	48	18	0
400	39	6	3	39	5	3	39	4	3	39	3	4	39	2	4
300	29	9	8	29	8	11	29	8	2	29	7	6	29	6	9
200	19	13	1	19	12	7	19	12	1	19	11	8	19	11	2
100	9	16	6	9	16	3	9	16	1	9	15	10	9	15	7
90	8	16	10	8	16	8	8	16	5	8	16	3	8	16	0
80	7	17	3	7	17	0	7	16	10	7	16	8	7	16	5
70	6	17	7	6	17	5	6	17	3	6	17	1	6	16	11
60	5	17	11	5	17	9	5	17	7	5	17	6	5	17	4
50	4	18	3	4	18	2	4	18	0	4	17	11	4	17	9
40	3	18	7	3	18	6	3	18	5	3	18	4	3	18	2
30	2	18	11	2	18	10	2	18	10	2	18	9	2	18	8
20	1	19	3	1	19	3	1	19	2	1	19	2	1	19	1
10	0	19	7	0	19	7	0	19	7	0	19	7	0	19	6
9	0	17	8	0	17	8	0	17	7	0	17	7	0	17	7
8	0	15	8	0	15	8	0	15	8	0	15	8	0	15	7
7	0	13	9	0	13	9	0	13	8	0	13	8	0	13	8
6	0	11	9	0	11	9	0	11	9	0	11	9	0	11	8
5	0	9	10	0	9	9	0	9	9	0	9	9	0	9	9
4	0	7	10	0	7	10	0	7	10	0	7	10	0	7	9
3	0	5	10	0	5	10	0	5	10	0	5	10	0	5	10
2	0	3	11	0	3	11	0	3	11	0	3	11	0	3	11
1	0	1	11	0	1	11	0	1	11	0	1	11	0	1	11
Stu 10	0	0	11	0	0	11	0	0	11	0	0	11	0	0	11
9	0	0	10	0	0	10	0	0	10	0	0	10	0	0	10
8	0	0	9	0	0	9	0	0	9	0	0	9	0	0	9
7	0	0	8	0	0	8	0	0	8	0	0	8	0	0	8
6	0	0	7	0	0	7	0	0	7	0	0	7	0	0	7
5	0	0	6	0	0	6	0	0	6	0	0	6	0	0	5
4	0	0	4	0	0	4	0	0	4	0	0	4	0	0	4
3	0	0	3	0	0	3	0	0	3	0	0	3	0	0	3
2	0	0	2	0	0	2	0	0	2	0	0	2	0	0	2
1	0	0	1	0	0	1	0	0	1	0	0	1	0	0	1
Pen 12	0	0	1	0	0	1	0	0	1	0	0	1	0	0	1
8	0	0	0	0	0	0	0	0	0	0	0	0	0	0	0

Eng.	34 *s.* 1½ *g.*			34 *s.* 2 *g.*			34 *s.* 2½ *g.*			34 *s.* 3 *g.*			34 *s.* 3½ *g.*		
£.	*G.*	*s.*	*p.*	*G.*	*s.*	*p.*	*G.*	*s.*	*p.*	*G.*	*s.*	*p.*	*G.*	*s.*	*p.*
1000	10237	10		10250			10262	10		10275	0		10287	10	
900	9213	15		9225			9236	5		9247	10		9258	15	
800	8190	0		8200			8210	0		8220	0		8230	0	
700	7166	5		7175			7183	15		7192	10		7201	5	
600	6142	10		6150			6157	10		6165	0		6172	10	
500	5118	15		5125			5131	5		5137	10		5143	15	
400	4095	0		4100			4105	0		4110	0		4115	0	
300	3071	5		3075			3078	15		3082	10		3086	5	
200	2047	10		2050			2052	10		2055	0		2057	10	
100	1023	15		1025			1026	5		1027	10		1028	15	
90	921	7	8	922	10		923	12	8	924	15		925	17	8
80	819	0	0	820	0		821	0	0	822	0		823	0	0
70	716	12	8	717	10		718	7	8	719	5		720	2	8
60	614	5	0	615	0		615	15	0	616	10		617	5	0
50	511	17	8	512	10		513	2	8	513	15		514	7	8
40	409	10	0	410	0		410	10	0	411	0		411	10	0
30	307	2	8	307	10		307	17	8	308	5		308	12	8
20	204	15	0	205	0		205	5	0	205	10		205	15	0
10	102	7	8	102	10		102	12	8	102	15		102	17	8
9	92	2	12	92	5		92	7	4	92	9	8	92	11	12
8	81	18	0	82	0		82	2	0	82	4	0	82	6	0
7	71	13	4	71	15		71	16	12	71	18	8	72	0	4
6	61	8	8	61	10		61	11	8	61	13	0	61	14	8
5	51	3	12	51	5		51	6	4	51	7	8	51	8	12
4	40	19	0	41	0		41	1	0	41	2	0	41	3	0
3	30	14	4	30	15		30	15	2	30	16	8	30	17	4
2	20	9	8	20	10		20	10	8	20	11	0	20	11	8
1	10	4	12	10	5		10	5	4	10	5	8	10	5	12
S. 10	5	2	0	5	2	8	5	2	10	5	2	12	5	2	14
9	4	12	2	4	12	5	4	12	6	4	12	8	4	12	9
8	4	1	14	4	2	0	4	2	2	4	2	3	4	2	5
7	3	11	11	3	11	12	3	11	13	3	11	15	3	12	0
6	3	1	7	3	1	8	3	1	9	3	1	10	3	1	12
5	2	11	3	2	11	4	2	11	5	2	11	6	2	11	7
4	2	0	15	2	1	0	2	1	1	2	1	2	2	1	2
3	1	10	11	1	10	12	1	10	13	1	10	13	1	10	14
2	1	0	8	1	0	8	1	0	8	1	0	9	1	0	9
1	0	10	4	0	10	4	0	10	4	0	10	4	0	10	5
D. 6	0	5	2	0	5	2	0	5	2	0	5	2	0	5	2
5	0	4	4	0	4	4	0	4	4	0	4	4	0	4	5
4	0	3	7	0	3	7	0	3	7	0	3	7	0	3	7
3	0	2	9	0	2	9	0	2	9	0	2	9	0	2	9
2	0	1	11	0	1	11	0	1	11	0	1	11	0	1	11
1	0	0	14	0	0	14	0	0	14	0	0	14	0	0	14

Dutch.	34 s. 1½ g.			34 s. 2 g.			34 s. 2½ g.			34 s. 3 g.			34 s. 3½ g.		
Guild.	£.	s.	d.	£.	s.	d.	£.	s.	d.	£.	s.	d.	£.	s.	d.
10000	976	16	0	975	12	2	974	8	5	973	4	8	972	1	0
5000	488	8	0	487	16	1	487	4	3	486	12	4	486	0	6
4000	390	14	4	390	4	10	389	15	4	389	5	10	388	16	5
3000	293	0	9	292	13	7	292	6	0	291	19	5	291	12	3
2000	195	7	2	195	2	5	194	17	8	194	12	11	194	8	2
1000	97	13	7	97	11	2	97	8	10	97	6	5	97	4	1
900	87	18	2	87	16	1	87	13	11	87	11	9	87	9	8
800	78	2	10	78	0	11	77	19	0	77	17	2	77	15	3
700	68	7	6	68	5	10	68	4	2	68	2	6	68	0	10
600	58	12	1	58	10	8	58	9	3	58	7	10	58	6	5
500	48	16	9	48	15	7	48	14	5	48	13	2	48	12	0
400	39	1	5	39	0	5	38	19	6	38	18	7	38	17	7
300	29	6	0	29	5	4	29	4	7	29	3	11	29	3	2
200	19	10	8	19	10	3	19	9	9	19	9	3	19	8	9
100	9	15	4	9	15	1	9	14	10	9	17	4	9	14	5
90	8	15	9	8	15	7	8	15	4	8	15	2	8	14	11
80	7	16	3	7	16	1	7	15	10	7	15	8	7	15	6
70	6	16	9	6	16	7	6	16	5	6	16	3	6	16	1
60	5	17	2	5	17	0	5	16	11	5	16	9	5	16	7
50	4	17	8	4	17	6	4	17	5	4	17	3	4	17	2
40	3	18	1	3	18	0	3	17	11	3	17	10	3	17	9
30	2	18	7	2	18	6	2	18	5	2	18	4	2	18	3
20	1	19	0	1	19	0	1	18	11	1	18	11	1	18	10
10	0	19	6	0	19	6	0	19	5	0	19	5	0	19	5
9	0	17	7	0	17	6	0	17	6	0	17	6	0	17	6
8	0	15	7	0	15	7	0	15	7	0	15	6	0	15	6
7	0	13	8	0	13	8	0	13	7	0	13	7	0	13	7
6	0	11	8	0	11	8	0	11	8	0	11	8	0	11	8
5	0	9	9	0	9	9	0	9	9	0	9	8	0	9	8
4	0	7	9	0	7	9	0	7	9	0	7	9	0	7	9
3	0	5	10	0	5	10	0	5	10	0	5	10	0	5	10
2	0	3	11	0	3	10	0	3	10	0	3	10	0	3	10
1	0	1	11	0	1	11	0	1	11	0	1	11	0	1	11
Stu. 10	0	0	11	0	0	11	0	0	11	0	0	11	0	0	11
9	0	0	10	0	0	10	0	0	10	0	0	10	0	0	10
8	0	0	9	0	0	9	0	0	9	0	0	9	0	0	9
7	0	0	8	0	0	8	0	0	8	0	0	8	0	0	8
6	0	0	7	0	0	7	0	0	7	0	0	7	0	0	7
5	0	0	5	0	0	5	0	0	5	0	0	5	0	0	5
4	0	0	4	0	0	4	0	0	4	0	0	4	0	0	4
3	0	0	3	0	0	3	0	0	3	0	0	3	0	0	3
2	0	0	2	0	0	2	0	0	2	0	0	2	0	0	2
1	0	0	1	0	0	1	0	0	1	0	0	1	0	0	1
Pen 12	0	0	1	0	0	1	0	0	0	0	0	0	0	0	0
8	0	0	0	0	0	0	0	0	0	0	0	0	0	0	0

Eng.	34 s. 4 g.			34 s. 4½ g.			34 s. 5 g.			34 s. 5½ g.			34 s. 6 g.		
£.	G.	s.	p.	G.	s.	p.	G.	s.	p.	G.	s.	p.	G.	s.	p.
1000	10300			10312	10		10325	0		10337	10		10350		
900	9270			9281	5		9292	10		9303	15		9315		
800	8240			8250	0		8260	0		8270	0		8280		
700	7210			7218	15		7227	10		7236	5		7245		
600	6180			6187	10		6195	0		6202	10		6210		
500	5150			5156	5		5162	10		5168	15		5175		
400	4120			4125	0		4130	0		4135	0		4140		
300	3090			3093	15		3097	10		3101	5		3105		
200	2060			2062	10		2065	0		2067	10		2070		
100	1030			1031	5		1032	10		1033	15		1035		
90	927			928	2	8	929	5		930	7	8	931	10	
80	824			825	0	0	826	0		827	0	0	828	0	
70	721			721	17	8	722	15		723	12	8	724	10	
60	618			618	15	0	619	10		620	5	0	621	0	
50	515			515	12	8	516	5		516	17	8	517	10	
40	412			412	10	0	413	0		413	10	0	414	0	
30	309			309	7	8	309	15		310	2	8	310	10	
20	206			206	5	0	206	10		206	15	0	207	0	
10	103			103	2	8	103	5		103	7	8	103	10	
9	92	14		92	16	4	92	18	8	93	0	12	93	3	
8	82	8		82	10	0	82	12	0	82	14	0	82	16	
7	72	2		72	3	12	72	5	8	72	7	4	72	9	
6	61	16		61	17	8	61	19	0	62	0	8	62	2	
5	51	10		51	11	4	51	12	8	51	13	12	51	15	
4	41	4		41	5	0	41	6	0	41	7	0	41	8	
3	30	18		30	18	12	30	19	8	31	0	4	31	1	
2	20	12		20	12	8	20	13	0	20	13	8	20	14	
1	10	6		10	6	4	10	6	8	10	6	12	10	7	
S. 10	5	3		5	3	2	5	3	4	5	3	6	5	3	8
9	4	12	11	4	12	13	4	12	15	4	13	1	4	13	2
8	4	2	6	4	2	8	4	2	10	4	2	11	4	2	13
7	3	12	1	3	12	3	3	12	4	3	12	6	3	12	7
6	3	1	13	3	1	14	3	1	15	3	2	0	3	2	2
5	2	11	8	2	11	9	2	11	10	2	11	11	2	11	12
4	2	1	3	2	1	4	2	1	5	2	1	6	2	1	6
3	1	10	15	1	10	15	1	11	0	1	11	0	1	11	1
2	1	0	10	1	0	10	1	0	10	1	0	11	1	0	11
1	0	10	5	0	10	5	0	10	5	0	10	6	0	10	6
D. 6	0	5	2	0	5	2	0	5	3	0	5	3	0	5	3
5	0	4	5	0	4	5	0	4	5	0	4	5	0	4	5
4	0	3	7	0	3	7	0	3	7	0	3	7	0	3	7
3	0	2	9	0	2	9	0	2	9	0	2	9	0	2	9
2	0	1	12	0	1	12	0	1	12	0	1	12	0	1	12
1	0	0	14	0	0	14	0	0	14	0	0	14	0	0	14

Dutch.	34 s. 4 g.			34 s. 4½ g.			34 s. 5 g.			34 s. 5½ g.			34 s. 6 g.		
Guild.	£.	s.	d.	£.	s.	d.	£.	s.	d.	£.	s.	d.	£.	s.	d.
10000	970	17	5	969	13	11	968	10	5	967	7	0	966	3	8
5000	485	8	8	487	16	11	484	5	6	483	13	6	483	1	10
4000	388	6	11	387	17	7	387	8	2	386	18	9	386	9	5
3000	291	5	2	290	18	2	290	11	1	290	4	1	289	17	1
2000	194	3	5	193	18	9	193	14	1	193	9	4	193	4	8
1000	97	1	9	96	19	4	96	17	0	96	14	8	96	12	4
900	87	7	6	87	5	5	87	3	4	87	1	2	86	19	1
800	77	13	4	77	11	6	77	9	7	77	7	9	77	5	10
700	67	19	2	67	17	7	67	15	11	67	14	3	67	12	7
600	58	5	2	58	3	7	58	2	2	58	0	9	57	19	5
500	48	10	10	48	9	8	48	8	6	48	7	4	48	6	2
400	38	16	8	38	15	9	38	14	9	38	13	10	38	12	11
300	29	2	6	29	1	9	29	1	1	29	0	5	28	19	8
200	19	8	4	19	7	10	19	7	5	19	6	11	19	6	5
100	9	14	2	9	13	11	9	13	8	9	13	5	9	13	2
90	8	14	9	8	14	6	8	14	4	8	14	1	8	13	11
80	7	15	4	7	15	1	7	14	11	7	14	9	7	14	7
70	6	15	11	6	15	9	6	15	7	6	15	5	6	15	3
60	5	16	6	5	16	4	5	16	2	5	16	1	5	15	11
50	4	17	1	4	16	11	4	16	10	4	16	8	4	16	7
40	3	17	8	3	17	7	3	17	5	3	17	4	3	17	3
30	2	18	3	2	18	2	2	18	1	2	18	0	2	17	11
20	1	18	10	1	18	9	1	18	9	1	18	8	1	18	7
10	0	19	5	0	19	4	0	19	4	0	19	4	0	19	3
9	0	17	5	0	17	5	0	17	5	0	17	5	0	17	4
8	0	15	6	0	15	6	0	15	6	0	15	5	0	15	5
7	0	13	7	0	13	7	0	13	6	0	13	6	0	13	6
6	0	11	7	0	11	7	0	11	7	0	11	7	0	11	7
5	0	9	8	0	9	8	0	9	8	0	9	8	0	9	8
4	0	7	9	0	7	9	0	7	9	0	7	8	0	7	8
3	0	5	10	0	5	9	0	5	9	0	5	9	0	5	9
2	0	3	10	0	3	10	0	3	10	0	3	10	0	3	10
1	0	1	11	0	1	11	0	1	11	0	1	11	0	1	11
Stu. 10	0	0	11	0	0	11	0	0	11	0	0	11	0	0	11
9	0	0	10	0	0	10	0	0	10	0	0	10	0	0	10
8	0	0	9	0	0	9	0	0	9	0	0	9	0	0	9
7	0	0	8	0	0	8	0	0	8	0	0	8	0	0	8
6	0	0	7	0	0	7	0	0	7	0	0	7	0	0	7
5	0	0	5	0	0	5	0	0	5	0	0	5	0	0	5
4	0	0	4	0	0	4	0	0	4	0	0	4	0	0	4
3	0	0	3	0	0	3	0	0	3	0	0	3	0	0	3
2	0	0	2	0	0	2	0	0	2	0	0	2	0	0	2
1	0	0	1	0	0	1	0	0	1	0	0	1	0	0	1
Pen 12	0	0	0	0	0	0	0	0	0	0	0	0	0	0	0
8	0	0	0	0	0	0	0	0	0	0	0	0	0	0	0

Eng.	34 s. 6½ g.			34 s. 7 g.			34 s. 7½ g.			33 s. 8 g.			34 s. 8½ g.		
£.	G.	s.	p.	G.	s.	p.	G.	s.	p.	G.	s.	p.	G.	s.	p.
1000	10362	10		10375	0		10387	10		10400			10412	10	
900	9326	5		9337	10		9348	15		9360			9371	5	
800	8290	0		8300	0		8310	0		8320			8330	0	
700	7253	15		7622	10		7271	5		7280			7288	15	
600	6217	10		6225	0		6232	10		6240			6247	10	
500	5181	5		5187	10		5193	15		5200			5206	5	
400	4145	0		4150	0		4155	0		4160			4165	0	
300	3108	15		3112	10		3116	5		3120			3123	15	
200	2072	10		2075	0		2077	10		2080			2082	10	
100	1036	5		1037	10		1038	15		1040			1041	5	
90	932	12	8	933	15		934	17	8	936			937	2	8
80	829	0	0	830	0		831	0	0	832			833	0	0
70	725	7	8	726	5		727	2	8	728			728	17	8
60	621	15	0	622	10		623	5	0	624			624	15	0
50	518	2	8	518	15		519	7	8	520			520	12	8
40	414	10	0	415	0		415	10	0	416			416	10	0
30	310	17	8	311	5		311	12	8	312			312	7	8
20	207	5	0	207	10		207	15	0	208			208	5	0
10	103	12	8	103	15		103	17	8	104			104	2	8
9	93	5	4	93	7	8	93	9	12	93	12		93	14	4
8	82	18	0	83	0	0	83	2	0	83	4		83	6	0
7	72	10	12	72	12	8	72	14	4	72	16		72	17	2
6	62	3	8	62	5	0	62	6	8	62	8		62	9	8
5	51	16	4	51	17	8	51	18	2	52	0		52	1	4
4	41	9	0	41	10	0	41	11	0	41	12		41	13	0
3	31	1	12	31	2	8	31	3	4	31	4		31	4	12
2	20	14	8	20	15	0	20	15	8	20	16		20	16	8
1	10	7	4	10	7	8	10	7	12	10	8		10	8	4
S. 10	5	3	10	5	3	12	5	3	14	5	4		5	4	2
9	4	13	4	4	13	6	4	13	8	4	13	10	4	13	11
8	4	2	14	4	3	0	4	3	2	4	3	3	4	3	5
7	3	12	9	3	12	10	3	12	11	3	12	13	3	12	14
6	3	2	3	3	2	4	3	2	5	3	2	6	3	2	8
5	2	11	13	2	11	14	2	11	15	2	12	0	2	12	1
4	2	1	7	2	1	8	2	1	9	2	1	10	2	1	10
3	1	11	1	1	11	2	1	11	3	1	11	3	1	11	4
2	1	0	12	1	0	12	1	0	12	1	0	13	1	0	13
1	0	10	6	0	10	6	0	10	6	0	10	6	0	10	7
D. 6	0	5	3	0	5	3	0	5	3	0	5	3	0	5	3
5	0	4	5	0	4	5	0	4	5	0	4	5	0	4	5
4	0	3	7	0	3	7	0	3	7	0	3	7	0	3	8
3	0	2	9	0	2	10	0	2	10	0	2	10	0	2	10
2	0	1	12	0	1	12	0	1	12	0	1	12	0	1	12
1	0	0	14	0	0	14	0	0	14	0	0	14	0	0	14

Dutch	34 s. 6½ g.			34 s. 7 g.			34 s. 7½ g.			34 s. 8 g.			34 s. 8½ g.		
Guild.	£.	s.	d.	£.	s.	d.	£.	s.	d.	£.	s.	d.	£.	s.	d.
10000	965	0	4	963	17	1	962	13	10	961	10	9	960	7	8
5000	482	10	2	481	18	6	481	6	11	480	15	4	480	3	10
4000	386	0	1	385	10	10	385	1	6	384	12	3	384	3	0
3000	289	10	1	289	3	1	288	16	2	288	9	2	288	2	3
2000	193	0	0	192	15	5	192	10	9	192	6	1	192	1	6
1000	96	10	0	96	7	8	96	5	4	96	3	1	96	0	9
900	86	17	0	86	14	11	86	12	10	86	10	9	86	8	8
800	77	4	0	77	2	2	77	0	3	76	18	5	76	16	7
700	67	11	0	67	9	4	67	7	9	67	6	1	67	4	6
600	57	18	0	57	16	7	57	15	2	57	13	10	57	12	5
500	48	5	0	48	3	10	48	2	8	48	1	6	48	0	4
400	38	12	0	38	11	1	38	10	1	38	9	2	38	8	3
300	28	19	0	28	18	3	28	7	7	28	16	11	28	16	2
200	19	6	0	19	5	6	19	5	1	19	4	7	19	4	1
100	9	13	0	9	12	9	9	12	6	9	12	3	9	12	1
90	8	13	8	8	13	6	8	13	3	8	13	1	8	12	10
80	7	14	4	7	14	2	7	14	0	7	13	10	7	13	8
70	6	15	1	6	14	11	6	14	9	6	14	7	6	14	5
60	5	15	9	5	15	8	5	15	6	5	15	4	5	15	3
50	4	16	6	4	16	4	4	16	3	4	16	1	4	16	0
40	3	17	2	3	17	1	3	17	0	3	16	11	3	16	10
30	2	17	10	2	17	10	2	17	9	2	17	8	2	17	7
20	1	18	7	1	18	6	1	18	6	1	18	5	1	18	5
10	0	19	3	0	19	3	0	19	3	0	19	2	0	19	2
9	0	17	4	0	17	4	0	17	4	0	17	3	0	17	3
8	0	15	5	0	15	5	0	15	4	0	15	4	0	15	4
7	0	13	6	0	13	6	0	13	5	0	13	5	0	13	5
6	0	11	7	0	11	6	0	11	6	0	11	6	0	11	6
5	0	9	7	0	9	7	0	9	7	0	9	7	0	9	7
4	0	7	8	0	7	8	0	7	8	0	7	8	0	7	8
3	0	5	9	0	5	9	0	5	9	0	5	9	0	5	9
2	0	3	10	0	3	10	0	3	10	0	3	10	0	3	10
1	0	1	11	0	1	11	0	1	11	0	1	11	0	1	11
Stu. 10	0	0	11	0	0	11	0	0	11	0	0	11	0	0	11
9	0	0	10	0	0	10	0	0	10	0	0	10	0	0	10
8	0	0	9	0	0	9	0	0	9	0	0	9	0	0	9
7	0	0	8	0	0	8	0	0	8	0	0	8	0	0	8
6	0	0	7	0	0	7	0	0	7	0	0	7	0	0	7
5	0	0	5	0	0	5	0	0	5	0	0	5	0	0	5
4	0	0	4	0	0	4	0	0	4	0	0	4	0	0	4
3	0	0	3	0	0	3	0	0	3	0	0	3	0	0	3
2	0	0	2	0	0	2	0	0	2	0	0	2	0	0	2
1	0	0	1	0	0	1	0	0	1	0	0	1	0	0	1
Pen 12	0	0	0	0	0	0	0	0	0	0	0	0	0	0	0
8	0	0	0	0	0	0	0	0	0	0	0	0	0	0	0

Eng.	34 s. 9 g.			34 s. 9½ g.			34 s. 10 g.			34 s. 10½ g.			34 s. 11 g.		
£.	G.	s.	p.	G.	s.	p.	G.	s.	p.	G.	s.	p.	G.	s.	p.
1000	10425	0		10437	10		10450			10462	10		10475	0	
900	9382	10		9393	15		9405			9416	5		9427	10	
800	8340	0		8350	0		8360			8370	0		8380	0	
700	7297	10		7306	5		7315			7323	15		7332	10	
600	6255	0		6262	10		6270			6277	10		6285	0	
500	5212	10		5218	15		5225			5231	5		5237	10	
400	4170	0		4175	0		4180			4185	0		4190	0	
300	3127	10		3131	5		3135			3138	15		3142	10	
200	2085	0		2087	10		2090			2092	10		2095	0	
100	1042	10		1043	15		1045			1046	5		1047	10	
90	938	5		939	7	8	940	10		941	12	8	942	15	
80	834	0		835	0	0	836	0		837	0	0	838	0	
70	729	15		730	12	8	731	10		732	7	8	733	5	
60	625	10		626	5	0	627	0		627	15	0	628	10	
50	521	5		521	17	8	522	10		523	2	8	523	15	
40	417	0		417	10	0	418	0		418	10	0	419	0	
30	312	15		313	2	8	313	10		313	17	8	314	5	
20	208	10		208	15	0	209	0		209	5	0	209	10	
10	104	5		104	7	8	104	10		104	12	8	104	15	
9	93	16	8	93	18	12	94	1		94	3	4	94	5	8
8	83	8	0	83	10	0	83	12		83	14	0	83	16	0
7	72	19	8	73	1	4	73	3		73	4	12	73	6	8
6	62	11	0	62	12	8	62	14		62	15	8	62	17	0
5	52	2	8	52	3	12	52	5		52	6	4	52	7	8
4	41	14	0	41	15	0	41	16		41	17	0	41	18	0
3	31	5	8	31	6	4	31	7		31	7	12	31	8	8
2	20	17	0	20	17	8	20	18		20	18	8	20	19	0
1	10	8	8	10	8	12	10	9		10	9	4	10	9	8
S. 10	5	4	4	5	4	6	5	4	8	5	4	10	5	4	12
9	4	13	13	4	13	15	4	14	1	4	14	3	4	14	4
8	4	3	6	4	3	8	4	3	10	4	3	11	4	3	13
7	3	13	0	3	13	1	3	13	2	3	13	4	3	13	5
6	3	2	9	3	2	10	3	2	11	3	2	12	3	2	14
5	2	12	2	2	12	3	2	12	4	2	12	5	2	12	6
4	2	1	11	2	1	12	2	1	13	2	1	14	2	1	14
3	1	11	4	1	11	5	1	11	6	1	11	6	1	11	7
2	1	0	14	1	0	14	1	0	14	1	0	15	1	0	15
1	0	10	7	0	10	7	0	10	7	0	10	7	0	10	8
D. 6	0	5	3	0	5	3	0	5	4	0	5	4	0	5	4
5	0	4	6	0	4	6	0	4	6	0	4	6	0	4	6
4	0	3	8	0	3	8	0	3	8	0	3	8	0	3	8
3	0	2	10	0	2	10	0	2	10	0	2	10	0	2	10
2	0	1	12	0	1	12	0	1	12	0	1	12	0	1	12
1	0	0	14	0	0	14	0	0	14	0	0	14	0	0	14

Dutch	34 s. 9 g.			34 s. 9½ g.			34 s. 10 g.			34 s. 10½ g.			34 s. 11 g.		
Guild.	£.	s.	d.	£.	s.	d.	£.	s.	d.	£.	s.	d.	£.	s.	d.
10000	959	4	7	958	1	8	956	18	9	955	15	10	954	13	0
5000	479	12	3	479	0	10	478	9	4	477	17	11	477	6	6
4000	383	13	10	383	4	8	382	15	6	382	6	4	381	17	2
3000	287	15	4	287	8	6	287	1	7	286	14	9	286	7	11
2000	191	16	11	191	12	4	191	7	9	191	3	2	190	18	7
1000	95	18	5	95	16	2	95	13	10	95	11	7	95	9	3
900	86	6	7	86	4	6	86	2	5	86	0	5	85	18	4
800	76	14	9	76	12	11	76	11	1	76	9	3	76	7	5
700	67	2	11	67	1	3	66	19	8	66	18	1	66	16	6
600	57	11	1	57	9	8	57	8	3	57	6	11	57	5	7
500	47	19	2	47	18	1	47	16	11	47	15	9	47	14	7
400	38	7	4	38	6	5	38	5	6	38	4	7	38	3	8
300	28	15	6	28	14	10	28	14	2	28	13	5	28	12	9
200	19	3	8	19	3	2	19	2	9	19	2	3	19	1	10
100	9	11	10	9	11	7	9	11	4	9	11	2	9	10	11
90	8	12	8	8	12	5	8	12	3	8	12	0	8	11	10
80	7	13	5	7	13	3	7	13	1	7	12	11	7	12	9
70	6	14	3	6	14	1	6	13	11	6	13	9	6	13	7
60	5	15	1	5	14	11	5	14	10	5	14	8	5	14	6
50	4	15	11	4	15	9	4	15	8	4	15	7	4	15	5
40	3	16	8	3	16	7	3	16	6	3	16	5	3	16	4
30	2	17	6	2	17	5	2	17	5	2	17	4	2	17	3
20	1	18	4	1	18	3	1	18	3	1	18	2	1	18	2
10	0	19	2	0	19	2	0	19	1	0	19	1	0	19	1
9	0	17	3	0	17	3	0	17	2	0	17	2	0	17	2
8	0	15	4	0	15	4	0	15	3	0	15	3	0	15	3
7	0	13	5	0	13	5	0	13	4	0	13	4	0	13	4
6	0	11	6	0	11	6	0	11	5	0	11	5	0	11	5
5	0	9	7	0	9	7	0	9	6	0	9	6	0	9	6
4	0	7	8	0	7	8	0	7	7	0	7	7	0	7	7
3	0	5	9	0	5	9	0	5	9	0	5	8	0	5	8
2	0	3	10	0	3	10	0	3	10	0	3	9	0	3	9
1	0	1	11	0	1	11	0	1	11	0	1	11	0	1	11
Stu. 10	0	0	11	0	0	11	0	0	11	0	0	11	0	0	11
9	0	0	10	0	0	10	0	0	10	0	0	10	0	0	10
8	0	0	9	0	0	9	0	0	9	0	0	9	0	0	9
7	0	0	8	0	0	8	0	0	8	0	0	8	0	0	8
6	0	0	7	0	0	7	0	0	7	0	0	7	0	0	7
5	0	0	5	0	0	5	0	0	5	0	0	5	0	0	5
4	0	0	4	0	0	4	0	0	4	0	0	4	0	0	4
3	0	0	3	0	0	3	0	0	3	0	0	3	0	0	3
2	0	0	2	0	0	2	0	0	2	0	0	2	0	0	2
1	0	0	1	0	0	1	0	0	1	0	0	1	0	0	1
Pen 12	0	0	0	0	0	0	0	0	0	0	0	0	0	0	0
8	0	0	0	0	0	0	0	0	0	0	0	0	0	0	0

Eng.	34 s. 11½ g.			35 s.			35 s. ½ g.			35 s. 1 g.			35 s. 1½ g.		
£.	G.	s.	p.	G.	s.	p.	G.	s.	p.	G.	s.	p.	G.	s.	p.
1000	10487	10		10500			10512	10		10525	0		10537	10	
900	9438	15		9450			9461	5		9472	10		9483	15	
800	8390	0		8400			8410	0		8420	0		8430	0	
700	7341	5		7350			7358	15		7367	10		7376	5	
600	6292	10		6300			6307	10		6315	0		6322	10	
500	5243	15		5250			5256	5		5262	10		5268	15	
400	4195	0		4200			4205	0		4210	0		4215	0	
300	3146	5		3150			3153	15		3157	10		3161	5	
200	2097	10		2100			2102	10		2105	0		2107	10	
100	1048	15		1050			1051	5		1052	10		1053	15	
90	943	17	8	945			946	2	8	947	5		948	7	8
80	839	0	0	840			841	0	0	842	0		843	0	0
70	734	2	8	735			735	17	0	736	15		737	12	8
60	629	5	0	630			630	15	0	631	10		632	5	0
50	524	7	8	525			525	12	8	526	5		526	17	8
40	419	10	0	420			420	10	0	421	0		421	10	0
30	314	12	8	315			315	7	8	315	15		316	2	8
20	209	15	0	210			210	5	0	210	10		210	15	0
10	104	17	8	105			105	2	8	105	5		105	7	8
9	94	7	12	94	10		94	12	4	94	14	8	94	16	12
8	83	18	0	84	0		84	2	0	84	4	0	84	6	0
7	73	8	4	73	10		73	11	12	73	13	8	73	15	4
6	62	18	8	63	0		63	1	8	63	3	0	63	4	8
5	52	8	12	52	10		52	11	4	52	12	8	52	13	12
4	41	19	0	42	0		42	1	0	42	2	0	42	3	0
3	31	9	4	31	10		31	10	12	31	11	8	31	12	4
2	20	19	8	21	0		21	0	8	21	1	0	21	1	8
1	10	9	12	10	10		10	10	4	10	10	8	10	10	12
S. 10	5	4	14	5	5	0	5	5	2	5	5	4	5	5	6
9	4	14	6	4	14	8	4	14	10	4	14	12	4	14	13
8	4	3	14	4	4	0	4	4	2	4	4	3	4	4	5
7	3	13	7	3	13	8	3	13	9	3	13	11	3	13	12
6	3	2	15	3	3	0	3	3	1	3	3	2	3	3	4
5	2	12	7	2	12	8	2	12	9	2	12	10	2	12	11
4	2	1	15	2	2	0	2	2	1	2	2	2	2	2	2
3	1	11	7	1	11	8	1	11	9	1	11	9	1	11	10
2	1	1	0	1	1	0	1	1	0	1	1	1	1	1	1
1	0	10	8	0	10	8	0	10	8	0	10	8	0	10	9
D. 6	0	5	4	0	5	4	0	5	4	0	5	4	0	5	4
5	0	4	6	0	4	6	0	4	6	0	4	6	0	4	6
4	0	3	8	0	3	8	0	3	8	0	3	8	0	3	8
3	0	2	10	0	2	10	0	2	10	0	2	10	0	2	10
2	0	1	12	0	1	12	0	1	12	0	1	12	0	1	12
1	0	0	14	0	0	14	0	0	14	0	0	14	0	0	14

Dutch	34 s. 11½ g.			35 s.			35 s. ½ g.			35 s. 1 g.			35 s. 1½ g.		
Guild.	£.	s.	d.	£.	s.	d.	£.	s.	d.	£.	s.	d.	£.	s.	d.
10000	953	10	3	952	7	7	951	4	11	950	2	4	948	19	10
5000	476	15	1	476	3	9	475	12	5	475	1	2	474	9	11
4000	381	8	1	380	19	0	380	9	11	380	0	11	379	11	11
3000	286	1	1	285	14	3	285	7	5	285	0	8	284	13	11
2000	190	14	0	190	9	6	190	4	11	190	0	5	189	15	11
1000	95	7	0	95	4	9	95	2	6	95	0	2	94	17	11
900	85	16	3	85	14	3	85	12	3	85	10	2	85	8	2
800	76	5	7	76	3	9	76	2	0	76	0	2	75	18	4
700	66	14	11	66	13	4	66	11	9	66	10	2	66	8	7
600	57	4	2	57	2	10	57	1	6	57	0	1	56	18	9
500	47	13	6	47	12	4	47	11	3	47	10	1	47	9	0
400	38	2	9	38	1	10	38	1	0	38	0	1	37	19	2
300	28	12	1	28	11	5	28	10	9	28	10	0	28	9	4
200	19	1	4	19	0	11	19	0	6	19	0	0	18	19	7
100	9	10	8	9	10	5	9	10	3	9	10	0	9	9	9
90	8	11	7	8	11	5	8	11	2	8	11	0	8	10	9
80	7	12	6	7	12	4	7	12	2	7	12	0	7	11	10
70	6	13	6	6	13	4	6	13	2	6	13	0	6	12	10
60	5	14	5	5	14	3	5	14	1	5	14	0	5	13	10
50	4	15	4	4	15	2	4	15	1	4	15	0	4	14	10
40	3	16	3	3	16	2	3	16	1	3	16	0	3	15	11
30	2	17	2	2	17	1	2	17	1	2	17	0	2	16	11
20	1	18	1	1	18	1	1	18	0	1	18	0	1	17	11
10	0	19	0	0	19	0	0	19	0	0	19	0	0	18	11
9	0	17	2	0	17	1	0	17	1	0	17	1	0	17	1
8	0	15	3	0	15	2	0	15	2	0	15	2	0	15	2
7	0	13	4	0	13	4	0	13	3	0	13	3	0	13	3
6	0	11	5	0	11	5	0	11	5	0	11	4	0	11	4
5	0	9	6	0	9	6	0	9	6	0	9	6	0	9	5
4	0	7	7	0	7	7	0	7	7	0	7	7	0	7	7
3	0	5	8	0	5	8	0	5	8	0	5	8	0	5	8
2	0	3	9	0	3	9	0	3	9	0	3	9	0	3	9
1	0	1	10	0	1	10	0	1	10	0	1	10	0	1	10
Stu. 10	0	0	11	0	0	11	0	0	11	0	0	11	0	0	11
9	0	0	10	0	0	10	0	0	10	0	0	10	0	0	10
8	0	0	9	0	0	9	0	0	9	0	0	9	0	0	9
7	0	0	8	0	0	8	0	0	8	0	0	8	0	0	8
6	0	0	6	0	0	6	0	0	6	0	0	6	0	0	6
5	0	0	5	0	0	5	0	0	5	0	0	5	0	0	5
4	0	0	4	0	0	4	0	0	4	0	0	4	0	0	4
3	0	0	3	0	0	3	0	0	3	0	0	3	0	0	3
2	0	0	2	0	0	2	0	0	2	0	0	2	0	0	2
1	0	0	1	0	0	1	0	0	1	0	0	1	0	0	1
Pen. 12	0	0	0	0	0	0	0	0	0	0	0	0	0	0	0
8	0	0	0	0	0	0	0	0	0	0	0	0	0	0	0

Eng.	35 s. 2 g.			35 s. 2½ g.			34 s. 3 g.			35 .s 3½ g.			35 s. 3 g.		
£.	G.	s.	p.	G.	s.	p.	G.	s.	p.	G.	s.	p.	G.	s.	p.
1000	10550			10562	10		10575	0		10587	10		10600		
900	9495			9506	5		9517	10		9528	15		9540		
800	8440			8450	0		8460	0		8470	0		8480		
700	7385			7393	15		7402	10		7411	5		7420		
600	6330			6337	10		6345	0		6352	10		6360		
500	5275			5281	5		5287	10		5293	15		5300		
400	4220			4225	0		4230	0		4235	0		4240		
300	3165			3168	15		3172	10		3176	5		3180		
200	2110			2112	10		2115	0		2117	10		2120		
100	1055			1056	5		1057	10		1058	15		1060		
90	949	10		950	12	8	951	15		952	17	8	954		
80	844	0		845	0	0	846	0		847	0	0	848		
70	738	10		739	7	8	740	5		741	2	8	742		
60	633	0		633	15	0	634	10		635	5	0	636		
50	527	10		528	2	8	528	15		529	7	8	530		
40	422	0		422	10	0	423	0		423	10	0	424		
30	316	10		316	17	8	317	5		317	12	8	318		
20	211	0		211	5	0	211	10		211	15	0	212		
10	105	10		105	12	8	105	15		105	17	8	106		
9	94	19		95	1	4	95	3	8	95	5	12	95	8	
8	84	8		84	10	0	84	12	0	84	14	0	84	16	
7	73	17		73	18	2	74	0	8	74	2	4	74	4	
6	63	6		63	7	8	63	9	0	63	10	8	63	12	
5	52	15		52	16	4	52	17	8	52	18	12	53	0	
4	42	4		42	5	0	42	6	0	42	7	0	42	8	
3	31	13		31	13	12	31	14	8	31	15	4	31	16	
2	21	2		21	2	8	21	3	0	21	3	8	21	4	
1	10	11		10	11	4	10	11	8	10	11	12	10	12	
S. 10	5	5	8	5	5	10	5	5	12	5	5	14	5	6	0
9	4	14	15	4	15	1	4	15	3	4	15	5	4	15	6
8	4	4	6	4	4	8	4	4	10	4	4	11	4	4	13
7	3	13	14	3	13	15	3	14	0	3	14	2	3	14	3
6	3	3	5	3	3	6	3	3	7	3	3	8	3	3	10
5	2	12	12	2	12	13	2	12	14	2	12	15	2	13	0
4	2	2	3	2	2	4	2	2	5	2	2	6	2	2	6
3	1	11	10	1	11	11	1	11	12	1	11	12	1	11	13
2	1	1	2	1	1	2	1	1	2	1	1	3	1	1	3
1	0	10	9	0	10	9	0	10	9	0	10	9	0	10	10
D. 6	0	5	4	0	5	4	0	5	5	0	5	5	0	5	5
5	0	4	6	0	4	6	0	4	7	0	4	7	0	4	7
4	0	3	8	0	3	8	0	3	8	0	3	8	0	3	8
3	0	2	10	0	2	10	0	2	10	0	2	10	0	2	10
2	0	1	12	0	1	12	0	1	12	0	1	12	0	1	12
1	0	0	14	0	0	14	0	0	14	0	0	14	0	0	14

Dutch	35 s. 2 g.			35 s. 2½ g.			35 s. 3 g.			35 s. 3½ g.			35 s. 4 g.		
Guild.	£.	s.	d.	£.	s.	d.	£.	s.	d.	£.	s.	d.	£.	s.	d.
10000	947	17	4	946	14	10	945	12	6	944	10	2	943	7	11
5000	473	18	8	473	7	5	472	16	3	472	5	1	471	13	11
4000	379	2	11	378	13	11	378	5	0	377	16	1	377	7	2
3000	284	7	2	284	0	5	283	13	9	283	7	0	283	0	4
2000	189	11	5	189	6	11	189	2	6	188	18	0	188	13	7
1000	94	15	8	94	13	5	94	11	3	94	9	0	94	6	9
900	85	6	1	85	4	1	85	2	1	85	0	1	84	18	1
800	75	16	11	75	14	9	75	13	0	75	11	2	75	9	5
700	66	7	0	66	5	5	66	3	10	66	2	3	66	0	9
600	56	17	5	56	16	1	56	14	9	56	13	4	56	12	0
500	47	7	10	47	6	9	47	5	7	47	4	6	47	3	4
400	37	18	3	37	17	4	37	16	6	37	15	7	37	14	8
300	28	8	8	28	8	0	28	7	4	28	6	8	28	6	0
200	18	19	1	18	8	8	18	18	3	18	17	9	18	17	4
100	9	9	6	9	9	4	9	9	1	9	8	10	9	8	8
90	8	10	7	8	10	5	8	10	2	8	10	0	8	9	9
80	7	11	8	7	11	5	7	11	3	7	11	1	7	10	11
70	6	12	8	6	12	6	6	12	4	6	12	2	6	12	1
60	5	13	9	5	13	7	5	13	5	5	13	4	5	13	2
50	4	14	9	4	14	8	4	14	6	4	14	5	4	14	4
40	3	15	10	3	15	8	3	15	7	3	15	6	3	15	5
30	2	16	10	2	16	9	2	16	8	2	16	8	2	16	7
20	1	17	11	1	17	10	1	17	10	1	17	9	1	17	8
10	0	18	11	0	18	11	0	18	11	0	18	10	0	18	10
9	0	17	0	0	17	0	0	17	0	0	17	0	0	16	11
8	0	15	2	0	15	1	0	15	1	0	15	1	0	15	1
7	0	13	3	0	13	3	0	13	2	0	13	2	0	13	2
6	0	11	4	0	11	4	0	11	4	0	11	4	0	11	3
5	0	9	5	0	9	5	0	9	5	0	9	5	0	9	5
4	0	7	7	0	7	6	0	7	6	0	7	6	0	7	6
3	0	5	8	0	5	8	0	5	8	0	5	8	0	5	8
2	0	3	9	0	3	9	0	3	9	0	3	9	0	3	9
1	0	1	10	0	1	10	0	1	10	0	1	10	0	1	10
Stu. 10	0	0	11	0	0	11	0	0	11	0	0	11	0	0	11
9	0	0	10	0	0	10	0	0	10	0	0	10	0	0	10
8	0	0	9	0	0	9	0	0	9	0	0	9	0	0	9
7	0	0	8	0	0	8	0	0	7	0	0	7	0	0	7
6	0	0	6	0	0	6	0	0	6	0	0	6	0	0	6
5	0	0	5	0	0	5	0	0	5	0	0	5	0	0	5
4	0	0	4	0	0	4	0	0	4	0	0	4	0	0	4
3	0	0	3	0	0	3	0	0	3	0	0	3	0	0	3
2	0	0	2	0	0	2	0	0	2	0	0	2	0	0	2
1	0	0	1	0	0	1	0	0	1	0	0	1	0	0	1
Pen. 12	0	0	0	0	0	0	0	0	0	0	0	0	0	0	0
8	0	0	0	0	0	0	0	0	0	0	0	0	0	0	0

Eng.	35 s. 4½ g.			35 s. 5 g.			35 s. 6 g.			35 s. 7 g.			35 s. 8 g.		
£.	G.	s.	p.	G.	s.	p.	G.	s.	p.	G.	s.	p.	G.	s.	p.
1000	10612	10		10625	0		10650			10675	0		10700		
900	9551	5		9562	10		9585			9607	10		9630		
800	8490	0		8500	0		8520			8540	0		8560		
700	7428	15		7437	10		7455			7472	10		7490		
600	6367	10		6375	0		6390			6405	0		6420		
500	5306	5		5312	10		5325			5337	10		5350		
400	4245	0		4250	0		4260			4270	0		4280		
300	3183	15		3187	10		3195			3202	10		3210		
200	2122	10		2125	0		2130			2135	0		2140		
100	1061	5		1062	10		1065			1067	10		1070		
90	955	2	8	956	5		958	10		960	15		963		
80	849	0	0	850	0		852	0		854	0		856		
70	742	17	8	743	15		748	10		747	5		749		
60	636	15	0	637	10		639	0		640	10		642		
50	530	12	8	531	5		532	10		533	15		535		
40	424	10	0	425	0		426	0		427	0		428		
30	318	7	8	318	15		319	10		320	5		321		
20	212	5	0	212	10		213	0		213	10		214		
10	106	2	8	106	5		106	10		106	15		107		
9	95	10	4	95	12	8	95	17		96	1	8	96	6	
8	84	18	0	85	0	0	85	4		85	8	0	85	12	
7	74	5	12	74	7	8	74	11		74	14	8	74	18	
6	63	13	8	63	15	0	63	18		64	1	0	64	4	
5	53	1	4	53	2	8	53	5		53	7	8	53	10	
4	42	9	0	42	10	0	42	12		42	14	0	42	16	
3	31	16	12	31	17	8	31	9		32	0	8	32	2	
2	21	4	8	21	5	0	21	6		21	7	0	21	8	
1	10	12	4	10	12	8	10	13		10	13	8	10	14	
S. 10	5	6	2	5	6	4	5	6	8	5	6	12	5	7	0
9	4	15	8	4	15	10	4	15	14	4	16	1	4	16	5
8	4	4	14	4	5	0	4	5	3	4	5	6	4	5	10
7	3	14	5	3	14	6	3	14	9	3	14	12	3	14	14
6	3	3	11	3	3	12	3	3	14	3	4	1	3	4	3
5	2	13	1	2	13	2	2	13	4	2	13	6	2	13	8
4	2	2	7	2	2	8	2	2	10	2	2	11	2	2	13
3	1	11	13	1	11	14	1	11	15	1	12	0	1	12	2
2	1	1	4	1	1	4	1	1	5	1	1	6	1	1	6
1	0	10	10	0	10	10	0	10	10	0	10	11	0	10	11
D. 6	0	5	5	0	5	5	0	5	5	0	5	5	0	5	6
5	0	4	7	0	4	7	0	4	7	0	4	7	0	4	7
4	0	3	9	0	3	9	0	3	9	0	3	9	0	3	9
3	0	2	10	0	2	11	0	2	11	0	2	11	0	2	11
2	0	1	12	0	1	12	0	1	12	0	1	12	0	1	12
1	0	0	14	0	0	14	0	0	14	0	0	14	0	0	14

Dutch	35 s. 4½ g.			35 s. 5 g.			35 s. 6 g.			35 s. 7 g.			35 s. 8 g.		
Guild.	£.	s.	d.	£.	s.	d.	£.	s.	d.	£.	s.	d.	£.	s.	d.
10000	942	5	8	941	3	6	938	19	4	936	15	4	934	11	7
5000	471	2	10	470	11	9	469	9	8	468	7	8	467	5	9
4000	376	18	3	376	9	4	375	11	8	374	14	1	373	16	7
3000	282	13	8	282	7	0	281	13	9	281	0	7	280	7	5
2000	188	9	1	188	4	8	187	15	10	187	7	0	186	18	3
1000	94	4	7	94	2	4	93	17	11	93	13	6	93	9	2
900	84	16	1	84	14	1	84	10	1	84	6	2	84	2	2
800	75	7	8	75	5	10	75	2	4	74	18	9	74	15	3
700	65	19	2	65	17	7	65	14	6	65	11	5	65	8	4
600	56	10	9	56	9	4	56	6	9	56	4	1	56	1	5
500	47	2	3	47	1	2	46	18	11	46	16	9	46	14	7
400	37	13	10	37	12	11	37	11	2	37	9	5	37	7	8
300	28	5	4	28	4	8	28	3	4	28	2	0	28	0	9
200	18	16	11	18	16	5	18	15	7	18	14	8	18	13	10
100	9	8	5	9	8	2	9	7	9	9	7	4	9	6	11
90	8	9	7	8	9	5	8	9	0	8	8	7	8	8	2
80	7	10	8	7	10	7	7	10	2	7	9	10	7	9	6
70	6	11	10	6	11	9	6	11	5	6	11	1	6	10	10
60	5	13	0	5	12	11	5	12	8	5	12	5	5	12	1
50	4	14	2	4	14	1	4	13	10	4	13	8	4	13	5
40	3	15	4	3	15	3	3	15	1	3	14	11	3	14	9
30	2	16	6	2	16	5	2	16	4	2	16	2	2	16	1
20	1	17	8	1	17	7	1	17	6	1	17	5	1	17	4
10	0	18	10	0	18	9	0	18	9	0	18	8	0	18	8
9	0	16	11	0	16	11	0	16	10	0	16	10	0	16	9
8	0	15	0	0	15	0	0	15	0	0	14	11	0	14	11
7	0	13	2	0	13	2	0	13	1	0	13	1	0	13	1
6	0	11	3	0	11	3	0	11	3	0	11	3	0	11	2
5	0	9	5	0	9	5	0	9	4	0	9	4	0	9	4
4	0	7	6	0	7	6	0	7	6	0	7	6	0	7	5
3	0	5	7	0	5	7	0	5	7	0	5	7	0	5	7
2	0	3	9	0	3	9	0	3	9	0	3	9	0	3	8
1	0	1	10	0	1	10	0	1	10	0	1	10	0	1	10
Stu 10	0	0	11	0	0	11	0	0	11	0	0	11	0	0	11
9	0	0	10	0	0	10	0	0	10	0	0	10	0	0	10
8	0	0	9	0	0	9	0	0	9	0	0	9	0	0	9
7	0	0	7	0	0	7	0	0	7	0	0	7	0	0	7
6	0	0	6	0	0	6	0	0	6	0	0	6	0	0	6
5	0	0	5	0	0	5	0	0	5	0	0	5	0	0	5
4	0	0	4	0	0	4	0	0	4	0	0	4	0	0	4
3	0	0	3	0	0	3	0	0	3	0	0	3	0	0	3
2	0	0	2	0	0	2	0	0	2	0	0	2	0	0	2
1	0	0	1	0	0	1	0	0	1	0	0	1	0	0	1
Pen 12	0	0	0	0	0	0	0	0	0	0	0	0	0	0	0
8	0	0	0	0	0	0	0	0	0	0	0	0	0	0	0

Eng.	35 s. 9 g.			35 s. 10 g.			35 s. 11 g.			36 s.			36 s. 1 g.		
£.	G.	s.	p.	G.	s.	p.	G.	s.	p.	G.	s.	p.	G.	s.	p.
1000	10725	0		10750			10775	0		10800			10825	0	
900	9652	10		9675			9697	10		9720			9742	10	
800	8580	0		8600			8620	0		8640			8660	0	
700	7507	10		7525			7542	10		7560			7577	10	
600	6435	0		6450			6465	0		6480			6495	0	
500	5362	10		5375			5387	10		5400			5412	10	
400	4290	0		4300			4310	0		4320			4330	0	
300	3217	10		3225			3232	10		3240			3247	10	
200	2145	0		2150			2155	0		2160			2165	0	
100	1072	10		1075			1077	10		1080			1082	10	
90	965	5		967	10		969	15		972			974	5	
80	858	0		860	0		862	0		864			866	0	
70	750	15		752	10		754	5		756			757	15	
60	643	10		645	0		646	10		648			649	10	
50	536	5		537	10		538	15		540			541	5	
40	429	0		430	0		431	0		432			433	0	
30	321	15		322	10		323	5		324			324	15	
20	214	10		215	0		215	10		216			216	10	
10	107	5		107	10		107	15		108			108	5	
9	96	10	8	96	15		96	19	8	97	4		97	8	8
8	85	16	0	86	0		86	4	0	86	8		86	12	0
7	75	1	8	75	5		75	8	8	75	12		75	15	8
6	64	7	0	64	10		64	13	0	64	16		64	19	0
5	53	12	8	53	15		53	17	8	54	0		54	2	8
4	42	18	0	43	0		43	2	0	43	4		43	6	0
3	32	3	8	32	5		32	6	8	32	8		32	9	8
2	21	9	0	21	10		21	11	0	21	12		21	13	0
1	10	14	8	10	15		10	15	8	10	16		10	16	8
S. 10	5	7	4	5	7	8	5	7	12	5	8	0	5	8	4
9	4	16	8	4	16	12	4	17	0	4	17	3	4	17	7
8	4	5	13	4	6	0	4	6	3	4	6	6	4	6	10
7	3	15	1	3	15	4	3	15	7	3	15	10	3	15	12
6	3	4	6	3	4	8	3	4	10	3	4	13	3	4	15
5	2	13	10	2	13	12	2	13	14	2	14	0	2	14	2
4	2	2	14	2	3	0	2	3	2	2	3	3	2	3	5
3	1	12	3	1	12	4	1	12	5	1	12	6	1	12	8
2	1	1	7	1	1	8	1	1	9	1	1	10	1	1	10
1	0	10	12	0	10	12	0	10	12	0	10	13	0	10	13
D. 6	0	5	6	0	5	6	0	5	6	0	5	6	0	5	7
5	0	4	7	0	4	8	0	4	8	0	4	8	0	4	8
4	0	3	9	0	3	9	0	3	9	0	3	10	0	3	10
3	0	2	11	0	2	11	0	2	11	0	2	11	0	2	11
2	0	1	12	0	1	13	0	1	13	0	1	13	0	1	13
1	0	0	14	0	0	14	0	0	14	0	0	14	0	0	14

Dutch.	35 s. 9 g.			35 s. 10 g.			35 s. 11 g.			36 s.			36 s. 1 g.		
Guild.	£.	s.	d.	£.	s.	d.	£.	s.	d.	£.	s.	d.	£.	s.	d.
10000	932	8	0	930	4	7	928	1	5	925	18	6	923	15	9
5000	466	4	0	465	2	3	464	0	8	462	19	3	461	17	10
4000	372	19	2	372	1	10	371	4	7	370	7	5	369	10	3
3000	279	14	4	279	1	4	278	8	5	277	15	6	277	2	8
2000	186	9	7	186	0	11	185	12	3	185	3	8	184	15	1
1000	93	4	9	93	0	5	92	16	1	92	11	10	92	7	7
900	83	18	3	83	14	5	83	10	6	83	6	8	83	2	9
800	74	11	10	74	8	4	74	4	11	74	1	5	73	18	0
700	65	5	4	65	2	3	64	19	3	64	16	3	64	13	3
600	55	18	10	55	16	3	55	13	8	55	11	1	55	8	6
500	46	12	4	46	10	2	46	8	0	46	5	11	46	3	9
400	37	5	11	37	4	2	37	2	5	37	0	9	36	19	0
300	27	19	5	27	18	1	27	16	10	27	15	6	27	14	3
200	18	12	11	18	12	1	18	11	2	18	10	4	18	9	6
100	9	6	5	9	6	0	9	5	7	9	5	2	9	4	9
90	8	7	10	8	7	5	8	7	0	8	6	8	8	6	3
80	7	9	2	7	8	10	7	8	6	7	8	1	7	7	9
70	6	10	6	6	10	2	6	9	11	6	9	7	6	9	4
60	5	11	10	5	11	7	5	11	4	5	11	1	5	10	10
50	4	13	2	4	13	0	4	12	9	4	12	7	4	12	4
40	3	14	7	3	14	5	3	14	3	3	14	1	3	13	10
30	2	15	11	2	15	9	2	15	8	2	15	6	2	15	5
20	1	17	3	1	17	2	1	17	1	1	17	0	1	16	11
10	0	18	7	0	18	7	0	18	6	0	18	6	0	18	5
9	0	16	9	0	16	9	0	16	8	0	16	8	0	16	7
8	0	14	11	0	14	10	0	14	10	0	14	9	0	14	9
7	0	13	0	0	13	0	0	13	0	0	12	11	0	12	11
6	0	11	2	0	11	2	0	11	1	0	11	1	0	11	1
5	0	9	3	0	9	3	0	9	3	0	9	3	0	9	2
4	0	7	5	0	7	5	0	7	5	0	7	5	0	7	4
3	0	5	7	0	5	7	0	5	6	0	5	6	0	5	6
2	0	3	8	0	3	8	0	3	8	0	3	8	0	3	8
1	0	1	10	0	1	10	0	1	10	0	1	10	0	1	10
Stu 10	0	0	11	0	0	11	0	0	11	0	0	11	0	0	11
9	0	0	10	0	0	10	0	0	10	0	0	10	0	0	10
8	0	0	9	0	0	9	0	0	9	0	0	9	0	0	8
7	0	0	7	0	0	7	0	0	7	0	0	7	0	0	7
6	0	0	6	0	0	6	0	0	6	0	0	6	0	0	6
5	0	0	5	0	0	5	0	0	5	0	0	5	0	0	5
4	0	0	4	0	0	4	0	0	4	0	0	4	0	0	4
3	0	0	3	0	0	3	0	0	3	0	0	3	0	0	3
2	0	0	2	0	0	2	0	0	2	0	0	2	0	0	2
1	0	0	1	0	0	1	0	0	1	0	0	1	0	0	1
Pen 12	0	0	0	0	0	0	0	0	0	0	0	0	0	0	0
8	0	0	0	0	0	0	0	0	0	0	0	0	0	0	0

Eng.	36 s. 2 g.			36 s. 3 g.			36 s. 4 g.			36 s. 5 g.			36 s. 6 g.		
£.	G.	s.	p.	G.	s.	p.	G.	s.	p.	G.	s.	p.	G.	s.	p.
1000	10850			10875	0		10900			10925	0		10950		
900	9765			9787	10		9810			9832	10		9855		
800	8680			8700	0		8720			8740	0		8760		
700	7595			7612	10		7630			7647	10		7665		
600	6510			6525	0		6540			6555	0		6570		
500	5425			5437	10		5450			5462	10		5475		
400	4340			4350	0		4360			4370	0		4380		
300	3255			3262	10		3270			3277	10		3285		
200	2170			2175	0		2180			2185	0		2190		
100	1085			1087	10		1090			1092	10		1095		
90	976	10		978	15		981			983	5		985	10	
80	868	0		870	0		872			874	0		876	0	
70	759	10		761	5		763			764	15		766	10	
60	651	0		652	10		654			655	10		657	0	
50	542	10		543	15		545			546	5		547	10	
40	434	0		435	0		436			437	0		438	0	
30	325	10		326	5		327			327	15		328	10	
20	217	0		217	10		218			218	10		219	0	
10	108	10		108	15		109			109	5		109	10	
9	97	13		97	17	8	98	2		98	6	8	98	11	
8	86	16		87	0	0	87	4		87	8	0	87	12	
7	75	19		76	2	8	76	6		76	9	8	76	13	
6	65	2		65	5	0	65	8		65	11	0	65	14	
5	54	5		54	7	8	54	10		54	12	8	54	15	
4	43	8		43	10	0	43	12		43	14	0	43	16	
3	32	11		32	12	8	32	14		32	15	8	32	17	
2	21	14		21	15	0	21	16		21	17	0	21	18	
1	10	17		10	17	8	10	18		10	18	8	10	19	
S. 10	5	8	8	5	8	12	5	9		5	9	4	5	9	8
9	4	17	10	4	17	14	4	18	2	4	18	5	4	18	9
8	4	6	13	4	7	0	4	7	3	4	7	6	4	7	10
7	3	15	15	3	16	2	3	16	5	3	16	8	3	16	10
6	3	5	2	3	5	4	3	5	6	3	5	9	3	5	11
5	2	14	4	2	14	6	2	14	8	2	14	10	2	14	12
4	2	3	6	2	3	8	2	3	10	2	3	11	2	3	13
3	1	12	9	1	12	10	1	12	11	1	12	12	1	12	14
2	1	1	11	1	1	12	1	1	13	1	1	14	1	1	14
1	0	10	14	0	10	14	0	10	14	0	10	15	0	10	15
D. 6	0	5	7	0	5	7	0	5	7	0	5	7	0	5	8
5	0	4	8	0	4	8	0	4	9	0	4	9	0	4	9
4	0	3	10	0	3	10	0	3	10	0	3	10	0	3	10
3	0	2	11	0	2	11	0	2	12	0	2	12	0	2	12
2	0	1	13	0	1	13	0	1	13	0	1	13	0	1	13
1	0	0	14	0	0	14	0	0	14	0	0	14	0	0	14

Dutch	36 s. 2 g.			36 s. 3 g.			36 s. 4 g.			36 s. 5 g.			36 s. 6 g.		
Guild.	£.	s.	d.	£.	s.	d.	£.	s.	d.	£.	s.	d.	£.	s.	d.
10000	921	13	2	919	10	9	917	8	7	915	6	7	913	4	10
5000	460	16	7	459	15	4	458	14	3	457	13	3	456	12	5
4000	368	13	3	367	16	3	366	19	5	366	2	7	365	5	11
3000	276	9	11	275	17	2	275	4	7	274	11	11	273	19	5
2000	184	6	7	183	18	2	183	9	8	183	1	3	182	12	11
1000	92	3	3	91	19	1	91	14	10	91	10	8	91	6	5
900	82	18	11	82	15	2	82	11	4	82	7	7	82	3	10
800	73	14	7	73	11	3	73	7	10	73	4	6	73	1	2
700	64	10	3	64	7	4	64	4	4	64	1	5	63	18	6
600	55	5	11	55	3	5	55	0	11	54	18	4	54	15	10
500	46	1	8	45	19	6	45	17	5	45	15	4	45	13	3
400	36	17	4	36	15	7	36	13	11	36	12	3	36	10	7
300	27	13	0	27	11	8	27	10	5	27	9	2	27	7	11
200	18	8	8	18	7	9	18	6	11	18	6	1	18	5	3
100	9	4	4	9	3	11	9	3	5	9	3	3	9	2	7
90	8	5	10	8	5	6	8	5	1	8	4	9	8	4	4
80	7	7	5	7	7	1	7	6	9	7	6	5	7	6	1
70	6	9	0	6	8	8	6	8	5	6	8	1	6	7	10
60	5	10	7	5	10	4	5	10	1	5	9	10	5	9	7
50	4	12	2	4	11	11	4	11	9	4	11	6	4	11	4
40	3	13	8	3	13	6	3	13	4	3	13	2	3	13	0
30	2	15	3	2	15	2	2	15	0	2	14	11	2	14	9
20	1	16	10	1	16	9	1	16	8	1	16	7	1	16	6
10	0	18	5	0	18	4	0	18	4	0	18	3	0	18	3
9	0	16	7	0	16	6	0	16	6	0	16	5	0	16	5
8	0	14	9	0	14	8	0	14	8	0	14	7	0	14	7
7	0	12	10	0	12	10	0	12	10	0	12	9	0	12	9
6	0	11	0	0	11	0	0	11	0	0	10	11	0	10	11
5	0	9	2	0	9	2	0	9	2	0	9	1	0	9	1
4	0	7	4	0	7	4	0	7	4	0	7	3	0	7	3
3	0	5	6	0	5	6	0	5	6	0	5	6	0	5	5
2	0	3	8	0	3	8	0	3	8	0	3	8	0	3	7
1	0	1	10	0	1	10	0	1	10	0	1	10	0	1	10
Stu. 10	0	0	11	0	0	11	0	0	11	0	0	11	0	0	11
9	0	0	10	0	0	10	0	0	10	0	0	10	0	0	9
8	0	0	8	0	0	8	0	0	8	0	0	8	0	0	8
7	0	0	7	0	0	7	0	0	7	0	0	7	0	0	7
6	0	0	6	0	0	6	0	0	6	0	0	6	0	0	6
5	0	0	5	0	0	5	0	0	5	0	0	5	0	0	5
4	0	0	4	0	0	4	0	0	4	0	0	4	0	0	4
3	0	0	3	0	0	3	0	0	3	0	0	3	0	0	3
2	0	0	2	0	0	2	0	0	2	0	0	2	0	0	2
1	0	0	1	0	0	1	0	0	1	0	0	1	0	0	1
Pen. 12	0	0	0	0	0	0	0	0	0	0	0	0	0	0	0
8	0	0	0	0	0	0	0	0	0	0	0	0	0	0	0

Eng.	36 s. 7 g.			36 s. 8 g.			36 s. 9 g.			36 s. 10 g.			36 s. 11 g.		
£.	G.	s.	p.	G.	s.	p.	G.	s.	p.	G.	s.	p.	G.	s.	p.
1000	10975	0		11000			11025	0		11050			11075	0	
900	9877	10		9900			9922	10		9945			9967	10	
800	8780	0		8800			8820	0		8840			8860	0	
700	7682	10		7700			7717	10		7735			7752	10	
600	6585	0		6600			6615	0		6630			6645	0	
500	5487	10		5500			5512	10		5525			5537	10	
400	4390	0		4400			4410	0		4420			4430	0	
300	3292	10		3300			3307	10		3315			3322	10	
200	2195	0		2200			2205	0		2210			2215	0	
100	1097	10		1100			1102	10		1105			1107	10	
90	987	15		990			992	5		994	10		996	15	
80	878	0		880			882	0		884	0		886	0	
70	768	5		770			771	15		773	10		775	5	
60	658	10		660			661	10		663	0		664	10	
50	548	15		550			551	5		552	10		553	15	
40	439	0		440			441	0		442	0		443	0	
30	329	5		330			330	15		331	10		332	5	
20	219	10		220			220	10		221	0		221	10	
10	109	15		110			110	5		110	10		110	15	
9	98	15	8	99			99	4	8	99	9		99	13	8
8	87	16	0	88			88	4	0	88	8		88	12	0
7	76	16	8	77			77	3	8	77	7		77	10	8
6	65	17	0	66			66	3	0	66	6		66	9	0
5	54	17	8	55			55	2	8	55	5		55	7	8
4	43	18	0	44			44	2	0	44	4		44	6	0
3	32	18	8	33			33	1	8	33	3		33	4	8
2	21	19	0	22			22	1	0	22	2		22	3	0
1	10	19	8	11			11	0	8	11	1		11	1	8
S. 10	5	9	12	5	10		5	10	4	5	10	8	5	10	12
9	4	18	12	4	19		4	19	4	4	19	7	4	19	11
8	4	7	13	4	8		4	8	3	4	8	6	4	8	10
7	3	16	13	3	17		3	17	3	3	17	6	3	17	8
6	3	5	14	3	6		3	6	2	3	6	5	3	6	7
5	2	14	14	2	15		2	15	2	2	15	4	2	15	6
4	2	3	14	2	4		2	4	2	2	4	3	2	4	5
3	1	12	15	1	13		1	13	1	1	13	2	1	13	5
2	1	1	15	1	2		1	2	1	1	2	2	1	2	2
1	0	11	0	0	11		0	11	1	0	11	1	0	11	1
D. 6	0	5	8	0	5	8	0	5	8	0	5	8	0	5	9
5	0	4	9	0	4	9	0	4	9	0	4	10	0	4	10
4	0	3	11	0	3	11	0	3	11	0	3	11	0	3	11
3	0	2	12	0	2	12	0	2	12	0	2	12	0	2	12
2	0	1	13	0	1	13	0	1	13	0	1	13	0	1	14
1	0	0	14	0	0	15	0	0	15	0	0	15	0	0	15

Dutch	36 s. 7 g.			36 s. 8 g.			36 s. 9 g.			36 s. 10 g.			36 s. 11 g.		
Guild.	£.	s.	d.	£.	s.	d.	£.	s.	d.	£.	s.	d.	£.	s.	d.
10000	911	3	2	909	1	9	907	0	7	904	19	6	902	18	8
5000	455	11	7	454	10	10	453	10	3	452	9	9	451	9	4
4000	364	9	3	363	12	8	362	16	2	361	19	9	361	3	5
3000	273	6	11	272	14	6	272	2	2	271	9	10	270	17	7
2000	182	4	7	181	16	4	181	8	1	180	19	10	180	11	8
1000	91	2	3	90	18	2	90	14	0	90	9	11	90	5	10
900	82	0	1	81	16	4	81	12	7	81	8	11	81	5	3
800	72	17	10	72	14	6	72	11	2	72	7	11	72	4	8
700	63	15	7	63	12	8	63	9	10	63	6	11	63	4	1
600	54	13	4	54	10	10	54	8	5	54	5	11	54	3	6
500	45	11	2	45	9	1	45	7	0	45	4	11	45	2	11
400	36	8	11	36	7	3	36	5	7	36	3	11	36	2	4
300	27	6	8	27	5	5	27	4	2	27	2	11	27	1	9
200	18	4	5	18	3	7	18	2	9	18	1	11	18	1	2
100	9	2	2	9	1	9	9	1	4	9	1	0	9	0	7
90	8	4	0	8	3	7	8	3	3	8	2	10	8	2	6
80	7	5	9	7	5	5	7	5	1	7	4	9	7	4	5
70	6	7	6	6	7	3	6	6	11	6	6	8	6	6	5
60	5	9	4	5	9	1	5	8	10	5	8	7	5	8	4
50	4	11	1	4	10	11	4	10	8	4	10	6	4	10	3
40	3	12	10	3	12	8	3	12	6	3	12	4	3	12	2
30	2	14	8	2	14	6	2	14	5	2	14	3	2	14	2
20	1	16	5	1	16	4	1	16	3	1	16	2	1	16	1
10	0	18	2	0	18	2	0	18	1	0	18	1	0	18	0
9	0	16	4	0	16	4	0	16	4	0	16	3	0	16	3
8	0	14	7	0	14	6	0	14	6	0	14	5	0	14	5
7	0	12	9	0	12	8	0	12	8	0	12	8	0	12	7
6	0	10	11	0	10	11	0	10	10	0	10	10	0	10	10
5	0	9	1	0	9	1	0	9	0	0	9	0	0	9	0
4	0	7	3	0	7	3	0	7	3	0	7	2	0	7	2
3	0	5	5	0	5	5	0	5	5	0	5	5	0	5	5
2	0	3	7	0	3	7	0	3	7	0	3	7	0	3	7
1	0	1	9	0	1	9	0	1	9	0	1	9	0	1	9
Stu. 10	0	0	11	0	0	11	0	0	11	0	0	10	0	0	10
9	0	0	9	0	0	9	0	0	9	0	0	9	0	0	9
8	0	0	8	0	0	8	0	0	8	0	0	8	0	0	8
7	0	0	7	0	0	7	0	0	7	0	0	7	0	0	7
6	0	0	6	0	0	6	0	0	6	0	0	6	0	0	6
5	0	0	5	0	0	5	0	0	5	0	0	5	0	0	5
4	0	0	4	0	0	4	0	0	4	0	0	4	0	0	4
3	0	0	3	0	0	3	0	0	3	0	0	3	0	0	3
2	0	0	2	0	0	2	0	0	2	0	0	2	0	0	2
1	0	0	1	0	0	1	0	0	1	0	0	1	0	0	1
Pen 12	0	0	0	0	0	0	0	0	0	0	0	0	0	0	0
8	0	0	0	0	0	0	0	0	0	0	0	0	0	0	0

Exchanges *between* England *and* Denmark.

The par with Hamburgh and Antwerp is 35 Schillings, 6 2-3 Groot or Pence Flemiſh, for 1*l.* Sterling.

Proportions of Money.

12 Pennings	— is —	1 Schilling-lub	— —	0	$1\frac{1}{8}$
16 Schilling-lubs	— is —	1 Mark	— —	1	6
2 Marks	— is —	1 Dollar	— —	3	0
3 Marks	— is —	1 Rix-dollar	— —	4	6
$6\frac{1}{4}$ Marks	— is —	1 Ducat	— —	9	$4\frac{1}{2}$
6 Pennings	— is —	1 Groot or Penny	— —	0	0.562
6 Schilling-lubs	— is —	1 Schilling	— —	0	6.75
1 Schilling-lub	— is —	2 Pence or Groots	— —	0	1.125
1 Mark	— is —	32 Pence or Groots	— —	1	6.
$7\frac{1}{2}$ Marks	— is —	1 Pound	— —	11	3.

The courſe of Exchange is from 32 Schs. $8\frac{1}{2}$ Grs. to 35 Schs. 4 Grs.

The common method of Calculation is by a Statement of the Rule of Three. As the Rate of Exchange is to one Pound Sterl. ſo is the Daniſh Money to the Engliſh; or, as one Pound Sterling is to the Rate, ſo is the Engliſh Money to the Daniſh.

Example.

How many Marks &c. muſt be received at Hamburgh, for 300*l.* Sterl. Exchange at 35 S. 3 *g.*

As 1*l.* is to 35*s.* 3*g.* ſo is 300*l.*

```
        35s. 3g.
        12
        ----
        423
         300
        ----
Groots in 1 Mark 32)126900(3965m. 10s.
        ----
Remainder  20
           16
        ----
        32)640
```

Reverſed, As 35*s.* 3*g.* is to 1*l.* ſo is 3965*m.* 10*s.*

```
35s. 3g.          3965m.  10s.
12                   32     2
----              -----   ----
423                7930   20d.
----              11897
                  -----
               423)126900(300l.
                   1269
                  -----
```

A TABLE

A TABLE of Decimal Multipliers, for *Danish* and *English* MONEY, at the several Rates of Exchange.

ENGLISH into DANISH.				DANISH into ENGLISH.			
RATE	Multpr.	RATE	Multpr.	RATE	Multpr.	RATE	Multpr.
32. 8h	12.2656	34. oh	12.7656	32. 8h	.08153	34. oh	.078335
32. 9	12.2812	34. 1	12.7812	32. 9	.081425	34. 1	.07824
32. 9h	12.2968	34. 1h	12.7968	32. 9h	.081321	34. 1h	.078144
32.10	12.3125	34. 2	12.8125	32.10	.081218	34. 2	.078048
32.10h	12.3281	34. 2h	12.8281	32.10h	.081115	34. 2h	.07798
32.11	12.3437	34. 3	12.8437	32.11	.081012	34. 3	.07786
32.11h	12.3593	34. 3h	12,8593	32.11h	.08091	34. 3h	.077765
33. 0	12.375	34. 4	12.875	33. 0	.080808	34. 4	.07767
33. oh	12.3906	34. 4h	12.8906	33. oh	.080758	34. 4h	.077575
33. 1	12.4062	34. 5	12.9061	33. 1	.080604	34. 5	.077481
33. 1h	12.4218	34. 5h	12.9218	33. 1h	.080502	34. 5h	.077388
33. 2	12.4375	34. 6	12.9375	33. 2	.080401	34. 6	.077295
33. 2h	12.4531	34. 6h	12.9531	33. 2h	.0803	34. 6h	.077201
33. 3	12.4687	34. 7	12.9687	33. 3	.0802	34. 7	.077108
33. 3h	12.4843	34. 7h	12.9843	33. 3h	.0801	34. 7h	.077015
33. 4	12.5	34. 8	13.	33. 4	.08	34. 8	.076923
33. 4h	12.5156	34. 8h	13.0156	33. 4h	.0799	34 8h	.07683
33. 5	12.5312	34. 9	13.0312	33. 5	.0798	34. 9	.076738
33. 5h	12.5468	34. 9h	13.0468	33. 5h	.0797	34. 9h	.076646
33. 6	12.5625	34.10	13.0625	33. 6	.079601	34.10	.076555
33. 6h	12.5781	34.10h	13.0781	33. 6h	.079503	34.10h	.076463
33. 7	12.5937	34.11	13.0937	33. 7	.079404	34.11	.076372
33. 7h	12.6093	34.11h	13.1096	33. 7h	.079305	34.11h	.076281
33. 8	12.625	35. 0	13.125	33. 8	.079207	35. 0	.07619
33. 8h	12.6406	35. oh	13.1406	33. 8h	.07911	35. oh	.0761
33. 9	12.6562	35. 1	13.1562	33. 9	.079012	35. 1	.07601
33. 9h	12.6718	35. 1h	13.1719	33. 9h	07892	35. 1h	.07592
33.10	12.6875	35. 2	13.1875	33.10	.078817	35. 2	.07583
33.10h	12.7031	35. 2h	13.2031	33.10h	.07872	35. 2h	.07574
33.11	12.7187	35. 3	13.2187	33 11	.078624	35. 3	.07565
33.11h	12.7343	35. 3h	13.2343	33.11h	.078527	35. 3h	.075556
34. 0	12.75	35. 4	13.25	34. 0	.078431	35. 4	.075471

A Decimal TABLE of *Schilling-lubs* and *Pennings*, 1 Mark being the Integer.

Schilling-lubs		Schilling-lubs		Pennigs	
1	.0625	11	.6875	4	.020833
2	.1250	12	.75	5	.026041
3	.1875	13	.8125	6	.03125
4	.25	14	.875	7	.036458
5	.3125	15	.9375	8	.041666
6	.372			9	.046874
7	.4375	Pennings		10	.052082
8	.5	1	.005208	11	.05729
9	.5625	2	.010416		
10	.625	3	.015625		

For the better underſtanding the foregoing Table of Multipliers, the reader will obſerve, that in the *Daniſh* Column, the Multiplier is no other than the Marks and Parts of a Mark contained in the Rate; and in the *Engliſh* Column, the Multiplier is the value of 1 Mark expreſſed in Parts of 1*l.* Sterl. at the ſeveral Rates; that is, (in the *Daniſh* Column) in 33 S. 4 G. there are 12 Marks 5 Parts, ſo that if any Sum of *Engliſh* Money be multiplied by 12 5 the Product will be Marks and Parts of a Mark at 33 S. 4 G. and in the *Engliſh* Column 33 S. 4 G. is .08 Parts of 1*l.* Sterl. ſo that if any ſum of *Daniſh* Money be multiplied by .08 the Product will be Pounds and Parts of a Pound Sterl. only remembring that the Schillings and Pennings muſt be expreſs'd as Decimal Parts of a Mark by the foregoing Table, and the Shillings and Pence as Parts of a Pound Sterl. by the table affixed to the Engliſh Exchanges.

Example.

What will be the value of 100*l* 10*s*. *Engliſh*, in *Daniſh* Money at 33*s*. 4*g*. per Pound Sterling.

*l.*100.5 parts Engliſh Money
12.5 Multiplier

5025
2010
1005

Marks 1256.25
16 Schillings per Mark

150
25

Schillings 4.00 Anſwer 1256 Ma. 4 Sch.

Reverſed.

What will be the value of 1256*m*. 4*s*. in Engliſh Money, at 33*s* 4*g* per Pound Sterling.

1256.25 Marks and Parts
.08 Multiplier

100.5000 Anſwer 100*l.* 5 Parts, or 100*l.* 10*s*

As ſome accounts are kept in Pounds Schillings and Groots, or Pence Flemiſh,—the proportions are,—

1 Groot	—	Value in Engliſh Sterl.	— —	*l.*0	0	0.562
12 Groots	— is —	1 Schilling	— —	0	0	6.75
20 Schilling	— is —	1 Pound Flemiſh	— —	0	11	3.

In

IN the foregoing Part of this Book I have given the Tables of Exchange with England, France and Holland, AT LARGE, *not only because our intercourse with them is more considerable than with most others, but also that the Reader might have a full opportunity of examining and proving the Tables of* DECIMAL MULTIPLIERS, *and other methods of calculation, which I have submitted to his judgment; and if they appear to him to be (as I believe they will) abundantly sufficient for all purposes of Trade, I hope a contraction of the following Tables will not lessen the utility of the Work.*

ENGLAND

Eng	32 s. 11 g.			33 s.			33 s. 1 g.			33 s. 2 g.			33 s. 3 g.		
£.	M.	s.	d.	M.	s.	d.	M.	s.	d.	M.	s.	d.	M.	s.	d.
1000	12343	12		12375	0		12406	4		12437	8		12468	12	
900	11109	6		11137	8		11165	10		11193	12		11221	14	
800	9875	0		9900	0		9925	0		9950	0		9975	0	
700	8640	10		8662	8		8684	6		8706	4		8728	2	
600	7406	4		7425	0		7443	12		7462	8		7481	4	
500	6171	14		6187	8		6203	2		6218	12		6234	6	
400	4937	8		4950	0		4962	8		4975	0		4987	8	
300	3703	2		3712	8		3721	14		3731	4		3740	10	
200	2468	12		2475	0		2481	4		2487	8		2493	12	
100	1234	6		1237	8		1240	10		1243	12		1246	14	
90	1110	15		1113	12		1116	9		1119	6		1122	3	
80	987	8		990	0		992	8		995	0		997	8	
70	864	1		866	4		868	7		870	10		872	13	
60	740	10		742	8		744	6		746	4		748	2	
50	617	3		618	12		620	5		621	14		623	7	
40	493	12		494	0		496	4		497	8		498	12	
30	370	5		371	4		372	3		373	2		374	1	
20	246	14		247	8		248	2		248	12		249	6	
10	123	7		123	12		124	1		124	6		124	11	
9	111	1	6	111	6		111	10	6	111	15		112	3	6
8	98	12	0	99	0		99	4	0	99	8		99	12	0
7	86	6	6	86	10		86	13	6	87	1		87	4	6
6	74	1	0	74	4		74	7	0	74	10		74	13	0
5	61	11	6	61	14		62	0	6	62	3		62	5	6
4	49	6	0	49	8		49	10	0	49	12		49	14	0
3	37	0	6	37	2		37	3	6	37	5		37	6	6
2	24	11	0	24	12		24	13	0	24	14		24	15	0
1	12	5	6	12	6		12	6	6	12	7		12	7	6
S. 10	6	2	9	6	3		6	3	3	6	3	6	6	3	9
9	5	8	11	5	9	1	5	9	4	5	9	7	5	9	9
8	4	15	0	4	15	2	4	15	5	4	15	7	4	15	10
7	4	5	2	4	5	4	4	5	6	4	5	8	4	5	10
6	3	11	3	3	11	5	3	11	7	3	11	8	3	11	10
5	3	1	5	3	1	6	3	1	8	3	1	9	3	1	11
4	2	7	6	2	7	7	2	7	8	2	7	10	2	7	11
3	1	13	8	1	13	8	1	13	9	1	13	10	1	13	11
2	1	3	9	1	3	10	1	3	10	1	3	11	1	3	11
1	0	9	11	0	9	11	0	9	11	0	9	11	0	10	0
D. 6	0	4	11	0	4	11	0	4	11	0	4	11	0	5	0
5	0	4	1	0	4	2	0	4	2	0	4	2	0	4	2
4	0	3	4	0	3	4	0	3	4	0	3	4	0	3	4
3	0	2	6	0	2	6	0	2	6	0	2	6	0	2	6
2	0	1	8	0	1	8	0	1	8	0	1	8	0	1	8
1	0	0	10	0	0	10	0	0	10	0	0	10	0	0	10

Dan.	32 s. 11 g.			33 s.			33 s. 1 g.			33 s. 2 g.			33 s. 3 g.		
Mks.	£.	s.	d.	£.	s.	d.	£.	s.	d.	£.	s.	d.	£.	s.	d.
10000	810	2	6	808	1	7	806	0	11	804	0	4	802	0	1
5000	405	1	3	404	0	9	403	0	5	402	0	2	401	0	0
4000	324	1	0	323	4	7	322	8	4	321	12	2	320	16	0
3000	243	0	9	242	8	5	241	16	3	241	4	1	240	12	0
2000	162	0	6	161	12	4	161	4	2	160	16	1	160	8	0
1000	81	0	3	80	16	2	80	12	1	80	8	0	80	4	0
900	72	18	2	72	14	6	72	10	10	72	7	3	72	3	7
800	64	16	2	64	12	11	64	9	8	64	6	5	64	3	2
700	56	14	2	56	11	3	56	8	5	56	5	7	56	2	9
600	48	12	1	48	9	8	48	7	3	48	4	10	48	2	4
500	40	10	1	40	8	1	40	6	0	40	4	0	40	2	0
400	32	8	1	32	6	5	32	4	10	32	3	2	32	1	7
300	24	6	1	24	4	10	24	3	7	24	2	5	24	1	2
200	16	4	0	16	3	2	16	2	5	16	1	7	16	0	9
100	8	2	0	8	1	7	8	1	2	8	0	9	8	0	4
90	7	5	10	7	5	5	7	5	1	7	4	8	7	4	4
80	6	9	7	6	9	3	6	8	11	6	8	7	6	8	3
70	5	13	5	5	13	1	5	12	10	5	12	6	5	12	3
60	4	17	2	4	16	11	4	16	8	4	16	5	4	16	3
50	4	1	0	4	0	9	4	0	7	4	0	4	4	0	2
40	3	4	9	3	4	7	3	4	5	3	4	3	3	4	2
30	2	8	7	2	8	5	2	8	4	2	8	3	2	8	1
20	1	12	4	1	12	4	1	12	3	1	12	2	1	12	1
10	0	16	2	0	16	2	0	16	1	0	16	1	0	16	0
9	0	14	7	0	14	6	0	14	6	0	14	5	0	14	5
8	0	12	11	0	12	11	0	12	10	0	12	10	0	12	0
7	0	11	4	0	11	3	0	11	3	0	11	3	0	11	2
6	0	9	8	0	9	8	0	9	8	0	9	7	0	9	7
5	0	8	1	0	8	1	0	8	0	0	8	0	0	8	0
4	0	6	5	0	6	5	0	6	5	0	6	5	0	6	5
3	0	4	10	0	4	10	0	4	10	0	4	10	0	4	9
2	0	3	3	0	3	2	0	3	2	0	3	2	0	3	2
1	0	1	7	0	1	7	0	1	7	0	1	7	0	1	7
Sch. 14	0	1	5	0	1	5	0	1	5	0	1	4	0	1	4
12	0	1	2	0	1	2	0	1	2	0	1	2	0	1	2
10	0	1	0	0	1	0	0	1	0	0	1	0	0	1	0
8	0	0	9	0	0	9	0	0	9	0	0	9	0	0	9
7	0	0	8	0	0	8	0	0	8	0	0	8	0	0	8
6	0	0	7	0	0	7	0	0	7	0	0	7	0	0	7
5	0	0	6	0	0	6	0	0	6	0	0	6	0	0	6
4	0	0	4	0	0	4	0	0	4	0	0	4	0	0	4
3	0	0	3	0	0	3	0	0	3	0	0	3	0	0	3
2	0	0	2	0	0	2	0	0	2	0	0	2	0	0	2
1	0	0	1	0	0	1	0	0	1	0	0	1	0	0	1
Pen 6	0	0	0	0	0	0	0	0	0	0	0	0	0	0	0

Eng.	33 s. 4 g.			33 s. 5 g.			33 s. 6 g.			33 s. 7 g.			33 s. 8 g.		
£.	M.	s.	d.	M.	s.	d	M.	s.	d	M.	s.	d.	M.	s.	d.
1000	12500			12531	4		12562	8		12593	12		12625	0	
900	11250			11278	2		11306	4		11334	6		11362	8	
800	10000			10025	0		10050	0		10075	0		10100	0	
700	8750			8771	14		8793	12		8815	10		8837	8	
600	7500			7518	12		7537	8		7556	4		7575	0	
500	6250			6265	10		6281	4		6296	14		6342	8	
400	5000			5012	8		5025	0		5037	8		5050	0	
300	3750			3759	6		3768	12		3778	2		3787	8	
200	2500			2506	4		2512	8		2518	12		2525	0	
100	1250			1253	2		1256	4		1259	6		1262	8	
90	1125			1127	13		1130	10		1133	7		1136	4	
80	1000			1002	8		1005	0		1007	8		1010	0	
70	875			877	3		879	6		881	9		883	12	
60	750			751	14		753	12		755	10		757	8	
50	625			626	9		628	2		629	11		631	4	
40	500			501	4		502	8		503	12		505	0	
30	375			375	15		376	14		377	13		378	12	
20	250			250	10		251	4		251	14		252	8	
10	125			125	5		125	10		125	15		126	4	
9	112	8		112	12	6	113	1		113	5	6	113	10	
8	100	0		100	4	0	100	8		100	12	0	101	0	
7	87	8		87	11	6	87	15		88	2	6	88	6	
6	75	0		75	3	0	75	6		75	9	0	75	12	
5	62	8		62	10	6	62	13		62	15	6	63	2	
4	50	0		52	2	0	50	4		50	6	0	50	8	
3	37	8		37	9	6	37	11		37	12	6	37	14	
2	25	0		25	1	0	25	2		25	3	0	25	4	
1	12	8		12	8	6	12	9		12	9	6	12	10	
S. 10	6	4		6	4	3	6	4	6	6	4	9	6	5	
9	5	10		5	10	3	5	10	5	5	10	8	5	10	11
8	5	0		5	0	2	5	0	5	5	0	7	5	0	10
7	4	6		4	6	2	4	6	[illegible]	4	6	6	4	6	8
6	3	12		3	12	2	3	12	[illegible]	3	12	5	3	12	7
5	3	2		3	2	2	3	2	[illegible]	3	2	5	3	2	6
4	2	8		2	8	1	2	8	[illegible]	2	8	4	2	8	5
3	1	14		1	14	1	1	14	2	1	14	3	1	14	4
2	1	4		1	4	1	1	4	1	1	4	2	1	4	2
1	0	10		0	10	0	0	10	1	0	10	1	0	10	1
D. 6	0	5		0	5	0	0	5	[illegible]	0	5	0	0	5	1
5	0	4	2	0	4	2	0	4	2	0	4	2	0	4	3
4	0	3	4	0	3	4	0	3	[illegible]	0	3	4	0	3	4
3	0	2	6	0	2	6	0	2	6	0	2	6	0	2	6
2	0	1	8	0	1	8	0	1	8	0	1	8	0	1	8
1	0	0	10	0	0	10	0	0	10	0	0	10	0	0	10

Dan.	33 s. 4 g.			33 s. 5 g.			33 s. 6 g.			33 s. 7 g.			33 s. 8 g.		
Mks.	£.	s.	d.	£.	s.	d.	£.	s.	d.	£.	s.	d.	£.	s.	d.
10000	800			798	0	1	796	0	4	794	0	10	792	1	7
5000	400			399	0	0	398	0	2	397	0	5	396	0	9
4000	320			319	4	0	318	8	2	317	12	4	316	16	7
3000	240			239	8	0	238	16	1	238	4	3	237	12	5
2000	160			159	12	0	159	4	1	158	16	2	158	8	3
1000	80			79	16	0	79	12	0	79	8	1	79	4	2
900	72			71	16	4	71	12	10	71	9	3	71	5	9
800	64			63	16	9	63	13	7	63	10	5	63	7	4
700	56			55	17	2	55	14	5	55	11	8	55	8	11
600	48			47	17	7	47	15	2	47	12	10	47	10	6
500	40			39	18	0	39	16	0	39	14	0	39	12	1
400	32			31	18	4	31	16	9	31	15	2	31	13	8
300	24			23	18	9	23	17	7	23	16	5	23	15	3
200	16			15	19	2	15	18	5	15	17	7	15	16	10
100	8			7	19	7	7	19	2	7	18	9	7	18	5
90	7	4		7	3	7	7	3	3	7	2	11	7	2	7
80	6	8		6	7	8	6	7	4	6	7	0	6	6	8
70	5	12		5	11	8	5	11	5	5	11	2	5	10	10
60	4	16		4	15	9	4	15	6	4	15	3	4	15	0
50	4	0		3	19	9	3	19	7	3	19	4	3	19	2
40	3	4		3	3	10	3	3	8	3	3	6	3	3	4
30	2	8		2	7	10	2	7	9	2	7	7	2	7	6
20	1	12		1	11	11	1	11	10	1	11	9	1	11	8
10	0	16		0	15	11	0	15	11	0	15	10	0	15	10
9	0	14	4	0	14	4	0	14	4	0	14	3	0	14	3
8	0	12	9	0	12	9	0	12	8	0	12	8	0	12	8
7	0	11	2	0	11	2	0	11	1	0	11	1	0	11	1
6	0	9	7	0	9	7	0	9	6	0	9	6	0	9	6
5	0	8	0	0	7	11	0	7	11	0	7	11	0	7	11
4	0	6	4	0	6	4	0	6	4	0	6	4	0	6	4
3	0	4	9	0	4	9	0	4	9	0	4	9	0	4	9
2	0	3	2	0	3	2	0	3	2	0	3	2	0	3	2
1	0	1	7	0	1	7	0	1	7	0	1	7	0	1	7
Sch. 14	0	1	4	0	1	4	0	1	4	0	1	4	0	1	4
12	0	1	2	0	1	2	0	1	2	0	1	2	0	1	2
10	0	1	0	0	1	0	0	1	0	0	1	0	0	1	0
8	0	0	9	0	0	9	0	0	9	0	0	9	0	0	9
7	0	0	8	0	0	8	0	0	8	0	0	8	0	0	8
6	0	0	7	0	0	7	0	0	7	0	0	7	0	0	7
5	0	0	6	0	0	6	0	0	6	0	0	6	0	0	6
4	0	0	4	0	0	4	0	0	4	0	0	4	0	0	4
3	0	0	3	0	0	3	0	0	3	0	0	3	0	0	3
2	0	0	2	0	0	2	0	0	2	0	0	2	0	0	2
1	0	0	1	0	0	1	0	0	1	0	0	1	0	0	1
Pen. 6	0	0	0	0	0	0	0	0	0	0	0	0	0	0	0

Eng.	33 s. 9 g.			33 s. 10 g.			33 s. 11 g.			34 s.			35 s.		
£.	M.	s.	d.	M.	s.	d.	M.	s.	d.	M.	s	d	M.	s.	d.
1000	12656	4		12687	8		12718	12		12750			13125	0	
900	11390	10		11418	12		11446	14		11475			11812	8	
800	10125	0		10150	0		10175	0		10200			10500	0	
700	8859	6		8881	4		8903	2		8925			9187	8	
600	7593	12		7612	8		7631	4		7650			7875	0	
500	6328	2		6343	12		6359	6		6375			6562	8	
400	5062	8		5075	0		5087	8		5100			5250	0	
300	3799	14		3806	4		3815	10		3825			3937	8	
200	2531	4		2537	8		2543	12		2550			2625	0	
100	1265	10		1268	12		1271	14		1275			1312	8	
90	1139	1		1141	14		1144	11		1147	8		1181	4	
80	1012	8		1015	0		1017	8		1020	0		1050	0	
70	885	15		888	2		890	5		892	8		918	12	
60	759	6		761	4		763	2		765	0		787	8	
50	632	13		634	6		635	15		637	8		656	4	
40	506	4		507	8		508	12		510	0		525	0	
30	379	1		380	10		381	9		382	8		393	12	
20	253	2		253	12		254	6		255	0		262	8	
10	126	9		126	14		127	3		127	8		131	4	
9	113	14	6	114	3		114	7	6	114	12		118	2	
8	101	4	0	101	8		101	12	0	102	0		105	0	
7	88	9	6	88	13		89	0	6	89	4		91	14	
6	75	15	0	76	2		76	5	0	76	8		78	12	
5	63	4	6	63	7		63	9	6	63	12		65	10	
4	50	10	0	50	12		50	14	0	51	0		52	8	
3	37	15	6	38	1		38	2	6	38	4		39	6	
2	25	5	0	25	6		25	7	0	25	8		26	4	
1	12	10	6	12	11		12	11	6	12	12		13	2	
S. 10	6	5	3	6	5	6	6	5	9	6	6	0	6	9	
9	5	11	2	5	11	4	5	11	7	5	11	10	5	14	6
8	5	1	0	5	1	2	5	1	5	5	1	7	5	4	0
7	4	6	11	4	7	1	4	7	3	4	7	5	4	9	6
6	3	12	9	3	12	11	3	13	1	3	13	2	3	15	0
5	3	[illegible]	8	3	2	9	3	2	11	3	3	0	3	4	6
4	2	8	6	2	8	7	2	8	8	2	8	10	2	10	0
3	1	14	5	1	14	5	1	14	6	1	14	7	1	15	6
2	1	4	3	1	4	4	1	4	[illegible]	1	4	5	1	5	0
1	0	10	2	0	10	2	0	10	2	0	10	2	0	10	6
D. 6	0	5	1	0	5	1	0	5	[illegible]	0	5	1	0	5	3
5	0	4	3	0	4	3	0	4	3	0	4	3	0	4	5
4	0	3	5	0	3	5	0	3	5	0	3	5	0	3	6
3	0	2	6	0	2	6	0	2	6	0	2	7	0	2	8
2	0	1	8	0	1	8	0	1	8	0	1	8	0	1	8
1	0	0	10	0	0	10	0	0	10	0	0	10	0	0	1

Dan.	33 s. 9 g.			33 s. 10 g.			33 s. 11 g.			43 s.			35 s.		
Mks.	£.	s.	d.	£.	s.	d.	£.	s.	d.	£.	s.	d.	£.	s.	d.
10000	790	2	5	788	3	6	786	4	9	784	6	3	761	18	1
5000	395	1	2	394	1	9	393	2	5	392	3	1	380	19	0
4000	316	0	11	315	5	5	314	9	11	313	14	6	304	15	2
3000	237	0	9	236	9	0	235	17	5	235	5	10	228	11	5
2000	158	0	6	157	12	8	157	4	11	156	17	3	152	7	7
1000	79	0	3	78	16	4	78	12	5	78	8	7	76	3	9
900	71	2	2	70	18	8	70	15	2	70	11	9	68	11	5
800	63	4	2	63	1	1	62	17	11	62	14	10	60	19	0
700	55	6	2	55	3	5	55	0	9	54	18	0	53	6	8
600	47	8	1	47	5	9	47	3	5	47	1	2	45	14	3
500	39	10	1	39	8	2	39	6	3	39	4	3	38	1	10
400	31	12	1	31	10	6	31	9	0	31	7	5	30	9	6
300	23	14	1	23	12	11	23	11	9	23	10	7	22	17	1
200	15	16	0	15	15	3	15	14	6	15	13	8	15	4	9
100	7	18	0	7	17	7	7	17	3	7	16	10	7	12	4
90	7	2	2	7	1	10	7	1	0	7	1	2	6	17	1
80	6	6	5	6	6	1	6	5	9	6	5	6	6	1	10
70	5	10	7	5	10	4	5	10	1	5	9	9	5	6	8
60	4	14	9	4	14	7	4	14	4	4	14	1	4	11	5
50	3	19	0	3	18	9	3	18	7	3	18	5	3	16	2
40	3	3	2	3	3	0	3	2	10	3	2	9	3	0	11
30	2	7	5	2	7	3	2	7	2	2	7	0	2	5	8
20	1	11	7	1	11	6	1	11	5	1	11	4	1	10	5
10	0	15	9	0	15	9	0	15	8	0	15	8	0	15	2
9	0	14	2	0	14	2	0	14	1	0	14	1	0	13	8
8	0	12	7	0	12	7	0	12	7	0	12	6	0	12	2
7	0	11	0	0	11	0	0	11	0	0	10	11	0	10	8
6	0	9	5	0	9	5	0	9	5	0	9	5	0	9	1
5	0	7	10	0	7	10	0	7	10	0	7	10	0	7	7
4	0	6	3	0	6	3	0	6	3	0	6	3	0	6	1
3	0	4	9	0	4	8	0	4	8	0	4	8	0	4	6
2	0	3	2	0	3	1	0	3	1	0	3	1	0	3	0
1	0	1	7	0	1	7	0	1	6	0	1	6	0	1	6
Sch 14	0	1	4	0	1	4	0	1	4	0	1	4	0	1	4
12	0	1	2	0	1	2	0	1	2	0	1	2	0	1	1
10	0	0	11	0	0	11	0	0	11	0	0	11	0	0	11
8	0	0	9	0	0	9	0	0	9	0	0	9	0	[illegible]	[illegible]
7	0	0	8	0	0	8	0	0	8	0	0	8	0	[illegible]	[illegible]
6	0	0	7	0	0	7	0	0	7	0	0	7	0	[illegible]	[illegible]
5	0	0	6	0	0	6	0	0	6	0	0	6	0	[illegible]	[illegible]
4	0	0	4	0	0	4	0	0	4	0	0	4	[illegible]	[illegible]	[illegible]
3	0	0	3	0	0	3	0	0	3	0	0	3	[illegible]	[illegible]	[illegible]
2	0	0	2	0	0	2	0	0	2	0	0	2	[illegible]	[illegible]	[illegible]
1	0	0	1	0	0	1	0	0	1	0	0	[illegible]	[illegible]	[illegible]	[illegible]
Pen 6	0	0	0	0	0	0	0	0	0	0	[illegible]	[illegible]	[illegible]	[illegible]	[illegible]

BANK MONEY, commonly called BANCO, on account of its undoubted security and convenience in Trade, generally exceeds the current money in value from 3 to 6 per Cent. which excess is called the *Agio*, and is determined by a station of the Rule of Three.

Example.

What will 2210 *guilders* in Bank Money amount to in Current Money, the Agio being 3⅛ per Cent.

As 100 is to 103⅛ so is 2210 *guilds.* to 2279 *guilds.* 1 *fl.* 4 *pen.* Current

Second Example.

What will 2430 *gs.* 6 *sts.* 5 *ds.* Current Money make in *Banco*, the Agio being 3⅝ per Cent.

As 103⅝ is to 100, so is 2430 *g.* 6 *fl.* 5 *d.* to 2345 *g.* 6 *fl.* Banco.

To save the trouble of a station by the Rule of Three, if any sum in Bank Money be multiplied by the tabular number affixed to the Rate in the left hand column of the following Table, it will give the value in Current Money—Guilders and Parts. Or if any sum in Current Money be multiplied by the tabular number affixed to the Rate in the right hand column, it will give the value in Banco.

BANCO into CURR. MONEY			CURR. MONEY into BANCO.		
Rate	8th	Multpr.	Rate	8th	Multpr.
3	0	1.03	3	0	·970873
	1	1.03125		1	·9697
	2	1.0325		2	·968525
	3	1.03375		3	·96735
	4	1.035		4	·966187
	5	1.03625		5	·965018
	6	1.0375		6	·963855
	7	1.03875		7	·962695
4	0	1.04	4	0	·961538
	1	1.04125		1	·960384
	2	1.0425		2	·959232
	3	1.04375		3	·958083
	4	1.045		4	·956937
	5	1.04625		5	·975794
	6	1.0475		6	·954654
	7	1.04875		7	·953516
5	0	1.05	5	0	·952381
	1	1.05125		1	·951248
	2	1.0525		2	·950118
	3	1.05375		3	·948991
	4	1.055		4	·947867
	5	1.05625		5	·946745
	6	1.0575		6	·945626
	7	1.05875		7	·94451
6	0	1.06	6	0	·543396

BANCO

Banco	At 3¼ p. Cent.			3½			4			5			6		
Guild.	G.	s.	p.	G.	s.	p.	G.	s.	p.	G.	s.	p.	G.	s.	p.
10000	10325	0		10350			10400			10500			10600		
5000	5162	10		5175			5200			5250			5300		
4000	4130	0		4140			4160			4200			4240		
3000	3097	10		3105			3120			3150			3180		
2000	2065	0		2070			2080			2100			2120		
1000	1032	10		1035			1040			1050			1060		
900	929	5		931	10		936			945			954		
800	826	0		823	0		832			840			848		
700	722	15		724	10		728			735			742		
600	619	10		621	0		624			630			636		
500	516	5		517	10		520			525			530		
400	413	0		410	0		416			420			424		
300	309	15		310	10		312			315			318		
200	206	10		207	0		208			210			212		
100	103	5		103	10		104			105			106		
90	92	18	8	93	3		93	12		94	10		95	8	
80	82	12	0	82	16		83	4		84	0		84	16	
70	72	5	8	72	9		72	16		73	10		74	4	
60	61	19	0	62	2		62	8		63	0		63	12	
50	51	12	8	51	15		52	0		52	10		53	0	
40	41	6	0	41	8		41	12		42	0		42	8	
30	30	19	8	31	1		31	4		31	10		31	16	
20	20	13	0	20	14		20	16		21	0		21	4	
10	10	6	8	10	7		10	8		10	10		10	12	
9	9	5	14	9	6	5	9	7	3	9	9		9	10	13
8	8	5	3	8	5	10	8	6	6	8	8		8	9	10
7	7	4	9	4	4	14	7	5	12	7	7		7	8	6
6	6	3	14	6	4	3	6	4	13	6	6		6	7	3
5	5	3	4	5	3	8	5	4	0	5	5		5	6	0
4	4	2	10	4	2	13	4	3	3	4	4		4	4	13
3	3	1	15	3	2	2	3	2	6	3	3		3	3	10
2	2	1	5	2	1	6	2	1	10	2	2		2	2	6
1	1	0	10	1	0	11	1	0	13	1	1		1	1	3
St. 10	0	10	5	0	10	6	0	10	6	0	10	8	0	10	10
9	0	9	5	0	9	5	0	9	6	0	9	7	0	9	9
8	0	8	4	0	8	4	0	8	5	0	8	6	0	8	8
7	0	7	4	0	7	4	0	7	4	0	7	6	0	7	7
6	0	6	3	0	6	3	0	6	4	0	6	5	0	6	6
5	0	5	3	0	5	3	0	5	3	0	5	4	0	5	5
4	0	4	2	0	4	2	0	4	3	0	4	3	0	4	4
3	0	3	2	0	3	2	0	3	2	0	3	2	0	3	3
2	0	2	1	0	2	1	0	2	1	0	2	1	0	2	2
1	0	1	1	0	1	1	0	1	1	0	1	1	0	1	1
Pen 12	0	0	12	0	0	12	0	0	12	0	0	12	0	0	13
8	0	0	8	0	0	8	0	0	8	0	0	8	0	0	8

Curt.	At 3¼ p.Cent			3½			4			5			6		
Guild.	G.	s.	p.	G.	s.	p.	G.	s.	p.	G.	s.	p.	G.	s.	p.
10000	9685	4	10	9661	16	11	9615	7	11	9523	16	3	9433	19	4
5000	4842	12	5	4830	18	6	4807	13	14	4761	18	2	4716	19	10
4000	3874	1	13	3864	14	11	3846	3	1	3809	10	8	3773	11	11
3000	2905	11	6	2898	11	0	2884	12	5	2857	2	14	2830	3	12
2000	1937	0	15	1932	7	5	1023	1	9	1904	15	4	1886	15	14
1000	968	10	7	966	3	11	961	10	12	952	7	10	943	7	15
900	871	13	7	869	11	5	865	7	11	857	2	14	849	1	2
800	774	16	6	772	18	15	769	4	10	761	18	2	754	14	5
700	677	19	5	676	6	9	673	1	9	666	13	5	660	7	9
600	581	2	4	579	14	3	576	18	7	571	8	9	566	0	12
500	484	5	4	483	1	13	480	15	6	476	3	13	471	13	15
400	387	8	3	386	9	7	384	12	5	380	19	1	377	7	3
300	290	11	2	289	17	2	288	9	4	285	14	5	283	0	6
200	193	14	1	193	4	12	192	6	2	190	9	8	188	13	9
100	96	17	1	96	12	6	96	3	1	95	4	12	94	6	13
90	87	3	6	86	19	2	86	10	12	85	14	5	84	18	2
80	77	9	10	77	5	14	76	18	7	76	3	13	75	9	7
70	67	15	15	67	12	10	67	6	2	66	13	5	66	0	12
60	58	2	4	57	19	7	57	13	4	57	2	14	56	12	1
50	48	8	8	48	6	3	48	1	9	47	12	6	47	3	6
40	38	14	13	38	12	15	38	9	4	38	1	14	37	14	11
30	29	1	2	28	19	11	28	16	15	28	11	7	28	6	1
20	19	7	7	19	6	8	19	4	10	19	0	15	18	17	6
10	9	13	11	9	13	4	9	12	5	9	10	8	9	8	11
9	8	14	5	8	13	15	8	13	1	8	11	7	8	9	13
8	7	14	15	7	14	9	7	13	12	7	12	6	7	10	15
7	6	15	9	6	15	4	6	14	10	6	13	5	6	12	1
6	5	16	4	5	15	15	5	15	6	5	14	5	5	13	3
5	4	16	4	4	16	10	4	16	2	4	15	4	4	14	5
4	3	17	8	3	17	5	3	16	15	3	16	3	3	15	8
3	2	18	2	2	18	0	2	17	11	2	17	2	2	16	10
2	1	18	12	1	18	10	1	18	7	1	18	2	1	17	12
1	0	19	6	0	19	5	0	19	4	0	19	1	0	18	14
St. 10	0	9	11	0	9	11	0	9	10	0	9	8	0	9	7
9	0	8	11	0	8	11	0	8	10	0	8	9	0	8	8
8	0	7	12	0	7	12	0	7	11	0	7	10	0	7	9
7	0	6	12	0	6	12	0	6	12	0	6	11	0	6	10
6	0	5	13	0	5	13	0	5	12	0	5	11	0	5	11
5	0	4	13	0	4	13	0	4	13	0	4	12	0	4	11
4	0	3	14	0	3	14	0	3	14	0	3	13	0	3	12
3	0	2	14	0	2	14	0	2	14	0	2	14	0	2	13
2	0	1	15	0	1	15	0	1	15	0	1	14	0	1	14
1	0	0	15	0	0	15	0	0	15	0	0	15	0	0	15
Pen. 12	0	0	12	0	0	12	0	0	12	0	0	12	0	0	11
8	0	0	8	0	0	8	0	0	8	0	0	8	0	0	8

EXCHANGE *between* England *and* Spain.

These Exchanges are rated on the Piaſtre. The *Par* is 43 pence Engliſh for a Piaſtre or Dollar of eight Rials, the courſe runs from 40 to 45 pence; and the relations of Spaniſh monies with England are as follows.

34 Mervadies	is	1 Rial	0s. $5\frac{3}{8}$*d.*	Sterling
8 Rials	is	1 Piaſtre	3 7	
375 Mervadies	is	1 Ducat	4 $11\frac{1}{4}$	

The uſual method of calculating theſe Exchanges, (like all others) is by a Station of the Rule of Three, *i. e.* as the Rate of Exchange is to one Piaſtre, ſo is the Engliſh Money to its value in Spaniſh; or as one Piaſtre is to the Rate of Exchange, ſo is the Spaniſh Money to its value in Engliſh.

Example.

What will be the value of 500*l.* Engliſh in Spaniſh Money at 43 pence the Piaſtre?

As 43 pence is to 1 Piaſtre, ſo is 500*l.* to 2790 *Pias.* 5 *Rial.* 10 *Merv.*

What will be the value of 2790 Piaſtres, 5 Rials, 10 Mervadies, in Engliſh Money at 43 pence the Piaſtre?

As 1 Piaſtre is to 43 pence, ſo is 2790 *Pias.* 5 *Rial* 10 *Mer.* to 500*l.* Sterl.

Theſe Exchanges (like the former) may alſo be determined with accuracy and expedition, by the following Table of Decimal Multipliers, remembering only, to expreſs the Rials and Mervadies as Decimal parts of a Piaſtre, (as per Table) and the Shillings and Pence as Decimal parts of a Pound Sterling, by the Table at the beginning of the Engliſh Exchanges.

A TABLE of MERVADIES, one PIASTRE being the Integer.

								RIALS.	
1	.0036	10	.0367	18	.0661	27	.0992		
2	.0073	11	.0404	19	.0698	28	.1029	1	.125
3	.011	12	.0441	20	.0735	29	.1066	2	.25
4	.0147	13	.0477	21	.0772	30	.1102	3	.375
5	.0183	14	.0514	22	.0808	31	.1139	4	.5
6	.022	15	.0551	23	.0845	32	.1176	5	.625
7	.0257	16	.0588	24	.0882	33	.1213	6	.75
8	.0294	17	.0625	25	.0919	34	.125	7	.875
9	.033			26	.0955			8	1.

A TABLE

A TABLE *of* DECIMAL MULTIPLIERS *for* SPANISH *and* ENGLISH MONEY, *at the ſeveral* RATES *of* EXCHANGE.

ENGLISH into SPANISH				SPANISH into ENGLISH			
RATE 8th	Multp.	Rate	Multr.	Rate	Multr.	Rate	Mulp.
40 —	6.	45—	5.3333	40—	.16666	45—	.1875
1	5.9812	1	5.3185	1	.16718	1	.18802
2	5.9627	2	5.3038	2	.16771	2	.18854
3	5.9442	3	5.2892	3	.16823	3	.18906
4	5.9259	4	5.2747	4	.16875	4	.18958
5	5.9077	5	5.2602	5	.16927	5	.1901
6	5.8893	6	5.1459	6	.16979	6	.19062
7	5.8715	7	5.2316	7	.17031	7	.19114
41 —	5.8536	46—	5.2173	41—	.17083	46—	.19167
1	5.8358	1	5.2032	1	.17135	1	.19219
2	5.8182	2	5.1891	2	.17187	2	.19271
3	5.8006	3	5.1752	3	.1724	3	.19323
4	5.7831	4	5.1613	4	.17292	4	.19375
5	5.7657	5	5.1474	5	.17344	5	.19427
6	5.7485	6	5.1337	6	.17396	6	.19479
7	5.7313	7	5.12	7	.17448	7	.19531
42 —	5.7143	47—	5.1063	42—	.175	47—	.19583
1	5.6973	1	5.0928	1	.17552	1	.19635
2	5.6804	2	5.0793	2	.17604	2	.19688
3	5.6637	3	5.0659	3	.17656	3	.1974
4	5.647	4	5.0526	4	.17708	4	.19791
5	5.6305	5	5.0393	5	.1776	5	.19844
6	5.614	6	5.0262	6	.17812	6	.19896
7	5.5977	7	5.013	7	.17864	7	.19948
43 —	5.5814	48—	5.	43—	.17917	48—	.2
1	5.5652	1	4.987	1	.17969	1	.20052
2	5.5491	2	4.9741	2	.18021	2	.20104
3	5.5331	3	4.9612	3	.18073	3	.20156
4	5.5172	4	4.9484	4	.18125	4	.20208
5	5.5014	5	4.9357	5	.18177	5	.2026
6	5.4857	6	4.923	6	.18229	6	.20312
7	5.47[illegible]	7	4.9105	7	.18281	7	.20364
44 —	5.4545	49—	4.8979	44—	.18333	49—	.20417
1	5.4391	1	4.8855	1	.18385	1	.20468
2	5.4237	2	4.8731	2	.18437	2	.20521
3	5.4084	3	4.8607	3	.1849	3	.20573
4	5.3932	4	4.8485	4	.18541	4	.20625
5	5.3781	5	4.8362	5	.18594	5	.20677
6	5.3631	6	4.8241	6	.18646	6	.20729
7	5.3482	7	4.812	7	.187	7	.20781
		50—	4.8			50—	.20833

Use of the foregoing Table.

If any Sum in English Money, be multiplied by the tabular number opposite the rate of Exchange in the Spanish column, the product will be Piastres and parts of a Piastre. Or if any sum in Spanish Money be multiplied by the tabular number opposite the Rate of Exchange in the right hand column, the product will be Pounds and parts of a Pound ster.

1st. Example.

What will be the value of £500 Engl. in Spanish Money, at 42⅝ pence the Piastre.

Tabular number for the Rate 5.6305
500 pounds sterl.

P. 2815.2500
Rials in the Piastre 8

2 | 00

Answer 2815 Piastres 2 Rials.

2d. Example.

What will be the value of £700 Engl. in Spanish Money, at 46⅞ pence the Piastre.

Tabular number for the Rate 5.12
700

P. 3584 | 00

Answer 3584 Piastres

3d. Example.

What will be the value of 1000 Piastres in English money at 43½ pence the Piastre

Tabular number for the Rate .18125
1000

£. 181 | 25 | 000
20

S. 5 | 00

Answer £.181 5

4th Example.

What will be the value of 2000 Piastres in English Money at 45 pence the Piastre

Tabular number for the Rate .1875
2000

£. 375 | 0000

Answer £.375

The following Tables are only given, to prove that this method by Decimal Multipliers is correct.

England

Eng.	At 40d.			40¼d.			40½d.			40¾d.			41d.		
£.	P.	r.	m	P.	r.	m.	P.	r.	m.	P.	r.	m.	P.	r.	m.
1000	6000			5962	5	29	5925	7	14	5889	4	19	5853	5	9
900	5400			5366	3	13	5333	2	23	5300	4	31	5268	2	12
800	4800			4770	1	17	4740	5	31	4711	5	9	4682	7	14
700	4200			4173	7	10	4148	1	6	4122	5	20	4097	4	17
600	3600			3577	7	4	3555	4	15	3533	5	32	3512	1	19
500	3000			2981	2	32	2962	7	24	2944	6	10	2926	6	22
400	2400			2385	0	25	2370	2	33	2355	6	21	2341	3	24
300	1800			1788	6	19	1777	6	8	1766	6	33	1756	0	27
200	1200			1192	4	13	1185	1	16	1177	7	11	1170	5	29
100	600			596	2	6	592	4	25	588	7	22	585	2	32
90	540			536	5	6	533	2	23	530	0	17	526	6	22
80	480			477	0	5	474	0	20	471	1	11	468	2	12
70	420			417	3	4	414	6	18	412	2	5	409	6	2
60	360			357	6	4	355	4	15	353	3	0	351	1	26
50	300			298	1	3	296	2	13	294	3	28	292	5	16
40	240			238	4	3	237	0	10	235	4	22	234	1	6
30	180			178	7	2	177	6	8	176	5	17	175	4	30
20	120			119	2	1	118	4	5	117	6	11	117	0	20
10	60			59	5	1	59	2	3	58	7	6	58	4	10
9	54			53	5	11	53	2	23	53	0	2	52	5	6
8	48			47	5	21	47	3	9	47	0	32	46	6	22
7	42			41	5	31	41	3	29	41	1	28	40	7	27
6	36			35	6	7	35	4	15	35	2	24	35	0	33
5	30			29	6	17	29	5	1	29	3	20	29	2	5
4	24			23	6	27	23	5	21	23	4	16	23	3	11
3	18			17	7	4	17	6	8	17	5	12	17	4	17
2	12			11	7	14	11	6	28	11	6	8	11	5	22
1	6			5	7	24	5	7	14	5	7	4	5	6	28
S. 10	3			2	7	29	2	7	24	2	7	19	2	7	14
9	2	5	20	2	5	16	2	5	11	2	5	7	2	5	2
8	2	3	6	2	3	3	2	2	33	2	2	29	2	2	25
7	2	0	27	2	0	24	2	0	20	2	0	17	2	0	13
6	1	6	13	1	6	11	1	6	8	1	6	5	1	6	2
5	1	4	0	1	3	31	1	3	29	1	3	26	1	3	24
4	1	1	20	1	1	18	1	1	16	1	1	14	1	1	12
3	0	7	7	0	7	5	0	7	4	0	7	2	0	7	1
2	0	4	27	0	4	26	0	4	25	0	4	24	0	4	23
1	0	2	13	0	2	13	0	2	13	0	2	12	0	2	12
D. 6	0	1	7	0	1	7	0	1	6	0	1	6	0	1	6
5	0	1	0	0	1	0	0	1	0	0	0	33	0	0	33
4	0	0	27	0	0	27	0	0	27	0	0	27	0	0	27
3	0	0	20	0	0	20	0	0	20	0	0	20	0	0	20
2	0	0	14	0	0	14	0	0	13	0	0	13	0	0	13
1	0	0	7	0	0	7	0	0	7	0	0	7	0	0	7

Span.	40d.			40¼d.			40½d.			40¾d.			41d.		
Piast.	£.	s.	d.	£.	s.	d.	£.	s.	d.	£.	s.	d.	£.	s.	d.
10000	1666	13	4	1677	1	8	1687	10		1697	18	4	1708	6	8
5000	833	6	8	838	10	10	843	15		848	19	2	854	3	4
4000	666	13	4	670	16	8	675	0		679	3	4	683	6	8
3000	500	0	0	503	2	6	506	5		509	7	6	512	10	0
2000	333	6	8	335	8	4	337	10		339	11	8	341	13	4
1000	166	13	4	167	14	2	168	15		169	15	10	170	16	8
900	150	0	0	150	18	9	151	17	6	152	16	3	153	15	0
800	133	6	8	134	3	4	135	0	0	135	16	8	136	13	4
700	116	13	4	117	7	11	118	2	6	118	17	1	119	11	8
600	100	0	0	100	12	6	101	5	0	101	17	6	102	10	0
500	83	6	8	83	17	1	84	7	6	84	17	11	85	8	4
400	66	13	4	67	1	8	67	10	0	67	18	4	68	6	8
300	50	0	0	50	6	3	50	12	6	50	18	9	51	5	0
200	33	6	8	33	10	10	33	15	0	33	19	2	34	3	4
100	16	13	4	16	15	5	16	17	6	16	19	7	17	1	8
90	15	0	0	15	1	10	15	3	9	15	5	7	15	7	6
80	13	6	8	13	8	4	13	10	0	13	11	8	13	3	4
70	11	13	4	11	14	9	11	16	3	11	17	8	11	19	2
60	10	0	0	10	1	3	10	2	6	10	3	9	10	5	0
50	8	6	8	8	7	8	8	8	9	8	9	9	8	10	10
40	6	13	4	6	14	2	6	15	0	6	15	11	6	16	8
30	5	0	0	5	0	7	5	1	3	5	1	10	5	2	6
20	3	6	8	3	7	1	3	7	6	3	7	11	3	8	4
10	1	13	4	1	13	6	1	13	9	1	13	11	1	14	2
9	1	10	0	1	10	2	1	10	4	1	10	6	1	10	9
8	1	6	8	1	6	10	1	7	0	1	7	2	1	7	4
7	1	3	4	1	3	5	1	3	7	1	3	9	1	3	11
6	1	0	0	1	0	1	1	0	3	1	0	4	1	0	6
5	0	16	8	0	16	9	0	16	10	0	16	11	0	17	1
4	0	13	4	0	13	5	0	13	6	0	13	7	0	13	8
3	0	10	0	0	10	0	0	10	1	0	10	2	0	10	3
2	0	6	8	0	6	8	0	6	9	0	6	9	0	6	10
1	0	3	4	0	3	4	0	3	4	0	3	4	0	3	5
R. 7	0	2	11	0	2	11	0	2	11	0	2	11	0	2	11
6	0	2	6	0	2	6	0	2	6	0	2	6	0	2	6
5	0	2	1	0	2	1	0	2	1	0	2	1	0	2	1
4	0	1	8	0	1	8	0	1	8	0	1	8	0	1	8
3	0	1	3	0	1	3	0	1	3	0	1	3	0	1	3
2	0	0	10	0	0	10	0	0	10	0	0	10	0	0	10
1	0	0	5	0	0	5	0	0	5	0	0	5	0	0	5
M. 25	0	0	3	0	0	3	0	0	3	0	0	3	0	0	3
17	0	0	2	0	0	2	0	0	2	0	0	2	0	0	2
8	0	0	1	0	0	1	0	0	1	0	0	1	0	0	1
4	0	0	½	0	0	½	0	0	½	0	0	½	0	0	½

Eng.	41½d.			42d.			42⅛d.			42⅜d.			43d.		
£.	P.	r.	m.	P.	r.	m.	P.	r.	m.	P.	r.	m.	P.	r.	m.
1000	5783	1	2	5714	2	10	5647	0	16	5630	4	0	5581	3	6
900	5204	6	19	5142	6	19	5082	2	28	5003	3	20	5023	2	2
800	4626	4	2	4571	3	15	4517	5	6	4504	3	6	4465	0	32
700	4048	1	18	4000	0	0	3952	7	18	3941	2	27	3906	7	28
600	3469	7	1	3428	4	19	3388	1	30	3378	2	13	3348	6	24
500	2891	4	18	2857	1	5	2823	4	8	2815	2	0	2790	5	10
400	2313	2	1	2285	5	24	2258	6	20	2252	1	20	2232	4	16
300	1734	7	17	1714	2	10	1694	0	32	1689	1	7	1674	3	12
200	1156	5	0	1142	6	29	1129	3	10	1126	0	27	1116	2	8
100	578	2	17	571	3	15	564	5	22	563	0	14	558	1	4
90	520	3	29	514	2	10	508	1	30	506	5	33	502	2	21
80	462	5	7	457	1	5	451	6	4	450	3	18	446	4	3
70	404	6	19	400	0	0	395	2	12	394	1	3	390	5	20
60	346	7	31	342	6	29	338	6	20	337	6	22	334	7	2
50	289	1	9	285	5	24	282	2	28	281	4	7	279	0	19
40	231	2	21	228	4	19	225	7	2	225	1	26	223	2	2
30	173	3	32	171	3	15	169	3	10	168	7	11	167	3	18
20	115	5	10	114	2	10	112	7	18	112	4	30	111	5	1
10	57	6	22	57	1	5	56	3	26	56	2	15	55	6	17
9	52	0	13	51	3	15	50	6	20	50	5	13	50	1	29
8	46	2	4	45	5	24	45	1	14	45	0	12	44	5	7
7	40	3	29	40	0	0	39	4	8	39	3	10	39	0	19
6	34	5	20	34	2	10	33	7	2	33	6	9	33	3	31
5	28	7	11	28	4	1	28	1	30	28	1	7	27	7	9
4	23	1	2	22	6	29	22	4	24	22	4	6	22	2	21
3	17	2	27	17	1	5	16	7	18	16	7	4	16	5	32
2	11	4	18	11	3	15	11	2	12	11	2	3	11	1	10
1	5	6	9	5	5	24	5	5	6	5	5	1	5	4	22
S. 10	2	7	5	2	6	29	2	6	20	2	6	18	2	6	11
9	2	4	28	2	4	19	2	4	11	2	4	9	2	4	3
8	2	2	17	2	2	10	2	2	2	2	2	1	2	1	29
7	2	0	7	2	0	0	1	7	28	1	7	26	1	7	21
6	1	5	30	1	5	24	1	5	19	1	5	17	1	5	13
5	1	3	19	1	3	15	1	3	10	1	3	9	1	3	6
4	1	1	9	1	1	5	1	1	1	1	1	0	1	0	32
3	0	6	32	0	6	29	0	6	26	0	6	26	0	6	24
2	0	4	21	0	4	19	0	4	18	0	4	17	0	4	16
1	0	2	11	0	2	10	0	2	9	0	2	9	0	2	8
D. 6	0	1	5	0	1	5	0	1	4	0	1	4	0	1	4
5	0	0	33	0	0	32	0	0	32	0	0	32	0	0	32
4	0	0	26	0	0	26	0	0	26	0	0	26	0	0	25
3	0	0	20	0	0	19	0	0	19	0	0	19	0	0	19
2	0	0	13	0	0	13	0	0	13	0	0	13	0	0	13
1	0	0	7	0	0	6	0	0	6	0	0	6	0	0	6

Span.	41½d.			42d.			42½d.			42⅝d.			43d.		
Piast.	£.	s.	d.	£.	s.	d.	£.	s.	d.	£.	s.	d.	£.	s.	d.
10000	1729	3	4	1750			1770	16	8	1776	0	10	1791	13	4
5000	864	11	8	875			885	8	4	888	0	5	895	16	8
4000	691	13	4	700			708	6	8	710	8	4	716	13	4
3000	518	15	0	525			531	5	0	532	16	3	537	10	0
2000	345	16	8	350			354	3	4	355	4	2	358	6	8
1000	172	18	4	175			177	1	8	177	12	1	179	3	4
900	155	12	6	157	10		159	7	6	159	16	10	161	5	0
800	138	6	8	140	0		141	13	4	142	1	8	143	6	8
700	121	0	10	122	10		123	19	2	124	6	5	125	8	4
600	103	15	0	105	0		106	5	0	106	11	3	107	10	0
500	86	9	2	87	10		88	10	10	88	16	0	89	11	8
400	69	3	4	70	0		70	16	8	71	0	10	71	13	4
300	51	17	6	52	10		53	2	6	53	5	7	53	15	0
200	34	11	8	35	0		35	8	4	35	10	5	35	16	8
100	17	5	10	17	10		17	14	2	17	15	2	17	18	4
90	15	11	3	15	15		15	18	9	15	19	8	16	2	6
80	13	16	8	14	0		14	3	4	14	4	2	14	6	8
70	12	2	1	12	5		12	7	11	12	8	7	12	10	10
60	10	7	6	10	10		10	12	6	10	13	1	10	15	0
50	8	12	11	8	15		8	17	1	8	17	7	8	19	2
40	6	18	4	7	0		7	1	8	7	2	1	7	3	4
30	5	3	9	5	5		5	6	3	5	6	6	5	7	6
20	3	9	2	3	10		3	10	10	3	11	0	3	11	8
10	1	14	7	1	15		1	15	5	1	15	6	1	15	10
9	1	11	1	1	11	6	1	11	10	1	11	11	1	12	3
8	1	7	8	1	8	0	1	8	4	1	8	5	1	8	8
7	1	4	2	1	4	6	1	4	9	1	4	10	1	5	1
6	1	0	9	1	1	0	1	1	3	1	1	3	1	1	6
5	0	17	3	0	17	6	0	17	8	0	17	9	0	17	11
4	0	13	10	0	14	0	0	14	2	0	14	2	0	14	4
3	0	10	4	0	10	6	0	10	7	0	10	7	0	10	9
2	0	6	11	0	7	0	0	7	1	0	7	1	0	7	2
1	0	3	5	0	3	6	0	3	6	0	3	6	0	3	7
R. 7	0	3	0	0	3	0	0	3	1	0	3	1	0	3	1
6	0	2	7	0	2	7	0	2	7	0	2	8	0	2	8
5	0	2	2	0	2	2	0	2	2	0	2	2	0	2	2
4	0	1	8	0	1	9	0	1	9	0	1	9	0	1	9
3	0	1	3	0	1	3	0	1	4	0	1	4	0	1	4
2	0	0	10	0	0	10	0	0	10	0	0	10	0	0	10
1	0	0	5	0	0	5	0	0	5	0	0	5	0	0	5
M. 25	0	0	3	0	0	3	0	0	4	0	0	4	0	0	4
17	0	0	2	0	0	2	0	0	2	0	0	2	0	0	2
8	0	0	1	0	0	1	0	0	1	0	0	1	0	0	1
4	0	0	½	0	0	½	0	0	½	0	0	½	0	0	½

Eng.	43½d.			44d.			44½d.			45d.			45½d.		
£.	P.	r.	m.	P.	r.	m.	P.	r.	m.	P.	r.	m.	P.	r.	m.
1000	5517	1	32	5454	4	12	5393	2	2	5333	2	23	5274	5	27
900	4965	4	5	4909	0	25	4853	7	16	4800	0	0	4747	2	1
800	4413	6	12	4363	5	3	4314	4	29	4266	5	11	4219	6	8
700	3862	0	19	3818	1	15	3775	2	8	3733	2	23	3692	2	16
600	3310	2	26	3272	5	28	3235	7	22	3200	0	0	3164	6	23
500	2758	4	33	2727	2	6	2696	5	1	2666	5	11	2637	2	31
400	2206	7	6	2181	6	19	2157	2	5	2133	2	23	2109	7	4
300	1655	1	13	1636	2	31	1617	7	28	1600	0	0	1582	3	12
200	1103	3	20	1090	7	9	1078	5	7	1066	5	11	1054	7	19
100	551	5	27	545	3	22	539	2	21	533	2	23	527	3	27
90	496	4	14	490	7	9	485	3	5	480	0	0	474	5	27
80	441	3	1	436	2	31	431	3	23	426	5	11	421	7	28
70	386	1	22	381	6	19	377	4	8	373	2	23	369	1	29
60	331	0	9	327	2	6	323	4	20	320	0	0	316	3	30
50	275	6	30	272	5	28	269	5	10	266	5	11	263	5	30
40	220	5	18	218	1	15	215	5	29	213	2	23	210	7	31
30	165	4	5	163	5	3	161	6	13	160	0	0	158	1	32
20	110	2	26	109	0	25	107	6	31	106	5	11	105	3	33
10	55	1	13	54	4	12	53	7	16	53	2	23	52	5	33
9	49	5	8	49	0	25	48	4	11	48	0	0	47	3	27
8	44	1	4	43	5	3	43	1	6	42	5	11	42	1	20
7	38	4	33	38	1	15	37	6	1	37	2	23	36	7	13
6	33	0	28	32	5	28	32	3	30	32	0	0	31	5	0
5	27	4	23	27	2	6	26	7	25	26	5	11	26	3	0
4	22	0	19	21	6	19	21	4	20	21	2	23	21	0	27
3	16	4	14	16	2	31	16	1	15	16	0	0	15	6	20
2	11	0	9	10	7	9	10	6	10	10	5	11	10	4	13
1	5	4	5	5	3	22	5	3	5	5	2	23	5	2	7
S. 10	2	6	2	2	5	28	2	5	19	2	5	11	2	5	3
9	2	3	29	2	3	22	2	3	14	2	3	7	2	3	0
8	2	1	22	2	1	15	2	1	9	2	1	2	2	0	30
7	1	7	15	1	7	9	1	7	3	1	6	32	1	6	26
6	1	5	8	1	5	3	1	4	32	1	4	27	1	4	22
5	1	3	1	1	2	3	1	2	27	1	2	23	1	2	19
4	1	0	28	1	0	25	1	0	21	1	0	18	1	0	15
3	0	6	21	0	6	19	0	6	16	0	6	14	0	6	11
2	0	4	14	0	4	12	0	4	11	0	4	9	0	4	7
1	0	2	7	0	2	6	0	2	5	0	2	5	0	2	4
D. 6	0	1	4	0	1	3	0	1	3	0	1	2	0	1	2
5	0	0	31	0	0	31	0	0	31	0	0	30	0	0	3[illegible]
4	0	0	25	0	0	25	0	0	24	0	0	24	0	0	24
3	0	0	19	0	0	19	0	0	18	0	0	18	0	0	18
2	0	0	12	0	0	12	0	0	12	0	0	12	0	0	12
1	0	0	6	0	0	6	0	0	6	0	0	6	0	0	6

Span.	At 43½d.			44d.			44½d			45d.			45½d.		
Piaſt.	£.	s.	d.	£.	s.	d.	£.	s.	d.	£.	s.	d.	£.	s.	d.
10000	1812	10		1833	6	8	1854	3	4	1875			1895	16	8
5000	906	5		916	13	4	927	1	8	937	10		947	13	4
4000	725	0		733	6	8	741	13	4	750	0		758	6	8
3000	543	15		550	0	0	556	5	0	562	10		568	15	0
200	362	10		366	13	4	370	16	8	375	0		379	3	4
1000	181	5		183	6	8	185	8	4	187	10		189	11	8
900	163	2	6	165	0	0	166	17	6	168	15		170	12	6
800	145	0	0	146	13	4	148	6	8	150	0		151	13	4
700	126	17	6	128	6	8	129	15	10	131	5		132	14	2
600	108	15	0	110	0	0	111	5	0	112	10		113	5	0
500	90	12	6	91	13	4	92	14	2	93	15		94	15	10
400	72	10	0	73	6	8	74	3	4	75	0		75	16	8
300	54	7	6	55	0	0	55	12	6	56	5		56	17	6
200	36	5	0	36	13	4	37	1	8	37	10		37	18	4
100	18	2	6	18	6	8	18	10	10	18	15		18	19	2
90	16	6	3	16	10	0	16	13	9	16	17	6	17	1	3
80	14	10	0	14	13	4	14	16	8	15	0	0	15	3	4
70	12	13	9	12	16	8	12	19	7	13	2	6	13	5	5
60	10	17	6	11	0	0	11	2	6	11	5	0	11	7	6
50	9	1	3	9	3	4	9	5	5	9	7	6	9	9	7
40	7	5	0	7	6	8	7	8	4	7	10	0	7	11	8
30	5	8	9	5	10	0	5	11	3	5	12	6	5	13	9
20	3	12	6	3	13	4	3	14	2	3	15	0	3	15	10
10	1	16	3	1	16	8	1	17	1	1	17	6	1	17	11
9	1	12	7	1	13	0	1	13	4	1	13	9	1	14	1
8	1	9	0	1	9	4	1	9	8	1	10	0	1	10	4
7	1	5	4	1	5	8	1	5	11	1	6	3	1	6	6
6	1	1	9	1	2	0	1	2	3	1	2	6	1	2	9
5	0	18	1	0	18	4	0	18	6	0	18	9	0	18	11
4	0	14	6	0	14	8	0	14	10	0	15	0	0	15	2
3	0	10	10	0	11	0	0	11	1	0	11	3	0	11	4
2	0	7	3	0	7	4	0	7	5	0	7	6	0	7	7
1	0	3	7	0	3	8	0	3	8	0	3	9	0	3	9
R. 7	0	3	2	0	3	2	0	3	3	0	3	3	0	3	3
6	0	2	8	0	2	9	0	2	9	0	2	9	0	2	10
5	0	2	3	0	2	3	0	2	3	0	2	4	0	2	4
4	0	1	9	0	1	10	0	1	10	0	1	10	0	1	10
3	0	1	4	0	1	4	0	1	4	0	1	4	0	1	5
2	0	0	10	0	0	11	0	0	11	0	0	11	0	0	11
1	0	0	5	0	0	5	0	0	5	0	0	5	0	0	5
M. 25	0	0	4	0	0	4	0	0	4	0	0	4	0	0	4
17	0	0	2	0	0	2	0	0	2	0	0	2	0	0	2
8	0	0	1	0	0	1	0	0	1	0	0	1	0	0	1
4	0	0	½	0	0	½	0	0	½	0	0	½	0	0	½

Eng.	*At 46d.*			46½*d.*			46⅞*d.*			47*d.*			47½*d.*		
£.	P.	*r.*	*m.*	P.	*r.*	*m.*	P.	*r.*	*m.*	P.	*r.*	*m.*	P.	*r.*	*m.*
1000	5217	3	4	5161	2	11	5120			5106	3	2	5052	5	2
900	4695	5	7	4645	1	10	4608			4595	5	33	4547	2	32
800	4173	7	10	4129	0	9	4096			2085	0	29	4042	0	29
700	3652	1	13	3612	7	8	3584			3574	3	25	3536	6	25
600	3130	3	16	3096	6	7	3072			3063	6	22	3031	4	2[illegible]
500	2608	5	19	2580	5	5	2560			2553	1	18	2526	2	18
400	2086	7	22	2064	4	4	2048			2042	4	14	2021	0	14
300	1565	1	25	1548	3	3	1536			1531	7	11	1515	6	11
200	1043	3	28	1032	2	2	1024			1021	2	7	1010	4	7
100	521	5	31	516	1	1	512			510	5	4	505	2	4
90	469	4	18	464	4	4	460	6	14	459	4	20	454	5	30
80	417	3	4	412	7	8	409	4	27	408	4	3	404	1	25
70	365	1	25	361	2	11	358	3	7	357	3	19	353	5	16
60	313	0	12	309	5	14	307	1	20	306	3	2	303	1	9
50	260	6	32	258	0	17	256	0	0	255	2	19	252	5	2
40	208	5	19	206	3	21	204	6	14	204	2	1	202	0	29
30	156	4	6	154	6	24	153	4	27	153	1	18	151	4	21
20	104	2	27	103	1	27	102	3	7	102	1	1	101	0	14
10	52	1	13	51	4	31	51	1	30	51	0	17	50	4	7
9	46	7	22	46	3	21	46	0	22	45	7	22	45	3	27
8	41	5	31	41	2	11	40	7	23	40	6	27	40	3	13
7	36	4	6	36	1	1	35	6	24	35	5	33	35	2	32
6	31	2	15	30	7	25	30	5	26	30	5	4	30	2	18
5	26	0	24	25	6	15	25	4	27	25	4	9	25	2	4
4	20	6	33	20	5	5	20	3	29	20	3	14	20	1	25
3	15	5	7	15	3	30	15	2	30	15	2	19	15	1	9
2	10	3	16	10	2	20	10	1	31	10	1	24	10	0	29
1	5	1	25	5	1	10	5	0	33	5	0	29	5	0	14
S. 10	2	4	30	2	4	22	2	4	16	2	4	14	2	4	7
9	2	2	27	2	2	20	2	2	15	2	2	13	2	2	6
8	2	0	24	2	0	18	2	0	13	2	0	12	2	0	6
7	1	6	21	1	6	15	1	6	11	1	6	10	1	6	5
6	1	4	18	1	4	13	1	4	10	1	4	9	1	4	4
5	1	2	15	1	2	11	1	2	8	1	2	7	1	2	4
4	1	0	12	1	0	9	1	0	7	1	0	6	1	0	3
3	0	6	9	0	6	7	0	6	5	0	6	4	0	6	2
2	0	4	6	0	4	4	0	4	3	0	4	3	0	4	1
1	0	2	3	0	2	2	0	2	2	0	2	2	0	2	1
D. 6	0	1	1	0	1	1	0	1	1	0	1	1	0	1	0
5	0	0	30	0	0	29	0	0	29	0	0	29	0	0	29
4	0	0	24	0	0	23	0	0	23	0	0	23	0	0	23
3	0	0	18	0	0	18	0	0	18	0	0	18	0	0	17
2	0	0	12	0	0	12	0	0	12	0	0	12	0	0	11
1	0	0	6	0	0	6	0	0	6	0	0	6	0	0	6

Span.	46d.			46½d.			46⅞d.			47d.			47½d.		
Piast.	£.	s.	d.	£.	s.	d.	£.	s.	d.	£.	s.	d.	£.	s.	d.
10000	1916	13	4	1937	10		1953	2	6	1958	6	8	1979	3	4
5000	958	6	8	968	15		976	11	3	979	3	4	989	11	8
4000	766	13	4	775	0		781	5	0	783	6	8	791	13	4
3000	575	0	0	581	5		585	18	9	587	10	0	593	15	0
2000	383	6	8	387	10		390	12	6	391	13	4	395	16	8
1000	191	13	4	193	15		195	6	3	195	16	8	197	18	4
900	172	10	0	174	7	6	175	15	7	176	5	0	178	2	6
800	153	6	8	155	0	0	156	5	0	156	13	4	158	6	8
700	134	3	4	135	12	6	136	14	4	137	1	8	138	10	10
600	115	0	0	116	5	0	117	3	9	117	10	0	118	15	0
500	95	16	8	96	17	6	97	13	1	97	18	4	98	19	2
400	76	13	4	77	10	0	78	2	6	78	6	8	79	3	4
300	57	10	0	58	2	6	58	11	10	58	15	0	59	7	6
200	38	6	8	38	15	0	39	1	3	39	3	4	39	11	8
100	19	3	4	19	7	6	19	10	7	19	11	8	19	15	10
90	17	5	0	17	8	9	17	11	6	17	12	6	17	16	3
80	15	6	8	15	10	0	15	12	6	15	13	4	15	16	8
70	13	8	4	13	11	3	13	13	5	13	14	2	13	17	1
60	11	10	0	11	12	6	11	14	4	11	15	0	11	17	6
50	9	11	8	9	13	9	9	15	3	9	15	10	9	17	11
40	7	13	4	7	15	0	7	16	3	7	16	8	7	18	4
30	5	15	0	5	16	3	5	17	2	5	17	6	5	18	9
20	3	16	8	3	17	6	3	18	1	3	18	4	3	19	2
10	1	18	4	1	18	9	1	19	0	1	19	2	1	19	7
9	1	14	6	1	14	10	1	15	1	1	15	3	1	15	7
8	1	10	8	1	11	0	1	11	3	1	11	4	1	11	8
7	1	6	10	1	7	1	1	7	4	1	7	5	1	7	8
6	1	3	0	1	3	3	1	3	5	1	3	6	1	3	9
5	0	19	2	0	19	4	0	19	6	0	19	7	0	19	9
4	0	15	4	0	15	6	0	15	7	0	15	8	0	15	10
3	0	11	6	0	11	7	0	11	8	0	11	9	0	11	10
2	0	7	8	0	7	9	0	7	9	0	7	10	0	7	11
1	0	3	10	0	3	10	0	3	10	0	3	11	0	3	11
R. 7	0	3	4	0	3	4	0	3	5	0	3	5	0	3	5
6	0	2	10	0	2	10	0	2	11	0	2	11	0	2	11
5	0	2	4	0	2	5	0	2	5	0	2	5	0	2	5
4	0	1	11	0	1	11	0	1	11	0	1	11	0	1	11
3	0	1	5	0	1	5	0	1	5	0	1	5	0	1	5
2	0	0	11	0	0	11	0	0	11	0	0	11	0	0	11
1	0	0	5	0	0	5	0	0	5	0	0	5	0	0	6
M. 25	0	0	4	0	0	4	0	0	4	0	0	4	0	0	4
17	0	0	2	0	0	2	0	0	2	0	0	2	0	0	3
8	0	0	1	0	0	1	0	0	1	0	0	1	0	0	1
4	0	0	½	0	0	½	0	0	½	0	0	½	0	0	¾

Eng.	At 48d.			48½d.			49d.			49½d.			50d.		
£.	P.	r.	m.	P.	r.	m.	P.	r.	m.	P.	r.	m.	P.	r.	m.
1000	5000			4948	3	21	4897	7	23	4848	3	30	4800		
900	4500			4453	4	29	4408	1	10	4363	5	3	4320		
800	4000			3958	6	4	3918	2	32	3878	6	10	3840		
700	3500			3463	7	12	3428	4	19	3393	7	18	3360		
600	3000			2969	0	20	2938	6	7	2909	0	25	2880		
500	2500			2474	1	25	2448	7	28	2424	1	32	2400		
400	2000			1979	3	2	1959	1	16	1939	3	5	1920		
300	1500			1484	4	10	1469	3	3	1454	4	12	1440		
200	1000			989	5	18	979	4	25	969	5	20	960		
100	500			494	6	26	489	6	12	484	6	27	480		
90	450			445	2	30	440	6	18	436	2	31	432		
80	400			395	7	0	391	6	24	387	7	1	384		
70	350			346	3	5	342	6	29	339	3	5	336		
60	300			296	7	9	293	7	1	290	7	9	288		
50	250			247	3	13	244	7	6	242	3	16	240		
40	200			197	7	17	195	7	12	193	7	17	192		
30	150			148	3	21	146	7	17	145	3	22	144		
20	100			98	7	26	97	7	23	96	7	26	96		
10	50			49	3	30	48	7	28	48	3	30	48		
9	45			44	4	10	44	0	22	43	5	3	43	1	20
8	40			39	4	24	39	1	16	38	6	10	38	3	7
7	35			34	5	4	34	2	10	33	7	18	33	4	27
6	30			29	5	18	29	3	3	29	0	25	28	6	14
5	25			24	5	32	24	3	31	24	1	32	24	0	0
4	20			19	6	12	19	4	25	19	3	5	19	1	20
3	15			14	6	26	14	5	19	14	4	12	14	3	7
2	10			9	7	6	9	6	12	9	5	20	9	4	27
1	5			4	7	20	4	7	6	4	6	27	4	6	14
S. 10	2	4	0	2	3	27	2	3	20	2	3	13	2	3	7
9	2	2	0	2	1	28	2	1	21	2	1	15	2	1	10
8	2	0	0	1	7	28	1	7	23	1	7	18	1	7	12
7	1	6	0	1	5	29	1	5	24	1	5	20	1	5	15
6	1	4	0	1	3	30	1	3	26	1	3	22	1	3	18
5	1	2	0	1	1	30	1	1	27	1	1	24	1	1	20
4	1	0	0	0	7	31	0	7	28	0	7	26	0	7	23
3	0	6	0	0	5	32	0	5	30	0	5	28	0	5	26
2	0	4	0	0	3	33	0	3	31	0	3	30	0	3	29
1	0	2	0	0	1	33	0	1	33	0	1	32	0	1	31
D. 6	0	1	0	0	1	0	0	0	33	0	0	33	0	0	33
5	0	0	28	0	0	28	0	0	28	0	0	27	0	0	27
4	0	0	23	0	0	22	0	0	22	0	0	22	0	0	22
3	0	0	17	0	0	17	0	0	17	0	0	16	0	0	16
2	0	0	11	0	0	11	0	0	11	0	0	11	0	0	11
1	0	0	6	0	0	6	0	0	6	0	0	5	0	0	5

Span.	48*d.*			48½*d.*			49*d.*			49½*d.*			50*d.*		
Piast.	£.	*s.*	*d.*	£.	*s.*	*d.*	£.	*s.*	*d.*	£.	*s.*	*d.*	£.	*s.*	*d.*
10000	2000			2020	16	8	2041	13	4	2062	10		2083	6	8
5000	1000			1010	8	4	1020	16	8	1031	5		1041	13	4
4000	800			808	6	8	816	13	4	825	0		833	6	8
3000	600			606	5	0	612	10	0	618	15		625	0	0
2000	400			404	3	4	408	6	8	412	10		416	13	4
1000	200			202	1	8	204	3	4	206	5		208	6	8
900	180			181	17	6	183	15	0	185	12	6	187	10	0
800	160			161	13	4	163	6	8	165	0	0	166	13	4
700	140			141	9	2	142	18	4	144	7	6	145	16	8
600	120			121	5	0	122	10	0	123	15	0	125	0	0
500	100			101	0	10	102	1	8	103	2	6	104	3	4
400	80			80	16	8	81	13	4	82	10	0	83	6	8
300	60			60	12	6	61	5	0	61	17	6	62	10	0
200	40			40	8	4	40	16	8	41	5	0	41	13	4
100	20			20	4	2	20	8	4	20	12	6	20	16	8
90	18			18	3	9	18	17	6	18	11	3	18	15	0
80	16			16	3	4	16	6	8	16	10	0	16	13	4
70	14			14	2	11	14	5	10	14	8	9	14	11	8
60	12			12	2	6	12	5	0	12	7	6	12	10	0
50	10			10	2	1	10	4	2	10	6	3	10	8	4
40	8			8	1	8	8	3	4	8	5	0	8	6	8
30	6			6	1	3	6	2	6	6	3	0	6	5	0
20	4			4	0	10	4	1	8	4	2	6	4	3	4
10	2			2	0	5	2	0	10	2	1	3	2	1	8
9	1	16		1	16	4	1	16	9	1	17	1	1	17	6
8	1	12		1	12	4	1	12	8	1	13	0	1	13	4
7	1	8		1	8	3	1	8	7	1	8	10	1	9	2
6	1	4		1	4	3	1	4	6	1	4	9	1	5	0
5	1	0		1	0	2	1	0	5	1	0	7	1	0	10
4	0	16		0	16	2	0	16	4	0	16	6	0	16	8
3	0	12		0	12	1	0	12	3	0	12	4	0	12	6
2	0	8		0	8	1	0	8	2	0	8	3	0	8	4
1	0	4		0	4	0	0	4	1	0	4	1	0	4	2
R. 7	0	3	6	0	3	6	0	3	6	0	3	7	0	3	7
6	0	3	0	0	3	0	0	3	0	0	3	1	0	3	1
5	0	2	6	0	2	6	0	2	6	0	2	7	0	2	7
4	0	2	0	0	2	0	0	2	0	0	2	0	0	2	1
3	0	1	6	0	1	6	0	1	6	0	1	6	0	1	6
2	0	1	0	0	1	0	0	1	0	0	1	0	0	1	0
1	0	0	6	0	0	6	0	0	6	0	0	6	0	0	6
M. 25	0	0	4	0	0	4	0	0	4	0	0	4	0	0	4
17	0	0	3	0	0	3	0	0	3	0	0	3	0	0	3
8	0	0	1	0	0	1	0	0	1	0	0	1	0	0	1
4	0	0	¾	0	0	¾	0	0	¾	0	0	¾	0	0	¾

EXCHANGE *between* England *and* Portugal.

Exchanges between Portugal and all other Nations are rated on the Millree, the par being 67½ pence Sterling, the course with England from 63*d.* to 68*d.* Sterl. per Millree.

The current Money, as follows, viz.

1 Ree is equal to	- -	£0	0	0.067 parts Sterl.
400 Rees ——— 1 Crusade	value - -		2	3
1000 Rees ——— 1 Millree	—— - -		5	7½

Tho' the value of a Crusade is given in this Table, yet accounts are kept only in Rees and Millrees, divided from each other by a dot, like a Decimal fraction, thus, 1247.234

Example,

What will be the value of 1247.234 Rees in English Money, at 65 pence Sterl. the Millree?

As 1000 Rees is to 65 pence, so is 1247.234 Rees to £337 15 10

```
                     65
               ————————
                6236170
               7483404
               ————————
        1000 | 81070 | 210 rejected
               ————————
          12 | 81070
               ————————
                675 | 5  10
               ————————
      Answer £337  15  10
```

This Station inverted, converts English into Portugal Money.

The following Table of Decimal Multipliers (like the former) is applicable to business, by multiplying the English Money by the Tabular number opposite the Rate in the Portugal columns, and the product will be Millrees and Rees. Or, by multiplying the Portugal Money by the Tabular number in the English columns, and the product will be Pounds and parts of a Pound Sterl.

Example,

What will be the value of 500*l* in Portugal Money, at 64½ pence the Millree?

Opposite 64½ the Tabular Number is 3.72093

```
                                          500
                                     ——————————
Answer M.1860.465 Rees               1860.465 | 00
```

Which Sum of 1860.465 Rees, multiplied by .26875, the Tabular Number opposite 64½ in the English column, brings it back again to 500*l*. Sterl.

A TABLE

A TABLE *of Decimal Multipliers for* PORTUGAL *and* ENGLISH MONEY, *at the several* RATES *of* EXCHANGE.

ENGLISH INTO PORTUGAL.				PORTUGAL INTO ENGLISH.			
Rate 8th	Multpr.	Rate	Multpr.	Rate 8th	Multpr.	Rate	Multpr.
60 —	4.	64—	3.75	60 —	.25	64—	.266666
1	3.991684	1	3.74269	1	.25052	1	.267183
2	3.983402	2	3.735409	2	.251042	2	.267704
3	3.975155	3	3.728155	3	.251562	3	.268229
4	3.966942	4	3.72093	4	.252084	4	.26875
5	3.958763	5	3.713733	5	.252604	5	.26927
6	3.950617	6	3.706564	6	.253125	6	.269792
7	3.942505	7	3.699422	7	.253646	7	.270612
61 —	3.934426	65—	3.692308	61 —	.254166	65—	.270834
1	3.92638	1	3.685221	1	.254688	1	.271354
2	3.918367	2	3.678161	2	.255208	2	.271875
3	3.910387	3	3.671128	3	.255729	3	.272396
4	4.902439	4	3.664122	4	.25625	4	.272916
5	3.894523	5	3.657143	5	.25677	5	.273438
6	3.88664	6	3.65019	6	.257292	6	.273958
7	3.878788	7	3.643264	7	.257812	7	.274479
62 —	3.870968	66—	3.636364	62 —	.258334	66—	.275
1	3.863179	1	3.62949	1	.258854	1	.27552
2	3.855422	2	3.622642	2	.259375	2	.276042
3	3.847695	3	3.615819	3	.259896	3	.276562
4	3.84	4	3.609023	4	.260416	4	.277084
5	3.832335	5	3.602251	5	.260934	5	.277604
6	3.824701	6	3.595506	6	.261458	6	.278125
7	3.817097	7	3.588785	7	.261979	7	.278646
63 —	3.809524	67—	3.58209	63 —	.2625	67—	.279162
1	3.80198	1	3.575419	1	.26302	1	.279688
2	3.794466	2	3.568773	2	.263542	2	.280208
3	3.786982	3	3.562152	3	.264062	3	.280729
4	3.779528	4	3.555556	4	.264584	4	.28125
5	3.772102	5	3.548983	5	.265104	5	.28177
6	3.764706	6	3.542435	6	.265625	6	.282292
7	3.757339	7	3.535911	7	.266146	7	.282812
		68—	3.529412			68—	.283334

A Table of Decimal Parts for Portugal Money would be useless, because Rees are no other than Decimals of a Milree, and therefore more convenient than any other Money in Europe, being always added up as Whole Numbers, only remembring to point of the last three Figures to the Right Hand as Rees.——☞ The following Tables are only given to prove the utility of the above.

ENGLAND

Eng.	At 60d.	60¼d.	60½d.	60¾d.	61d.
£.	M. R.	M. R.	M. R.	M. R.	M. R
1000	4000.	3983.492	3966.942	3950.617	3934.426
900	3600.	3585.062	3570.248	3555.556	3541.984
800	3200.	3186.722	3173.554	3160.494	3147.541
700	2800.	2788.382	2776.860	2765.432	2754.098
600	2400.	2390.041	2380.165	2370.370	2360.656
500	2000.	1991.701	1983.471	1975.309	1967.213
400	1600.	1593.361	1586.777	1580.247	1573.770
300	1200.	1195.021	1190.083	1185.185	1180.328
200	800.	796.680	793.388	790.123	786.885
100	400.	398.340	396.694	395.062	393.443
90	360.	358.506	357.025	355.556	354.098
80	320.	318.672	317.355	316.049	314.754
70	280.	278.838	277.686	276.543	275.410
60	240.	239.004	238.017	237.037	236.066
50	200.	199.170	198.347	197.531	196.721
40	160.	159.336	158.678	158.025	157.377
30	120.	119.502	119.008	118.519	118.033
20	80.	79.668	79.339	79.012	78.689
10	40.	39.834	39.669	39.506	39.344
9	36.	35.851	35.702	35.556	35.410
8	32.	31.867	31.736	31.605	31.475
7	28.	27.884	27.769	27.654	27.541
6	24.	23.900	23.802	23.704	23.607
5	20.	19.917	19.835	19.753	19.672
4	16.	15.934	15.868	15.802	15.738
3	12.	11.950	11.901	11.852	11.803
2	8.	7.967	7.934	7.901	7.869
1	4.	3.983	3.967	3.951	3.934
S. 10	2.	1.992	1.983	1.975	1.967
9	1.800	1.793	1.783	1.778	1.770
8	1.600	1.593	1.587	1.580	1.574
7	1.400	1.394	1.388	1.383	1.377
6	1.200	1.195	1.190	1.185	1.180
5	1.000	0.996	0.992	0.988	0.984
4	0.800	0.797	0.793	0.790	0.787
3	0.600	0.598	0.595	0.593	0.590
2	0.400	0.398	0.397	0.395	0.393
1	0.200	0.199	0.108	0.198	0.197
D. 6	0.100	0.100	0. 99	0. 99	0. 98
5	0. 83	0. 83	0. 83	0. 82	0. 82
4	0. 67	0. 67	0. 66	0. 66	0. 66
3	0. 50	0. 50	0. 50	0. 49	0. 49
2	0. 33	0. 33	0. 33	0. 33	0. 33
1	0. 17	0. 17	0. 17	0. 16	0. 16

Port.	At 60d.			60¼d.			60½d.			60¾d.			61d.		
Mill.	£.	s.	d.	£.	s.	d.	£.	s.	d.	£.	s.	d.	£.	s.	d.
4000	1000			1004	3	4	1008	6	8	1012	10		1016	13	4
3000	750			753	2	6	756	5	0	759	7	6	762	10	0
2000	500			502	1	8	504	3	4	506	5	0	508	6	8
1000	250			251	0	10	252	1	8	253	2	6	254	3	4
900	225			225	18	9	226	17	6	227	16	3	228	15	0
800	200			200	16	8	201	13	4	202	10	0	203	6	8
700	175			175	14	7	176	9	2	177	3	9	177	18	4
600	150			150	12	6	151	5	0	151	17	6	152	10	0
500	125			125	10	5	126	0	10	126	11	3	127	1	8
400	100			100	8	4	100	16	8	101	5	0	101	13	4
300	75			75	6	3	75	12	6	75	18	9	76	5	0
200	50			50	4	2	50	8	4	50	12	6	50	16	8
100	25			25	2	1	25	4	2	25	6	3	25	8	4
90	22	10		22	11	10	22	13	9	22	15	7	22	17	6
80	20	0		20	1	8	20	3	4	20	5	0	20	6	8
70	17	10		17	11	5	17	12	11	17	14	4	17	15	10
60	15	0		15	1	3	15	2	6	15	3	9	15	5	0
50	12	10		12	11	0	12	12	1	12	13	1	12	14	2
40	10	0		10	0	10	10	1	8	10	2	6	10	3	4
30	7	10		7	10	7	7	11	3	7	11	10	7	12	6
20	5	0		5	0	5	5	0	10	5	1	3	5	1	8
10	2	10		2	10	2	2	10	5	2	10	7	2	10	10
9	2	5		2	5	2	2	5	4	2	5	6	2	5	9
8	2	0		2	0	2	2	0	4	2	0	6	2	0	8
7	1	15		1	15	1	1	15	3	1	15	5	1	15	7
6	1	10		1	10	1	1	10	3	1	10	4	1	10	6
5	1	5		1	5	1	1	5	2	1	5	3	1	5	5
4	1	0		1	0	1	1	0	2	1	0	3	1	0	4
3	0	15		0	15	0	0	15	1	0	15	2	0	15	3
2	0	10		0	10	0	0	10	1	0	10	1	0	10	2
1	0	5		0	5	0	0	5	0	0	5	0	0	5	1
R.900	0	4	6	0	4	6	0	4	6	0	4	6	0	4	6
800	0	4	0	0	4	0	0	4	0	0	4	0	0	4	0
700	0	3	6	0	3	6	0	3	6	0	3	6	0	3	6
600	0	3	0	0	3	0	0	3	0	0	3	0	0	3	0
500	0	2	6	0	2	6	0	2	6	0	2	6	0	2	6
400	0	2	0	0	2	0	0	2	0	0	2	0	0	2	
300	0	1	6	0	1	6	0	1	6	0	1	6	0	1	6
200	0	1	0	0	1	0	0	1	0	0	1	0	0	1	0
100	0	0	6	0	0	6	0	0	6	0	0	6	0	0	6
50	0	0	3	0	0	3	0	0	3	0	0	3	0	0	3
40	0	0	2	0	0	2	0	0	2	0	0	2	0	0	2
30	0	0	1	0	0	1	0	0	1	0	0	1	0	0	1
20	0	0	1	0	0	1	0	0	1	0	0	1	0	0	1
10	0	0	½	0	0	½	0	0	½	0	0	½	0	0	½

Eng.	At 61¼d.	61½d.	62d.	62½d.	63d.
£.	M. R.	M. R.	M. R.	M. R.	M. R.
1000	3918.367	3902.439	3870.968	3840.	3809.524
900	3526.531	3512.195	3483.871	3456.	3428.571
800	3134.694	3121.951	3096.774	3072.	3047.619
700	2742.857	2731.707	2709.677	2688.	2666.667
600	2351.020	2341.463	2322.581	2304.	2285.714
500	1959.184	1951.220	1935.484	1920.	1904.762
400	1567.347	1560.976	1548.387	1536.	1523.810
300	1175.510	1170.732	1161.290	1152.	1142.857
200	783.673	780.488	774.194	768.	761.905
100	391.837	390.244	387.097	384.	380.952
90	352.653	351.220	348.387	345.600	342.857
80	313.469	312.195	309.677	307.200	304.762
70	274.286	273.171	270.968	268.800	266.667
60	235.102	234.146	232.258	230.400	228.571
50	195.918	195.122	193.548	192.0	190.476
40	156.735	156.098	154.839	153.600	152.381
30	117.551	117.073	116.129	115.200	114.286
20	78.367	78.049	77.419	76.800	76.191
10	39.184	39.024	38.710	38.400	38.095
9	35.261	35.122	34.839	34.560	34.286
8	31.347	31.220	30.968	30.720	30.476
7	27.429	27.317	27.097	26.880	26.667
6	23.510	23.415	23.226	23.040	22.875
5	19.592	19.512	19.355	19.200	19.048
4	15.673	15.610	15.484	15.360	15.238
3	11.755	11.707	11.613	11.520	11.429
2	7.837	7.805	7.742	7.680	7.619
1	3.918	3.902	3.871	3.840	3.810
S. 10	1.959	1.951	1.935	1.920	1.905
9	1.763	1.756	1.742	1.728	1.714
8	1.567	1.561	1.548	1.536	1.524
7	1.371	1.366	1.355	1.344	1.333
6	1.176	1.171	1.161	1.152	1.143
5	0.980	0.976	0.968	0.960	0.952
4	0.784	0.780	0.774	0.768	0.762
3	0.588	0.585	0.581	0.576	0.571
2	0.392	0.390	0.387	0.384	0.381
1	0.196	0.195	0.194	0.192	0.190
D. 6	0. 98	0. 98	0. 97	0. 96	0. 95
5	0. 82	0. 81	0. 81	0. 80	0. 79
4	0. 65	0. 65	0. 65	0. 64	0. 64
3	0. 49	0. 49	0. 48	0. 48	0. 48
2	0. 33	0. 33	0. 32	0. 32	0. 32
1	0. 16	0. 16	0. 16	0. 16	0. 16

Port.	At 61¼*d.*			61½*d.*			62*d.*			62½*d.*			63*d.*		
Mill	£.	*s.*	*d.*	£.	*s.*	*d.*	£.	*s.*	*d.*	£.	*s.*	*d.*	£.	*s.*	*d.*
4000	1020	16	8	1025	0		1033	6	8	1041	13	4	1050	0	
3000	765	12	6	768	15		775	0	0	781	15	0	787	10	
2000	510	8	4	512	10		516	13	4	520	16	8	525	0	
1000	255	4	2	256	5		258	6	8	260	8	4	262	10	
900	229	13	9	230	12	6	232	10	0	234	7	6	236	5	
800	204	3	4	205	0	0	206	13	4	208	6	8	210	0	
700	178	12	11	179	7	6	180	16	8	182	5	10	183	15	
600	153	2	6	153	15	0	155	0	0	156	5	0	157	10	
500	127	12	1	128	2	6	129	3	4	130	4	2	131	5	
400	102	1	8	102	10	0	103	6	8	104	3	4	105	0	
300	76	11	3	76	17	6	77	10	0	78	2	6	78	15	
200	51	0	10	51	5	0	51	13	4	52	1	8	52	10	
100	25	10	5	25	12	6	25	16	8	26	0	10	26	5	
90	22	19	4	23	1	3	23	5	0	23	8	9	23	12	6
80	20	8	4	20	10	0	20	13	4	20	16	8	21	0	0
70	17	17	3	17	18	9	18	1	8	18	4	7	18	7	6
60	15	6	3	15	7	6	15	10	0	15	12	6	15	15	0
50	12	15	2	12	16	3	12	18	4	13	0	5	13	2	6
40	10	4	2	10	5	0	10	6	8	10	8	4	10	10	0
30	7	13	1	7	13	9	7	15	0	7	16	3	7	17	6
20	5	2	1	5	2	6	5	3	4	5	4	2	5	5	0
10	2	11	0	2	11	3	2	11	8	2	12	1	2	12	6
9	2	5	11	2	6	1	2	6	6	2	6	10	2	7	3
8	2	0	10	2	1	0	2	1	4	2	1	8	2	2	0
7	1	15	8	1	15	10	1	16	2	1	16	5	1	16	9
6	1	10	7	1	10	9	1	11	0	1	11	3	1	11	6
5	1	5	6	1	5	7	1	5	10	1	6	0	1	6	3
4	1	0	5	1	0	6	1	0	8	1	0	10	1	1	0
3	0	15	3	0	15	4	0	15	6	0	15	7	0	15	9
2	0	10	2	0	10	3	0	10	4	0	10	5	0	10	6
1	0	5	1	0	5	1	0	5	2	0	5	2	0	5	3
*R.*900	0	4	7	0	4	7	0	4	7	0	4	8	0	4	8
800	0	4	1	0	4	1	0	4	1	0	4	2	0	4	2
700	0	3	6	0	3	6	0	3	6	0	3	7	0	3	8
600	0	3	0	0	3	0	0	3	0	0	3	1	0	3	1
500	0	2	6	0	2	6	0	2	6	0	2	7	0	2	7
400	0	2	0	0	2	0	0	2	0	0	2	1	0	2	1
300	0	1	6	0	1	6	0	1	6	0	1	6	0	1	6
200	0	1	0	0	1	0	0	1	0	0	1	0	0	1	0
100	0	0	6	0	0	6	0	0	6	0	0	6	0	0	6
50	0	0	3	0	0	3	0	0	3	0	0	3	0	0	3
40	0	0	2	0	0	2	0	0	2	0	0	2	0	0	2
30	0	0	1	0	0	1	0	0	1	0	0	1	0	0	1
20	0	0	1	0	0	1	0	0	1	0	0	1	0	0	1
10	0	0	½	0	0	½	0	0	½	0	0	½	0	0	½

Eng.	At 63½d.	64d.	64½d.	65d.	65½d.
£.	M. R.	M. R.	M. R.	M. R.	M. R.
1000	3779.528	3750.	3720.930	3692.308	3664.122
900	3401.575	3375	3348.837	3333.077	3297.710
800	3023.622	3000.	2976.744	2953.846	2931.298
700	2645.669	2625.	2604.650	2584.615	2564.885
600	2267.717	2250.	2232.558	2215.385	2198.473
500	1889.764	1875.	1860.465	1846.154	1832.061
400	1511.811	1509.	1488.372	1476.923	1465.649
300	1133.858	1125.	1116.279	1107.692	1099.237
200	755.906	750.	744.186	738.462	732.824
100	377.953	375.	372.093	369.231	366.412
90	340.158	337.	334.884	332.308	329.771
80	302.362	300.	297.674	295.385	293.130
70	264.567	262.500	260.465	258.462	256.488
60	226.772	225.	223.256	221.538	219.847
50	188.976	187.500	186.047	184.615	183.206
40	151.181	150.	148.837	147.692	146.565
30	113.386	112.500	111.628	110.769	109.924
20	75.591	75.	74.419	73.846	73.282
10	37.795	37.500	37.209	36.923	36.641
9	34.016	33.750	33.488	33.231	32.977
8	30.236	30.	29.767	29.538	29.313
7	26.457	26.250	26.047	25.846	25.649
6	22.677	22.500	22.326	22.154	21.985
5	18.898	18.750	18.605	18.462	18.321
4	15.118	15.	14.884	14.769	14.656
3	11.339	11.250	11.163	11.077	10.992
2	7.559	7.500	7.442	7.385	7.328
1	3.780	3.750	3.721	3.692	3.664
S. 10	1.890	1.875	1.860	1.846	1.832
9	1.701	1.687	1.674	1.662	1.649
8	1.512	1.500	1.488	1.477	1.466
7	1.323	1.312	1.302	1.292	1.282
6	1.134	1.125	1.116	1.108	1.099
5	0.945	0.937	0.930	0.923	0.916
4	0.756	0.750	0.744	0.738	0.733
3	0.567	0.562	0.558	0.554	0.550
2	0.378	0.375	0.372	0.369	0.366
1	0.189	0.187	0.186	0.185	0.183
D. 6	0. 94	0. 94	0. 93	0. 92	0. 92
5	0. 79	0. 78	0. 78	0. 77	0. 76
4	0. 63	0. 62	0. 62	0. 62	0. 61
3	0. 47	0. 47	0. 47	0. 46	0. 46
2	0. 31	0. 31	0. 31	0. 31	0. 31
1	0. 16	0. 16	0. 16	0. 15	0. 15

Port.	At 63½d. £.	s.	d.	64d. £.	s.	d.	64½d £.	s.	d.	65d. £.	s.	d.	65½d. £.	s.	d.
Mill.															
4000	1058	6	8	1066	13	4	1075	0	0	1083	6	8	1091	13	4
3000	793	15	0	800	0	0	806	5	0	811	10	0	818	15	0
20 0	529	3	4	533	6	8	537	10	0	541	13	4	545	16	8
1000	264	11	8	266	13	4	268	15	0	270	16	8	272	18	4
900	238	2	6	240	0	0	241	17	6	243	15	0	245	12	6
800	211	13	4	213	6	8	215	0	0	216	13	4	218	6	8
700	185	4	2	186	13	4	188	2	6	189	11	8	191	0	10
600	158	15	0	160	0	0	161	5	0	162	10	0	163	15	0
500	132	5	10	133	6	8	134	7	6	135	8	4	136	9	2
400	105	16	8	106	13	4	107	10	0	108	6	8	109	3	4
300	79	7	6	80	0	0	80	12	6	81	5	0	81	17	6
200	52	18	4	53	6	8	53	15	0	54	3	4	54	11	8
100	26	9	2	26	13	4	26	17	6	27	1	8	27	5	10
90	23	16	3	24	0	0	24	3	9	24	7	6	24	11	3
80	21	3	4	21	6	8	21	10	0	21	13	4	21	16	8
70	18	10	5	18	13	4	18	16	3	18	19	2	19	2	1
60	15	17	6	16	0	0	16	2	6	16	5	0	16	7	6
50	13	4	7	13	6	8	13	8	9	13	10	10	13	12	11
40	10	11	8	10	13	4	10	15	0	10	16	8	10	18	4
30	7	18	9	8	0	0	8	1	3	8	2	6	8	3	9
20	5	5	10	5	6	8	5	7	6	5	8	4	5	9	2
10	2	12	11	2	13	4	2	13	9	2	14	2	2	14	7
9	2	7	7	2	8	0	2	8	4	2	8	9	2	9	1
8	2	2	4	2	2	8	2	3	0	2	3	4	2	3	8
7	1	17	0	1	17	4	1	17	7	1	17	11	1	18	2
6	1	11	9	1	12	0	1	12	3	1	12	6	1	12	9
5	1	6	5	1	6	8	1	6	10	1	7	1	1	7	3
4	1	1	2	1	1	4	1	1	6	1	1	8	1	1	10
3	0	15	10	0	16	0	0	16	1	0	16	3	0	16	4
2	0	10	7	0	10	8	0	10	9	0	10	10	0	10	11
1	0	5	3	0	5	4	0	5	4	0	5	5	0	5	5
R.900	0	4	9	0	4	9	0	4	10	0	4	10	0	4	11
800	0	4	2	0	4	3	0	4	3	0	4	4	0	4	4
700	0	3	8	0	3	8	0	3	9	0	3	9	0	3	9
600	0	3	2	0	3	2	0	3	2	0	3	3	0	3	3
500	0	2	7	0	2	8	0	2	8	0	2	8	0	2	8
400	0	2	1	0	2	1	0	2	1	0	2	2	0	2	2
300	0	1	7	0	1	7	0	1	7	0	1	7	0	1	7
200	0	1	0	0	1	0	0	1	0	0	1	1	0	1	1
100	0	0	6	0	0	6	0	0	6	0	0	6	0	0	6
50	0	0	3	0	0	3	0	0	3	0	0	3	0	0	3
40	0	0	2	0	0	2	0	0	2	0	0	2	0	0	2
30	0	0	1	0	0	1	0	0	1	0	0	1	0	0	1
20	0	0	1	0	0	1	0	0	1	0	0	1	0	0	1
10	0	0	½	0	0	½	0	0	½	0	0	½	0	0	½

Eng.	At 66d.	66½d.	67d.	67½d.	68d.
£.	M. R.	M. R.	M. R.	M. R.	M. R.
1000	3636.364	3609.023	3582.090	3555.556	3529.412
900	3272.727	3248.120	3223.881	3200.	3176.471
800	2909.091	2887.218	2865.672	2844.444	2823.529
700	2545.455	2526.316	2507.463	2488.889	2470.588
600	2181.818	2165.414	2149.254	2133.333	2117.647
500	1818.182	1804.511	1791.045	1777.778	1764.706
400	1454.545	1443.609	1432.836	1422.222	1411.765
300	1090.909	1082.707	1074.627	1066.667	1058.824
200	727.273	721.805	716.418	711.111	705.882
100	363.636	360.902	358.209	355.556	352.941
90	327.273	324.822	322.388	320.	317.647
80	290.909	28[illegible]7[illegible]2	28[illegible].567	284.444	282.353
70	254.545	25[illegible].632	2[illegible]0.7[illegible]6	248.889	247.259
60	218.182	216.541	21[illegible]25	2[illegible]3.333	211.765
50	181.818	180.451	179.104	177.778	176.471
40	145.455	144.361	143.284	142.222	141.177
30	109.091	108.271	107.463	106.667	105.882
20	72.727	72.180	71.642	71.111	70.588
10	36.364	36.090	35.821	35.556	35.294
9	32.727	32.481	32.239	32.	31.765
8	29.091	28.872	28.657	28.444	28.235
7	25.455	25.263	25.075	24.889	24.706
6	21.818	21.654	21.493	21.333	21.176
5	18.182	18.045	17.910	17.778	17.647
4	14.545	14.436	14.328	14.222	14.118
3	10.909	10.827	10.746	10.667	10.588
2	7.273	7.218	7.164	7.111	7.059
1	3.636	3.609	3.582	3.556	3.529
S. 10	1.818	1.805	1.791	1.778	1.765
9	1.636	1.624	1.612	1.600	1.588
8	1.455	1.444	1.433	1.422	1.412
7	1.273	1.263	1.254	1.244	1.235
6	1.091	1.083	1.075	1.067	1.059
5	0.909	0.902	0.896	0.889	0.882
4	0.727	0.722	0.716	0.711	0.706
3	0.545	0.541	0.537	0.533	0.529
2	0.364	0.361	0.358	0.356	0.353
1	0.182	0.180	0.179	0.178	0.176
D. 6	0. 91	0. 90	0. 90	0. 89	0. 88
5	0. 76	0. 75	0. 75	0. 74	0. 74
4	0. 61	0. 60	0. 60	0. 59	0. 59
3	0. 45	0. 45	0. 45	0. 44	0. 44
2	0. 30	0. 30	0. 30	0. 30	0. 30
1	0. 15	0. 15	0. 15	0. 15	0. 15

Portu.	At 66*d.*			66½*d.*			67*d.*			67½*d.*			68*d.*		
Mill.	£.	*s.*	*d.*	£.	*s.*	*d.*	£.	*s.*	*d.*	£.	*s.*	*d.*	£.	*s.*	*d.*
4000	1100			1108	6	8	1116	13	4	1125			1133	6	8
3000	825			831	5	0	837	10	0	843	15		850	0	0
2000	550			554	3	4	558	6	8	562	10		566	13	4
1000	275			277	1	8	279	3	4	281	5		283	6	8
900	247	10		249	7	6	251	5	0	253	2	6	255	0	0
800	220	0		221	13	4	223	6	8	225	0	0	226	13	4
700	192	10		193	19	2	195	8	4	196	17	6	198	6	8
600	165	0		166	5	0	167	10	0	168	15	0	170	0	0
500	137	10		138	10	10	139	11	8	140	12	6	141	13	4
400	110	0		110	16	8	111	13	4	112	10	0	113	6	8
300	82	10		83	2	6	83	15	0	84	7	6	85	0	0
200	55	0		55	8	4	55	16	8	56	5	0	56	13	4
100	27	10		27	14	2	27	18	4	28	2	6	28	6	8
90	24	15		24	18	9	25	2	6	25	6	3	25	10	0
80	22	0		22	3	4	22	6	8	22	10	0	22	13	4
70	19	5		19	7	11	19	10	10	19	13	9	19	16	8
60	16	10		16	12	6	16	15	0	16	17	6	17	0	0
50	13	15		13	17	11	13	19	2	14	1	3	14	3	4
40	11	0		11	1	8	11	3	4	11	5	0	11	6	8
30	8	5		8	6	3	8	7	6	8	8	9	8	10	0
20	5	10		5	10	10	5	11	8	5	12	6	5	13	4
10	2	15		2	15	5	2	15	10	2	16	3	2	16	8
9	2	9	6	2	9	10	2	10	3	2	10	7	2	11	0
8	2	4	0	2	4	4	2	4	8	2	5	0	2	5	4
7	1	18	6	1	18	9	1	19	1	1	19	4	1	19	8
6	1	13	0	1	13	3	1	13	6	1	13	9	1	14	0
5	1	7	6	1	7	8	1	7	11	1	8	1	1	8	4
4	1	2	0	1	2	2	1	2	4	1	2	6	1	2	8
3	0	16	6	0	16	7	0	16	9	0	16	10	0	17	0
2	0	11	0	0	11	1	0	11	2	0	11	3	0	11	4
1	0	5	6	0	5	6	0	5	7	0	5	7	0	5	8
*R.*900	0	4	11	0	4	11	0	5	0	0	5	0	0	5	1
800	0	4	4	0	4	5	0	4	5	0	4	6	0	4	6
700	0	3	10	0	3	10	0	3	10	0	3	11	0	3	11
600	0	3	3	0	3	3	0	3	4	0	3	4	0	3	4
500	0	2	9	0	2	9	0	2	9	0	2	9	0	2	10
400	0	2	2	0	2	2	0	2	2	0	2	3	0	2	3
300	0	1	7	0	1	8	0	1	8	0	1	8	0	1	8
200	0	1	1	0	1	1	0	1	1	0	1	1	0	1	1
100	0	0	6	0	0	6	0	0	6	0	0	6	0	0	6
50	0	0	3	0	0	3	0	0	3	0	0	3	0	0	3
40	0	0	2	0	0	2	0	0	2	0	0	2	0	0	2
30	0	0	2	0	0	2	0	0	2	0	0	2	0	0	2
20	0	0	1	0	0	1	0	0	1	0	0	1	0	0	1
10	0	0	½	0	0	½	0	0	½	0	0	½	0	0	½

If, in the Use of the foregoing Table of Exchanges with Portugal, it should be required to ascertain the Value of any Sum, at a Rate of Exchange, which does not appear at the Head of any Column, it may be done according to the following,

Example.

What will be the Value of 500l. English at 64⅛ Pence.

I find the Value of 64 to be		1875
	At 64½	1860.465
	Difference	14.535
one fourth part	-	3.634
Subtracted from	-	1875.
leaves the value at 64⅛		1871.366

2nd. Example.

What will be the value of 1000 Millrees, at 64⅛ pence?

	£	s.	d.
I find the value at 64½ to be	£.268	15	
at 64 - -	266	13	4
Difference - -	2	1	8
one fourth part - -		10	5
added to - -	266	13	4
value at 64⅛	£ 267	3	9

Exchange *between* England *and* Venice.

In Venice the Bank Money is twenty per Cent better than the Banco current, and the Banco current is twenty per Cent better than the Picoli Money. Exchanges are on the Ducat Banco, the par being at 4s. 2¼d. Sterling. The Monies are as follows

5¼ Soldi makes 1 Gros.
24 Gros makes 1 Ducat value 50¼ pence Sterling.

Bankers and Merchants for ease of Computation, reckon

12 Deniers d'or to 1 Sol d'or
20 Sols d'or - - to 1 Ducat value 50¼ pence Sterling.

The course of Exchange is from 45 to 50 pence Sterl. the Ducat.

Calculation.

As 49 pence is to 1 Ducat, so is 40l. to 195 Ducats, 22 Gros
As 1 Ducat is to 49 pence, so is 200 Ducats to £.40 16 8

Bank Money is brought into Current Money, thus

As 100 is to 120, so is Bank Money to Current Money and the contrary by reversing the operation

100 Ducats Banco Venice

In Leghorn	93 Pezzos	In Lucca	77 Crowns
In Rome	68½ Crowns	In Frankfort	139½ Florins

A TABLE

A TABLE of *Gros's*, one Ducat the Integer.

1	.0416	5	.2083	9	.375	13	.5416	17	.7084	21	.875
2	.0833	6	.25	10	.4166	14	.5832	18	.75	22	.9166
3	.125	7	.2916	11	.4583	15	.6249	19	.7916	23	.9584
4	.1666	8	.3332	12	.5	16	.6665	20	.8333	24	1.

A TABLE *of Decimal Multipliers for* VENETIAN *and* ENGLISH MONEY, *at the several* RATES *of* EXCHANGE.

ENGLISH INTO VENETIAN.				VENETIAN INTO ENGLISH.			
Rate	Mulpr	Rate	Mulpr	Rate	Mulpr	Rate	Mulpr
45 *d.*	5.3333	47 5	5.0393	45 *d.*	.1875	47 5	.19844
1	5.3185	6	5.0261	1	.188	6	.19896
2	5.3038	7	5.013	2	.18854	7	.19948
3	5.2892	48—	5.	3	.1891	48—	.2
4	5.2747	1	4.987	4	.18958	1	.20052
5	5.2602	2	4.9741	5	.1901	2	.20104
6	5.2458	3	4.9612	6	.1906	3	.20156
7	5.2315	4	4.9484	7	.1911	4	.20208
46—	5.2173	5	4.9357	46—	.19162	5	.2026
1	5.2032	6	4.9231	1	.19218	6	.20312
2	5.1891	7	4.9104	2	.19271	7	.20364
3	5.1751	49—	4.8975	3	.19323	49—	.20416
4	5.1613	1	4.8854	4	.19375	1	.20469
5	5.1474	2	4.873	5	.19427	2	.20521
6	5.1336	3	4.8607	6	.19479	3	.20573
7	5.12	4	4.8484	7	.19531	4	.20625
47—	5.1063	5	4.8362	47—	.19583	5	.20677
1	5.0928	6	4.8241	1	.19635	6	.20729
2	5.0793	7	4.812	2	.19687	7	.20781
3	5.0659	50—	4.8	3	.1974	50—	.20833
4	5.0526			4	.19791		

Use of the above Table.

Any ſum of Engliſh Money multiplied by the tabular Number oppoſite the Rate in the Venetian Column, the Product will be Ducats and Parts. —— Or, any ſum of Venetian Money multiplied by the tabular Number in the Engliſh Column, the Product will be Pounds, and Parts of a Pound ſterl.

Examples.

What will be the value of £.500 in Ven. Money, at 46⅞ per Ducat?

Tabular Number 5.12
500

Anſwer in Ducats 2560 | 00

What will be the value of 4000 Ducats in Engliſh Money, at 46½ pence per Ducat?

Tabular Number .19375
4000

Anſwer £.775 | 00000

Eng.	At 46¼d.		46½d.		46⅞d.		47d.		47½d.	
£.	D.	G.	D.	G.	D.	G.	D.	G.	D.	G.
1000	5189	4	5161	7	5120		5106	9	5052	15
900	4670	6	4645	4	4608		4595	8	4547	8
800	4151	8	4129	1	4096		4085	2	4042	2
700	3632	10	3612	22	3584		3574	11	3536	20
600	3113	12	3096	18	3072		3063	10	3031	14
500	2594	14	2580	15	2560		2553	4	2526	7
400	2075	16	2064	12	2048		2042	13	2021	1
300	1556	18	1548	9	1536		1531	22	1515	19
200	1037	20	1032	6	1024		1021	6	1010	12
100	518	22	516	3	512		510	15	505	6
90	467	0	464	12	460	19	459	13	454	17
80	415	3	412	21	409	14	408	12	404	5
70	363	5	361	7	358	9	357	10	353	16
60	311	8	309	16	307	4	306	9	303	4
50	259	11	258	1	256	0	255	7	252	15
40	207	13	206	10	204	19	204	6	202	2
30	155	16	154	20	153	14	153	4	151	13
20	103	18	103	5	102	9	102	3	101	1
10	51	21	51	14	51	4	51	1	50	12
9	46	16	46	10	46	1	45	23	45	11
8	41	12	41	7	40	23	40	20	40	10
7	36	7	36	3	35	20	35	17	35	8
6	31	3	30	23	30	17	30	15	30	7
5	25	22	25	19	25	14	25	12	25	6
4	20	18	20	15	20	11	20	10	20	5
3	15	13	15	11	15	8	15	7	15	3
2	10	9	10	7	10	5	10	5	10	2
1	5	4	5	3	5	2	5	2	5	1
S. 10	2	14	2	14	2	13	2	13	2	12
9	2	8	2	7	2	7	2	7	2	6
8	2	1	2	1	2	1	2	1	2	0
7	1	19	1	19	1	19	1	18	1	18
6	1	13	1	13	1	12	1	12	1	12
5	1	7	1	7	1	6	1	6	1	[illegible]
4	1	0	1	0	1	0	1	0	1	0
3	0	18	0	18	0	18	0	18	0	18
2	0	12	0	12	0	12	0	12	0	12
1	0	6	0	6	0	6	0	6	0	6
D. 6	0	3	0	3	0	3	0	3	0	3
5	0	2	0	2	0	2	0	2	0	2
4	0	2	0	2	0	2	0	2	0	2
3	0	1	0	1	0	1	0	1	0	1
2	0	1	0	1	0	1	0	1	0	1
1	0	½	0	½	0	½	0	½	[illegible]	½

Venice	At 46¼d.			46½d.			45⅞d.			47d.			47½d.		
Ducats	£.	s.	d.	£.	s.	d.	£.	s.	d.	£.	s.	d.	£.	s.	d.
10000	1927	1	8	1937	10		1953	2	6	1958	6	8	1979	3	4
5000	963	10	10	968	15		976	11	3	979	3	4	989	11	8
4000	770	16	8	775	0		781	5	0	783	6	8	791	13	4
3000	578	2	6	581	5		585	18	9	587	10	0	593	15	0
2000	385	8	4	387	10		390	12	6	391	13	4	395	16	8
1000	192	14	2	193	15		195	6	3	195	16	8	197	18	4
900	173	8	9	174	7	6	175	15	7	176	5	0	178	2	6
800	154	3	4	155	0	0	156	5	0	156	13	4	158	6	8
700	134	17	11	135	12	6	136	14	4	137	1	8	138	10	10
600	115	12	6	116	5	0	117	3	9	117	10	0	118	15	0
500	96	7	1	96	17	6	97	13	1	97	18	4	98	19	2
400	77	1	8	77	10	0	78	2	6	78	6	8	79	3	4
300	57	16	3	58	2	6	58	11	10	58	15	0	59	7	6
200	38	10	10	38	15	0	39	1	3	39	3	4	39	11	8
100	19	5	5	19	7	6	19	10	7	19	11	8	19	15	10
90	17	6	10	17	8	9	17	11	6	17	12	6	17	16	3
80	15	8	4	15	10	0	15	12	6	15	13	4	15	16	8
70	13	9	9	13	11	3	13	13	5	13	14	2	13	17	1
60	11	11	3	11	12	6	11	14	4	11	15	0	11	17	6
50	9	12	8	9	13	9	9	15	3	9	15	10	9	17	11
40	7	14	2	7	15	0	7	16	3	7	16	8	7	18	4
30	5	15	7	5	16	3	5	17	2	5	17	6	5	18	9
20	3	17	1	3	17	6	3	18	1	3	18	4	3	19	2
10	1	18	6	1	18	9	1	19	0	1	19	2	1	19	7
9	1	14	8	1	14	10	1	15	1	1	15	3	1	15	7
8	1	10	10	1	11	0	1	11	3	1	11	4	1	11	8
7	1	6	11	1	7	1	1	7	4	1	7	5	1	7	8
6	1	3	1	1	3	3	1	3	5	1	3	6	1	3	9
5	0	19	3	0	19	4	0	19	6	0	19	7	0	19	9
4	0	15	5	0	15	6	0	15	7	0	15	8	0	15	10
3	0	11	6	0	11	7	0	11	8	0	11	9	0	11	10
2	0	7	8	0	7	9	0	7	9	0	7	10	0	7	11
1	0	3	10	0	3	10	0	3	10	0	3	11	0	3	11
Gr. 12	0	1	11	0	1	11	0	1	11	0	1	11	0	1	11
11	0	1	9	0	1	9	0	1	9	0	1	9	0	1	9
10	0	1	7	0	1	7	0	1	7	0	1	7	0	1	7
9	0	1	5	0	1	5	0	1	5	0	1	5	0	1	5
8	0	1	3	0	1	3	0	1	3	0	1	3	0	1	3
7	0	1	1	0	1	1	0	1	1	0	1	1	0	1	1
6	0	0	11	0	0	11	0	0	11	0	0	11	0	0	11
5	0	0	9	0	0	9	0	0	9	0	0	9	0	0	9
4	0	0	7	0	0	7	0	0	7	0	0	7	0	0	7
3	0	0	5	0	0	5	0	0	5	0	0	5	0	0	6
2	0	0	3	0	0	3	0	0	3	0	0	3	0	0	4
1	0	0	1	0	0	1	0	0	1	0	0	1	0	0	2

Eng.	At 48d.		48½d.		49d.		49½d.		50d.	
£.	D.	G.	D.	G.	D.	G.	D.	G.	D.	G.
1000	5000		4948	11	4897	13	4848	11	4800	
900	4500		4453	14	4408	4	4363	15	4320	
800	4000		3958	18	3918	9	3878	19	3840	
700	3500		3463	21	3428	13	3393	22	3360	
600	3000		2969	1	2938	18	2909	2	2880	
500	2500		2474	5	2448	23	2424	5	2400	
400	2000		1979	9	1959	4	1939	9	1920	
300	1500		1484	12	1469	9	1454	13	1440	
200	1000		989	16	979	14	969	15	960	
100	500		494	20	489	19	484	20	480	
90	450		445	8	440	19	436	8	432	
80	400		395	21	391	20	387	21	384	
70	350		346	9	342	20	339	9	336	
60	300		296	21	293	21	290	21	288	
50	250		247	10	244	21	242	10	240	
40	200		197	22	195	22	193	22	192	
30	150		148	10	146	22	145	10	144	
20	100		98	23	97	23	96	23	96	
10	50		49	11	48	23	48	11	48	
9	45		44	12	44	2	43	15	43	4
8	40		39	14	39	4	38	19	38	9
7	35		34	15	34	6	33	22	33	14
6	30		29	16	29	9	29	2	28	19
5	25		24	17	24	11	24	5	24	0
4	20		19	19	19	14	19	9	19	4
3	15		14	20	14	16	14	13	14	9
2	10		9	21	9	19	9	16	9	14
1	5		4	22	4	21	4	20	4	19
S. 10	2	12	2	11	2	10	2	10	2	9
9	2	6	2	5	2	4	2	4	2	3
8	2	0	1	23	1	23	1	22	1	22
7	1	18	1	17	1	17	1	16	1	16
6	1	12	1	11	1	11	1	10	1	10
5	1	6	1	5	1	5	1	5	1	4
4	1	0	0	23	0	23	0	23	0	23
3	0	18	0	17	0	17	0	17	0	17
2	0	12	0	11	0	11	0	11	0	11
1	0	6	0	6	0	6	0	6	0	6
D. 6	0	3	0	3	0	3	0	3	0	3
5	0	2	0	2	0	2	0	2	0	2
4	0	2	0	2	0	2	0	2	0	2
3	0	1	0	1	0	1	0	1	0	1
2	0	1	0	1	0	1	0	1	0	1
1	0	½	0	½	0	½	0	½	0	½

Venice	At 48d.			48½d.			49d.			49½d.			50d.		
Duc.	£.	s.	d.	£.	s.	d.	£.	s.	d.	£.	s.	d.	£.	s.	d.
10000	2000			2020	16	8	2041	13	4	2062	10		2083	6	8
5000	1000			1010	8	4	1020	16	8	1031	5		1041	13	4
4000	800			808	6	8	816	13	4	825	0		833	6	8
3000	600			606	5	0	612	10	0	618	15		625	0	0
2000	400			404	3	4	408	6	8	412	10		416	13	4
1000	200			202	1	8	204	3	4	206	5		208	6	8
900	180			181	17	6	183	15	0	185	12	6	187	10	0
800	160			161	13	4	163	6	8	165	0	0	166	13	4
700	140			141	9	2	142	18	4	144	7	6	145	16	8
600	120			121	5	0	122	10	0	123	15	0	125	0	0
500	100			101	0	10	102	1	8	103	2	6	104	3	4
400	80			80	16	8	81	13	4	82	10	0	83	6	8
300	60			60	12	6	61	5	0	61	17	6	62	10	0
200	40			40	8	4	40	16	8	41	5	0	41	13	4
100	20			20	4	2	20	8	4	20	12	6	20	16	8
90	18			18	3	9	18	7	6	18	11	3	18	15	0
80	16			16	3	4	16	6	8	16	10	0	16	13	4
70	14			14	2	11	14	5	10	14	8	9	14	11	8
60	12			12	2	6	12	5	0	12	7	6	12	10	0
50	10			10	2	1	10	4	2	10	6	3	10	8	4
40	8			8	1	8	8	3	4	8	5	0	8	6	8
30	6			6	1	3	6	2	6	6	3	9	6	5	0
20	4			4	0	10	4	1	8	4	2	6	4	3	4
10	2			2	0	5	2	0	10	2	1	3	2	1	8
9	1	16		1	16	4	1	16	9	1	17	1	1	17	6
8	1	12		1	12	4	1	12	8	1	13	0	1	13	4
7	1	8		1	8	3	1	8	7	1	8	10	1	9	2
6	1	4		1	4	3	1	4	6	1	4	9	1	5	0
5	1	0		1	0	2	1	0	5	1	0	7	1	0	10
4	0	16		0	16	2	0	16	4	0	16	6	0	16	8
3	0	12		0	12	1	0	12	3	0	12	4	0	12	6
2	0	8		0	8	1	0	8	2	0	8	3	0	8	4
1	0	4		0	4	0	0	4	1	0	4	1	0	4	2
G. 12	0	2		0	2	0	0	2	0	0	2	0	0	2	1
11	0	1	10	0	1	10	0	1	10	0	1	10	0	1	10
10	0	1	8	0	1	8	0	1	8	0	1	8	0	1	8
9	0	1	6	0	1	6	0	1	6	0	1	6	0	1	6
8	0	1	4	0	1	4	0	1	4	0	1	4	0	1	4
7	0	1	2	0	1	2	0	1	2	0	1	2	0	1	2
6	0	1	0	0	1	0	0	1	0	0	1	0	0	1	0
5	0	0	10	0	0	10	0	0	10	0	0	10	0	0	10
4	0	0	8	0	0	8	0	0	8	0	0	8	0	0	8
3	0	0	6	0	0	6	0	0	6	0	0	6	0	0	6
2	0	0	4	0	0	4	0	0	4	0	0	4	0	0	4
1	0	0	2	0	0	2	0	0	2	0	0	2	0	0	2

These Tables of Exchanges being abbreviated, (because the Tables of Decimal Multipliers will answer every purpose) if any Gentleman should rather choose to make use of the common Tables, and not find in them the Rate of Exchange which he may want, the deficiency may be supplied by the Rule at the end of the Portugal Exchanges, which I now repeat once for all:

Make out the Exchange at the two Rates nearest to the Rate required, and subtract the one from the other, (if the distinction of the Columns be one half-penny, and the Rate required be at one-eighth) take one-fourth of the remainder, and subtract it from the amount at the Rate next less, and this last Remainder will be the answer in foreign Money—Or, add it to the amount at the Rate next less, and the sum will be the answer in English Money.—Always remembering to subtract for Foreign Money, and to add for English.

Examples of this Rule have been given at the beginning of the Dutch, and at the end of the Portugal Exchanges.

Exchange *between* England, Genoa, *and* Leghorn.

Their Monies are Pezzos or Lires, Soldi, and Denari.

12 Denari	is	1 Soldi
20 Soldi	—	1 Pezzo, value 4s. 6d. English.

These Pezzos are frequently called Dollars.—The course of Exchange runs from 47 to 56 pence sterl. the Pezzo.

Example.

What will be the value of £.500 in the Money of Genoa, at 56 pence the Pezzo?

As 56 pence is to 20 Soldi, so is 500*l.* to 2142 *Pez.* 17 *sol.* 2 *den.*

As 20 Soldi is to 56 pence, so is 3000 *den.* to 700*l.*

In the use of the following Table of Decimal Multipliers, as Pezzos, Soldis, and Denaris, and Pounds, Shillings, and Pence, are in the same proportions, there will not be any occasion for a Table of Decimal Parts, only multiply the sum to be exchanged by the Multiplier opposite the given Rate.

Examples.

What will be the value of £.500 at 52¼ pence?

Tabular Number	- -	4.5933	
multiplied by	- - -	500	
Pezzos	- -	2296,6500	— to 2296 P. 13 S.

What will be the value of 4000 Pezzos, at 52½ pence?

Tabular Number	- -	.21875
multiplied by	- - - -	4000
Answer	- -	£.875,0000

A TABLE *of* DECIMAL MULTIPLIERS, *fitted to every* RATE *of* EXCHANGE *between* ENGLAND, GENOA, *and* LEGHORN.

ENGLISH INTO GENOESE.				GENOESE INTO ENGLISH.			
Rate	Mulpr	Rate	Mulpr	Rate	Mulpr	Rate	Mulpr
47—	5·1064	51 5	4·6489	47—	·19583	51 5	·2151
1	5·0928	6	4·6377	1	·19635	6	·21562
2	5·0794	7	4·6265	2	·19687	7	·21614
3	5·066	52—	4·6154	3	·1974	52—	·21666
4	5·0526	1	4·6043	4	·19792	1	·21719
5	5·0394	2	4·5933	5	·19844	2	·21771
6	5·0262	3	4·5823	6	·19896	3	·21823
7	5·0131	4	4·5714	7	·19948	4	·21875
48—	5·	5	4·5606	48—	·2	5	·21927
1	4·987	6	4·5498	1	·20052	6	·21979
2	4·9741	7	4·539	2	·20104	7	·22031
3	4·9612	53—	4·5283	3	·20156	53—	·22083
4	4·9485	1	4·5176	4	·20208	1	·22135
5	4·9357	2	4·507	5	·2026	2	·22187
6	4·9231	3	4·4965	6	·20312	3	·2224
7	4·9105	4	4·486	7	·20365	4	·22291
49—	4·898	5	4·4755	49—	·20417	5	·22344
1	4·8855	6	4·4651	1	·20469	6	·22396
2	4·8721	7	4·4548	2	·20521	7	·22448
3	4·8607	54—	4·4444	3	·20573	54—	·225
4	4·8485	1	4·4342	4	·20625	1	·22552
5	4·8363	2	4·424	5	·20677	2	·22604
6	4·8241	3	4·4138	6	·20729	3	·22656
7	4·812	4	4·4037	7	·20781	4	·22708
50—	4·8	5	4·3936	50—	·20833	5	·2276
1	4·788	6	4·3836	1	·20885	6	·22812
2	4·7761	7	4·3736	2	·20937	7	·22865
3	4·7642	55—	4·3636	3	·2099	55—	·22917
4	4·7525	1	4·3537	4	·21042	1	·22969
5	4·7407	2	4·3439	5	21094	2	·23021
6	4·729	3	4·3341	6	·21146	3	·23073
7	4·7174	4	4·3243	7	·21198	4	·23125
51—	4·7059	5	4·3146	51—	·2125	5	·23177
1	4·6944	6	4·3049	1	·21302	6	·23229
2	4·6829	7	4·2953	2	·21354	7	·23281
3	4·6715	56—	4·2857	3	·21406	56—	·23333
4	4·6602			4	·21458		

Eng.	At 47d.			47½d.			48d.			48½d.			49d.		
£.	P.	s.	d.	P.	s.	d.	P.	s.	d.	l.	s.	d.	P.	s.	d.
1000	5106	7	8	5052	12	8	5000			4938	9	1	4897	19	2
900	4595	14	11	4547	7	4	4500			4453	12	2	4408	3	3
800	4085	2	2	4042	2	1	4000			3958	15	3	3918	7	4
700	3574	9	4	3536	16	10	3500			3463	18	4	3428	11	5
600	3063	16	7	3031	11	7	3000			2969	1	5	2938	15	6
500	2553	3	10	2526	6	4	2500			2474	4	6	2448	19	7
400	2042	11	1	2021	1	1	2000			1979	7	7	1959	3	8
300	1531	18	3	1515	15	9	1500			1484	10	9	1469	7	9
200	1021	5	6	1010	10	6	1000			989	13	10	979	11	10
100	510	12	9	505	5	3	500			494	16	11	489	15	11
90	459	11	6	454	14	9	450			445	7	3	440	16	4
80	408	10	3	404	4	3	400			395	17	6	391	16	9
70	357	8	11	353	13	8	350			346	7	10	342	17	2
60	306	7	8	303	3	2	300			296	18	2	293	17	7
50	255	6	5	252	12	8	250			247	8	5	244	18	0
40	204	5	1	202	2	1	200			197	18	9	195	18	4
30	153	3	10	151	11	7	150			148	9	1	146	18	9
20	102	2	7	101	1	1	100			98	19	5	97	19	2
10	51	1	3	50	10	6	50			49	9	8	48	19	7
9	45	19	2	45	9	6	45			44	10	8	44	1	8
8	40	17	0	40	8	5	40			39	11	9	39	3	8
7	35	14	11	35	7	4	35			34	12	9	34	5	9
6	30	12	9	30	6	4	30			29	13	10	29	7	9
5	25	10	8	25	5	3	25			24	14	4	24	9	9
4	20	8	6	20	4	3	20			19	15	11	19	11	10
3	15	6	5	15	3	2	15			14	16	11	14	13	11
2	10	4	3	10	2	1	10			9	17	11	9	15	11
1	5	2	2	5	1	1	5			4	19	0	4	18	0
S. 10	2	11	1	2	10	6	2	10		2	9	6	2	9	0
9	1	5	11	2	5	6	2	.5		2	4	6	2	4	1
8	2	9	10	2	0	5	2	0		1	19	7	1	19	2
7	1	15	9	1	15	4	1	15		1	14	8	1	14	3
6	1	10	8	1	10	4	1	10		1	9	8	1	9	5
5	1	5	6	1	5	3	1	5		1	4	9	1	4	6
4	1	0	5	1	0	3	1	0		0	19	10	0	19	7
3	0	15	4	0	15	2	0	15		0	14	10	0	14	8
2	0	10	3	0	10	1	0	10		0	9	11	0	9	10
1	0	5	1	0	5	1	0	5		0	4	11	0	4	11
D. 6	0	2	7	0	2	6	0	2	6	0	2	6	0	2	5
5	0	2	2	0	2	1	0	2	1	0	2	1	0	2	1
4	0	1	8	0	1	8	0	1	8	0	1	8	0	1	8
3	0	1	3	0	1	3	0	1	3	0	1	3	0	1	3
2	0	0	10	0	0	10	0	0	10	0	0	10	0	0	10
1	0	0	5	0	0	5	0	0	5	0	0	5	0	0	5

Genc.	At 47*d.*			47½*d.*			48*d.*			48½*d.*			49*d.*		
Pez.	£.	s.	d.	£.	s.	d.	£.	s.	d.	£.	s.	d.	£.	s.	d.
10000	1958	6	8	1979	3	4	2000			2020	16	8	2041	13	4
5000	979	3	4	989	11	8	1000			1010	8	4	1020	16	8
4000	783	6	8	791	13	4	800			808	6	8	816	13	4
3000	587	10	0	593	15	0	600			606	5	0	612	10	0
2000	391	13	4	395	16	8	400			404	3	4	408	6	8
1000	195	16	8	197	18	4	200			202	1	8	204	3	4
900	176	5	0	178	2	6	180			181	17	6	183	15	0
800	156	13	4	158	6	8	160			161	13	4	163	6	8
700	137	1	8	138	10	10	140			141	9	2	142	18	4
600	117	10	0	118	15	0	120			121	5	0	122	10	0
500	97	18	4	98	19	2	100			101	0	10	102	1	8
400	78	6	8	79	3	4	80			80	16	8	81	13	4
300	58	15	0	56	7	6	60			60	12	6	61	5	0
200	39	3	4	39	11	8	40			40	8	4	40	16	8
100	19	11	8	19	15	10	20			20	4	2	20	8	4
90	17	12	6	17	16	3	18			18	3	9	18	7	6
80	15	13	4	15	16	8	16			16	3	4	16	6	8
70	13	14	2	13	17	1	14			14	2	11	14	5	10
60	11	15	0	11	17	6	12			12	2	6	12	5	0
50	9	15	10	9	17	11	10			10	2	1	10	4	2
40	7	16	8	7	18	4	8			8	1	8	8	3	4
30	5	17	6	5	18	9	6			6	1	3	6	2	6
20	3	18	4	3	19	2	4			4	0	10	4	1	8
10	1	19	2	1	19	7	2			2	0	5	2	0	10
9	1	15	3	1	15	7	1	16		1	16	4	1	16	9
8	1	11	4	1	11	8	1	12		1	12	4	1	12	8
7	1	7	5	1	7	8	1	8		1	8	3	1	8	7
6	1	3	6	1	3	9	1	4		1	4	3	1	4	6
5	0	19	7	0	19	9	1	0		1	0	2	1	0	5
4	0	15	8	0	15	10	0	16		0	16	2	0	16	4
3	0	11	9	0	11	10	0	12		0	12	1	0	12	3
2	0	7	10	0	7	11	0	8		0	8	1	0	8	2
1	0	3	11	0	3	11	0	4		0	4	0	0	4	1
S. 10	0	1	11	0	1	11	0	2		0	2	0	0	2	0
9	0	1	9	0	1	9	0	1	9	0	1	9	0	1	10
8	0	1	6	0	1	7	0	1	7	0	1	7	0	1	7
7	0	1	4	0	1	4	0	1	4	0	1	4	0	1	5
6	0	1	2	0	1	2	0	1	2	0	1	2	0	1	2
5	0	0	11	0	0	11	0	1	0	0	1	0	0	1	0
4	0	0	9	0	0	9	0	0	9	0	0	9	0	0	9
3	0	0	7	0	0	7	0	0	7	0	0	7	0	0	7
2	0	0	4	0	0	4	0	0	4	0	0	4	0	0	4
1	0	0	2	0	0	2	0	0	2	0	0	2	0	0	2
D. 6	0	0	1	0	0	1	0	0	1	0	0	1	0	0	1
3	0	0	½	0	0	½	0	0	½	0	0	½	0	0	½

Eng.	At 49½d.			50d			50½d.			51d.			51½d.		
£.	P.	s.	d.	P.	s.	d.	P.	s.	d.	P.	s.	d.	P.	s.	d.
1000	4848	9	5	4800			4752	9	6	4705	17	8	4660	3	11
900	4363	12	9	4320			4277	4	7	4235	5	11	4194	3	6
800	3878	15	9	3840			3801	19	7	3764	14	1	3728	3	1
700	3393	18	9	3360			3326	14	8	3294	2	4	3262	2	9
600	2909	1	10	2880			2851	9	8	2823	10	7	2796	2	4
500	2424	4	10	2400			2376	4	9	2352	18	10	1330	1	11
400	1939	7	11	1920			1900	19	10	1882	7	1	1864	1	7
300	1454	10	11	1440			1425	14	10	1411	15	4	1398	1	2
200	969	13	11	960			950	9	11	941	3	6	932	0	9
100	484	17	0	480			475	4	11	470	11	9	466	0	5
90	436	7	3	432			427	14	5	423	10	7	419	8	4
80	387	17	7	384			380	4	0	376	9	5	372	16	4
70	339	7	11	336			332	13	6	329	8	3	326	4	3
60	290	18	2	288			285	3	0	282	7	1	279	12	3
50	242	8	6	240			237	12	6	235	5	11	233	0	2
40	193	18	9	192			190	2	0	188	4	8	186	8	2
30	145	9	1	144			142	11	6	141	3	6	139	16	1
20	96	19	5	96			95	1	0	94	2	4	93	4	1
10	48	9	8	48			47	10	6	47	1	2	46	12	0
9	43	12	9	43	4		42	15	5	42	7	1	41	18	10
8	38	15	9	38	8		35	0	5	37	12	11	37	5	8
7	33	18	9	33	12		33	5	4	32	18	10	32	12	5
6	29	1	10	28	16		28	10	4	28	4	8	27	19	3
5	24	4	10	24	0		23	15	3	23	10	7	23	6	0
4	19	7	11	19	4		19	0	2	18	16	6	18	12	10
3	14	10	11	14	8		14	5	2	14	2	4	13	19	7
2	9	13	1	9	12		9	10	1	9	8	3	9	6	5
1	4	17	0	4	16		4	15	1	4	14	1	4	3	2
S. 10	2	8	6	2	8		2	7	6	2	7	1	2	6	7
9	2	3	8	2	3	2	2	2	9	2	2	4	2	1	11
8	1	18	9	1	18	5	1	18	0	1	17	8	1	17	3
7	1	13	11	1	13	7	1	13	3	1	12	11	1	12	7
6	1	9	1	1	8	10	1	8	6	1	8	3	1	8	0
5	1	4	3	1	4	0	1	3	9	1	3	6	1	3	4
4	0	19	5	0	19	2	0	19	0	0	18	10	0	18	8
3	0	14	7	0	14	5	0	14	3	0	14	1	0	14	0
2	0	9	8	0	9	7	0	9	6	0	9	5	0	9	4
1	0	4	10	0	4	9	0	4	9	0	4	8	0	4	8
D. 6	0	2	5	0	2	5	0	2	5	0	2	4	0	2	4
5	0	2	0	0	2	0	0	2	0	0	2	0	0	1	11
4	0	1	7	0	1	7	0	1	7	0	1	7	0	1	7
3	0	1	3	0	1	2	0	1	2	0	1	2	0	1	2
2	0	0	10	0	0	10	0	0	10	0	0	9	0	0	9
1	0	0	5	0	0	5	0	0	5	0	0	5	0	0	5

Geno.	At 49½d.			50d.			50½d.			51d.			51½d.		
Pez.	£.	s.	d.	£.	s.	d.	£.	s.	d.	£.	s.	d.	£.	s.	d.
10000	2062	10	0	2083	6	8	2104	3	4	2125	0		2145	16	8
5000	1031	5	0	1041	13	4	1052	1	8	1062	10		1072	18	4
4000	825	0	0	833	6	8	841	13	4	850	0		858	6	8
3000	618	15	0	625	0	0	631	5	0	637	10		643	15	0
2000	412	10	0	416	13	4	420	16	8	425	0		429	3	4
1000	206	5	0	208	6	8	210	8	4	212	10		214	11	8
900	185	12	6	187	10	0	189	7	6	191	5		193	2	6
800	165	0	0	166	13	4	168	6	8	170	0		171	13	4
700	144	7	6	145	16	8	147	5	10	148	15		150	4	2
600	123	15	0	125	0	0	126	5	0	127	10		128	15	0
500	103	2	6	104	3	4	105	4	2	106	5		107	5	10
400	82	10	0	83	6	8	84	3	4	85	0		85	16	8
300	61	17	6	62	10	0	63	2	6	63	15		64	7	6
200	41	5	0	41	13	4	42	1	8	42	10		42	18	4
100	20	12	6	20	16	8	21	0	10	21	5		21	19	2
90	18	11	3	18	15	0	18	18	9	19	2	6	19	6	3
80	16	10	0	16	13	4	16	16	8	17	0	0	17	3	4
70	14	8	9	14	11	8	14	14	7	14	17	6	15	0	5
60	12	7	6	12	10	0	12	12	6	12	15	0	12	17	6
50	10	6	3	10	8	4	10	10	5	10	12	6	10	17	6
40	8	5	0	8	6	8	8	8	4	8	10	0	8	11	8
30	6	3	9	6	5	0	6	6	3	6	7	6	6	8	9
20	4	2	6	4	3	4	4	4	2	4	5	0	4	5	10
10	2	1	3	2	1	8	2	2	1	2	2	6	2	2	11
9	1	17	1	1	17	6	1	17	10	1	18	3	1	18	7
8	1	13	0	1	13	4	1	13	8	1	14	0	1	14	4
7	1	8	10	1	9	2	1	9	5	1	9	9	1	10	0
6	1	4	9	1	5	0	1	5	3	1	5	6	1	5	9
5	1	0	7	1	0	10	1	1	0	1	1	3	1	1	5
4	0	16	6	0	16	8	0	16	10	0	17	0	0	17	2
3	0	12	4	0	12	6	0	12	7	0	12	9	0	12	10
2	0	8	3	0	8	4	0	8	5	0	8	6	0	8	7
1	0	4	1	0	4	2	0	4	2	0	4	3	0	4	3
S. 10	0	2	0	0	2	1	0	2	1	0	2	1	0	2	1
9	0	1	10	0	1	10	0	1	10	0	1	11	0	1	11
8	0	1	7	0	1	8	0	1	8	0	1	8	0	1	8
7	0	1	5	0	1	5	0	1	5	0	1	5	0	1	5
6	0	1	2	0	1	3	0	1	3	0	1	3	0	1	3
5	0	1	0	0	1	0	0	1	0	0	1	0	0	1	0
4	0	0	9	0	0	10	0	0	10	0	0	10	0	0	10
3	0	0	7	0	0	7	0	0	7	0	0	7	0	0	7
1	0	0	5	0	0	5	0	0	5	0	0	5	0	0	5
2	0	0	2	0	0	2	0	0	2	0	0	2	0	0	2
D. 6	0	0	1	0	0	1	0	0	1	0	0	1	0	0	1
3	0	0	½	0	0	½	0	0	½	0	0	½	0	0	½

Eng.	*At* 52*d.*			52½*d.*			53*d.*			53½*d.*			54*d.*		
£.	*P.*	*s.*	*d.*	*P.*	*s.*	*d.*	*P.*	*s.*	*d.*	*P.*	*s.*	*d.*	*P.*	*s.*	*d.*
1000	4615	7	8	4571	8	7	4528	6	0	4485	19	7	4444	8	11
900	4153	16	11	4114	5	9	4075	9	5	4037	7	8	4000	0	0
800	3692	6	2	3657	2	10	3622	12	10	3588	15	9	3555	11	1
700	3230	15	4	3200	0	0	3169	16	3	3140	3	9	3111	2	3
600	2769	4	7	2742	17	2	2716	19	7	2691	11	9	2666	13	4
500	2307	13	10	2285	14	3	2264	3	0	2242	19	9	2222	4	5
400	1846	3	1	1828	11	5	1811	6	5	1794	7	10	1777	15	7
300	1384	12	4	1371	8	7	1358	9	10	1345	15	11	1333	6	8
200	923	1	6	914	5	9	905	13	3	897	3	11	888	17	9
100	461	10	9	457	2	10	452	16	7	448	12	0	444	8	11
90	415	7	8	411	8	7	407	10	11	403	14	9	400	0	0
80	369	4	7	365	14	3	362	5	3	358	17	7	355	11	1
70	323	1	6	320	0	0	316	19	7	314	0	4	311	2	3
60	276	18	6	274	5	9	271	14	0	269	3	2	266	13	4
50	230	15	5	228	11	5	226	8	4	224	6	0	222	4	5
40	184	12	4	182	17	2	181	2	8	179	8	9	177	15	7
30	138	9	3	137	2	10	135	17	0	134	11	7	133	9	8
20	92	6	2	91	8	7	90	11	4	89	14	5	88	17	9
10	46	3	1	45	14	3	45	5	8	44	17	2	44	8	11
9	41	10	9	41	2	10	40	15	1	40	7	6	40	0	0
8	36	18	6	36	11	5	36	4	6	35	17	9	35	11	1
7	32	6	2	32	0	0	31	14	0	31	8	0	31	2	3
6	27	13	10	27	8	7	27	3	5	26	18	4	26	13	4
5	23	1	6	22	17	2	22	12	10	22	8	7	22	4	5
4	18	9	3	18	5	9	18	2	3	17	18	11	17	15	7
3	13	16	11	13	14	3	13	11	8	13	9	2	13	6	8
2	9	4	7	9	2	10	9	1	2	8	19	5	8	17	9
1	4	12	4	4	11	5	4	10	7	4	9	9	4	8	11
S. 10	2	6	2	2	5	9	2	5	3	2	4	10	2	4	5
9	2	1	6	2	1	2	2	0	9	2	0	4	2	0	0
8	1	16	11	1	16	7	1	16	3	1	15	11	1	15	7
7	1	12	4	1	12	0	1	11	8	1	11	5	1	11	1
6	1	7	8	1	7	5	1	7	2	1	6	11	1	6	8
5	1	3	1	1	2	10	1	2	8	1	2	5	1	2	3
4	0	18	6	0	18	3	0	18	1	0	17	11	0	17	9
3	0	13	10	0	13	9	0	13	7	0	13	5	0	13	4
2	0	9	3	0	9	2	0	9	1	0	9	0	0	8	11
1	0	4	7	0	4	7	0	4	6	0	4	6	0	4	5
D. 6	0	2	4	0	2	3	0	2	3	0	2	3	0	2	3
5	0	1	11	0	1	11	0	1	11	0	1	10	0	1	10
4	0	1	6	0	1	6	0	1	6	0	1	6	0	1	6
3	0	1	2	0	1	2	0	1	2	0	1	1	0	1	1
2	0	0	9	0	0	9	0	0	9	0	0	9	0	0	9
1	0	0	5	0	0	5	0	0	5	0	0	4	0	0	4

Genoe.	At 52d.			52½d.			53d.			53½d.			54d.		
Pez.	£.	s.	d.	£.	s.	d.	£.	s.	d.	£.	s.	d.	£.	s.	d.
10000	2166	13	4	2187	10		2208	6	8	2229	3	4	2250		
5000	1083	6	8	1093	15		1104	3	4	1114	11	8	1125		
4000	866	13	4	875	0		883	6	8	891	13	4	900		
3000	650	0	0	656	5		662	10	0	668	15	0	675		
2000	433	6	8	437	10		441	13	4	445	16	8	450		
1000	216	13	4	218	15		220	16	8	222	18	4	225		
900	195	0	0	196	17	6	198	15	0	200	12	6	202	10	
800	173	6	8	175	0	0	176	13	4	178	6	8	180	0	
700	151	13	4	153	2	6	154	11	8	156	0	10	157	10	
600	130	0	0	131	5	0	132	10	0	133	15	0	135	0	
500	108	6	8	109	7	6	110	8	4	111	9	2	112	10	
400	86	13	4	87	10	0	88	6	8	89	3	4	90	0	
300	65	0	0	65	12	6	66	5	0	66	17	6	67	10	
200	43	6	8	43	15	0	44	3	4	44	11	8	45	0	
100	21	13	4	21	17	6	22	1	8	22	5	10	22	10	
90	19	10	0	19	13	9	19	17	6	20	1	3	20	5	
80	17	6	8	17	10	0	17	13	4	17	6	8	18	0	
70	15	3	4	15	6	3	15	9	2	15	12	1	15	15	
60	13	0	0	13	2	6	13	5	0	13	7	6	13	10	
50	10	16	8	10	18	9	11	0	10	11	2	11	11	5	
40	8	13	4	8	15	0	8	16	8	8	18	4	9	0	
30	6	10	0	6	11	3	6	12	6	6	13	9	6	15	
20	4	6	8	4	7	6	4	8	4	4	9	2	4	10	
10	2	3	4	2	3	9	2	4	2	2	4	7	2	5	
9	1	19	0	1	19	4	1	19	9	2	0	1	2	0	6
8	1	14	8	1	15	0	1	15	4	1	15	8	1	16	0
7	1	10	4	1	10	7	1	10	11	1	11	2	1	11	6
6	1	6	0	1	6	3	1	6	6	1	6	9	1	7	0
5	1	1	8	1	1	10	1	2	1	1	2	3	1	2	6
4	0	17	4	0	17	6	0	17	8	0	17	10	0	18	0
3	0	13	0	0	13	1	0	13	3	0	13	4	0	13	6
2	0	8	8	0	8	9	0	8	10	0	8	11	0	9	0
1	0	4	4	0	4	4	0	4	5	0	4	5	0	4	6
S. 10	0	2	2	0	2	2	0	2	2	0	2	2	0	2	3
9	0	1	11	0	1	11	0	1	11	0	2	0	0	2	0
8	0	1	8	0	1	9	0	1	9	0	1	9	0	1	9
7	0	1	6	0	1	6	0	1	6	0	1	6	0	1	6
6	0	1	3	0	1	3	0	1	3	0	1	4	0	1	4
5	0	1	1	0	1	1	0	1	1	0	1	1	0	1	1
4	0	0	10	0	0	10	0	0	10	0	0	10	0	0	10
3	0	0	7	0	0	7	0	0	8	0	0	8	0	0	8
2	0	0	5	0	0	5	0	0	5	0	0	5	0	0	5
1	0	0	2	0	0	2	0	0	2	0	0	2	0	0	[illegible]
D. 6	0	0	1	0	0	1	0	0	1	0	0	1	0	0	1
3	0	0	½	0	0	½	0	0	½	0	0	½	0	0	[illegible]

Eng.	At 54½d.			55d.			55½d.			55¾d.			56d.		
£.	P.	s.	d.	P.	s.	d.	P.	s.	d.	P.	s.	d.	P.	s.	d.
1000	4403	13	4	4363	12	9	4324	6	6	4304	18	8	4285	14	3
900	3963	6	1	3927	5	5	3891	17	10	3874	8	9	3857	2	10
800	3522	18	9	3490	18	2	3459	9	2	3443	18	11	3428	11	5
700	3082	11	5	3054	10	11	3027	0	6	3013	9	1	3000	0	0
600	2642	4	0	2618	3	8	2594	11	11	2582	19	2	2571	8	7
500	2201	16	8	2181	16	4	2162	3	3	2152	9	4	2142	17	2
400	1761	9	4	1745	9	1	1729	14	7	1721	19	6	1714	5	9
300	1321	2	0	1309	1	10	1297	5	11	1291	9	7	1285	14	3
200	880	14	8	872	14	7	864	17	4	860	19	9	857	2	10
100	440	7	4	436	7	3	432	8	8	430	9	10	428	11	5
90	396	6	7	392	14	7	389	3	9	387	8	11	385	14	3
80	352	5	10	349	1	10	345	18	11	344	7	11	342	17	2
70	308	5	2	305	9	1	302	14	1	301	6	11	300	0	0
60	264	4	5	261	16	4	259	2	9	258	5	11	257	2	1
50	220	3	8	218	3	8	216	4	4	215	4	11	214	5	9
40	176	2	11	174	10	11	172	19	5	172	3	11	171	8	7
30	132	2	2	130	18	2	129	14	7	129	3	0	128	11	5
20	88	1	6	87	5	5	86	9	9	86	2	0	85	14	3
10	44	0	9	43	12	9	43	4	10	43	1	0	42	17	2
9	39	12	8	39	5	5	38	18	5	38	14	11	38	11	5
8	35	4	7	34	18	2	34	11	11	34	8	9	34	5	9
7	30	16	6	30	10	11	30	5	5	30	2	8	30	0	0
6	26	8	5	26	3	8	25	18	11	25	16	7	25	14	3
5	22	0	4	21	16	4	21	12	5	21	10	6	21	8	7
4	17	12	4	17	9	1	17	5	11	17	4	5	17	2	10
3	13	4	3	13	1	10	12	19	6	12	18	4	12	17	2
2	8	16	2	8	14	7	8	13	0	8	12	2	8	11	5
1	4	8	1	4	7	3	4	6	6	4	6	1	4	5	9
S. 10	2	4	0	2	3	8	2	3	3	2	3	1	2	2	10
9	1	19	8	1	19	3	1	18	11	1	18	9	1	18	7
8	1	15	3	1	14	11	1	14	7	1	14	5	1	14	3
7	1	10	10	1	10	7	1	10	3	1	10	2	1	10	0
6	1	6	5	1	6	2	1	5	11	1	5	10	1	5	9
5	1	2	0	1	1	10	1	1	7	1	1	6	1	1	5
4	0	17	7	0	17	5	0	17	4	0	17	3	0	17	2
3	0	13	3	0	13	1	0	13	0	0	12	11	0	12	10
2	0	8	10	0	8	9	0	8	8	0	8	7	0	8	7
1	0	4	5	0	4	4	0	4	4	0	4	4	0	4	3
D. 6	0	2	2	0	2	2	0	2	2	0	2	2	0	2	2
5	0	1	10	0	1	10	0	1	10	0	1	10	0	1	10
4	0	1	6	0	1	5	0	1	5	0	1	5	0	1	5
3	0	1	1	0	1	1	0	1	1	0	1	1	0	1	1
2	0	0	9	0	0	9	0	0	9	0	0	9	0	0	9
1	0	0	4	0	0	4	0	0	4	0	0	4	0	0	4

Gen.	At 54½d.			55d.			55½d.			55¾d.			56d.		
Pcz.	£.	s.	d.	£.	s.	d.	£.	s.	d.	£	s.	d.	£.	s.	d.
10000	2270	16	8	2291	13	4	2312	10		2322	18	4	2333	6	8
5000	1135	8	4	1145	16	8	1156	5		1161	9	2	1166	13	4
4000	908	6	8	916	13	4	925	0		929	3	4	933	6	8
3000	681	5	0	687	10	0	693	15		696	17	6	700	0	0
2000	454	3	4	458	6	8	462	10		464	11	8	466	13	4
1000	227	1	8	229	3	4	231	5		232	5	10	233	6	8
900	204	7	6	206	5	0	208	2	6	209	1	3	210	0	0
800	181	13	4	183	6	8	185	0	0	185	16	8	186	13	4
700	158	19	2	160	8	4	161	17	6	162	12	1	163	6	8
600	136	5	0	137	10	0	138	15	0	139	7	6	140	0	0
500	113	10	10	114	11	8	115	12	6	116	2	11	116	13	4
400	90	16	8	91	13	4	92	10	0	92	18	4	93	6	8
300	68	2	6	68	15	0	69	7	6	69	13	9	70	0	0
200	45	8	4	45	16	8	46	5	0	46	9	2	46	13	4
100	22	14	2	22	18	4	23	2	6	23	4	7	23	6	8
90	20	8	9	20	12	6	20	16	3	20	18	1	21	0	0
80	18	3	4	18	6	8	18	10	0	18	11	8	18	13	4
70	15	17	11	16	0	10	16	3	9	16	5	2	16	6	8
60	13	12	6	13	15	0	13	17	6	13	18	9	14	0	0
50	11	7	1	11	9	2	11	11	3	11	12	3	11	13	4
40	9	1	8	9	3	4	9	5	0	9	5	10	9	6	8
30	6	16	3	6	17	6	6	18	9	6	19	4	7	0	0
20	4	10	10	4	11	8	4	12	6	4	12	11	4	13	4
10	2	5	5	2	5	10	2	6	3	2	6	5	2	6	8
9	2	0	10	2	1	3	2	1	7	2	1	9	2	2	0
8	1	16	4	1	16	8	1	17	0	1	17	2	1	17	4
7	1	11	9	1	12	1	1	12	4	1	12	6	1	12	8
6	1	7	3	1	7	6	1	7	9	1	7	10	1	8	0
5	1	2	8	1	2	11	1	3	1	1	3	2	1	3	4
4	0	18	2	0	18	4	0	18	6	0	18	7	0	18	8
3	0	13	7	0	13	9	0	13	10	0	13	11	0	14	0
2	0	9	1	0	9	2	0	9	3	0	9	3	0	9	4
1	0	4	6	0	4	7	0	4	7	0	4	7	0	4	8
S. 10	0	2	3	0	2	3	0	2	3	0	2	3	0	2	4
9	0	2	0	0	2	0	0	2	1	0	2	1	0	2	1
8	0	1	9	0	1	10	0	1	10	0	1	10	0	1	10
7	0	1	7	0	1	7	0	1	7	0	1	7	0	1	7
6	0	1	4	0	1	4	0	1	4	0	1	4	0	1	4
5	0	1	1	0	1	1	0	1	1	0	1	1	0	1	2
4	0	0	10	0	0	11	0	0	11	0	0	11	0	0	11
3	0	0	8	0	0	8	0	0	8	0	0	8	0	0	8
2	0	0	5	0	0	5	0	0	5	0	0	5	0	0	5
1	0	0	2	0	0	2	0	0	2	0	0	2	0	0	2
D. 6	0	0	1	0	0	1	0	0	1	0	0	1	0	0	1
3	0	0	½	0	0	½	0	0	½	0	0	½	0	0	½

Exchange *between* England *and* Germany.

The course of Exchange is from 541 to 572 Rix-dollars per 100 Pounds Sterling; and the common method of Calculation is by a Statement of the Rule of Three.

Example.

What will be the value in English Money, of 5000 Rix-dollars, at 560 per 100 Pounds Sterling?

As 560 R. D. is to 100*l.* so is 5000 R. D. to *l.*892 17 1

Or, As 100*l.* is to 560 R. D. so is 100*l.* to 5600 R. Dollars.

A TABLE *of Decimal Multipliers fitted to the several* Rates *of* Exchange *between* ENGLAND *and* GERMANY.

ENGLISH INTO GERMAN.				GERMAN INTO ENGLISH.			
Rate	Mulpr	Rate	Mulpr	Rate	Mulpr	Rate	Mulpr
540	5.40	556	5.56	540	.18518	556	.17986
541	5.41	557	5.57	541	.18484	557	.17953
542	5.42	558	5.58	542	.1845	558	.17921
543	5.43	559	5.59	543	.18416	559	.17889
544	5.44	560	5.60	544	.18382	560	.17857
545	5.45	561	5.61	545	.18348	561	.17825
546	5.46	562	5.62	546	.18315	562	.17794
547	5.47	563	5.63	547	.18281	563	.1776
548	5.48	564	5.64	548	.18248	564	.1773
549	5.49	565	5.65	549	.18215	565	.17699
550	5.50	566	5.66	550	.18182	566	.17668
551	5.51	567	5.67	551	.18149	567	.17637
552	5.52	568	5.68	552	.18116	568	.17606
553	5.53	569	5.69	553	.18083	569	.17575
554	5.54	570	5.70	554	.1805	570	.17544
555	5.55	571	5.71	555	.18018	571	.17513
		572	5.72			572	.17482

Use of this Table.

Any Sum of English Money, multiplied by the Tabular Number in the German Columns, will give Rix dollars and parts.—Or, any Sum of German Money, multiplied by the Tabular Number in the English Columns, will give Pounds Sterling and parts.

The Exchanges with Germany are so easily calculated, that Tables in the usual way would be superfluous.—I shall now present the Reader with the Par of Exchange between England and most of the other places in Europe.

Rome	—	1 Crown	value	—	£0	6*s.*	1½*d.*
Naples	—	1 Ducat	——	—		3	4½
Florence	—	1 Crown	——	—		5	4½
Milan	—	1 Ducat	——	—		4	7
Bologna	—	1 Dollar	——	—		4	3

Sicily	—	1 Crown	value	—	£.0	5s.	0d.
Vienna	—	1 Rix-dollar	——	—	0	4	8
Ausburg	—	1 Florin	——	—	0	3	1½
Frankfort	—	1 Florin	——	—	0	3	0
Bremen	—	1 Rix-dollar	——	—	0	3	6
Breslaw	—	1 Rix-dollar	——	—	0	3	3
Berlin	—	1 Rix-dollar	——	—	0	4	0
Stetin	—	1 Mark	——	—	0	1	6
Embden	—	1 Rix dollar	——	—	0	3	6
Bolsenna	—	1 Rix-dollar	——	—	0	3	8
Dantzick	—	13½ Florins	——	—	1	0	0
Stockholm	—	34½ Dollars	——	—	1	0	0
Russia	—	1 Ruble	——	—	0	4	5
Turkey	—	1 Asper	——	—	0	4	6

The following places, viz. Switzerland, Nuremburg, Leipsic, Dresden, Osnaburg, Brunswick, Cologn, Leige, Strasburg, Cracow, Denmark, Norway, Riga, Revel and Narva, exchanges with England on the Rix-dollar, the Par being 4*s.* 6*d.* Sterling.

Exchange *between* England *and* America.

The Federal or Bank Monies of America, are Eagles, Dollars, Dismes, Cents, and Mills.

1 Mille	—	value in English sterl.		£.0	0	0.054 parts
10 Milles	make	1 Cent	value	0	0	0.54
10 Cents	——	1 Disme	——	0	0	5.4
10 Dismes	——	1 Dollar	——	0	4	6
10 Dollars	——	1 Eagle	——	2	5	0

England however Exchanges with America and the West-Indies in Pounds, Shillings and Pence, commonly called American, or West-India Currency, at various Rates per Cent,——And like all other Exchanges, is determined by a Station of the Rule of Three.—The Par is as follows,

£.100 English sterl. is equal to—

£.166	13	4	Currency of New Jersey, Pensylvania, Delaware and Maryland.
177	15	6⅔	Currency of New York, and North Carolina.
103	14	1	Currency of South Carolina, and Georgia.
133	6	8	Currency of New Hampshire, Massachusetts, Rhode-Island, Connecticut and Virginia.

Or 44 Eagles, 4, Dollars, 4 Dismes, 4 Cents, 3 Mills, Federal Money.

The following Table of Decimal Multipliers will readily convert any Sum of English Money into American, or American into English; only remembering always to consider Shillings and Pence as Decimal Parts of a Pound sterl.

DECIMAL

DECIMAL MULTIPLIERS *between* ENGLAND *and* AMERICA.

Exchange at Par.

	English *into* American.	American *into* English.
New Jersey, Pensylvania, Delaware and Maryland.	1.66662	.6
New York, and North Carolina,	1.77775	.56246
South Carolina, and Georgia.	1.037	.96432
New Hampshire, Massachusetts, Rhode-Island, Connecticut and Virginia.	1.33303	.75092

Tables of this kind having been annexed to each of the foregoing Exchanges, the Reader will easily recollect their use.

Having gone thro' the Monies and Exchanges of the several Christian Nations of Europe and America, I shall give the Reader some account of those of Turkey in Europe, of Asia and Africa, with their several values in English Money, i. e. Pounds, Shillings and Pence, and the Decimal Parts of a Penny.

IN TURKEY, that is, *in Greece, Candia, Cyprus, &c.*

		£.	s.	d.			£.	s.	d.
1 Mangar		£.0	0	0.15	20 Aspers	1 Solota	£.0	1	0
4 Ditto	1 Asper	0	0	0.6	80 Ditto	1 Piastre	0	4	0
3 Aspers	1 Parec	0	0	1.8	100 Ditto	1 Caragrouche		5	0
5 Ditto	1 Bestic	0	0	3	200 Ditto	1 Xeriff	0	10	0
10 Ditto	1 Ostic	0	0	6					

A S I A.

IN ARABIA, that is, *in Medina, Mecca, &c.*

		£.	s.	d.			£.	s.	d.
1 Carret		£.0	0	0.128	60 Comashees	1 Piastre	£.0	4	6
5¼ Ditto	1 Caveer	0	0	0.675	80 Caveers	1 Dollar	0	4	6
7 Ditto	1 Comashee	0	0	0.9	100 Comashees	1 Sequin	0	7	6
80 Ditto	1 Larin	0	0	10.125	80 Larins	1 Tomond	3	7	6
18 Comash.	1 Abyss	0	1	4.2					

IN PERSIA, that is, *in Ispahan, Ormus, &c.*

		£.	s.	d.			£.	s.	d.
1 Coz		£.0	0	0.4	4 Shahees	1 Abashee	£.0	1	4
4 Ditto	1 Bisti	0	0	1.6	5 Abashees	1 Or	0	6	8
10 Ditto	1 Shahee	0	0	4	12 Ditto	1 Bovelo	0	16	0
20 Ditto	1 Mamooda	0	0	8	50 Ditto	1 Tomond	3	6	8
25 Ditto	1 Larin	0	0	10					

EAST-INDIES, that is, *in Surat, Cambay, &c.*

		£.	s.	d.			£.	s.	d.
1 Fecka		£.0	0	0.234	4 Anas	1 Rupee	£.0	2	6
2 Ditto	1 [illegible]	[illegible]	0	0.469	2 Rupees	1 Crown	0	5	[illegible]
4 Pices	1 [illegible]		0	1.875	14 Anas	1 Pagoda	0	8	[illegible]
5 Pices	1 Viz	0	0	2.344	4 Pagoda	1 Gold Rupee	1	15	[illegible]
10 Ditto	1 Ana	[illegible]	0	7.5					

MALABAR, *Bombay*, *Dabul*, &c.

		£	s	d			£	s	d
1 Budgrook		£.0	0	0.0337	240 Rez	1 Xeraphim	£.0	0	4.17
2 Ditto	1 Rez	0	0	0.0674	4 Quart.	1 Rupee	0	2	4
5 Rez	1 Pice	0	0	0.337	14 Ditto	1 Pagoda	0	8	2
16 Pices	1 Laree	0	0	5.4	60 Ditto	1 GoldRupee	1	15	0
20 Ditto	1 Quarter	0	0	7					

Goa, *Visapour*, &c.

		£	s	d			£	s	d
1 Rez		£.0	0	0.067	3 Larees	1 Xeraphim	£.0	1	4.2
2 Ditto	1 Bazaraco		0	0.134	42 Vintins	1 Tangu	0	4	4.5
2 Bazaraco	1 Pecka	0	0	0.27	4 Tangus	1 Paru	0	17	6
20 Rez	1 Vintin	0	0	1.35	8 Ditto	1 GoldRupee	1	15	0
4 Vintin	1 Laree	0	0	5.4					

COROMANDEL, *Madras*, *Pondicherry*, &c.

		£	s	d			£	s	d
1 Cash		£.0	0	0.094	10 Fanams	1 Rupee	£.0	2	6
2 Ditto	1 Viz	0	0	0.187	2 Rupees	1 Crown	0	5	0
2 Viz	1 Pice	0	0	0.375	35 Fanams	1 Pagoda	0	8	9
6 Pices	1 Pical	0	0	2.25	4 Pagodas	1 Gold Rupee	1	15	0
8 Ditto	1 Fanam	0	0	3					

BENGAL, *Callicut*, *Fort-William*, &c.

		£	s	d			£	s	d
1 Pice		£.0	0	0.156	10 Ana	1 Piano	£.0	1	6.75
4 Ditto	1 Fanam	0	0	0.625	16 Ditto	1 Rupee	0	2	6
6 Ditto	1 Viz	0	0	0.937	2 Rupees	1 Crown	0	5	0
12 Ditto	1 Ana	0	0	1.875	56 Anas	1 Pagoda	0	8	9

SIAM, *Pegu*, *Malacco*, *Cambodia*, *Sumatra*, *Java*, *Borneo*, &c.

		£	s	d			£	s	d
1 Cori		£.0	0	0.0008	900 Fettees	1 Dollar	£.0	4	6
800 Ditto	1 Fettee	0	0	0.06	2 Tutals	1 Rial	0	5	0
125 Fettees	1 Sataleer		0	7.5	4 Soocos	1 Crown	0	5	0
250 Ditto	1 Sooco	0	1	3	8 Sataleers	1 Ditto	0	5	0
500 Ditto	1 Tutal	0	2	6					

CHINA, *Pekin*, *Canton*, &c.

		£	s	d			£	s	d
1 Caxa		£.0	0	0.08	35 Candareens	1 Rupee	£.0	2	3
10 Ditto	1 Candareen		0	0.8	2 Rupees	1 Dollar	0	4	6
10 Candar.	1 Mace	0	0	8	10 Maces	1 Tale	0	6	8

JAPAN, *Jeddo*, *Macoa*, &c.

		£	s	d			£	s	d
1 Piti		£.0	0	0.2	30 Maces	1 Ingot	£.0	10	0
20 Pitis	1 Mace	0	0	0	13 Oz. Silver	1 Oz. Gold	3	3	0
15 Maces	1 Oz. Silver	0	4	10.15	2 Oz. Gold	1 Japanese	6	6	0
20 Ditto	1 Tale	0	6	8	20 Oz. Gold	1 Cattee	66	3	0

AFRICAN MONIES.

EGYPT, *Cairo, Alexandria, &c.*

		£	s	d			£	s	d
1 Asper		£.0	0	0.58	30 Medins	1 Dollar	£.0	4	6
3 Ditto	1 Medin	0	0	1.74	96 Aspers	1 Crown	0	5	0
24 Medins	1 Ital. Ducato		3	4	192 Ditto	1 Sultanin	0	10	0
80 Aspers	1 Piastre	0	4	0	72 Medins	1 Pargo-dollar		10	6

BARBARY, *Algier, Tunis, Tripoli, &c.*

		£	s	d			£	s	d
1 Asper		£.0	0	0.57	24 Medins	1 Chequin	£.0	3	4
3 Ditto		0	0	1.71	32 Ditto	1 Dollar	0	4	6
10 Ditto	1 Rial	0	0	6.71	180 Aspers	1 Zequin	0	8	10
2 Rials	1 Double	0	1	1.5	15 Doubles	1 Pistole	0	16	9
4 Doubles	1 Dollar	0	4	6					

MOROCCO, *Santa-Cruz, Mequinez, Fez, &c.*

		£	s	d			£	s	d
1 Fluce		£.0	0	0.08	2 Quartos	1 Media	L.0	4	8
24 Ditto	1 Blanquil	0	0	2	24 Blanquils	1 Dollar	0	4	6
4 Blanquils	1 Ounce	0	0	8	57 Ditto	1 Xequin	0	9	[illegible]
7 Ditto	1 Octavo	0	1	2	100 Ditto	1 Pistole	0	16	0
14 Ditto	1 Quarto	0	2	4					

The Monies and Exchanges of the different Nations of the Earth, being now sufficiently explained; for the information of the Readers of History, I shall in this place give some account of the Monies of the Antients,——And first of—

JEWISH MONIES.

		£	s	d			£	s	d
1 Gerah		L.0	0	1.37	60 Mina	1 Tal. Silv.	L.342	3	9
10 Ditto	1 Bekah	0	1	1.7	1 Sextula	Gold	0	12	2
2 Bekah	1 Shekel	0	2	3.2	3 Ditto	1 Siculus	1	16	6.
50 Shekel	1 Mina	5	14	0	3000 Do.	1 Tal. Gold	5475	0	0

GRECIAN MONIES.

		£	s	d			£	s	d
1 Chalcus		L.0	0	0.322	2 Diabol.	1 Tetrabolum	L.0	0	5.16
2 Ditto	1 Dichalchus	0	0	0.645	1½ Tetrabol.	1 Drachma	0	0	7.75
2 Hemibolum	1 Obolus	0	0	1.29	100 Drachma	1 Mina	3	4	7.
2 Obolus	1 Diabolum	0	0	2.58	60 Mina	1 Talent	193	15	0

ROMAN MONIES.

		£	s	d			£	s	d
1 Teruncius		L.0	0	0.2	2 Sestertius	1 Victoriatus	L.0	0	4
2 Ditto	1 Semilibella	0	0	0.4	2 Victoriatus	1 Denarius	0	0	7.75
2 Semilib.	1 Libella	0	0	0.8	1000 Sester.	1 Sestertium	8	1	6
2½ Libella	1 Sestertius	0	0	2	100 Sestertia	1 Decies	8072	18	4

Having

AND here I conclude an account of the different Monies of the World, which I hope will be found full and satisfactory.

MONEY is an article of Commerce of more general use than any, because it is (almost universally) considered as an equivalent for every other; but it is an article that has done more mischief, than all the rest put together.—If Poisons and strong-drinks have killed their thousands, this has killed its ten thousands; for it has been the cause of almost all the strifes and contentions, wars and fightings that have been since the World began, and it has been equally destructive to the Souls of Men, by enabling them to gratify their lusts, and by lifting them up in pride, has sunk them into perdition.

It is called in Scripture "*the God of this World*" and our Saviour calls the Devil "*the Prince of this World,*" perhaps the terms are nearly synonymous. —— We read of Indians who sacrifice to the Devil, thinking thereby to prevail on him not to hurt them; but almost all the world are ready to sacrifice every thing for Money, without the least regard to any evil consequences or dangers whatever, that may attend the possession of it; — Tho' our LORD expresly says, that "*it is easier for a Camel to go through the eye of a Needle, than for a rich Man to enter the Kingdom of God.*" — But in his infinite mercy he has also given us a Recipe, that will not only effectually purge it from all its pestilential malignity, but at the same time greatly increase the quantity in possession.—"*Give, and it shall be given you, good measure, pressed down, heaped together and running over, shall Men give into your Bosom.*"

I cannot help observing, that as MEN are to be the givers, the fulfilling of this promise is to be expected in this life.

A Comparative View of *Weights* and *Measures*, &c.

Weight, in Commerce, denotes a Body of a known Weight, appointed to be put in the Balance, against other Bodies, whose Weight is required.

The Security of Commerce depending very much on the Justness of Weights, which are usually of Lead, Iron or Brass; most Nations have taken care to prevent frauds, by Stamping or Marking them by proper Officers, who are with us called Clerks of the Market.

All the Weights made Use of in Great Britain and Ireland, are appointed by the twenty seventh Chapter of Magna Charta, and are of two Sorts, viz. Troy Weight, and Avoirdupoise Weight. The origin from which they are both raised, is a Grain of Wheat taken from the middle of the Ear.

In Troy Weight, twenty four of these Grains make a Penny-weight Sterl. twenty Penny-weights make one Ounce, and twelve Ounces one Pound. By this Weight, Gold, Silver, Jewels, Grains and Liquors are Weighed. The Apothecaries also use the Troy-pound, Ounce and Grain: but they differ from the rest in the intermediate Divisions; they divide the Ounce into eight Drachms, the Drachm into three Scruples, and the Scruple into twenty Grains. And to this Weight Corn measures are reducible; as 8 *lbs.* make a Gallon. 16 *lbs*, a Peck, and 64 *lbs.* a Bushel. Liquid measures also depend upon Troy Weight, their contents corresponding thereto in their different Sizes, from a Pint consisting of 12 Ounces, (or 1 Pound) up to a Ton containing 252 Gallons, and weighing 2016 *lbs.* or 1890 *lbs.* Avoirdupoise.

In Avoirdupoise Weight, the Pound contains sixteen Ounces, but the Ounce is less by near one-twelfth than the Troy ounce, this latter containing 490 Grains, and the former only 448. The Ounce containing 16 Drachms. 80 Ounces are only equal to 73 Ounces Troy, and 17 pounds Troy, equal to 14 Pounds Avoirdupoise; by this weight all gross Goods and base Metals are weighed; such as Grocery, Rosin, Pitch, Tar, Tobacco, Tallow, Soap, Butter, Cheese, Iron, Lead, Copper, Allum, &c.

The Proportions of these Weights will be,

Troy Weight.		Apothecaries Wt.	Avoirdupoise Wt. *lbs.*	*oz.*
24 Grs. —	1 Penny-wt. —	1 Scruple 4 Grs. —	0.	0.0535 Parts
20 Py-wts. —	1 Ounce —	1 Oz. or 8 Drachms	0.	1.71
12 Oz. —	1 Pound —	1 Pound — —	0.	13.176

Avoirdupoise Weight. *lbs.*	*oz.*		Troy Weight. *lbs.*	*oz.*
0.	1	—— —— is equal to —— ——	0.	0.953 Parts
1.	0	———	1.	3 Nearly

All the comparative Views of Foreign Weights and Meaſures that I have met with, have conſidered 100 Pounds of London, Amſterdam or Paris, as the Standard to which all others were made equal. I have thought that it would facilitate the Calculation of an Invoice, rather to ſhew, how many of our Pounds and Parts of a Pound, are equal to 100 Pounds of the ſeveral Places abroad. I accordingly preſent the Reader with the following.

TABLE, Shewing how many Pounds and Parts of a Pound Avoirdupoiſe, are equal to 100 Pounds in the following Places.

Foreign Pounds.	Cities or Towns.	Nations.	Engliſh Pounds.
100	Amſterdam	Holland	109.
—	Alicant	Spain	100.9
—	Antwerp	Brabant	103.8
—	Archangel	Ruſſia	90.75
—	Arſchot	Brabant	103.8
—	Avignon	France	90.75
—	Baſil	Switzerland	111.22
—	Bayonne	France	109.
—	Biſancon	Do.	109.
—	Bilboa	Spain	109.
—	Bergen-op-zome	Brabant	112.3
— Small	Bergamo	Italy	65.46
— Great	Do.	Do.	160.3
—	Bergen	Norway	113.9
—	Bern	Switzerland	98.15
—	Boiſleduc	Brabant	103.8
—	Bologna	Italy	72.
—	Bordeaux	France	109.
—	Bourg-en-breſs	Do.	104.8
—	Bremen	Germany	105.81
—	Breſlaw	Bohemia	87.1
—	Bruges	Flanders	103.8
—	Bruſſels	Brabant	103.8
—	Cadiz	Spain	103.8
—	Cologn	Germany	103.8
—	Coningſberg	Pruſſia	87.1
—	Copenhagan	Denmark	101.46
— Rottos	Conſtantinople	Greece	125.4
—	Dantzick	Poland	96.
—	Dort	Holland	109.
— Small	Florence	Italy	76.2
— Great	Do.	Do.	117.2
—	Elbing	Poland	96.5
—	Erford	Germany	100.25
—	Frankfort-main	Do.	111.22
—	Frankfort-oder	Do.	111.22
—	Ghent	Flanders	103.8
—	Geneva	Savoy	122.8

Foreign Pounds.	Cities or Towns.	Nations.	English Pound.
100			
-cash-wt	Genoa	Italy	67.6
-com-wt	Do.	Do.	109.
-grt-wt.	Do.	Do.	120.4
—	Hamburg	Denmark	106.8
—	Koningsberg	Poland	87.14
—	Leyden	Holland	102.8
—	Leipsick	Germany	103.8
—	Liege	Low Countries	103.3
—	Lisle	Flanders	96.
—Sm al	Leghorn	Tuscany	76.07
—Great	Do.	Do.	117.2
—	Lisbon	Portugal	102.3
—	Lovain	Brabant	103.8
—	Lubeck	Denmark	103.8
—Small	Lucca	Italy	76.8
—Great	Do.	Do.	115.34
-city-wt.	Lyons	France	94.
-silk-wt.	Do.	Do.	101.5
—	Madrid	Spain	96
—	Marlines	France	103.8
—	Marseilles	Do.	88.2
—	Messina	Italy	73.85
—	Milan	Do.	65.2
—	Montpelier	France	91.
— or	Bercherocts of	Muscovy	87.14
—	Naumberg	Germany	104.3
—	Nantes	France	109.
—	Nancy	Do.	103.3
—	Naples	Italy	64.3
—	Nurenburg	Germany	111.22
—	Paris and Rochelle	France	109.
—Small	Palermo	Italy	71.
—Great	Do.	Do.	154.3
—	Revel	Russia	96.83
—	Riga	Do.	100.
—	Rome	Italy	75.
—	Rotterdam	Holland	109.
—	Rouen	France	113.5
—	St. Malos	Do.	109.
—	St. Sebastion	Spain	109.
—	Saragosa	Do.	69.
—	Seville	Do.	102.8
—	Smyrna	Lesser Asia	96.
—	Stetin	Germany	99.
—	Tholouse	France	135.2
—	Turin	Piedmont	72.
—	Valencia	Spain	69.
—Small	Venice	Italy	60.16
—Great	Do.	Do.	114.13

By

By the foregoing Table, the Proportion of one Pound may be known as easily as 100, by moving the decimal Dot two figures farther to the left Hand; for Example. I wish to know how much one Pound at Bergen in Norway will weigh in England. I find 100 Pounds in Bergen is equal to 113.9 Pounds in England; consequently 1 Pound in Bergen will weigh 1.139 Pounds and Parts in England.

Particular *Weights* of FOREIGN NATIONS.

Divisions of the *Paris Pound*, for GOLD, SILVER, &c.

French Weights.		Avoirdupoise.		Troy Weight.			
		lb.	*oz. pts.*	*lb.*	*oz.*	*pwts.*	*grs. pts.*
1 Penny-wt.		0	0.04541	0	0	0	19.82
3 Do.	1 Gros	0	0.13625	0	0	2	10.72
8 Gros	1 Ounce	0	1·09	0	0	19	20.16
8 Ounces	1 Mark	0	8.72	0	7	18	18.24
2 Marks	1 Pound	1	1.44	1	3	17	12.48

For Goods of less Value.

French Wt.		Avoirdupoise.		
		lb.	*oz.*	
1 Pound	——	1	1.44	Parts
½ Pound	——	0	8.72	
¼ Pound	——	0	1.09	

For the different *Pounds* of LYONS, THOULOUSE, and ROUEN, see the foregoing Table,

SPANISH Wt.				Avoirdupoise	
				lb.	*oz. pts.*
1 Adarme		——	——	0	0.06
16 Do.	1 Ounce		——	0	0.96
16 Ounces	1 Pound		——	0	15.36
25 Pounds	1 Arroba		——	24	
4 Arrobas	1 Quintal		——	96	
6 Do.		——	——	144	

Gold Weights of *Spain* compared with Troy Weight.

				lb.	*oz.*	*pwts.*	*grs. pts.*
1 Tomin		——	——	0	0	0	8,29
8 Do.	1 Castilian		——	0	0	2	19.16
100 Castilian	1 Pound		——	1	1	19	20.16

Weights of PORTUGAL.

			Avoirdupoise.	
			lb.	*oz. pts.*
1 Arratal or Pound		——	1	0.368
2 Do.	1 Faratella	——	2	0.736
12 Do.	1 Rottoli	——	12	4.416
32 Do.	1 Arroba	——	32	11.776

Weights

WEIGHTS of ITALY.

				Avoirdupoise	
				lb.	*oz.pts.*
1 Pound	—		—	1	2.26
30 Ditto	—	1 Mirre	—	34	3.82
4 Mirre	—	1 Migliaro	—	136	15.29
Rotollo of Genoa		—	—	24	

In GERMANY, FLANDERS, HOLLAND, SWEDEN, DENMARK, &c.

One Schippondt is equal to—

			Avoirdupoise	
			lb.	*oz.pts.*
300 Pounds	at Antwerp	—	311	6.4
300 ———	at Hamburg	—	329	6.4
320 ———	at Lubeck	—	332	2.56
400 ———	at Cuningsberg	—	348	9.
320 ———	in Sweden for Copper	—	324	10.72
400 ———	in Ditto for Provisions	—	405	13.44
400 ———	at Riga	—	400	
400 ———	at Revel	—	387	5.12
340 ———	at Dantzic	—	326	6.4
300 ———	in Norway	—	341	11.2
300 ———	at Amsterdam	—	341	
1 Lyspondt of Amsterdam		—	16	5.6

WEIGHTS of MUSCOVY.

				Avoirdupoise	
				lb.	*oz.pts.*
1 Poede	—		—	8	11.42
10 Ditto	—	1 Berkewits	—	87	3.24

WEIGHTS of TURKEY.

Great Weight.

				Avoirdupoise	
				lb.	*oz.pts.*
1 Occo	—		—	3	12.8
6 Ditto	—	1 Batman	—	22	12.8
44 Ditto	—	1 Quintal	—	167	3.2

Small Weight.

				lb.	*oz.pts.*
1 Occo	—		—	0	15.
6 Ditto	—	1 Batman	—	5	10.
Rottoli	of Egypt	144 Drachms		1	6.4
Large Ditto	of Aleppo	720 Ditto		7	
Small Ditto	of Ditto	624 Ditto		6	1.22
Ditto	of Seyda	600 Ditto		5	13.28

Weights of PERSIA.

			King's Weight.		comm. wt.	
			lb.	*oz. pts.*	*lb.*	*oz. pts.*
1 Dung			0	0.324	0	0.173
6 Ditto	1 Meſchal	—	0	2.18	0	1.04
2 Meſchal	1 Derhem	—	0	4.36	0	2.08
50 Derhem	1 Batman	—	13	10.	6	8.
1 Ratel		—	0	13.625	0	6.5
16 Ditto	1 Batman	—	13	10.	6	8.
The Sah Cheray	1170 to a Derham		—		0	0.00[illegible]
The Vakie			—		0	1.24

Weights of the MOGUL EMPIRE.

Great Weight.

				lb.	*oz. pts.*
1 Seer or Indian Pound			—	1	1.44
40 Ditto	—	1 Maun	—	43	9.6

Small Weight.

				lb.	*oz. pts.*
1 Seer			—	0	13.08
40 Ditto	—	1 Maun	—	32	11.2

Weights of SIAM.

				lb.	*oz. pts.*
1 Clam			—	0	0.272
2 Ditto	—	1 Paye	—	0	0.544
4 Paye	—	1 Fouang	—	0	2.176
2 Fouangs	—	1 Mayon	—	0	4.352
4 Mayons	—	1 Baat	—	1	1.44
4 Baat	—	1 Tael	—	4	5.76
10 Taels	—	1 Catti	—	43	9.6
2 Cattis	—	1 Piece	—	87	3.2
				lb.	*oz. pts.*
The Gantan	—	of Java	—	3	4.32
The Metricol	—	of Golconda	—	0	0.166
The Rotolo	—	of Ditto	—	0	14.25
The Furatella	—	of Ditto	—	1	14.
The Mangelin	—	of Ditto	—	0	0.01

Weights of CHINA.

				lb.	*oz. pts.*
1 Tael	—		—	0	1.37
16 Ditto	—	1 Cati	—	1	6.
100 Catis	—	1 Piece	—	137	0.
66¾ Ditto	—	1 Picol for Silk	—	91	7.16
300 Catis	—	1 Bakaire	—	411	0.

As

As the foregoing account of the weights commonly uſed in moſt Nations, will (I hope) be found ſatisfactory and uſeful; before I enter upon meaſures of capacity and length, I ſhall preſent the Reader with ſome obſervations of a *Right Reverend Prelate*, who has honored this Work with his Name.——His words are,

" It has been deſirable to have ſome one ſtandard for meaſures of length, which ſhould be the ſame at all times and in all places: and yet ſo ſimple and obvious, that the moſt illiterate Perſon of common underſtanding could have recourſe to it, as well as the moſt refined and ſcientific ſpeculator.

" Sir John Miller, a member of the laſt Britiſh Parliament, applied to the Houſe of Commons, for leave to bring in a bill to anſwer this deſirable end, and he conſulted the moſt ingenious and able Philoſophers, both in Britain and France, how to find ſome certain Standard; but they could not think of any thing better than what was deduced from the vibrations of the Pendulum, or from meaſuring a portion of a Degree on the great Circle of the Globe, &c. But at the diſſolution of that Parliament, the whole ſubject fell to the Ground: and ſir John, not being a member of the ſucceeding Parliament, it was not reſumed.

" But in a Book publiſhed in London 1745, Octavo, entitled *the Natural Hiſtory of Bees*, (by way of Dialogue) the Author aſſerts, that the width or diameter of the Cells of the common working honey Bee, is the ſame in them all throughout the World, and therefore may be preſumed to have been the ſame in all ages, and that therefore formed from ſo many breadths or diameters of Cells in a Honey-comb (three of which always make an Inch) would be obvious, ſimple, eaſy to be applied to in all Ages and Countries, as a ſtandard for meaſures of length."

If this had been known to the Antients, and recorded in any of their writings, it would have given us a much better Idea of the meaſures we meet with in Hiſtory, than we can poſſibly have at preſent; but as that has not been the caſe, we muſt be content to compare Antient with Modern; and thoſe of one Nation with another, according to the commonly received opinion.

But with all due deference to the Author of *the Natural Hiſtory of Bees*, ſhould the diameters of Cells in an Honey-comb be ever ſo uniformly equal in all Ages and Nations: I can't help thinking that ſuch a diameter is rather too ſmall to be a ſtandard for meaſures of length: for unleſs that diameter be taken with a degree of exactneſs, which the beſt *Geometrician*, furniſhed with the niceſt inſtruments, can hardly be ſuppoſed equal to; there will appear in a long length, a very material deviation from the truth.

To prove this, let us premiſe that the meaſure called a *Line* is the twelfth part of an Inch, and let us ſuppoſe that in taking the diameter of a Cell, I exceed one tenth part of a Line. A Mile meaſured by this ſtandard, ſo taken, would exceed the truth by two Perches and 14 Feet; and I believe I may be allowed to ſay, that it would be almoſt impoſſible to avoid ſo ſmall an error, either over or under.

A ſtill greater objection will lie againſt the Barley-corn, applied either *length-ways or* breadth-ways, from the uncertainty of their ſize, tho' taken with ever ſo much care out of the middle of the Ear.

Upon

Upon the whole then I muſt conclude, that meaſures taken from the greater to the leſs, will be found much more exact than from the leſs to the greater; and conſequently, that a *portion of a degree on the great Circle on the Globe*, will be found a much better ſtandard, than even the vibrations of the Pendulum; tho' that muſt be allowed to be infinitely better than either of the former. We are now however only talking of the buſineſs: and it is, and will be to very little purpoſe, unleſs parliament ſhould (ſome time or other) think it a ſubject worthy their conſideration.

Till then we muſt be content with meaſures as we find them, and compare them one with another, ſo as to come at the neareſt ratio they bear with our own; and if Inches, Feet, Yards, &c. be exactly copied from one another, this kind of traditional knowledge, may anſwer our purpoſe tolerably well; and we may found upon it, a ſtandard for meaſures of capacity by their cubes; and alſo a ſtandard for weights, by the weight of a quantity of any liquid, whoſe ſpecific gravity is known, that can be contained in a given cube. For inſtance a cubic foot of ſpring water, will be found to weigh 1000 ounces Avoirdupoiſe: conſequently a cube whoſe ſide is equal to one tenth of a foot, will contain one ounce, and as our ounce Avoirdupoiſe is the ſame that was uſed by the antient Romans, and by them introduced among us, we find here a key to the knowledge of the antient weights and meaſures, and alſo our own; the Engliſh wine-gallon being 231, their beer gallon 282, and the Iriſh gallon 217.6 cubic Inches. But not to detain the Reader any longer with obſervations, I ſhall now proceed to reduce foreign meaſures of length into Yards, Feet, Inches and Parts; and laſtly to reduce foreign meaſures of capacity, whether liquid or dry, into gallons and parts.

MEASURES OF LENGTH IN EUROPE.

Measures	Nations	Cities	observations	Yards	Feet	Inches	Parts
Aune of	France	Abbeville					
		Bayone					
		Bordeaux					
		Caen					
		Calais					
		Elberuf					
		Havre deGrace	– –	1	0	6.	
		Nantz					
		Paris					
		St. Quintins					
		Rochelle					
		Rouen					
		Sedan					
		Cambray	– –	0	2	4.8	
		Lyons	– –	1	0	8.5	
	Brabant	Abo					
		Bergen-op-Z.					
		Bois-le-Duc					
		Breda					
		Bruſſels					
		Lovain	– .	0	2	3.4	
		Maeſtrict					
		Malines					
		Narva					
		Straſburg					
		Antwerp	– .	0	2	3.6	
	Holland	Amſterdam					
		Campvier					
		Delft					
		Hague	–	0	2	3.	
		Haerlem					
		Leyden					
		Rotterdam					
		Guelders	. --		2	2.1	
	Zeland	Fluſhing					
		Middleburg	– --	0	2	3.	
	LowCountr.	Nimeguen	– –	0	2	2.1	
		Liege	– --	0	2	0.1	
		Ruremond	– --	0	2	3.	
	Hainault	Mons	– –	0	2	1.2	
	Germany	Fribourg	– –	0	2	6.6	
	Italy	Geneva	– --	1	0	8.5	
	Spain	Cadiz	– –	0	2	3.4	
	Denmark	Altona	– ..	0	2	3.0	

Meaſures

MEASURES OF LENGTH IN EUROPE.

Meaſures	Nations	Cities	obſervations	Yards	Feet	Inches Parts
Aune of	Flanders	Arras	– –	0	2	3.7
		Bruges St. Omers Oſtend	– –	0	2	2.3
		Liſle	– –	0	2	4.8
		Dovay Ypres	– –	0	2	4.
		Dunkirk Ghent	– –	0	2	2.6
		Namur	– –	0	2	2.1
		Tournay	– –	0	2	0.
		Valenciennes	– –	0	2	2.
Arſheen containing 16 Veſhoves	Ruſſia Muſcovy Courland	Archangel Narva Peterſburg Moſcow Mitaw	– –	0	2	1.6
Barras, containing $2\frac{1}{3}$ Palmas	Spain	Almeira	– –	0	2	3.4
		St. Andero Bilboa St. Sebaſtian	– –	0	2	9.3
		Cadiz	for Silk	0	2	8.4
			for Linen	0	2	9.8
		Carthagena Saley	– –	0	2	8.4
		Corunna MADRID	– –	0	2	9.1
	Portugal	LISBON	– –	1	0	8.3
Brazzas of containing 2 Palmas	Italy	Bergamo Bologna	– –	0	2	2.5
		Milan	Silk	0	1	8.9
			Cloth	0	2	2.5
		Venice	Silk	0	1	10.5
			Cloth	0	2	2.5
		Rome Ferrara	– –	1	0	0.
		Florence Lucca	– –	0	1	11.4
		Genoa	– –	0	1	10.3
		Parma Mantua Modena Placentia	– –	0	2	2.8

Meaſures

MEASURES OF LENGTH IN EUROPE.

Measures	Nations	Cities	observations	Yards	Feet	Inches Parts
Cames containing 8 Pams	France	Alby	– –	1	2	10.2
		Avignon, Marseilles, Toulon	– –	2	0	4.7
		Montpelier	– –	2	0	5.4
		Toulouse	– –	1	2	11.6
Camas containing 8 Palmas, or 4 Brazzes	Italy	Capua, Gaieta, Messina, Naples, St Remo, Salerno, Savona	– –	2	1	4.3
		Rome, Civita-Vecch.	– –	2	0	9.4
		Florence	– –	2	1	9.6
		Genoa	Woollen	2	1	4.3
			Linen	2	2	2.1
	Sicily	Palermo, Syracusa	– –	2	1	4.2
	Minorca	– –	– –	1	2	3.0
	Majorca	– –	– –	1	0	1.8
	Malta	– –	– –	2	1	4.2
Camos containing 8 Palmes	Spain	Alicant, Valencia	– –	1	0	1.6
		Barcelona	– –	1	2	3.
		Saragosa, Tortosa	– –	1	2	6.
Cavidos	Portugal	Lisbon	– –	0	2	3.
Crocas	Poland	Dantzic	48 Ells	32	0	0.
Chain containing 4 Perches	England	Surveying	– –	22	0	0.
	Ireland		– –	28	0	0.
	Scotland		– –	24	0	0,
Ell of	Germany	Aix-la-Chapp., Dusseldorp, Mentz	– –	0	1	9.6
		Augsburg	Linen	0	2	11.
			Woollen	0	2	7.7
		Bonn, Coblentz, Cologn, Manheim, Philipsburg, Triers	– –	0	1	10.
		Nuremburg	– –	0	2	3.
		Osnaburg	– –	1	0	8.7

MEASURES OF LENGTH IN EUROPE.

Meaſures	Nations	Cities	obſervations	Yards	Feet	Inches Parts
Ell of	Sweden	Abo, Chriſtianople	– –	0	1	11.4
	Switzerland	Bazil, Bern	– –	0	1	10.7
		St. Gall	Woollen	0	2	0.1
			Linen	0	2	7.3
	Saxony	Bremen, Liepſig, Naumberg	– –	0	1	11.
		Dreſden, Wiſmar	– –	0	1	9.2
	Sileſia	Breſlaw	– –	0	1	9.6
	Auſtria	Vienna	– –	0	1	10.
		Inſpruck, Bolſano	– –	0	1	9.6
	Bavaria	Munich	– –	0	1	9.2
		Ratiſbon, Saltſburg	– –	0	1	9.6
	Brandenbur.	Potſdam	– –	0	1	11.4
	Bohemia	Prague	– –	0	1	9.6
	Denmark	Copenhagen	– –	0	2	0.3
		Altona, Lubeck	– –	0	1	10.4
		Kiel	– –	0	1	10.
	Franconia	Frankfort	– –	0	1	10.3
	Hanover	Zell	– –	0	1	9.6
	Hungary	Preſburg	– –	0	1	10.
	Italy	Ravena	– –	0	2	2.5
		Trent	– –	0	1	9.6
	Livonia	Revel, Riga	– –	0	1	11.4
	Norway	Bergen, Chriſtigna, Drontheim	– –	0	2	0.3
	Poland	Warſaw, Cracow	– –	0	1	9.6
		Thorn	– –	0	1	11.
		Dantzig	– –	0	2	0.
	Pruſſia	Berlin	– –	0	1	11.4
	Pomerania	Stetin	– –	0	1	9.6
		Emden, Paderborn	– –	0	1	9.2
		Mimſter		0	1	9.6

Meaſures

MEASURES OF LENGTH IN EUROPE.

Meaſures	Nations	Cities	obſervations	Yards	Feet	Inches Parts
Foot of	England, Ireland, Scotland	– –	– –	0	0	12.
	France	– –	– –	0	1	0.8
Fathom	England	– –	– –	2	0	0.
Furlong	England	– –	– –	220	0	0,
	Ireland	– –	– –	280	0	0.
	Scotland	– –	– –	240	0	0.
League	Denmark	– –	5000 Paces	8340	0	0.
	England	– –	– –	5280	0	0.
	Ireland	– –	– –	6720	0	0.
	Scotland	– –	– –	5760	0	0.
	France	– –	2000 Toiſes	4260	0	0.
	Spain	– –	3428 Paces	6000	0	0.
	Portugal	– –	3428 Paces	6000	0	0.
	Sweden	– –	5000 Paces	8400	0	0.
	Switzerland	– –	5000 Paces	8400	0	0.
Mile	England	8 Furlongs	– –	1760	0	0.
	Ireland	8 Furlongs	– –	2240	0	0.
	Scotland	8 Furlongs	– –	1920	0	0.
	Germany	– –	4000 Paces	6700	0	0.
	Holland	– –	– –	1340	0	0.
	Hungary	– –	6000 Paces	10000	0	0.
	Poland	– –	3000 Paces	5050	0	0.
	Italy	– –	8 Stadas	1680	0	0.
		Rome	8 Stadas	1696	0	0.
Pace	generally	about	– –	0	5	0.
Perch	England	– –	– –	0	16	6.
	Ireland	– –	– –	0	21	0.
	Scotland	– –	– –	0	18	0.
	France	– –	3 Toiſes	0	19	2.
Palmas	Italy	Gaieta, Meſſina, Naples	– –	0	0	11.
		Genoa	– –	0	0	9.8
		Civita-vecchia	– –	0	0	10.2
		Savona	– –	0	0	10.
Palmos	Spain	Valencia, Alicant	– –	0	0	4.7
		Saragoſa, Tortoſa, Barcelona	– –	0	0	7.8
	Majorca	– –	– –	0	0	4.7
	Minorca	– –	– –	0	0	7.8

MEASURES

MEASURES OF LENGTH IN EUROPE, GREECE, ASIA AND AFRICA.

Meaſures	Nations	Cities	obſervations	Yards	Feet	Inches Parts
Pams	France	Alby	– –	0	0	8.8
		Toulouſe	– –	0	0	9.
		Avignon, Marſeilles, Montpelier, Toulon	– –	0	0	9.6
Raz	Sardinia	Cagliari	– –	0	1	9.6
	France	Chamberry				
	Savoy	Nice				
	Italy	Raconis, Turin, Villafranca				
Shocks	Poland	Cracow	for Linen	36	0	0.
			narrow Do.	72	0	0
		Dantzig	for Linen	40	0	2
			narrow Do.	80	0	4.
Stadas	Italy	Rome	125 Paces	210	0	0.
Toiſe	France	– –	6 French ft.	0	6	4.7
Voerſt	Ruſſia, Muſcovy	– –	750 Paces	1300	0	0.
Veſhove	Ruſſia, &c.	– –	– –	0	0	1.6

SQUARE MEASURE.

Meaſures	Nations	Cities	obſervations	Yards	Feet	Inches Parts
Acres	England	– –	10 ſq.Chains	880	0	0.
	Ireland	– –	Ditto.	1120	0	0.
	Scotland	– –	Ditto.	960	0	0.
Arpents	France	– –	100ſq.Perch.	639	0	0.
Barras	Barbary	Oran	– –	0	2	8.4
		Tangier	– –	0	2	9.1
Cavid	Java	Batavia, Bantam	– –	0	1	7.8
	Malabar	Bombay, Callicut	– –	0	1	6.
		Cambay	– –	0	1	6.4
	Sumatra	Bencoolen	– –	0	1	6.
	Eaſt Indies	Bengal	– –	0	1	6.6
	China	Canton, Pekin	– –	0	1	2.4
	Coromandel	Madraſs, Pondicherry	– –	0	1	6.
	Siam	Malucca, Queda, Tanaſſareen	– –	0	1	6.

MEASURES

MEASURES OF LENGTH IN GREECE, ASIA, AND AFRICA.

Measures	Nations	Cities	observations	Yards	Feet	Inches	Parts
Cavid	Guzaret	Surat	– –	0	1	6.	4
	Persia		usually	0	2	0.	
	Mog. Emp.		usually	0	2	3.	
	Arabia	Mocka	– –	0	2	3.	
Cavidos		Goa	– –	0	2	3.	
	Persia		– –	0	3	1.	
Coffee	Mog. Emp.	– –	2400 Paces	4010	0	0.	
Goffee	Do. Do.	– –	– –	8020	0	0.	
Ichan	Japan	– –	– –	0	7	7.	8
Lys	China	– –	240 Paces	405	0	0.	
Pus	Do.	– –	10 Lys	4050	0	0.	
Purizangas	Persia	– –	30 Stadias	6300	0	0.	
Pace	China, &c.	– –	about	0	5	0.	
Pico	Palestine	Jerusalem, Acre	– –	0	2	0.	
	Syria	Aleppo	– –	0	2	0.	
		Damascus	– –	0	2	3.	
		Scanderoon	– –	0	2	0.	
	Egypt	Alexandria	– –	0	2	0.	
		Sayde	– –	0	2	3.	
	Arabia	Bassora	– –	0	2	0.	
		Mecca, Medina, Suez	– –	0	2	3.	
	Africa	Tunis and Tripoly	for cloth	0	2	3.	
			linen	0	2	6.	
			silk	0	1	6.	
		Oran	– –	0	2	3.	
	Greece	Athens, Lacedemon	– –	0	1	6.	
	Barbary	Algier	– –	0	2	3.	
	Africa	Barca	for cloth	0	2	0.	
			silk	0	1	6.	
	Lesser Asia	Ephesus, Smyrna	– –	0	2	0.	
	Romania	Adrianople	– –	0	2	3.	
		Gallipoli	– –	0	1	6.	
	Candia	– –	for cloth	0	2	6.	
			silk	0	1	6.	
	Persia	Gombroon	– –	0	2	6.	
Stadias	Moria	– –		0	0	0.	
	Persia	– –	125 Paces	210	0	0.	
	Egypt	– –		0	0	0.	
Schoenus	Egypt	– –	40 Stadia	8400	0	0.	

Liquid

LIQUID MEASURES AS USED IN HOLLAND AND GERMANY.

				Galls. pts
1 Stope	—		—	0.125
2 Do.	—	1 Mingle	—	0.25
8 Mingles	—	1 Veertel or Verge	—	2.
2½ Veertel	—	1 Steckan	—	5.
2 Steckans	—	1 Ancker	—	10.
4 Anckers	—	1 Aum	—	40.
6 Aums	—	1 Tun of 2 Pipes	—	240.
14 Do.	—	1 Woeder	—	560.

AS USED IN FRANCE.

1 Poiſſon	—		—	.0312[illegible]
2 Poiſſons	—	1 Demi-ſetier	—	.625
2 Demi-ſetiers	—	1 Chopin	—	.125
2 Chopins	—	1 Pint	—	.25
2 Pints	—	1 Quart	—	.5
4 Quarts	—	1 Setier	—	2.
8 Setiers	—	1 Millerole	—	16.
36 Do.	—	1 Muid or poin con	—	72.

Hogſhead of	Embden	in Germany	54.
	Hamburg	in Denmark	60.
	Lubeck	in Ditto	60.
	Holland		60.
	Guienne	in France	64.
	Bretagne	in Ditto	58.
	Rochelle	in Ditto	54.
	England		63.

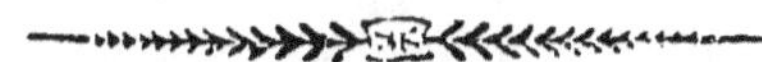

LIQUID MEASURES OF THE ANTIENTS.

JEWISH.

		Galls. pts.
1 Caph	—	0.078
1⅓ Ditto	1 Logg	0.104
4 Log	1 Cab	0.416
3 Cab	1 Hin	1.248
2 Hin	1 Seah	2.496
3 Seah	1 Bath or Epha	7.488
10 Bath	1 Coran or Chomer	74.88

GREEK.

1 Cochliarion	—	0.001
2 Ditto	1 Cheme	0.002
1½ Cheme	1 Myſtron	0.003
2 Myſtron	1 Conche	0.006
2 Conche	1 Cyathos	0.012
2 Cyathos	1 Oxybaphon	0.024
4 Oxybaphon	1 Cotyle	0.096
2 Cotyle	1 Xyſtus	0.192
6 Xyſtus	1 Chous	1.152
10 Chous	1 Metretis	11.52

ROMAN.

1 Ligula	—	0.003
4 Ditto	1 Cyathus	0.012
1½ Cyathus	1 Acetabulum	0.018
2 Acetabulum	1 Quartarius	0.032
2 Quartarius	1 Hemine	0.064
2 Hemine	1 Sextarius	0.125
2 Sextarius	1 Congius	0.25
6 Congius	1 Urna	1.5
4 Urna	1 Amphora	6.
20 Amphora	1 Culeus	120.

The

THE following Table of Dry Meaſures, is taken from *La Bibliotheque des Jeunes Negocians*; only in that Work the SEXTIER of Paris is the Standard, but in *this* the Iriſh GALLON, containing 217.6 Cubic Inches.

	Gal.pts
ASNEE of	
Lyons	40.—
Macon	53.32
ALQURE of	
Liſbon	2.44
BUSHEL of	
Amboiſe	2.30
Aubiterre	6.4
Auray	8.—
Avignon	19.2
Amſterdam	16.—
Barbevieux	6.4
Blois	16.—
Bordeaux	16.—
Eſtafort	18.—
Havre de Grace	6.32
La Rochel	14.48
Maram	25.32
Miramban	18.24
Mirandous	18.24
Montandre	20.—
Perigueux	6.4
Roane	4.—
Tours	2.30
Villen de Agen	16.96
CARTIERES of	
Breau	21.28
CARTES of	
Cahers	6.08
CONQUES of	
Bayone	9.14
EMINE of	
Taraſcon	21.32
Toulon	21.32
FENEGAS of	
Cadiz	13.2
Seville	13.21
HORDT of	
Bruges	34.8[illegible]
HALSTER of	
Ghent	10.86
LAST of	
Amſterdam	608.—
Coningſberg	709.32
Dantzick	320.—
England	640.—

	Gal.pts
LOAD of	
Marſeilles	32.—
Saint Gilles	15.2
LOOPEN of	
Riga	13.2
MOUVER of	
Bois le Duc	28.68
Nimeguen	27.64
Doesbourgh	27.64
MUID of	
Orleans	608.—
Paris	384.—
MUD of	
Amſterdam	22.56
Campen	24.30
Deventer	16.88
Edam	22.52
Groeninguen	18.41
Harderwyck	20.4
Harlingen	18.41
Leeuwarden	18.41
Lovain	22.52
Montfort	34.—
Munickendam	22.5
Purmerent	22.52
Tongres	40.52
Utrecht	24.32
Yſſelſtein	34.—
Zwol	25.46
MINE of	
Dieppe	34.—
PIPE of	
Bergerac	112.—
Caſtle Mauron	112.—
Limuel	120.—
Ribeyrac	112.—
QUARTER of	
Caſtenau Medoc	20.48
Royen	22.—
RAZIERE of	
Dixmude	20.—
Dunkirk	3[illegible].64
Gravelines	27.—
Liſle	14.82
Saint Omers	27.—

Sack of	Gal.pts	Sack continued	Gal.pts
Agen	18.08	Nerac	18.24
Alcmaer	23.38	Puymeral	18.24
Beaumont	16.—	Realville	24.32
Bommel	21.72	Rotterdam	21.—
Bourret	21.28	St. Lieurade	16.96
Brussells	24.32	Schudam	21.—
Cadillac	18.24	Talemont	19.2
Canville	18.24	Thiel	21.7
Castle Jaloux	17.28	Tonniens	15.68
Castle Sarazin	23.44	Valence	20.—
Caude Coste	18.72	Verdun	21.44
Clairac	17.92	Villemur	20.48
Condom	15.36	Weesop	14.—
Creon	20.—	Zirick Zee	15.2
Delft	21.—	Sextier of	
Dort	25.4	Abbeville	26.66
Dunes	18.24	Alby	24.—
Eguillon	15.36	Amiens	8.—
Enchuyson	14.—	Beaucaire	8.88
Espersack	16.—	Bologne	20.—
Flessing	15.2	Calais	34.66
Fronsac	21.28	Paris	32.—
Fronton	21.44	Castres	24.—
Gensac	22.—	Caillac	27.68
Gimond	31.68	Leige	6.32
Goes	15.2	Lisle d'Albegeois	41.6
Goudres	21.72	Montaubon	44.8
Grenada	20.48	Montpellier	11.2
Grisoles	20.48	Negrepelsse	25.28
Haerlem	16.—	Rabastens	30.88
Hoorn	14.—	Realmont	26.56
La Brille	15.4	Realville	24.32
La Guerre	17.28	Rouen	37.32
La Magistire	17.92	St. Valery	32.—
La Reolle	20.—	Saumur	32.—
Lavaur	24.32	Toulouse	18.88
Layrac	19.2	Staro of	
Le Mas d'Agenois	16.8	Venice	16.—
Le Mas d'Verdun	21.44	Schepel of	
Les Pare	21.44	Amersfort	9.5
Leghorn	16.—	Bremen	15.2
Leyden	14.—	Hamburg	6.76
Leyloure	18.24	Lubeck	6.4
Leybourne	17.92	Ruremond	8.94
Middleburgh	14.26	Turtolen	6.52
Moisac	20.—	Tervere	16.—
Montcassin	17.28	Ton of	
Montaubon	22.4	Audienne	320.—
Muyden	14.—	Beauvais	400.—
Narden	14.—	Brest	320.—
Narbonne	30.4	Concarneau	228.—
Negrepelesse	25.28	Copenhagen	14.48

Embden

Ton continued	Gal. pts.	Ton continued	Gal. pts.
Embden	40.—	Quimperlay	400.—
Hennebon	404.—	Redon	336 —
Lanion	320.—	Rennes	304.—
La Roche	280.—	St. Brieu	320.—
Les Adrieus	288.—	St. Cadou	304.—
Lisle Dieu	320.—	St. Malos	288.—
Morlaix	288.—	Stockholm	26.44
Nantes	288.—	Vannes	320.—
Narmoutier	304.—	Verteel of	
Pain d'Avaine	288.—	Antwerp	18.70
Pont le Able	304.—	Bergen op Zoom	17.88
Port Louis	304.—	Breda	18.16
Quiberon	304.—	Malines	21.—
Quinpercorantin	304.—		

Tho' the foregoing Table has been esteemed more full and correct than any other yet published in Europe, and is here reduced into Irish Gallons, yet to make this work as useful as possible, I shall consider these Measures with respect to their Divisions or Multiples.

The Last used on Ship-board contains 2 Tons, or 8 Hogsheads of Wine, or 5 Pieces of Brandy, or 12 Barrels of Herrings, or 13 Barrels of Pitch, or 4 Pipes or Butts of Olive-oil, or 7 Quarters of Fish-oil. The Weight is generally supposed to be 4000lb. But of Wool, because bulky, only 2000lb. and so of other Goods in proportion to the room they occupy in the Ship.

Note,—tho' these measures, both the foregoing and the following, are commonly used for Corn, yet their weight cannot be given with any degree of precision, because of its different states of humidity, however the common weight of the *Last* is from 4200 to 4800*lb.* for Wheat, from 4000 *lb.* to 4200 for Rye, and from 3200 *lb.* to 3400 *lb.* for Barley.

Divisions

Diviſions of DUTCH *and* FLEMISH MEASURES.		*Gal pts.*
In AMSTERDAM.		
1 Scheppel		5.54
3 Do.	1 Sack	16.61
36 Sacks	1 Laſt	608.
alſo		
1 Scheppel		5.54
4 Do.	1 Mud	22.15
27 Muds	1 Laſt	608.
In HOORN, ENCHUYSON, MUYDEN, NAARDEN, and WEESCOP.		
1 Scheppel		7.
2 Do.	1 Sack	14.
44 Sacks	1 Laſt	616.
In ROTTERDAM, DELFT, SCHEUDAM, & TERGOW		
1 Scheppel		7.05
3 Do.	1 Sack	21.38
10¼ Sack	1 Hoedt	219.
29 Do.	1 Laſt	620.
The Laſt here is 2 pr. Ct. more than at Amſterdam.		
In HAERLEM.		
1 Scheppel		8.
2 Do.	1 Sack	16.
38 Sacks	1 Laſt	608.
In ALCKMAER.		
1 Scheppel		7.79
3 Do.	1 Sack	23.38
26 Sacks	1 Laſt	608.
In UTRECHT.		
1 Mud		24.32
25 Do.	1 Laſt	608.
In AMERSFORT.		
1 Scheppel		9.5
64 Do.	1 Laſt	608.
In MONTFORT, VIANEN, and YSELSTEIN.		
1 Scheppel		8.5
4 Do.	1 Mud	34.
18 Muds	1 Laſt	612.
In FRISELAND.		
1 Mud		18.41
33 Do.	1 Laſt	607.53

In NIMEGUEN, ARNHEIM, and DRESBURG.		*Gal.pts.*
1 Scheppel		6.91
4 Do.	1 Mouver	27.64
22 Mouvers	1 Laſt	608.
In CAMPEN.		
1 Mud		24.3
25 Do.	1 Laſt	607.5
In DEVENTER.		
1 Scheppel		8.44
2 Do.	1 Mud	16.88
36 Mud	1 Laſt	607.68
In MIDDLEBURG.		
1 Scheppel		7.13
2 Do.	1 Sack	14.26
42½ Sacks	1 Laſt	606.
In ANTWERP.		
1 Muken		4.67
4 Do.	1 Verteel	18.7
32½ Verteels	1 Laſt	608.
In BRUSSELS.		
1 Sack		24.32
25 Do.	1 Laſt	608.
In MALINES.		
1 Verteel		21.
29 Do.	1 Laſt	609.
In LOVAIN.		
1 Halfter		2.81
8 Do.	1 Mud	22.52
27 Mud	1 Laſt	608.
In BREDA, and STEENBERGEN.		
1 Verteel		18.16
33½ Do.	1 Laſt	609.
In BERGEN OP ZOOM.		
1 Verteel		17.88
34 Do.	1 Laſt	608.
In BOIS LE DUC.		
1 Mouver		28.68
21 Do.	1 Laſt	602.28
In GHENT.		
1 Halfter		10.86
2 Do.	1 Sack	21.72
6 Sacks	1 Mud	130.32
28 Do.	1 Laſt	608.16
19 Do.	for Oats	412.6[illegible]

In

In Bruges.		Gal.pts.
1 Hoedt		34.86
17½ Do.	1 Last	606.
14½ Do.	for Oats	488.
In St. Omers.		
1 Razier		27.
22½ Do.	1 Last	607.5
In Dixmude.		
1 Razier		20.
30½ Do.	1 Last	610.
24 Do. for Oats		480.
In Lisle.		
1 Razier		14.82
41 Do.	1 Last	607.62
30 Do. for Oats		444.6
In Gravelines.		
1 Razier		27.
22½ Do.	1 Last	607.5
18¾ Do. for Oats		505.75
In Liege.		
1 Sextiere		6.32
96 Do.	1 Last	606.72
In Tongres.		
1 Mud		40.52
15 Do.	1 Last	607.8
14 Do. for Oats		567.28
In Dantzick.		
1 Scheppel		8.88
36 Do.	1 Last	608.
In Coningsberg.		
1 Last		709.32
In Riga.		
1 Looper		16.88
36 Do.	1 Last	608.
In Stockholm.		
1 Barrel or Ton		26.44
23 Do.	1 Last	608.
In Copenhagen.		
1 Scheppel		7.24

Copenhagen continued		Gal.pts
80 Do.	1 Last	579.2
96 Do.	1 Do.	695.
also		
1 Barrel or Ton		14.48
42 Do.	1 Last	608.16
In Hamburg.		
1 Scheppel		6.76
90 Do.	1 Last	608.4
In Bremen.		
1 Scheppel		15.2
40 Do.	1 Last	608.
In Embden.		
1 Barrel or Ton		40.
15½ Do.	1 Last	620.
Divisions of French Measures.		
In Paris.		
1 Bushel		2.66
12 Do.	1 Sextier	32.
12 Sexteir	1 Mud	384.
In Rouen.		
1 Bushel		4.15
9 Ditto	1 Sextier	37.32
12 Sextiers	1 Mud	447.84
In Oleans.		
1 Mine		50.6
12 Ditto	1 Mud	608.
In Lyons.		
1 Bushel		6.66
6 Ditto	1 Asnee	40.
In Montpelier.		
1 Quarter		2.8
2 Ditto	1 Emine	2.6
2 Emine	1 Sextier	11.2
In Castres.		
1 Petit		.75
16 Ditto	1 Emine	12.
2 Emine	1 Sextier	24.

HAVING

HAVING now taken a comparative view of such foreign Weights and Measures, as I thought would be most useful in mercantile business; I have to say, that the farther I proceeded in the search, the wider I found the field; and so fitted with an immense, and almost inexplicable variety, that I believe it would be impossible to reduce such a babel of confusion into any order. — Even in one Nation, and in Towns or Cities very near each other, one name is frequently given to very different quantities, and one and the same quantities called by very different names.

How absurd is it to find among ourselves, two kind of Weights; one for the Goldsmith and Apothecary, and another for the Merchant; without any agreement either in their pounds or ounces. — Would not one system of weights, sufficiently divided or multiplied, answer every purpose much better, and give more ease to business? —— Ought not our Monies of account, and our current Monies be the same?—one piece for a pound, and another for a shilling; instead of having one piece at £.1 2s. 9d. and another at 13 pence. —— Why should not our statute and geometrical mile be the same? I cannot see any reason for a difference. But of this I shall make some further observations when I come to shew how the latter may be applied as a rational and just standard for all weights and Measures.

Such a scheme was beginning to be set on foot in France, at, or a little before the commencement of this unhappy war; and the interruption of it was one, among many other of its unhappy effects.—For how desirable and useful would it be, to have the weights and measures of Europe, deduced from one natural or mathematical standard; and the same in every place: — Indeed the nations of Europe, as they are all Christian, ought to be only one great family or republic, having the same laws, customs and manners. And as our holy religion was given us by an infinitely wise and good God, and affords us all necessary knowledge for our temporal as well as spiritual happiness; it might be reasonably expected that our laws, customs and manners should be perfect, and without fault: and that Christians in every part of the globe, wherever scattered, but more especially where collected under national governments, should *think and speak the same thing, should walk according to the one divine rule*, and then, as Saint Paul expresses it, "*Peace should be on them, and Mercy, and upon the Israel of God.*"

I hope none of my readers will be displeased at the appearance of the word *republic* in the last paragraph; I would not be understood to mean, that it is better for a nation than any other system of government; I am perfectly well convinced that a *Monarchial*, an *Aristocratical*, or a *Democratical*, will be equally good and happy, when the governors, whether one or many, make the good of the people (and not their own aggrandizement) the object of their study and endeavour: — for the happiness of the people is not founded on their mode of government, but on the excellence of their laws, and the impartiality of their execution: my meaning is only this, that the several nations of Europe, whether under kingly or republican governments, or both, should altogether form one great family or republic, and maintain a friendly, and not an hostile intercourse; and this might be easily effected, and an uniformity of laws, customs

customs and manners obtain a prevalency, if instead of determining every national difference on the point of the bayonet, a general council or diet were held once every two or three years in some central city of Europe, to which every nation should send an ambassador; not only for the amicable settlement of national differences, but for the mutual improvement of their laws, customs and manners; by the universal adoption of every thing that might be found good and useful in any nation, and by the universal rejection of whatever might be found otherwise.

It was in this manner (by general councils) that the church for several ages endeavoured to preserve peace and uniformity in doctrine, and discipline; and it would certainly have had the desired effect, had it not been for the influence and ambition of kings, popes, cardinals, &c. assuming a *dominion over our faith*, instead of *being helpers of our joy*: yet even now if such councils were restored, and held with freedom and impartiality, there might be some hope that our divisions would be healed, and Christians united in one bond of charity.

It is time now to return to our weights and measures. I have said in a former paragraph that it seems rather absurd that the statute and geometrical mile should not agree, *Mr. Norwood* and *Mr. Picart* assert that 69 English miles make a degree of 60 miles or minutes on the equator: it should however be remembered, that as the earth is an oblate spheroid, a degree on the equator must be some small matter more than a degree on the meridian; this last might be measured with sufficient exactness, by two altitudes of the sun taken at proper distances, by two observers exactly north and south of each other: a degree so measured may be divided into as many parts as convenience may require for measures of length;—superficial measures may be obtained by the squares of these parts; measures of capacity from their cubes; and weights from such a quantity of any well known liquid, as can be contained in one of those cubes.

These hints I have only presumed to throw out, in hopes that if attended to by such as have inclination and ability, they may some time or other contribute to the general good.

A TABLE of Simple Interest at one per Cent for 365 Days; also monthly for 12 Months, and yearly for 7 Years; in Pounds, Shillings, Pence, and Parts of a Penny.

Prin.	1 Day.			2 Days.			3 Days.			4 Days.			5 Days.		
£.	£.	s.	d.pts	£.	s.	d.pts	£.	s.	d.pts	£.	s.	d.pts	£.	s.	d.pts
1	0	0	0.00	0	0	0.01	0	0	0.02	0	0	0.02	0	0	0.03
2	—		—.01	—		—.02	—		—.03	—		—.05	—		—.06
3	—		—.01	—		—.03	—		—.05	—		—.07	—		—.09
4	—		—.02	—		—.05	—		—.07	—		—.10	—		—.13
5	—		—.03	—		—.06	—		—.09	—		—.13	—		—.16
6	—		—.03	—		—.07	—		—.11	—		—.15	—		—.19
7	—		—.04	—		—.09	—		—.13	—		—.18	—		—.23
8	—		—.05	—		—.10	—		—.15	—		—.21	—		—.26
9	—		—.06	—		—.12	—		—.17	—		—.23	—		—.29
10	—		—.0[illegible]	—		—.13	—		—.19	—		—.26	—		—.32
11	—		—.07	—		—.14	—		—.21	—		—.29	—		—.36
12	—		—.08	—		—.15	—		—.23	—		—.31	—		—.39
13	—		—.08	—		—.17	—		—.25	—		—.34	—		—.42
14	—		—.09	—		—.18	—		—.27	—		—.36	—		—.46
15	—		—.10	—		—.19	—		—.29	—		—.39	—		—.49
16	—		—.10	—		—.21	—		—.31	—		—.42	—		—.52
17	—		—.11	—		—.22	—		—.33	—		—.44	—		—.55
18	—		—.11	—		—.23	—		—.35	—		—.47	—		—.59
19	—		—.12	—		—.25	—		—.37	—		—.50	—		—.62
20	—		—.13	—		—.26	—		—.39	—		—.52	—		—.65
21	—		—.14	—		—.27	—		—.41	—		—.55	—		—.69
22	—		—.14	—		—.29	—		—.43	—		—.57	—		—.72
23	—		—.15	—		—.30	—		—.45	—		—.60	—		—.75
24	—		—.15	—		—.31	—		—.47	—		—.63	—		—.78
25	—		—.16	—		—.33	—		—.49	—		—.65	—		—.82
26	—		—.17	—		—.34	—		—.51	—		—.68	—		—.85
27	—		—.1[illegible]	—		—.35	—		—.53	—		—.71	—		—.88
28	—		—.18	—		—.37	—		—.55	—		—.73	—		—.92
29	—		—.19	—		—.38	—		—.57	—		—.76	—		—.95
30	—		—.1[illegible]	—		—.39	—		—.59	—		—.79	—		—.98
40	—		—.2[illegible]	—		—.52	—		—.79	—		1.05	—		1.31
50	—		—.3[illegible]	—		—.65	—		—.99	—		1.31	—		1.64
60	—		—.4[illegible]	—		—.79	—		1.18	—		1.57	—		1.97
70	—		—.4[illegible]	—		—.92	—		1.38	—		1.84	—		2.30
80	—		—.5[illegible]	—		1.04	—		1.57	—		2.10	—		2.63
90	—		—.5[illegible]	—		1.18	—		1.77	—		2.36	—		2.95
100	—		—.65	—		1.31	—		1.97	—		2.63	—		3.28
200	—		1.31	—		2.63	—		3.94	—		5.26	—		6.57
300	—		2.—	—		3.94	—		5.91	—		7.89	—		9.86
400	—		2.63	—		5.26	—		7.80	—		10.52	—	1	1.15
500	—		3.28	—		6.57	—		9.86	—	1	1.15	—	1	4.43
600	—		4.—	—		8.—	—		11.83	—	1	3.78	—	1	7.72
700	—		4.60	—		9.20	—	1	1.80	—	1	6.41	—	1	11.01
800	—		5.26	—		10.52	—	1	3.78	—	1	9.04	—	2	2.30
900	—		6.—	—		11.34	—	1	5.75	—	1	11.67	—	2	5.58
1000	—		6.57	—	1	1.15	—	1	7.72	—	2	2.30	—	2	8.87
2000	—	1	1.15	—	2	2.30	—	3	3.45	—	4	4.60	—	5	5.75
3000	—	1	7.72	—	3	3.45	—	4	11.17	—	6	6.90	—	8	2.63
4000	—	2	2.30	—	4	4.60	—	6	6.90	—	8	9.20	—	10	11.50
5000	—	2	8.87	—	5	5.75	—	8	2.63	—	10	11.50	—	13	8.38

Prin.	6 Days.			7 Days.			8 Days.			9 Days.			10 Days.		
£.	£.	s.	d.pts	£.	s.	d.pts	£.	s.	d.pts	£.	s.	d.pts	£.	s.	d.pts
1	0	0	0.04	0	0	0.04	0	0	0.05	0	0	0.06	0	0	0.06
2	—	—	.08	—	—	.09	—	—	.10	—	—	.12	—	—	.13
3	—	—	.12	—	—	.13	—	—	.15	—	—	.17	—	—	.19
4	—	—	.15	—	—	.18	—	—	.21	—	—	.23	—	—	.26
5	—	—	.19	—	—	.23	—	—	.26	—	—	.29	—	—	.32
6	—	—	.23	—	—	.27	—	—	.31	—	—	.35	—	—	.39
7	—	—	.27	—	—	.32	—	—	.36	—	—	.41	—	—	.46
8	—	—	.31	—	—	.36	—	—	.42	—	—	.47	—	—	.52
9	—	—	.35	—	—	.41	—	—	.47	—	—	.53	—	—	.59
10	—	—	.39	—	—	.46	—	—	.52	—	—	.59	—	—	.65
11	—	—	.43	—	—	.50	—	—	.57	—	—	.65	—	—	.72
12	—	—	.47	—	—	.55	—	—	.63	—	—	.71	—	—	.78
13	—	—	.51	—	—	.59	—	—	.68	—	—	.77	—	—	.85
14	—	—	.55	—	—	.64	—	—	.73	—	—	.82	—	—	.92
15	—	—	.59	—	—	.69	—	—	.78	—	—	.88	—	—	.98
16	—	—	.63	—	—	.73	—	—	.84	—	—	.94	—	—	1.05
17	—	—	.67	—	—	.78	—	—	.89	—	—	1.—	—	—	1.11
18	—	—	.71	—	—	.82	—	—	.94	—	—	1.06	—	—	1.18
19	—	—	.75	—	—	.87	—	—	1.—	—	—	1.12	—	—	1.24
20	—	—	.79	—	—	.92	—	—	1.05	—	—	1.18	—	—	1.31
21	—	—	.83	—	—	.96	—	—	1.10	—	—	1.24	—	—	1.38
22	—	—	.86	—	—	1.01	—	—	1.15	—	—	1.30	—	—	1.44
23	—	—	.90	—	—	1.05	—	—	1.20	—	—	1.36	—	—	1.51
24	—	—	.94	—	—	1.10	—	—	1.26	—	—	1.42	—	—	1.57
25	—	—	.98	—	—	1.15	—	—	1.31	—	—	1.48	—	—	1.64
26	—	—	1.02	—	—	1.19	—	—	1.36	—	—	1.53	—	—	1.70
27	—	—	1.06	—	—	1.24	—	—	1.42	—	—	1.59	—	—	1.77
28	—	—	1.10	—	—	1.28	—	—	1.47	—	—	1.65	—	—	1.84
29	—	—	1.14	—	—	1.33	—	—	1.52	—	—	1.71	—	—	1.90
30	—	—	1.18	—	—	1.38	—	—	1.57	—	—	1.77	—	—	1.97
40	—	—	1.57	—	—	1.84	—	—	2.10	—	—	2.36	—	—	2.63
50	—	—	1.97	—	—	2.30	—	—	2.63	—	—	2.95	—	—	3.28
60	—	—	2.36	—	—	2.76	—	—	3.15	—	—	3.55	—	—	3.94
70	—	—	2.76	—	—	3.22	—	—	3.68	—	—	4.14	—	—	4.60
80	—	—	3.15	—	—	3.68	—	—	4.20	—	—	4.73	—	—	5.26
90	—	—	3.55	—	—	4.14	—	—	4.73	—	—	5.32	—	—	5.91
100	—	—	3.94	—	—	4.60	—	—	5.26	—	—	5.91	—	—	6.57
200	—	—	7.89	—	—	9.20	—	—	10.52	—	—	11.83	—	1	1.15
300	—	—	11.83	—	1	1.80	—	1	3.78	—	1	5.75	—	1	7.72
400	—	1	3.78	—	1	6.41	—	1	9.04	—	1	11.67	—	2	2.30
500	—	1	7.72	—	1	11.01	—	2	2.30	—	2	5.58	—	2	8.87
600	—	1	11.67	—	2	3.61	—	2	7.56	—	2	11.50	—	3	3.45
700	—	2	3.61	—	2	8.21	—	3	0.82	—	3	5.42	—	3	10.02
800	—	2	7.56	—	3	0.82	—	3	6.08	—	3	11.34	—	4	4.60
900	—	2	11.50	—	3	5.42	—	3	11.34	—	4	5.26	—	4	11.17
1000	—	3	3.45	—	3	10.02	—	4	4.60	—	4	11.17	—	5	5.75
2000	—	6	6.90	—	7	8.05	—	8	9.20	—	9	10.35	—	10	11.50
3000	—	9	10.35	—	11	6.08	—	13	1.80	—	14	9.53	—	16	5.26
4000	—	13	1.80	—	15	4.10	—	17	6.41	—	19	8.71	1	1	11.01
5000	—	16	5.26	—	19	2.13	1	1	11.01	1	4	7.89	1	7	4.76

Prin.	11 Days.			12 Days.			13 Days.			14 Days.			15 Days.		
£.	£.	s.	d.pts	£.	s.	d.pts	£.	s.	d.pts	£.	s.	d.pts	£.	s.	d.pts
1	0	0	0.07	0	0	0.08	0	0	0.08	0	0	0.09	0	0	0.09
2	—		—.14	—		—.15	—		—.17	—		—.18	—		—.19
3	—		—.21	—		—.23	—		—.25	—		—.27	—		—.29
4	—		—.28	—		—.31	—		—.34	—		—.36	—		—.39
5	—		—.36	—		—.39	—		—.42	—		—.46	—		—.49
6	—		—.43	—		—.47	—		—.51	—		—.55	—		—.59
7	—		—.50	—		—.55	—		—.59	—		—.64	—		—.69
8	—		—.57	—		—.63	—		—.68	—		—.73	—		—.78
9	—		—.65	—		—.71	—		—.76	—		—.82	—		—.88
10	—		—.72	—		—.78	—		—.85	—		—.92	—		—.98
11	—		—.79	—		—.86	—		—.94	—		1.01	—		1.08
12	—		—.86	—		—.94	—		1.03	—		1.10	—		1.18
13	—		—.94	—		1.02	—		1.12	—		1.19	—		1.28
14	—		1.01	—		1.10	—		1.20	—		1.28	—		1.37
15	—		1.08	—		1.18	—		1.29	—		1.38	—		1.47
16	—		1.15	—		1.26	—		1.37	—		1.47	—		1.57
17	—		1.21	—		1.34	—		1.46	—		1.56	—		1.67
18	—		1.29	—		1.42	—		1.54	—		1.65	—		1.78
19	—		1.36	—		1.49	—		1.63	—		1.74	—		1.87
20	—		1.43	—		1.57	—		1.70	—		1.84	—		1.97
21	—		1.50	—		1.65	—		1.79	—		1.93	—		2.07
22	—		1.58	—		1.73	—		1.88	—		2.02	—		2.16
23	—		1.65	—		1.81	—		1.96	—		2.11	—		2.26
24	—		1.72	—		1.89	—		2.05	—		2.20	—		2.36
25	—		1.79	—		1.97	—		2.13	—		2.30	—		2.46
26	—		1.87	—		2.05	—		2.22	—		2.39	—		2.56
27	—		1.94	—		2.12	—		2.30	—		2.48	—		2.66
28	—		2.01	—		2.20	—		2.39	—		2.57	—		2.76
29	—		2.08	—		2.28	—		2.47	—		2.66	—		2.86
30	—		2.15	—		2.36	—		2.56	—		2.76	—		2.95
40	—		2.88	—		3.15	—		3.41	—		3.68	—		3.94
50	—		3.60	—		3.94	—		4.27	—		4.60	—		4.93
60	—		4.32	—		4.73	—		5.12	—		5.52	—		5.91
70	—		5.05	—		5.52	—		5.98	—		6.44	—		6.90
80	—		5.77	—		6.31	—		6.83	—		7.36	—		7.89
90	—		6.49	—		7.10	—		7.69	—		8.28	—		8.87
100	—		7.23	—		7.89	—		8.54	—		9.20	—		9.86
200	—	1	2.46	—	1	3.78	—	1	5.09	—	1	6.41	—	1	7.72
300	—	1	9.69	—	1	11.67	—	2	1.64	—	2	3.61	—	2	5.58
400	—	2	4.93	—	2	7.56	—	2	10.19	—	3	0.82	—	3	3.45
500	—	3	0.16	—	3	3.45	—	3	6.73	—	3	10.02	—	4	1.31
600	—	3	7.39	—	3	11.34	—	4	3.28	—	4	7.23	—	4	11.17
700	—	4	2.63	—	4	7.23	—	4	11.83	—	5	4.43	—	5	9.04
800	—	4	9.86	—	5	3.12	—	5	8.38	—	6	1.64	—	6	6.90
900	—	5	5.09	—	5	11.01	—	6	4.93	—	6	10.84	—	7	4.76
1000	—	6	0.32	—	6	6.90	—	7	1.47	—	7	8.05	—	8	2.63
2000	—	12	0.65	—	13	1.80	—	14	2.95	—	15	4.10	—	16	5.26
3000	—	18	0.98	—	19	8.71	1	1	4.43	1	3	0.16	1	4	7.89
[illegible]	1	4	1.21	1	6	3.61	1	8	5.91	1	10	8.21	1	12	10.52
[illegible]	1	10	1.54	1	12	10.52	1	15	7.39	1	18	4.27	2	1	1.15

Prin.	16 Days.			17 Days.			18 Days.			19 Days.			20 Days.		
£.	£.	s.	d.pts	£.	s.	d.pts	£.	s.	d.pts	£.	s.	d.pts	£.	s.	d.pts
1	0	0	0.11	0	0	0.11	0	0	0.11	0	0	0.12	0	0	0.13
2	—		—.21	—		—.22	—		—.23	—		—.24	—		—.26
3	—		—.31	—		—.33	—		—.35	—		—.37	—		—.39
4	—		—.42	—		—.44	—		—.47	—		—.49	—		—.52
5	—		—.52	—		—.55	—		—.59	—		—.62	—		—.65
6	—		—.63	—		—.67	—		—.71	—		—.74	—		—.78
7	—		—.73	—		—.78	—		—.82	—		—.87	—		—.92
8	—		—.84	—		—.89	—		—.94	—		1.—	—		1.05
9	—		—.94	—		1.—	—		1.06	—		1.12	—		1.18
10	—		1.05	—		1.11	—		1.18	—		1.24	—		1.31
11	—		1.15	—		1.22	—		1.30	—		1.37	—		1.44
12	—		1.26	—		1.34	—		1.42	—		1.50	—		1.57
13	—		1.36	—		1.45	—		1.53	—		1.62	—		1.70
14	—		1.47	—		1.56	—		1.65	—		1.74	—		1.84
15	—		1.57	—		1.67	—		1.77	—		1.87	—		1.97
16	—		1.68	—		1.78	—		1.89	—		2.—	—		2.10
17	—		1.79	—		1.90	—		2.01	—		2.12	—		2.23
18	—		1.89	—		2.01	—		2.13	—		2.24	—		2.36
19	—		2.—	—		2.12	—		2.24	—		2.37	—		2.49
20	—		2.10	—		2.23	—		2.36	—		2.49	—		2.63
21	—		2.20	—		2.34	—		2.48	—		2.62	—		2.76
22	—		2.31	—		2.45	—		2.60	—		2.74	—		2.89
23	—		2.41	—		2.57	—		2.72	—		2.87	—		3.02
24	—		2.52	—		2.68	—		2.84	—		3.—	—		3.15
25	—		2.63	—		2.79	—		2.95	—		3.12	—		3.28
26	—		2.73	—		2.90	—		3.07	—		3.24	—		3.41
27	—		2.83	—		3.01	—		3.19	—		3.37	—		3.55
28	—		2.93	—		3.12	—		3.31	—		3.49	—		3.68
29	—		3.04	—		3.24	—		3.43	—		3.62	—		3.81
30	—		3.15	—		3.35	—		3.55	—		3.74	—		3.94
40	—		4.20	—		4.47	—		4.73	—		5.—	—		5.26
50	—		5.20	—		5.58	—		5.91	—		6.24	—		6.57
60	—		6.31	—		6.70	—		7.10	—		7.49	—		7.89
70	—		7.36	—		7.82	—		8.28	—		8.74	—		9.20
80	—		8.41	—		8.94	—		9.46	—		10.—	—		10.52
90	—		9.46	—		10.06	—		10.65	—		11.24	—		11.83
100	—		10.52	—		11.17	—		11.83	—		12.49	—	1	1.15
200	—	1	9.04	—	1	10.35	—	1	11.67	—	2	1.—	—	2	2.30
300	—	2	7.56	—	2	9.53	—	2	11.50	—	3	1.47	—	3	3.45
400	—	3	6.08	—	3	8.71	—	3	11.34	—	4	2.—	—	4	4.60
500	—	4	4.60	—	4	7.89	—	4	11.17	—	5	2.46	—	5	5.75
600	—	5	3.12	—	5	7.06	—	5	11.01	—	6	3.—	—	6	6.90
700	—	6	1.64	—	6	6.24	—	6	10.84	—	7	3.45	—	7	8.05
800	—	7	0.16	—	7	5.42	—	7	10.68	—	8	4.—	—	8	9.20
900	—	7	10.68	—	8	4.60	—	8	10.52	—	9	4.43	—	9	10.35
1000	—	8	9.20	—	9	3.78	—	9	10.35	—	10	5.—	—	10	11.50
2000	—	17	6.41	—	18	7.56	—	19	8.71	1	0	9.86	1	1	11.01
3000	1	6	3.61	1	7	11.34	1	9	7.09	1	11	2.79	1	12	10.51
4000	1	15	0.82	1	17	3.12	1	19	5.42	2	1	7.72	2	3	10.02
5000	2	3	10.02	2	6	6.90	2	9	3.78	2	12	0.65	2	14	9.53

Prin	21 Days.			22 Days.			23 Days.			24 Days.			25 Days.		
£.	£.	s.	d.pts	£.	s.	d.pts	£.	s.	d.pts	£.	s.	d.pts	£.	s.	d.pts
1	0	0	0.13	0	0	0.14	0	0	0.15	0	0	0.15	0	0	0.16
2	—	—	.27	—	—	.28	—	—	.30	—	—	.31	—	—	.32
3	—	—	.41	—	—	.43	—	—	.45	—	—	.47	—	—	.49
4	—	—	.55	—	—	.57	—	—	.60	—	—	.63	—	—	.65
5	—	—	.69	—	—	.72	—	—	.75	—	—	.78	—	—	.82
6	—	—	.82	—	—	.86	—	—	.90	—	—	.94	—	—	.98
7	—	—	.96	—	—	1.01	—	—	1.05	—	—	1.10	—	—	1.15
8	—	—	1.10	—	—	1.15	—	—	1.20	—	—	1.26	—	—	1.31
9	—	—	1.24	—	—	1.30	—	—	1.36	—	—	1.42	—	—	1.47
10	—	—	1.38	—	—	1.44	—	—	1.51	—	—	1.57	—	—	1.64
11	—	—	1.51	—	—	1.59	—	—	1.66	—	—	1.73	—	—	1.80
12	—	—	1.65	—	—	1.73	—	—	1.81	—	—	1.89	—	—	1.97
13	—	—	1.79	—	—	1.88	—	—	1.96	—	—	2.05	—	—	2.13
14	—	—	1.93	—	—	2.02	—	—	2.11	—	—	2.20	—	—	2.30
15	—	—	2.07	—	—	2.16	—	—	2.26	—	—	2.36	—	—	2.46
16	—	—	2.20	—	—	2.31	—	—	2.41	—	—	2.52	—	—	2.63
17	—	—	2.34	—	—	2.45	—	—	2.57	—	—	2.68	—	—	2.79
18	—	—	2.48	—	—	2.60	—	—	2.72	—	—	2.84	—	—	2.95
19	—	—	2.62	—	—	2.74	—	—	2.87	—	—	3.—	—	—	3.12
20	—	—	2.76	—	—	2.89	—	—	3.02	—	—	3.15	—	—	3.28
21	—	—	2.89	—	—	3.03	—	—	3.17	—	—	3.31	—	—	3.45
22	—	—	3.03	—	—	3.18	—	—	3.32	—	—	3.47	—	—	3.61
23	—	—	3.17	—	—	3.32	—	—	3.41	—	—	3.62	—	—	3.78
24	—	—	3.31	—	—	3.47	—	—	3.62	—	—	3.78	—	—	3.94
25	—	—	3.45	—	—	3.61	—	—	3.78	—	—	3.94	—	—	4.10
26	—	—	3.59	—	—	3.76	—	—	3.93	—	—	4.10	—	—	4.27
27	—	—	3.72	—	—	3.90	—	—	4.08	—	—	4.26	—	—	4.43
28	—	—	3.86	—	—	4.05	—	—	4.23	—	—	4.41	—	—	4.60
29	—	—	4.—	—	—	4.19	—	—	4.38	—	—	4.57	—	—	4.76
30	—	—	4.14	—	—	4.33	—	—	4.53	—	—	4.73	—	—	4.93
40	—	—	5.52	—	—	5.78	—	—	6.04	—	—	6.31	—	—	6.57
50	—	—	6.90	—	—	7.23	—	—	7.56	—	—	7.89	—	—	8.21
60	—	—	8.28	—	—	8.67	—	—	9.07	—	—	9.46	—	—	9.86
70	—	—	9.66	—	—	10.12	—	—	10.58	—	—	11.04	—	—	11.50
80	—	—	11.04	—	—	11.57	—	1	0.09	—	1	0.62	—	1	1.15
90	—	—	12.42	—	1	1.01	—	1	1.61	—	1	2.20	—	1	2.79
100	—	1	1.80	—	1	1.46	—	1	3.12	—	1	3.78	—	1	4.43
200	—	2	3.61	—	2	4.95	—	2	6.24	—	2	7.56	—	2	8.87
300	—	3	5.42	—	3	7.59	—	3	9.36	—	3	11.34	—	4	1.31
400	—	4	7.23	—	4	9.86	—	5	0.49	—	5	3.12	—	5	5.75
500	—	5	9.04	—	6	0.32	—	6	3.61	—	6	6.90	—	6	10.19
600	—	6	10.84	—	7	2.79	—	7	6.73	—	7	10.68	—	8	2.62
700	—	8	0.65	—	8	5.25	—	8	9.86	—	9	2.46	—	9	7.06
800	—	9	2.46	—	9	7.72	—	10	0.98	—	10	6.24	—	10	11.50
900	—	10	4.27	—	10	10.19	—	11	4.10	—	11	10.02	—	12	3.94
1000	—	11	6.08	—	12	0.65	—	12	7.23	—	13	1.80	—	13	8.38
2000	1	3	0.16	1	4	1.31	1	5	2.46	1	6	3.61	1	7	4.76
3000	1	14	6.24	1	6	1.97	1	17	9.69	1	19	5.42	2	1	1.14
4000	2	6	0.32	2	8	2.62	2	10	4.92	2	12	7.13	2	14	9.52
5000	2	17	6.40	3	0	3.28	3	3	0.15	3	5	9.04	3	8	5.90

Prin.	26 Days.			27 Days.			28 Days.			29 Days.			30 Days.		
£.	£.	s.	d. pts	£.	s.	d. pts	£.	s.	d. pts	£.	s.	d. pts	£.	s.	d. pts
1	0	0	0.17	0	0	0.17	0	0	0.18	0	0	0.19	0	0	0.19
2	——		—.34	——		—.35	——		—.36	——		—.38	——		—.39
3	——		—.51	——		—.53	——		—.55	——		—.57	——		—.59
4	——		—.68	——		—.71	——		—.73	——		—.76	——		—.78
5	——		—.85	——		—.88	——		—.92	——		—.95	——		—.98
6	——		1.02	——		1.06	——		1.10	——		1.14	——		1.18
7	——		1.19	——		1.24	——		1.28	——		1.33	——		1.38
8	——		1.36	——		1.42	——		1.47	——		1.52	——		1.57
9	——		1.53	——		1.59	——		1.65	——		1.71	——		1.77
10	——		1.70	——		1.77	——		1.84	——		1.90	——		1.97
11	——		1.88	——		1.95	——		2.02	——		2.09	——		2.16
12	——		2.05	——		2.13	——		2.20	——		2.28	——		2.36
13	——		2.22	——		2.30	——		2.39	——		2.47	——		2.56
14	——		2.39	——		2.48	——		2.57	——		2.66	——		2.76
15	——		2.56	——		2.66	——		2.76	——		2.86	——		2.95
12	——		2.73	——		2.84	——		2.94	——		3.05	——		3.15
17	——		2.90	——		3.01	——		3.12	——		3.24	——		3.35
18	——		3.07	——		3.19	——		3.31	——		3.43	——		3.55
19	——		3.24	——		3.37	——		3.49	——		3.62	——		3.74
20	——		3.41	——		3.55	——		3.68	——		3.81	——		3.94
21	——		3.59	——		3.72	——		3.86	——		4.—	——		4.14
22	——		3.76	——		3.90	——		4.05	——		4.19	——		4.33
23	——		3.93	——		4.08	——		4.23	——		4.38	——		4.53
24	——		4.10	——		4.26	——		4.41	——		4.57	——		4.73
25	——		4.27	——		4.43	——		4.60	——		4.76	——		4.93
26	——		4.44	——		4.61	——		4.78	——		4.95	——		5.12
27	——		4.61	——		4.79	——		4.97	——		5.14	——		5.32
28	——		4.78	——		4.97	——		5.15	——		5.33	——		5.52
29	——		4.95	——		5.14	——		5.33	——		5.52	——		5.72
30	——		5.12	——		5.32	——		5.52	——		5.72	——		5.91
40	——		6.83	——		7.10	——		7.36	——		7.62	——		7.89
50	——		8.54	——		8.87	——		9.20	——		9.53	——		9.86
60	——		10.25	——		10.65	——		11.04	——		11.44	——		11.83
70	——		11.96	—	1	0.42	—	1	0.88	—	1	1.34	—	1	1.80
80	—	1	1.67	—	1	2.20	—	1	2.72	—	1	3.25	—	1	3.78
90	—	1	3.38	—	1	3.97	—	1	4.56	—	1	5.16	—	1	5.75
100	—	1	5.09	—	1	5.75	—	1	6.41	—	1	7.06	—	1	7.72
200	—	2	10.19	—	2	11.50	—	3	0.82	—	3	2.13	—	3	3.45
300	—	4	3.28	—	4	5.25	—	4	7.23	—	4	9.20	—	4	11.17
400	—	5	8.38	—	5	11.01	—	6	1.64	—	6	4.27	—	6	6.90
500	—	7	1.47	—	7	4.76	—	7	8.05	—	7	11.34	—	8	2.63
600	—	8	6.57	—	8	10.51	—	9	2.46	—	9	6.40	—	9	10.35
700	—	9	11.67	—	10	4.27	—	10	8.87	—	11	1.47	—	11	6.08
800	—	11	4.76	—	11	10.02	—	12	3.28	—	12	8.54	—	13	1.80
900	—	12	9.86	—	13	3.77	—	13	9.69	—	14	3.61	—	14	9.53
1000	—	14	2.95	—	14	9.53	—	15	4.11	—	15	10.68	—	16	5.26
2000	1	8	5.91	1	9	7.06	1	10	8.22	1	11	9.36	1	12	10.52
3000	2	2	8.87	2	4	4.59	2	6	0.33	2	7	8.04	2	9	3.78
4000	2	16	11.83	2	19	2.12	3	1	4.44	3	3	6.72	3	5	9.04
5000	3	11	2.79	3	13	11.53	3	17	4.55	3	19	5.40	4	2	2.30

Prin.	31 Days.			32 Days.			33 Days.			34 Days.			35 Days.		
£.	£.	s.	d.pts	£.	s.	d.pts	£.	s.	d.pts	£.	s.	d.pts	£.	s.	d.pts
1	0	0	0.20	0	0	0.21	0	0	0.21	0	0	0.22	0	0	0.23
2	—	—	.40	—	—	.42	—	—	.43	—	—	.44	—	—	.46
3	—	—	.61	—	—	.63	—	—	.65	—	—	.67	—	—	.69
4	—	—	.81	—	—	.84	—	—	.86	—	—	.89	—	—	.92
5	—	—	1.01	—	—	1.05	—	—	1.08	—	—	1.11	—	—	1.15
6	—	—	1.22	—	—	1.26	—	—	1.30	—	—	1.34	—	—	1.38
7	—	—	1.42	—	—	1.47	—	—	1.51	—	—	1.56	—	—	1.61
8	—	—	1.63	—	—	1.68	—	—	1.73	—	—	1.78	—	—	1.84
9	—	—	1.83	—	—	1.89	—	—	1.95	—	—	2.01	—	—	2.07
10	—	—	2.03	—	—	2.10	—	—	2.16	—	—	2.23	—	—	2.30
11	—	—	2.24	—	—	2.31	—	—	2.38	—	—	2.45	—	—	2.53
12	—	—	2.44	—	—	2.52	—	—	2.60	—	—	2.68	—	—	2.76
13	—	—	2.64	—	—	2.73	—	—	2.82	—	—	2.90	—	—	3.—
14	—	—	2.85	—	—	2.94	—	—	3.03	—	—	3.12	—	—	3.22
15	—	—	3.05	—	—	3.15	—	—	3.25	—	—	3.35	—	—	3.45
16	—	—	3.26	—	—	3.66	—	—	3.47	—	—	3.57	—	—	3.68
17	—	—	3.46	—	—	3.57	—	—	3.68	—	—	3.80	—	—	3.91
18	—	—	3.66	—	—	3.78	—	—	3.90	—	—	4.02	—	—	4.14
19	—	—	3.87	—	—	4.—	—	—	4.12	—	—	4.24	—	—	4.37
20	—	—	4.07	—	—	4.20	—	—	4.33	—	—	4.47	—	—	4.60
21	—	—	4.28	—	—	4.41	—	—	4.55	—	—	4.69	—	—	4.83
22	—	—	4.48	—	—	4.62	—	—	4.77	—	—	4.91	—	—	5.06
23	—	—	4.68	—	—	4.83	—	—	5.—	—	—	5.14	—	—	5.29
24	—	—	4.89	—	—	5.04	—	—	5.20	—	—	5.36	—	—	5.52
25	—	—	5.09	—	—	5.26	—	—	5.42	—	—	5.58	—	—	5.75
26	—	—	5.29	—	—	5.47	—	—	5.64	—	—	5.81	—	—	6.—
27	—	—	5.50	—	—	5.68	—	—	5.85	—	—	6.03	—	—	6.21
28	—	—	5.70	—	—	5.89	—	—	6.07	—	—	6.25	—	—	6.44
29	—	—	5.91	—	—	6.10	—	—	6.29	—	—	6.48	—	—	6.67
30	—	—	6.11	—	—	6.31	—	—	6.50	—	—	6.70	—	—	6.90
40	—	—	8.15	—	—	8.41	—	—	8.67	—	—	8.94	—	—	9.20
50	—	—	10.19	—	—	10.52	—	—	10.84	—	—	11.17	—	—	11.50
60	—	1	0.22	—	1	0.62	—	1	1.01	—	1	1.41	—	1	1.80
70	—	1	2.26	—	1	2.72	—	1	3.18	—	1	3.64	—	1	4.10
80	—	1	4.30	—	1	4.83	—	1	5.35	—	1	5.88	—	1	6.41
90	—	1	6.34	—	1	6.93	—	1	7.52	—	1	8.12	—	1	8.71
100	—	1	8.38	—	1	9.04	—	1	9.69	—	1	10.35	—	1	11.01
200	—	3	4.76	—	3	6.08	—	3	7.39	—	3	8.71	—	3	10.02
300	—	5	1.14	—	5	3.12	—	5	5.09	—	5	7.06	—	5	9.03
400	—	6	9.53	—	7	0.16	—	7	2.79	—	7	5.42	—	7	8.05
500	—	8	5.91	—	8	9.20	—	9	0.49	—	9	3.78	—	9	7.06
600	—	10	2.29	—	10	6.24	—	10	10.18	—	11	2.13	—	11	6.07
700	—	11	10.68	—	12	3.28	—	12	7.88	—	13	0.49	—	13	5.09
800	—	13	7.06	—	14	0.32	—	14	5.58	—	14	10.84	—	15	4.16
900	—	15	3.44	—	15	9.36	—	16	3.28	—	16	9.20	—	17	3.11
1000	—	16	11.83	—	17	6.41	—	18	1.	—	18	7.56	—	19	2.13
2000	1	13	11.66	1	15	0.82	1	16	2.	1	17	3.12	1	18	4.26
3000	2	10	11.49	2	11	9.23	2	14	3.	2	15	10.68	2	17	6.39
4000	3	7	11.32	3	10	1.64	3	12	4.	3	14	6.24	3	16	8.52
5000	4	4	11.15	4	7	8.05	4	10	5.	4	13	1.80	4	15	10.65

Prin.	36 Days.			37 Days.			38 Days.			39 Days.			40 Days.		
£.	£.	s.	d.pts	£.	s.	d.pts	£.	s.	d.pts	£.	s.	d.pts	£.	s.	d.pts
1	0	0	0.23	0	0	0.24	0	0	0.24	0	0	0.25	0	0	0.26
2	—	—	.47	—	—	.48	—	—	.49	—	—	.51	—	—	.52
3	—	—	.71	—	—	.72	—	—	.75	—	—	.76	—	—	.78
4	—	—	.94	—	—	.97	—	—	1.—	—	—	1.02	—	—	1.05
5	—	—	1.13	—	—	1.21	—	—	1.25	—	—	1.28	—	—	1.31
6	—	—	1.42	—	—	1.45	—	—	1.50	—	—	1.53	—	—	1.57
7	—	—	1.65	—	—	1.70	—	—	1.74	—	—	1.79	—	—	1.84
8	—	—	1.89	—	—	1.94	—	—	2.—	—	—	2.05	—	—	2.10
9	—	—	2.13	—	—	2.18	—	—	2.24	—	—	2.30	—	—	2.36
10	—	—	2.36	—	—	2.42	—	—	2.50	—	—	2.56	—	—	2.63
11	—	—	2.60	—	—	2.67	—	—	2.74	—	—	2.82	—	—	2.89
12	—	—	2.81	—	—	2.91	—	—	3.—	—	—	3.07	—	—	3.15
13	—	—	3.07	—	—	3.16	—	—	3.24	—	—	3.33	—	—	3.41
14	—	—	3.31	—	—	3.40	—	—	3.49	—	—	3.59	—	—	3.68
15	—	—	3.55	—	—	3.64	—	—	3.74	—	—	3.84	—	—	3.94
16	—	—	3.78	—	—	3.89	—	—	4.—	—	—	4.10	—	—	4.20
17	—	—	4.02	—	—	4.13	—	—	4.24	—	—	4.35	—	—	4.47
18	—	—	4.26	—	—	4.37	—	—	4.49	—	—	4.61	—	—	4.73
19	—	—	4.49	—	—	4.62	—	—	4.74	—	—	4.87	—	—	4.99
20	—	—	4.73	—	—	4.86	—	—	5.—	—	—	5.12	—	—	5.26
21	—	—	4.97	—	—	5.10	—	—	5.24	—	—	5.38	—	—	5.52
22	—	—	5.20	—	—	5.35	—	—	5.49	—	—	5.64	—	—	5.78
23	—	—	5.44	—	—	5.59	—	—	5.74	—	—	5.89	—	—	6.04
24	—	—	5.68	—	—	5.83	—	—	6.—	—	—	6.15	—	—	6.31
25	—	—	5.91	—	—	6.08	—	—	6.24	—	—	6.41	—	—	6.57
26	—	—	6.15	—	—	6.32	—	—	6.49	—	—	6.66	—	—	6.83
27	—	—	6.39	—	—	6.56	—	—	6.74	—	—	6.92	—	—	7.10
28	—	—	6.62	—	—	6.81	—	—	7.—	—	—	7.18	—	—	7.36
29	—	—	6.86	—	—	7.05	—	—	7.24	—	—	7.43	—	—	7.62
30	—	—	7.10	—	—	7.29	—	—	7.49	—	—	7.69	—	—	7.89
40	—	—	9.46	—	—	9.73	—	—	10.—	—	—	10.25	—	—	10.52
50	—	—	11.83	—	1	0.16	—	1	0.49	—	1	0.82	—	1	1.15
60	—	1	2.20	—	1	2.59	—	1	3.—	—	1	3.38	—	1	3.78
70	—	1	4.56	—	1	5.02	—	1	5.40	—	1	5.95	—	1	6.41
80	—	1	6.93	—	1	7.46	—	1	8.—	—	1	8.51	—	1	9.04
90	—	1	9.30	—	1	9.89	—	1	10.48	—	1	11.07	—	1	11.67
100	—	1	11.67	—	2	0.32	—	2	1.—	—	2	1.62	—	2	2.30
200	—	3	11.34	—	4	0.65	—	4	2.—	—	4	3.28	—	4	4.60
300	—	5	11.01	—	6	1.—	—	6	3.—	—	6	5.—	—	6	6.90
400	—	7	10.68	—	8	1.31	—	8	4.—	—	8	6.57	—	8	9.20
500	—	9	10.35	—	10	1.64	—	10	5.—	—	10	8.21	—	10	11.50
600	—	11	10.02	—	12	2.—	—	12	6.—	—	12	9.85	—	13	1.80
700	—	13	9.69	—	14	2.29	—	14	7.—	—	14	11.50	—	15	4.10
800	—	15	9.36	—	16	2.62	—	16	8.—	—	17	1.14	—	17	6.40
900	—	17	9.03	—	18	3.—	—	18	9.—	—	19	2.78	—	19	8.70
1000	—	19	8.71	1	0	3.25	1	0	10.—	1	1	4.43	1	1	11.01
2000	1	19	5.42	2	0	6.56	2	1	7.72	2	2	8.86	2	3	10.02
3000	2	19	2.13	3	0	9.82	3	2	5.58	3	4	1.29	3	5	9.03
4000	3	18	10.84	4	1	1.12	4	3	3.41	4	5	5.72	4	7	8.04
5000	4	18	7.55	5	1	4.40	5	4	1.30	5	6	10.15	5	9	7.05

Prin.	41 Days.			42 Days.			43 Days.			44 Days			45 Days.		
£.	£.	s.	d.pts	£.	s.	d.pts	£.	s.	d.pts	£.	s.	d.pts	£.	s.	d.pts
1	0	0	0.27	0	0	0.27	0	0	0.28	0	0	0.28	0	0	0.29
2	—	—	—.53	—	—	—.55	—	—	—.56	—	—	—.57	—	—	—.59
3	—	—	—.80	—	—	—.82	—	—	—.84	—	—	—.86	—	—	—.88
4	—	—	1.07	—	—	1.10	—	—	1.13	—	—	1.15	—	—	1.18
5	—	—	1.34	—	—	1.38	—	—	1.41	—	—	1.44	—	—	1.47
6	—	—	1.61	—	—	1.65	—	—	1.69	—	—	1.73	—	—	1.77
7	—	—	1.88	—	—	1.93	—	—	1.97	—	—	2.02	—	—	2.07
8	—	—	2.15	—	—	2.20	—	—	2.26	—	—	2.31	—	—	2.36
9	—	—	2.42	—	—	2.48	—	—	2.54	—	—	2.60	—	—	[illegible]
10	—	—	2.69	—	—	2.76	—	—	2.82	—	—	2.89	—	—	2.95
11	—	—	2.96	—	—	3.03	—	—	3.11	—	—	3.18	—	—	3.25
12	—	—	3.23	—	—	3.31	—	—	3.39	—	—	3.47	—	—	3.55
13	—	—	3.50	—	—	3.59	—	—	3.67	—	—	3.76	—	—	3.84
14	—	—	3.77	—	—	3.86	—	—	3.95	—	—	4.05	—	—	4.14
15	—	—	4.04	—	—	4.14	—	—	4.24	—	—	4.33	—	—	4.43
16	—	—	4.31	—	—	4.41	—	—	4.52	—	—	4.62	—	—	4.73
17	—	—	4.58	—	—	4.69	—	—	4.80	—	—	4.91	—	—	5.03
18	—	—	4.85	—	—	4.97	—	—	5.08	—	—	5.20	—	—	5.32
19	—	—	5.12	—	—	5.24	—	—	5.37	—	—	5.49	—	—	5.62
20	—	—	5.39	—	—	5.52	—	—	5.65	—	—	5.78	—	—	5.91
21	—	—	5.66	—	—	5.80	—	—	5.93	—	—	6.07	—	—	6.21
22	—	—	5.93	—	—	6.07	—	—	6.22	—	—	6.36	—	—	6.50
23	—	—	6.20	—	—	6.35	—	—	6.50	—	—	6.65	—	—	6.80
24	—	—	6.46	—	—	6.62	—	—	6.78	—	—	6.94	—	—	7.10
25	—	—	6.73	—	—	6.90	—	—	7.06	—	—	7.23	—	—	7.39
26	—	—	7.—	—	—	7.18	—	—	7.35	—	—	7.52	—	—	7.69
27	—	—	7.27	—	—	7.45	—	—	7.63	—	—	7.81	—	—	7.98
28	—	—	7.54	—	—	7.73	—	—	7.91	—	—	8.10	—	—	8.28
29	—	—	7.81	—	—	8.—	—	—	8.19	—	—	8.38	—	—	8.58
30	—	—	8.08	—	—	8.28	—	—	8.48	—	—	8.67	—	—	8.87
40	—	—	10.78	—	—	11.04	—	—	11.30	—	—	11.57	—	—	11.83
50	—	1	1.47	—	1	1.80	—	1	2.13	—	1	2.46	—	1	2.79
60	—	1	4.17	—	1	4.56	—	1	4.96	—	1	5.35	—	1	5.75
70	—	1	6.87	—	1	7.33	—	1	7.79	—	1	8.25	—	1	8.71
80	—	1	9.56	—	1	10.08	—	1	10.61	—	1	11.14	—	1	11.67
90	—	2	0.26	—	2	0.85	—	2	1.44	—	2	2.03	—	2	2.63
100	—	2	3.—	—	2	3.61	—	2	4.27	—	2	4.93	—	2	5.58
200	—	4	6.—	—	4	7.23	—	4	8.54	—	4	9.86	—	4	11.17
300	—	6	8.87	—	6	10.84	—	7	0.82	—	7	2.79	—	7	4.71
400	—	8	11.83	—	9	2.46	—	9	5.09	—	9	7.72	—	9	10.3
500	—	11	2.79	—	11	6.08	—	11	9.37	—	12	0.65	—	12	3.9
600	—	13	5.74	—	13	9.69	—	14	1.64	—	14	5.58	—	14	9.5
700	—	15	8.70	—	16	1.31	—	16	5.91	—	16	10.51	—	17	3.1
800	—	17	11.66	—	18	4.92	—	18	10.19	—	19	3.41	—	19	8.7
900	1	0	2.62	1	0	8.54	1	1	2.46	1	1	8.37	1	2	2.31
1000	1	2	5.58	1	3	0.1[illegible]	1	3	6.74	1	4	1.31	1	4	7.89
2000	2	4	11.16	2	6	0.32	2	7	1.48	2	8	2.62	2	9	3.78
3000	3	7	4.74	3	9	0.46	3	10	8.22	3	12	3.93	3	13	11.67
4000	4	9	10.32	4	12	0.64	4	14	2.96	4	16	5.24	4	18	7.56
5000	5	12	3.90	5	15	0.80	5	17	9.70	6	0	6.55	6	3	3.45

Prin.	46 Days.			47 Days.			48 Days.			49 Days.			50 Days.		
£.	£.	s.	d pts	£.	s.	d.pts	£.	s.	d.pts	£.	s.	d.pts	£.	s.	d.pts
1	0	0	0.30	0	0	0.31	0	0	0.31	0	0	0.32	0	0	0.32
2	——		—.60	——		—.61	——		—.63	——		—.64	——		—.65
3	——		—.90	——		—.92	——		—.94	——		—.96	——		—.98
4	——		1.20	——		1.23	——		1.26	——		1.28	——		1.31
5	——		1.51	——		1.54	——		1.57	——		1.61	——		1.64
6	——		1.81	——		1.85	——		1.89	——		1.93	——		1.97
7	——		2.11	——		2.16	——		2.20	——		2.25	——		2.30
8	——		2.41	——		2.47	——		2.52	——		2.57	——		2.63
9	——		2.72	——		2.78	——		2.84	——		2.89	——		2.95
10	——		3.02	——		3.09	——		3.15	——		3.22	——		3.28
11	——		3.32	——		3.39	——		3.47	——		3.54	——		3.61
12	——		3.62	——		3.70	——		3.78	——		3.86	——		3.94
13	——		3.93	——		4.01	——		4.10	——		4.18	——		4.27
14	——		4.23	——		4.32	——		4.41	——		4.51	——		4.60
15	——		4.53	——		4.63	——		4.73	——		4.83	——		4.93
16	——		4.83	——		4.94	——		5.04	——		5.15	——		5.26
17	——		5.14	——		5.25	——		5.36	——		5.47	——		5.58
18	——		5.44	——		5.56	——		5.68	——		5.79	——		5.91
19	——		5.74	——		5.87	——		6.—	——		6.12	——		6.24
20	——		6.04	——		6.18	——		6.31	——		6.44	——		6.57
21	——		6.35	——		6.48	——		6.62	——		6.76	——		6.90
22	——		6.65	——		6.79	——		6.94	——		7.08	——		7.23
23	——		6.95	——		7.10	——		7.25	——		7.41	——		7.56
24	——		7.25	——		7.41	——		7.57	——		7.73	——		7.89
25	——		7.56	——		7.72	——		7.89	——		8.05	——		8.21
26	——		7.86	——		8.03	——		8.20	——		8.37	——		8.54
27	——		8.16	——		8.34	——		8.52	——		8.69	——		8.87
28	——		8.46	——		8.65	——		8.83	——		9.02	——		9.20
29	——		8.77	——		8.96	——		9.15	——		9.34	——		9.53
30	——		9.07	——		9.27	——		9.46	——		9.66	——		9.86
40	—	1	0.09	—	1	0.36	—	1	0.62	—	1	0.88	—	1	1.15
50	—	1	3.12	—	1	3.45	—	1	3.78	—	1	4.10	—	1	4.43
60	—	1	6.14	—	1	6.54	—	1	7.—	—	1	7.33	—	1	7.72
70	—	1	9.17	—	1	9.63	—	1	10.09	—	1	10.53	—	1	11.01
80	—	2	0.19	—	2	0.72	—	2	1.24	—	2	1.77	—	2	2.30
90	—	2	3.22	—	2	3.81	—	2	4.40	—	2	4.99	—	2	5.58
100	—	2	6.24	—	2	6.90	—	2	7.56	—	2	8.21	—	2	8.87
200	—	5	0.49	—	5	1.8[illegible]	—	5	3.12	—	5	4.43	—	5	5.75
300	—	7	6.73	—	7	8.71	—	7	10.68	—	8	0.63	—	8	2.62
400	—	10	1.—	—	10	3.61	—	10	6.24	—	10	8.87	—	10	11.50
500	—	12	7.23	—	12	10.52	—	13	1.80	—	13	5.09	—	15	8.38
600	—	15	1.47	—	15	5.42	—	15	9.36	—	16	1.31	—	16	[illegible]
700	—	17	7.72	—	18	0.32	—	18	4.92	—	18	9.53	—	19	2.13
800	1	0	1.96	1	0	7.23	1	1	0.48	1	1	5.75	1	1	[illegible]
900	1	2	8.21	1	3	2.13	1	3	8.04	1	4	1.97	1	4	7.8[illegible]
1000	1	5	2.46	1	5	9.04	1	6	3.61	1	6	10.19	1	7	[illegible]
2000	2	10	4.92	2	11	6.08	2	12	7.22	2	13	8.38	2	14	9.52
3000	3	15	7.38	3	17	3.12	3	18	10.83	4	0	6.57	4	[illegible]	2.2[illegible]
4000	5	0	9.84	5	3	0.16	5	5	2.44	5	7	4.7[illegible]	5	9	7.04
5000	6	6	0.30	6	8	9.20	6	11	6.05	6	14	[illegible]	6	1[illegible]	11.[illegible]

Prin.	51 Days.			52 Days.			53 Days.			54 Days.			55 Days.		
£.	£.	s.	d.pts	£.	s.	d.pts	£.	s.	d.pts	£.	s.	d.pts	£.	s.	d.pts
1	0	0	0.33	0	0	0.34	0	0	0.34	0	0	0.35	0	0	0.36
2	—	—	.67	—	—	.68	—	—	.69	—	—	.71	—	—	.72
3	—	—	1.—	—	—	1.02	—	—	1.04	—	—	1.06	—	—	1.08
4	—	—	1.34	—	—	1.36	—	—	1.39	—	—	1.42	—	—	1.44
5	—	—	1.67	—	—	1.70	—	—	1.74	—	—	1.77	—	—	1.80
6	—	—	2.01	—	—	2.05	—	—	2.09	—	—	2.13	—	—	2.16
7	—	—	2.34	—	—	2.39	—	—	2.43	—	—	2.48	—	—	2.53
8	—	—	2.68	—	—	2.73	—	—	2.78	—	—	2.84	—	—	2.89
9	—	—	3.0	—	—	3.07	—	—	3.13	—	—	3.19	—	—	3.25
10	—	—	3.35	—	—	3.41	—	—	3.4[illegible]	—	—	3.55	—	—	3.61
11	—	—	3.68	—	—	3.76	—	—	3.83	—	—	3.90	—	—	3.97
12	—	—	4.0[illegible]	—	—	4.10	—	—	4.18	—	—	4.26	—	—	4.33
13	—	—	4.35	—	—	4.44	—	—	4.53	—	—	4.61	—	—	4.70
14	—	—	4.69	—	—	4.78	—	—	4.87	—	—	4.97	—	—	5.06
15	—	—	5.03	—	—	5.12	—	—	5.22	—	—	5.32	—	—	5.42
16	—	—	5.36	—	—	5.47	—	—	5.57	—	—	5.68	—	—	5.78
17	—	—	5.70	—	—	5.81	—	—	5.92	—	—	6.03	—	—	6.14
18	—	—	6.03	—	—	6.15	—	—	6.27	—	—	6.39	—	—	6.50
19	—	—	6.37	—	—	6.49	—	—	6.62	—	—	6.74	—	—	6.87
20	—	—	6.70	—	—	6.83	—	—	6.96	—	—	7.10	—	—	7.23
21	—	—	7.04	—	—	7.18	—	—	7.31	—	—	7.45	—	—	7.59
22	—	—	7.37	—	—	7.52	—	—	7.66	—	—	7.81	—	—	7.95
23	—	—	7.71	—	—	7.86	—	—	8.01	—	—	8.16	—	—	8.31
24	—	—	8.04	—	—	8.20	—	—	8.36	—	—	8.52	—	—	8.67
25	—	—	8.38	—	—	8.54	—	—	8.71	—	—	8.8[illegible]	—	—	9.04
26	—	—	8.71	—	—	8.88	—	—	9.06	—	—	9.23	—	—	9.40
27	—	—	9.05	—	—	9.23	—	—	9.40	—	—	9.58	—	—	9.76
28	—	—	9.38	—	—	9.57	—	—	9.75	—	—	9.94	—	—	10.12
29	—	—	9.72	—	—	9.91	—	—	10.10	—	—	10.29	—	—	10.48
30	—	—	10.05	—	—	10.25	—	—	10.45	—	—	10.65	—	—	10.84
40	—	1	1.4	—	1	1.67	—	1	1.93	—	1	2.2[illegible]	—	1	2.46
50	—	1	4.76	—	1	5.09	—	1	5.42	—	1	5.75	—	1	6.08
60	—	1	8.1	—	1	8.51	—	1	8.90	—	1	9.30	—	1	9.69
70	—	1	11.47	—	1	11.93	—	2	0.39	—	2	0.85	—	2	1.31
80	—	2	2.82	—	2	3.35	—	2	3.87	—	2	4.40	—	2	4.93
90	—	2	6.1[illegible]	—	2	6.77	—	2	7.36	—	2	8.—	—	2	8.54
100	—	2	9.53	—	2	10.19	—	2	10.84	—	2	11.50	—	3	0.16
200	—	5	7.0[illegible]	—	5	8.38	—	5	9.69	—	5	11.0[illegible]	—	6	0.32
300	—	8	4 6	—	8	6.57	—	8	8.54	—	8	10.51	—	9	0.49
400	—	11	2.1[illegible]	—	11	4.76	—	11	7.3[illegible]	—	11	10.02	—	12	0.65
500	—	13	11.6[illegible]	—	14	2.95	—	14	6.2[illegible]	—	14	9.55	—	15	0.82
600	—	16	9.2[illegible]	—	17	1.14	—	16	5.69	—	17	9.03	—	18	0.98
700		19	9.75	—	19	11.33	1	0	3.9[illegible]	1	0	8.54	1	1	1.14
800	1	2	4.27	1	2	9.52	1	3	2.70	1	3	8.04	1	4	1.31
900	1	5	1.[illegible]	1	5	7.71	1	6	1.64	1	6	7.55	1	7	1.47
1000	1	7	11.34	1	8	5.91	1	9	0.49	1	9	7.0[illegible]	1	10	1.64
2000	2	15	10.[illegible]	2	16	11.8[illegible]	2	18	0.98	2	19	2.12	3	0	3.28
3000	4	3	10.[illegible]	4	5	5.73	4	7	1.47	4	8	9.18	4	10	4.92
4000	5	11	9.36	5	13	11.64	5	16	1.96	5	18	4.24	6	0	6.56
5000	6	19	8.7[illegible]	7	2	5.55	7	5	2.45	7	7	11.36	7	10	8.20

Prin.	56 Days.			57 Days.			58 Days.			59 Days.			60 Days.		
£.	£.	s.	d.pts	£.	s.	d.pts	£.	s.	d.pts	£.	s.	d.pts	£.	s.	d.pts
1	0	0	0.36	0	0	0.37	0	0	0.38	0	0	0.38	0	0	0,39
2	——	——	.73	——	——	.74	——	——	.76	——	——	.77	——	——	,78
3	——	——	1.10	——	——	1.12	——	——	1.14	——	——	1.16	——	——	1,18
4	——	——	1.47	——	——	1.49	——	——	1.52	——	——	1.55	——	——	1,57
5	——	——	1.84	——	——	1.87	——	——	1.90	——	——	1.93	——	——	1,97
6	——	——	2.20	——	——	2.24	——	——	2.28	——	——	2.32	——	——	2,36
7	——	——	2.57	——	——	2.62	——	——	2.66	——	——	2.71	——	——	2,76
8	——	——	2.94	——	——	3.—	——	——	3.05	——	——	3.10	——	——	3,15
9	——	——	3.31	——	——	3.37	——	——	3.43	——	——	3.49	——	——	3,55
10	——	——	3.68	——	——	3.74	——	——	3.81	——	——	3.87	——	——	3,94
11	——	——	4.05	——	——	4.12	——	——	4.19	——	——	4.26	——	——	4,33
12	——	——	4.41	——	——	4.49	——	——	4.57	——	——	4.65	——	——	4,73
13	——	——	4.78	——	——	4.87	——	——	4.95	——	——	5.04	——	——	5,12
14	——	——	4.15	——	——	5.24	——	——	5.33	——	——	5.43	——	——	5,52
15	——	——	5.52	——	——	5.62	——	——	5.72	——	——	5.81	——	——	5,91
16	——	——	5.89	——	——	6.—	——	——	6.10	——	——	6.20	——	——	6,31
17	——	——	6.25	——	——	6.37	——	——	6.48	——	——	6.59	——	——	6,70
18	——	——	6.62	——	——	6.74	——	——	6.86	——	——	5.98	——	——	7,10
19	——	——	7.—	——	——	7.12	——	——	7.24	——	——	7.37	——	——	7,49
20	——	——	7.36	——	——	7.49	——	——	7.62	——	——	7.75	——	——	7,89
21	——	——	7.73	——	——	7.87	——	——	8.—	——	——	8.14	——	——	8,28
22	——	——	8.10	——	——	8.24	——	——	8.39	——	——	8.53	——	——	8,67
23	——	——	8.46	——	——	8.62	——	——	8.77	——	——	8.92	——	——	9,07
24	——	——	8.83	——	——	9.—	——	——	9.15	——	——	9.31	——	——	9,46
25	——	——	9.20	——	——	9.37	——	——	9.53	——	——	9.69	——	——	9,86
26	——	——	9.57	——	——	9.74	——	——	9.91	——	——	10.08	——	——	10,25
27	——	——	9.94	——	——	10.11	——	——	10.29	——	——	10.47	——	——	10,65
28	——	——	10t30	——	——	10.49	——	——	10.67	——	——	10.86	——	——	11,04
29	——	——	10.67	——	——	10.86	——	——	11.05	——	——	11.25	——	——	11,44
30	——	——	11.04	——	——	11.24	——	——	11.44	——	——	11.63	——	——	11,83
40	——	1	2.72	——	1	3.—	——	1	3.25	——	1	3.51	——	1	3,78
50	——	1	6.41	——	1	6.73	——	1	7.06	——	1	7.39	——	1	7,72
60	——	1	10.99	——	1	10.48	——	1	10.88	——	1	11.27	——	1	11,67
70	——	2	1.77	——	2	2.23	——	2	2.69	——	2	3.15	——	2	3,61
80	——	2	5.45	——	2	6.—	——	2	6.50	——	2	7.03	——	2	7,56
90	——	2	9.13	——	2	9.73	——	2	10.32	——	2	10.91	——	2	11,50
100	——	3	0.82	——	3	1.47	——	3	2.13	——	3	2.79	——	3	3,45
200	——	6	1.64	——	6	2.95	——	6	4.27	——	6	5.58	——	6	6,90
300	——	9	2.46	——	9	4.43	——	9	6.40	——	9	8.38	——	9	10,35
400	——	12	3.28	——	12	5.91	——	12	8,54	——	12	11.17	——	13	1,80
500	——	15	4.10	——	15	7.39	——	15	10.68	——	16	1.97	——	16	5,26
600	——	18	4.92	——	18	8.87	——	19	0.81	——	19	4.76	——	19	8,71
700	1	1	5.74	1	1	10.35	1	2	2.95	1	2	7.55	1	3	0,16
800	1	4	6.56	1	4	11.83	1	5	5.08	1	5	10.35	1	6	3,61
900	1	7	7.38	1	8	1.31	1	8	7.22	1	9	1.14	1	9	7,06
1000	1	10	8.21	1	11	2.47	1	11	9.36	1	12	3.94	1	12	10,52
2000	3	1	4.42	3	2	5.58	3	3	6.72	3	4	7.88	3	5	9,04
3000	4	12	0.63	4	13	8.37	4	15	4.08	4	16	11.82	4	18	7,56
4000	6	2	8.84	6	4	11.16	6	7	1.44	6	9	3.76	6	11	6,08
5000	7	13	5.05	7	16	1.95	7	18	10.80	8	1	7.70	8	4	4,60

Prin.	61 Days.			62 Days.			63 Days.			64 Days.			65 Days.		
£.	£.	s.	d.pts	£.	s.	d.pts	£.	s.	d.pts	£.	s.	d.pts	£.	s.	d.pts
1	0	0	0.40	0	0	0.40	0	0	0.41	0	0	0.42	0	0	0.43
2	—		—.80	—		—.81	—		—.82	—		—.84	—		—.85
3	—		1.20	—		1.22	—		1.24	—		1.26	—		1,28
4	—		1.60	—		1.63	—		1.65	—		1.68	—		1,70
5	—		2.—	—		2.03	—		2.07	—		2.10	—		2,13
6	—		2.40	—		2.44	—		2.48	—		2.52	—		2,56
7	—		2.80	—		2.85	—		2.89	—		2,94	—		3,—
8	—		3.20	—		3.26	—		3.31	—		3.36	—		3,41
9	—		3.60	—		3.66	—		3.72	—		3.78	—		3.84
10	—		4.01	—		4.07	—		4.14	—		4.20	—		4,27
11	—		4.41	—		4.48	—		4.55	—		4.62	—		4,70
12	—		4.81	—		4.89	—		4.97	—		5.04	—		5,12
13	—		5.21	—		5.29	—		5.38	—		5.47	—		5,55
14	—		5.61	—		5.70	—		5.79	—		5.89	—		5,98
15	—		6.01	—		6.11	—		6.21	—		6.31	—		6,41
16	—		6.41	—		6.52	—		6.62	—		6.73	—		6.83
17	—		6.81	—		6.93	—		7.04	—		7.15	—		7,26
18	—		7.21	—		7.33	—		7.45	—		7.57	—		7,69
19	—		7.62	—		7.74	—		7.87	—		8.—	—		8,12
20	—		8.02	—		8.15	—		8.28	—		8.41	—		8.54
21	—		8.42	—		8.56	—		8.69	—		8.83	—		8,97
22	—		8.82	—		8.96	—		9.11	—		9.25	—		9,40
23	—		9.22	—		9.37	—		9.52	—		9.67	—		9,82
24	—		9.62	—		9.78	—		9.94	—		10.09	—		10,25
25	—		10.02	—		10.19	—		10.35	—		10.52	—		10,68
26	—		10.42	—		10.59	—		10.77	—		10.94	—		11.11
27	—		10.82	—		11.—	—		11.18	—		11.36	—		11.53
28	—		11.23	—		11.41	—		11.59	—		11.78	—		11.96
29	—		11.63	—		11.82	—	1	0.01	—	1	0.20	—	1	0,39
30	—	1	0.03	—	1	0.23	—	1	0.42	—	1	0.62	—	1	0,82
40	—	1	4.94	—	1	4.30	—	1	4.56	—	1	4.83	—	1	5.09
50	—	1	8.05	—	1	8.38	—	1	8.71	—	1	9.04	—	1	9,36
60	—	2	0.06	—	2	0.46	—	2	0.85	—	2	1.24	—	2	1,04
70	—	2	4.07	—	2	4.55	—	2	5.—	—	2	5.45	—	2	5.91
80	—	2	8.08	—	2	8.61	—	2	9.13	—	2	9.66	—	2	10,19
90	—	3	0.09	—	3	0.69	—	3	1.28	—	3	1.87	—	3	2.46
100	—	3	4.10	—	3	4.76	—	3	5.42	—	3	6.08	—	3	6,73
200	—	6	8.21	—	6	9.53	—	6	10.84	—	7	0.16	—	7	1,47
300	—	10	0.32	—	10	2.30	—	10	4.27	—	10	6.24	—	10	8,21
400	—	13	4.43	—	13	7.06	—	13	9.69	—	14	0.32	—	14	2,95
500	—	16	8.54	—	16	11.83	—	17	3.12	—	17	6.41	—	17	9,69
600	1	0	0.65	1	0	4.60	1	0	8.54	1	1	0.49	1	1	4,43
700	1	3	4.76	1	3	9.36	1	4	1.96	1	4	6.57	1	4	11,17
800	1	6	8.87	1	7	2.13	1	7	7.39	1	8	0.65	1	8	5.91
900	1	10	0.98	1	10	6.90	1	11	0.81	1	11	6.73	1	12	0,65
1000	1	13	5.09	1	13	11.67	1	14	6.24	1	15	0.82	1	15	7,39
2000	3	6	10.18	3	7	11.34	3	9	0.48	3	10	1.64	3	11	2,78
3000	5	0	3.27	5	1	11.01	5	3	6.72	5	5	2.46	5	6	10,17
4000	6	13	8.36	6	15	10.68	6	18	0.96	7	0	3.28	7	2	5,56
5000	8	7	1.45	8	9	10.35	8	12	7.20	8	15	4.10	8	18	0,95

Prin.	66 Days.			67 Days.			68 Days.			69 Days.			70 Days.		
£.	£.	s.	d.pts	£.	s.	d.pts	£.	s.	d.pts	£.	s.	d.pts	£.	s.	d.pts
1	0	0	0,43	0	0	0,44	0	0	0.44	0	0	0,45	0	0	0,46
2	—		—,86	—		—,88	—		—,89	—		—,90	—		—,92
3	—		1,30	—		1,32	—		1,34	—		1,36	—		1,38
4	—		1,73	—		1,76	—		1,78	—		1,81	—		1,84
5	—		2,16	—		2,20	—		2,23	—		2,26	—		2,30
6	—		2,60	—		2,64	—		2,68	—		2,77	—		2,76
7	—		3,03	—		3,08	—		3,12	—		3,17	—		3,22
8	—		3,47	—		3,52	—		3,57	—		3,62	—		3,68
9	—		3,90	—		3,96	—		4,02	—		4,08	—		4,14
10	—		4,33	—		4,40	—		4,47	—		4,53	—		4,60
11	—		4,77	—		4,84	—		4,91	—		5,—	—		5,06
12	—		5,20	—		5,28	—		5,36	—		5,45	—		5,52
13	—		5,64	—		5,72	—		5,81	—		5,89	—		5,98
14	—		6,07	—		6,16	—		6,25	—		6,35	—		6,44
15	—		6,50	—		6,60	—		6,70	—		6,80	—		6,90
16	—		6,94	—		7,04	—		7,15	—		7.25	—		7,36
17	—		7,37	—		7,48	—		7,60	—		7,71	—		7,82
18	—		7,81	—		7,92	—		8,04	—		8,16	—		8,28
19	—		8,24	—		8,37	—		8,49	—		8,62	—		8,74
20	—		8,67	—		8,81	—		8,94	—		9,07	—		9,20
21	—		9,11	—		9,25	—		9,38	—		9,52	—		9,66
22	—		9,54	—		8,69	—		9,83	—		9,98	—		10,12
23	—		9,98	—		10,13	—		10.28	—		10,43	—		10,58
24	—		10,41	—		10,57	—		10,73	—		10,88	—		11,04
25	—		10,84	—		11,01	—		11,17	—		11,34	—		11,50
26	—		11,28	—		11,45	—		11,62	—		11,79	—		11,96
27	—		11,71	—		11,89	—	1	0,07	—	1	0,24	—	1	0,42
28	—	1	0,1	—	1	0,33	—	1	0,51	—	1	0,70	—	1	0,88
29	—	1	0,5	—	1	0,77	—	1	0,96	—	1	1,15	—	1	1,34
30	—	1	1,01	—	1	1,21	—	1	1,41	—	1	1,61	—	1	1,80
40	—	1	5,33	—	1	5,62	—	1	5,88	—	1	6,14	—	1	6,41
50	—	1	9,69	—	1	10,02	—	1	10,35	—	1	10,68	—	1	11,01
60	—	2	2,03	—	2	2,43	—	2	2,82	—	2	3,22	—	2	3,61
70	—	2	6,37	—	2	6,83	—	2	7,29	—	2	7,75	—	2	8,21
80	—	2	10,71	—	2	11,24	—	2	11,76	—	3	0,29	—	3	0,82
90	—	3	3,05	—	3	3,64	—	3	4,24	—	3	4,83	—	3	5,42
100	—	3	7,39	—	3	8,05	—	3	8,71	—	3	9,36	—	3	10,02
200	—	7	2,78	—	7	4,10	—	7	5,42	—	7	6,73	—	7	8,05
300	—	10	10,17	—	11	0,16	—	11	2,13	—	11	4,10	—	11	6,08
400	—	14	5,58	—	14	8,21	—	14	5,84	—	15	1,47	—	15	4,10
500	—	18	0,98	—	18	4,27	—	18	7.56	—	18	10,84	—	19	2,13
600	1	1	8,35	1	2	0,32	1	2	4,27	1	2	8,21	1	3	0,16
700	1	5	3,77	1	5	8.37	1	6	0.98	1	6	5,58	1	6	10,18
800	1	8	11,17	1	9	4,43	1	9	9,69	1	10	2,95	1	10	8,21
900	1	12	6,57	1	13	0,48	1	13	6,40	1	14	0,32	1	14	6,24
1000	1	16	1,97	1	16	8.54	1	17	3,12	1	17	9,69	1	18	4,27
2000	3	12	3,94	3	13	5,08	3	14	6,24	3	15	7,38	3	16	8,54
3000	5	8	5,91	5	10	1,62	5	11	9,36	5	13	5,07	5	15	0.81
4000	7	4	7,88	7	6	10,16	7	9	0,48	7	11	2,76	7	13	5,08
5000	9	0	9,85	9	3	6,70	9	6	3,60	9	9	0,45	9	11	9.35

Prin.	71 Days.			72 Days.			73 Days.			74 Days.			75 Days.		
£.	£.	s.	d. pts	£.	s.	d. pts	£.	s.	d. pts	£.	s.	d. pts	£.	s.	d. pts
1	0	0	0,46	0	0	0,47	0	0	0,48	0	0	0,48	0	0	0,49
2	—	—	,93	—	—	,94	—	—	,96	—	—	,97	—	—	,98
3	—	—	1,40	—	—	1,42	—	—	1,44	—	—	1,45	—	—	1,47
4	—	—	1,86	—	—	1,89	—	—	1,92	—	—	1,94	—	—	1,97
5	—	—	2,33	—	—	2,36	—	—	2,40	—	—	2,43	—	—	2,46
6	—	—	2,80	—	—	2,84	—	—	2,88	—	—	2,91	—	—	2,95
7	—	—	3,26	—	—	3,31	—	—	3,36	—	—	3,40	—	—	3,4[illegible]
8	—	—	3,73	—	—	3,78	—	—	3,84	—	—	3,89	—	—	3,94
9	—	—	4,2[illegible]	—	—	4,26	—	—	4,32	—	—	4,37	—	—	4,43
10	—	—	4,66	—	—	4,73	—	—	4,80	—	—	4,86	—	—	4,93
11	—	—	5,13	—	—	5,20	—	—	5,28	—	—	5,35	—	—	5,42
12	—	—	5,6[illegible]	—	—	5,68	—	—	5,76	—	—	5,83	—	—	5,91
13	—	—	6,06	—	—	6,15	—	—	6,24	—	—	6,32	—	—	6,41
14	—	—	6,53	—	—	6,62	—	—	6,72	—	—	6,81	—	—	6,9[illegible]
15	—	—	7,—	—	—	7,10	—	—	7,20	—	—	7,29	—	—	7,39
16	—	—	7,46	—	—	7,57	—	—	7,68	—	—	7,78	—	—	7,8[illegible]
17	—	—	7,93	—	—	8,04	—	—	8,16	—	—	8,27	—	—	8,38
18	—	—	8,40	—	—	8,52	—	—	8,64	—	—	8,75	—	—	8,8[illegible]
19	—	—	8,86	—	—	9,—	—	—	9,12	—	—	9,24	—	—	9,36
20	—	—	9,33	—	—	9,46	—	—	9,60	—	—	9,73	—	—	9,86
21	—	—	9,80	—	—	9,94	—	—	10,08	—	—	10,21	—	—	10,35
22	—	—	10,27	—	—	10,41	—	—	10,56	—	—	10,70	—	—	10,84
23	—	—	10,73	—	—	10,88	—	—	11,04	—	—	11,19	—	—	11,34
24	—	—	11,20	—	—	11,36	—	—	11,52	—	—	11,67	—	—	11,83
25	—	—	11,67	—	—	11,83	—	1	0,—	—	1	0,16	—	1	0,3[illegible]
26	—	1	0,13	—	1	0,30	—	1	0,48	—	1	0,65	—	1	0,82
27	—	1	0,60	—	1	0,78	—	1	0,96	—	1	1,13	—	1	1,31
28	—	1	1,07	—	1	1,25	—	1	1,44	—	1	1,62	—	1	1,80
29	—	1	1,53	—	1	1,72	—	1	1,92	—	1	2,11	—	1	2,3[illegible]
30	—	1	2,—	—	1	2,20	—	1	2,40	—	1	2,59	—	1	2,79
40	—	1	6,66	—	1	6,93	—	1	7,20	—	1	7,46	—	1	7,73
50	—	1	11,34	—	1	11,67	—	2	0,—	—	2	0,32	—	2	0,65
60	—	2	4,01	—	2	4,49	—	2	4,80	—	2	5,19	—	2	5,58
70	—	2	8,67	—	2	9,13	—	2	9,60	—	2	10,05	—	2	10,53
80	—	3	1,34	—	3	1,87	—	3	2,40	—	3	2,92	—	3	3,45
90	—	3	6,01	—	3	6,60	—	3	7,20	—	3	7,70	—	3	8,3[illegible]
100	—	3	10,68	—	3	11,34	—	4	0,—	—	4	0,65	—	4	1,31
200	—	7	9,36	—	7	10,68	—	8	0,—	—	8	1,31	—	8	2,6[illegible]
300	—	11	8,05	—	11	10,02	—	12	0,—	—	12	1,97	—	12	3,94
400	—	15	6,73	—	15	9,36	—	16	0,—	—	16	2,62	—	16	5,26
500	—	19	5,42	—	19	8,71	1	0	0,—	1	0	3,28	1	0	6,57
600	1	3	4,10	1	3	8,05	1	4	0,—	1	4	3,94	1	4	7,89
700	1	7	2,78	1	7	7,39	1	8	0,—	1	8	4,59	1	8	9,20
800	1	11	1,47	1	11	6,73	1	12	0,—	1	12	5,25	1	12	10,52
900	1	15	0,15	1	15	6,07	1	16	0,—	1	16	5,91	1	16	11,83
1000	1	18	10,84	1	19	5,42	2	0	0,—	2	0	6,57	2	1	1,15
2000	3	17	9,68	3	18	10,84	4	0	0,—	4	1	1,14	4	2	2,3[illegible]
3000	5	16	8,52	5	18	4,26	6	0	0,—	6	1	7,71	6	3	3,45
4000	7	15	7,36	7	17	9,68	8	0	0,—	8	2	2,28	8	4	4,60
5000	9	14	6,20	9	17	3,10	10	0	0,—	10	2	8,85	10	5	5,7[illegible]

Prin.	76 Days.			77 Days.			78 Days.			79 Days.			80 Days.		
£.	£.	s.	d.pts	£.	s.	d.pts	£.	s.	d.pts	£.	s.	d.pts	£.	s.	d.pts
1	0	0	0.49	0	0	0.50	0	0	0.51	0	0	0.52	0	0	0.52
2	—	—	.96	—	—	1.01	—	—	1.02	—	—	1.03	—	—	1.05
3	—	—	1.49	—	—	1.51	—	—	1.53	—	—	1.55	—	—	1.57
4	—	—	1.99	—	—	2.02	—	—	2.05	—	—	2.07	—	—	2.10
5	—	—	2.49	—	—	2.53	—	—	2.56	—	—	2.59	—	—	2.63
6	—	—	2.99	—	—	3.03	—	—	3.07	—	—	3.11	—	—	3.15
7	—	—	3.49	—	—	3.54	—	—	3.59	—	—	3.63	—	—	3.68
8	—	—	3.99	—	—	4.0[illegible]	—	—	4.10	—	—	4.15	—	—	4.20
9	—	—	4.49	—	—	4.55	—	—	4.61	—	—	4.67	—	—	4.73
10	—	—	4.99	—	—	5.06	—	—	5.12	—	—	5.19	—	—	5.26
11	—	—	5.49	—	—	5.56	—	—	5.64	—	—	5.71	—	—	5.78
12	—	—	5.99	—	—	6.07	—	—	6.15	—	—	6.23	—	—	6.31
13	—	—	6.49	—	—	6.58	—	—	6.66	—	—	6.75	—	—	6.83
14	—	—	6.99	—	—	7.08	—	—	7.18	—	—	7.27	—	—	7.36
15	—	—	7.49	—	—	7.59	—	—	7.69	—	—	7.79	—	—	7.89
16	—	—	7.99	—	—	8.10	—	—	8.20	—	—	8.31	—	—	8.41
17	—	—	8.49	—	—	8.60	—	—	8.71	—	—	8.83	—	—	8.94
18	—	—	8.99	—	—	9.11	—	—	9.23	—	—	9.35	—	—	9.46
19	—	—	9.49	—	—	9.61	—	—	9.74	—	—	9.86	—	—	10.—
20	—	—	9.99	—	—	10.12	—	—	10.25	—	—	10.38	—	—	10.52
21	—	—	10.49	—	—	10.63	—	—	10.77	—	—	10.90	—	—	11.04
22	—	—	10.99	—	—	11.13	—	—	11.28	—	—	11.42	—	—	11.57
23	—	—	11.49	—	—	11.64	—	—	11.79	—	—	11.94	—	1	0.09
24	—	—	11.99	—	1	0.15	—	1	0.30	—	1	0.46	—	1	0.62
25	—	1	0.49	—	1	0.65	—	1	0.62	—	1	0.98	—	1	1.15
26	—	1	0.99	—	1	1.16	—	1	1.33	—	1	1.50	—	1	1.67
27	—	1	1.49	—	1	1.67	—	1	1.84	—	1	2.02	—	1	2.20
28	—	1	1.99	—	1	2.17	—	1	2.36	—	1	2.54	—	1	2.72
29	—	1	2.49	—	1	2.68	—	1	2.87	—	1	3.06	—	1	3.25
30	—	1	2.99	—	1	3.18	—	1	3.38	—	1	3.58	—	1	3.78
40	—	1	7.98	—	1	3.25	—	1	8.51	—	1	8.77	—	1	9.04
50	—	2	0.98	—	2	1.31	—	2	1.64	—	2	1.97	—	2	2.30
60	—	2	5.98	—	2	6.37	—	2	6.77	—	2	7.16	—	2	7.56
70	—	2	10.98	—	2	11.44	—	2	11.93	—	3	0.36	—	3	0.82
80	—	3	3.97	—	3	4.50	—	3	5.02	—	3	5.55	—	3	6.08
90	—	3	8.97	—	3	9.56	—	3	10.15	—	3	10.75	—	3	11.34
100	—	4	1.97	—	4	2.63	—	4	3.28	—	4	3.94	—	4	4.60
200	—	8	3.94	—	8	5.26	—	8	6.57	—	8	7.89	—	8	9.2[illegible]
300	—	12	5.91	—	12	7.89	—	12	9.86	—	12	11.83	—	13	1.80
400	—	16	7.88	—	16	10.52	—	17	1.14	—	17	3.78	—	17	6.40
500	1	0	9.86	1	1	1.15	1	1	4.43	1	1	7.72	1	1	11.[illegible]
600	1	4	11.83	1	5	3.78	1	5	7.72	1	5	11.67	1	6	3.61
700	1	9	1.80	1	9	6.41	1	9	1[illegible]	1	10	3.61	1	10	8.21
800	1	13	3.77	1	13	9.04	1	14	2.29	1	14	7.56	1	15	0.31
900	1	17	5.74	1	17	11.67	1	18	5.58	1	18	11.50	1	19	5.41
1000	2	1	7.72	2	2	2.30	2	2	8.87	2	3	3.45	2	3	10.02
2000	4	3	3.44	4	4	4.60	4	5	5.74	4	6	6.90	4	7	8.04
3000	6	4	11.16	6	6	6.90	6	8	2.61	6	9	10.35	6	11	6.06
4000	8	6	6.88	8	8	9.20	8	10	11.48	8	13	1.80	8	15	4.[illegible]
5000	10	8	2.60	10	10	11.50	10	13	8.25	10	16	5.35	10	19	2.10

Prin.	81 Days.			82 Days.			83 Days.			84 Days.			85 Days.		
£.	£.	s.	d.pts	£.	s.	d.pts	£.	s.	d.pts	£.	s.	d.pts	£.	s.	d.pts
1	0	0	0.53	0	0	0.53	0	0	0.54	0	0	0.55	0	0	0.55
2	——		1.06	——		1.07	——		1.09	——		1.10	——		1.11
3	——		1.59	——		1.61	——		1.63	——		1.65	——		1.67
4	——		2.13	——		2.15	——		2.18	——		2.20	——		2.23
5	——		2.66	——		2.69	——		2.72	——		2.76	——		2.79
6	——		3.19	——		3.23	——		3.27	——		3.31	——		3.35
7	——		3.72	——		3.77	——		3.82	——		3.86	——		3.91
8	——		4.26	——		4.31	——		4.36	——		4.41	——		4.47
9	——		4.79	——		4.85	——		4.91	——		4.97	——		5.03
10	——		5.32	——		5.39	——		5.45	——		5.52	——		5.58
11	——		5.85	——		5.93	——		6.—	——		6.07	——		6.14
12	——		6.39	——		6.47	——		6.54	——		6.62	——		6.70
13	——		6.92	——		7.—	——		7.09	——		7.18	——		7.26
14	——		7.45	——		7.54	——		7.64	——		7.73	——		7.82
15	——		7.98	——		8.08	——		8.18	——		8.28	——		8.38
16	——		8.52	——		8.62	——		8.73	——		8.83	——		8.94
17	——		9.05	——		9.16	——		9.27	——		9.38	——		9.50
18	——		9.58	——		9.70	——		9.82	——		9.94	——		10.06
19	——		10.11	——		10.24	——		10.36	——		10.49	——		10.61
20	——		10.65	——		10.78	——		10.91	——		11.04	——		11.17
21	——		11.18	——		11.32	——		11.46	——		11.55	——		11.73
22	——		11.71	——		11.86	—	1	0.—	—	1	0.15	—	1	0.29
23	—	1	0.24	—	1	0.40	—	1	0.55	—	1	0.70	—	1	0.85
24	—	1	0.78	—	1	0.94	—	1	1.09	—	1	1.25	—	1	1.41
25	—	1	1.31	—	1	1.47	—	1	1.64	—	1	1.80	—	1	1.97
26	—	1	1.84	—	1	2.01	—	1	2.18	—	1	2.36	—	1	2.53
27	—	1	2.38	—	1	2.55	—	1	2.73	—	1	2.91	—	1	3.09
28	—	1	2.91	—	1	3.09	—	1	3.28	—	1	3.46	—	1	3.64
29	—	1	3.44	—	1	3.63	—	1	3.82	—	1	4.01	—	1	4.20
30	—	1	3.97	—	1	4.17	—	1	4.37	—	1	4.56	—	1	4.76
40	—	1	9.30	—	1	9.56	—	1	9.83	—	1	10.09	—	1	10.35
50	—	2	2.63	—	2	2.95	—	2	3.28	—	2	3.61	—	2	3.94
60	—	2	7.95	—	2	8.35	—	2	8.74	—	2	9.13	—	2	9.53
70	—	3	1.28	—	3	1.74	—	3	2.20	—	3	2.66	—	3	3.12
80	—	3	6.60	—	3	7.13	—	3	7.66	—	3	8.18	—	3	8.71
90	—	3	11.93	—	4	0.52	—	4	1.11	—	4	1.70	—	4	2.30
100	—	4	5.26	—	4	5.91	—	4	6.57	—	4	7.23	—	4	7.89
200	—	8	10.52	—	8	11.83	—	9	1.15	—	9	2.46	—	9	3.78
300	—	13	3.78	—	13	5.75	—	13	7.72	—	13	9.69	—	13	11.67
400	—	17	9.04	—	17	11.66	—	18	2.30	—	18	4.92	—	18	7.56
500	1	2	2.30	1	2	5.58	1	2	8.87	1	3	0.16	1	3	3.45
600	1	6	7.56	1	6	11.50	1	7	3.45	1	7	7.39	1	7	11.34
700	1	11	0.82	1	11	5.41	1	11	10.02	1	12	2.62	1	12	7.23
800	1	15	6.08	1	15	11.33	1	16	4.60	1	16	9.85	1	17	3.12
900	1	19	11.34	2	0	5.25	2	0	11.17	2	1	5.08	2	1	11.01
1000	2	4	4.60	2	4	11.17	2	5	5.75	2	6	0.32	2	6	6.90
2000	4	8	9.20	4	9	10.34	4	10	11.50	4	12	0.64	4	13	1.80
3000	6	13	1.80	6	14	9.51	6	16	5.25	6	18	0.96	6	19	8.70
4000	8	17	6.40	8	19	8.68	9	1	11.—	9	4	1.28	9	6	3.60
5000	11	1	11.—	11	4	7.85	11	7	4.75	11	10	1.60	11	12	10.50

Prin.	86 Days.			87 Days.			88 Days.			89 Days.			90 Days.		
£.	£.	s.	d.pts	£.	s.	d.pts	£.	s.	d.pts	£.	s.	d.pts	£.	s.	d.pts
1	0	0	0.56	0	0	0.57	0	0	0.57	0	0	0.58	0	0	0.59
2	—		1.13	—		1.14	—		1.15	—		1.17	—		1.18
3	—		1.69	—		1.71	—		1.73	—		1.75	—		1.77
4	—		2.26	—		2.28	—		2.31	—		2.34	—		2.36
5	—		2.82	—		2.86	—		2.89	—		2.92	—		2.95
6	—		3.39	—		3.43	—		3.47	—		3.51	—		3.55
7	—		3.95	—		4.—	—		4.05	—		4.09	—		4.14
8	—		4.52	—		4.57	—		4.62	—		4.68	—		4.73
9	—		5.08	—		5.14	—		5.20	—		5.26	—		5.32
10	—		5.65	—		5.72	—		5.78	—		5.85	—		5.91
11	—		6.22	—		6.29	—		6.36	—		6.43	—		6.50
12	—		6.78	—		6.86	—		6.94	—		7.02	—		7.10
13	—		7.35	—		7.43	—		7.52	—		7.60	—		7.69
14	—		7.91	—		8.—	—		8.10	—		8.19	—		8.28
15	—		8.48	—		8.58	—		8.67	—		8.77	—		8.87
16	—		9.04	—		9.15	—		9.25	—		9.36	—		9.46
17	—		9.61	—		9.72	—		9.83	—		9.94	—		10.06
18	—		10.17	—		10.29	—		10.41	—		10.53	—		10.65
19	—		10.74	—		10.86	—		11.—	—		11.11	—		11.24
20	—		11.31	—		11.44	—		11.57	—		11.70	—		11.83
21	—		11.87	—	1	0.01	—	1	0.15	—	1	0.28	—	1	0.42
22	—	1	0.44	—	1	0.58	—	1	0.72	—	1	0.87	—	1	1.01
23	—	1	1.—	—	1	1.15	—	1	1.30	—	1	1.45	—	1	1.61
24	—	1	1.57	—	1	1.72	—	1	1.88	—	1	2.04	—	1	2.20
25	—	1	2.13	—	1	2.30	—	1	2.46	—	1	2.63	—	1	2.79
26	—	1	2.70	—	1	2.87	—	1	3.04	—	1	3.21	—	1	3.38
27	—	1	3.26	—	1	3.44	—	1	3.62	—	1	3.80	—	1	3.97
28	—	1	3.83	—	1	4.01	—	1	4.20	—	1	4.38	—	1	4.56
29	—	1	4.39	—	1	4.58	—	1	4.78	—	1	4.97	—	1	5.16
30	—	1	4.96	—	1	5.16	—	1	5.35	—	1	5.55	—	1	5.75
40	—	1	10.61	—	1	10.88	—	1	11.14	—	1	11.40	—	1	11.67
50	—	2	4.27	—	2	4.60	—	2	4.93	—	2	5.26	—	2	5.58
60	—	2	9.92	—	2	10.32	—	2	10.71	—	2	11.11	—	2	11.50
70	—	3	3.58	—	3	4.04	—	3	4.50	—	3	4.96	—	3	5.42
80	—	3	9.23	—	3	9.76	—	3	10.20	—	3	10.81	—	3	11.34
90	—	4	2.89	—	4	3.48	—	4	4.07	—	4	4.66	—	4	5.26
100	—	4	8.54	—	4	9.20	—	4	9.86	—	4	10.52	—	4	11.17
200	—	9	5.09	—	9	6.41	—	9	7.72	—	9	9.04	—	9	10.35
300	—	14	1.64	—	14	3.61	—	14	5.58	—	14	7.56	—	14	9.53
400	—	18	10.18	—	19	0.82	—	19	3.45	—	19	6.08	—	19	8.71
500	1	3	6.73	1	3	10.02	1	4	1.31	1	4	4.60	1	4	7.89
600	1	8	3.28	1	8	7.23	1	8	11.17	1	9	3.12	1	9	7.06
700	1	12	11.82	1	13	4.43	1	13	9.04	1	14	1.64	1	14	6.24
800	1	17	8.37	1	18	1.67	1	18	6.90	1	19	0.16	1	19	5.42
900	2	2	4.92	2	2	10.84	2	3	4.76	2	3	10.68	2	4	4.60
1000	2	7	1.47	2	7	8.05	2	8	2.63	2	8	9.20	2	9	3.78
2000	4	14	2.94	4	15	4.10	4	16	5.26	4	17	6.40	4	18	7.56
3000	7	1	4.41	7	3	0.15	7	4	7.80	7	6	3.60	7	7	11.34
4000	9	8	5.88	9	10	8.20	9	12	10.52	9	15	0.80	9	17	3.12
5000	11	15	7.35	11	18	4.25	12	1	1.15	12	3	10.—	12	6	6.90

Prin.	91 Days.			92 Days.			93 Days.			94 Days.			95 Days.		
£.	£.	s.	d.pts	£.	s.	d.pts	£.	s.	d.pts	£.	s.	d.pts	£.	s.	d.pts
1	0	0	0.59	0	0	0.60	0	0	0.61	0	0	0.61	0	0	0.62
2	—	—	1.19	—	—	1.20	—	—	1.22	—	—	1.23	—	—	1.24
3	—	—	1.79	—	—	1.81	—	—	1.83	—	—	1.85	—	—	1.87
4	—	—	2.39	—	—	2.41	—	—	2.44	—	—	2.47	—	—	2.49
5	—	—	3.—	—	—	3.02	—	—	3.05	—	—	3.00	—	—	3.12
6	—	—	3.59	—	—	3.62	—	—	3.66	—	—	3.7[illegible]	—	—	3.74
7	—	—	4.18	—	—	4.23	—	—	4.28	—	—	4.3[illegible]	—	—	4.37
8	—	—	4.78	—	—	4.83	—	—	4.89	—	—	4.94	—	—	5.—
9	—	—	5.38	—	—	5.44	—	—	5.50	—	—	5.56	—	—	5.62
10	—	—	5.98	—	—	6.04	—	—	6.11	—	—	6.18	—	—	6.24
11	—	—	6.58	—	—	6.65	—	—	6.72	—	—	6.79	—	—	6.[illegible]
12	—	—	7.18	—	—	7.25	—	—	7.33	—	—	7.4	—	—	7.[illegible]
13	—	—	7.77	—	—	7.86	—	—	7.94	—	—	8.0[illegible]	—	—	8.12
14	—	—	8.37	—	—	8.46	—	—	8.56	—	—	8.65	—	—	8.74
15	—	—	8.97	—	—	9.07	—	—	9.17	—	—	9.2[illegible]	—	—	9.3[illegible]
16	—	—	9.57	—	—	9.67	—	—	9.78	—	—	9.88	—	—	10.—
17	—	—	10.17	—	—	10.28	—	—	10.39	—	—	[illegible]	—	—	10.61
18	—	—	10.77	—	—	10.88	—	—	11.—	—	—	11.[illegible]	—	—	11.24
19	—	—	11.36	—	—	11.49	—	—	11.61	—	—	11.74	—	—	11.86
20	—	1	0.—	—	1	0.09	—	1	0.23	—	1	0.36	—	1	0.49
21	—	1	0.56	—	1	0.70	—	1	0.84	—	1	0.97	—	1	1.11
22	—	1	1.16	—	1	1.30	—	1	1.45	—	1	1.59	—	1	1.74
23	—	1	1.76	—	1	1.91	—	1	2.06	—	1	2.21	—	1	2.36
24	—	1	2.36	—	1	2.51	—	1	2.67	—	1	2.8[illegible]	—	1	3.—
25	—	1	2.95	—	1	3.12	—	1	3.28	—	1	3.45	—	1	3.61
26	—	1	3.55	—	1	3.72	—	1	3.89	—	1	4.07	—	1	4.24
27	—	1	4.15	—	1	4.33	—	1	4.51	—	1	4.68	—	1	4.86
28	—	1	4.75	—	1	4.93	—	1	5.12	—	1	5.30	—	1	5.49
29	—	1	5.35	—	1	5.54	—	1	5.73	—	1	5.9[illegible]	—	1	6.11
30	—	1	5.95	—	1	6.14	—	1	6.34	—	1	6.54	—	1	6.73
40	—	1	11.93	—	2	0.19	—	2	0.46	—	2	0.7[illegible]	—	2	0.93
50	—	2	5.91	—	2	6.24	—	2	6.57	—	2	6.90	—	2	7.23
60	—	2	11.90	—	3	0.29	—	3	0.69	—	3	1.08	—	3	1.47
70	—	3	5.88	—	3	6.3[illegible]	—	3	6.80	—	3	7.26	—	3	7.72
80	—	3	11.86	—	4	0.39	—	4	0.92	—	4	1.44	—	4	1.97
90	—	4	5.85	—	4	6.44	—	4	7.03	—	4	7.64	—	4	8.21
100	—	4	11.83	—	5	0.49	—	5	1.15	—	5	1.80	—	5	2.46
200	—	9	11.67	—	10	0.98	—	10	2.30	—	10	3.61	—	10	4.93
300	—	14	11.50	—	15	1.47	—	15	3.45	—	15	5.42	—	15	6.39
400	—	19	11.34	1	0	1.97	1	0	4.60	1	0	7.23	1	0	9.86
500	1	4	11.17	1	5	2.46	1	5	5.75	1	5	9.04	1	6	0.32
600	1	9	11.01	1	10	2.95	1	10	6.90	1	10	10.84	1	11	2.79
700	1	14	10.84	1	15	3.45	1	15	8.05	1	16	0.65	1	16	5.26
800	1	19	10.68	2	0	3.94	2	0	9.20	2	1	2.46	2	1	7.72
900	2	4	10.51	2	5	4.43	2	5	10.35	2	6	4.27	2	6	10.19
1000	2	9	10.35	2	10	4.93	3	10	11.5[illegible]	2	11	6.08	2	12	0.65
2000	4	19	8.70	5	0	9.86	5	1	11.01	5	3	0.16	5	4	1.31
3000	7	9	0.05	7	11	2.79	7	12	10.57	7	14	6.24	7	16	1.97
4000	9	19	5.40	10	1	7.72	10	3	10.03	10	6	0.32	10	8	2.62
5000	12	9	3.75	12	12	6.6[illegible]	12	14	9.53	12	17	6.41	13	0	3.28

Prin.	96 Days.			97 Days.			98 Days.			99 Days.			100 Days.		
£.	£.	s.	d.pts	£.	s.	d.pts	£.	s.	d.pts	£.	s	d.pts	£.	s.	d.pts
1	0	0	0.63	0	0	0.63	0	0	0.64	0	0	0.65	0	0	0.65
2	—	—	1.26	—	—	1.27	—	—	1.28	—	—	1.30	—	—	1.31
3	—	—	1.89	—	—	1.91	—	—	1.93	—	—	1.95	—	—	1.97
4	—	—	2.52	—	—	2.55	—	—	2.57	—	—	2.60	—	—	2.63
5	—	—	3.15	—	—	3.18	—	—	3.22	—	—	3.25	—	—	3.28
6	—	—	3.78	—	—	3.82	—	—	3.86	—	—	3.90	—	—	3.94
7	—	—	4.41	—	—	4.46	—	—	4.51	—	—	4.55	—	—	4.60
8	—	—	5.0[illegible]	—	—	5.10	—	—	5.15	—	—	5.20	—	—	5.26
9	—	—	5.68	—	—	5.74	—	—	5.80	—	—	5.85	—	—	5.91
10	—	—	6.31	—	—	6.37	—	—	6.44	—	—	6.5[illegible]	—	—	6.57
11	—	—	6.94	—	—	7.01	—	—	7.08	—	—	7.01	—	—	7.23
12	—	—	7.57	—	—	7.65	—	—	7.73	—	—	7.81	—	—	7.89
13	—	—	8.2[illegible]	—	—	8.29	—	—	8.37	—	—	8.46	—	—	8.54
14	—	—	8.8[illegible]	—	—	8.92	—	—	9.02	—	—	9.11	—	—	9.20
15	—	—	9.4[illegible]	—	—	9.56	—	—	9.66	—	—	9.76	—	—	9.86
16	—	—	10.09	—	—	10.20	—	—	10.31	—	—	10.41	—	—	10.52
17	—	—	10.73	—	—	10.84	—	—	10.95	—	—	11.06	—	—	11.17
18	—	—	11.36	—	—	11.48	—	—	11.59	—	—	11.71	—	—	11.83
19	—	1	0.[illegible]	—	1	0.11	—	1	0.24	—	1	0.36	—	1	0.49
20	—	1	0.62	—	1	0.75	—	1	0.88	—	1	1.01	—	1	1.15
21	—	1	1.25	—	1	1.39	—	1	1.53	—	1	1.66	—	1	1.80
22	—	1	1.88	—	1	2.03	—	1	2.17	—	1	2.32	—	1	2.46
23	—	1	2.5[illegible]	—	1	2.66	—	1	2.82	—	1	2.97	—	1	3.12
24	—	1	3.41	—	1	3.30	—	1	3.46	—	1	3.62	—	1	3.78
25	—	1	3.78	—	1	3.94	—	1	4.10	—	1	4.27	—	1	4.43
26	—	1	4.4[illegible]	—	1	4.58	—	1	4.75	—	1	4.92	—	1	5.09
27	—	1	5.04	—	1	5.22	—	1	5.39	—	1	5.57	—	1	5.75
28	—	1	5.6[illegible]	—	1	5.85	—	1	6.04	—	1	6.22	—	1	6.41
29	—	1	6.3[illegible]	—	1	6.49	—	1	6.68	—	1	6.87	—	1	7.06
30	—	1	6.9[illegible]	—	1	7.13	—	1	7.33	—	1	7.52	—	1	7.72
40	—	2	1.2[illegible]	—	2	1.51	—	2	1.77	—	2	2.03	—	2	2.50
50	—	2	7.5[illegible]	—	2	7.89	—	2	8.21	—	2	8.54	—	2	8.87
60	—	3	1.8[illegible]	—	3	2.26	—	3	2.66	—	3	3.05	—	3	3.45
70	—	3	8.1[illegible]	—	3	8.64	—	3	9.10	—	3	9.56	—	3	10.02
80	—	4	2.4[illegible]	—	4	3.[illegible]2	—	4	3.55	—	4	4.07	—	4	4.60
90	—	4	8.8[illegible]	—	4	9.4[illegible]	—	4	9.99	—	5	10.58	—	4	11.17
100	—	5	3.12	—	5	3.78	—	5	4.43	—	5	5.09	—	5	5.75
200	—	10	6.2[illegible]	—	10	7.56	—	10	8.87	—	10	10.19	—	10	11.15
300	—	15	9.3[illegible]	—	15	11.34	—	16	1.31	—	16	3.28	—	16	5.26
400	1	1	0.[illegible]9	1	1	3.12	1	1	5.75	1	1	8.38	1	1	11.01
500	1	6	3.6[illegible]	1	6	6.9[illegible]	1	6	10.19	1	7	1.47	1	7	4.76
600	1	11	6.73	1	1[illegible]	10.68	1	12	2.62	1	12	6.57	1	12	10.52
700	1	16	9.86	1	17	2.46	1	17	7.06	1	17	11.66	1	18	4.27
800	2	2	0.98	2	2	[illegible].24	2	2	11.50	2	3	4.76	2	3	10.02
900	2	7	4.10	2	7	10.02	2	8	3.94	2	8	9.85	2	9	2.77
1000	2	12	7.23	2	13	1.80	2	13	8.35	2	14	2.95	2	14	9.53
2000	5	5	2.46	5	6	3.61	5	7	4.76	5	8	5.91	5	9	7.06
3000	7	17	9.69	7	19	5.42	8	1	1.15	8	2	8.87	8	4	4.60
4000	10	10	4.93	10	12	7.23	10	14	9.53	10	16	11.83	10	19	2.13
5000	13	3	0.16	13	5	9.04	13	8	5.91	13	11	2.79	13	13	11.67

Prin.	101 Days.			102 Days.			103 Days.			104 Days.			105 Days.		
£.	£.	s.	d. pts	£.	s.	d. pts	£.	s.	d. pts	£.	s.	d. pts	£.	s.	d. pts
1	0	0	0.66	0	0	0.67	0	0	0.67	0	0	0.68	0	9	0.69
2	—		1,32	—		1.34	—		1.35	—		1.36	—		1.38
3	—		2.—	—		2.01	—		2.03	—		2.05	—		2.07
4	—		2.65	—		2.68	—		2.70	—		2.73	—		2.76
5	—		3.32	—		3.35	—		3.38	—		3.41	—		3.45
6	—		4.—	—		4.02	—		4.06	—		4.10	—		4.14
7	—		4.64	—		4.69	—		4.74	—		4.78	—		4.83
8	—		5.31	—		5.36	—		5.41	—		5.47	—		5.52
9	—		5.97	—		6.03	—		6.09	—		6.15	—		6.21
10	—		6.64	—		6.70	—		6.77	—		6.83	—		6.90
11	—		7.30	—		7.37	—		7.44	—		7.52	—		7.59
12	—		7.96	—		8.04	—		8.12	—		8.20	—		8.28
13	—		8.63	—		8.71	—		8.80	—		8.88	—		8.9[illegible]
14	—		9.29	—		9.38	—		9.48	—		9.57	—		9.66
15	—		9.9[illegible]	—		10.06	—		10.15	—		10.25	—		10.[illegible]
16	—		10.62	—		10.73	—		10.83	—		10.94	—		11.[illegible]
17	—		11.28	—		11.40	—		11.51	—		11.62	—		11.[illegible]
18	—		11.95	—	1	0.07	—	1	0.19	—	1	0.30	—	1	0.[illegible]
19	—	1	0.61	—	1	0.74	—	1	0.86	—	1	1 —	—	1	1.[illegible]
20	—	1	1.28	—	1	1.41	—	1	1.54	—	1	1.67	—	1	1.80
21	—	1	1.94	—	1	2.08	—	1	2.22	—	1	2.36	—	1	2.49
22	—	1	2.61	—	1	2.75	—	1	2.89	—	1	3.04	—	1	3.18
23	—	1	3.27	—	1	3.42	—	1	3.57	—	1	3.72	—	1	3.87
24	—	1	3.93	—	1	4.09	—	1	4.25	—	1	4.41	—	1	4.56
25	—	1	4.60	—	1	4.76	—	1	4.93	—	1	5.09	—	1	5.26
26	—	1	5.26	—	1	5.43	—	1	5.60	—	1	5.77	—	1	5.95
27	—	1	5.93	—	1	6.10	—	1	6.28	—	1	6.46	—	1	6.64
28	—	1	6.59	—	1	6.77	—	1	6.96	—	1	7.14	—	1	7.33
29	—	1	7.25	—	1	7.44	—	1	7.64	—	1	7.83	—	1	8.02
30	—	1	7.92	—	1	8.12	—	1	8.31	—	1	8.51	—	1	8.71
40	—	2	2.56	—	2	2.82	—	2	3.09	—	2	3.35	—	2	3.61
50	—	2	9.20	—	2	9.53	—	2	9.86	—	2	10.19	—	2	10.52
60	—	3	3.84	—	3	4.24	—	3	4.63	—	3	5.03	—	3	5.42
70	—	3	10.48	—	3	10.94	—	3	11.40	—	3	11.86	—	4	0.32
80	—	4	5.12	—	4	5.65	—	4	6.18	—	4	6.70	—	4	7.23
90	—	4	11.76	—	5	0.36	—	5	.95	—	5	1.54	—	5	2.13
100	—	5	6.41	—	5	7.06	—	5	7.72	—	5	8.38	—	5	9.04
200	—	11	0.82	—	11	2.13	—	11	3.45	—	11	4.76	—	11	6.08
300	—	16	7.23	—	16	9.20	—	16	11.17	—	17	1.15	—	17	3.12
400	1	2	1.64	1	2	4.27	1	2	6.90	1	2	9.53	1	3	0.16
500	1	7	8.05	1	7	11.34	1	8	2.63	1	8	5.91	1	8	9.20
600	1	13	2.46	1	13	6.41	1	13	10.35	1	14	2.30	1	14	6.24
700	1	18	8.87	1	19	1.47	1	19	6.08	1	19	10.68	2	0	3.28
800	2	4	3.28	2	4	8.54	2	5	1.80	2	5	7.06	2	6	0.32
900	2	9	9.69	2	10	3.61	2	10	9.53	2	11	3.44	2	11	9.36
1000	2	15	4.10	2	15	10.68	2	16	5.26	1	16	11.83	2	17	6.41
2000	5	10	8.21	5	11	9.36	5	12	10.52	5	13	11.67	5	15	0.82
3000	8	6	0.32	8	7	8.[illegible]5	8	9	3.78	8	10	11.50	8	12	7.23
4000	11	1	4.45	11	3	6.73	11	5	9.04	11	7	11.34	11	10	1.64
5000	13	16	8.54	13	19	5.42	14	2	2.30	14	7	8.05	14	7	8.0[illegible]

Prin.	106 Days.			107 Days.			108 Days.			109 Days.			110 Days.		
£.	£.	s.	d.pts	£.	s.	d.pts	£.	s.	d.pts	£.	s.	d.pts	£.	s.	d.pts
1	0	0	0.69	0	0	0.70	0	0	0.71	0	0	0.71	0	0	0.72
2	—		1.39	—		1.40	—		1.42	—		1.43	—		1.44
3	—		2.09	—		2.11	—		2.13	—		2.15	—		2.16
4	—		2.78	—		2.81	—		2.84	—		2.86	—		2.89
5	—		3.48	—		3.51	—		3.55	—		3.58	—		3.61
6	—		4.81	—		4.22	—		4.26	—		4.30	—		4.33
7	—		4.87	—		4.92	—		4.97	—		5.01	—		5.06
8	—		5.57	—		5.62	—		5.68	—		5.73	—		5.78
9	—		6.27	—		6.33	—		6.39	—		6.45	—		6.50
10	—		6.96	—		7.03	—		7.10	—		7.16	—		7.23
11	—		7.66	—		7.73	—		7.81	—		7.88	—		7.95
12	—		8.36	—		8.44	—		8.52	—		8.60	—		8.67
13	—		9.06	—		9.14	—		9.23	—		9.31	—		9.40
14	—		9.75	—		9.84	—		9.94	—		10.03	—		10.12
15	—		10.45	—		10.55	—		10.65	—		10.75	—		10.84
16	—		11.15	—		11.25	—		11.36	—		11.46	—		11.57
17	—		11.84	—		11.96	—	1	0.07	—	1	0.18	—	1	0.29
18	—	1	0.54	—	1	0.66	—	1	0.78	—	1	0.90	—	1	1.01
19	—	1	1.24	—	1	1.36	—	1	1.49	—	1	1.61	—	1	1.74
20	—	1	1.93	—	1	2.07	—	1	2.20	—	1	2.33	—	1	2.46
21	—	1	2.63	—	1	2.77	—	1	2.91	—	1	3.05	—	1	3.18
22	—	1	3.33	—	1	3.47	—	1	3.62	—	1	3.76	—	1	3.91
23	—	1	4.03	—	1	4.18	—	1	4.33	—	1	4.4[illegible]	—	1	4.63
24	—	1	4.72	—	1	4.88	—	1	5.04	—	1	5.20	—	1	5.35
25	—	1	5.42	—	1	5.58	—	1	5.75	—	1	5.91	—	1	6.08
26	—	1	6.12	—	1	6.29	—	1	6.46	—	1	6.63	—	1	6.80
27	—	1	6.81	—	1	7.—	—	1	7.17	—	1	7.35	—	1	7.52
28	—	1	7.51	—	1	7.70	—	1	7.88	—	1	8.06	—	1	8.25
29	—	1	8.21	—	1	8.40	—	1	8.59	—	1	8.78	—	1	8.97
30	—	1	8.90	—	1	9.10	—	1	9.30	—	1	9.50	—	1	9.69
40	—	2	3.87	—	2	4.14	—	2	4.40	—	2	4.66	—	2	4.93
50	—	2	10.84	—	2	11.17	—	2	11.50	—	2	11.83	—	3	0.16
60	—	3	5.81	—	3	6.21	—	3	6.60	—	3	7.—	—	3	7.39
70	—	4	0.78	—	4	1.24	—	4	1.70	—	4	2.16	—	4	2.62
80	—	4	7.75	—	4	8.28	—	4	8.81	—	4	9.33	—	4	9.86
90	—	5	2,72	—	5	3.32	—	5	3.91	—	5	4.50	—	5	5.09
100	—	5	9.69	—	5	10.35	—	5	11.01	—	5	11.67	—	6	0.32
200	—	11	7.39	—	11	8.71	—	11	10.02	—	11	11.34	—	12	0.65
300	—	17	5.09	—	17	8.06	—	17	9.04	—	17	11.01	—	18	0.98
400	1	3	2.79	1	3	5.42	1	3	8.05	1	3	10.68	1	4	1.31
500	1	9	0.49	1	9	3.78	1	9	7.06	1	9	10.35	1	10	1.64
600	1	14	10.19	1	15	2.13	1	15	6.08	1	15	10.02	1	16	1.97
700	2	0	7.88	2	1	0.49	2	1	5.09	2	1	9.69	2	2	2.29
800	2	6	5.58	2	6	10.84	2	7	4.10	2	7	9.36	2	8	2.62
900	1	12	3.28	2	12	9.20	2	13	3.12	2	13	9.04	2	14	2.95
1000	2	18	0.98	2	18	7.56	2	19	2.13	2	19	8.71	3	0	3.28
2000	5	16	1.97	5	17	3.12	5	18	4.27	5	19	5.42	6	0	6 57
3000	8	14	2.95	8	15	10.68	8	17	6.41	8	19	2.13	9	0	9.86
4000	11	12	3.94	11	14	6.24	11	16	8.54	11	18	10.84	12	1	1.15
5000	14	10	4.93	14	13	1.80	14	15	10.62	14	18	7.5[illegible]	15	1	4.43

Prin.	111 Days.			112 Days.			113 Days.			114 Days.			115 Days.		
£.	£.	s.	d.pts	£.	s.	d.pts	£.	s.	d.pts	£.	s.	d.pts	£.	s.	d.pts
1	0	0	0,72	0	0	0,73	0	0	0,74	0	0	0,74	0	0	0,75
2	—		1,45	—		1,47	—		1,48	—		1,49	—		1,51
3	—		2,18	—		2,20	—		2,22	—		2,24	—		2,26
4	—		2,91	—		2,94	—		2,97	—		3,—	—		3,02
5	—		3,64	—		3,68	—		3,71	—		3,74	—		3,78
6	—		4,37	—		4,41	—		4,45	—		4,49	—		4,53
7	—		5,10	—		5,15	—		5,20	—		5,24	—		5,29
8	—		5,83	—		5,89	—		5,94	—		6,—	—		6,04
9	—		6,56	—		6,62	—		6,68	—		6,74	—		6,80
10	—		7,29	—		7,36	—		7,43	—		7,49	—		7,56
11	—		8,02	—		8,10	—		8,17	—		8,24	—		8,31
12	—		8,75	—		8,83	—		8,91	—		9,—	—		9,07
13	—		9,48	—		9,57	—		9,65	—		9,74	—		9,83
14	—		10,21	—		10,31	—		10,40	—		10,49	—		10,58
15	—		10,94	—		11,04	—		11,14	—		11,24	—		11,34
16	—		11,67	—		11,78	—		11,88	—	1	0,—	—	1	0,09
17	—	1	0,40	—	1	0,51	—	1	0,63	—	1	0,74	—	1	0,85
18	—	1	1,13	—	1	1,25	—	1	1,37	—	1	1,49	—	1	1,61
19	—	1	1,86	—	1	2,—	—	1	2,11	—	1	2,24	—	1	2,36
20	—	1	2,59	—	1	2,72	—	1	2,86	—	1	3,—	—	1	3,12
21	—	1	3,32	—	1	3,46	—	1	3,60	—	1	3,74	—	1	3,87
22	—	1	4,05	—	1	4,20	—	1	4,34	—	1	4,49	—	1	4,63
23	—	1	4,78	—	1	4,93	—	1	5,08	—	1	5,24	—	1	5,39
24	—	1	5,51	—	1	5,67	—	1	5,83	—	1	6,—	—	1	6,14
25	—	1	6,64	—	1	6,41	—	1	6,57	—	1	6,74	—	1	6,90
26	—	1	6,97	—	1	7,14	—	1	7,31	—	1	7,48	—	1	7,66
27	—	1	7,70	—	1	7,88	—	1	8,06	—	1	8,23	—	1	8,41
28	—	1	8,43	—	1	8,62	—	1	8,80	—	1	9,—	—	1	9,17
29	—	1	9,16	—	1	9,35	—	1	9,54	—	1	9,74	—	1	9,92
30	—	1	9,89	—	1	10,09	—	1	10,29	—	1	10,48	—	1	10,68
40	—	2	5,19	—	2	5,45	—	2	5,72	—	2	6,—	—	2	6,24
50	—	3	0,49	—	3	0,82	—	3	1,15	—	3	1,47	—	3	1,80
60	—	3	7,79	—	3	8,18	—	3	8,58	—	3	9,—	—	3	9,36
70	—	4	3,09	—	4	3,55	—	4	4,01	—	4	4,47	—	4	4,93
80	—	4	10,38	—	4	10,91	—	4	11,44	—	4	11,—	—	5	0,49
90	—	5	5,68	—	5	6,27	—	5	6,87	—	5	7,47	—	5	8,05
100	—	6	0,98	—	6	1,64	—	6	2,30	—	6	3,—	—	6	3,61
200	—	12	1,97	—	12	3,28	—	12	4,60	—	12	6,—	—	12	7,23
300	—	18	2,95	—	18	4,93	—	18	6,90	—	18	8,87	—	18	10,84
400	1	4	3,94	1	4	6,57	1	4	9,20	1	4	11,83	1	5	2,46
500	1	10	4,93	1	10	8,21	1	10	11,50	1	11	2,79	1	11	6,08
600	1	16	5,91	1	16	9,86	1	17	1,80	1	17	5,75	1	17	9,69
700	2	2	6,90	2	2	11,50	2	3	4,10	2	3	8,71	2	4	1,31
800	2	8	7,88	2	9	1,14	2	9	6,40	2	9	11,66	2	10	4,93
900	2	14	[illegible],87	2	15	2,79	2	15	8,71	2	16	2,62	2	16	8,54
1000	3	0	9,87	4	1	4,43	3	1	11,01	3	2	5,58	3	3	0,[illegible]
2000	6	1	7,7[illegible]	6	2	8,87	6	3	10,02	6	4	11,17	6	6	0,3[illegible]
3000	9	2	5,5[illegible]	9	4	1,31	9	5	9,04	9	7	4,76	9	9	0,4[illegible]
4000	12	3	5,45	12	5	5,75	12	7	8,05	12	9	10,35	12	12	0,[illegible]
5000	15	4	1,3[illegible]	15	6	10,19	15	9	7,06	15	12	3,94	15	15	0,[illegible]2

Prin	116 Days.			117 Days.			118 Days.			119 Days.			120 Days.		
L.	L.	s.	d.pts	L.	s.	d.pts	L.	s.	d.pts	L.	s.	d.pts	L.	s.	d.pts
1	o	o	0,76	o	o	0,76	o	o	0,77	o	o	0,78	o	o	0,78
2	——		1,52	——		1,53	——		1,55	——		1,56	——		1,57
3	——		2,28	——		2,30	——		2,32	——		2,34	——		2,36
4	——		3,05	——		3,07	——		3,10	——		3,12	——		3,15
5	——		3,81	——		3,84	——		3,87	——		3,91	——		3,94
6	——		4,57	——		4,61	——		4,65	——		4,69	——		4,73
7	——		5,33	——		5,38	——		5,43	——		5,47	——		5,52
8	——		6,10	——		6,15	——		6,20	——		6,25	——		6,31
9	——		6,86	——		6,92	——		6,98	——		7,04	——		7,10
10	——		7,62	——		7,69	——		7,75	——		7,82	——		7,89
11	——		8,39	——		8,46	——		8,53	——		8,60	——		8,67
12	——		9,15	——		9,23	——		9,31	——		9,38	——		9,46
13	——		9,91	——		10,—	——		10,08	——		10,17	——		10,25
14	——		10,67	——		10,77	——		10,86	——		10,95	——		11,04
15	——		11,43	——		11,53	——		11,63	——		11,73	——		11,83
16	—	1	0,20	—	1	0,30	—	1	0,41	—	1	0,51	—	1	0,62
17	—	1	0,96	—	1	1,07	—	1	1,19	—	1	1,30	—	1	1,41
18	—	1	1,72	—	1	1,84	—	1	1,96	—	1	2,08	—	1	2,20
19	—	1	2,49	—	1	2,61	—	1	2,74	—	1	2,86	—	1	3,—
20	—	1	3,25	—	1	3,38	—	1	3,51	—	1	3,64	—	1	3,78
21	—	1	4,01	—	1	4,15	—	1	4,29	—	1	4,43	—	1	4,56
22	—	1	4,78	—	1	4,92	—	1	5,06	—	1	5,21	—	1	5,35
23	—	1	5,54	—	1	5,69	—	1	5,84	—	1	6,—	—	1	6,14
24	—	1	6,30	—	1	6,46	—	1	6,62	—	1	6,77	—	1	6,93
25	—	1	7,06	—	1	7,23	—	1	7,39	—	1	7,56	—	1	7,72
26	—	1	7,83	—	1	8,—	—	1	4,17	—	1	8,34	—	1	8,51
27	—	1	8,59	—	1	8,77	—	1	8,94	—	1	9,12	—	1	9,30
28	—	1	9,35	—	1	9,54	—	1	9,72	—	1	9,90	—	1	10,09
29	—	1	10,11	—	1	10,31	—	1	10,50	—	1	10,69	—	1	10,88
30	—	1	10,88	—	1	11,07	—	1	11,27	—	1	11,47	—	1	11,67
40	—	2	6,50	—	2	6,77	—	2	7,03	—	2	7,29	—	2	7,56
50	—	3	2,13	—	3	2,46	—	3	2,79	—	3	3,12	—	3	3,45
60	—	3	9,76	—	3	10,15	—	3	10,55	—	3	10,94	—	3	11,34
70	—	4	5,39	—	4	5,85	—	4	6,31	—	4	6,77	—	4	7,23
80	—	5	1,01	—	5	1,54	—	5	2,07	—	5	2,59	—	5	3,12
90	—	5	8,64	—	5	9,23	—	5	9,83	—	5	10,42	—	5	11,01
100	—	6	4,27	—	6	4,93	—	6	5,58	—	6	6,24	—	6	6,9
200	—	12	8,54	—	12	9,86	—	12	11,17	—	13	0,49	—	13	1,80
300	—	19	0,82	—	19	2,79	—	19	4,76	—	19	6,73	—	19	8,71
400	1	5	5,0	1	5	7,72	1	5	10,35	1	6	0,98	1	6	3,61
500	1	11	9,36	1	12	0,65	1	12	3,94	1	12	7,23	1	12	10,52
600	1	18	1,64	1	18	5,58	1	18	9,53	1	19	1,47	1	19	5,42
700	2	4	5,91	2	4	10,51	2	5	3,12	2	5	7,72	2	6	0,32
800	2	10	10,18	2	11	3,45	2	11	8,71	2	12	1,97	2	12	7,23
900	2	17	2,46	2	17	8,38	2	18	2,30	2	18	8,21	2	19	2,13
1000	3	3	6,73	3	4	1,31	3	4	7,89	3	5	2,46	3	5	9,04
2000	6	7	1,47	6	8	2,63	6	9	3,78	6	10	4,93	6	11	6,08
3000	9	10	8,21	9	12	3,94	9	13	11,67	9	15	7,39	9	17	3,12
4000	12	14	2,95	12	16	5,26	12	18	7,56	13	0	9,86	13	3	0,16
5000	15	17	9,69	16	0	6,57	16	3	3,45	16	6	0,32	16	8	9,2

2 B

Prin.	121 Days.			122 Days.			123 Days.			124 Days.			125 Days.		
£.	£.	s.	d.pts	£.	s.	d.pts	£.	s.	d.pts	£.	s.	d.pts	£.	s.	d.pts
1	0	0	0.79	0	0	0.80	0	0	0.80	0	0	0.81	0	0	0.82
2	—	—	1.59	—	—	1.60	—	—	1.61	—	—	1.63	—	—	1.64
3	—	—	2.38	—	—	2.41	—	—	2.42	—	—	2.44	—	—	2.46
4	—	—	3.18	—	—	3.20	—	—	3.23	—	—	3.26	—	—	3.28
5	—	—	3.97	—	—	4.01	—	—	4.04	—	—	4.07	—	—	4.10
6	—	—	4.77	—	—	4.81	—	—	4.85	—	—	4.89	—	—	4.93
7	—	—	5.56	—	—	5.61	—	—	5.66	—	—	5.70	—	—	5.75
8	—	—	6.36	—	—	6.41	—	—	6.47	—	—	6.52	—	—	6.57
9	—	—	7.16	—	—	7.21	—	—	7.27	—	—	7.33	—	—	7.39
10	—	—	7.95	—	—	8.02	—	—	8.08	—	—	8.15	—	—	8.21
11	—	—	8.75	—	—	8.82	—	—	8.89	—	—	8.96	—	—	9.04
12	—	—	9.54	—	—	9.62	—	—	9.70	—	—	9.78	—	—	9.86
13	—	—	10.34	—	—	10.42	—	—	10.51	—	—	10.59	—	—	10.68
14	—	—	11.13	—	—	11.23	—	—	11.32	—	—	11.41	—	—	11.50
15	—	—	11.93	—	1	0.03	—	1	0.13	—	1	0.23	—	1	0.32
16	—	1	0.72	—	1	0.83	—	1	0.94	—	1	1.04	—	1	1.15
17	—	1	1.52	—	1	1.63	—	1	1.74	—	1	1.86	—	1	1.97
18	—	1	2.32	—	1	2.43	—	1	2.55	—	1	2.67	—	1	2.79
19	—	1	3.11	—	1	3.24	—	1	3.36	—	1	3.49	—	1	3.61
20	—	1	3.91	—	1	4.04	—	1	4.17	—	1	4.30	—	1	4.43
21	—	1	4.70	—	1	4.84	—	1	4.98	—	1	5.12	—	1	5.26
22	—	1	5.50	—	1	5.64	—	1	5.79	—	1	5.93	—	1	6.08
23	—	1	6.29	—	1	6.45	—	1	6.60	—	1	6.75	—	1	6.90
24	—	1	7.09	—	1	7.25	—	1	7.41	—	1	7.56	—	1	7.52
25	—	1	7.89	—	1	8.05	—	1	8.21	—	1	8.38	—	1	8.54
26	—	1	8.68	—	1	8.85	—	1	9.09	—	1	9.19	—	1	9.36
27	—	1	9.48	—	1	9.65	—	1	9.83	—	1	10.01	—	1	10.19
28	—	1	10.27	—	1	10.46	—	1	10.64	—	1	10.82	—	1	11.01
29	—	1	11.07	—	1	11.26	—	1	11.45	—	1	11.64	—	1	11.83
30	—	1	11.86	—	2	0.06	—	2	0.26	—	2	0.46	—	2	0.65
40	—	2	7.82	—	2	8.08	—	2	8.35	—	2	8.61	—	2	8.87
50	—	3	3.78	—	3	4.10	—	3	4.43	—	3	4.76	—	3	5.09
60	—	3	11.73	—	4	0.13	—	4	0.52	—	4	0.92	—	4	1.31
70	—	4	7.69	—	4	8.15	—	4	8.61	—	4	9.07	—	4	9.53
80	—	5	3.64	—	5	4.17	—	5	4.70	—	5	5.22	—	5	5.75
90	—	5	11.60	—	6	0.19	—	6	0.78	—	6	1.38	—	6	1.97
100	—	6	7.56	—	6	8.21	—	6	8.87	—	6	9.53	—	6	10.19
200	—	13	3.12	—	13	4.43	—	13	5.75	—	13	7.06	—	13	8.38
300	—	19	10.68	1	0	0.65	1	0	2.63	1	0	4.60	1	0	6.47
400	1	6	6.24	1	6	8.87	1	6	11.50	1	7	2.13	1	7	4.76
500	1	13	1.80	1	13	5.09	1	13	8.38	1	13	11.67	1	4	2.95
600	1	19	9.36	2	1	0.31	2	0	5.25	2	0	9.20	2	1	1.14
700	2	6	4.93	2	6	9.53	2	7	2.13	2	7	6.73	2	7	11.34
800	2	13	0.49	2	13	5.75	2	13	11.01	2	14	4.27	2	14	9.53
900	2	19	8.05	3	0	1.97	3	0	7.88	3	1	1.85	3	1	7.72
1000	3	6	3.62	3	6	10.19	3	7	4.76	3	7	11.34	3	8	5.91
2000	6	12	7.08	6	13	8.38	6	14	9.53	6	15	10.68	6	16	11.83
3000	9	18	10.84	10	0	0.57	10	2	2.30	10	3	10.02	10	5	4.75
4000	13	5	2.46	13	7	4.76	13	9	7.06	13	11	9.36	13	13	11.66
5000	16	11	6.08	16	14	2.95	16	16	11.83	16	19	8.71	17	2	5.58

Prin.	126 Days.			127 Days.			128 Days.			129 Days.			130 Days.		
£.	£.	s.	d.pts	£.	s.	d.pts	£.	s.	d.pts	£.	s.	d.pts	£.	s.	d.pts
1	0	0	0.82	0	0	0,83	0	0	0,84	0	0	0,84	0	0	0,85
2	—	—	1.65	—	—	1.67	—	—	1.68	—	—	1.69	—	—	1.70
3	—	—	2.48	—	—	2.50	—	—	2.52	—	—	2.54	—	—	2.56
4	—	—	3.31	—	—	3.34	—	—	3.36	—	—	3.39	—	—	3.41
5	—	—	4.14	—	—	4.17	—	—	4.20	—	—	4.24	—	—	4.27
6	—	—	4.97	—	—	5.01	—	—	5.04	—	—	5.08	—	—	5.12
7	—	—	5.80	—	—	5.84	—	—	5.89	—	—	5.93	—	—	5.98
8	—	—	6.62	—	—	6.68	—	—	6.73	—	—	6.78	—	—	6.83
9	—	—	7.45	—	—	7.51	—	—	7.57	—	—	7.63	—	—	7.69
10	—	—	8.28	—	—	8.35	—	—	8.41	—	—	8.48	—	—	8.54
11	—	—	9.11	—	—	9.18	—	—	9.25	—	—	9.33	—	—	9.40
12	—	—	9.94	—	—	10.02	—	—	10.10	—	—	10.17	—	—	10.25
13	—	—	10.77	—	—	10.85	—	—	10.94	—	—	11.02	—	—	11.11
14	—	—	11.59	—	—	11.69	—	—	11.78	—	—	11.87	—	—	11.96
15	—	1	0.42	—	1	0.52	—	1	0.62	—	1	0.72	—	1	0.82
16	—	1	1.25	—	1	1.36	—	1	1.46	—	1	1.57	—	1	1.67
17	—	1	2.08	—	1	2.19	—	1	2.30	—	1	2.41	—	1	2.53
18	—	1	2.91	—	1	3.03	—	1	3.14	—	1	3.26	—	1	3.38
19	—	1	3.74	—	1	3.86	—	1	4.—	—	1	4.11	—	1	4.24
20	—	1	4.56	—	1	4.70	—	1	4.83	—	1	4.96	—	1	5.09
21	—	1	5.39	—	1	5.53	—	1	5.67	—	1	5.81	—	1	5.95
22	—	1	6.22	—	1	6.37	—	1	6.51	—	1	6.66	—	1	6.80
23	—	1	7.05	—	1	7.20	—	1	7.35	—	1	7.50	—	1	7.66
24	—	1	7.88	—	1	8.04	—	1	8.20	—	1	8.35	—	1	8.51
25	—	1	8.71	—	1	8.87	—	1	9.04	—	1	9.20	—	1	9.36
26	—	1	9.54	—	1	9.71	—	1	9.88	—	1	10.05	—	1	10.22
27	—	1	10.36	—	1	10.5	—	1	10.72	—	1	10.90	—	1	11.07
28	—	1	11.19	—	1	11.38	—	1	11.56	—	1	11.74	—	1	11.93
29	—	2	0.02	—	2	0.21	—	2	0.40	—	2	0.59	—	2	0.78
30	—	2	0.85	—	2	1.05	—	2	1.24	—	2	1.44	—	2	1.64
40	—	2	9.13	—	2	9.40	—	2	9.66	—	2	9.92	—	2	10.19
50	—	3	5.42	—	3	5.75	—	3	6.08	—	3	6.41	—	3	6.73
60	—	4	1.70	—	4	2.10	—	4	2.49	—	4	2.89	—	4	3.28
70	—	4	10.—	—	4	10.45	—	4	10.91	—	4	11.37	—	4	11.83
80	—	5	5.27	—	5	6.80	—	5	7.33	—	5	7.85	—	5	8.38
90	—	6	2.56	—	6	3.15	—	6	3.74	—	6	4.33	—	6	4.93
100	—	6	10.84	—	6	11.59	—	7	0.16	—	7	0.82	—	7	1.47
200	—	13	9.69	—	13	11.01	—	14	0.32	—	14	1.64	—	14	2.95
300	1	0	8.54	1	0	10.52	1	1	0.49	1	1	2.46	1	1	4.43
400	1	7	7.39	1	7	10.03	1	8	0.65	1	8	3.28	1	8	5.91
500	1	14	6.24	1	14	9.53	1	15	0.82	1	15	4.10	1	15	7.39
600	2	1	5.09	2	1	9.04	2	2	0.98	2	2	4.93	2	2	8.87
700	2	8	3.94	2	8	8.54	2	9	1.14	2	9	5.75	2	9	10.35
800	2	15	2.79	2	15	8.05	2	16	1.31	2	16	6.57	2	16	11.83
900	3	2	1.64	3	2	7.55	3	3	1.47	3	3	7.39	3	4	1.31
1000	3	9	0.49	3	9	7.06	3	10	1.64	3	10	8.21	3	11	2.79
2000	6	18	0.98	6	19	2.13	7	0	3.28	7	1	4.43	7	2	5.58
3000	10	7	1.47	10	8	9.20	10	10	4.93	10	12	0.65	10	13	8.38
4000	13	16	1.97	13	13	4.27	14	0	6.57	14	2	8.87	14	4	11.17
5000	17	5	2.46	17	7	11.34	17	10	8.21	17	13	5.21	17	16	1.97

Prin.	131 Days.			132 Days.			133 Days.			134 Days.			135 Days.		
L.	L.	s.	d.pts	L.	s.	d.pts	L.	s.	d.pts	L.	s.	d.pts	L.	s.	d.pts
1	0	0	0.86	0	0	0.86	0	0	0.87	0	0	0.88		0	0.88
2	—		1.72	—		1.73	—		1.74	—		1.76	—		1.77
3	—		2.58	—		2.60	—		2.62	—		2.64	—		2.66
4	—		3.44	—		3.47	—		3.49	—		3.5[illegible]	—		3.55
5	—		4.3[illegible]	—		4.33	—		4.37	—		4.4[illegible]	—		4.4[illegible]
6	—		5.16	—		5.20	—		5.24	—		5.2[illegible]	—		5.3[illegible]
7	—		6.02	—		6.07	—		6.12	—		6.16	—		6.21
8	—		6.89	—		6.94	—		7.—	—		7.04	—		7.10
9	—		7.75	—		7.81	—		7.87	—		7.92	—		7.[illegible]
10	—		8.61	—		8.67	—		8.74	—		8.8	—		8.8
11	—		9.47	—		9.54	—		9.61	—		9.69	—		9.[illegible]
12	—		10.33	—		10.41	—		10.49	—		10.5[illegible]	—		10.6[illegible]
13	—		11.19	—		11.28	—		11.36	—		11.45	—		11.5[illegible]
14	—	1	0.05	—	1	0.15	—	1	0.24	—	1	0.33	—	1	0.4[illegible]
15	—	1	0.92	—	1	1.01	—	1	1.11	—	1	1.21	—	1	[illegible].31
16	—	1	1.78	—	1	1.88	—	1	2 —	—	1	2.09	—	1	2.20
17	—	1	2.64	—	1	2.75	—	1	2.86	—	1	2.97	—	1	3.09
18	—	1	3.50	—	1	3.62	—	1	3.74	—	1	3.86	—	1	3.97
19	—	1	4.36	—	1	4.79	—	1	4.61	—	1	4.74	—	1	4.86
20	—	1	5.22	—	1	5.35	—	1	5.49	—	1	5.62	—	1	5.75
21	—	1	6.08	—	1	6.22	—	1	6.36	—	1	6.50	—	1	6.64
22	—	1	6.94	—	1	7.09	—	1	7.23	—	1	7.38	—	1	7.52
23	—	1	7.81	—	1	7.96	—	1	8.11	—	1	8.26	—	1	8.41
24	—	1	8.67	—	1	8.83	—	1	9 —	—	1	9.14	—	1	9.30
25	—	1	9.53	—	1	9.69	—	1	9.86	—	1	10.02	—	1	10.19
26	—	1	10.39	—	1	10.56	—	1	10.73	—	1	10.9[illegible]	—	1	11.07
27	—	1	11.25	—	1	11.43	—	1	11.61	—	1	11.7[illegible]	—	1	11.96
28	—	2	0.11	—	2	0.30	—	2	0.48	—	2	0.67	—	2	0.85
29	—	2	0.97	—	2	1.17	—	2	1.36	—	2	1.55	—	2	1.74
30	—	2	1.84	—	2	2.03	—	2	2.23	—	2	2.43	—	2	2.[illegible]3
40	—	2	10.45	—	2	10.71	—	2	10.98	—	2	11.24	—	2	11.50
50	—	3	7.0[illegible]	—	3	7.39	—	3	7.72	—	3	8.05	—	3	8.38
60	—	4	3.68	—	4	4.07	—	4	4.47	—	4	4.8[illegible]	—	4	5.26
70	—	5	0.29	—	5	0.75	—	5	1.21	—	5	1.67	—	5	2.13
80	—	5	6.90	—	5	9.43	—	5	9.9[illegible]	—	5	10.48	—	5	11.01
90	—	6	5.52	—	6	6.11	—	6	6.70	—	6	7.29	—	6	7.89
100	—	7	2.13	—	7	2.79	—	7	3.45	—	7	4.10	—	7	4.76
200	—	14	4.27	—	14	5.58	—	14	6.90	—	14	8.21	—	14	9.53
300	1	1	6.41	1	1	8.38	1	1	10.35	1	2	0.32	1	2	2.30
400	1	8	8.54	1	8	11.17	1	9	1.80	1	9	4.43	1	9	7.06
500	1	15	10.68	1	16	1.97	1	16	5.26	1	16	8.54	1	16	11.83
600	2	3	0.82	2	3	4.76	2	3	8.71	2	4	0.65	2	4	4.60
700	2	10	2.95	2	10	7.56	2	11	0.16	2	11	4.76	2	11	9.36
800	2	17	5.09	2	17	10.35	2	18	3.61	2	18	8.87	2	19	2.13
900	3	4	7.2[illegible]	3	5	1.14	3	5	7.06	3	6	0.98	3	6	6.9[illegible]
1000	3	11	9.3[illegible]	3	12	3.94	3	12	10.52	3	13	5.09	3	13	11.67
2000	7	3	6.73	7	4	7.89	7	5	9.94	7	6	10.19	7	7	11.34
3000	10	15	4.10	10	16	11.83	10	18	7.56	11	0	3.28	11	1	11.01
4000	14	7	1.47	14	9	3.78	14	11	6.08	14	13	8.38	14	15	10.68
5000	17	18	10.84	18	1	7.72	18	4	4.60	18	7	1.47	18	9	10.35

Prin.	136 Days.			137 Days.			138 Days.			139 Days.			140 Days.		
L.	L.	s.	d.pts	L.	s.	d.pts	L.	s.	d.pts	L.	s.	d.pts	L.	s.	d.pts
1	0	0	0.89	0	0	0.90	0	0	0.90	0	0	0.91	0	0	0.92
2	—		1.78	—		1.80	—		1.81	—		1.82	—		1.84
3	—		2.68	—		2.70	—		2.72	—		2.74	—		2.76
4	—		3.57	—		3.60	—		3.62	—		3.65	—		3.68
5	—		4.47	—		4.50	—		4.53	—		4.56	—		4.60
6	—		5.36	—		5.40	—		5.44	—		5.48	—		5.52
7	—		6.25	—		6.30	—		6.35	—		6.39	—		6.44
8	—		7.15	—		7.20	—		7.25	—		7.31	—		7.36
9	—		8.04	—		8.10	—		8.16	—		8.22	—		8.28
10	—		8.94	—		9.—	—		9.07	—		9.13	—		9.20
11	—		9.83	—		9.90	—		9.98	—		10.05	—		10.12
12	—		10.73	—		10.80	—		10.88	—		10.96	—		11.04
13	—		11.62	—		11.71	—		11.79	—		11.88	—		11.96
14	—	1	0.5	—	1	0.61	—	1	0.70	—	1	0.79	—	1	0.88
15	—	1	1.41	—	1	1.51	—	1	1.61	—	1	1.70	—	1	1.80
16	—	1	2.30	—	1	2.41	—	1	2.51	—	1	2.62	—	1	2.72
17	—	1	3.20	—	1	3.31	—	1	3.42	—	1	3.53	—	1	3.64
18	—	1	4.09	—	1	4.21	—	1	4.33	—	1	4.45	—	1	4.56
19	—	1	5.—	—	1	5.11	—	1	5.24	—	1	5.36	—	1	5.49
20	—	1	5.88	—	1	6.01	—	1	6.14	—	1	6.27	—	1	6.41
21	—	1	6.77	—	1	6.91	—	1	7.05	—	1	7.19	—	1	7.33
22	—	1	7.67	—	1	7.81	—	1	7.96	—	1	8.10	—	1	8.25
23	—	1	8.56	—	1	8.71	—	1	8.87	—	1	9.02	—	1	9.15
24	—	1	9.46	—	1	9.61	—	1	9.77	—	1	9.93	—	1	10.09
25	—	1	10.35	—	1	10.52	—	1	10.68	—	1	10.84	—	1	11.01
26	—	1	11.25	—	1	11.42	—	1	11.59	—	1	11.76	—	1	11.93
27	—	2	0.14	—	2	0.32	—	2	0.49	—	2	0.67	—	2	0.85
28	—	2	1.03	—	2	1.22	—	2	1.40	—	2	1.59	—	2	1.77
29	—	2	1.93	—	2	2.12	—	2	2.31	—	2	2.50	—	2	2.69
30	—	2	2.82	—	2	3.02	—	2	3.22	—	2	3.41	—	2	3.61
40	—	2	11.76	—	3	0.03	—	3	0.29	—	3	0.55	—	3	0.82
50	—	3	8.71	—	3	9.04	—	3	9.36	—	3	9.69	—	3	10.02
60	—	4	5.65	—	4	6.04	—	4	6.44	—	4	6.83	—	4	7.23
70	—	5	2.79	—	5	3.65	—	5	3.51	—	5	3.97	—	5	4.43
80	—	5	11.53	—	6	0.06	—	6	0.59	—	6	1.11	—	6	1.64
90	—	6	8.48	—	6	9.07	—	6	9.66	—	6	10.25	—	6	10.84
100	—	7	5.42	—	7	6.08	—	7	6.73	—	7	7.39	—	7	8.05
200	—	14	10.84	—	15	0.16	—	15	1.47	—	15	2.79	—	15	4.10
300	1	2	4.27	1	2	6.24	1	2	8.21	1	2	10.19	1	3	0.16
400	1	9	9.69	1	10	0.32	1	10	2.95	1	10	5.58	1	10	8.21
500	1	17	3.12	1	17	6.41	1	17	9.69	1	18	0.98	1	18	4.27
600	2	4	8.54	2	5	0.49	2	5	4.43	2	5	8.38	2	6	0.32
700	2	12	1.97	2	12	6.57	2	12	11.17	2	13	3.78	2	13	8.38
800	2	19	7.39	3	0	0.65	3	0	5.91	3	0	11.17	3	1	4.43
900	3	7	0.81	3	7	6.73	3	8	0.65	3	8	6.57	3	9	0.49
1000	3	14	6.24	3	15	0.82	3	15	7.39	3	16	1.97	3	16	8.54
2000	7	9	0.49	7	10	1.64	7	11	2.79	7	12	3.94	7	13	5.09
3000	11	3	6.73	11	5	2.46	11	6	10.19	11	8	5.91	11	10	1.64
4000	14	18	0.98	15	0	3.28	15	2	5.58	15	4	7.88	15	6	10.19
5000	18	12	7.23	18	15	4.10	18	18	0.98	19	0	9.36	19	3	6.74

Prin.	141 Days.			142 Days.			143 Days.			144 Days.			145 Days.		
£.	£.	s.	d.pts	£.	s.	d.pts	£.	s.	d.pts	£.	s.	d.pts	£.	s.	d.pts
1	0	0	0.94	0	0	0.93	0	0	0.94	0	0	0.94	0	0	0.95
2	—	—	1.85	—	—	1.86	—	—	1.88	—	—	1.89	—	—	1,90
3	—	—	2.78	—	—	2.80	—	—	2.82	—	—	2.84	—	—	2,86
4	—	—	3.70	—	—	3.73	—	—	3.76	—	—	3.78	—	—	3,81
5	—	—	4.63	—	—	4.66	—	—	4.70	—	—	4.73	—	—	4,76
6	—	—	5.56	—	—	5.60	—	—	5.64	—	—	5.68	—	—	5,72
7	—	—	6.48	—	—	6.53	—	—	6.58	—	—	6.62	—	—	6,67
8	—	—	7.41	—	—	7.46	—	—	7.52	—	—	7.57	—	—	7,62
9	—	—	8.34	—	—	8.40	—	—	8.46	—	—	8.52	—	—	8,58
10	—	—	9.27	—	—	9.33	—	—	9.40	—	—	9.46	—	—	9,53
11	—	—	10.19	—	—	10.27	—	—	10.34	—	—	10.41	—	—	10,48
12	—	—	11.12	—	—	11.20	—	—	11.28	—	—	11.36	—	—	11,44
13	—	1	0.05	—	1	0.13	—	1	0.22	—	1	0.30	—	1	0,39
14	—	1	0.97	—	1	1.07	—	1	1.16	—	1	2.25	—	1	1,34
15	—	1	1.90	—	1	2.—	—	1	2.10	—	1	2.20	—	1	2,30
16	—	1	2.83	—	1	2.93	—	1	3.04	—	1	3.14	—	1	3,25
17	—	1	3.76	—	1	3.87	—	1	3.98	—	1	4.09	—	1	4,20
18	—	1	4.68	—	1	4.80	—	1	4.92	—	1	5.04	—	1	5,16
19	—	1	5.61	—	1	5.74	—	1	5.86	—	1	6.—	—	1	6,11
20	—	1	6.54	—	1	6.67	—	1	6.80	—	1	6.93	—	1	7,06
21	—	1	7.46	—	1	7.60	—	1	7.74	—	1	7.88	—	1	8,02
22	—	1	8.39	—	1	8.54	—	1	8.68	—	1	8.83	—	1	8,97
23	—	1	9.32	—	1	9.47	—	1	9.62	—	1	9.77	—	1	9,92
24	—	1	10.25	—	1	10.40	—	1	10.56	—	1	10.72	—	1	10,88
25	—	1	11.17	—	1	11.34	—	1	11.50	—	1	11.67	—	1	11,83
26	—	2	0.10	—	2	0.27	—	2	0.44	—	2	0.61	—	2	0,78
27	—	2	1.03	—	2	1.20	—	2	1.38	—	2	1.56	—	2	1,74
28	—	2	1.95	—	2	2.14	—	2	2.32	—	2	2.51	—	2	2,69
29	—	2	2.88	—	2	3.07	—	2	3.26	—	2	3.45	—	2	3,64
30	—	2	3.81	—	2	4.01	—	2	4.20	—	2	4.40	—	2	4,60
40	—	3	1.08	—	3	1.34	—	3	1.61	—	3	1.87	—	3	2,13
50	—	3	10.35	—	3	10.68	—	3	11.01	—	3	11.34	—	3	11,67
60	—	4	7.62	—	4	8.02	—	4	8.41	—	4	8.81	—	4	9,20
70	—	5	4.89	—	5	5.35	—	5	5.81	—	5	6.27	—	5	6,73
80	—	6	2.16	—	6	2.69	—	6	3.22	—	6	3.74	—	6	4,27
90	—	6	11.44	—	7	0.03	—	7	0.62	—	7	1.21	—	7	1,80
100	—	7	8.71	—	7	9.36	—	7	10.02	—	7	10.68	—	7	11,34
200	—	15	5.42	—	15	6.73	—	15	8.05	—	15	9.36	—	15	10,08
300	1	3	2.13	1	3	4.10	1	3	6.[illegible]	1	3	8.[illegible]	1	3	10,0[illegible]
400	1	10	10.84	1	11	1.47	1	11	4.10	1	11	6.73	1	11	0 36
500	1	18	7.56	1	18	10.84	1	19	2.1[illegible]	1	19	5 42	1	19	[illegible].71
600	2	6	4.27	2	6	8.21	2	7	0.16	2	7	4.1[illegible]	2	7	8,05
700	2	14	0.98	2	14	5.58	2	14	10.16	2	15	2.79	2	15	7.39
800	3	1	9.69	3	2	2.95	3	2	8.21	3	3	1.47	3	3	6,78
900	3	9	6.[illegible]	3	10	0.32	3	10	6.2[illegible]	3	11	0.16	3	11	6,08
1000	3	17	3.12	3	17	9.69	3	18	4.27	3	18	10.8[illegible]	3	19	5,44
2000	7	14	6.24	7	15	7.39	7	16	8.54	7	17	9.6[illegible]	7	18	10.84
3000	11	11	9 37	11	13	5.[illegible]	11	15	0.82	11	16	8.54	11	18	4.27
4000	15	9	0.49	15	11	2.79	15	13	5.[illegible]	15	15	7.3[illegible]	15	17	9,[illegible]
5000	19	6	3.61	19	9	0.49	19	11	0.36	19	14	6.24	19	17	3.1[illegible]

Prin.	146 Days.			147 Days.			148 Days.			149 Days.			150 Days.		
£.	£.	s.	d.pts	£.	s.	d.pts	£.	s.	d.pts	£.	s.	d.pts	£.	s.	d.pts
1	0	0	0.96	0	0	0.96	0	0	0.97	0	0	0.97	0	0	0.98
2	—	—	1.92	—	—	1.93	—	—	1.94	—	—	1.95	—	—	1.97
3	—	—	2.88	—	—	2.89	—	—	2.91	—	—	2.93	—	—	2.95
4	—	—	3.84	—	—	3.86	—	—	3.89	—	—	3.91	—	—	3.94
5	—	—	4.80	—	—	4.83	—	—	4.86	—	—	4.89	—	—	4.93
6	—	—	5.76	—	—	5.80	—	—	5.83	—	—	5.87	—	—	5.91
7	—	—	6.72	—	—	6.76	—	—	6.81	—	—	6.85	—	—	6.90
8	—	—	7.68	—	—	7.73	—	—	7.78	—	—	7.83	—	—	7.89
9	—	—	8.64	—	—	8.69	—	—	8.75	—	—	8.81	—	—	8.87
10	—	—	9.60	—	—	9.66	—	—	9.73	—	—	9.79	—	—	9.85
11	—	—	10.56	—	—	10.63	—	—	10.70	—	—	10.77	—	—	10.84
12	—	—	11.52	—	—	11.59	—	—	11.67	—	—	11.75	—	—	11.83
13	—	1	0.48	—	1	0.56	—	1	0.65	—	1	0.73	—	1	0.82
14	—	1	1.44	—	1	1.53	—	1	1.62	—	1	1.71	—	1	1.80
15	—	1	2.40	—	1	2.49	—	1	2.59	—	1	2.69	—	1	2.79
16	—	1	3.36	—	1	3.46	—	1	3.57	—	1	3.67	—	1	3.78
17	—	1	4.32	—	1	4.43	—	1	4.54	—	1	4.65	—	1	4.76
18	—	1	5.28	—	1	5.39	—	1	5.51	—	1	5.63	—	1	5.75
19	—	1	6.24	—	1	6.36	—	1	6.48	—	1	6.61	—	1	6.73
20	—	1	7.20	—	1	7.33	—	1	7.46	—	1	7.59	—	1	7.72
21	—	1	8.16	—	1	8.29	—	1	8.43	—	1	8.57	—	1	8.71
22	—	1	9.12	—	1	9.26	—	1	9.40	—	1	9.55	—	1	9.69
23	—	1	10.08	—	1	10.23	—	1	10.38	—	1	10.53	—	1	10.68
24	—	1	11.04	—	1	11.19	—	1	11.35	—	1	11.51	—	1	11.67
25	—	2	0.—	—	2	0.16	—	2	0.32	—	2	0.49	—	2	0.65
26	—	2	0.96	—	2	1.13	—	2	1.30	—	2	1.47	—	2	1.64
27	—	2	1.92	—	2	2.09	—	2	2.27	—	2	2.45	—	2	2.63
28	—	2	2.88	—	2	3.06	—	2	3.24	—	2	3.43	—	2	3.61
29	—	2	3.84	—	2	4.03	—	2	4.22	—	2	4.41	—	2	4.60
30	—	2	4.80	—	2	5.—	—	2	5.19	—	2	5.39	—	2	5.58
40	—	3	2.40	—	3	2.66	—	3	2.92	—	3	3.18	—	3	3.45
50	—	4	0.—	—	4	0.32	—	4	0.65	—	4	1.—	—	4	1.31
60	—	4	9.60	—	4	10.—	—	4	10.38	—	4	10.73	—	4	11.17
70	—	5	7.20	—	5	7.66	—	5	8.12	—	5	8.58	—	5	9.04
80	—	6	4.80	—	6	5.32	—	6	5.85	—	6	6.37	—	6	6.90
90	—	7	2.40	—	7	3.—	—	7	3.58	—	7	4.17	—	7	4.76
100	—	8	0.	—	8	0.65	—	8	1.31	—	8	2.—	—	8	2.63
200	—	16	0.	—	16	1.31	—	16	2.63	—	16	4.—	—	16	5.26
300	1	4	0.	1	4	2.—	1	4	3.94	1	4	5.91	1	4	7.89
400	1	12	0.	1	12	2.63	1	12	5.26	1	12	7.89	1	12	10.52
500	2	0	0.	2	0	3.28	2	0	6.57	2	0	9.86	2	1	1.15
600	2	8	0.	2	8	4.—	2	8	7.89	2	8	11.83	2	9	3.78
700	2	16	0.	2	16	4.60	2	16	9.20	2	17	1.80	2	17	6.41
800	3	4	0.	3	4	5.25	3	4	10.52	3	5	3.77	3	5	9.04
900	3	12	0.	3	12	6.—	1	12	11.83	3	13	5.75	3	13	11.67
1000	4	0	0.	4	0	6.57	4	1	1.15	4	1	7:72	4	2	2.30
2000	8	0	0.	8	1	1.15	8	2	2.30	8	3	3.45	8	4	4.60
3000	12	0	0.	12	1	7.72	12	3	3.45	12	4	11.17	12	6	6.90
4000	16	0	0.	16	2	2.30	16	4	4.60	16	6	6.90	16	8	9.20
5000	20	0	0.	20	2	8.87	20	5	5.75	20	8	2.63	20	10	11.50

Prin.	151 Days.			152 Days.			153 Days.			154 Days.			155 Days.		
L.	L.	s.	d.pts	L.	s.	d.pts	L.	s.	d.pts	L.	s.	d.pts	L.	s.	d.pts
1	0	0	1.—	0	0	1.—	0	0	1.—	0	0	1.01	0	0	1.01
2	—		1.98	—		2.—	—		2.01	—		2.02	—		2,03
3	—		2.97	—		3.—	—		3.01	—		3.03	—		3,05
4	—		3.97	—		4.—	—		4.02	—		4.05	—		4,07
5	—		4.96	—		5.—	—		5.03	—		5.06	—		5,09
6	—		5.95	—		6.—	—		6.03	—		6.07	—		6,11
7	—		6.95	—		7.—	—		7.04	—		7.08	—		7,13
8	—		7.94	—		8.—	—		8.04	—		8.10	—		8,15
9	—		8.93	—		9.—	—		9.05	—		9.11	—		9,17
10	—		9.93	—		10.—	—		10.06	—		10.12	—		10,19
11	—		10.92	—		11.—	—		11.06	—		11.13	—		11,21
12	—		11.91	—	1	0.—	—	1	0.07	—	1	0.15	—	1	0,23
13	—	1	0.90	—	1	1.—	—	1	1.07	—	1	1.16	—	1	1,24
14	—	1	1.90	—	1	2.—	—	1	2.08	—	1	2.17	—	1	2,26
15	—	1	2.89	—	1	3.—	—	1	3.09	—	1	3.18	—	1	3,28
16	—	1	3.88	—	1	4.—	—	1	4.09	—	1	4.20	—	1	4,30
17	—	1	4.87	—	1	5.—	—	1	5.10	—	1	5.21	—	1	5,32
18	—	1	5.87	—	1	6.—	—	1	6.10	—	1	6.22	—	1	6,34
19	—	1	6.86	—	1	7.—	—	1	7.11	—	1	7.33	—	1	7,36
20	—	1	7.85	—	1	8.—	—	1	8.12	—	1	8.25	—	1	8,38
21	—	1	8.85	—	1	9.—	—	1	9.12	—	1	9.26	—	1	9,40
22	—	1	9.84	—	1	10.—	—	1	10.13	—	1	10.27	—	1	10,42
23	—	1	10.83	—	1	11.—	—	1	11.13	—	1	11.28	—	1	11,44
24	—	1	11.82	—	2	0 —	—	2	0.14	—	2	0.30	—	2	0,46
25	—	2	0.82	—	2	1.—	—	2	1.15	—	2	1.31	—	2	1,47
26	—	2	1.81	—	2	2.—	—	2	2.15	—	2	2.32	—	2	2,49
27	—	2	2.80	—	2	3.—	—	2	3.16	—	2	3.34	—	2	3,51
28	—	2	3.80	—	2	4.—	—	2	4.16	—	2	4.35	—	2	4,53
29	—	2	4.79	—	2	5.—	—	2	5.17	—	2	5.36	—	2	5,55
30	—	2	5.78	—	2	6.—	—	2	6.18	—	2	6.37	—	2	6,57
40	—	3	3.71	—	3	4.—	—	3	4.24	—	3	4.50	—	3	4,76
50	—	4	1.64	—	4	2.—	—	4	2.30	—	4	2.63	—	4	3,—
60	—	4	11.57	—	5	0.—	—	5	0.36	—	5	0.75	—	5	1,15
70	—	5	9.50	—	5	10.—	—	5	10.42	—	5	10.88	—	5	11,34
80	—	6	7.42	—	6	8.—	—	6	8.48	—	6	9.—	—	6	9,53
90	—	7	5.35	—	7	6.—	—	7	6.54	—	7	7.13	—	7	7,72
100	—	8	3.28	—	8	4.—	—	8	4.60	—	8	5.26	—	8	5,91
200	—	16	6.57	—	16	7.89	—	16	9.20	—	16	10.52	—	16	11,83
300	1	4	9.86	1	4	11.85	1	5	1.80	1	5	3.78	1	5	5,75
400	1	13	1.15	1	13	3.78	1	13	6,41	1	13	9.04	1	13	11,67
500	2	1	4.43	2	1	7.72	2	1	11.01	2	2	2.30	2	2	5,58
600	2	9	7.72	2	9	11.67	2	10	3.61	2	10	7.56	2	10	11,50
700	2	17	11.01	2	18	3.61	2	18	8.21	2	19	0.82	2	19	5,42
800	3	6	2.29	3	6	7.56	3	7	0.81	3	7	6.08	3	7	11,34
900	3	14	5.58	3	14	11.50	3	15	5.42	3	15	11.34	3	16	5,25
1000	4	2	8.87	4	3	3.45	4	3	10.02	4	4	4.60	4	4	11,17
2000	8	5	5.75	8	6	6.90	8	7	8.05	8	8	9.20	8	9	10,35
3000	12	8	2.63	12	9	10.35	12	11	6.08	12	13	1.80	12	14	9,53
4000	16	10	11.50	16	13	1.80	16	15	4.10	16	17	6.40	16	19	8,71
5000	20	13	8.38	20	16	5.26	20	19	2.13	21	1	11.01	21	4	7,89

Prin.	156 Days.			157 Days.			158 Days.			159 Days.			160 Days.		
L.	*L.*	*s.*	*d.pts*	*L.*	*s.*	*d.pts*	*L.*	*s.*	*d.pts*	*L.*	*s.*	*d.pts*	*L.*	*s.*	*d.pts*
1	0	0	1.02	0	0	1.03	0	0	1.03	0	0	1.04	0	0	1.05
2	—		2.05	—		2.06	—		2.07	—		2.09	—		2.10
3	—		3.07	—		3.09	—		3.11	—		3.13	—		3.15
4	—		4.10	—		4.12	—		4.15	—		4.18	—		4.20
5	—		5.12	—		5.16	—		5.19	—		5.22	—		5.26
6	—		6.15	—		6.19	—		6.23	—		6.27	—		6.31
7	—		7.18	—		7.22	—		7.27	—		7.31	—		7.36
8	—		8.20	—		8.25	—		8.31	—		8.36	—		8.41
9	—		9.23	—		9.29	—		9.35	—		9.40	—		9.46
10	—		10.25	—		10.32	—		10.38	—		10.45	—		10.52
11	—		11.28	—		11.35	—		11.42	—		11.50	—		11.57
12	—	1	0.30	—	1	0.38	—	1	0.46	—	1	0.54	—	1	0.62
13	—	1	1.33	—	1	1.42	—	1	1.50	—	1	1.59	—	1	1.67
14	—	1	2.36	—	1	2.45	—	1	2.54	—	1	2.63	—	1	2.72
15	—	1	3.38	—	1	3.48	—	1	3.58	—	1	3.68	—	1	3.78
16	—	1	4.41	—	1	4.51	—	1	4.62	—	1	4.72	—	1	4.83
17	—	1	5.43	—	1	5.54	—	1	5.66	—	1	5.77	—	1	5.88
18	—	1	6.46	—	1	6.58	—	1	6.70	—	1	6.81	—	1	6.93
19	—	1	7.48	—	1	7.61	—	1	7.73	—	1	7.86	—	1	7.98
20	—	1	8.51	—	1	8.64	—	1	8.77	—	1	8.90	—	1	9.04
21	—	1	9.54	—	1	9.67	—	1	9.81	—	1	9.95	—	1	10.09
22	—	1	10.56	—	1	10.71	—	1	10.85	—	1	11.—	—	1	11.04
23	—	1	11.59	—	1	11.74	—	1	11.89	—	2	0.04	—	2	0.19
24	—	2	0.61	—	2	0.77	—	2	0.9[illegible]	—	2	1.09	—	2	1.24
25	—	2	1.64	—	2	1.80	—	2	1.97	—	2	2.13	—	2	2.30
26	—	2	2.66	—	2	2.84	—	2	3.01	—	2	3.18	—	2	3.35
27	—	2	3.69	—	2	3.87	—	2	4.05	—	2	4.22	—	2	4.40
28	—	2	4.72	—	2	4.90	—	2	5.08	—	2	5.27	—	2	5.45
29	—	2	5.74	—	2	5.93	—	2	6.12	—	2	6.31	—	2	6.50
30	—	2	6.77	—	2	6.96	—	2	7.16	—	2	7.36	—	2	7.56
40	—	3	5.03	—	3	5.29	—	3	5.55	—	3	5.81	—	3	6.08
50	—	4	3.2[illegible]	—	4	3.61	—	4	3.9[illegible]	—	4	4.2[illegible]	—	4	4.6[illegible]
60	—	5	1.5[illegible]	—	5	1.9[illegible]	—	5	2.33	—	5	2.72	—	5	3.12
70	—	5	11.8[illegible]	—	6	0.[illegible]	—	6	0.7[illegible]	—	6	1.18	—	6	1.64
80	—	6	10.0[illegible]	—	6	10.5[illegible]	—	6	11.11	—	6	11.63	—	7	0.16
90	—	7	8.31	—	7	8.9[illegible]	—	7	9.5[illegible]	—	7	10.00	—	7	10.68
100	—	8	6.57	—	8	7.2[illegible]	—	8	7.89	—	8	8.54	—	8	9.20
200	—	17	1.15	—	17	2.4[illegible]	—	17	3.78	—	17	5.09	—	17	6.41
300	1	5	7.7[illegible]	1	5	9.09	1	5	11.[illegible]7	1	0	1.64	1	6	3.61
400	1	14	2.3[illegible]	1	14	4.93	1	14	7.56	1	14	10.19	1	15	0.82
500	2	[illegible]	8.8[illegible]	2	3	0.16	2	3	3.45	2	3	6.73	2	3	10.02
600	2	11	3.45	2	11	7.39	2	11	11.34	2	12	3.28	2	12	7.23
700	2	19	10.02	3	0	2.[illegible]	3	0	7.23	3	0	11.83	3	1	4.43
800	3	8	2.6[illegible]	3	8	9.86	3	9	3.12	3	9	8.38	3	10	1.64
900	3	16	11.17	3	17	5.09	3	17	11.01	3	18	4.93	3	18	10.84
1000	4	5	5.75	4	6	0.32	4	6	6.9[illegible]	4	7	1.47	4	7	8.05
2000	8	10	11.5[illegible]	8	12	0.65	8	13	1.80	8	14	2.95	8	15	4.10
3000	12	16	5.25	12	18	0.98	12	19	8.71	13	1	4.43	13	3	0.16
4000	17	1	11.01	17	4	1.31	17	6	3.61	17	8	5.91	17	10	8.21
5000	21	7	4.76	21	10	1.04	21	12	10.52	21	15	7.39	21	18	4.27

Prin.	161 Days.			162 Days.			163 Days.			164 Days.			165 Days.		
£.	£.	s.	d.pts	£.	s.	d.pts	£.	s.	d.pts	£.	s.	d.pts	£.	s.	d.pts
1	0	0	1.05	0	0	1.06	0	0	1.07	0	0	1.07	0	0	1,08
2	—		2.11	—		2.13	—		2.14	—		2.15	—		2.16
3	—		3.17	—		3.19	—		3.21	—		3.23	—		3.25
4	—		4.23	—		4.26	—		4.28	—		4.31	—		4.33
5	—		5.29	—		5.32	—		5.35	—		5.39	—		5.42
6	—		6.35	—		6.39	—		6.43	—		6.47	—		6.50
7	—		7.41	—		7.45	—		7.50	—		7.55	—		7.59
8	—		8.46	—		8.52	—		8.57	—		8.62	—		8.67
9	—		9.52	—		9.58	—		9.64	—		9.75	—		9.76
10	—		10.58	—		10.65	—		10.71	—		10.78	—		10.84
11	—		11.64	—		11.71	—		11.78	—		11.86	—		11.93
12	—	1	0.70	—	1	0.78	—	1	0.86	—	1	1.—	—	1	1.01
13	—	1	1.76	—	1	1.84	—	1	1.93	—	1	2.01	—	1	2.10
14	—	1	2.82	—	1	2.91	—	1	3.—	—	1	3.09	—	1	3.18
15	—	1	3.87	—	1	3.97	—	1	4.07	—	1	4.17	—	1	4.27
16	—	1	4.93	—	1	5.04	—	1	5.14	—	1	5.25	—	1	5.35
17	—	1	6.—	—	1	6.10	—	1	6.22	—	1	6.33	—	1	6.44
18	—	1	7.05	—	1	7.17	—	1	7.29	—	1	7.41	—	1	7.52
19	—	1	8.11	—	1	8.23	—	1	8.36	—	1	8.48	—	1	8.61
20	—	1	9.17	—	1	9.30	—	1	9.43	—	1	9.56	—	1	9.69
21	—	1	10.23	—	1	10.36	—	1	10.50	—	1	10.64	—	1	10.78
22	—	1	11.28	—	1	11.43	—	1	11.57	—	1	11.72	—	1	11.86
23	—	2	0.34	—	2	0.49	—	2	0.65	—	2	0.80	—	2	1.—
24	—	2	1.40	—	2	1.56	—	2	1.72	—	2	1.88	—	2	2.03
25	—	2	2.46	—	2	2.63	—	2	2.79	—	2	2.95	—	2	3.12
26	—	2	3.52	—	2	3.69	—	2	3.86	—	2	4.03	—	2	4.20
27	—	2	4.48	—	2	4.76	—	2	4.93	—	2	5.11	—	2	5.29
28	—	2	5.64	—	2	5.82	—	2	6.—	—	2	6.19	—	2	6.37
29	—	2	6.70	—	2	6.89	—	2	7.08	—	2	7.27	—	2	7.46
30	—	2	7.75	—	2	7.95	—	2	8.15	—	2	8.35	—	2	8.54
40	—	3	6.34	—	3	6.60	—	3	6.87	—	3	7.13	—	3	7.39
50	—	4	5.—	—	4	5.26	—	4	5.58	—	4	5.91	—	4	6.24
60	—	5	3.51	—	5	3.91	—	5	4.30	—	5	4.70	—	5	5.09
70	—	6	2.10	—	6	2.56	—	6	3.02	—	6	3.48	—	6	4.
80	—	7	0.69	—	7	1.21	—	7	1.74	—	7	2.26	—	7	2.79
90	—	7	11.27	—	7	11.86	—	8	0.46	—	8	1.05	—	8	1.64
100	—	8	9.86	—	8	10.52	—	8	11.17	—	8	11.83	—	9	0.49
200	—	17	7.72	—	17	9.04	—	17	10.35	—	17	11.67	—	18	1.—
300	1	6	5.58	1	6	7.56	1	6	9.53	1	6	11.50	1	7	1.47
400	1	15	3.45	1	15	6.08	1	15	8.71	1	15	11.34	1	16	2.—
500	2	4	1.31	2	4	4.60	2	4	7.89	2	4	11.17	2	5	2.46
600	2	12	11.17	2	13	3.12	2	13	7.06	2	13	11.01	2	14	3.—
700	3	1	9.04	3	2	1.64	3	2	6.24	3	2	10.84	3	3	3.45
800	3	10	6.90	3	11	0.16	3	11	5.42	3	11	10.68	3	12	4.—
900	3	19	4.76	3	19	10.68	4	0	4.60	4	0	10.51	4	1	4.43
1000	4	8	2.63	4	8	9.20	4	9	3.78	4	9	10.35	4	10	5.—
2000	8	16	5.26	8	17	6.41	8	18	7.56	8	19	8.71	9	0	10.—
3000	13	4	7.89	13	16	3.61	13	7	11.34	13	9	7.06	13	11	2.79
4000	17	12	10.52	17	15	0.82	17	17	3.12	17	19	5.42	18	1	7.72
5000	22	1	1.15	22	3	10.02	22	6	8.90	22	9	3.78	22	12	0.65

Prin.	166 Days.			167 Days.			168 Days.			169 Days.			170 Days.		
£.	£.	s.	d.pts	£.	s.	d.pts	£.	s.	d.pts	£.	s.	d.pts	£.	s.	d.pts
1	0	0	1.09	0	0	1.09	0	0	1.10	0	0	1.11	0	0	1.11
2	—		2.18	—		2.19	—		2.20	—		2.22	—		2.23
3	—		3.27	—		3.29	—		3.31	—		3.33	—		3.35
4	—		4.36	—		4.39	—		4.41	—		4.44	—		4.47
5	—		5.45	—		5.49	—		5.52	—		5.55	—		5.58
6	—		6.54	—		6.58	—		6.62	—		6.66	—		6.70
7	—		7.64	—		7.68	—		7.73	—		7.77	—		7.82
8	—		8.73	—		8.78	—		8.83	—		8.88	—		9.—
9	—		9.82	—		9.88	—		9.94	—		10.—	—		10.06
10	—		10.91	—		11.—	—		11.04	—		11.11	—		11.17
11	—	1	0.—	—	1	0.07	—	1	0.15	—	1	0.22	—	1	0.29
12	—	1	1.00	—	1	1.17	—	1	1.25	—	1	1.33	—	1	1.41
13	—	1	2.18	—	1	2.27	—	1	2.36	—	1	2.44	—	1	2.53
14	—	1	3.28	—	1	3.37	—	1	3.46	—	1	3.55	—	1	3.64
15	—	1	4.37	—	1	4.47	—	1	4.56	—	1	4.66	—	1	4.76
16	—	1	5.46	—	1	5.56	—	1	5.67	—	1	5.77	—	1	5.88
17	—	1	6.55	—	1	6.66	—	1	6.77	—	1	7.—	—	1	7.01
18	—	1	7.64	—	1	7.76	—	1	7.88	—	1	8.—	—	1	8.12
19	—	1	8.73	—	1	8.86	—	1	8.98	—	1	9.11	—	1	9.23
20	—	1	9.83	—	1	10.—	—	1	10.09	—	1	10.22	—	1	10.35
21	—	1	10.92	—	1	11.05	—	1	11.19	—	1	11.33	—	1	11.47
22	—	2	0.01	—	2	0.15	—	2	0.30	—	2	0.44	—	2	0.59
23	—	2	1.10	—	2	1.25	—	2	1.40	—	2	1.55	—	2	1.70
24	—	2	2.19	—	2	2.35	—	2	2.51	—	2	2.66	—	2	2.82
25	—	2	3.28	—	2	3.45	—	2	3.61	—	2	3.78	—	2	3.94
26	—	2	4.37	—	2	4.55	—	2	4.72	—	2	5.—	—	2	5.06
27	—	2	5.47	—	2	5.64	—	2	5.82	—	2	6.—	—	2	6.18
28	—	2	6.56	—	2	6.74	—	2	6.93	—	2	7.11	—	2	7.29
29	—	2	7.65	—	2	7.84	—	2	8.03	—	2	8.22	—	2	8.41
30	—	2	8.74	—	2	8.94	—	2	9.13	—	2	9.33	—	2	9.53
40	—	3	7.66	—	3	7.92	—	3	8.18	—	3	8.44	—	3	8.71
50	—	4	6.57	—	4	6.90	—	4	7.23	—	4	7.56	—	4	7.89
60	—	5	5.49	—	5	5.88	—	5	6.27	—	5	6.67	—	5	7.06
70	—	6	4.40	—	6	4.86	—	6	5.32	—	6	5.78	—	6	6.24
80	—	7	3.32	—	7	3.84	—	7	4.37	—	7	5.—	—	7	5.42
90	—	8	2.23	—	8	2.82	—	8	3.41	—	8	4.01	—	8	4.60
100	—	9	1.15	—	9	1.80	—	9	2.46	—	9	3.12	—	9	3.78
200	—	18	2.30	—	18	3.61		18	4.93	—	18	6.24		18	7.56
300	1	7	3.45	1	7	5.42	1	7	7.39	1	7	9.36	1	7	11.34
400	1	16	4.60	1	16	7.23	1	16	9.86	1	17	0.49	1	17	3.1[illegible]
500	2	5	5.75	2	5	9.04	2	6	0.32	2	6	3.61	2	6	6.9[illegible]
600	2	14	6.90	2	14	10.84	2	15	2.79	2	15	6.73	2	15	10.68
700	3	3	8.05	3	4	0.65	3	4	5.25	3	4	9.86	3	5	2.4[illegible]
800	3	12	9.20	3	13	2.46	3	13	7.72	3	14	1.—	3	14	6.24
600	4	1	10.35	4	2	4.27	4	2	10.18	4	3	4.10	4	3	10.02
1000	4	10	11.50	4	11	6.08	4	12	0.65	4	12	7.23	4	13	1.80
2000	9	1	11.01	9	3	0.16	9	4	1.31	9	5	2.46	9	6	3.61
3000	13	12	10.51	13	14	6.24	13	16	2.—	13	17	9.69	13	19	5.42
4000	18	3	10.02	18	6	0.32	18	8	2.62	18	10	4.92	18	12	7.23
5000	22	14	9.53	22	17	6.41	23	0	3.28	23	3	0.16	23	5	9.04

Prin.	171 Days.			172 Days.			173 Days.			174 Days.			175 Days.		
£.	£.	s.	d.pts	£.	s.	d.pts	£.	s.	d.pts	£.	s.	d.pts	£.	s.	d.pts
1	0	0	1.12	0	0	1.13	0	0	1.13	0	0	1.14	0	0	1.15
2	—		2.24	—		2.26	—		2.27	—		2.28	—		2.30
3	—		3.37	—		3.39	—		3.41	—		3.43	—		3.45
4	—		4.49	—		4.52	—		4.55	—		4.57	—		4.60
5	—		5.62	—		5.65	—		5.68	—		5.7[illegible]	—		5.75
6	—		6.74	—		6.78	—		6.82	—		6.86	—		6.90
7	—		7.87	—		7.91	—		7.96	—		8.—	—		8.05
8	—		9.—	—		9.04	—		9.10	—		9.15	—		9.20
9	—		10.11	—		10.17	—		10.23	—		10.29	—		10.35
10	—		11.24	—		11.30	—		11.37	—		11.44	—		11.50
11	—	1	0.36	—	1	0.44	—	1	0.51	—	1	0.58	—	1	0.65
12	—	1	1.49	—	1	1.57	—	1	1.65	—	1	1.72	—	1	1.80
13	—	1	2.61	—	1	2.70	—	1	2.78	—	1	2.87	—	1	2.95
14	—	1	3.74	—	1	3.83	—	1	3.92	—	1	4.01	—	1	4.10
15	—	1	4.86	—	1	4.96	—	1	5.06	—	1	5.16	—	1	5.26
16	—	1	6.—	—	1	6.09	—	1	6.20	—	1	6.3[illegible]	—	1	6.41
17	—	1	7.11	—	1	7.22	—	1	7.33	—	1	7.44	—	1	7.56
18	—	1	8.23	—	1	8.35	—	1	8.47	—	1	8.59	—	1	8.71
19	—	1	9.36	—	1	9.48	—	1	9.61	—	1	9.73	—	1	9.86
20	—	1	10.48	—	1	10.61	—	1	10.75	—	1	10.88	—	1	11.01
21	—	1	11.61	—	1	11.74	—	1	11.88	—	2	0.02	—	2	0.16
22	—	2	0.73	—	2	0.88	—	2	1.02	—	2	1.17	—	2	1.31
23	—	2	1.86	—	2	2.01	—	2	2.16	—	2	2.31	—	2	2.46
24	—	2	2.98	—	2	3.14	—	2	3.30	—	2	3.45	—	2	3.61
25	—	2	4.10	—	1	4.27	—	2	4.43	—	2	4.60	—	2	4.76
26	—	2	5.23	—	2	5.40	—	2	5.57	—	2	5.74	—	2	5.91
27	—	2	6.35	—	2	6.54	—	2	6.71	—	2	6.89	—	2	7.06
28	—	2	7.48	—	2	7.68	—	2	7.85	—	2	8.03	—	2	8.21
29	—	2	8.60	—	2	8.8[illegible]	—	2	8.98	—	2	9.17	—	2	9.36
30	—	2	9.73	—	2	9.94	—	2	10.[illegible]	—	2	10.3[illegible]	—	2	10.52
40	—	3	8.97	—	3	9.23	—	3	9.50	—	3	9.76	—	3	10.02
50	—	4	8.21	—	5	8.54	—	4	8.87	—	4	[illegible]	—	4	9.53
60	—	5	7.46	—	5	7.85	—	5	8.25	—	5	8.6[illegible]	—	5	9.04
70	—	6	6.70	—	6	7.16	—	6	7.62	—	6	8.08	—	6	8.54
80	—	7	5.95	—	7	6.47	—	7	7.—	—	7	7.5[illegible]	—	7	8.05
90	—	8	5.19	—	8	5.78	—	8	6.37	—	8	6.96	—	8	7.56
100	—	9	4.43	—	9	5.[illegible]	—	9	5.75	—	9	6.4[illegible]	—	9	7.06
200	—	18	8.87	—	18	10.19	—	18	11.5[illegible]	—	19	0.8[illegible]	—	19	2.13
300	1	8	1.31	1	8	3.28	1	8	5.26	1	8	7.23	1	8	9.20
400	1	17	5.75	1	17	8.38	1	17	11.01	1	18	1.64	1	18	4.27
500	2	6	10.19	2	7	1.47	2	7	4.76	2	7	8.05	2	7	11.34
600	2	16	2.62	2	16	6.57	2	16	10.52	2	17	2.46	2	17	6.41
700	3	5	7.06	3	5	11.[illegible]	3	6	4.27	3	6	8.87	3	7	1.47
800	3	14	11.50	3	15	4.76	3	15	10.[illegible]	3	16	3.28	3	16	8.54
900	4	4	3.94	4	4	9.85	4	5	3.77	4	5	9.69	4	6	3.01
1000	4	13	8.38	4	14	2.95	4	14	9.53	4	15	4.10	4	15	10.68
2000	9	7	4.76	9	8	5.91	9	9	7.[illegible]	9	10	8.21	9	11	9.36
3000	14	1	1.15	14	2	8.87	14	4	4.[illegible]	14	6	0.3[illegible]	14	7	8.05
4000	18	14	9.53	18	16	11.85	18	19	2.13	19	1	4.43	19	3	6.73
5000	23	8	5.9[illegible]	23	11	2.79	23	13	11.67	23	16	8.54	23	19	5.42

Prin.	176 Days.			177 Days.			178 Days.			179 Days.			180 Days.		
£.	£.	s.	d.pts	£.	s.	d.pts	£.	s	d.pts	£.	s.	d.pts	£.	s.	d.pts
1	0	0	1.15	0	0	1.16	0	0	1.17	0	0	1.17	0	0	1.18
2	—		2.31	—		2.32	—		2.34	—		2.35	—		2.36
3	—		3.47	—		3.49	—		3.51	—		3.53	—		3.55
4	—		4.62	—		4.65	—		4.68	—		4.70	—		4.73
5	—		5.78	—		5.81	—		5.85	—		5.88	—		5.91
6	—		6.94	—		6.98	—		7.02	—		7.06	—		7.10
7	—		8.10	—		8.14	—		8.19	—		8.23	—		8.28
8	—		9.25	—		9.34	—		9.36	—		9.41	—		9.46
9	—		10.41	—		10.47	—		10.53	—		10.59	—		10.65
10	—		11.57	—		11.63	—		11.70	—		11.76	—		11.83
11	—	1	0.72	—	1	0.80	—	1	0.87	—	1	0.94	—	1	1.01
12	—	1	1.88	—	1	1.96	—	1	2.04	—	1	2.12	—	1	2.20
13	—	1	3.04	—	1	3.12	—	1	3.21	—	1	3.30	—	1	3.38
14	—	1	4.20	—	1	4.29	—	1	4.38	—	1	4.47	—	1	4.56
15	—	1	5.35	—	1	5.45	—	1	5.55	—	1	5.65	—	1	5.75
16	—	1	6.51	—	1	6.62	—	1	6.72	—	1	6.83	—	1	6.93
17	—	1	7.67	—	1	7.78	—	1	7.89	—	1	8.—	—	1	8.12
18	—	1	8.83	—	1	8.94	—	1	9.06	—	1	9.18	—	1	9.30
19	—	1	9.98	—	1	10.11	—	1	10.23	—	1	10.36	—	1	10.48
20	—	1	11.14	—	1	11.27	—	1	11.40	—	1	11.53	—	1	11.67
21	—	2	0.30	—	2	0.44	—	2	0.57	—	2	0.71	—	2	0.85
22	—	2	1.45	—	2	1.60	—	2	1.74	—	2	1.89	—	2	2.03
23	—	2	2.61	—	2	2.76	—	2	2.91	—	2	3.07	—	2	3.22
24	—	2	3.77	—	2	3.93	—	2	4.08	—	2	4.24	—	2	4.40
25	—	2	4.93	—	2	5.09	—	2	5.26	—	2	5.42	—	2	5.58
26	—	2	6.08	—	2	6.25	—	2	6.43	—	2	6.60	—	2	6.77
27	—	2	7.24	—	2	7.42	—	2	7.60	—	2	7.77	—	2	7.95
28	—	2	8.40	—	2	8.58	—	2	8.77	—	2	8.95	—	2	9.13
29	—	2	9.56	—	2	9.75	—	2	9.94	—	2	10.13	—	2	10.32
30	—	2	10.71	—	2	10.91	—	2	11.11	—	2	11.30	—	2	11.50
40	—	3	10.29	—	3	10.55	—	3	10.81	—	3	11.07	—	3	11.34
50	—	4	9.86	—	4	10.19	—	4	10.52	—	4	10.84	—	4	11.17
60	—	5	9.43	—	5	9.83	—	5	10.22	—	5	10.61	—	5	11.01
70	—	6	9.--	—	6	9.46	—	6	9.92	—	6	10.38	—	6	10.84
80	—	7	8.58	—	7	9.10	—	7	9.63	—	7	10.15	—	7	10.68
90	—	8	8.15	—	8	8.74	—	8	9.33	—	8	9.92	—	8	10.52
100	—	9	7.72	—	9	8.38	—	9	9.04	—	9	9.69	—	9	10.35
200	—	19	3.45	—	19	4.76	—	19	6.08	—	19	7.39	—	19	8.71
300	1	8	11.17	1	9	1.15	1	9	3.12	1	9	5.29	1	9	7.06
400	1	18	6.90	1	18	9.53	1	19	0.16	1	19	2.79	1	19	5.42
500	2	8	2.63	2	8	5.91	2	8	9.20	2	9	0.49	2	9	3.78
600	2	17	10.35	2	18	2.30	2	18	6.24	2	18	10.19	2	19	2.13
700	3	7	6.08	3	7	10.68	3	8	3.28	3	8	7.88	3	9	0.49
800	3	17	1.80	3	17	7.06	3	18	0.32	3	18	5.58	3	18	10.84
900	4	6	9.53	4	7	3.44	4	7	9.36	4	8	3.28	4	8	9.20
1000	4	16	5.26	4	16	11.83	4	17	6.41	4	18	0.98	4	18	7.56
2000	9	12	10.52	9	13	11.67	9	15	0.82	9	16	1.97	9	17	3.12
3000	14	9	3.78	14	10	11.50	14	12	7.23	14	14	2.95	14	15	10.68
4000	19	5	9.04	19	7	11.34	19	10	1.64	19	12	3.94	19	14	6.24
5000	24	2	2.30	24	4	11.17	24	7	8.05	24	10	4.03	24	13	1.80

Prin.	181 Days.			182 Days.			183 Days.			184 Days.			185 Days.		
£.	£.	s.	d.pts	£.	s.	d.pts	£.	s.	d.pts	£.	s.	d.pts	£.	s.	d.pts
1	0	0	1,19	0	0	1,19	0	0	1,20	0	0	1,20	0	0	1,21
2	—		2,38	—		2,39	—		2,40	—		2,41	—		2,43
3	—		3,57	—		3,59	—		3,60	—		3,62	—		3,64
4	—		4,76	—		4,78	—		4,81	—		4,83	—		4,86
5	—		5,95	—		5,98	—		6,01	—		6,04	—		6,08
6	—		7,14	—		7,18	—		7,21	—		7,25	—		7,29
7	—		8,33	—		8,37	—		8,42	—		8,46	—		8,51
8	—		9,52	—		9,57	—		9,62	—		9,67	—		9,73
9	—		10,71	—		10,77	—		10,82	—		10,88	—		10,94
10	—		11,90	—		11,96	—	1	0,03	—	1	0,09	—	1	0,16
11	—	1	1,09	—	1	1,16	—	1	1,23	—	1	1,30	—	1	1,38
12	—	1	2,28	—	1	2,36	—	1	2,43	—	1	2,51	—	1	2,59
13	—	1	3,47	—	1	3,55	—	1	3,64	—	1	3,72	—	1	3,81
14	—	1	4,36	—	1	4,75	—	1	4,84	—	1	4,93	—	1	5,03
15	—	1	5,85	—	1	5,95	—	1	6,04	—	1	6,14	—	1	6,24
16	—	1	7,04	—	1	7,14	—	1	7,25	—	1	7,35	—	1	7,46
17	—	1	8,23	—	1	8,34	—	1	8,45	—	1	8,56	—	1	8,67
18	—	1	9,42	—	1	9,54	—	1	9,65	—	1	9,77	—	1	9,89
19	—	1	10,61	—	1	10,73	—	1	10,86	—	1	10,98	—	1	11,11
20	—	1	11,80	—	1	11,93	—	2	0,06	—	2	0,19	—	2	0,32
21	—	2	1,—	—	2	1,13	—	2	1,26	—	2	1,40	—	2	1,54
22	—	2	2,18	—	2	2,32	—	2	2,47	—	2	2,61	—	2	2,76
23	—	2	3,37	—	2	3,52	—	2	3,67	—	8	3,82	—	2	3,97
24	—	2	4,56	—	2	4,72	—	2	4,87	—	2	5,03	—	2	5,19
25	—	2	5,75	—	2	5,91	—	2	6,08	—	2	6,24	—	2	6,41
26	—	2	6,94	—	2	7,11	—	2	7,28	—	2	7,45	—	2	7,62
27	—	2	8,13	—	2	8,31	—	2	8,48	—	2	8,66	—	2	8,84
28	—	2	9,32	—	2	9,50	—	2	9,69	—	2	9,87	—	2	10,06
29	—	2	10,51	—	2	10,70	—	2	10,89	—	2	11,08	—	2	11,27
30	—	2	11,70	—	2	11,92	—	3	0,09	—	3	0,29	—	3	0,49
40	—	3	11,60	—	3	11,86	—	4	0,13	—	4	0,39	—	4	0,65
50	—	4	11,50	—	4	11,83	—	5	0,16	—	5	0,49	—	5	0,82
60	—	5	11,40	—	5	11,80	—	6	0,19	—	6	0,59	—	6	0,98
70	—	6	11,30	—	6	11,76	—	7	0,22	—	7	0,69	—	7	1,15
80	—	7	11,21	—	7	11,73	—	8	0,26	—	8	0,78	—	8	1,31
90	—	8	11,11	—	8	11,70	—	9	0,29	—	9	0,88	—	9	1,47
100	—	9	11,01	—	9	11,67	—	10	0,32	—	10	0,98	—	10	1,64
200	—	19	10,02	—	19	11,34	1	0	0,65	1	0	1,91	1	0	3,25
300	1	9	9,04	1	9	11,01	1	10	0,98	1	10	2,95	1	10	4,93
400	1	19	8,05	1	19	10,68	2	0	1,31	2	0	3,94	2	0	6,57
500	2	9	7,06	2	9	10,35	2	10	1,64	2	10	4,93	3	10	8,21
600	2	19	6,08	2	19	10,02	3	0	1,97	3	0	5,91	3	0	9,86
700	3	9	5,09	3	9	9,69	3	10	2,29	3	10	6,90	3	10	11,50
800	3	19	4,10	3	19	9,36	4	0	0,62	4	0	7,89	4	1	1,14
900	4	9	3,12	4	9	9,04	4	10	2,95	4	10	8,87	4	11	2,79
1000	4	19	2,13	4	19	8,71	5	0	3,28	5	0	9,86	5	1	4,43
2000	9	18	4,27	9	19	5,42	10	0	6,57	10	1	7,72	10	2	8,87
3000	14	17	6,40	14	19	2,13	15	0	9,86	15	2	5,58	15	4	1,31
4000	19	16	8,54	19	18	10,84	20	1	1,44	20	3	3,44	20	5	5,75
5000	24	15	10,68	24	18	7,56	25	4	1,41	25	4	1,31	25	6	10,19

Prin.	186 Days.			187 Days.			188 Days.			189 Days.			190 Days.		
L.	L.	s.	d.pts	L.	s.	d.pts	L.	s.	d.pts	L.	s.	d.pts	L.	s.	d.pts
1	0	0	1.22	0	0	1.22	0	0	1.23	0	0	1.24	0	0	1.24
2	—		2.44	—		2.45	—		2.47	—		2.48	—		2.49
3	—		3.66	—		3.68	—		3.70	—		3.72	—		3.74
4	—		4.89	—		4.91	—		4.94	—		4.97	—		5.—
5	—		6.11	—		6.14	—		6.18	—		6.21	—		6.24
6	—		7.33	—		7.37	—		7.41	—		7.45	—		7.49
7	—		8.56	—		8.60	—		8.65	—		8.69	—		8.74
8	—		9.78	—		9.83	—		9.88	—		9.94	—		10.—
9	—		11.—	—		11.06	—		11.12	—		11.18	—		11.24
10	—	1	0.23	—	1	0.29	—	1	0.36	—	1	0.42	—	1	0.49
11	—	1	1.45	—	1	1.52	—	1	1.59	—	1	1.67	—	1	1.74
12	—	1	2.67	—	1	2.75	—	1	2.83	—	1	2.91	—	1	2.—
13	—	1	3.89	—	1	3.98	—	1	4.07	—	1	4.15	—	1	4.24
14	—	1	5.12	—	1	5.21	—	1	5.30	—	1	5.39	—	1	5.49
15	—	1	6.34	—	1	6.44	—	1	6.54	—	1	6.64	—	1	6.73
16	—	1	7.56	—	1	7.67	—	1	7.77	—	1	7.88	—	1	7.98
17	—	1	8.79	—	1	8.90	—	1	9.01	—	1	9.12	—	1	9.23
18	—	1	10.01	—	1	10.13	—	1	10.25	—	1	10.36	—	1	10.48
19	—	1	11.23	—	1	11.36	—	1	11.48	—	1	11.61	—	1	11.73
20	—	2	0.46	—	2	0.59	—	2	0.72	—	2	0.85	—	2	1.—
21	—	2	1.68	—	2	1.82	—	2	1.95	—	2	2.09	—	2	2.23
22	—	2	2.90	—	2	3.05	—	2	3.19	—	2	3.34	—	2	3.48
23	—	2	4.12	—	2	4.28	—	2	4.43	—	2	4.58	—	2	4.73
24	—	2	5.35	—	2	5.50	—	2	5.66	—	2	5.82	—	2	6.—
25	—	2	6.57	—	2	6.73	—	2	6.90	—	2	7.06	—	2	7.23
26	—	2	7.79	—	2	7.96	—	2	8.14	—	2	8.31	—	2	8.48
27	—	2	9.02	—	2	9.19	—	2	9.37	—	2	9.55	—	2	9.73
28	—	2	10.24	—	2	10.42	—	2	10.61	—	2	10.79	—	2	11.—
29	—	2	11.45	—	2	11.65	—	2	11.84	—	3	0.03	—	3	0.23
30	—	3	0.68	—	3	0.88	—	3	1.08	—	3	1.28	—	3	1.47
40	—	4	0.92	—	4	1.18	—	4	1.44	—	4	1.70	—	4	1.97
50	—	5	1.15	—	5	1.47	—	5	1.80	—	5	2.13	—	5	2.46
60	—	6	1.37	—	6	1.77	—	6	2.16	—	6	2.56	—	6	2.95
70	—	7	1.61	—	7	2.07	—	7	2.53	—	7	3.—	—	7	3.45
80	—	8	1.84	—	8	2.37	—	8	2.89	—	8	3.41	—	8	3.94
90	—	9	2.07	—	9	2.66	—	9	3.25	—	9	3.84	—	9	4.43
100	—	10	2.30	—	10	2.96	—	10	3.61	—	10	4.27	—	10	4.93
200	1	0	4.60	1	0	5.91	1	0	7.23	1	0	8.54	1	0	9.86
300	1	10	6.90	1	10	8.87	1	10	10.84	1	11	0.82	1	11	2.79
400	2	0	9.20	2	0	11.83	2	1	2.46	2	1	5.09	2	1	7.72
500	2	10	11.50	2	11	2.79	2	11	6.08	2	11	9.36	2	12	0.05
600	3	1	1.80	3	1	5.75	3	1	9.69	3	2	1.64	3	2	5.58
700	3	11	4.10	3	11	8.71	3	12	1.31	3	12	5.91	3	12	10.51
800	4	1	6.40	4	1	11.66	4	2	4.93	4	2	10.18	4	3	3.45
900	4	11	8.71	4	12	2.62	4	12	8.54	4	13	2.46	4	13	8.38
1000	5	1	11.01	5	2	5.58	5	3	0.16	5	3	6.73	5	4	1.31
2000	10	3	10.02	10	4	11.17	10	6	0.32	10	7	1.47	10	8	2.63
3000	15	5	9.03	15	7	4.76	15	9	0.49	15	10	8.21	15	12	3.94
4000	20	7	8.05	20	9	10.35	20	12	0.65	20	14	2.95	20	16	5.26
5000	25	9	7.06	25	12	3.94	25	15	0.82	25	17	9.69	26	0	6.57

Prin.	191 Days.			192 Days.			193 Days.			194 Days.			195 Days.		
£.	£.	s.	d.pts	£.	s.	d.pts	£.	s.	d.pts	£.	s.	d.pts	£.	s.	d.pts
1	0	9	1.25	0	0	1.26	0	0	1.26	0	0	1.27	0	0	1.28
2	——		2.51	——		2.52	——		2.53	——		2.55	——		2.56
3	——		3.76	——		3.78	——		3.80	——		3.82	——		3.84
4	——		5.02	——		5.04	——		5.07	——		5.10	——		5.12
5	——		6.27	——		6.31	——		6.34	——		6.37	——		6.41
6	——		7.53	——		7.57	——		7.61	——		7.65	——		7.69
7	——		8.79	——		8.83	——		8.88	——		8.92	——		8.97
8	——		10.04	——		10.09	——		10.15	——		10.20	——		10.25
9	——		11.30	——		11.36	——		11.42	——		11.48	——		11.53
10	—	1	0.55	—	1	0.62	—	1	0.69	—	1	0.75	—	1	0.82
11	—	1	1.81	—	1	1.88	—	1	1.95	—	1	2.03	—	1	2.10
12	—	1	3.07	—	1	3.14	—	1	3.22	—	1	3.30	—	1	3.38
13	—	1	4.32	—	1	4.41	—	1	4.49	—	1	4.58	—	1	4.66
14	—	1	5.58	—	1	5.67	—	1	5.76	—	1	5.85	—	1	5.95
15	—	1	6.83	—	1	6.93	—	1	7.03	—	1	7.13	—	1	7.23
16	—	1	8.09	—	1	8.19	—	1	8.30	—	1	8.40	—	1	8.51
17	—	1	9.35	—	1	9.46	—	1	9.57	—	1	9.68	—	1	9.79
18	—	1	10.60	—	1	10.72	—	1	10.84	—	1	10.96	—	1	11.07
19	—	1	11.86	—	1	11.98	—	2	0.11	—	2	0.23	—	2	0.36
20	—	2	1.11	—	2	1.24	—	2	1.38	—	2	1.51	—	2	1.64
21	—	2	2.37	—	2	2.51	—	2	2.64	—	2	2.78	—	2	2.92
22	—	2	3.62	—	2	3.77	—	2	3.91	—	2	4.06	—	2	4.20
23	—	2	4.88	—	2	5.03	—	2	5.18	—	2	5.33	—	2	5.49
24	—	2	6.14	—	2	6.29	—	2	6.45	—	2	6.59	—	2	6.77
25	—	2	7.39	—	2	7.56	—	2	7.72	—	2	7.87	—	2	8.05
26	—	2	8.65	—	2	8.82	—	2	9.—	—	2	9.14	—	2	9.35
27	—	2	9.91	—	2	10.08	—	2	10.26	—	2	10.42	—	2	10.61
28	—	2	11.16	—	2	11.34	—	2	11.53	—	2	11.69	—	2	11.90
29	—	3	0.42	—	3	0.61	—	3	0.80	—	3	0.97	—	3	1.18
30	—	3	1.67	—	3	1.87	—	3	2.07	—	3	2.24	—	3	2.46
40	—	4	2.23	—	4	2.49	—	4	2.76	—	4	3.02	—	4	3.28
50	—	5	2.79	—	5	3.12	—	5	3.45	—	5	3.78	—	5	4.10
60	—	6	3.35	—	6	3.74	—	6	4.14	—	6	4.53	—	6	4.93
70	—	7	3.91	—	7	4.37	—	7	4.83	—	7	5.29	—	7	5.75
80	—	8	4.47	—	8	5.—	—	8	5.52	—	8	6.04	—	8	6.57
90	—	9	5.03	—	9	5.62	—	9	6.21	—	9	6.80	—	9	7.39
100	—	10	5.58	—	10	6.24	—	10	6.90	—	10	7.56	—	10	8.21
200	1	0	11.17	1	1	0.49	1	1	1.80	1	1	3.12	1	1	4.43
300	1	11	4.76	1	11	6.73	1	11	8.71	1	11	10.68	1	12	0.65
400	2	1	10.35	2	2	1.—	2	2	3.61	2	2	6.24	2	2	8.87
500	2	12	3.94	2	12	7.23	2	12	10.52	2	13	1.80	2	13	5.09
600	3	2	9.53	3	3	1.47	3	3	5.47	3	3	9.36	3	4	1.31
700	3	13	3.12	3	13	7.72	3	14	0.32	3	14	4.93	3	14	9.53
800	4	3	8.71	4	4	1.97	4	4	7.23	4	5	0.49	4	5	5.75
900	4	14	2.30	4	14	8.21	4	15	2.13	4	15	8.05	4	16	1.97
1000	5	4	7.89	5	5	2.46	5	5	9.04	5	6	3.61	5	6	10.19
2000	10	9	3.78	10	10	4.9	10	11	6.08	10	12	7.23	10	13	8.38
3000	15	13	11.67	15	15	7.39	15	17	3.12	15	18	10.82	16	0	7.57
4000	20	18	7.56	21	0	9.86	21	3	0.16	21	5	2.46	21	7	4.76
5000	16	3	3.45	26	6	0.32	26	8	9.20	26	11	6.05	26	14	2.95

Prin.	196 Days.			197 Days.			198 Days.			199 Days.			200 Days.		
L.	L.	s.	d.pts	L.	s.	d.pts	L.	s.	d.pts	L.	s.	d.pts	L.	s.	d.pts
1	0	0	1.28	0	0	1.29	0	0	1.30	0	0	1.30	0	0	1.31
2	—		2.57	—		2.59	—		2.60	—		2.61	—		2.63
3	—		3.86	—		3.88	—		3.90	—		3.92	—		3.94
4	—		5.15	—		5.18	—		5.20	—		5.23	—		5.26
5	—		6.44	—		6.47	—		6.50	—		6.54	—		6.57
6	—		7.73	—		7.77	—		7.81	—		7.85	—		7.89
7	—		9.02	—		9.06	—		9.11	—		9.15	—		9.20
8	—		10.31	—		10.36	—		10.41	—		10.46	—		10.52
9	—		11.59	—		11.65	—		11.71	—		11.77	—		11.83
10	—	1	0.88	—	1	0.95	—	1	1.01	—	1	1.08	—	1	1.15
11	—	1	2.17	—	1	2.24	—	1	2.32	—	1	2.39	—	1	2.46
12	—	1	3.46	—	1	3.54	—	1	3.62	—	1	3.70	—	1	3.78
13	—	1	4.75	—	1	4.83	—	1	4.92	—	1	5.01	—	1	5.09
14	—	1	6.04	—	1	6.13	—	1	6.22	—	1	6.31	—	1	6.41
15	—	1	7.33	—	1	7.43	—	1	7.52	—	1	7.62	—	1	7.72
16	—	1	8.62	—	1	8.72	—	1	8.83	—	1	8.93	—	1	9.04
17	—	1	9.90	—	1	10.02	—	1	10.13	—	1	10.24	—	1	10.35
18	—	1	11.19	—	1	11.31	—	1	11.43	—	1	11.55	—	1	11.67
19	—	2	0.48	—	2	0.61	—	2	0.73	—	2	0.86	—	2	0.98
20	—	2	1.77	—	2	1.90	—	2	2.03	—	2	2.16	—	2	2.30
21	—	2	3.06	—	2	3.20	—	2	3.34	—	2	3.47	—	2	3.61
22	—	2	4.35	—	2	4.49	—	2	4.64	—	2	4.78	—	2	4.93
23	—	2	5.64	—	2	5.79	—	2	5.94	—	2	6.09	—	2	6.24
24	—	2	6.93	—	2	7.08	—	2	7.24	—	2	7.40	—	2	7.56
25	—	2	8.21	—	2	8.38	—	2	8.54	—	2	8.71	—	2	8.87
26	—	2	9.50	—	2	9.67	—	2	9.84	—	2	10.02	—	2	10.19
27	—	2	10.79	—	2	10.97	—	2	11.15	—	2	11.32	—	2	11.50
28	—	3	0.08	—	3	0.26	—	3	0.45	—	3	0.63	—	3	0.82
29	—	3	1.37	—	3	1.56	—	3	1.75	—	3	1.94	—	3	2.13
30	—	3	2.66	—	3	2.86	—	3	3.05	—	3	3.25	—	3	3.45
40	—	4	3.55	—	4	3.81	—	4	4.0[illegible]	—	4	4.33	—	4	4.60
50	—	5	4.43	—	5	4.76	—	5	5.0[illegible]	—	5	5.42	—	5	5.75
60	—	6	5.32	—	6	5.71	—	6	6.01	—	6	6.5[illegible]	—	6	6.90
70	—	7	6.21	—	7	6.6[illegible]	—	7	7.1[illegible]	—	7	7.59	—	7	8.0[illegible]
80	—	8	7.10	—	8	7.62	—	8	8.15	—	8	8.5[illegible]	—	8	9.20
90	—	9	7.98	—	9	8.57	—	9	[illegible]	—	9	9.76	—	9	10.35
100	—	10	8.8[illegible]	—	10	9.5[illegible]	—	10	10.19	—	10	10.54	—	10	11.5[illegible]
200	1	1	5.75	1	1	7.06	1	1	8.38	1	1	9.69	1	1	11.01
300	1	12	2.63	1	12	4.59	1	12	6.57	1	12	8.54	1	12	10.52
400	2	2	11.50	2	3	2.12	2	3	4.76	2	3	7.39	2	3	10.02
500	2	13	8.38	2	13	11.66	2	14	2.95	2	14	6.24	2	14	9.53
600	3	4	5.25	3	4	9.19	3	5	1.14	3	5	5.0[illegible]	3	5	9.04
700	3	15	2.13	3	15	6.72	3	17	11.34	3	16	3.94	3	16	8.54
800	4	5	11.01	4	6	4.26	4	6	9.53	4	7	2.79	4	7	8.05
900	4	16	7.88	4	17	1.79	4	17	7.74	4	18	1.64	4	18	7.55
1000	5	7	4.75	5	7	11.3[illegible]	5	8	5.91	5	0	0.49	5	9	7.06
2000	10	14	9.53	10	15	10.68	10	16	11.53	10	18	0.98	10	19	2.1[illegible]
3000	16	2	2.30	16	3	9.92	16	5	5.7[illegible]	16	7	1.47	16	8	9.20
4000	21	9	7.06	21	11	9.26	21	13	11.6[illegible]	21	16	1.97	21	18	4.27
5000	26	16	11.83	26	19	8.61	27	2	5.58	27	5	2.46	27	7	11.24

2 D

Prin.	201 Days.			202 Days.			203 Days.			204 Days.			205 Days.		
L.	L.	s.	d.pts	L.	s.	d.pts	L.	s.	d.pts	L.	s.	d.pts	L.	s.	d.pts
1	0	0	1.32	0	0	1.32	0	0	1.33	0	0	1.34	0	0	1.34
2	—		2.64	—		2.65	—		2.66	—		2.68	—		2.69
3	—		3.96	—		3.98	—		4.—	—		4.02	—		4.04
4	—		5.28	—		5.31	—		5.33	—		5.36	—		5.39
5	—		6.60	—		6.64	—		6.67	—		6.70	—		6.73
6	—		7.92	—		7.96	—		8.—	—		8.04	—		8.08
7	—		9.25	—		9.29	—		9.34	—		9.38	—		9.4[illegible]
8	—		10.57	—		10.62	—		10.67	—		10.7[illegible]	—		10.[illegible]
9	—		11.89	—		11.95	—	1	0.01	—	1	0.07	—	1	0.1[illegible]
10	—	1	1.21	—	1	1.28	—	1	1.34	—	1	1.41	—	1	1.4[illegible]
11	—	1	2.53	—	1	2.61	—	1	2.68	—	1	2.75	—	1	2.82
12	—	1	3.85	—	1	3.93	—	1	4.01	—	1	4.0[illegible]	—	1	4.1[illegible]
13	—	1	5.18	—	1	5.26	—	1	5.35	—	1	5.43	—	1	5.52
14	—	1	6.50	—	1	6.59	—	1	6.68	—	1	6.77	—	1	6.8[illegible]
15	—	1	7.82	—	1	7.92	—	1	8.02	—	1	8.12	—	1	8.21
16	—	1	9.14	—	1	9.25	—	1	9.35	—	1	9.46	—	1	9.56
17	—	1	10.46	—	1	10.57	—	1	10.6[illegible]	—	1	10.80	—	1	10.[illegible]1
18	—	1	11.78	—	1	11.90	—	2	0.02	—	2	0.14	—	2	0.26
19	—	2	1.11	—	2	1.23	—	2	1.36	—	2	1.48	—	2	1.61
20	—	2	2.43	—	2	2.56	—	2	2.6[illegible]	—	2	2.82	—	2	2.95
21	—	2	3.75	—	2	3.89	—	2	4.03	—	2	4.16	—	2	4.30
22	—	2	5.07	—	2	5.22	—	2	5.36	—	2	5.50	—	2	5.65
23	—	2	6.39	—	2	6.54	—	2	6.70	—	2	6.85	—	2	7.—
24	—	2	7.71	—	2	7.87	—	2	8.03	—	2	8.19	—	2	8.35
25	—	2	9.04	—	2	9.20	—	2	0.36	—	2	9.53	—	2	9.60
26	—	2	10.36	—	2	10.53	—	2	10.70	—	2	10.87	—	2	11.04
27	—	2	11.68	—	2	11.86	—	3	0.03	—	3	0.21	—	3	0.30
28	—	3	1.—	—	3	1.18	—	3	1.37	—	3	1.55	—	3	1.74
29	—	3	2.32	—	3	2.51	—	3	2.70	—	3	2.89	—	3	3.09
30	—	3	3.64	—	3	3.84	—	3	4.04	—	3	4.24	—	3	4.43
40	—	4	4.86	—	4	5.12	—	4	5.39	—	4	5.[illegible]	—	4	5.91
50	—	5	6.08	—	5	6.41	—	5	6.7[illegible]	—	5	7.06	—	5	7.39
60	—	6	7.29	—	6	7.6[illegible]	—	6	8.08	—	6	8.48	—	6	8.8[illegible]
70	—	7	8.51	—	7	8.97	—	7	9.4[illegible]	—	7	9.89	—	7	10.35
80	—	8	9.73	—	8	10.25	—	8	10.7[illegible]	—	8	11.30	—	8	11.8[illegible]
90	—	9	10.94	—	9	11.53	—	10	0.13	—	10	0.72	—	10	1.[illegible]
100	—	11	0.16	—	11	0.82	—	11	1.47	—	11	2.13	—	11	2.79
200	1	2	0.32	1	2	1.64	1	2	2.95	1	2	4.27	1	2	5.58
300	1	13	0.49	1	13	2.46	1	13	4.43	1	13	6.41	1	13	8.38
400	2	4	0.65	2	4	3.28	2	4	5.91	2	4	8.54	2	4	11.17
500	2	15	0.82	2	15	4.10	2	15	7.39	2	15	10.68	2	16	1.9[illegible]
600	3	6	0.98	3	6	4.9	3	6	8.8[illegible]	3	7	0.82	3	7	4.[illegible]6
700	3	17	1.14	3	17	5.75	3	17	10.35	3	18	2.95	3	18	7.56
800	4	8	1.31	4	8	6.57	4	8	11.8[illegible]	4	9	5.0[illegible]	4	9	10.5[illegible]
900	4	19	1.47	4	19	7.39	5	0	1.31	5	0	7.22	5	1	1.14
1000	5	10	1.64	5	10	8.21	5	11	2.79	5	11	9.36	5	12	3.94
2000	11	0	3.28	11	1	4.4[illegible]	11	2	5.58	11	3	6.7[illegible]	11	4	7.89
3000	16	10	4.92	16	12	0.65	16	13	8.38	16	15	4.10	16	16	11.83
4000	22	0	6.57	22	2	8.8[illegible]	22	4	11.1[illegible]	22	7	1.47	22	9	3.7[illegible]
5000	27	10	8.21	27	13	5.09	27	16	1.9[illegible]	27	18	10.84	28	1	7.7[illegible]

Prin.	206 Days.			207 Days.			208 Days.			209 Days.			210 Days.		
L.	L.	s.	d.pts	L.	s.	d.pts	L.	s.	d.pts	L.	s.	d.pts	L.	s.	d.pts
1	0	0	1.35	0	0	1.36	0	0	1.36	0	0	1.37	0	0	1.38
2	—		2.70	—		2.72	—		2.73	—		2.74	—		2.76
3	—		4.06	—		4.08	—		4.10	—		4.12	—		4.14
4	—		5.41	—		5.44	—		5.47	—		5.49	—		5.52
5	—		6.77	—		6.80	—		6.83	—		6.87	—		6.90
6	—		8.12	—		8.16	—		8.20	—		8.24	—		8.28
7	—		9.48	—		9.52	—		9.57	—		9.61	—		9.66
8	—		10.83	—		10.88	—		10.94	—		11.—	—		11.04
9	—	1	0.19	—	1	0.24	—	1	0.30	—	1	0.36	—	1	0.42
10	—	1	1.54	—	1	1.61	—	1	1.67	—	1	1.74	—	1	1.80
11	—	1	2.89	—	1	2.97	—	1	3.04	—	1	3.11	—	1	3.18
12	—	1	4.25	—	1	4.33	—	1	4.41	—	1	4.49	—	1	4.56
13	—	1	5.60	—	1	5.69	—	1	5.77	—	1	5.86	—	1	5.95
14	—	1	6.96	—	1	7.05	—	1	7.14	—	1	7.23	—	1	7.33
15	—	1	8.31	—	1	8.41	—	1	8.51	—	1	8.61	—	1	8.71
16	—	1	9.67	—	1	9.77	—	1	9.88	—	1	9.98	—	1	10.09
17	—	1	11.02	—	1	11.13	—	1	11.25	—	1	11.36	—	1	11.47
18	—	2	0.38	—	2	0.49	—	2	0.61	—	2	0.73	—	2	0.85
19	—	2	1.73	—	2	1.86	—	2	1.98	—	2	2.11	—	2	2.23
20	—	2	3.09	—	2	3.22	—	2	3.35	—	2	3.48	—	2	3.61
21	—	2	4.44	—	2	4.58	—	2	4.72	—	2	4.85	—	2	5.—
22	—	2	5.79	—	2	5.94	—	2	6.08	—	2	6.23	—	2	6.37
23	—	2	7.15	—	2	7.30	—	2	7.45	—	2	7.60	—	2	7.75
24	—	2	8.50	—	2	8.66	—	2	8.82	—	2	8.98	—	2	9.13
25	—	2	9.86	—	2	10.02	—	2	10.19	—	2	10.35	—	2	10.52
26	—	2	11.21	—	2	11.38	—	2	11.55	—	3	0.73	—	2	11.90
27	—	3	0.57	—	3	0.74	—	3	0.92	—	3	1.10	—	3	1.28
28	—	3	1.92	—	3	2.11	—	3	2.29	—	3	2.47	—	3	2.66
29	—	3	3.28	—	3	3.47	—	3	3.66	—	3	3.85	—	3	4.04
30	—	3	4.63	—	3	4.83	—	3	5.03	—	3	5.22	—	3	5.42
40	—	4	6.18	—	4	6.44	—	4	6.70	—	4	6.96	—	4	7.23
50	—	5	7.72	—	5	8.05	—	5	8.38	—	5	8.71	—	5	9.04
60	—	6	9.27	—	6	9.66	—	6	10.06	—	6	10.45	—	6	10.84
70	—	7	10.81	—	7	11.27	—	7	11.73	—	8	0.19	—	8	0.65
80	—	9	0.36	—	9	0.88	—	9	1.41	—	9	1.93	—	9	2.46
90	—	10	1.90	—	10	2.49	—	10	3.09	—	10	3.68	—	10	4.27
100	—	11	3.45	—	11	4.1[illegible]	—	11	4.76	—	11	5.42	—	11	6.08
200	1	2	6.90	1	2	8.21	1	2	9.53	1	2	10.84	1	3	0.1[illegible]
300	1	13	10.35	1	14	0.[illegible]2	1	14	2.30	1	14	4.27	1	14	[illegible]
400	2	5	1.80	2	5	4.43	2	5	7.06	2	5	9.69	2	6	0.3[illegible]
500	2	16	5.26	2	16	8.54	2	16	11.83	2	17	3.12	2	17	6.4[illegible]
600	3	7	8.71	3	8	0.65	3	8	4.60	3	8	8.54	3	9	0.49
700	3	19	0.16	3	19	4.76	3	19	9.36	4	0	1.97	4	0	6.57
800	4	10	3.61	4	10	8.87	4	11	2.13	4	11	7.39	4	12	0.[illegible]
900	5	1	7.06	5	2	0.98	5	2	6.90	5	3	0.81	5	3	6.7[illegible]
1000	5	12	10.52	5	13	5.09	5	13	11.67	5	14	6.2[illegible]	5	15	[illegible]
2000	11	5	9.04	11	6	10.10	11	7	11.34	11	9	0.49	11	10	1.6[illegible]
3000	16	18	7.56	17	0	3.28	17	1	11.01	17	3	6.7	17	5	2.46
4000	22	11	6.08	22	13	8.38	22	15	10.68	22	18	0.9[illegible]	23	0	3.08
5000	28	4	4.60	28	7	1.47	28	9	10.35	28	12	7.2[illegible]	28	15	4.1[illegible]

Prin.	211 Days.			212 Days.			213 Days.			214 Days.			215 Days.		
£.	£.	s.	d.pts	£.	s.	d.pts	£.	s.	d.pts	£.	s.	d.pts	£.	s.	d.pts
1	0	0	1.38	0	0	1.39	0	0	1.40	0	0	1.40	0	0	1.41
2	—	—	2.77	—	—	2.78	—	—	2.80	—	—	2.81	—	—	2.82
3	—	—	4.16	—	—	4.18	—	—	4.20	—	—	4.22	—	—	4.24
4	—	—	5.54	—	—	5.57	—	—	5.60	—	—	5.62	—	—	5.65
5	—	—	6.93	—	—	6.96	—	—	7.—	—	—	7.03	—	—	7.06
6	—	—	8.32	—	—	8.36	—	—	8.40	—	—	8.44	—	—	8.48
7	—	—	9.71	—	—	9.75	—	—	9.80	—	—	9.84	—	—	9.89
8	—	—	11.09	—	—	11.15	—	—	11.20	—	—	11.25	—	—	11.30
9	—	1	0.48	—	1	0.54	—	1	0.60	—	1	0.66	—	1	0.72
10	—	1	1.87	—	1	1.93	—	1	2.—	—	1	2.07	—	1	2.13
11	—	1	3.26	—	1	3.33	—	1	3.40	—	1	3.47	—	1	3.55
12	—	1	4.64	—	1	4.72	—	1	4.80	—	1	4.88	—	1	4.96
13	—	1	6.03	—	1	6.12	—	1	6.20	—	1	6.29	—	1	6.37
14	—	1	7.42	—	1	7.51	—	1	7.60	—	1	7.69	—	1	7.79
15	—	1	8.81	—	1	8.90	—	1	9.—	—	1	9.10	—	1	9.20
16	—	1	10.19	—	1	10.30	—	1	10.40	—	1	10.51	—	1	10.61
17	—	1	11.58	—	1	11.69	—	1	11.80	—	1	11.92	—	2	0.03
18	—	2	0.97	—	2	1.09	—	2	1.20	—	2	1.32	—	2	1.44
19	—	2	2.36	—	2	2.48	—	2	2.61	—	2	2.73	—	2	2.86
20	—	2	3.74	—	2	3.87	—	2	4.01	—	2	4.14	—	2	4.27
21	—	2	5.13	—	2	5.27	—	2	5.41	—	2	5.54	—	2	5.68
22	—	2	6.52	—	2	6.66	—	2	6.81	—	2	6.95	—	2	7.10
23	—	2	7.91	—	2	8.06	—	2	8.21	—	2	8.36	—	2	8.51
24	—	2	9.29	—	2	9.45	—	2	9.61	—	2	9.77	—	2	9.92
25	—	2	10.68	—	2	10.84	—	2	11.01	—	2	11.17	—	2	11.34
26	—	3	0.07	—	3	0.24	—	3	0.41	—	3	0.58	—	3	0.75
27	—	3	1.45	—	3	1.63	—	3	1.81	—	3	2.—	—	3	2.16
28	—	3	2.84	—	3	3.03	—	3	3.21	—	3	3.40	—	3	3.58
29	—	3	4.23	—	3	4.42	—	3	4.61	—	3	4.80	—	3	5.—
30	—	3	5.62	—	3	5.81	—	3	6.01	—	3	6.21	—	3	6.41
40	—	4	7.49	—	4	7.75	—	4	8.02	—	4	8.28	—	4	8.54
50	—	5	9.36	—	5	9.69	—	5	10.02	—	5	10.35	—	5	10.68
60	—	6	11.24	—	6	11.63	—	7	0.03	—	7	0.42	—	7	0.82
70	—	8	1.11	—	8	1.57	—	8	2.03	—	8	2.49	—	8	2.95
80	—	9	3.—	—	9	3.51	—	9	4.04	—	9	4.56	—	9	5.09
90	—	10	4.86	—	10	5.45	—	10	6.04	—	10	6.64	—	10	7.23
100	—	11	6.73	—	11	7.39	—	11	8.05	—	11	8.71	—	11	9.26
200	1	3	1.47	1	3	2.79	1	3	4.10	1	3	5.42	1	3	6.73
300	1	14	8.21	1	14	10.19	1	15	0.16	1	15	2.13	1	15	4.10
400	2	6	2.95	2	6	5.58	2	6	8.21	2	6	10.84	2	7	1.47
500	2	17	9.69	2	18	0.98	2	18	4.27	2	18	7.56	2	18	10.84
600	3	9	4.43	3	9	8.38	3	10	0.32	3	10	4.27	3	10	8.21
700	4	0	11.17	4	1	3.78	4	1	8.38	4	2	0.98	4	2	5.58
800	4	12	5.91	4	12	11.17	4	13	4.43	4	13	9.69	4	14	2.95
900	5	4	0.65	5	4	6.17	5	5	0.49	5	5	6.40	5	6	0.32
1000	5	15	7.30	5	16	1.97	5	16	8.54	5	17	3.12	5	17	9.69
2000	11	11	2.79	11	12	3.94	11	13	5.09	11	14	6.24	11	15	7.39
3000	17	6	10.19	17	8	5.91	17	10	1.64	17	11	9.36	17	13	5.09
4000	23	2	5.58	23	4	7.88	23	6	10.18	23	9	0.49	23	11	2.79
5000	28	18	0.98	29	0	8.86	29	3	6.73	29	6	3.61	29	9	0.49

Prin.	216 Days.			217 Days.			218 Days.			219 Days.			220 Days.		
L.	L.	s.	d.pts	L.	s.	d.pts	L.	s.	d.pts	L.	s.	d.pts	L.	s.	d.pts
1	0	0	1.42	0	0	1.42	0	0	1.43	0	0	1.44	0	0	1.44
2	—		2.84	—		2.85	—		2.86	—		2.88	—		2.89
3	—		4.26	—		4.28	—		4.30	—		4.31	—		4.33
4	—		5.68	—		5.70	—		5.73	—		5.76	—		5.78
5	—		7.10	—		7.13	—		7.16	—		7.20	—		7.23
6	—		8.52	—		8.56	—		8.60	—		8.64	—		8.67
7	—		9.94	—		9.98	—		10.03	—		10.08	—		10.12
8	—		11.36	—		11.41	—		11.46	—		11.52	—		11.57
9	–	1	0.78	–	1	0.84	–	1	0.90	–	1	0.96	–	1	1.01
10	–	1	2.20	–	1	2.26	–	1	2.33	–	1	2.40	–	1	2.46
11	–	1	3.62	–	1	3.69	–	1	3.76	–	1	3.84	–	1	3.91
12	–	1	5.04	–	1	5.12	–	1	5.20	–	1	5.28	–	1	5.35
13	–	1	6.46	–	1	6.64	–	1	6.63	–	1	6.72	–	1	6.80
14	–	1	7.88	–	1	7.97	–	1	8.06	–	1	8.16	–	1	8.25
15	–	1	9.30	–	1	9.40	–	1	9.50	–	1	9.60	–	1	9.69
16	–	1	10.72	–	1	10.82	–	1	10.93	–	1	11.04	–	1	11.14
17	–	2	0.14	–	2	0.25	–	2	0.36	–	2	0.48	–	2	0.59
18	–	2	1.56	–	2	1.68	–	2	1.80	–	2	1.92	–	2	2.03
19	–	2	2.98	–	2	3.11	–	2	3.23	–	2	3.36	–	2	3.48
20	–	2	4.40	–	2	4.53	–	2	4.66	–	2	4.80	–	2	4.93
21	–	2	5.82	–	2	5.96	–	2	6.10	–	2	6.24	–	2	6.37
22	–	2	7.24	–	2	7.39	–	2	7.53	–	2	7.68	–	2	7.82
23	–	2	8.66	–	2	8.81	–	2	8.96	–	2	9.12	–	2	9.27
24	–	2	10.08	–	2	10.24	–	2	10.40	–	2	10.56	–	2	10.71
25	–	2	11.50	–	2	11.67	–	2	11.83	–	3	0.—	–	3	0.16
26	–	3	0.92	–	3	1.09	–	3	1.26	–	3	1.43	–	3	1.60
27	–	3	2.34	–	3	2.52	–	3	2.70	–	3	2.88	–	3	3.05
28	–	3	3.76	–	3	3.95	–	3	4.13	–	3	4.32	–	3	4.50
29	–	3	5.18	–	3	5.37	–	3	5.56	–	3	5.76	–	3	5.94
30	–	3	6.60	–	3	6.80	–	3	7.—	–	3	7.20	–	3	7.40
40	–	4	8.81	–	4	9.07	–	4	9.33	–	4	9.60	–	4	9.86
50	–	5	11.01	–	5	11.34	–	5	11.67	–	6	0.—	–	6	0.32
60	–	7	1.21	–	7	1.61	–	7	2.—	–	7	2.40	–	7	2.79
70	–	8	3.41	–	8	3.87	–	8	4.33	–	8	4.30	–	8	5.26
80	–	9	5.62	–	9	6.14	–	9	6.67	–	9	7.20	–	9	7.72
90	–	10	7.82	–	10	8.41	–	10	9.—	–	10	9.60	–	10	10.19
100	–	11	10.02	–	11	10.68	–	11	11.34	–	12	0.—	–	12	0.65
200	1	3	8.05	1	3	8.36	1	3	10.68	1	4	0.—	1	4	1.31
300	1	15	6.08	1	15	8.05	1	15	10.02	1	16	0.—	1	16	1.97
400	2	7	4.10	2	7	6.73	2	7	9.36	2	8	0.—	2	8	2.63
500	2	19	2.13	2	19	5.42	2	19	8.71	3	0	0.—	3	0	3.28
600	3	11	0.16	3	11	4.10	3	11	8.05	3	12	0.—	3	12	3.94
700	4	2	10.19	4	3	2.79	4	3	7.39	4	4	0.—	4	4	4.60
800	4	14	8.21	4	15	1.47	4	15	6.73	4	16	0.—	4	16	5.25
900	5	6	6.24	5	7	0.16	5	7	6.08	5	8	0.—	5	8	5.91
1000	5	18	4.27	5	18	10.84	5	19	5.42	6	0	0.—	6	0	6.57
2000	11	16	8.54	11	17	9.69	11	18	10.84	12	0	0.—	12	1	1.15
3000	17	15	0.81	17	16	8.54	17	18	4.27	18	0	0.—	18	1	7.72
4000	23	13	5.09	23	15	7.39	23	17	9.69	24	0	0.—	24	2	2.30
5000	29	11	9.36	29	14	6.24	29	17	3.12	30	0	0.—	30	2	8.87

Prin.	221 Days.			222 Days.			223 Days.			224 Days.			225 Days.		
L.	L.	s.	d.pts	L.	s.	d.pts	L.	s.	d.pts	L.	s.	d.pts	L.	s.	d.pts
1	0	0	1,45	0	0	1,45	0	0	1,46	0	0	1,47	0	0	1,47
2	—	—	2,90	—	—	2,91	—	—	2,93	—	—	2,94	—	—	2,95
3	—	—	4,35	—	—	4,37	—	—	4,39	—	—	4,41	—	—	4,43
4	—	—	5,81	—	—	5,8[illegible]	—	—	5,86	—	—	5,88	—	—	5,91
5	—	—	7,26	—	—	7,29	—	—	7,33	—	—	7,36	—	—	7,39
6	—	—	8,71	—	—	8,75	—	—	8,79	—	—	8,83	—	—	8,87
7	—	—	10,17	—	—	10,21	—	—	10 26	—	—	10,31	—	—	10,35
8	—	—	11,62	—	—	11,67	—	—	11,73	—	—	11,78	—	—	11,83
9	—	1	1,07	—	1	1,13	—	1	1,19	—	1	1,25	—	1	1,31
10	—	1	2,53	—	1	2,59	—	1	2,66	—	1	2,72	—	1	2,79
11	—	1	3,98	—	1	4,05	—	1	4,12	—	1	4,20	—	1	4,27
12	—	1	5,43	—	1	5,51	—	1	5,59	—	1	5,67	—	1	5,75
13	—	1	6,89	—	1	6,97	—	1	7,06	—	1	7,14	—	1	7,23
14	—	1	8,34	—	1	8,43	—	1	8,52	—	1	8,62	—	1	8,71
15	—	1	9,79	—	1	9,89	—	1	10,—	—	1	10,09	—	1	10,19
16	—	1	11,25	—	1	11,35	—	1	11,46	—	1	11,56	—	1	11,67
17	—	2	0,70	—	2	0,81	—	2	0,92	—	2	1,04	—	2	1,15
18	—	2	2,15	—	2	2,27	—	2	2,39	—	2	2,51	—	2	2,63
19	—	2	3,61	—	2	3,73	—	2	3,85	—	2	3,98	—	2	4,10
20	—	2	5,06	—	2	5,19	—	2	5,32	—	2	5,45	—	2	5,59
21	—	2	6,51	—	2	6,65	—	2	6,79	—	2	6,93	—	2	7,06
22	—	2	7,97	—	2	8,11	—	2	8,25	—	2	8,40	—	2	8,54
23	—	2	9,42	—	2	9,57	—	2	9,72	—	2	9,87	—	2	10,02
24	—	2	10,87	—	2	11,03	—	2	11,19	—	2	11,34	—	2	11,50
25	—	3	0,33	—	3	0,49	—	3	0,65	—	3	0,82	—	3	0,98
26	—	3	1,78	—	3	1,95	—	3	2,12	—	3	2,29	—	3	2,46
27	—	3	3,23	—	3	3,41	—	3	3,59	—	3	3,76	—	3	3,94
28	—	3	4,69	—	3	4,87	—	3	5,05	—	3	5,24	—	3	5,42
29	—	3	6,14	—	3	6,33	—	3	6,52	—	3	6,71	—	3	6,90
30	—	3	7,59	—	3	7,79	—	3	8,—	—	3	8,18	—	3	8,30
40	—	4	10,12	—	4	10,38	—	4	10,65	—	4	10,91	—	4	11,17
50	—	6	0,65	—	6	1,—	—	6	1,31	—	6	1,64	—	6	2,—
60	—	7	3,18	—	7	3,58	—	7	3,97	—	7	4,37	—	7	4,76
70	—	8	5,74	—	8	6,18	—	8	6,64	—	8	7,10	—	8	7,56
80	—	9	8,25	—	9	8,77	—	9	9,30	—	9	9,82	—	9	10,35
90	—	10	10,78	—	10	11,37	—	10	11,96	—	11	0,55	—	11	1,15
100	—	12	1,31	—	12	1,97	—	12	2,63	—	12	3,28	—	12	3,94
200	1	4	2,63	1	4	3,94	1	4	5,26	1	4	6,57	1	4	7,89
300	1	16	3,94	1	16	5,91	1	16	7,8	1	16	9,86	1	16	11,83
400	2	8	5,26	2	8	7,89	2	8	10,52	2	9	1,15	2	9	3,78
500	3	0	6,57	3	0	9,8	3	1	1,15	3	1	4,43	3	1	7,72
600	3	12	7,89	3	12	11,83	3	13	3,78	3	13	7,72	3	13	11,67
700	4	4	9,20	4	5	1,80	4	5	6,41	4	5	11,01	4	6	3,61
800	4	16	10,52	4	17	3,77	4	17	9,01	4	18	2,29	4	18	7,56
900	5	8	11,83	5	9	5,75	5	9	11,67	5	10	5,58	5	10	11,50
1000	6	1	1,15	6	1	7,72	6	2	2,30	6	2	8,87	6	3	3,45
2000	12	2	2,30	12	3	3,45	12	4	4,60	12	5	5,75	12	6	6,90
3000	18	3	3,45	18	4	11,17	18	6	6,90	18	8	2,62	18	9	10,35
4000	24	4	4,60	24	6	6,90	24	8	9,20	24	10	11,50	24	13	1,80
5000	30	5	5,75	30	8	2,63	30	10	11,50	30	13	8,38	30	16	5,25

Prin.	226 Days			227 Days.			228 Days.			229 Days.			230 Days.		
L.	L.	s.	d.pts	L.	s.	d.pts	L.	s.	d.pts	L.	s.	d.pts	L.	s.	d.pts
1	0	0	1.48	0	0	1.49	0	0	1.49	0	0	1.50	0	0	1.51
2	—	—	2.97	—	—	2.98	—	—	3.—	—	—	3.01	—	—	3.02
3	—	—	4.45	—	—	4.47	—	—	4.49	—	—	4.51	—	—	4.53
4	—	—	5.94	—	—	5.97	—	—	6.—	—	—	6.02	—	—	6.04
5	—	—	7.43	—	—	7.46	—	—	7.49	—	—	7.52	—	—	7.56
6	—	—	8.91	—	—	8.95	—	—	9.—	—	—	9.03	—	—	9.07
7	—	—	10.40	—	—	10.44	—	—	10.49	—	—	10.54	—	—	10.58
8	—	—	11.88	—	—	11.94	—	1	0.—	—	1	0.04	—	1	0.09
9	—	1	1.37	—	1	1.43	—	1	1.49	—	1	1.55	—	1	1.61
10	—	1	2.86	—	1	2.92	—	1	3.—	—	1	3.05	—	1	3.12
11	—	1	4.34	—	1	4.41	—	1	4.49	—	1	4.56	—	1	4.63
12	—	1	5.83	—	1	5.91	—	1	6.—	—	1	6.06	—	1	6.14
13	—	1	7.31	—	1	7.40	—	1	7.48	—	1	7.57	—	1	7.66
14	—	1	8.80	—	1	8.89	—	1	9.—	—	1	9.08	—	1	9.17
15	—	1	10.29	—	1	10.38	—	1	10.48	—	1	10.58	—	1	10.68
16	—	1	11.77	—	1	11.88	—	2	0.—	—	2	0.09	—	2	0.19
17	—	2	1.26	—	2	1.37	—	2	1.48	—	2	1.59	—	2	1.70
18	—	2	2.74	—	2	2.86	—	2	3.—	—	2	3.10	—	2	3.22
19	—	2	4.23	—	2	4.35	—	2	4.48	—	2	4.60	—	2	4.73
20	—	2	5.72	—	2	5.85	—	2	6.—	—	2	6.11	—	2	6.24
21	—	2	7.20	—	2	7.34	—	2	7.48	—	2	7.62	—	2	7.75
22	—	2	8.69	—	2	8.83	—	2	9.—	—	2	9.12	—	2	9.27
23	—	2	10.17	—	2	10.32	—	2	10.48	—	2	10.63	—	2	10.78
24	—	2	11.66	—	2	11.82	—	3	0.—	—	3	0.13	—	3	0.29
25	—	3	1.15	—	3	1.31	—	3	1.48	—	3	1.64	—	3	1.80
26	—	3	2.63	—	3	2.80	—	3	3.—	—	3	3.14	—	3	3.32
27	—	3	4.12	—	3	4.30	—	3	4.48	—	3	4.65	—	3	4.83
28	—	3	5.60	—	3	5.79	—	3	6.—	—	3	6.16	—	3	6.34
29	—	3	7.09	—	3	7.28	—	3	7.48	—	3	7.66	—	3	7.85
30	—	3	8.58	—	3	8.77	—	3	9.—	—	3	9.17	—	3	9.36
40	—	4	11.44	—	4	11.70	—	5	0.—	—	5	0.23	—	5	0.40
50	—	6	2.30	—	6	2.63	—	6	3.—	—	6	3.28	—	6	3.61
60	—	7	5.16	—	7	5.55	—	7	6.—	—	7	6.34	—	7	6.73
70	—	8	8.02	—	8	8.48	—	8	9.—	—	8	9.40	—	8	9.86
80	—	9	10.88	—	9	11.40	—	10	0.—	—	10	0.46	—	10	1.—
90	—	11	1.74	—	11	2.33	—	11	3.—	—	11	3.51	—	11	4.10
100	—	12	4.60	—	12	5.26	—	12	6.—	—	12	6.57	—	12	7.23
200	1	4	9.20	1	4	10.52	1	4	11.83	1	5	1.15	1	5	2.46
300	1	17	1.80	1	17	3.78	1	17	5.75	1	17	7.72	1	17	9.69
400	2	9	6.41	2	9	9.04	2	9	11.67	2	10	2.30	2	10	4.93
500	3	1	11.01	3	2	2.30	3	2	5.58	3	2	8.87	3	3	0.16
600	3	14	3.61	3	14	7.56	3	14	11.49	3	15	3.45	3	15	7.39
700	4	6	8.21	4	7	0.82	4	7	5.41	4	7	10.02	4	8	2.62
800	4	19	0.81	4	19	6.08	4	19	11.33	5	0	4.60	5	0	9.85
900	5	11	5.42	5	11	11.34	5	12	5.24	5	12	11.17	5	13	5.08
1000	6	3	10.02	6	4	4.60	6	4	11.16	6	5	5.75	6	6	0.32
2000	12	7	8.05	12	8	9.20	12	9	10.53	12	10	11.50	12	12	0.65
3000	18	11	6.08	18	13	1.80	18	14	9.50	18	16	5.25	18	18	0.98
4000	24	15	4.10	24	17	6.40	24	19	8.71	25	1	11.—	25	4	1.31
5000	30	19	2.13	31	1	11.—	31	4	7.89	31	7	4.75	31	10	1.64

Pen.	231 Days.			232 Days.			233 Days.			234 Days.			235 Days.		
L.	L.	s.	d.pts	L.	s.	d.pts	L.	s.	d.pts	L.	s.	d.pts	L.	s.	d.pts
1	0	0	1.51	0	0	1.52	0	0	1.53	0	0	1.53	0	0	1.54
2	—		3.03	—		3.05	—		3.06	—		3.07	—		3.09
3	—		4.55	—		4.57	—		4.59	—		4.61	—		4.63
4	—		6.07	—		6.10	—		6.12	—		6.15	—		6.18
5	—		7.59	—		7.62	—		7.66	—		7.69	—		7.72
6	—		9.11	—		5.15	—		9.19	—		9.23	—		9.27
7	—		10.63	—		10.67	—		10.72	—		10.77	—		10.81
8	–	1	0.15	–	1	0.20	–	1	0.25	–	1	0.30	–	1	0.36
9	–	1	1.67	–	1	1.72	–	1	1.78	–	1	1.84	–	1	1.90
10	–	1	3.18	–	1	3.25	–	1	3.32	–	1	3.38	–	1	3.45
11	–	1	4.70	–	1	4.78	–	1	4.85	–	1	4.92	–	1	5.—
12	–	1	6.22	–	1	6.30	–	1	6.38	–	1	6.46	–	1	6.54
13	–	1	7.74	–	1	7.83	–	1	7.91	–	1	8.—	–	1	8.08
14	–	1	9.26	–	1	9.35	–	1	9.44	–	1	9.54	–	1	9.63
15	–	1	10.78	–	1	10.88	–	1	11.—	–	1	11.07	–	1	11.17
16	–	2	0.30	–	2	0.40	–	2	0.51	–	2	0.61	–	2	0.72
17	–	2	1.82	–	2	1.93	–	2	2.04	–	2	2.15	–	2	2.26
18	–	2	3.34	–	2	3.45	–	2	3.57	–	2	3.69	–	2	3.81
19	–	2	4.85	–	2	4.98	–	2	5.10	–	2	5.23	–	2	5.35
20	–	2	6.37	–	2	6.50	–	2	6.64	–	2	6.77	–	2	6.90
21	–	2	7.89	–	2	8.03	–	2	8.17	–	2	8.31	–	2	8.44
22	–	2	9.41	–	2	9.56	–	2	9.70	–	2	9.84	–	2	10.—
23	–	2	10.93	–	2	11.08	–	2	11.23	–	2	11.38	–	2	11.54
24	–	3	0.45	–	3	0.61	–	3	0.76	–	3	0.92	–	3	1.08
25	–	3	1.97	–	3	2.13	–	3	2.30	–	3	2.46	–	3	2.63
26	–	3	3.49	–	3	3.66	–	3	3.83	–	3	4.—	–	3	4.17
27	–	3	5.01	–	3	5.18	–	3	5.36	–	3	5.54	–	3	5.72
28	–	3	6.52	–	3	6.71	–	3	6.89	–	3	7.08	–	3	7.26
29	–	3	8.04	–	3	8.23	–	3	8.42	–	3	8.62	–	3	8.81
30	–	3	9.56	–	3	9.76	–	3	9.96	–	3	10.15	–	3	10.35
40	–	5	0.75	–	5	1.01	–	5	1.28	–	5	1.54	–	5	1.80
50	–	6	3.94	–	6	4.27	–	6	4.61	–	6	4.93	–	6	5.26
60	–	7	7.13	–	7	7.52	–	7	7.92	–	7	8.31	–	7	8.71
70	–	8	10.32	–	8	10.78	–	8	11.23	–	8	11.70	–	9	0.16
80	–	10	1.51	–	10	2.05	–	10	2.56	–	10	3.09	–	10	3.61
90	–	11	4.70	–	11	5.29	–	11	5.88	–	11	6.47	–	11	7.06
100	–	12	7.89	–	12	8.54	–	12	9.20	–	12	9.86	–	12	10.52
200	1	5	3.78	1	5	5.09	1	5	6.41	1	5	7.72	1	5	9.04
300	1	17	11.67	1	18	1.64	1	18	3.61	1	18	5.58	1	18	7.56
400	2	10	7.56	2	10	10.18	2	11	0.82	2	11	3.45	2	11	6.08
500	3	3	3.45	3	3	6.74	3	3	10.02	3	4	1.31	3	4	4.60
600	3	15	11.34	3	16	3.28	3	16	7.23	3	16	11.17	3	17	3.12
700	4	8	7.23	4	8	11.82	4	9	4.41	4	9	9.04	4	10	1.64
800	5	1	3.12	5	1	8.37	5	2	1.64	5	2	6.90	5	3	0.16
900	5	13	11.01	5	14	4.92	5	14	10.84	5	15	4.76	5	15	10.68
1000	6	6	6.90	6	7	1.47	6	7	8.05	6	8	2.63	6	8	9.21
2000	12	13	1.80	12	14	2.94	12	15	4.10	12	16	5.26	12	17	6.42
3000	18	19	8.70	19	1	4.41	19	3	0.15	19	4	7.89	19	6	3.63
4000	25	6	3.60	25	8	5.88	25	10	8.20	25	12	10.52	25	15	0.84
5000	31	12	10.50	31	15	7.45	31	18	4.25	32	1	1.15	32	3	10.05

Prin.	236 Days.			237 Days.			238 Days.			239 Days.			240 Days.		
£.	£.	s.	d.pts	£.	s.	d.pts	£.	s.	d.pts	£.	s.	d.pts	£.	s.	d.pts
1	0	0	1.55	0	0	1.55	0	0	1.56	0	0	1.57	0	0	1.57
2	——		3.10	——		3.11	——		3.12	——		3.14	——		3.15
3	——		4.65	——		4.67	——		4.69	——		4.71	——		4.73
4	——		6.20	——		6.23	——		6.25	——		6.28	——		6.31
5	——		7.75	——		7.79	——		7.82	——		7.85	——		7.89
6	——		9.31	——		9.35	——		9.38	——		9.42	——		9.46
7	——		10.86	——		10.90	——		10.95	——		11.—	——		11.04
8	–	1	0.41	–	1	0.46	–	1	0.51	–	1	0.57	–	1	0.62
9	–	1	1.96	–	1	2.02	–	1	2.08	–	1	2.14	–	1	2.20
10	–	1	3.51	–	1	3.58	–	1	3.64	–	1	3.71	–	1	3.78
11	–	1	5.06	–	1	5.14	–	1	5.21	–	1	5.28	–	1	5.35
12	–	1	6.62	–	1	6.70	–	1	6.77	–	1	6.85	–	1	6.93
13	–	1	8.07	–	1	8.25	–	1	8.34	–	1	8.42	–	1	8.51
14	–	1	9.72	–	1	9.81	–	1	9.90	–	1	10.—	–	1	10.09
15	–	1	11.27	–	1	11.37	–	1	11.47	–	1	11.57	–	1	11.67
16	–	2	0.82	–	2	0.93	–	2	1.03	–	2	1.14	–	2	1.24
17	–	2	2.38	–	2	2.49	–	2	2.60	–	2	2.71	–	2	2.82
18	–	2	3.93	–	2	4.05	–	2	4.16	–	2	4.28	–	2	4.40
19	–	2	5.48	–	2	5.60	–	2	5.73	–	2	5.85	–	2	5.98
20	–	2	7.03	–	2	7.16	–	2	7.29	–	2	7.43	–	2	7.56
21	–	2	8.78	–	2	8.72	–	2	8.86	–	2	9.—	–	2	9.13
22	–	2	10.13	–	2	10.28	–	2	10.42	–	2	10.57	–	2	10.71
23	–	2	11.69	–	2	11.84	–	3	0.—	–	3	0.14	–	3	0.29
24	–	3	1.24	–	3	1.40	–	3	1.55	–	3	1.71	–	3	1.87
25	–	3	2.79	–	3	2.95	–	3	3.12	–	3	3.28	–	3	3.45
26	–	3	4.34	–	3	4.51	–	3	4.68	–	3	4.85	–	3	5.03
27	–	3	5.89	–	3	6.07	–	3	6.25	–	3	6.43	–	3	6.60
28	–	3	7.44	–	3	7.63	–	3	7.81	–	3	8.—	–	3	8.18
29	–	3	9.—	–	3	9.19	–	3	9.38	–	3	9.57	–	3	9.76
30	–	3	10.55	–	3	10.75	–	3	10.94	–	3	11.14	–	3	11.34
40	–	5	2.07	–	5	2.33	–	5	2.59	–	5	2.86	–	5	3.12
50	–	6	5.58	–	6	5.91	–	6	6.24	–	6	6.57	–	6	6.90
60	–	7	9.10	–	7	9.50	–	7	9.89	–	7	10.29	–	7	10.68
70	–	9	0.62	–	9	1.08	–	9	1.54	–	9	2.—	–	9	2.46
80	–	10	4.14	–	10	4.66	–	10	5.19	–	10	5.72	–	10	6.24
90	–	11	7.66	–	11	8.25	–	11	8.84	–	11	9.43	–	11	10.02
100	–	12	11.17	–	12	11.83	–	13	0.49	–	13	1.15	–	13	1.80
200	1	5	10.35	1	5	11.67	1	6	0.98	1	6	2.30	1	6	3.61
300	1	18	9.53	1	18	11.50	1	19	1.47	1	19	3.45	1	19	5.42
400	2	11	8.71	2	11	11.33	2	12	1.97	2	12	4.60	2	12	7.23
500	3	4	7.89	3	4	11.17	3	5	2.46	3	5	5.75	3	5	9.04
600	3	17	7.06	3	17	11.01	3	18	2.95	3	18	6.90	3	18	10.84
700	4	10	6.24	4	10	10.84	4	11	3.45	4	11	8.05	4	12	0.65
800	5	3	5.42	5	3	10.68	5	4	3.94	5	4	9.20	5	5	2.46
900	5	16	4.60	5	16	10.51	5	17	4.43	5	17	10.35	5	18	4.24
1000	6	9	3.78	6	9	10.35	6	10	4.9	6	10	11.50	6	11	6.08
2000	12	18	7.56	12	19	8.70	13	0	9.86	13	1	11.—	13	3	0.16
3000	19	7	11.34	19	9	7.05	19	11	2.79	19	12	10.50	19	14	6.24
4000	25	17	3.12	25	19	5.40	26	1	7.72	26	3	10.—	26	6	0.32
5000	32	6	6.90	32	9	3.75	32	12	0.65	32	14	9.59	32	17	6.40

Prin.	241 Days.			242 Days.			243 Days.			244 Days.			245 Days.		
L.	L.	s.	d.pts	L.	s.	d.pts	L.	s.	d.pts	L.	s.	d.pts	L.	s.	d.pts
1	0	0	1.58	0	0	1.59	0	0	1.59	0	0	1.60	0	0	1.61
2	—		3,16	—		3,18	—		3.19	—		3,20	—		3,22
3	—		4,75	—		4,77	—		4,79	—		4,81	—		4,83
4	—		6,33	—		6,36	—		6,39	—		6,41	—		6,44
5	—		7,92	—		7,95	—		7,98	—		8,02	—		8,05
6	—		9,50	—		9,54	—		9,58	—		9,62	—		9,66
7	—		11,09	—		11,13	—		11,18	—		11,23	—		11,27
8	—	1	0,67	—	1	0,72	—	1	0,78	—	1	0,83	—	1	0,88
9	—	1	2,26	—	1	2,32	—	1	2,38	—	1	2,43	—	1	2,49
10	—	1	3,84	—	1	3,91	—	1	3,97	—	1	4,04	—	1	4,10
11	—	1	5,43	—	1	5,50	—	1	5,57	—	1	5,64	—	1	5,72
12	—	1	7,01	—	1	7,09	—	1	7,17	—	1	7,25	—	1	7,33
13	—	1	8,60	—	1	8,68	—	1	8,77	—	1	8,85	—	1	8,94
14	—	1	10,18	—	1	10,27	—	1	10,36	—	1	10,46	—	1	10,55
15	—	1	11,76	—	1	11,86	—	1	11,96	—	2	0,06	—	2	0,16
16	—	2	1,35	—	2	1,45	—	2	1,56	—	2	1,67	—	2	1,77
17	—	2	2,93	—	2	3,05	—	2	3,16	—	2	3,27	—	2	3,38
18	—	2	4,52	—	2	4,64	—	2	4,76	—	2	4,87	—	2	5,—
19	—	2	6,10	—	2	6,23	—	2	6,35	—	2	6,48	—	2	6,60
20	—	2	7,69	—	2	7,82	—	2	7,95	—	2	8,08	—	2	8,21
21	—	2	9,27	—	2	9,41	—	2	9,55	—	2	9,69	—	2	9,82
22	—	2	10,86	—	2	11,—	—	2	11,15	—	2	11,29	—	2	11,44
23	—	3	0,43	—	3	0,59	—	3	0,74	—	3	0,90	—	3	1,05
24	—	3	2,03	—	3	2,18	—	3	2,34	—	3	2,50	—	3	2,66
25	—	3	3,61	—	3	3,77	—	3	3,94	—	3	4,10	—	3	4,27
26	—	3	5,02	—	3	5,36	—	3	5,54	—	3	5,71	—	3	5,88
27	—	3	6,78	—	3	6,95	—	3	7,14	—	3	7,31	—	3	7,49
28	—	3	8,37	—	3	8,54	—	3	8,73	—	3	8,92	—	3	9,10
29	—	3	9,95	—	3	10,13	—	3	10,33	—	3	10,52	—	3	10,71
30	—	3	11,53	—	3	11,72	—	3	11,93	—	4	0,13	—	4	0,32
40	—	5	3,38	—	5	3,64	—	5	3,91	—	5	4,17	—	5	4,43
50	—	6	7,23	—	6	7,56	—	6	7,89	—	6	8,21	—	6	8,54
60	—	7	11,07	—	7	11,47	—	7	11,93	—	8	0,26	—	8	0,05
70	—	9	2,92	—	9	3,38	—	9	3,84	—	9	4,30	—	9	4,76
80	—	10	6,77	—	10	7,29	—	10	7,82	—	10	8,35	—	10	8,87
90	—	11	10,61	—	11	11,21	—	11	11,80	—	12	0,39	—	12	1,—
100	—	13	2,46	—	13	3,12	—	13	3,78	—	13	4,43	—	13	5,09
200	1	6	4,93	1	6	6,24	1	6	7,56	1	6	8,87	1	6	10,19
300	1	19	7,39	1	19	9,36	1	19	11,34	2	0	1,31	2	0	3,28
400	2	12	9,86	2	13	0,49	2	13	3,12	2	13	5,75	2	13	8,38
500	3	6	0,32	3	6	3,61	3	6	6,90	3	6	10,19	3	7	1,47
600	3	19	2,79	3	19	6,73	3	19	10,68	4	0	2,62	4	0	6,57
700	4	12	5,25	4	12	9,86	4	13	2,40	4	13	7,06	4	13	11,66
800	5	5	7,72	5	6	0,98	5	6	6,24	5	6	11,50	5	7	4,76
900	5	18	10,18	5	19	4,10	5	19	8,02	6	0	3,94	6	0	9,85
1000	6	12	0,65	6	12	7,23	6	13	1,80	6	13	8,36	6	14	2,95
2000	13	4	1,30	13	5	2,46	13	6	3,60	13	7	4,70	13	8	5,90
3000	19	16	1,95	19	17	9,60	19	19	5,40	20	1	1,14	20	2	8,85
4000	26	8	2,60	26	10	4,92	26	12	7,20	26	14	6,52	26	16	11,80
5000	33	0	3,25	33	3	0,15	33	5	9,—	33	8	5,90	33	11	2,75

Prin.	246 Days.			247 Days.			248 Days.			249 Days.			250 Days.		
£.	£.	s.	d.pts	£.	s.	d.pts	£.	s.	d.pt.	£.	s.	d.pt.	£.	s.	d.pt.
1	0	0	1.61	0	0	1.62	0	0	1.62	0	0	1.63	0	0	1.64
2	—		3.23	—		3.24	—		3.26	—		3.2[illegible]	—		3.28
3	—		4.85	—		4.87	—		4.86	—		4.91	—		4.93
4	—		6.47	—		6.49	—		6.52	—		6.54	—		6.57
5	—		8.0	—		8.12	—		8.15	—		8.18	—		[illegible]
6	—		9.70	—		9.74	—		9.78	—		9.82	—		9.80
7	—		11.32	—		11.36	—		11.41	—		11.46	—		11.50
8	—	1	0.94	—	1	1.—	—	1	1.04	—	1	1.0[illegible]	—	1	1.15
9	—	1	2.55	—	1	2.62	—	1	2.67	—	1	2.73	—	1	2.79
10	—	1	4.17	—	1	4.24	—	1	4.30	—	1	4.37	—	1	[illegible]
11	—	1	5.79	—	1	5.86	—	1	5.93	—	1	6.—	—	1	6.08
12	—	1	7.41	—	1	7.48	—	1	7.56	—	1	7.63	—	1	7.72
13	—	1	9.02	—	1	9.11	—	1	9.19	—	1	9.28	—	1	9.36
14	—	1	10.64	—	1	10.73	—	1	10.82	—	1	10.92	—	1	11.01
15	—	2	0.26	—	2	0.36	—	2	0.46	—	2	0.55	—	2	0.65
16	—	2	1.88	—	2	2.—	—	2	2.09	—	2	2.19	—	2	2.30
17	—	2	3.49	—	2	3.61	—	2	3.72	—	2	3.83	—	2	3.94
18	—	2	5.11	—	2	5.23	—	2	5.35	—	2	5.47	—	2	5.58
19	—	2	6.73	—	2	6.85	—	2	6.98	—	2	7.10	—	2	7.20
20	—	2	8.35	—	2	8.48	—	2	8.61	—	2	8.74	—	2	8.87
21	—	2	9.96	—	2	10.10	—	2	10.24	—	2	10.38	—	2	10.52
22	—	2	11.58	—	2	11.73	—	2	11.87	—	3	0.01	—	3	0.16
23	—	3	1.20	—	3	1.35	—	3	1.50	—	3	1.65	—	3	1.80
24	—	3	2.82	—	3	2.97	—	3	3.13	—	3	3.29	—	3	3.45
25	—	3	4.43	—	3	4.60	—	3	4.76	—	3	4.93	—	3	5.09
26	—	3	6.05	—	3	6.22	—	3	6.39	—	3	6.56	—	3	6.73
27	—	3	7.67	—	3	7.85	—	3	8.03	—	3	8.20	—	3	8.38
28	—	3	9.29	—	3	9.47	—	3	9.65	—	3	9.84	—	3	10.02
29	—	3	10.90	—	3	11.09	—	3	11.28	—	3	11.48	—	3	11.67
30	—	4	0.52	—	4	0.72	—	4	0.92	—	4	1.11	—	4	1.31
40	—	5	4.70	—	5	4.96	—	5	5.22	—	5	5.49	—	5	5.75
50	—	6	6.84	—	6	9.20	—	6	9.53	—	6	9.86	—	6	10.19
60	—	8	1.05	—	8	1.44	—	8	1.84	—	8	2.23	—	8	2.62
70	—	9	5.22	—	9	5.68	—	9	6.14	—	9	6.60	—	9	7.06
80	—	10	9.40	—	10	9.92	—	10	10.45	—	10	10.98	—	10	11.50
90	—	12	1.57	—	12	2.16	—	12	2.75	—	12	3.35	—	12	3.94
100	—	13	5.75	—	13	6.41	—	13	7.06	—	13	7.72	—	13	8.38
200	1	6	11.50	1	7	0.82	1	7	2.13	1	7	3.45	1	7	4.76
300	2	0	5.25	2	0	7.63	2	0	9.20	2	0	11.17	2	1	1.14
400	2	13	11.01	2	14	1.64	2	14	4.27	2	14	6.90	2	14	9.53
500	3	7	4.76	3	7	8.05	3	7	11.34	3	8	2.63	3	8	5.91
600	4	0	10.51	4	1	2.46	4	[illegible]	6.40	4	1	10.35	4	2	2.29
700	4	14	4.27	4	14	8.87	4	15	1.47	4	15	6.08	4	15	10.68
800	5	7	10.02	5	8	3.28	5	8	8.54	5	9	1.80	5	9	7.06
900	6	1	3.77	6	1	9.69	6	2	3.61	6	2	9.53	6	3	3.44
1000	6	14	9.53	6	15	4.10	6	15	10.68	6	16	5.26	6	16	11.83
2000	13	9	7.06	13	10	8.20	13	11	9.30	13	12	10.52	13	13	11.66
3000	20	4	4.59	20	6	0.30	20	7	8.04	20	9	3.78	20	10	11.49
4000	26	19	2.12	27	1	4.40	27	3	6.72	27	5	9.04	27	7	11.32
5000	33	13	11.65	33	16	8.50	33	19	5.40	34	2	2.30	34	4	11.15

Prin	251 Days.			252 Days.			253 Days.			254 Days.			255 Days.		
£.	£.	s.	d.pts	£.	s.	d.pts	£.	s.	d.pts	£.	s.	d.pts	£.	s.	d.pts
1	0	0	1.6[illegible]	0	0	1.65	0	0	1.66	0	0	1.67	0	0	1.67
2	—		[illegible]	—		3,3[illegible]	—		3,32	—		3,34	—		3,35
3	—		4,95	—		4,97	—		5,—	—		5,01	—		5,03
4	—		6,60	—		6,62	—		6,65	—		6,6[illegible]	—		6,70
5	—		8,25	—		8,28	—		8,31	—		8,3[illegible]	—		8,38
6	—		9,90	—		9.94	—		9,98	—		10,0[illegible]	—		10,06
7	—		11,55	—		11,59	—		11,64	—		11,6[illegible]	—		11,73
8	—	1	1,20	—	1	1,25	—	1	1,30	—	1	1,39	—	1	1,41
9	—	1	2,85	—	1	2,91	—	1	2,07	—	1	3,03	—	1	3,09
10	—	1	4,50	—	1	4,56	—	1	4,63	—	1	4,70	—	1	4,76
11	—	1	6,15	—	1	6,22	—	1	6,29	—	1	6,3[illegible]	—	1	6,44
12	—	1	7,80	—	1	7,88	—	1	7,96	—	1	8,0	—	1	8,12
13	—	1	6,45	—	1	9.54	—	1	9,62	—	1	9,71	—	1	9,79
14	—	1	11,10	—	1	11,19	—	1	11,28	—	1	11,38	—	1	11,47
15	—	2	0,73	—	2	0,85	—	2	0,95	—	2	1,05	—	2	1,15
16	—	2	2,47	—	2	2,51	—	2	2,61	—	2	2,72	—	2	2,82
17	—	2	4,05	—	2	4,16	—	2	4,28	—	2	4,39	—	2	4,50
18	—	2	5,70	—	2	5,82	—	2	5,94	—	2	6,06	—	2	6,18
19	—	2	7,35	—	2	7,48	—	2	7,60	—	2	7,73	—	2	7,85
20	—	2	9,—	—	2	9,13	—	2	9,27	—	2	9,40	—	2	9,53
21	—	2	10,65	—	2	10,79	—	2	10,93	—	2	11,07	—	2	11,21
22	—	3	0,30	—	3	0,45	—	3	0,59	—	3	0,74	—	3	0,88
23	—	3	1,95	—	3	2,11	—	3	2,26	—	3	2,41	—	3	2,56
24	—	3	3,60	—	3	3,76	—	3	3,92	—	3	4,08	—	3	4,24
25	—	3	5,26	—	3	5,42	—	3	5,58	—	3	5,75	—	3	5,91
26	—	3	6,91	—	3	7,08	—	3	7,25	—	3	7,42	—	3	7,59
27	—	3	8,56	—	3	8,75	—	3	8,91	—	3	9,09	—	3	9,27
28	—	3	10,21	—	3	10,39	—	3	10,57	—	3	10,76	—	3	10,94
29	—	3	11,86	—	4	0,05	—	4	0,24	—	4	0,43	—	4	0,62
30	—	4	1,51	—	4	1,70	—	4	1,90	—	4	2,10	—	4	2,30
40	—	5	6,[illegible]1	—	5	6,27	—	5	6,54	—	5	6,80	—	5	7,06
50	—	6	10,42	—	6	10,8[illegible]	—	6	11,17	—	6	11,1[illegible]	—	6	11,83
60	—	8	3,02	—	8	3,41	—	8	3,81	—	8	4,20	—	8	4,60
70	—	9	7,52	—	9	8,—	—	9	8,44	—	9	8,9[illegible]	—	9	9,36
80	—	11	0,8[illegible]	—	11	0,55	—	11	1,08	—	11	1,61	—	11	2,1[illegible]
90	—	12	4,5	—	12	5,12	—	12	5,72	—	12	6,31	—	12	6,9[illegible]
100	—	13	9,04	—	13	9,69	—	13	10,[illegible]5	—	13	11,01	—	13	11,67
200	1	7	6,0[illegible]	1	7	7,3	1	7	8,71	1	7	10,02	1	7	11,34
300	2	1	[illegible]	2	1	5,0[illegible]	2	1	7,06	2	1	9,02	2	1	11,01
400	2	15	[illegible],16	2	15	2,[illegible]	2	15	5,42	2	15	8,05	2	15	10,68
500	3	[illegible]	[illegible],20	3	9	[illegible]	3	9	3,78	3	9	7,06	3	9	10,35
600	4	2	[illegible]	4	2	10,1[illegible]	4	3	2,13	4	3	6,07	4	3	10,02
700	4	16	3,2[illegible]	4	1[illegible]	[illegible]	4	17	0,49	4	17	5,09	4	17	9,69
800	5	10	[illegible]	5	10	5,5[illegible]	5	10	10,84	5	11	4,10	5	11	9,[illegible]
900	6	3	[illegible]	6	4	[illegible],28	6	4	9,20	6	5	3,11	6	5	0,0[illegible]
1000	6	17	[illegible]	6	18	[illegible]	6	18	7,5[illegible]	9	19	2,02	6	19	8,71
2000	13	15	[illegible]	13	16	1,[illegible]	13	17	3,12	13	18	4,20	13	19	5,42
3000	20	12	7,2[illegible]	20	14	2,9[illegible]	20	15	10,68	20	17	6,[illegible]9	20	19	2,13
4000	27	10	1,6[illegible]	27	12	[illegible]	27	14	[illegible]	27	16	8,52	27	18	10,84
5000	[illegible]	7	8,0[illegible]	34	10	4,0[illegible]	34	13	1,80	34	15	10,65	34	18	7,65

Prin	256 Days.			257 Days.			258 Days.			259 Days.			260 Days.		
£.	£.	s.	d.pts	£.	s.	d.pts	£.	s.	d.pts	£.	s.	d.pts	£.	s.	d.pts
1	0	0	1,68	0	0	1.68	0	0	1.69	0	0	1.70	0	0	1.70
2	——		3.36	——		3.37	——		3.39	——		3.40	——		3.41
3	——		5.04	——		5.06	——		5.08	——		5.10	——		5.12
4	——		6.7	——		6.75	——		6.78	——		6.81	——		6.83
5	——		8.41	——		8.44	——		8.48	——		8.51	——		8.54
6	——		10.09	——		10 13	——		10 17	——		10.21	——		10.25
7	——		11.78	——		11 82	——		11.87	——		11.02	——		11.96
8	—	1	1.46	—	1	1.51	—	1	1.57	—	1	1.62	—	1	1.67
9	—	1	3.14	—	1	3.20	—	1	3.26	—	1	3.32	—	1	3.38
10	—	1	4.83	—	1	4.80	—	1	4.96	—	1	5.03	—	1	5.09
11	—	1	6.51	—	1	6.58	—	1	6.66	—	1	6.73	—	1	6.80
12	—	1	8.19	—	1	8.27	—	1	8.35	—	1	8.43	—	1	8.51
13	—	1	9 88	—	1	9.96	—	1	10.05	—	1	10 13	—	1	10.22
14	—	1	11.56	—	1	11.65	—	1	11.75	—	1	11.84	—	1	11.93
15	—	2	1.24	—	2	1.34	—	2	1.44	—	2	1.54	—	2	1.64
16	—	2	2.93	—	2	3.03	—	2	3.14	—	2	3.24	—	2	3.35
17	—	2	4.61	—	2	4.72	—	2	4.83	—	2	4.95	—	2	5.06
18	—	2	6.29	—	2	6.41	—	2	6.53	—	2	6.65	—	2	6.77
19	—	2	7.98	—	2	8.10	—	2	8.23	—	2	8.35	—	2	8.48
20	—	2	9.66	—	2	9.79	—	2	9.92	—	2	10.05	—	2	10.19
21	—	2	11.34	—	2	11.48	—	2	11.62	—	2	11.76	—	2	11.90
22	—	3	1.03	—	3	1.17	—	3	1.32	—	3	1.46	—	3	1.61
23	—	3	2.71	—	3	2.86	—	3	3.01	—	3	3.16	—	3	3.32
24	—	3	4.39	—	3	4.55	—	3	4.71	—	3	4.87	—	3	5.02
25	—	3	6.08	—	3	6.24	—	3	6.41	—	3	6.57	—	3	6.73
26	—		7.76	—	3	7.93	—	3	8.10	—	3	8.27	—	3	8.44
27	—	3	9.44	—	3	9.63	—	3	9.80	—	3	9.98	—	3	10.15
28	—	3	11.13	—	3	11.31	—	3	11.50	—	3	11.60	—	3	11.86
29	—	4	0.81	—	4	1.—	—	4	1.19	—	4	1.39	—	4	1.57
30	—	4	2.49	—	4	2.69	—	4	2.89	—	4	3.09	—	4	3.28
40	—	5	7.33	—	5	7.59	—	5	7.85	—	5	8.12	—	5	8.38
50	—	7	0.16	—	7	0.49	—	7	0.82	—	7	1.15	—	7	1.47
60	—	8	5.—	—	8	5.39	—	8	5.78	—	8	6.18	—	8	6.57
70	—	9	9.82	—	9	10.29	—	9	10.75	—	9	11.21	—	9	11.67
80	—	11	2.66	—	11	3 18	—	11	3.71	—	11	4.24	—	11	4.7
90	—	12	7.49	—	12	8.08	—	12	8.67	—	12	9.27	—	12	9.86
100	—	14	0.32	—	14	0.98	—	14	1.64	—	14	2.30	—	14	2.95
200	1	8	0.65	1	8	1.97	1	8	3.28	1	8	4.60	1	8	5.91
300	2	2	0.91	2	2	2.95	2	2	4.92	2	2	6.90	2	2	8.87
400	2	16	1.31	2	16	3.94	2	16	6.57	2	16	9.20	2	16	11.83
500	3	10	1.64	3	10	4.93	3	10	8.21	3	10	11.50	3	11	2.79
600	4	4	1.96	4	4	5.91	4	4	9.85	4	5	1.80	4	5	5.74
700	4	18	2.29	4	18	6.92	4	18	11.50	4	19	4.10	4	19	8.70
800	5	12	2.62	5	12	7.88	5	13	1.14	5	13	6.40	5	13	11.66
900	6	6	2.95	6	6	8.87	6	7	2.78	6	7	8.70	6	8	2.72
1000	7	0	3.28	7	0	9.86	7	1	4.43	7	1	11.01	7	2	5.58
2000	14	0	6.56	14	1	7.72	14	2	8.86	14	3	10.62	14	4	11.16
3000	21	0	9 84	21	2	5.58	21	4	1 29	21	5	9.03	21	7	4.74
4000	28	1	1.12	28	3	3.44	28	5	5.72	28	7	8.04	28	9	10.32
5000	35	1	4.40	35	4	1.30	35	6	10. 5	35	9	7.05	35	12	3.90

Prin.	261 Days.			262 Days.			263 Days.			264 Days.			265 Days.		
£.	£.	s.	d.pts	£.	s.	d.pts	£.	s.	d.pts	£.	s.	d.pts	£.	s.	d.pts
1	0	0	1.71	0	0	1.72	0	0	1.72	0	0	1.73	0	0	1.74
2	—		3.43	—		3.44	—		3.45	—		3.47	—		3.48
3	—		5.14	—		5.16	—		5.18	—		5.20	—		5.22
4	—		6.86	—		6.89	—		6.91	—		6.94	—		6.96
5	—		8.58	—		8.61	—		8.64	—		8.67	—		8.71
6	—		10.29	—		10.33	—		10.37	—		10.41	—		10.45
7	—	1	0.01	—	1	0.05	—	1	0.10	—	1	0.15	—	1	0.19
8	—	1	1.72	—	1	1.78	—	1	1.83	—	1	1.88	—	1	1.93
9	—	1	3.44	—	1	3.50	—	1	3.56	—	1	3.62	—	1	3.68
10	—	1	5.16	—	1	5.22	—	1	5.29	—	1	5.35	—	1	5.42
11	—	1	6.87	—	1	6.95	—	1	7.02	—	1	7.09	—	1	7. 6
12	—	1	8.59	—	1	8.67	—	1	8.75	—	1	8.83	—	1	8.90
13	—	1	10.31	—	1	10.39	—	1	10.48	—	1	10.56	—	1	10.65
14	—	2	0.02	—	2	0.11	—	2	0.21	—	2	0.30	—	2	0.39
15	—	2	1.74	—	2	1.84	—	2	1.93	—	2	2.03	—	2	2.13
16	—	2	3.45	—	2	3.56	—	2	3.66	—	2	3.77	—	2	3.87
17	—	2	5.17	—	2	5.28	—	2	5.39	—	2	5.51	—	2	5.62
18	—	2	6.89	—	2	7.—	—	2	7.12	—	2	7.24	—	2	7.36
19	—	2	8.60	—	2	8.73	—	2	8.85	—	2	8.98	—	2	9.10
20	—	2	10.32	—	2	10.45	—	2	10.58	—	2	10.71	—	2	10.84
21	—	3	0.03	—	3	0.17	—	3	0.31	—	3	0.45	—	3	0.59
22	—	3	1.75	—	3	1.90	—	3	2.04	—	3	2.18	—	3	2.33
23	—	3	3.47	—	3	3.62	—	3	3.77	—	3	3.92	—	3	4.07
24	—	3	5.18	—	3	5.34	—	3	5.50	—	3	5.66	—	3	5.81
25	—	3	6.90	—	3	7.06	—	3	7.23	—	3	7.39	—	3	7.56
26	—	3	8.62	—	3	8.79	—	3	8.96	—	3	9.13	—	3	9.30
27	—	3	10.33	—	3	10.51	—	3	10.69	—	3	10.86	—	3	11.04
28	—	4	0.05	—	4	0.23	—	4	0.42	—	4	0.60	—	4	0.78
29	—	4	1.76	—	4	1.95	—	4	2.15	—	4	2.34	—	4	2.53
30	—	4	3.48	—	4	3.68	—	4	3.87	—	4	4.07	—	4	4.27
40	—	5	8.64	—	5	8.90	—	5	9.17	—	5	9.43	—	5	9.69
50	—	7	1.80	—	7	2.13	—	7	2.46	—	7	2.79	—	7	3.12
60	—	8	6.96	—	8	7.36	—	8	7.75	—	8	8.15	—	8	8.54
70	—	10	0.13	—	10	0.59	—	10	1.05	—	10	1.51	—	10	1.97
80	—	11	5.29	—	11	5.81	—	11	6.34	—	11	6.87	—	11	7.39
90	—	12	10.45	—	12	11.04	—	12	11.63	—	13	[illegible]	—	13	0.82
100	—	14	3.61	—	14	4.27	—	14	4.93	—	14	5.58	—	14	6.24
200	1	8	7.23	1	8	8.54	1	8	9.86	1	8	11.17	1	9	0.49
300	2	2	10.84	2	3	0.81	2	3	2.79	2	3	4.76	2	3	6.73
400	2	17	2.46	2	17	5.09	2	17	7.72	2	17	10.35	2	18	0.98
500	3	11	6.08	3	11	9.36	3	12	0.65	3	12	3.94	3	12	7.23
600	4	5	9.69	4	6	1.63	4	6	5.58	4	6	9.53	4	7	1.47
700	5	0	1.31	5	0	5.91	5	0	10.51	5	1	3.12	5	1	7.92
800	5	14	4.92	5	14	10.18	5	15	3.44	5	15	8.71	5	16	1.96
900	6	8	8.54	6	9	2.45	6	9	8.37	6	10	2.30	6	10	8.21
1000	7	3	0.16	7	3	6.73	7	4	1.31	7	4	7.89	7	5	2.46
2000	14	6	0.32	14	7	1.40	14	8	2.62	14	9	3.78	14	10	4.92
3000	21	9	0.48	21	10	8.19	21	12	3.93	21	13	11.67	21	15	7.38
4000	28	12	0.64	28	14	2.92	28	16	5.24	28	18	7.56	29	0	9.84
5000	35	15	0.80	35	17	9.65	36	0	6.55	36	3	3.45	36	6	0.30

Prin.	266 Days.			267 Days.			268 Days.			269 Days.			270 Days.		
£.	£.	s.	d.pts	£.	s.	d.pts	£.	s.	d.pts	£.	s.	d.pts	£.	s.	d.pts
1	0	9	1.74	0	0	1.75	0	0	1.76	0	0	1.76	0	0	1.77
2	——		3.49	——		3.51	——		3.52	——		3.53	——		3.55
3	——		5.24	——		5.26	——		5.28	——		5.30	——		5.32
4	——		7.—	——		7.02	——		7.04	——		7.07	——		7.10
5	——		8.74	——		8.77	——		8.81	——		8.84	——		8.87
6	——		10.49	——		10.53	——		10.57	——		10.61	——		10.65
7	—	1	0.24	—	1	0.28	—	1	0.33	—	1	0.38	—	1	0.42
8	—	1	2.—	—	1	2.04	—	1	2.09	—	1	2.15	—	1	2.20
9	—	1	3.74	—	1	3.80	—	1	3.85	—	1	3.91	—	1	3.97
10	—	1	5.49	—	1	5.55	—	1	5.62	—	1	5.68	—	1	5.75
11	—	1	7.24	—	1	7.31	—	1	7.38	—	1	7.45	—	1	7.52
12	—	1	9.—	—	1	9.06	—	1	9.14	—	1	9.22	—	1	9.30
13	—	1	10.74	—	1	10.82	—	1	10.90	—	1	11.—	—	1	11.07
14	—	2	0.49	—	2	0.57	—	2	0.67	—	2	0.76	—	2	0.85
15	—	2	2.24	—	2	2.33	—	2	2.43	—	2	2.53	—	2	2.63
16	—	2	4.—	—	2	4.08	—	2	4.19	—	2	4.30	—	2	4.40
17	—	2	5.73	—	2	5.84	—	2	5.95	—	2	6.06	—	2	6.18
18	—	2	7.48	—	2	7.60	—	2	7.71	—	2	7.83	—	2	7.95
19	—	2	9.23	—	2	9.35	—	2	9.48	—	2	9.60	—	2	9.73
20	—	2	10.98	—	2	11.11	—	2	11.24	—	2	11.37	—	2	11.50
21	—	3	0.72	—	3	0.86	—	3	1.—	—	3	1.14	—	3	1.28
22	—	3	2.47	—	3	2.62	—	3	2.76	—	3	2.91	—	3	3.05
23	—	3	4.22	—	3	4.37	—	3	4.53	—	3	4.68	—	3	4.83
24	—	3	5.97	—	3	6.13	—	3	6.29	—	3	6.45	—	3	6.60
25	—	3	7.72	—	3	7.89	—	3	8.05	—	3	8.21	—	3	8.38
26	—	3	9.47	—	3	9.64	—	3	9.81	—	3	9.98	—	3	10.15
27	—	3	11.22	—	3	11.40	—	3	11.57	—	3	11.75	—	3	11.93
28	—	4	0.97	—	4	1.15	—	4	1.34	—	4	1.52	—	4	1.70
29	—	4	2.72	—	4	2.91	—	4	3.10	—	4	3.29	—	4	3.48
30	—	4	4.47	—	4	4.66	—	4	4.86	—	4	5.06	—	4	5.26
40	—	5	9.96	—	5	10.22	—	5	10.48	—	5	10.75	—	5	11.01
50	—	7	3.45	—	7	3.78	—	7	4.10	—	7	4.43	—	7	4.76
60	—	8	8.94	—	8	9.33	—	8	9.73	—	8	10.12	—	8	10.52
70	—	10	2.43	—	10	2.89	—	10	3.35	—	10	3.81	—	10	4.27
80	—	11	7.92	—	11	8.44	—	11	8.97	—	11	9.59	—	11	10.02
90	—	13	1.41	—	13	2.—	—	13	2.59	—	13	3.18	—	13	3.78
100	—	14	6.90	—	14	7.56	—	14	8.21	—	14	8.87	—	14	9.53
200	1	9	1.80	1	9	3.12	1	9	4.43	1	9	5.75	1	9	7.06
300	2	3	8.71	2	3	10.66	2	4	0.65	2	4	2.62	2	4	4.60
400	2	18	3.61	2	18	6.24	2	18	8.87	2	18	11.50	2	19	2.13
500	3	12	10.52	3	13	1.80	3	13	5.09	3	13	8.38	3	13	11.67
600	4	7	5.42	4	7	9.36	4	8	1.31	4	8	5.25	4	8	9.20
700	5	2	0.32	5	2	4.92	5	2	9.52	5	3	2.13	5	3	6.73
800	5	16	7.23	5	17	0.48	5	17	5.75	5	17	11.—	5	18	4.27
900	6	11	2.13	6	11	8.04	6	12	1.97	6	12	7.88	6	13	1.80
1000	7	5	9.04	7	6	3.61	7	6	10.19	7	7	4.76	7	7	11.34
2000	14	11	6.08	14	12	7.22	14	13	8.38	14	14	9.52	14	15	10.68
3000	21	17	3.12	21	18	10.83	22	0	6.57	22	2	2.28	22	3	10.02
4000	29	3	0.16	29	5	2.44	29	7	4.76	29	9	7.04	29	11	9.36
5000	36	8	9.20	36	11	6.05	36	14	2.95	36	16	11.80	36	19	8.70

Prin	271 Days.			272 Days.			273 Days.			274 Days.			275 Days.		
L.	L.	s.	d.pts	L.	s.	d.pts	L.	s.	d.pts	L.	s.	d.pts	L.	s.	d.pts
1	0	0	1.78	0	0	1.78	0	0	1.79	0	0	1.80	0	0	1.80
2	—		3.56	—		3.57	—		3.59	—		3.60	—		3.61
3	—		5.34	—		5.36	—		5.38	—		5.40	—		5.42
4	—		7.12	—		7.15	—		7.18	—		7.20	—		7.2
5	—		8.91	—		8.94	—		8.97	—		9.00	—		9.04
6	—		10.69	—		10.73	—		11.77	—		10.80	—		10.84
7	—	1	0.47	—	1	0.51	—	1	0.55	—	1	0.61	—	1	0.65
8	—	1	2.25	—	1	2.30	—	1	2.36	—	1	2.41	—	1	2.46
9	—	1	4.03	—	1	4.09	—	1	4.15	—	1	4.21	—	1	4.27
10	—	1	5.81	—	1	5.88	—	1	5.95	—	1	6.01	—	1	6.08
11	—	1	7.6	—	1	7.67	—	1	7.74	—	1	7.81	—	1	7.89
12	—	1	9.38	—	1	9.46	—	1	9.53	—	1	9.61	—	1	9.69
13	—	1	11.16	—	1	11.25	—	1	11.33	—	1	11.42	—	1	11.50
14	—	2	0.94	—	2	1.03	—	2	1.13	—	2	1.22	—	2	1.31
15	—	2	2.72	—	2	2.82	—	2	2.92	—	2	3.02	—	2	3.12
16	—	2	4.51	—	2	4.61	—	2	4.72	—	2	4.82	—	2	4.93
17	—	2	6.29	—	2	6.40	—	2	6.51	—	2	6.62	—	2	6.73
18	—	2	8.07	—	2	8.19	—	2	8.31	—	2	8.42	—	2	8.54
19	—	2	9.85	—	2	9.98	—	2	10.10	—	2	10.23	—	2	10.35
20	—	2	11.63	—	2	11.76	—	2	11.90	—	3	0.03	—	3	0.16
21	—	3	1.42	—	3	1.55	—	3	1.69	—	3	1.83	—	3	1.97
22	—	3	3.20	—	3	3.34	—	3	3.49	—	3	3.63	—	3	3.78
23	—	3	4.98	—	3	5.13	—	3	5.28	—	3	5.43	—	3	5.58
24	—	3	6.76	—	3	6.92	—	3	7.08	—	3	7.23	—	3	7.39
25	—	3	8.54	—	3	8.71	—	3	8.87	—	3	9.04	—	3	9.20
26	—	3	10.32	—	3	10.50	—	3	10.67	—	3	10.84	—	3	11.01
27	—	4	0.11	—	4	0.28	—	4	0.46	—	4	0.64	—	4	0.82
28	—	4	1.89	—	4	2.07	—	4	2.26	—	4	2.44	—	4	2.62
29	—	4	3.67	—	4	3.86	—	4	4.05	—	4	4.24	—	4	4.43
30	—	4	5.45	—	4	5.65	—	4	5.85	—	4	6.04	—	4	6.24
40	—	5	11.27	—	5	11.53	—	5	11.80	—	6	0.06	—	6	0.32
50	—	7	5.09	—	7	5.42	—	7	5.75	—	7	6.08	—	7	6.41
60	—	8	10.91	—	8	11.30	—	8	11.70	—	9	0.09	—	9	0.49
70	—	10	4.73	—	10	5.19	—	10	5.65	—	10	6.11	—	10	6.57
80	—	11	10.55	—	11	11.07	—	11	11.60	—	12	0.13	—	12	0.65
90	—	13	4.37	—	13	4.96	—	13	5.55	—	13	6.14	—	13	6.73
100	—	14	10.19	—	14	10.84	—	14	11.50	—	15	0.16	—	15	0.82
200	1	9	8.38	1	9	9.69	1	9	11.01	1	10	0.32	1	10	1.64
300	2	4	6.57	2	4	8.54	2	4	10.51	2	5	0.48	2	5	2.46
400	2	19	4.76	2	19	7.39	2	19	10.02	3	0	0.65	3	0	3.28
500	3	14	2.15	3	14	6.24	3	14	9.53	3	15	0.82	3	15	4.10
600	4	9	1.14	4	9	5.09	4	9	9.04	4	10	0.99	4	10	4.92
700	5	3	11.33	5	4	3.94	5	4	8.54	5	5	1.14	5	5	5.74
800	5	18	9.52	5	19	2.79	5	19	8.04	6	0	1.31	6	0	6.50
900	6	13	7.71	6	14	1.64	6	14	7.55	6	15	1.47	6	15	7.38
1000	7	8	5.91	7	9	0.49	7	9	7.09	7	10	1.64	7	10	8.21
2000	14	16	11.82	14	18	0.98	14	19	2.12	15	0	3.28	15	1	4.42
3000	22	5	5.73	22	7	1.47	22	8	9.18	22	10	4.92	22	12	0.65
4000	29	13	11.64	29	16	1.96	29	18	4.21	30	0	6.51	30	2	8.84
5000	37	2	5.55	37	5	2.45	37	7	11.39	37	10	8.20	37	13	5.05

Prin.	276 Days.			277 Days.			278 Days.			279 Days.			280 Days.		
£.	£.	s.	d.pts	£.	s.	d.pts	£.	s.	d.pts	£.	s.	d.pts	£.	s.	d.pts
1	0	0	1.81	0	0	1.82	0	0	1.82	0	0	1.83	0	0	1.84
2	——		3.62	——		3.64	——		3.65	——		3.66	——		3.68
3	——		5.44	——		5.46	——		5.48	——		5.50	——		5.52
4	——		7.25	——		7.28	——		7.31	——		7.33	——		7.36
5	——		9.07	——		9.10	——		9.13	——		9.17	——		9.20
6	——		10.88	——		10.92	——		10.96	——		11.—	——		11.04
7	—	1	0.70	—	1	0.74	—	1	0.79	—	1	0.84	—	1	0.88
8	—	1	2.51	—	1	2.57	—	1	2.62	—	1	2.67	—	1	2.72
9	—	1	4.33	—	1	4.39	—	1	4.45	—	1	4.51	—	1	4.56
10	—	1	6.14	—	1	6.21	—	1	6.27	—	1	6.34	—	1	6.41
11	—	1	7.96	—	1	8.03	—	1	8.10	—	1	8.17	—	1	8.25
12	—	1	9.77	—	1	9.83	—	1	9.93	—	1	10.01	—	1	10.09
13	—	1	11.59	—	1	11.67	—	1	11.76	—	1	11.84	—	1	11.93
14	—	2	1.40	—	2	1.50	—	2	1.59	—	2	1.68	—	2	1.77
15	—	2	3.22	—	2	3.32	—	2	3.41	—	2	3.51	—	2	3.61
16	—	2	5.03	—	2	5.14	—	2	5.24	—	2	5.35	—	2	5.45
17	—	2	6.85	—	2	6.96	—	2	7.07	—	2	7.18	—	2	7.29
18	—	2	8.66	—	2	8.78	—	2	8.90	—	2	9.02	—	2	9.13
19	—	2	10.48	—	2	10.60	—	2	10.53	—	2	10.85	—	2	10.98
20	—	3	0.29	—	3	0.42	—	3	0.55	—	3	0.69	—	3	0.82
21	—	3	2.10	—	3	2.24	—	3	2.38	—	3	2.52	—	3	2.66
22	—	3	3.92	—	3	4.06	—	3	4.21	—	3	4.35	—	3	4.50
23	—	3	5.73	—	3	5.89	—	3	6.04	—	3	6.19	—	3	6.34
24	—	3	7.55	—	3	7.71	—	3	7.87	—	3	8.02	—	3	8.18
25	—	3	9.36	—	3	9.53	—	3	9.69	—	3	9.86	—	3	10.02
26	—	3	11.18	—	3	11.35	—	3	11.52	—	3	11.69	—	3	11.86
27	—	4	1.—	—	4	1.17	—	4	1.35	—	4	1.53	—	4	1.70
28	—	4	2.81	—	4	3.—	—	4	3.18	—	4	3.36	—	4	3.55
29	—	4	4.62	—	4	4.81	—	4	5.01	—	4	5.20	—	4	5.39
30	—	4	6.44	—	4	6.64	—	4	6.83	—	4	7.03	—	4	7.23
40	—	6	0.59	—	6	0.85	—	6	1.11	—	6	1.38	—	6	1.64
50	—	7	6.73	—	7	7.06	—	7	7.39	—	7	7.72	—	7	8.05
60	—	9	0.88	—	9	1.28	—	9	1.67	—	9	2.07	—	9	2.46
70	—	10	7.03	—	10	7.49	—	10	7.95	—	10	8.41	—	10	8.87
80	—	12	1.18	—	12	1.70	—	12	2.23	—	12	2.76	—	12	3.28
90	—	13	7.33	—	13	7.92	—	13	8.51	—	13	9.10	—	13	9.69
100	—	15	1.47	—	15	2.13	—	15	2.79	—	15	3.45	—	15	4.10
200	1	10	2.95	1	10	4.27	1	10	5.58	1	10	6.90	1	10	8.21
300	2	5	4.43	2	5	6.40	2	5	8.38	2	5	10.35	2	6	0.32
400	3	0	5.91	3	0	8.54	3	0	11.17	3	1	1.80	3	1	4.43
500	3	15	7.39	3	15	10.68	3	16	3.97	3	16	7.25	3	16	10.54
600	4	10	8.87	4	11	0.81	4	11	4.76	4	11	8.71	4	12	0.65
700	5	5	10.35	5	6	2.95	5	6	7.55	5	7	0.16	5	7	4.76
800	6	0	11.83	6	1	5.08	6	1	10.35	6	2	3.61	6	2	8.87
900	6	16	1.31	6	16	7.22	6	17	1.14	6	17	7.06	6	18	0.98
1000	7	11	2.79	7	11	9.36	7	12	3.94	7	12	10.52	7	13	5.09
2000	15	2	5.58	15	3	6.72	15	4	7.88	15	5	9.04	15	6	10.18
3000	22	13	8.37	22	15	4.08	22	16	11.82	22	18	7.56	23	0	3.27
4000	30	4	11.16	30	7	1.44	30	9	3.76	30	11	6.09	30	13	8.36
5000	37	16	1.95	37	18	10.80	38	1	7.70	38	4	4.60	38	7	1.45

Prin.	281 Days.			282 Days.			283 Days.			284 Days.			285 Days.		
L.	L.	s.	d.pts	L.	s.	d.pts	L.	s.	d.pts	L.	s.	d.pts	L.	s.	d.pts
1	0	0	1.84	0	0	1.85	0	0	1.86	0	0	1.86	0	0	1.8[illegible]
2	——		3.69	——		3.70	——		3.72	——		3.73	——		3.7[illegible]
3	——		5.54	——		5.56	——		5.58	——		5.60	——		5.6[illegible]
4	——		7.39	——		7.41	——		7.44	——		7.46	——		7.4[illegible]
5	——		9.23	——		9.27	——		9.30	——		9.33	——		9.3[illegible]
6	——		11.08	——		11.12	——		11.16	——		11.20	——		11.24
7	—	1	0.93	—	1	0.97	—	1	1.02	—	1	1.07	—	1	1.11
8	—	1	2.78	—	1	2.83	—	1	2.88	—	1	2.93	—	1	3.—
9	—	1	4.62	—	1	4.68	—	1	4.74	—	1	4.80	—	1	4.8[illegible]
10	—	1	6.47	—	1	6.54	—	1	6.60	—	1	6.67	—	1	6.73
11	—	1	8.32	—	1	8.39	—	1	8.46	—	1	8.54	—	1	8.61
12	—	1	10.17	—	1	10.25	—	1	10.32	—	1	10.40	—	1	10.48
13	—	2	0.01	—	2	0.10	—	2	0.19	—	2	0.27	—	2	0.36
14	—	2	1.86	—	2	1.95	—	2	2.05	—	2	2.14	—	2	2.23
15	—	2	3.71	—	2	3.81	—	2	3.91	—	2	4.01	—	2	4.10
16	—	2	5.56	—	2	5.66	—	2	5.77	—	2	5.87	—	2	5.98
17	—	2	7.41	—	2	7.52	—	2	7.63	—	2	7.74	—	2	7.85
18	—	2	9.25	—	2	9.37	—	2	9.49	—	2	9.61	—	2	9.73
19	—	2	11.10	—	2	11.23	—	2	11.35	—	2	11.48	—	2	11.6[illegible]
20	—	3	0.95	—	3	1.08	—	3	1.21	—	3	1.34	—	3	1.47
21	—	3	2.80	—	3	2.93	—	3	3.07	—	3	3.21	—	3	3.35
22	—	3	4.64	—	3	4.79	—	3	4.93	—	3	5.08	—	3	5.22
23	—	3	6.49	—	3	6.64	—	3	6.79	—	3	6.94	—	5	7.10
24	—	3	8.34	—	3	8.50	—	3	8.65	—	3	8.81	—	3	8.97
25	—	3	10.19	—	3	10.35	—	3	10.52	—	3	10.68	—	3	10.84
26	—	4	0.03	—	4	0.20	—	4	0.38	—	4	0.55	—	4	0.72
27	—	4	1.88	—	4	2.06	—	4	2.24	—	4	2.41	—	4	2.59
28	—	4	3.73	—	4	3.91	—	4	4.10	—	4	4.28	—	4	4.47
29	—	4	5.58	—	4	5.77	—	4	5.96	—	4	6.15	—	4	6.34
30	—	4	7.43	—	4	7.62	—	4	7.82	—	4	8.02	—	4	8.21
40	—	6	1.90	—	6	2.16	—	6	2.43	—	6	2.69	—	6	2.95
50	—	7	8.38	—	7	8.71	—	7	9.03	—	7	9.36	—	7	9.6[illegible]
60	—	9	2.86	—	9	3.25	—	9	3.64	—	9	4.04	—	9	4.4[illegible]
70	—	10	9.33	—	10	9.79	—	10	10.25	—	10	10.71	—	10	11.1[illegible]
80	—	12	3.81	—	12	4.33	—	12	4.85	—	12	5.38	—	12	5.9[illegible]
90	—	13	10.29	—	13	10.87	—	13	11.47	—	14	0.06	—	14	0.65
100	—	15	4.70	—	15	5.42	—	15	6.08	—	15	6.7[illegible]	—	15	7.3[illegible]
200	1	10	9.53	1	10	10.84	1	11	0.16	1	11	1.4[illegible]	1	11	2.7[illegible]
300	2	6	2.30	2	6	4.26	2	6	6.24	2	6	8.21	2	6	10.18
400	3	1	7.06	3	1	9.68	3	2	0.3[illegible]	3	2	2.94	3	2	5.5[illegible]
500	3	17	1.83	3	17	5.11	3	17	8.40	3	17	11.68	3	18	0.9[illegible]
600	4	12	4.60	4	12	8.53	4	13	0.48	4	13	4.42	4	13	8.3[illegible]
700	5	7	9.36	5	8	1.95	5	8	6.56	5	8	11.15	5	9	3.7[illegible]
800	6	3	2.13	6	3	7.37	6	4	0.64	6	4	5.89	6	4	11.1[illegible]
900	6	18	6.92	6	19	0.79	6	19	6.72	7	0	0.63	7	0	6.55
1000	7	13	11.67	7	14	6.21	7	15	0.8[illegible]	7	15	7.37	7	16	1.95
2000	15	7	11.54	15	9	0.44	15	10	1.[illegible]	15	11	2.74	15	12	3.9[illegible]
3000	23	1	11.01	23	3	0.66	23	5	2.4[illegible]	23	6	10.11	23	8	5.8[illegible]
4000	30	15	10.68	30	18	0.88	31	0	3.2[illegible]	31	2	5.48	31	4	7.8
5000	38	9	10.35	38	12	7.3[illegible]	38	15	4.—	38	18	0.85	39	0	9.75

Prin.	286 Days.			287 Days.			288 Days.			289 Days.			290 Days.		
L.	L.	s.	d.pts	L.	s.	d.pts	L.	s.	d.pts	L.	s.	d.pts	L.	s.	d.pts
1	0	0	1.88	0	0	1.88	0	0	1.89	0	0	1.90	0	0	1.90
2	——		3.76	——		3.77	——		3.78	——		3.80	——		3.81
3	——		5.64	——		5.66	——		5.68	——		5.70	——		5.72
4	——		7.52	——		7.54	——		7.57	——		7.60	——		7.62
5	——		9.40	——		9.43	——		9.46	——		9.50	——		9.53
6	——		11.28	——		11.32	——		11.36	——		11.40	——		11.44
7	—	1	1.16	—	1	1.20	—	1	1.25	—	1	1.30	—	1	1.34
8	—	1	3.04	—	1	3.09	—	1	3.14	—	1	3.20	—	1	3.25
9	—	1	4.92	—	1	4.98	—	1	5.04	—	1	5.10	—	1	5.16
10	—	1	6.80	—	1	6.87	—	1	6.93	—	1	7.—	—	1	7.06
11	—	1	8.68	—	1	8.75	—	1	8.83	—	1	8.90	—	1	8.97
12	—	1	10.56	—	1	10.64	—	1	10.72	—	1	10.80	—	1	10.88
13	—	2	0.44	—	2	0.53	—	2	0.61	—	2	0.70	—	2	0.78
14	—	2	2.32	—	2	2.41	—	2	2.51	—	2	2.60	—	2	2.69
15	—	2	4.20	—	2	4.30	—	2	4.40	—	2	4.50	—	2	4.60
16	—	2	6.08	—	2	6.19	—	2	6.29	—	2	6.40	—	2	6.50
17	—	2	7.96	—	2	8.08	—	2	8.19	—	2	8.30	—	2	8.41
18	—	2	9.84	—	2	9.96	—	2	10.08	—	2	10.20	—	2	10.32
19	—	2	11.72	—	2	11.85	—	2	11.97	—	3	0.10	—	3	0.22
20	—	3	1.61	—	3	1.74	—	3	1.87	—	3	2.—	—	3	2.13
21	—	3	3.49	—	3	3.62	—	3	3.76	—	3	3.90	—	3	4.04
22	—	3	5.37	—	3	5.51	—	3	5.66	—	3	5.80	—	3	5.95
23	—	3	7.25	—	3	7.40	—	3	7.55	—	3	7.70	—	3	7.85
24	—	3	9.13	—	3	9.29	—	3	9.44	—	3	9.60	—	3	9.76
25	—	3	11.01	—	3	11.17	—	3	11.34	—	3	11.50	—	3	11.67
26	—	4	0.89	—	4	1.06	—	4	1.23	—	4	1.40	—	4	1.57
27	—	4	2.77	—	4	2.95	—	4	3.12	—	4	3.30	—	4	3.48
28	—	4	4.65	—	4	4.83	—	4	5.02	—	4	5.20	—	4	5.39
29	—	4	6.53	—	4	6.72	—	4	6.91	—	4	7.10	—	4	7.29
30	—	4	8.41	—	4	8.61	—	4	8.81	—	4	9.—	—	4	9.20
40	—	6	3.22	—	6	3.48	—	6	3.75	—	6	4.01	—	6	4.27
50	—	7	10.02	—	7	10.35	—	7	10.68	—	7	11.01	—	7	11.34
60	—	9	4.83	—	9	5.22	—	9	5.62	—	9	6.01	—	9	6.40
70	—	10	11.63	—	11	0.09	—	11	0.55	—	11	1.01	—	11	1.47
80	—	12	6.44	—	12	6.96	—	12	7.48	—	12	8.01	—	12	8.54
90	—	14	1.22	—	14	1.83	—	14	2.45	—	14	3.02	—	14	3.61
100	—	15	8.05	—	15	8.71	—	15	9.38	—	15	10.02	—	15	10.68
200	1	11	4.10	1	11	5.42	1	11	6.75	1	11	8.05	1	11	9.36
300	2	7	0.15	2	7	2.13	2	7	4.10	2	7	6.07	2	7	8.04
400	3	2	8.20	3	2	10.84	3	3	1.46	3	3	4.10	3	3	6.72
500	3	18	4.26	3	18	7.55	3	18	10.83	3	19	2.12	3	19	5.41
600	4	14	0.31	4	14	4.26	4	14	8.22	4	15	0.13	4	15	4.09
700	5	9	8.36	5	10	0.97	5	10	5.56	5	10	10.15	5	11	2.77
800	6	5	4.41	6	5	9.68	6	6	2.95	6	6	8.18	6	7	1.45
900	7	1	0.46	7	1	6.39	7	2	0.30	7	2	6.20	7	3	0.13
1000	7	16	8.52	7	17	2.10	7	17	0.67	7	18	4.25	7	18	10.82
2000	15	13	5.04	15	14	6.20	15	15	7.34	15	16	8.50	15	17	9.64
3000	23	10	1.56	23	11	9.30	23	13	5.01	23	15	0.75	23	16	8.46
4000	31	6	10.08	31	9	0.40	31	11	2.68	31	13	5.—	31	15	7.28
5000	39	3	6.60	39	6	3.50	39	9	0.35	39	11	9.25	39	14	6.10

Prin.	291 Days.			292 Days.			293 Days.			294 Days.			295 Days.		
£.	£.	s.	d.pts	£.	s.	d.pts	£.	s.	d.pts	£.	s.	d.pts	£.	s.	d.pts
1	0	0	1.91	0	0	1.92	0	0	1.92	0	0	1.93	0	0	1.93
2	—		3.82	—		3.84	—		3.85	—		3.86	—		3.87
3	—		5.74	—		5.76	—		5.77	—		5.79	—		5.81
4	—		7.65	—		7.68	—		7.70	—		7.73	—		7.75
5	—		9.56	—		9.60	—		9.63	—		9.66	—		9.69
6	—		11.48	—		11.52	—		11.55	—		11.59	—		11.63
7	—	1	1.39	—	1	1.44	—	1	1.48	—	1	1.53	—	1	1.57
8	—	1	3.30	—	1	3.36	—	1	3.41	—	1	3.46	—	1	3.51
9	—	1	5.22	—	1	5.28	—	1	5.35	—	1	5.39	—	1	5.45
10	—	1	7.13	—	1	7.20	—	1	7.26	—	1	7.33	—	1	7.39
11	—	1	9.04	—	1	9.12	—	1	9.19	—	1	9.26	—	1	9.33
12	—	1	10.96	—	1	11.04	—	1	11.11	—	1	11.19	—	1	11.27
13	—	2	0.87	—	2	0.96	—	2	1.04	—	2	1.13	—	2	1.21
14	—	2	2.78	—	2	2.88	—	2	2.97	—	2	3.06	—	2	3.15
15	—	2	4.70	—	2	4.80	—	2	4.89	—	2	5.—	—	2	5.09
16	—	2	6.61	—	2	6.72	—	2	6.82	—	2	6.93	—	2	7.03
17	—	2	8.52	—	2	8.64	—	2	8.75	—	2	8.86	—	2	8.97
18	—	2	10.44	—	2	10.56	—	2	10.67	—	2	10.79	—	2	10.91
19	—	3	0.35	—	3	0.48	—	3	0.60	—	3	0.72	—	3	0.85
20	—	3	2.26	—	3	2.40	—	3	2.52	—	3	2.66	—	3	2.79
21	—	3	4.18	—	3	4.32	—	3	4.45	—	3	4.59	—	3	4.73
22	—	3	6.09	—	3	6.24	—	3	6.38	—	3	6.52	—	3	6.67
23	—	3	8.—	—	3	8.16	—	3	8.31	—	3	8.46	—	3	8.61
24	—	3	9.91	—	3	10.08	—	3	10.23	—	3	10.39	—	3	10.55
25	—	3	11.83	—	4	0.—	—	4	0.16	—	4	0.32	—	4	0.49
26	—	4	1.74	—	4	1.92	—	4	2.09	—	4	2.26	—	4	2.43
27	—	4	3.66	—	4	3.84	—	4	4.01	—	4	4.19	—	4	4.37
28	—	4	5.57	—	4	5.76	—	4	5.94	—	4	6.12	—	4	6.31
29	—	4	7.48	—	4	7.68	—	4	7.87	—	4	8.06	—	4	8.25
30	—	4	9.40	—	4	9.60	—	4	9.79	—	4	10.—	—	4	10.19
40	—	6	4.5[illegible]	—	6	4.80	—	6	5.06	—	6	5.32	—	6	5.58
50	—	7	11.6[illegible]	—	8	0.—	—	8	0.32	—	8	0.65	—	8	0.98
60	—	9	6.80	—	9	7.2[illegible]	—	9	7.59	—	9	8.—	—	9	8.38
70	—	11	1.9	—	11	2.40	—	11	2.85	—	11	3.32	—	11	3.77
80	—	12	9.07	—	12	9.6[illegible]	—	12	10.1[illegible]	—	12	10.65	—	12	11.17
90	—	14	4.2[illegible]	—	14	4.8[illegible]	—	14	5.39	—	14	5.98	—	14	6.57
100	—	15	11.34	—	16	0.—	—	16	0.65	—	16	1.31	—	16	1.97
200	1	11	10.68	1	12	0.—	1	12	1.31	1	12	2.63	1	12	3.94
300	2	7	10.02	2	8	0.—	2	8	1.97	2	8	3.54	2	8	5.91
400	3	3	9.36	3	4	0.—	3	4	2.62	3	4	5.26	3	4	7.88
500	3	19	8.7[illegible]	4	0	0.—	4	0	3.28	4	0	6.57	4	0	9.86
600	4	15	8.[illegible]	4	16	0.—	4	16	3.94	4	16	7.89	4	16	11.82
700	5	11	7.38	5	12	0.—	5	12	4.59	5	12	9.20	5	13	1.79
800	6	7	6.7[illegible]	6	8	0.—	6	8	5.25	6	8	10.52	6	9	3.76
900	7	3	6.06	7	4	0.—	7	4	5.91	7	4	11.83	7	5	5.73
1000	7	19	5.40	8	0	0.—	8	0	6.57	8	1	1.15	8	1	7.72
2000	15	18	10.80	16	0	0.—	16	1	1.14	16	2	2.30	16	3	3.44
3000	23	18	4.20	24	0	0.—	24	1	7.71	24	3	3.45	24	4	11.16
4000	31	17	9.60	32	0	0.—	32	2	2.28	32	4	4.60	32	6	6.88
5000	39	17	3.—	40	0	0.—	40	2	8.85	40	5	5.75	40	8	2.60

Prin.	296 Days.			297 Days.			298 Days.			299 Days.			300 Days.		
L.	L.	s.	d.pts	L.	s.	d.pts	L.	s.	d.pts	L.	s.	d.pts	L.	s.	d.pts
1	0	0	1.94	0	0	1.95	0	0	1.95	0	0	1.96	0	0	1.42
2	—		3.89	—		3.90	—		3.91	—		3.93	—		3.94
3	—		5.83	—		5.85	—		5.87	—		5.89	—		5.91
4	—		7.78	—		7.81	—		7.83	—		7.86	—		7.89
5	—		9.73	—		9.76	—		9.79	—		9.83	—		9.86
6	—		11.67	—		11.71	—		11.75	—		11.79	—		11.83
7	–	1	1.62	–	1	1.67	–	1	1.71	–	1	1.76	–	1	1.80
8	–	1	3.57	–	1	3.62	–	1	3.67	–	1	3.72	–	1	3.78
9	–	1	5.51	–	1	5.57	–	1	5.63	–	1	5.69	–	1	5.75
10	–	1	7.46	–	1	7.52	–	1	7.59	–	1	7.66	–	1	7.72
11	–	1	9.40	–	1	9.48	–	1	9.55	–	1	9.62	–	1	9.69
12	–	1	11.35	–	1	11.43	–	1	11.51	–	1	11.59	–	1	11.67
13	–	2	1.30	–	2	1.38	–	2	1.47	–	2	1.55	–	2	1.64
14	–	2	3.24	–	2	3.34	–	2	3.43	–	2	3.52	–	2	3.61
15	–	2	5.19	–	2	5.29	–	2	5.39	–	2	5.49	–	2	5.58
16	–	2	7.14	–	2	7.24	–	2	7.35	–	2	7.45	–	2	7.56
17	–	2	9.08	–	2	9.19	–	2	9.31	–	2	9.42	–	2	9.53
18	–	2	11.03	–	2	11.15	–	2	11.27	–	2	11.38	–	2	11.50
19	–	3	0.97	–	3	1.10	–	3	1.22	–	3	1.35	–	3	1.47
20	–	3	2.92	–	3	3.05	–	3	3.18	–	3	3.32	–	3	3.45
21	–	3	4.87	–	3	5.01	–	3	5.14	–	3	5.28	–	3	5.42
22	–	3	6.81	–	3	7.—	–	3	7.10	–	3	7.25	–	3	7.39
23	–	3	8.76	–	3	8.94	–	4	9.06	–	3	9.21	–	3	9.36
24	–	3	10.71	–	3	10.86	–	3	11.02	–	3	11.18	–	3	11.34
25	–	4	0.65	–	4	0.82	–	4	1.—	–	4	1.15	–	4	1.31
26	–	4	2.60	–	4	2.77	–	4	2.94	–	4	3.11	–	4	3.28
27	–	4	4.55	–	4	4.72	–	4	4.90	–	4	5.08	–	4	5.26
28	–	4	6.49	–	4	6.68	–	4	6.86	–	4	7.04	–	4	7.23
29	–	4	8.44	–	4	8.63	–	4	8.82	–	4	9.01	–	4	9.20
30	–	4	10.38	–	4	10.58	–	4	10.78	–	4	10.98	–	4	11.17
40	–	6	5.85	–	6	6.11	–	6	6.37	–	6	6.64	–	6	6.90
50	–	8	1.31	–	8	1.64	–	8	1.97	–	8	2.30	–	8	2.63
60	–	9	8.77	–	9	9.17	–	9	9.76	–	9	9.96	–	9	10.35
70	–	11	4.24	–	11	4.70	–	11	5.16	–	11	5.62	–	11	6.08
80	–	12	11.70	–	13	0.22	–	13	0.75	–	13	1.28	–	13	1.80
90	–	14	7.16	–	14	7.75	–	14	8.35	–	14	8.94	–	14	9.53
100	–	16	2.63	–	16	3.28	–	16	3.94	–	16	4.60	–	16	5.26
200	1	12	5.26	1	12	6.57	1	12	7.89	1	12	9.20	1	12	10.52
300	2	8	7.89	2	8	9.86	2	8	11.83	2	9	1.80	2	9	3.78
400	3	4	10.52	3	5	1.14	3	5	3.78	3	5	6.40	3	5	9.04
500	4	1	1.15	4	1	4.43	4	1	7.72	4	1	11.01	4	2	2.30
600	4	17	3.78	4	17	7.72	4	17	11.67	4	18	3.61	4	18	7.56
700	5	13	6.41	5	13	11.—	5	14	3.61	5	14	8.21	5	15	0.82
800	6	9	9.04	6	10	2.20	6	10	7.56	6	11	0.81	6	11	6.08
900	7	5	11.67	7	6	5.58	7	6	11.50	7	7	5.41	7	7	11.34
1000	8	2	2.30	8	2	8.87	8	3	3.45	8	3	10.02	8	4	4.60
2000	16	4	4.60	16	5	5.74	16	6	6.90	16	7	8.04	16	8	9.20
3000	24	6	6.90	24	8	2.61	24	9	10.35	24	11	6.06	24	13	1.80
4000	32	8	8.20	32	10	10.48	32	13	0.80	32	15	3.08	32	17	6.40
5000	40	10	10.50	40	13	7.35	40	16	4.25	40	19	1.10	41	1	11.—

Dist.	301 Days.			302 Days.			303 Days.			304 Days.			305 Days.		
L.	L.	s.	d.pts	L.	s.	d.pts	L.	s.	d.pts	L.	s.	d.pts	L.	s.	d.pts
1	0	0	1,97	0	0	1,98	0	0	1,99	0	0	1,99	0	0	2.—
2	——		3,95	——		3,97	——		3,98	——		3,99	——		4,01
3	——		5,93	——		5,95	——		5,97	——		5,99	——		6,01
4	——		7,91	——		7,94	——		7,96	——		7,99	——		8,02
5	——		9,88	——		9,92	——		9,96	——		9,99	——		10,02
6	——		11,86	——		11,91	——		11,95	——		11,99	—	1	0,03
7	—	1	1,84	—	1	1,90	—	1	1,94	—	1	1,99	—	1	2,03
8	—	1	3,82	—	1	3,88	—	1	3,93	—	1	3,99	—	1	4,04
9	—	1	5,80	—	1	5,87	—	1	5,93	—	1	5,99	—	1	6,04
10	—	1	7,78	—	1	7,85	—	1	7,92	—	1	7,98	—	1	8,05
11	—	1	9,76	—	1	9,84	—	1	9,91	—	1	9,98	—	1	10,06
12	—	1	11,74	—	1	11,82	—	1	11,90	—	1	11,98	—	2	0,06
13	—	2	1,71	—	2	1,81	—	2	1,90	—	2	1,98	—	2	2,07
14	—	2	3,69	—	2	3,80	—	2	3,89	—	2	3,98	—	2	4,07
15	—	2	5,67	—	2	5,78	—	2	5,88	—	2	5,98	—	2	6,08
16	—	2	7,65	—	2	7,77	—	2	7,87	—	2	7,98	—	2	8,08
17	—	2	9,63	—	2	9,75	—	2	9,86	—	2	9,98	—	2	10,09
18	—	2	11,61	—	2	11,74	—	2	11,86	—	2	11,98	—	3	0,09
19	—	3	1,59	—	3	1,72	—	3	1,85	—	3	1,97	—	3	2,10
20	—	3	3,58	—	3	3,71	—	3	3,84	—	3	3,97	—	3	4,10
21	—	3	5,56	—	3	5,70	—	3	5,83	—	3	5,97	—	3	6,11
22	—	3	7,54	—	3	7,68	—	3	7,83	—	3	7,97	—	3	8,12
23	—	3	9,52	—	3	9,67	—	3	9,82	—	3	9,97	—	3	10,12
24	—	3	11,50	—	3	11,65	—	3	11,81	—	3	11,97	—	4	0,13
25	—	4	1,47	—	4	1,64	—	4	1,80	—	4	1,97	—	4	2,13
26	—	4	3,45	—	4	3,62	—	4	3,80	—	4	3,97	—	4	4,14
27	—	4	5,43	—	4	5,61	—	4	5,79	—	4	5,97	—	4	6,14
28	—	4	7,41	—	4	7,60	—	4	7,78	—	4	7,96	—	4	8,15
29	—	4	9,39	—	4	9,58	—	4	9,77	—	4	9,96	—	4	10,18
30	—	4	11,37	—	4	11,57	—	4	11,76	—	4	11,96	—	5	0,19
40	—	6	7,16	—	6	7,43	—	6	7,69	—	6	7,95	—	6	8,21
50	—	8	2,85	—	8	3,28	—	8	3,61	—	8	3,94	—	8	4,27
60	—	9	10,65	—	9	11,14	—	9	11,5[illegible]	—	9	11,93	—	10	0,32
70	—	11	6,44	—	11	7,—	—	11	7,4[illegible]	—	11	7,92	—	11	8,38
80	—	13	2,23	—	13	2,8[illegible]	—	13	[illegible]	—	13	3,91	—	13	4,45
90	—	14	10,92	—	14	[illegible]	—	14	11,30	—	14	[illegible]	—	15	0,49
100	—	16	5,31	—	16	6,37	—	16	7,2[illegible]	—	16	7,39	—	16	8,54
200	1	12	11,80	1	13	1,15	1	13	2,4[illegible]	1	13	3,78	1	13	5,09
300	2	9	5,75	2	9	7,72	2	9	9,[illegible]	2	9	11,67	2	10	1,64
400	3	5	11,66	3	6	2,3[illegible]	3	6	4,92	3	6	7,56	3	6	10,18
500	4	2	5,58	4	2	9,37	4	3	0,1[illegible]	4	3	3,45	4	3	6,73
600	4	18	11,50	4	19	4,45	4	19	7,3[illegible]	4	19	11,[illegible]4	5	0	3,28
700	5	15	5,41	5	15	11,02	5	16	2,6[illegible]	5	16	7,2[illegible]	5	16	11,82
800	6	11	11,33	6	12	4,00	6	12	9,85	6	13	3,12	6	13	8,37
900	7	8	5,25	[illegible]	[illegible]	11,17	7	9	5,0[illegible]	7	9	11,01	7	10	4,92
1000	8	4	11,17	8	5	5,75	8	6	0,3[illegible]	8	6	6,90	8	7	1,47
2000	16	9	10,34	16	10	11,50	16	12	0,64	16	13	1,80	16	14	2,94
3000	24	14	9,51	24	16	5,25	24	18	0,96	24	19	8,70	25	1	4,41
4000	32	19	7,68	33	1	10,—	33	4	1,28	33	6	3,60	33	8	5,83
5000	41	4	5,85	41	7	2,75	41	10	1,60	41	12	10,50	41	15	7,35

Prin.	306 Days.			307 Days.			308 Days.			309 Days.			310 Days.		
L.	L.	s.	d.pts	L.	s.	d.pts	L.	s.	d.pts	L.	s.	d.pts	L.	s.	d.pts
1	0	0	2.01	0	0	2.01	0	0	2.02	0	0	2.03	0	0	2.05
2	—		4.02	—		4.03	—		4.03	—		4.06	—		4.07
3	—		6.03	—		6.05	—		6.07	—		6.09	—		6.11
4	—		8.04	—		8.07	—		8.10	—		8.12	—		8.15
5	—		10.06	—		10.09	—		10.12	—		10.15	—		10.19
6	—	1	0.07	—	1	0.11	—	1	0.15	—	1	0.19	—	1	0.23
7	—	1	2.08	—	1	2.13	—	1	2.17	—	1	2.22	—	1	2.26
8	—	1	4.09	—	1	4.14	—	1	4.20	—	1	4.25	—	1	4.30
9	—	1	6.11	—	1	6.16	—	1	6.22	—	1	6.28	—	1	6.34
10	—	1	8.12	—	1	8.18	—	1	8.25	—	1	8.31	—	1	8.45
11	—	1	10.13	—	1	10.20	—	1	10.27	—	1	10.34	—	1	10.42
12	—	2	0.14	—	2	0.22	—	2	0.30	—	2	0.38	—	2	0.46
13	—	2	2.15	—	2	2.24	—	2	2.32	—	2	2.41	—	2	2.49
14	—	2	4.16	—	2	4.26	—	2	4.35	—	2	4.44	—	2	4.53
15	—	2	6.18	—	2	6.27	—	2	6.37	—	2	6.47	—	2	6.57
16	—	2	8.19	—	2	8.29	—	2	8.40	—	2	8.50	—	2	8.61
17	—	2	10.14	—	2	10.31	—	2	10.42	—	2	10.54	—	2	10.65
18	—	3	0.21	—	3	0.33	—	3	0.45	—	3	0.57	—	3	0.69
19	—	3	2.22	—	3	2.35	—	3	2.47	—	3	2.60	—	3	2.72
20	—	3	4.24	—	3	4.37	—	3	4.50	—	3	4.63	—	3	4.76
21	—	4	6.25	—	3	6.39	—	3	6.52	—	3	6.66	—	3	6.80
22	—	3	8.26	—	3	8.40	—	3	8.55	—	3	8.69	—	3	8.84
23	—	3	10.27	—	3	10.42	—	3	10.57	—	3	10.73	—	3	10.88
24	—	4	0.28	—	4	0.44	—	4	0.60	—	4	0.76	—	4	0.92
25	—	4	2.30	—	4	2.46	—	4	2.63	—	4	2.79	—	4	2.95
26	—	4	4.31	—	4	4.48	—	4	4.65	—	4	4.82	—	4	5.—
27	—	4	6.32	—	4	6.50	—	4	6.68	—	4	6.85	—	4	7.03
28	—	4	8.33	—	4	8.52	—	4	8.70	—	4	8.89	—	4	9.07
29	—	4	10.34	—	4	10.54	—	4	10.73	—	4	9.92	—	4	11.11
30	—	5	0.36	—	5	0.55	—	5	0.75	—	5	0.95	—	5	1.15
40	—	6	8.48	—	6	8.74	—	6	9.—	—	6	9.27	—	6	9.53
5	—	8	4.60	—	8	4.93	—	8	5.26	—	8	5.58	—	8	5.91
60	—	10	0.72	—	10	1.11	—	10	1.51	—	10	1.90	—	10	2.3[illegible]
70	—	11	8.84	—	11	9.30	—	11	9.76	—	11	10.2[illegible]	—	11	10.68
80	—	13	4.96	—	13	5.49	—	13	6.02	—	13	6.54	—	13	7.06
90	—	15	1.08	—	15	1.67	—	15	2.29	—	15	2.86	—	15	3.45
100	—	16	9.20	—	16	9.85	—	16	10.52	—	16	11.17	—	16	11.83
200	1	13	6.41	1	13	7.72	1	13	9.04	1	13	10.35	1	13	11.67
300	2	10	3.61	2	10	5.58	2	10	7.56	2	10	9.5[illegible]	2	10	11.50
400	3	7	0.82	3	7	3.45	3	7	6.08	3	7	8.7[illegible]	3	7	11.34
500	4	3	10.02	4	4	1.31	4	4	4.60	4	4	7.8[illegible]	4	4	11.17
600	5	0	7.23	5	0	11.17	5	1	3.12	5	1	7.06	5	1	11.01
700	5	17	4.43	5	17	9.04	5	18	1.64	5	18	6.24	5	18	10.84
800	6	14	1.64	6	14	6.90	6	15	0.16	6	15	5.41	6	15	10.68
900	7	10	10.84	7	11	4.76	7	11	10.68	7	12	4.61	7	12	10.51
1000	8	7	8.05	8	8	2.63	8	8	9.20	8	9	3.78	8	9	10.35
2000	16	15	4.1[illegible]	16	16	5.26	16	17	6.40	16	18	7.56	16	19	8.70
3000	25	3	0.15	25	4	7.89	25	6	3.6	25	7	11.3[illegible]	25	9	7.05
4000	33	10	8.20	33	12	10.52	33	15	0.80	33	17	3.12	33	19	5.40
5000	41	18	4.25	42	1	1.15	42	3	10.—	42	6	6.9[illegible]	42	9	3.75

Prin.	311 Days.			312 Days.			313 Days.			314 Days.			315 Days.		
L.	L.	s.	d.pts	L.	s.	d.pts	L.	s.	d.pts	L.	s.	d.pts	L.	s.	d.pts
1	0	0	2.04	0	0	2.05	0	0	2.05	0	0	2.06	0	0	2.07
2	—		4.08	—		4.10	—		4.11	—		4.12	—		4.14
3	—		6.13	—		6.15	—		6.17	—		6.19	—		6.21
4	—		8.17	—		8.20	—		8.23	—		8.25	—		8.28
5	—		10.22	—		10.25	—		10.29	—		10.32	—		10.35
6	—	1	0.26	—	1	0.30	—	1	0.34	—	1	0.38	—	1	0.42
7	—	1	2.31	—	1	2.36	—	1	2.40	—	1	2.45	—	1	2.49
8	—	1	4.35	—	1	4.41	—	1	4.46	—	1	4.51	—	1	4.56
9	—	1	6.40	—	1	6.46	—	1	6.52	—	1	6.58	—	1	6.64
10	—	1	8.44	—	1	8.51	—	1	8.58	—	1	8.64	—	1	8.71
11	—	1	10.49	—	1	10.56	—	1	10.63	—	1	10.71	—	1	10.78
12	—	2	0.53	—	2	0.61	—	2	0.69	—	2	0.77	—	2	0.85
13	—	2	2.58	—	2	2.66	—	2	2.75	—	2	2.84	—	2	2.92
14	—	2	4.62	—	2	4.72	—	2	4.81	—	2	4.90	—	2	5.—
15	—	2	6.67	—	2	6.77	—	2	6.87	—	2	6.96	—	2	7.06
16	—	2	8.71	—	2	8.82	—	2	8.92	—	2	9.03	—	2	9.13
17	—	2	10.76	—	2	10.87	—	2	10.98	—	2	11.09	—	2	11.21
18	—	3	0.80	—	3	0.92	—	3	1.04	—	3	1.16	—	3	1.28
19	—	3	2.85	—	3	2.97	—	3	3.10	—	3	3.22	—	3	3.35
20	—	3	4.89	—	3	5.03	—	3	5.16	—	3	5.29	—	3	5.42
21	—	3	6.94	—	3	7.08	—	3	7.21	—	3	7.35	—	3	7.49
22	—	3	8.98	—	3	9.13	—	3	9.27	—	3	9.42	—	3	9.56
23	—	3	11.03	—	3	11.18	—	3	11.33	—	3	11.48	—	3	11.63
24	—	4	1.07	—	4	1.23	—	4	1.39	—	4	1.55	—	4	1.70
25	—	2	2.12	—	4	3.28	—	4	3.45	—	4	3.61	—	4	3.78
26	—	4	5.16	—	4	5.33	—	4	5.51	—	4	5.68	—	4	5.85
27	—	4	7.21	—	4	7.39	—	4	7.56	—	4	7.74	—	4	7.92
28	—	4	9.25	—	4	9.44	—	4	9.62	—	4	9.81	—	4	10.—
29	—	4	11.30	—	4	11.49	—	4	11.68	—	4	11.87	—	5	0.06
30	—	5	1.34	—	5	1.54	—	5	1.74	—	5	1.93	—	5	2.13
40	—	6	9.79	—	6	10.06	—	6	10.32	—	6	10.58	—	6	10.84
50	—	8	6.24	—	8	6.57	—	8	6.90	—	8	7.13	—	8	7.56
60	—	10	2.69	—	10	3.09	—	10	3.48	—	10	3.87	—	10	4.27
70	—	11	11.14	—	11	11.60	—	12	0.06	—	12	0.52	—	12	1.—
80	—	13	7.59	—	13	8.12	—	13	8.64	—	13	9.17	—	13	9.07
90	—	15	4.04	—	15	4.63	—	15	5.22	—	15	5.81	—	15	6.41
100	—	17	0.49	—	17	1.15	—	17	1.80	—	17	2.46	—	17	3.12
200	1	14	0.98	1	14	2.30	1	14	3.61	1	14	4.93	1	14	6.24
300	2	11	1.47	2	11	3.45	2	11	5.42	2	11	7.39	2	11	9.36
400	3	8	1.97	3	8	4.60	3	8	7.23	3	8	9.86	3	9	0.49
500	4	5	2.46	4	5	5.75	4	5	9.04	4	6	0.32	4	6	3.61
600	5	2	2.95	5	2	6.90	5	2	10.84	5	3	2.79	5	3	6.73
700	5	19	3.45	5	19	8.05	6	0	0.65	6	0	5.25	6	0	9.86
800	6	16	3.94	6	16	9.20	6	17	2.46	6	17	7.72	6	18	0.98
900	7	13	4.43	7	13	10.35	7	14	4.27	7	14	10.18	7	15	4.10
1000	8	10	4.92	8	10	11.50	8	11	6.08	8	12	0.65	8	12	7.23
2000	17	0	9.84	17	1	11.—	17	3	0.16	17	4	1.30	17	5	[illegible]
3000	25	11	2.75	25	12	10.50	25	14	6.24	25	16	1.95	25	17	9.67
4000	34	1	7.72	34	3	10.—	34	6	0.82	34	8	2.60	34	10	4.94
5000	42	12	0.65	42	14	9.50	42	17	6.40	43	0	3.25	43	3	0.15

Prin.	316 Days.			317 Days.			318 Days.			319 Days.			320 Days.		
L.	L.	s.	d.pts	L.	s.	d.pts	L.	s.	d.pts	L.	s.	d.pts	L.	s.	d.pts
1	0	0	2.07	0	0	2.08	0	0	2.09	0	0	2.09	0	0	2.10
2	—		4.15	—		4.16	—		4.18	—		4.19	—		4.20
3	—		6.23	—		6.25	—		6.27	—		6.29	—		6.31
4	—		8.31	—		8.33	—		8.36	—		8.39	—		8.41
5	—		10.38	—		10.42	—		10.45	—		10.48	—		10.52
6	—	1	0.46	—	1	0.50	—	1	0.54	—	1	0.58	—	1	0.62
7	—	1	2.54	—	1	2.59	—	1	2.63	—	1	2.68	—	1	2.72
8	—	1	4.62	—	1	4.67	—	1	4.72	—	1	4.78	—	1	4.83
9	—	1	6.70	—	1	6.75	—	1	6.81	—	1	6.87	—	1	6.93
10	—	1	8.77	—	1	8.84	—	1	8.90	—	1	8.97	—	1	9.04
11	—	1	10.85	—	1	10.92	—	1	11.—	—	1	11.07	—	1	11.14
12	—	2	0.93	—	2	1.01	—	2	1.09	—	2	1.17	—	2	1.24
13	—	2	3.01	—	2	3.09	—	2	3.18	—	2	3.26	—	2	3.35
14	—	2	5.08	—	2	5.18	—	2	5.27	—	2	5.36	—	2	5.45
15	—	2	7.16	—	2	7.26	—	2	7.36	—	2	7.46	—	2	7.56
16	—	2	9.24	—	2	9.35	—	2	9.45	—	2	9.56	—	2	9.66
17	—	2	11.32	—	2	11.43	—	2	11.54	—	2	11.65	—	2	11.76
18	—	3	1.40	—	3	1.51	—	3	1.63	—	3	1.75	—	3	1.87
19	—	3	3.47	—	3	3.60	—	3	3.72	—	3	3.85	—	3	3.97
20	—	3	5.55	—	3	5.68	—	3	5.81	—	3	5.95	—	3	6.08
21	—	3	7.63	—	3	7.77	—	3	7.90	—	3	8.04	—	3	8.18
22	—	3	9.71	—	3	9.85	—	3	10.—	—	3	10.14	—	3	10.29
23	—	3	11.78	—	3	11.94	—	4	0.09	—	4	0.24	—	4	0.39
24	—	4	1.86	—	4	2.02	—	4	2.18	—	4	2.34	—	4	2.49
25	—	4	3.94	—	4	4.10	—	4	4.27	—	4	4.43	—	4	4.60
26	—	4	6.02	—	4	6.19	—	4	6.36	—	4	6.53	—	4	6.70
27	—	4	8.10	—	4	8.27	—	4	8.45	—	4	8.63	—	4	8.81
28	—	4	10.17	—	4	10.36	—	4	10.54	—	4	10.72	—	4	10.91
29	—	5	0.25	—	5	0.44	—	5	0.63	—	5	0.82	—	5	1.01
30	—	5	2.33	—	5	2.53	—	5	2.72	—	5	2.92	—	5	3.12
40	—	6	11.11	—	6	11.37	—	6	11.63	—	6	11.90	—	7	0.16
50	—	8	7.89	—	8	8.21	—	8	8.54	—	8	8.87	—	8	9.20
60	—	10	4.66	—	10	5.06	—	10	5.45	—	10	5.85	—	10	6.24
70	—	12	1.44	—	12	1.90	—	12	2.36	—	12	2.82	—	12	3.28
80	—	13	10.22	—	13	10.75	—	13	11.27	—	13	11.80	—	14	0.32
90	—	15	7.—	—	15	7.59	—	15	8.18	—	15	8.77	—	15	9.36
100	—	17	3.78	—	17	4.43	—	17	5.09	—	17	5.75	—	17	6.41
200	1	14	7.56	1	14	8.87	1	14	10.19	1	14	11.50	1	15	0.82
300	2	11	11.34	2	12	1.31	2	12	3.28	2	12	5.25	2	12	7.23
400	3	9	3.12	3	9	5.75	3	9	8.38	3	9	11.01	3	10	1.64
500	4	6	6.90	4	6	10.19	4	7	1.47	4	7	4.76	4	7	8.05
600	5	3	10.68	5	4	2.62	5	4	6.57	5	4	10.51	5	5	2.46
700	6	1	6.46	6	1	7.06	6	1	11.66	6	2	4.27	6	2	8.87
800	6	18	6.24	6	18	11.50	6	19	4.70	6	19	10.02	7	0	3.28
900	7	15	10.02	7	16	3.04	7	16	9.85	7	17	3.77	7	17	9.69
1000	8	13	1.80	8	13	8.36	8	14	2.97	8	14	9.5	8	15	4.10
2000	17	6	3.60	17	7	4.70	17	8	5.90	17	9	7.00	17	10	8.20
3000	25	19	5.40	26	1	1.14	26	2	8.85	26	4	4.50	26	6	0.30
4000	34	12	7.20	34	14	9.52	34	16	11.80	34	9	2.1·	35	1	4.40
5000	43	5	9.—	43	8	7.90	43	11	2.75	43	13	11.65	43	16	8.50

Prin.	321 Days.			322 Days.			323 Days.			324 Days.			325 Days.		
L.	L.	s.	d.pts	L.	s.	d.pts	L.	s.	d.pts	L.	s.	d.pts	L.	s.	d.pts
1	0	0	2.11	0	0	2.11	0	0	2.12	0	0	2.13	0	0	2.13
2	——		4.22	——		4.23	——		4.24	——		4.26	——		4.27
3	——		6.33	——		6.35	——		6.37	——		6.39	——		6.41
4	——		8.44	——		8.46	——		8.49	——		8.52	——		8.54
5	——		10.55	——		10.58	——		10.61	——		10.65	——		10.68
6	—	1	0.66	—	1	0.70	—	1	0.74	—	1	0.78	—	1	0.82
7	—	1	2.77	—	1	2.82	—	1	2.86	—	1	2.91	—	1	2.95
8	—	1	4.88	—	1	4.93	—	1	5.—	—	1	5.04	—	1	5.09
9	—	1	6.99	—	1	7.05	—	1	7.12	—	1	7.17	—	1	7.23
10	—	1	9.10	—	1	9.17	—	1	9.23	—	1	9.30	—	1	9.36
11	—	1	11.21	—	1	11.28	—	1	11.36	—	1	11.43	—	1	11.50
12	—	2	1.32	—	2	1.40	—	2	1.48	—	2	1.56	—	2	1.64
13	—	2	3.43	—	2	3.52	—	2	3.60	—	2	3.69	—	2	3.78
14	—	2	5.54	—	2	5.64	—	2	5.73	—	2	5.82	—	2	5.91
15	—	2	7.66	—	2	7.75	—	2	7.85	—	2	7.95	—	2	8.05
16	—	2	9.77	—	2	9.87	—	2	10.—	—	2	10.08	—	2	10.19
17	—	2	11.88	—	3	0.—	—	3	0.11	—	3	0.21	—	3	0.32
18	—	3	1.99	—	3	2.11	—	3	2.22	—	3	2.34	—	3	2.46
19	—	3	4.10	—	3	4.22	—	3	4.35	—	3	4.47	—	3	4.60
20	—	3	6.21	—	3	6.34	—	3	6.47	—	3	6.60	—	3	6.73
21	—	3	8.32	—	3	8.46	—	3	8.60	—	3	8.73	—	3	8.87
22	—	3	10.43	—	3	10.57	—	3	10.72	—	3	10.86	—	3	11.01
23	—	4	0.54	—	4	0.69	—	4	0.84	—	4	1.—	—	4	1.15
24	—	4	2.65	—	4	2.81	—	4	2.97	—	4	3.13	—	4	3.28
25	—	4	4.76	—	4	4.93	—	4	5.09	—	4	5.26	—	4	5.42
26	—	4	6.87	—	4	7.04	—	4	7.21	—	4	7.39	—	4	7.56
27	—	4	8.98	—	4	9.16	—	4	9.34	—	4	9.52	—	4	9.69
28	—	4	11.09	—	4	11.28	—	4	11.46	—	4	11.65	—	4	11.83
29	—	5	1.20	—	5	1.40	—	5	1.59	—	5	1.78	—	5	1.97
30	—	5	3.32	—	5	3.51	—	5	3.71	—	5	3.91	—	5	4.10
40	—	7	0.42	—	7	0.69	—	7	0.95	—	7	1.21	—	7	1.47
50	—	8	9.53	—	8	9.86	—	8	10.19	—	8	10.52	—	8	10.84
60	—	10	6.64	—	10	7.03	—	10	7.42	—	10	7.82	—	10	8.21
70	—	12	3.74	—	12	4.20	—	12	4.66	—	12	5.12	—	12	5.58
80	—	14	0.85	—	14	1.38	—	14	1.90	—	14	2.43	—	14	2.95
90	—	15	9.96	—	15	10.55	—	15	11.14	—	15	11.73	—	16	0.32
100	—	17	7.06	—	17	7.71	—	17	8.38	—	17	9.04	—	17	9.69
200	1	15	2.[illegible]3	1	15	3.45	1	15	4.76	1	15	6.08	1	15	7.39
300	2	12	9.20	2	12	11.17	2	13	1.14	2	13	3.12	2	13	5.09
400	3	10	4.27	3	10	6.90	3	10	9.53	3	11	0.16	3	11	2.79
500	4	7	11.34	4	8	2.63	4	8	5.91	4	8	9.20	4	9	0.49
600	5	5	6.40	5	5	10.35	5	6	2.29	5	6	6.24	5	6	10.18
700	6	3	1.47	6	3	6.08	6	3	10.68	6	4	3.28	6	4	7.88
800	7	0	8.54	7	1	1.80	7	1	7.06	7	2	0.32	7	2	5.58
900	7	18	3.61	7	18	9.53	7	19	3.44	7	19	9.36	8	0	3.28
1000	8	15	10.68	8	16	5.26	8	16	11.83	8	17	6.41	8	18	0.98
2000	17	11	9.36	17	12	10.52	17	13	11.66	17	15	0.82	17	16	1.96
3000	26	7	8.04	26	9	3.78	26	10	11.49	26	12	7.23	26	14	2.94
4000	35	3	6.72	35	5	9.04	35	7	11.32	35	10	1.64	35	12	3.92
5000	43	19	5.40	44	2	2.30	44	4	11.15	44	7	8.05	44	10	4.90

Prin.	326 Days.			327 Days.			328 Days.			329 Days.			330 Days.		
£.	£.	*s.*	*d.pts*	£.	*s.*	*d.pts*	£.	*s.*	*d.pts*	£.	*s.*	*d.pts*	£.	*s.*	*d.pts*
1	0	0	2.14	0	0	2.15	0	0	2.15	0	0	2.16	0	0	2.16
2	—		4.28	—		4.30	—		4.31	—		4.32	—		4.33
3	—		6.43	—		6.45	—		6.47	—		6.48	—		6.50
4	—		8.57	—		8.60	—		8.62	—		8.65	—		8.67
5	—		10.71	—		10.75	—		10.78	—		10.81	—		10.84
6	—	1	0.86	—	1	0.90	—	1	0.94	—	1	0.97	—	1	1.01
7	—	1	3.—	—	1	3.05	—	1	3.09	—	1	3.14	—	1	3.18
8	—	1	5.14	—	1	5.20	—	1	5.25	—	1	5.30	—	1	5.35
9	—	1	7.29	—	1	7.35	—	1	7.41	—	1	7.46	—	1	7.52
10	—	1	9.43	—	1	9.5	—	1	9.56	—	1	9.63	—	1	9.69
11	—	1	11.57	—	1	11.65	—	1	11.72	—	1	11.79	—	1	11.86
12	—	2	1.72	—	2	1.80	—	2	1.88	—	2	1.95	—	2	2.03
13	—	2	3.86	—	2	3.95	—	2	4.03	—	2	4.12	—	2	4.20
14	—	2	6.—	—	2	6.10	—	2	6.19	—	2	6.28	—	2	6.37
15	—	2	8.15	—	2	8.25	—	2	8.35	—	2	8.44	—	2	8.54
16	—	2	10.29	—	2	10.40	—	2	10.50	—	2	10.61	—	2	10.71
17	—	3	0.44	—	3	0.55	—	3	0.66	—	3	0.77	—	3	0.88
18	—	3	2.58	—	3	2.70	—	3	2.82	—	3	2.93	—	3	3.05
19	—	3	4.72	—	3	4.85	—	3	4.97	—	3	5.10	—	3	5.22
20	—	3	6.87	—	3	7.—	—	3	7.13	—	3	7.26	—	3	7.39
21	—	3	9.01	—	3	9.15	—	3	9.29	—	3	9.49	—	3	9.56
22	—	3	11.15	—	3	11.30	—	3	11.44	—	3	11.59	—	3	11.73
23	—	4	1.30	—	4	1.45	—	4	1.60	—	4	1.75	—	4	1.90
24	—	4	3.44	—	4	3.60	—	4	3.76	—	4	3.91	—	4	4.07
25	—	4	5.58	—	4	5.75	—	4	5.91	—	4	6.08	—	4	6.24
26	—	4	7.73	—	4	7.90	—	4	8.07	—	4	8.24	—	4	8.41
27	—	4	9.87	—	4	10.05	—	4	10.23	—	4	10.40	—	4	10.58
28	—	5	0.01	—	5	0.20	—	5	0.38	—	5	0.57	—	5	0.75
29	—	5	2.16	—	5	2.35	—	5	2.54	—	5	2.73	—	5	2.92
30	—	5	4.30	—	5	4.50	—	5	4.70	—	5	4.89	—	5	5.09
40	—	7	1.74	—	7	2.—	—	7	2.26	—	7	2.53	—	7	2.79
50	—	8	11.17	—	8	11.50	—	8	11.83	—	9	0.16	—	9	0.49
60	—	10	8.61	—	10	9.—	—	10	9.40	—	10	9.79	—	10	10.19
70	—	12	6.04	—	12	6.50	—	12	6.96	—	12	7.42	—	12	7.89
80	—	14	3.48	—	14	4.01	—	14	4.53	—	14	5.06	—	14	5.58
90	—	16	0.92	—	16	1.51	—	16	2.10	—	16	2.69	—	16	3.28
100	—	17	10.35	—	17	11.01	—	17	11.67	—	18	0.32	—	18	0.98
200	1	15	8.71	1	15	10.02	1	15	11.34	1	16	0.65	1	16	1.97
300	2	13	7.06	2	13	9.03	2	13	11.01	2	14	0.98	2	14	2.95
400	3	11	5.42	3	11	8.05	3	11	10.68	3	12	1.31	3	12	3.94
500	4	9	3.78	4	9	7.06	4	9	10.35	4	10	1.64	4	10	4.93
600	5	7	2.13	5	7	6.07	5	7	10.02	5	8	1.96	5	8	5.91
700	6	5	0.49	6	5	5.09	6	5	9.69	6	6	2.29	6	6	6.90
800	7	2	10.84	7	3	4.10	7	3	9.36	7	4	2.62	7	4	7.88
900	8	0	9.20	8	1	3.11	8	1	9.03	8	2	2.95	8	2	8.87
1000	8	18	7.56	8	19	2.13	8	19	8.7	9	0	3.28	9	0	9.86
2000	17	17	3.12	17	18	4.26	17	19	5.42	18	0	5.56	18	1	7.72
3000	26	15	10.68	26	17	6.39	26	19	2.13	27	0	9.84	27	2	5.58
4000	35	14	6.24	35	16	8.52	35	18	10.84	36	1	1.12	36	3	3.44
5000	44	13	1.80	44	15	10.65	44	18	7.55	45	1	4.40	45	4	1.30

Prin.	331 Days.			332 Days.			333 Days.			334 Days.			335 Days.		
£.	£.	s.	d.pts	£.	s.	d.pts	£.	s.	d.pts	£.	s.	d.pts	£.	s.	d.pts
1	0	0	2.17	0	0	2.18	0	0	2.18	0	0	2.19	0	0	2.20
2	—		4.35	—		4.36	—		4.37	—		4.39	—		4.40
3	—		6.52	—		6.54	—		6.56	—		6.58	—		6.60
4	—		8.70	—		8.73	—		8.75	—		8.78	—		8.81
5	—		10.88	—		10.91	—		10.94	—		10.98	—		11.01
6	—	1	1.05	—	1	1.09	—	1	1.13	—	1	1.17	—	1	1.21
7	—	1	3.23	—	1	3.28	—	1	3.32	—	1	3.37	—	1	3.41
8	—	1	5.41	—	1	5.46	—	1	5.51	—	1	5.56	—	1	5.62
9	—	1	7.58	—	1	7.64	—	1	7.70	—	1	7.76	—	1	7.82
10	—	1	9.7[illegible]	—	1	9.83	—	1	9.89	—	1	9.96	—	1	10.02
11	—	1	11.94	—	2	0.01	—	2	0.08	—	2	0.15	—	2	0.23
12	—	2	2.11	—	2	2.19	—	2	2.27	—	2	2.35	—	2	2.43
13	—	2	4.29	—	2	4.37	—	2	4.46	—	2	4.55	—	2	4.63
14	—	2	6.47	—	2	6.56	—	2	6.65	—	2	6.74	—	2	6.83
15	—	2	8.64	—	2	8.74	—	2	8.84	—	2	8.94	—	2	9.04
16	—	2	10.82	—	2	10.92	—	2	11.03	—	2	11.13	—	2	11.24
17	—	3	1.—	—	3	1.11	—	3	1.22	—	3	1.33	—	3	1.44
18	—	3	3.17	—	3	3.29	—	3	3.41	—	3	3.53	—	3	3.64
19	—	3	5.35	—	3	5.47	—	3	5.60	—	3	5.72	—	3	5.85
20	—	3	7.52	—	3	7.66	—	3	7.79	—	3	7.92	—	3	7.05
21	—	3	9.7[illegible]	—	3	9.84	—	3	9.98	—	3	10.11	—	3	10.25
22	—	3	11.88	—	4	0.92	—	4	0.17	—	4	0.31	—	4	0.46
23	—	4	2.05	—	4	2.20	—	4	2.36	—	4	2.51	—	4	2.66
24	—	4	4.23	—	4	4.39	—	4	4.54	—	4	4.70	—	4	4.86
25	—	4	6.41	—	4	6.57	—	4	6.73	—	4	6.90	—	4	7.06
26	—	4	8.58	—	4	8.75	—	4	8.92	—	4	9.10	—	4	9.27
27	—	4	10.76	—	4	10.94	—	4	11.11	—	4	11.29	—	4	11.47
28	—	5	0.94	—	5	1.12	—	5	1.30	—	5	1.49	—	5	1.67
29	—	5	3.11	—	5	3.30	—	5	3.49	—	5	3.68	—	5	3.87
30	—	5	5.29	—	5	5.49	—	5	5.68	—	5	5.88	—	5	6.08
40	—	7	3.05	—	7	3.32	—	7	3.58	—	7	3.84	—	7	4.10
50	—	9	0.8[illegible]	—	9	1.15	—	9	1.47	—	9	1.80	—	9	2.13
60	—	10	10.5[illegible]	—	10	10.98	—	10	11.37	—	10	11.76	—	11	0.16
70	—	12	8.35	—	12	8.81	—	12	9.27	—	12	9.73	—	12	10.19
80	—	14	6.1	—	14	6.64	—	14	7.16	—	14	7.69	—	14	8.21
90	—	16	3.87	—	16	4.47	—	16	5.06	—	16	5.65	—	16	6.24
100	—	18	1.64	—	18	2.30	—	18	2.95	—	18	3.61	—	18	4.27
200	1	16	3.28	1	16	4.60	1	16	5.91	1	16	7.23	1	16	8.54
300	2	14	4.92	2	14	6.90	2	14	8.87	2	14	10.84	2	15	0.81
400	3	12	6.57	3	12	9.20	3	12	11.83	3	13	2.46	3	13	5.09
500	4	10	8.21	4	10	11.50	4	11	2.79	4	11	6.08	4	11	9.36
600	5	8	9.85	5	9	1.80	5	9	5.74	5	9	9.69	5	10	1.63
700	6	6	11.50	6	7	4.10	6	7	8.70	6	8	1.31	6	8	5.91
800	7	5	1.14	7	5	6.40	7	5	11.66	7	6	4.92	7	6	10.18
900	8	3	2.78	8	3	8.70	8	4	2.62	8	4	8.54	8	5	2.45
1000	9	1	4.43	9	1	11.01	9	2	5.58	9	3	0.16	9	3	6.73
2000	18	2	8.86	18	3	10.02	18	4	11.16	18	6	0.32	18	7	1.46
3000	27	4	1.29	27	5	9.03	27	7	4.74	27	9	0.48	27	10	8.19
4000	36	5	5.72	36	7	8.04	36	9	10.32	36	12	0.64	36	14	2.92
5000	45	6	10.15	45	9	7.05	45	12	3.90	45	15	0.80	45	17	9.65

Prin.	336 Days.			337 Days.			338 Days.			339 Days.			340 Days.		
£.	£.	s.	d.pts	£.	s.	d.pts	£.	s.	d.pts	£.	s.	d.pts	£.	s.	d.pts
1	0	0	2.20	0	0	2.21	0	0	2.22	0	0	2.22	0	0	2.23
2	——		4.41	——		4.43	——		4.44	——		4.45	——		4.47
3	——		6.62	——		6.64	——		6.66	——		6.68	——		6.70
4	——		8.83	——		8.86	——		8.88	——		8.91	——		8.94
5	——		11.04	——		11.07	——		11.11	——		11.14	——		11.17
6	–	1	1.25	–	1	1.29	–	1	1.33	–	1	1.37	–	1	1.41
7	–	1	3.46	–	1	3.51	–	1	3.55	–	1	3.60	–	1	3.64
8	–	1	5.67	–	1	5.72	–	1	5.77	–	1	5.83	–	1	5.88
9	–	1	7.88	–	1	7.94	–	1	8.—	–	1	8.06	–	1	8.12
10	–	1	10.09	–	1	10.15	–	1	10.22	–	1	10.29	–	1	10.35
11	–	2	0.3[illegible]	–	2	0.37	–	2	0.44	–	2	0.51	–	2	0.59
12	–	2	2.51	–	2	2.5[illegible]	–	2	2.66	–	2	2.74	–	2	2.82
13	–	2	4.72	–	2	4.80	–	2	4.89	–	2	4.97	–	2	5.06
14	–	2	6.93	–	2	7.02	–	2	7.11	–	2	7.2[illegible]	–	2	7.29
15	–	2	9.13	–	2	9.23	–	2	9.33	–	2	9.43	–	2	9.53
16	–	2	11.34	–	2	11.45	–	2	11.55	–	2	11.66	–	2	11.76
17	–	3	1.55	–	3	1.67	–	3	1.78	–	3	1.89	–	3	2.—
18	–	3	3.76	–	3	3.88	–	3	4.—	–	3	4.12	–	3	4.24
19	–	3	5.97	–	3	6.10	–	3	6.22	–	3	6.35	–	3	6.47
20	–	3	8.18	–	3	8.31	–	3	8.44	–	3	8.58	–	3	8.71
21	–	3	10.39	–	3	10.53	–	3	10.67	–	3	10.80	–	3	10.94
22	–	4	0.6[illegible]	–	4	0.74	–	4	0.89	–	4	1.03	–	4	1.18
23	–	4	2.8[illegible]	–	4	2.96	–	4	3.11	–	4	3.26	–	4	3.41
24	–	4	5.02	–	4	5.18	–	4	5.33	–	4	5.49	–	4	5.65
25	–	4	7.23	–	4	7.39	–	4	7.56	–	4	7.72	–	4	7.89
26	–	4	9.44	–	4	9.61	–	4	9.78	–	4	9.95	–	4	10.12
27	–	4	11.65	–	4	11.83	–	5	0.—	–	5	0.18	–	5	0.36
28	–	5	1.86	–	5	2.04	–	5	2.22	–	5	2.41	–	5	2.59
29	–	5	4.06	–	5	4.2[illegible]	–	5	4.45	–	5	4.64	–	5	4.83
30	–	5	6.27	–	5	6.47	–	5	6.67	–	5	6.87	–	5	7.06
40	–	7	4.37	–	7	4.63	–	7	4.89	–	7	5.16	–	7	5.42
50	–	9	2.46	–	9	2.79	–	9	3.12	–	9	3.45	–	9	3.78
60	–	11	0.55	–	11	0.95	–	11	1.34	–	11	1.74	–	11	2.13
70	–	12	10.65	–	12	11.11	–	12	11.57	–	13	0.03	–	13	0.49
80	–	14	8.74	–	14	9.27	–	14	9.79	–	14	10.32	–	14	10.84
90	–	16	6.83	–	15	7.46	–	16	8.02	–	16	8.61	–	16	9.20
100	–	18	4.93	–	18	5.58	–	18	6.24	–	18	6.90	–	18	7.56
200	1	16	9.86	1	16	11.17	1	17	0.49	1	17	1.80	1	17	3.12
300	2	15	2.79	2	15	4.76	2	15	6.73	1	15	8.71	2	15	10.68
400	3	13	7.72	3	13	10.35	3	14	0.98	3	14	3.61	3	14	6.24
500	4	12	0.65	4	12	3.94	4	12	7.23	4	12	10.52	4	13	1.80
600	5	10	5.58	5	10	9.53	5	11	1.47	5	11	5.42	5	11	9.36
700	6	8	10.51	6	9	3.12	6	9	7.72	6	10	0.32	6	10	4.92
800	7	7	3.44	7	7	8.71	7	8	1.96	7	8	7.23	7	9	0.48
900	8	5	8.37	8	6	2.30	8	6	8.21	8	7	2.13	8	7	8.04
1000	9	4	1.31	9	4	7.89	9	5	2.46	9	5	9.04	9	6	3.21
2000	18	8	2.62	18	9	3.75	18	10	4.92	18	11	6.08	18	12	7.22
3000	27	12	3.93	27	13	11.67	27	15	7.38	27	17	3.12	27	18	10.83
4000	36	16	5.24	36	18	7.56	37	0	9.84	37	3	0.16	37	5	2.44
5000	46	0	6.55	46	3	3.45	46	6	0.30	46	8	9.20	46	11	6.05

Prin.	341 Days.			342 Days.			343 Days.			344 Days.			345 Days.		
£.	£.	s.	d.pts	£.	s.	d.pts	£.	s.	d.pts	£.	s.	d.pts	£.	s.	d.pts
1	0	0	2.24	0	0	2.24	0	0	2.25	0	0	2.26	0	0	2.26
2	——		4.48	——		4.49	——		4.51	——		4.52	——		4.53
3	——		6.72	——		6.74	——		6.76	——		6.78	——		6.80
4	——		8.96	——		9.—	——		9.02	——		9.04	——		9.07
5	——		11.21	——		11.24	——		11.27	——		11.30	——		11.34
6	—	1	1.45	—	1	1.49	—	1	1.53	—	1	1.57	—	1	1.61
7	—	1	3.69	—	1	3.74	—	1	3.78	—	1	3.83	—	1	3.87
8	—	1	5.93	—	1	6.—	—	1	6.04	—	1	6.09	—	1	6.14
9	—	1	8.17	—	1	8.23	—	1	8.29	—	1	8.35	—	1	8.41
10	—	1	10.42	—	1	10.48	—	1	10.55	—	1	10.61	—	1	10.68
11	—	2	0.66	—	2	0.73	—	2	0.80	—	2	0.88	—	2	0.95
12	—	2	2.90	—	2	3.—	—	2	3.06	—	2	3.14	—	2	3.22
13	—	2	5.14	—	2	5.23	—	2	5.31	—	2	5.40	—	2	5.49
14	—	2	7.39	—	2	7.48	—	2	7.57	—	2	7.66	—	2	7.75
15	—	2	9.63	—	2	9.73	—	2	9.83	—	2	9.92	—	2	10.02
16	—	2	11.87	—	3	0.—	—	3	0.08	—	3	0.19	—	3	0.26
17	—	3	2.11	—	3	2.22	—	3	2.34	—	3	2.45	—	3	2.56
18	—	3	4.35	—	3	4.47	—	3	4.59	—	3	4.71	—	3	4.83
19	—	3	6.60	—	3	6.72	—	3	6.85	—	3	6.97	—	3	7.10
20	—	3	8.84	—	3	9.—	—	3	9.10	—	3	9.23	—	3	9.36
21	—	3	11.08	—	3	11.22	—	3	11.36	—	3	11.50	—	3	11.63
22	—	4	1.32	—	4	1.47	—	4	1.61	—	4	1.76	—	4	1.90
23	—	4	3.57	—	4	3.72	—	4	3.87	—	4	4.02	—	4	4.17
24	—	4	5.81	—	4	6.—	—	4	6.12	—	4	6.28	—	4	6.44
25	—	4	8.05	—	4	8.21	—	4	8.38	—	4	8.54	—	4	8.71
26	—	4	10.29	—	4	10.46	—	4	10.63	—	4	10.80	—	4	10.97
27	—	5	0.53	—	5	0.71	—	5	0.89	—	5	1.07	—	5	1.24
28	—	5	2.78	—	5	3.—	—	5	3.14	—	5	3.33	—	5	3.51
29	—	5	5.02	—	5	5.21	—	5	5.40	—	5	5.59	—	5	5.78
30	—	5	7.26	—	5	7.45	—	5	7.66	—	5	7.85	—	5	8.05
40	—	7	5.68	—	7	6.—	—	7	6.21	—	7	6.47	—	7	6.73
50	—	9	4.10	—	9	4.43	—	9	4.76	—	9	5.05	—	9	5.42
60	—	11	2.53	—	11	2.92	—	11	3.32	—	11	3.71	—	11	4.10
70	—	13	0.95	—	13	1.41	—	13	1.87	—	13	2.33	—	13	2.79
80	—	14	11.37	—	14	11.90	—	15	0.42	—	15	0.95	—	15	1.47
90	—	16	9.79	—	16	10.38	—	16	10.98	—	16	11.57	—	17	0.16
100	—	18	8.2	—	18	8.87	—	18	9.53	—	18	10.19	—	18	10.84
200	1	17	4.43	1	17	5.75	1	17	7.06	1	17	8.38	1	17	9.69
300	2	16	0.65	2	16	2.62	2	16	4.60	2	16	6.57	2	16	8.54
400	3	14	8.87	3	14	11.50	3	15	2.13	3	15	4.76	3	15	7.39
500	4	13	5.09	4	13	8.38	4	13	11.67	4	14	2.95	4	14	6.24
600	5	12	1.31	5	12	5.25	5	12	9.20	5	13	1.14	5	13	5.09
700	6	10	9.53	6	11	2.13	6	11	6.73	6	11	11.33	6	12	3.94
800	7	9	5.75	7	9	11.—	7	10	4.27	7	10	9.52	7	11	2.79
900	8	8	1.97	8	8	7.88	8	9	1.80	8	9	7.71	8	10	1.64
1000	9	6	10.19	9	7	4.76	9	7	11.34	9	8	5.91	9	9	0.46
2000	18	13	8.38	18	14	9.52	18	15	10.68	18	16	11.82	18	18	0.98
3000	28	0	6.57	28	2	2.28	28	3	10.02	28	5	5.73	28	7	1.47
4000	37	7	4.76	37	9	7.04	37	11	9.36	37	13	11.64	37	16	1.96
5000	46	14	2.95	46	16	11.85	46	19	8.75	47	2	5.55	47	5	2.45

Prin.	346 Days.			347 Days.			348 Days.			349 Days.			350 Days.		
£.	£.	s.	d.pts	£.	s.	d.pts	£.	s.	d.pts	£.	s.	d.pts	£.	s.	d.pts
1	0	0	2.27	0	0	2.28	0	0	2.28	0	0	2.29	0	0	2.30
2	—		4.55	—		4.56	—		4.57	—		4.58	—		4.60
3	—		6.82	—		6.84	—		6.86	—		6.88	—		9.90
4	—		9.10	—		9.12	—		9.15	—		9.17	—		9.20
5	—		11.37	—		11.40	—		11.44	—		11.47	—		11.50
6	—	1	1.65	—	1	1.68	—	1	1.72	—	1	1.76	—	1	1.80
7	—	1	3.92	—	1	3.97	—	1	4.01	—	1	4.06	—	1	4.10
8	—	1	6.20	—	1	6.25	—	1	6.30	—	1	6.35	—	1	6.41
9	—	1	8.47	—	1	8.53	—	1	8.59	—	1	8.65	—	1	8.71
10	—	1	10.75	—	1	10.81	—	1	10.88	—	1	10.94	—	1	11.01
11	—	2	1.02	—	2	1.09	—	2	1.17	—	2	1.24	—	2	1.31
12	—	2	3.30	—	2	3.37	—	2	3.45	—	2	3.53	—	2	3.61
13	—	2	5.57	—	2	5.66	—	2	5.74	—	2	5.83	—	2	5.91
14	—	2	7.85	—	2	7.94	—	2	8.03	—	2	8.12	—	2	8.21
15	—	2	10.12	—	2	10.22	—	2	10.32	—	2	10.42	—	2	10.52
16	—	3	0.40	—	3	0.50	—	3	0.61	—	3	0.71	—	3	0.82
17	—	3	2.67	—	3	2.78	—	3	2.89	—	3	3.01	—	3	3.12
18	—	3	4.95	—	3	5.06	—	3	5.18	—	3	5.30	—	3	5.42
19	—	3	7.22	—	3	7.35	—	3	7.47	—	3	7.60	—	3	7.72
20	—	3	9.50	—	3	9.63	—	3	9.76	—	3	9.89	—	3	10.02
21	—	3	11.77	—	3	11.91	—	4	0.05	—	4	0.19	—	4	0.32
22	—	4	2.05	—	4	2.19	—	4	2.34	—	4	2.48	—	4	2.62
23	—	4	4.32	—	4	4.47	—	4	4.62	—	4	4.78	—	4	4.93
24	—	4	6.60	—	4	6.75	—	4	6.91	—	4	7.07	—	4	7.23
25	—	4	9.87	—	4	9.04	—	4	9.20	—	4	9.36	—	4	9.53
26	—	4	11.15	—	4	11.32	—	4	11.49	—	4	11.66	—	4	11.83
27	—	5	1.42	—	5	1.60	—	5	1.78	—	5	1.95	—	5	2.13
28	—	5	3.70	—	5	3.88	—	5	4.06	—	5	4.25	—	5	4.43
29	—	5	5.97	—	5	6.16	—	5	6.35	—	5	6.54	—	5	6.73
30	—	5	8.25	—	5	8.44	—	5	8.64	—	5	8.84	—	5	9.04
40	—	7	7.—	—	7	7.26	—	7	7.52	—	7	7.79	—	7	8.05
50	—	9	5.75	—	9	6.08	—	9	6.41	—	9	6.73	—	9	7.06
60	—	11	4.50	—	11	4.89	—	11	5.2[illegible]	—	11	5.68	—	11	6.08
70	—	13	3.25	—	13	3.71	—	13	4.17	—	13	4.63	—	13	5.09
80	—	15	2.—	—	15	2.53	—	15	3.05	—	15	3.58	—	15	4.10
90	—	17	0.75	—	17	1.34	—	17	1.93	—	17	2.53	—	17	3.12
100	—	18	11.50	—	19	0.16	—	19	0.82	—	19	1.47	—	19	2.13
200	1	17	11.01	1	18	0.32	1	18	1.64	1	18	2.95	1	18	4.27
300	2	16	10.51	2	17	0.49	2	17	2.46	2	17	4.43	2	17	6.40
400	3	15	10.02	3	16	0.55	3	16	3.28	3	16	5.91	3	16	8.54
500	4	14	9.53	4	15	0.82	4	15	4.10	4	15	7.39	4	15	10.68
600	5	13	9.03	5	14	0.89	5	14	4.92	5	14	8.87	5	15	0.81
700	6	12	8.54	6	13	1.14	6	13	5.74	6	13	10.35	6	14	2.95
800	7	11	8.04	7	12	1.31	7	12	6.56	7	12	11.83	7	13	5.08
900	8	10	7.55	8	11	1.47	8	11	7.38	8	12	1.31	8	12	7.22
1000	9	9	7.06	9	10	1.64	9	10	8.21	9	11	2.79	9	11	9.36
2000	18	19	2.12	19	0	3.28	19	1	4.42	19	2	5.58	19	3	6.72
3000	28	8	9.18	28	10	4.92	28	12	0.63	28	13	8.37	28	15	4.08
4000	37	18	4.24	38	0	6.56	38	2	8.84	38	4	11.16	38	7	1.44
5000	47	7	11.30	47	10	8.20	47	13	5.05	47	16	1.95	47	18	10.80

Prin.	351 Days.			352 Days.			353 Days.			354 Days.			355 Days.		
L.	L.	s.	d.pts	L.	s.	d.pts	L.	s.	d.pts	L.	s.	d.pts	L.	s.	d.pts
1	0	0	2.30	0	0	2.31	0	0	2.32	0	0	2.32	0	0	2.33
2	——		4.61	——		4.62	——		4.64	——		4.65	——		4.66
3	——		6.92	——		6.94	——		6.96	——		6.98	——		7.—
4	——		9.23	——		9.25	——		9.28	——		9.31	——		9.33
5	——		11.53	——		11.57	——		11.60	——		11.63	——		11.67
6	—	1	1.84	—	1	1.88	—	1	1.92	—	1	1.96	—	1	2.—
9	—	1	4.15	—	1	4.22	—	1	4.24	—	1	4.29	—	1	4.33
7	—	1	6.46	—	1	6.51	—	1	6.56	—	1	6.62	—	1	6.67
8	—	1	8.77	—	1	8.83	—	1	8.88	—	1	8.94	—	1	9.—
10	—	1	11.07	—	1	11.14	—	1	11.21	—	1	11.27	—	1	11.34
11	—	2	1.38	—	2	1.45	—	2	1.53	—	2	1.60	—	2	1.67
12	—	2	3.69	—	2	3.77	—	2	3.85	—	2	3.93	—	2	4.01
13	—	2	6.—	—	2	6.08	—	2	6.17	—	2	6.25	—	2	6.34
14	—	2	8.3	—	2	8.40	—	2	8.49	—	2	8.58	—	2	8.67
15	—	2	10.61	—	2	10.71	—	2	10.81	—	2	10.91	—	2	11.01
16	—	3	0.92	—	3	1.03	—	3	1.13	—	3	1.24	—	3	1.34
17	—	3	3.23	—	3	3.34	—	3	3.45	—	3	3.57	—	3	3.68
18	—	3	5.54	—	3	5.66	—	3	5.77	—	3	5.89	—	3	6.01
19	—	3	7.85	—	3	7.97	—	3	8.10	—	3	8.22	—	3	8.35
20	—	3	10.15	—	3	10.29	—	3	10.42	—	3	10.55	—	3	10.68
21	—	4	0.46	—	4	0.60	—	4	0.74	—	4	0.88	—	4	1.01
22	—	4	2.77	—	4	2.91	—	4	3.06	—	4	3.20	—	4	3.35
23	—	4	5.08	—	4	5.23	—	4	5.38	—	4	5.53	—	4	5.68
24	—	4	7.39	—	4	7.54	—	4	7.70	—	4	7.86	—	4	8.02
25	—	4	9.69	—	4	9.86	—	4	10.02	—	4	10.19	—	4	10.35
26	—	5	0.—	—	5	0.17	—	5	0.34	—	5	0.51	—	5	0.69
27	—	5	2.31	—	5	2.49	—	5	2.66	—	5	2.84	—	5	3.02
28	—	5	4.62	—	5	4.80	—	5	5.—	—	5	5.17	—	5	5.35
29	—	5	6.93	—	5	7.12	—	5	7.31	—	5	7.10	—	5	7.69
30	—	5	9.24	—	5	9.43	—	5	9.63	—	5	9.83	—	5	10.02
40	—	7	8.31	—	7	8.58	—	7	8.84	—	7	9.10	—	7	9.36
50	—	9	7.39	—	9	7.72	—	9	8.05	—	9	8.38	—	9	8.71
60	—	11	6.47	—	11	6.87	—	11	7.26	—	11	7.66	—	11	8.05
70	—	13	5.55	—	13	6.01	—	13	6.47	—	13	6.93	—	13	7.39
80	—	15	5.55	—	15	5.16	—	15	5.68	—	15	6.21	—	15	6.73
90	—	17	3.71	—	17	4.30	—	17	4.89	—	17	5.49	—	17	6.08
100	—	19	2.79	—	19	3.45	—	19	4.10	—	19	4.76	—	19	5.42
200	1	18	5.58	1	18	6.90	1	18	8.21	1	18	9.53	1	18	10.84
300	2	17	8.38	2	17	10.35	2	18	0.32	2	18	2.30	2	18	4.27
400	3	16	11.17	3	17	1.80	3	17	4.43	3	17	7.06	3	17	9.69
500	4	16	1.97	4	16	5.26	4	16	8.54	4	16	11.83	4	17	3.12
600	5	15	4.76	5	15	8.71	5	16	0.65	5	16	4.60	5	16	8.54
700	6	14	7.55	6	15	0.16	6	15	4.76	6	15	9.36	6	16	1.96
800	7	13	10.35	7	14	3.61	7	14	8.87	7	15	2.13	7	15	7.39
900	8	13	1.14	8	13	7.06	8	14	0.98	8	14	6.90	8	15	0.81
1000	9	12	3.94	9	12	10.52	9	13	5.09	9	13	11.67	9	14	6.24
2000	19	4	7.88	19	5	9.04	19	6	10.18	19	7	11.34	19	9	0.48
3000	28	16	11.82	28	18	7.56	29	0	3.27	29	1	11.01	29	3	6.72
4000	38	9	3.76	38	11	6.08	38	13	8.36	38	15	10.68	38	18	0.96
5000	48	1	7.76	48	4	4.60	48	7	1.45	48	9	10.35	48	12	7.20

Prin.	356 Days.			357 Days.			358 Days.			359 Days.			360 Days.		
£.	£.	s.	d.pts	£.	s.	d.pts	£.	s.	d.pts	£.	s.	d.pts	£.	s.	d.pts
1	0	0	2.34	0	0	2.34	0	0	2.35	0	0	2.36	0	0	2.36
2	—		4,68	—		4,69	—		4,70	—		4,72	—		4,73
3	—		7,02	—		7,04	—		7,06	—		7,08	—		7,10
4	—		9,36	—		9,38	—		9,41	—		9.44	—		9,46
5	—		11,70	—		11,73	—		11,76	—		11,80	—		11,83
6	—	1	2,04	—	1	2,08	—	1	2,12	—	1	2,16	—	1	2,20
7	—	1	4,38	—	1	4,73	—	1	4,47	—	1	4,52	—	1	4,56
8	—	1	6,72	—	1	6,77	—	1	6,83	—	1	6,88	—	1	6,93
9	—	1	9,06	—	1	9,12	—	1	9,18	—	1	9.24	—	1	9,30
10	—	1	11,40	—	1	11,47	—	1	11,53	—	1	11,60	—	1	11,67
11	—	2	1,74	—	2	1,82	—	2	1,89	—	2	1,96	—	2	2,03
12	—	2	4,08	—	2	4.16	—	2	4,24	—	2	4.32	—	2	4:40
13	—	2	6,43	—	2	6,51	—	2	6,60	—	2	6,68	—	2	6,77
14	—	2	8,77	—	2	8,86	—	2	8,95	—	2	9,04	—	2	9.13
15	—	2	11,11	—	2	11,21	—	2	11,30	—	2	11,40	—	2	11,50
16	—	3	1,45	—	3	1,55	—	3	1,60	—	3	1,76	—	3	1,87
17	—	3	3,79	—	3	3,90	—	3	4,01	—	3	4,12	—	3	4,24
18	—	3	6,13	—	3	6,25	—	3	6,37	—	3	6,48	—	3	6,60
19	—	3	8,47	—	3	8,60	—	3	8,72	—	3	8,85	—	3	8,97
20	—	3	10,81	—	3	10,94	—	3	11,07	—	3	11,21	—	3	11,34
21	—	4	1,15	—	4	1,29	—	4	1,43	—	4	1,57	—	4	1,70
22	—	4	3,49	—	4	3,64	—	4	3.78	—	4	3,93	—	4	4,07
23	—	4	5,83	—	4	5,98	—	4	6,14	—	4	6,29	—	4	6,44
24	—	4	8,17	—	4	8,33	—	4	8,49	—	4	8,65	—	4	8,81
25	—	4	10,52	—	4	10,68	—	4	10,84	—	4	11,01	—	4	11,17
26	—	5	0,86	—	5	1,03	—	5	1,20	—	5	1,37	—	5	1,54
27	—	5	3,20	—	5	3,37	—	5	3,55	—	5	3,73	—	5	3,91
28	—	5	5,54	—	5	5,72	—	5	5,91	—	5	6,09	—	5	6,27
29	—	5	7,88	—	5	8,07	—	5	8,26	—	5	8,45	—	5	8,64
30	—	5	10,22	—	5	10,42	—	5	10,61	—	5	10,81	—	5	11,01
40	—	7	9,63	—	7	9,89	—	7	10,15	—	7	10,42	—	7	10,68
50	—	9	9,04	—	9	9,36	—	9	9,69	—	9	10,02	—	9	10,35
60	—	11	8,44	—	11	8,84	—	11	9,23	—	11	9,63	—	11	10,02
70	—	13	7,85	—	13	8,31	—	13	8,77	—	13	9,23	—	13	9,69
80	—	15	7,26	—	15	7,79	—	15	8,31	—	15	8,84	—	15	9,36
90	—	17	6,67	—	17	7,26	—	17	7,85	—	17	8,44	—	17	9,04
100	—	19	6,08	—	19	6,73	—	19	7,39	—	19	8,05	—	19	8,71
200	1	19	0,16	1	19	1,47	1	19	2,79	1	19	4,10	1	19	5,42
300	2	18	6,24	2	18	8,21	2	18	10,19	2	19	0,16	2	19	2,13
400	3	18	0,32	3	18	2,95	3	18	5,58	3	18	8,21	3	18	10,84
500	4	17	6,41	4	17	9,69	4	18	0,98	4	18	4,27	4	18	7.56
600	5	17	0,49	5	17	4,43	5	17	8,38	5	18	0,32	5	18	4 27
700	6	16	6,57	6	16	11,17	6	17	3,77	6	17	8,37	6	18	0,98
800	7	16	0,65	7	16	5,91	7	16	11,17	7	17	4,43	7	17	9,69
900	8	15	6,73	8	16	0,65	8	16	6,57	8	17	0,48	8	17	6,40
1000	9	15	0,82	9	15	7,39	9	16	1,97	9	16	8,54	9	17	3,12
2000	19	10	1,64	19	11	2,78	19	12	3,9[illegible]	19	13	5,08	19	14	6,24
3000	29	5	2,46	29	6	10,17	29	8	5,91	29	10	1,62	29	11	9,36
4000	39	0	3,28	39	2	5,56	39	4	7,88	39	6	10,16	39	9	0,48
5000	48	15	4,10	48	18	0,95	49	0	9,85	49	3	6.7[illegible]	49	6	3,6[illegible]

Prin.	361 Days.			362 Days.			363 Days.			364 Days.			365 Days.		
L.	L.	s.	d.pts	L.	s.	d.pts	L.	s.	d.pts	L.	s.	d.pts	L.	s.	d.pts
1	0	0	2.37	0	0	2.38	0	0	2.38	0	0	2.39	0	0	2.40
2	—		4.74	—		4,76	—		4,77	—		4,78	—		4,80
3	—		7,12	—		7,14	—		7,16	—		7,18	—		7,20
4	—		9,49	—		9,52	—		9,54	—		9,57	—		9,60
5	—		11,86	—		11,90	—		11,93	—		11,96	—	1	0,—
6	—	1	2,24	—	1	2,28	—	1	2,32	—	1	2,36	—	1	2,40
7	—	1	4,61	—	1	4,66	—	1	4,70	—	1	4,75	—	1	4,80
8	—	1	6,98	—	1	7,04	—	1	7,09	—	1	7,14	—	1	7,20
9	—	1	9,36	—	1	9,42	—	1	9,48	—	1	9,54	—	1	9,60
10	—	1	11,73	—	1	11,80	—	1	11,86	—	1	11,93	—	2	0,—
11	—	2	2,11	—	2	2,18	—	2	2,25	—	2	2,32	—	2	2,40
12	—	2	4,48	—	2	4,56	—	2	4,64	—	2	4,72	—	2	4,80
13	—	2	6,85	—	2	6,94	—	2	7,02	—	2	7,11	—	2	7,20
14	—	2	9,23	—	2	9,32	—	2	9,41	—	2	9,50	—	2	9,60
15	—	2	11,60	—	2	11,79	—	2	11,80	—	2	11,90	—	3	0—
16	—	3	1,97	—	3	2,08	—	3	2,18	—	3	2,29	—	3	2,40
17	—	3	4,35	—	3	4,46	—	3	4,57	—	3	4,68	—	3	4.80
18	—	3	6,72	—	3	6,84	—	3	6,96	—	3	7,08	—	3	7,20
19	—	3	9,10	—	3	9,22	—	3	9,34	—	3	9,47	—	3	9,60
20	—	3	11,47	—	3	11,60	—	3	11,73	—	3	11,86	—	4	0,—
21	—	4	1,84	—	4	1,98	—	4	2,12	—	4	2,26	—	4	2,40
22	—	4	4,22	—	4	4,36	—	4	4,51	—	4	4,65	—	4	4,80
23	—	4	6,59	—	4	6,74	—	4	6,89	—	4	7,04	—	4	7,20
24	—	4	8,96	—	4	9,12	—	4	9,28	—	4	9,44	—	4	9,60
25	—	4	11,34	—	4	11,50	—	4	11,67	—	4	11,83	—	5	0,—
26	—	5	1,71	—	5	1,88	—	5	2,05	—	5	2,22	—	5	2,40
27	—	5	4,08	—	5	4,26	—	5	4,44	—	5	4,62	—	5	4,80
28	—	5	6,46	—	5	6,64	—	5	6,83	—	5	7,01	—	5	7,20
29	—	5	8,8[illegible]	—	5	9,02	—	5	9,21	—	5	9,40	—	5	9,60
30	—	5	11,21	—	5	11,40	—	5	11,60	—	5	11,80	—	6	0,—
40	—	7	10,94	—	7	11,21	—	7	11,47	—	7	11,73	—	8	0,—
50	—	9	10,68	—	9	11,01	—	9	11,34	—	9	11,67	—	10	0,—
60	—	11	10,42	—	11	10,81	—	11	11,21	—	11	11,60	—	12	0,—
70	—	13	10,15	—	13	10,61	—	13	11,07	—	13	11,53	—	14	0,—
80	—	15	9,89	—	15	10,42	—	15	10,94	—	15	11,47	—	16	0,—
90	—	17	9,63	—	17	10,22	—	17	10,81	—	17	11,40	—	18	0,—
100	—	19	9,36	—	19	10,02	—	19	10,68	—	19	11,34	1	0	0,—
200	1	19	6,73	1	19	8,05	1	19	9,36	1	19	10,68	2	0	0,—
300	2	19	4,10	2	19	6,68	2	19	8,05	2	19	10,02	3	0	0,—
400	3	19	1,47	3	19	4,1[illegible]	3	19	6,73	3	19	9,36	4	0	0,—
500	4	18	10,84	4	19	2,13	4	19	5,42	4	19	8,71	5	0	0,—
600	5	18	8,21	5	19	[illegible],16	5	19	4,10	5	19	8,05	6	0	0,—
700	6	18	5,58	6	18	10,18	6	19	2,78	6	19	7,39	7	0	0,—
800	7	18	2,95	7	18	8,21	7	19	1,47	7	19	6,73	8	0	0,—
900	8	18	[illegible],32	8	18	6,24	8	19	0,15	8	19	6,07	9	0	0,—
1000	9	17	9,69	9	18	4,27	9	18	10,84	9	19	5,42	10	0	0,—
2000	19	15	7,38	19	16	8,54	19	17	9,68	19	18	10,84	20	0	0,—
3000	29	13	5,[illegible]	29	15	[illegible],81	29	16	8,52	29	18	4,26	30	0	0,—
4000	39	11	2,76	39	13	5,08	39	15	7,36	39	17	9,68	40	0	0,—
5000	49	9	0,45	49	11	9,35	49	14	6,20	49	17	3,10	50	0	0,—

Prin.	1 Month.			2 Months.			3 Months.			4 Months.			5 Months.			6 Months		
L.	*L.*	*s.*	*d.ps*	*L.*	*s.*	*d.ps*	*L.*	*s.*	*d.ps*	*L.*	*s.*	*d.pts*	*L.*	*s.*	*d.ps*	*L.*	*s.*	*d.ps*
1	0	0	0.2	0	0	0.4	0	0	0.6	0	0	0.8	0	0	1.0	0	0	1.2
2	——		0.4	——		0.8	——		1.2	——		1.6	——		2.0	——		2.4
3	——		0.6	——		1.2	——		1.8	——		2.4	——		3.0	——		3.6
4	——		0.8	——		1.6	——		2.4	——		3.2	——		4.0	——		4.8
5	——		1.0	——		1.6	——		3.0	——		4.0	——		5.0	——		6.0
6	——		1.2	——		2.4	——		3.6	——		4.8	——		6.0	——		7.2
7	——		1.4	——		2.8	——		4.2	——		5.6	——		7.0	——		8.4
8	——		1.6	——		3.2	——		4.8	——		6.4	——		8.0	——		9.6
9	——		1.8	——		3.6	——		5.4	——		7.2	——		9.0	——		10.8
10	——		2.0	——		4.0	——		6.0	——		8.0	——		10.0	–	1	0.0
11	——		2.2	——		4.4	——		6.6	——		8.8	——		11.0	–	1	1.2
12	——		2.4	——		4.8	——		7.2	——		9.6	–	1	0.0	–	1	2.4
13	——		2.6	——		5.2	——		7.8	——		10.4	–	1	1.0	–	1	3.6
14	——		2.8	——		5.6	——		8.4	——		11.2	–	1	2.0	–	1	4.8
15	——		3.0	——		6.0	——		9.0	–	1	0.0	–	1	3.0	–	1	6.0
16	——		3.2	——		6.4	——		9.6	–	1	0.8	–	1	4.0	–	1	7.2
17	——		3.4	——		6.8	——		10.2	–	1	1.6	–	1	5.0	–	1	8.4
18	——		3.6	——		7.2	——		10.8	–	1	2.4	–	1	6.0	–	1	9.6
19	——		3.8	——		7.6	——		11.4	–	1	3.2	–	1	7.0	–	1	10.8
20	——		4.0	——		8.0	–	1	0.0	–	1	4.0	–	1	8.0	–	2	0.0
21	——		4.2	——		8.4	–	1	0.6	–	1	4.8	–	1	9.0	–	2	1.2
22	——		4.4	——		8.8	–	1	1.2	–	1	5.6	–	1	10.0	–	2	2.4
23	——		4.6	——		9.2	–	1	1.8	–	1	6.4	–	1	11.0	–	2	3.6
24	——		4.8	——		9.6	–	1	2.4	–	1	7.2	–	2	0.0	–	2	4.8
25	——		5.0	——		10.0	–	1	3.0	–	1	8.0	–	2	1.0	–	2	6.0
26	——		5.2	——		10.4	–	1	3.6	–	1	8.8	–	2	2.0	–	2	7.4
27	——		5.4	——		10.8	–	1	4.2	–	1	9.6	–	2	3.0	–	2	8.4
28	——		5.6	——		11.2	–	1	4.8	–	1	10.4	–	2	4.0	–	2	9.6
29	——		5.8	——		11.6	–	1	5.4	–	1	11.2	–	2	5.0	–	2	10.8
30	——		6.0	–	1	0.0	–	1	6.0	–	2	0.0	–	2	6.0	–	3	0.0
40	——		8.0	–	1	4.0	–	2	0.0	–	2	8.0	–	3	4.0	–	4	0.0
5	——		10.0	–	1	8.0	–	2	6.0	–	3	4.0	–	4	2.0	–	5	0.0
60	–	1	0.0	–	2	0.0	–	3	0.0	–	4	0.0	–	5	0.0	–	6	0.0
70	–	1	2.0	–	2	4.0	–	3	6.0	–	4	8.0	–	5	10.0	–	7	0.0
80	–	1	4.0	–	2	8.0	–	4	0.0	–	5	4.0	–	6	8.0	–	8	0.0
90	–	1	6.0	–	3	0.0	–	4	6.0	–	6	0.0	–	7	6.0	–	9	0.0
100	–	1	8.0	–	3	4.0	–	5	0.0	–	6	8.0	–	8	4.0	–	10	0.0
200	–	3	4.0	–	6	8.0	–	10	0.0	–	13	4.0	–	16	8.0	1	0	0.0
300	–	5	0.0	–	10	0.0	–	15	0.0	1	0	0.0	1	5	0.0	1	10	0.0
400	–	6	8.0	–	13	4.0	1	0	0.0	1	6	8.0	1	13	4.0	2	0	0.0
500	–	8	4.0	–	16	8.0	1	5	0.0	1	13	4.0	2	1	8.0	2	10	0.0
600	–	10	0.0	1	0	0.0	1	10	0.0	2	0	0.0	2	10	0.0	3	0	0.0
700	–	11	8.0	1	3	4.0	1	15	0.0	2	6	8.0	2	18	4.0	3	10	0.0
800	–	13	4.0	1	6	8.0	2	0	0.0	2	13	4.0	3	6	8.0	4	0	0.0
900	–	15	0.0	1	10	0.0	2	5	0.0	3	0	0.0	3	15	0.0	4	10	0.0
1000	–	16	8.0	1	13	4.0	2	10	0.0	3	6	8.0	4	3	4.0	5	0	0.0
2000	1	13	4.0	3	6	8.0	5	0	0.0	6	13	4.0	8	6	8.0	10	0	0.0
3000	2	10	0.0	5	0	0.0	7	10	0.0	10	0	0.0	12	10	0.0	15	0	0.0
4000	3	6	8.0	6	13	4.0	10	0	0.0	13	6	8.0	16	13	4.0	20	0	0.0
5000	4	3	4.0	8	6	8.0	12	10	0.0	16	13	4.0	20	16	8.0	25	0	0.0

Prin.	7 Months.			8 Months.			9 Months.			10 Months.			11 Months.		
£.	£.	s.	d.pts	£.	s.	d.pts	£.	s.	d.pts	£.	s.	d.pts	£.	s.	d.pts
1	0	0	1.4	0	0	1.6	0	0	1.8	0	0	2.0	0	0	2.2
2	—		2.8	—		3.2	—		3.6	—		4.0	—		4.4
3	—		4.2	—		4.8	—		5.4	—		6.0	—		6.6
4	—		5.6	—		6.4	—		7.2	—		8.0	—		8.8
5	—		7.0	—		8.0	—		9.0	—		10.0	—		11.0
6	—		8.4	—		9.6	—		10.8	—	1	0.0	—	1	1.4
7	—		9.8	—		11.2	—	1	0.6	—	1	2.0	—	1	3.2
8	—		11.2	—	1	0.8	—	1	2.4	—	1	4.0	—	1	5.6
9	—	1	0.6	—	1	2.4	—	1	4.2	—	1	6.0	—	1	7.[illegible]
10	—	1	2.0	—	1	4.0	—	1	6.0	—	1	8.[illegible]	—	1	10.0
11	—	1	3.4	—	1	5.6	—	1	7.8	—	1	10.[illegible]	—	2	[illegible]
12	—	1	4.8	—	1	7.2	—	1	9.6	—	2	0.0	—	2	[illegible]
13	—	1	6.2	—	1	8.8	—	1	11.4	—	2	2.0	—	[illegible]	[illegible]
14	—	1	7.6	—	1	10.4	—	2	1.2	—	2	4.0	—	[illegible]	[illegible]
15	—	1	9.0	—	2	0.0	—	2	3.0	—	2	6.0	—	[illegible]	[illegible]
16	—	1	10.4	—	2	1.6	—	2	4.8	—	2	8.0	—	2	[illegible]
17	—	1	11.8	—	2	3.2	—	2	6.6	—	2	10.0	—	3	1.4
18	—	2	1.2	—	2	4.8	—	2	8.4	—	3	0.0	—	3	[illegible]
19	—	2	2.6	—	2	6.4	—	2	10.2	—	3	2.0	—	3	5.8
20	—	2	4.0	—	2	8.0	—	3	0.0	—	3	4.0	—	3	8.0
21	—	2	5.4	—	2	9.6	—	3	1.8	—	3	6.0	—	3	10.2
22	—	2	6.8	—	2	11.2	—	3	3.6	—	3	8.0	—	4	0.4
23	—	2	8.2	—	3	0.8	—	3	5.4	—	3	10.0	—	4	2.6
24	—	2	9.6	—	3	2.4	—	3	7.2	—	4	0.0	—	4	4.8
25	—	2	11.0	—	3	4.0	—	3	9.0	—	4	2.0	—	4	7.0
26	—	3	0.4	—	3	5.6	—	3	10.8	—	4	4.0	—	4	9.2
27	—	3	1.8	—	3	7.2	—	4	0.6	—	4	6.0	—	4	11.4
28	—	3	3.2	—	3	8.8	—	4	2.4	—	4	8.0	—	5	1.6
29	—	3	4.6	—	3	10.4	—	4	4.2	—	4	10.0	—	5	3.8
30	—	3	6.0	—	4	0.0	—	4	6.0	—	5	0.0	—	5	6.0
40	—	4	8.0	—	5	4.0	—	6	0.0	—	6	8.0	—	7	4.0
50	—	5	10.0	—	6	8.0	—	7	6.0	—	8	4.0	—	9	2.0
60	—	7	0.0	—	8	0.0	—	9	0.0	—	10	0.0	—	11	0.0
70	—	8	2.0	—	9	4.0	—	10	6.0	—	11	8.0	—	12	10.0
80	—	9	4.0	—	10	8.0	—	12	0.0	—	13	4.0	—	14	8.0
90	—	10	6.0	—	12	0.0	—	13	6.0	—	15	0.0	—	16	6.0
100	—	11	8.0	—	13	4.0	—	15	0.0	—	16	8.0	—	18	4.0
200	1	3	4.0	1	6	8.0	1	10	0.0	1	13	4.0	1	16	8.0
300	1	15	0.0	2	0	0.0	2	5	0.0	2	10	0.0	2	15	0.0
400	2	6	8.0	2	13	4.0	3	0	0.0	3	6	8.0	3	13	4.0
500	2	18	4.0	3	6	8.0	3	15	0.0	4	3	4.0	4	11	8.0
600	3	10	0.0	4	0	0.0	4	10	0.0	5	0	0.0	5	10	0.0
700	4	1	8.0	4	13	4.0	5	5	0.0	5	16	8.0	6	8	4.0
800	4	13	4.0	5	6	8.0	6	0	0.0	6	13	4.0	7	6	4.0
600	5	5	0.0	6	0	0.0	6	15	0.0	7	10	0.0	8	5	0.0
1000	5	16	8.0	6	13	4.0	7	10	0.0	8	6	8.0	9	3	4.0
2000	11	13	4.0	13	6	8.0	15	0	0.0	16	13	4.0	18	6	8.0
3000	17	10	0.0	20	0	0.0	22	10	0.0	25	0	0.0	27	10	0.0
4000	23	6	8.0	26	13	4.0	30	0	0.0	33	6	8.0	36	13	4.0
5000	29	3	4.0	33	6	8.0	37	10	0.0	41	13	4.0	45	16	8.0

Prin.	2 Years.			3 Years.			4 Years.			5 Years.			6 Years.		
£.	£.	s.	d.pts	£.	s.	d.pts	£.	s.	d.pts	£.	s.	d.pts	£.	s.	d.pts
1	0	0	4.8	0	0	7.2	0	0	9.6	0	1	0.0	0	1	2.4
2	—		9.6	—	1	2.4	—	1	7.2	—	2	0.0	—	2	4.8
3	—	1	2.4	—	1	9.6	—	2	4.8	—	3	0.0	—	3	7.2
4	—	1	7.2	—	2	4.8	—	3	2.4	—	4	0.0	—	4	9.6
5	—	2	0.0	—	3	0.0	—	4	0.0	—	5	0.0	—	6	0.0
6	—	2	4.8	—	3	7.2	—	4	9.6	—	6	0.0	—	7	2.4
7	—	2	9.6	—	4	2.4	—	5	7.2	—	7	0.0	—	8	4.8
8	—	3	2.4	—	4	9.6	—	6	4.8	—	8	0.0	—	9	7.2
9	—	3	7.2	—	5	4.8	—	7	2.4	—	9	0.0	—	10	9.6
10	—	4	0.0	—	6	0.0	—	8	0.0	—	10	0.0	—	12	0.0
11	—	4	4.8	—	6	7.2	—	8	9.6	—	11	0.0	—	13	2.4
12	—	4	9.6	—	7	2.4	—	9	7.2	—	12	0.0	—	14	4.8
13	—	5	2.4	—	7	9.6	—	10	4.8	—	13	0.0	—	15	7.2
14	—	5	7.2	—	8	4.8	—	11	2.4	—	14	0.0	—	16	9.6
15	—	6	0.0	—	9	0.0	—	12	0.0	—	15	0.0	—	18	0.0
16	—	6	4.8	—	9	7.2	—	12	9.6	—	16	0.0	—	19	2.4
17	—	6	9.6	—	10	2.4	—	13	7.2	—	17	0.0	1	0	4.8
18	—	7	2.4	—	10	9.6	—	14	4.8	—	18	0.0	1	1	7.2
19	—	7	7.2	—	11	2.8	—	15	2.4	—	19	0.0	1	2	9.6
20	—	8	0.0	—	12	0.0	—	16	0.0	1	0	0.0	1	4	0.0
21	—	8	4.0	—	12	7.2	—	16	9.6	1	1	0.0	1	5	2.4
22	—	8	9.6	—	13	2.4	—	17	7.2	1	2	0.0	1	6	4.8
23	—	9	2.4	—	13	9.6	—	18	4.8	1	3	0.0	1	7	7.2
24	—	9	7.2	—	14	4.8	—	19	2.4	1	4	0.0	1	8	9.6
25	—	10	0.0	—	15	0.0	1	0	0.0	1	5	0.0	1	10	0.0
26	—	10	4.8	—	15	7.2	1	0	0.0	1	6	0.0	1	11	2.4
27	—	10	9.6	—	16	2.4	1	1	7.2	1	7	0.0	1	12	4.8
28	—	11	2.4	—	16	9.6	1	2	4.8	1	8	0.0	1	13	7.2
29	—	11	9.2	—	17	4.8	1	3	2.4	1	9	0.0	1	14	9.6
3	—	12	0.0	—	18	0.0	1	4	0.0	1	10	0.0	1	16	0.0
40	—	16	0.0	1	4	0.0	1	12	0.0	2	0	0.0	2	8	0.0
50	1	0	0.0	1	10	0.0	2	0	0.0	2	10	0.0	3	0	0.0
60	1	4	0.0	1	16	0.0	2	8	0.0	3	0	0.0	3	12	0.0
70	1	8	0.0	2	2	0.0	2	16	0.0	3	10	0.0	3	4	0.0
80	1	12	0.0	2	8	0.0	3	4	0.0	4	0	0.0	4	16	0.0
90	1	16	0.0	2	14	0.0	3	12	0.0	4	10	0.0	5	8	0.0
100	2	0	0.0	3	0	0.0	4	0	0.0	5	0	0.0	6	0	0.0
200	4	0	0.0	6	0	0.0	8	0	0.0	10	0	0.0	12	0	0.0
300	6	0	0.0	9	0	0.0	12	0	0.0	15	0	0.0	18	0	0.0
400	8	0	0.0	12	0	0.0	16	0	0.0	20	0	0.0	24	0	0.0
500	16	0	0.0	15	0	0.0	20	0	0.0	25	0	0.0	30	0	0.0
600	12	0	0.0	18	0	0.0	24	0	0.0	30	0	0.0	36	0	0.0
700	14	0	0.0	21	0	0.0	28	0	0.0	35	0	0.0	42	0	0.0
800	16	0	0.0	24	0	0.0	32	0	0.0	40	0	0.0	48	0	0.0
900	18	0	0.0	27	0	0.0	36	0	0.0	45	0	0.0	54	0	0.0
1000	20	0	0.0	30	0	0.0	40	0	0.0	50	0	0.0	60	0	0.0
2000	40	0	0.0	60	0	0.0	80	0	0.0	100	0	0.0	120	0	0.0
3000	60	0	0.0	90	0	0.0	120	0	0.0	150	0	0.0	180	0	0.0
4000	80	0	0.0	120	0	0.0	160	0	0.0	200	0	0.0	240	0	0.0
5000	100	0	0.0	150	0	0.0	200	0	0.0	250	0	0.0	300	0	0.0

Use *of the foregoing* TABLE.

What will be the Interest of 260*l.* 15*s.* for 286 days, at 5 per Cent?

I find by the Table,

*L.*200 for 286 days	is	*L.*1	11	4.1
60	is	0	9	4.83
0 15	is	0	0	1.41
*L.*260 15	Interest at one per Cent	2	0	10.34
	Multiplied by 5			5
Answer 10*l.* 4*s.* 3¾*d.*		*L.*10	4	3.7

What will be the balance of Interest on the following account at 5 per Cent?

Debtor. Sums. *L.*	*s.*	*d.*	Days	Interest *L.*	*s.*	*d.pts*		Creditor. Sums. *L.*	*s.*	*d*	Days	Interest *L.*	*s.*	*d.pts*
140	10	0	375	1	8	10.41		100	0	0	407	1	2	3.6
60	9	6	288	0	9	6.52		80	0	0	284	0	12	5.38
260	15	0	286	2	0	10.34		227	0	0	273	1	13	11.47
80	12	0	161	0	7	1.32		50	0	0	246	0	6	8.84
170	8	0	206	0	19	2.8		200	0	0	208	1	2	9.53
77	14	0	192	0	8	2.04		70	0	0	172	0	6	7.16
260	15	0	119	0	17	0.02		250	0	0	129	0	17	8.05
99	10	0	141	0	7	8.24		227	10	0	110	0	13	8.53
110	14	0	121	0	7	4.06		50	0	0	60	0	1	7.72
128	12	6	104	0	7	3.95		100	0	0	41	0	2	3.—
58	10	0	2	0	0	0.75		150	0	0	2	0	0	1.96
214	6	0	45	0	5	3.32								
												7	0	3.24
				*L.*7	17	11.77		balance at 1 per Cent.					17	8.53
												*L.*7	17	11.77

Which balance of *l.*0 17 8.53 multiplied by 5, gives the true balance at 5 per Cent,—*l.*4. 8 6½.

What will be the amount of Commission on 5400*l.* at 2½ per Cent?

5000*l.* by the table at 1 per Cent	*l.*50	0	0
400 by Ditto	4	0	0
	54	0	0
multiplied by	2	0	0
	108	0	0
add one half	27	0	0
Answer	135	0	0

I hope

I HOPE the foregoing Table of Simple Intereſt at one per Cent, will anſwer every purpoſe that can be deſired.—It only remains to conſider under what circumſtances Intereſt (or rather ſomething equivalent, which might be called by another name) ſhould, or ſhould not be taken.

If a Trader borrows money to employ it in his trade, the lender may be conſidered as a kind of partner, and conſequently intitled to a proportionate ſhare of the profits, which, what is called legal Intereſt may be ſuppoſed to be ——— But the ſame juſtice which intitles him to a proportion of the profit, ought to ſubject him to the ſame proportion of loſs; if ſuch ſhould happen. For it is quite inconſiſtent with every idea of equity, that the lender, who has not any thing to do with the management of the money, after he lends it; ſhould have a rate per Cent. certain to him: while the borrower, who has the whole care and trouble of the buſineſs, and runs every riſk, muſt pay to the lender a certain gain, whether he gains or loſes.

If a Trader borrows money to extricate him from an impending difficulty, and will pay it as ſoon as poſſible, after that difficulty is over, the lender ought not to take any Intereſt at all, as the borrower (ſo long as the difficulty laſts) muſt be claſſed among poor men, who ought not to be charged with Intereſt in any caſe whatever, as will appear demonſtratively at the cloſe of theſe obſervations. Indeed, I could wiſh the word Intereſt, expunged from our vocabulary, there is too much of uſury in the ſound of it.

With reſpect to the diſcounting of bills and notes, however great the convenience may ſeem, or however lucrative to the diſcounter; it would have been happy for the trading world, if no ſuch practice had ever been; as it is only a temptation to the Trader, to extend his trade farther and farther; till at laſt, he finds himſelf ſo much out of his depth, that he cannot by any means whatever, recover firm footing. If, (as in the former caſe) Traders would only get a few bills diſcounted, when ſome unexpected difficulty had ſurprized them, and redouble their endeavours to avoid ſuch difficulties in future, it would then be a real convenience. But when one difficulty is overcome, and trade is extended with a vain dependance on the ſame reſource, it only ſerves as an *Ignis-fatuus*, to lead the unwary traveller from leſſer difficulties to greater, 'till he is irrecoverably loſt in the quagmires of bankruptcy; and then every one will know that it was the diſcounter, and not the trader, who gave the credits, and that all his eminence in trade was only fictitious: How aptly does that text in the 39th Pſalm apply in this caſe, "*Surely ſuch men walk in a vain ſhew, they are diſquieted in vain.*"

I ſhall now put a caſe which I ſuppoſe never happens, only becauſe the reader will thereby more eaſily ſee, that a trade carried on by continual diſcounts, will probably, in the end be ruinous. For tho' bills and notes be diſcounted at 5 per Cent. yet it will appear plainly, that continual diſcounts will amount to a rate much larger than is generally imagined. Suppoſe then, that I begin with a ware houſe ſtocked with goods bought for ready money, and that in 30 days I ſell the whole for bills at 61 days, which I immediately get caſh for at 5 per Cent. and with that caſh purchaſe more, which I alſo ſell in 30 days, for bills at 61 days, and go on as before; what rate per Cent. will be found chargeable on my original ſtock? As I pay but 5 per Cent. for all the diſcounts, the firſt month of this buſineſs is chargeable with no more; but as the ſecond parcel of bills go in a month before the firſt are at maturity, the

ſecond

ſecond, and every following month, will be at 10 per Cent. I know it may be ſaid that this is a falſe ſtatement, becauſe I pay no more than 5 per Cent. for the money I receive for the ſeveral parcels of bills diſcounted, yet, granting this to be true; as the original capital is my only ſtake, which muſt bear all burthens, and ſtand againſt every aſſault, it is certainly to be charged with all the diſcounts I pay, and the more frequently the money is turned in this way, the heavier the charge, ſo that the diſcounts on my original capital, may, (by ſuch a trade) amount to 15, or even to 20 per Cent. To this, however, it may be anſwered, that the profits on ſuch frequent turnings of money, would bear the payments of the diſcounts very well; this indeed, would overſet my whole argument, if the hazards of trade were not proportionate to its increaſe; but as they too frequently exceed: the returning of bills proteſted, and other caſualties, may probably take away from the original capital, much more than the heavy diſcounts it has already paid. It would take up too much of the reader's time, to lead him through the intricacies of a real caſe in trade; but there cannot be any, ſo favourable to the man who diſcounts all the papers he receives, as the above.

I ſhall here preſent the reader with an extract from a work, perhaps the beſt on the ſubject of trade that has been written. The author concludes his obſervations on Intereſt in theſe words, "Intereſt money is a "canker-worm upon the trader's profit; it conſumes him unawares; not "one trader in fifty, ſtates to himſelf the true nature of it; it eats "through his ready money, for it takes nothing for payment but its own "kind, it makes no defalcation or abatement for bad debts, or diſaſters "of any kind: whatever loſs the trader meets with, the *uſurer* muſt be "paid; whoever the trader compounds with, he makes no compoſition, "unleſs it is at the very laſt, when he is forced, by the ruin of the "trader, to compound both for principal and intereſt; when perhaps by "the mere intereſt, he has had his principal two or three times over." And at the concluſion of his thoughts on diſcounts, he ſays, "Nothing "can be more needful than to poſſeſs the trader's mind with an abhor- "rence of this fatal practice of diſcounting; and therefore, I recommend "it to them with the greateſt earneſtneſs, to enter into its particular "conſequences in their own thoughts, and make themſelves maſters of "the whole ſcheme, and avoid it, as they would an houſe infected with "the plague."

I ſhall now take the liberty, to make one ſhort obſervation on the etymology of the word *Diſcount*: the firſt ſyllable *Dis*, ſignifies evil; and among the old Heathens, was the name of one of their infernal deities, ſo that the true meaning of the word *Diſcount* is, *an evil, or infernal manner of counting.*

Having promiſed to prove, that Intereſt ought neither to be paid nor received; that the word ſhould be expunged from our language; at leaſt in this application of it: and that the thing itſelf can only be juſtifiable under the idea of a partnerſhip, ſubject to all its conſequences. I ſhall offer the following Scriptures to the reader's conſideration. In the 35th chapter of Leviticus, 35th, 36th and 37th verſes, it is written, "*If thy brother be waxen poor and fallen in decay with thee, then thou ſhalt relieve him; yea, tho' he be a ſtranger or a ſojourner; that he may live with thee. Take thou no uſury of him, or increaſe, but fear thy God; that thy brother may live with thee. Thou ſhalt not give him thy money upon uſury, nor lend him thy victuals for increaſe.*" the equity of this command is evident, for as the borrower

borrower is supposed to be a poor man; his subsistence ought not to be made more chargeable to him (by the payment of usury, or, which is the same thing, interest) than the lender's, who has enough and to spare. I know it will be said, "*if no interest money was to be paid, we should not be able to borrow any, were our securities ever so good, or our exigencies ever so great:*" the interest to be paid and received, being the main, perhaps the only inducement with the lender. I answer, I believe it is, with such lenders as do not think themselves under any obligation to obey the commands of GOD; and this HE, who knows the secret thoughts and motives of every man, has guarded against by an express and indispensable command, in the 15th chapter of Deuteronomy, 7th, 8th, 9th and 10th verses. *If there be among you a poor man, of one of thy brethren, within any of thy gates, in thy land which the* LORD *thy* GOD *giveth thee, thou shalt not harden thy heart, nor shut thy hand from thy poor brother. But thou shalt open thy hand wide unto him, and shalt surely lend him sufficient for his need, in that which he wanteth. Beware that there be not a thought in thy wicked heart, saying, the seventh year, the year of release is at hand, and thine eye be evil against thy poor brother, and thou givest him nought, and he cry unto the* LORD *against thee, and it be sin unto thee. Thou shalt surely give him, and thy heart shall not be grieved when thou givest unto him, because that for this thing, the* LORD *thy* GOD *shall bless thee in all thy works, and in all that thou puttest thine hand unto.*" The case alluded to in this scripture, is evidently that of a mortgage; because, in the "*year of release,*" lands were to return to the original proprietor, whether redeemed or not: so that by comparing these two quotations together, we find interest was not to be paid, even in the case of a mortgage. In the 22d chapter of Exodus, 25th, 26th and 27th verses, it is written, "*If thou lend money to any of thy people that is poor by thee, thou shalt not be to him as an usurer, neither shalt thou lay upon him usury. If thou at all take thy neighbour's raiment to pledge, thou shalt deliver it unto him by that the sun goeth down.*" How many articles of *wearing apparel*, are now lying in pledge in this city, not for one day only, but for months; does not these scriptures most expressly forbid, not only the payment of interest, but also all manner of *Pawn-broking*, and yet in a country where the bible is believed to be the *word of* GOD, and published as such by authority of government; both the one and the other, are made legal by act of parliament. But we find that these scriptures just now quoted, are verily, and indeed, commandments, they are expressed in the same language as the Decalogue, *thou shalt*, and *thou shalt not*; and therefore, the one must be as binding on us christians, as the other: and it would be absurd to say, that they are only a part of the Mosaic dispensation, done away by the Christian; unless we can suppose, that the latter is less merciful, and gives a larger license to covetousness than the former; and that cannot be supposed, when we consider that Christianity was founded on an equality of property, when an apostle tells us that *covetousness is idolatry*; when our LORD expressly directs us, to "*sell that we have and give alms,*" that we may "*provide ourselves bags which wax not old, a treasure in the Heavens that faileth not;*" freely and liberally to "*give to him that asketh, and from him that would borrow of us not to turn away;*" and concludes with this dreadful sentence on the covetous worldling, "*Depart from me ye cursed into everlasting fire, prepared for the Devil and his angels,*" a sentence not unlike that of the prophet *Ezekiel*, 18th chapter, 13th verse, "*Hath he given forth upon usury; hath he taken increase; shall he then live, he shall not live, he shall surely die.*"

A TABLE *of the Value of* GOODS, *ready caſt up and carefully corrected.*

EXPLANATION *and* USE *of the following* TABLE

As the value of an hundred weight and its diviſions is often neceſſary to be known, and alſo, what any particular ſum per day, will amount to per year; to direct the eye the more readily, the proper numbers are incloſed in hooks: as [365] being the days in one year, [112] being the pounds in one hundred weight, [84] being the pounds in three quarters of an hundred, [56] thoſe in half an hundred, and [28] thoſe in one quarter; ſo that if it ſhould be required to know what 6 ſhillings and 4 pence per day, will amount to per year, I find in the column under 6*s.* 4*d.* and oppoſite to 365, £115 11 8. If it ſhould be required to know the value of one hundred and three quarters of any goods ſold by weight, at 15½ pence per pound, I find in the column under 15½ pence, and oppoſite to 112*lb.* or 1 Cwt. £. 7 4 8.

and oppoſite to 84*lb.* or ¾ - - - 5 8 6

ſo that the value of 1¾ Cwt. at 15½ pence is £. 12 13 2

If the rate of any goods per hundred, be given, and it is required to know the value per pound; ſearch in the table oppoſite 112, till you find the rate per hundred, and the rate at the head of that column, will be the rate per pound.

EXAMPLE.—If any goods be £. 4 18*s.* per hundred, what will that be per pound? having found £. 4 18*s.* oppoſite 112; I find at the head of that column, 10½*d.* the rate per pound.

It would be needleſs to give any further examples, as the uſe of this Table muſt be obvious.

	1 Farthing			2 Farthings			3 Farthings			1 Penny			1¼ Pence		
Value of	L.	s.	d.f.	L.	s.	d.f.	L.	s.	d.f.	L.	s.	d.	L.	s.	d.f.
2	0	0	0½	0	0	1	0	0	1½	0	0	2	0	0	2½
3	—	—	0¾	—	—	1½	—	—	2¼	—	—	3	—	—	3¾
4	—	—	1	—	—	2	—	—	3	—	—	4	—	—	5
5	—	—	1¼	—	—	2½	—	—	3¾	—	—	5	—	—	6¼
6	—	—	1½	—	—	3	—	—	4½	—	—	6	—	—	7½
7	—	—	1¾	—	—	3½	—	—	5¼	—	—	7	—	—	8¾
8	—	—	2	—	—	4	—	—	6	—	—	8	—	—	10
9	—	—	2¼	—	—	4½	—	—	6¾	—	—	9	—	—	11¼
10	—	—	2½	—	—	5	—	—	7½	—	—	10	—	1	0½
11	—	—	2¾	—	—	5½	—	—	8¼	—	—	11	—	1	1¾
12	—	—	3	—	—	6	—	—	9	—	1	0	—	1	3
13	—	—	3¼	—	—	6½	—	—	9¾	—	1	1	—	1	4¼
14	—	—	3½	—	—	7	—	—	10½	—	1	2	—	1	5½
15	—	—	3¾	—	—	7½	—	—	11¼	—	1	3	—	1	6¾
16	—	—	4	—	—	8	—	1	0	—	1	4	—	1	8
17	—	—	4¼	—	—	8½	—	1	0¾	—	1	5	—	1	9¼
18	—	—	4½	—	—	9	—	1	1½	—	1	6	—	1	10½
19	—	—	4¾	—	—	9½	—	1	2¼	—	1	7	—	1	11¾
20	—	—	5	—	—	10	—	1	3	—	1	8	—	2	1
[28]	—	—	7	—	1	2	—	1	9	—	2	4	—	2	11
30	—	—	7½	—	1	3	—	1	10½	—	2	6	—	3	1½
40	—	—	10	—	1	8	—	2	6	—	3	4	—	4	2
50	—	1	0½	—	2	1	—	3	1½	—	4	2	—	5	2½
[56]	—	1	2	—	2	4	—	3	6	—	4	8	—	5	10
60	—	1	3	—	2	6	—	3	9	—	5	0	—	6	3
70	—	1	5½	—	2	11	—	4	4½	—	5	10	—	7	3½
80	—	1	8	—	3	4	—	5	0	—	6	8	—	8	4
[84]	—	1	9	—	3	6	—	5	3	—	7	0	—	8	9
90	—	1	10½	—	3	9	—	5	7½	—	7	6	—	9	4½
100	—	2	1	—	4	2	—	6	3	—	8	4	—	10	5
[112]	—	2	4	—	4	8	—	7	0	—	9	4	—	11	8
200	—	4	2	—	8	4	—	12	6	—	16	8	1	0	10
300	—	6	3	—	12	6	—	18	9	1	5	0	1	11	3
[365]	—	7	7¼	—	15	2½	1	2	9¾	1	10	5	1	18	0¼
400	—	8	4	—	16	8	1	5	0	1	13	4	2	1	8
500	—	10	5	1	0	10	1	11	3	2	1	8	2	12	1
600	—	12	6	1	5	0	1	17	6	2	10	0	3	2	6
700	—	14	7	1	9	2	2	3	9	2	18	4	3	12	11
800	—	16	8	1	13	4	2	10	0	3	6	8	4	3	4
900	—	18	9	1	17	6	2	16	3	3	15	0	4	13	9
1000	1	0	10	2	1	8	3	2	6	4	3	4	5	4	2
2000	2	1	8	4	3	4	6	5	0	8	6	8	10	8	4
3000	3	2	6	6	5	0	9	7	6	12	10	0	15	12	6
4000	4	3	4	8	6	8	12	10	0	16	13	4	20	16	8
5000	5	4	2	10	8	4	15	12	6	20	16	8	26	0	10
6000	6	5	0	12	10	0	18	15	0	25	0	0	31	5	0
7000	7	5	10	14	11	8	21	17	6	29	3	4	36	9	2
8000	8	6	8	16	13	4	25	0	0	33	6	8	41	13	4
9000	9	7	6	18	15	0	28	2	6	37	10	0	46	17	6
10000	10	8	4	20	16	8	31	5	0	41	13	4	52	1	8

	1½ Pence			1¾ Pence			2 Pence			2¼ Pence			2½ Pence		
Value	L.	s.	d.	L.	s.	d.f.	L.	s.	d.	L.	s.	d.f.	L.	s.	d.f.
of 2	0	0	3	—	—	3½	0	0	4	0	0	4½	0	0	5
3	—	—	4½	—	—	5¼	—	—	6	—	—	6¾	—	—	7½
4	—	—	6	—	—	7	—	—	8	—	—	9	—	—	10
5	—	—	7½	—	—	8¾	—	—	10	—	—	11¼	—	1	0½
6	—	—	9	—	—	10½	—	1	0	—	1	1½	—	1	3
7	—	—	10½	—	1	0¼	—	1	2	—	1	3¾	—	1	5½
8	—	1	0	—	1	2	—	1	4	—	1	6	—	1	8
9	—	1	1½	—	1	3¾	—	1	6	—	1	8¼	—	1	10½
10	—	1	3	—	1	5½	—	1	8	—	1	10½	—	2	1
11	—	1	4½	—	1	7¼	—	1	10	—	2	0¾	—	2	3½
12	—	1	6	—	1	9	—	2	0	—	2	3	—	2	6
13	—	1	7½	—	1	10¾	—	2	2	—	2	5¼	—	2	8½
14	—	1	9	—	2	0½	—	2	4	—	2	7½	—	2	11
15	—	1	10½	—	2	2¼	—	2	6	—	2	9¾	—	3	1½
16	—	2	0	—	2	4	—	2	8	—	3	0	—	3	4
17	—	2	1½	—	2	5¾	—	2	10	—	3	2¼	—	3	6½
18	—	2	3	—	2	7½	—	3	0	—	3	4½	—	3	9
19	—	2	4½	—	2	9¼	—	3	2	—	3	6¾	—	3	11½
20	—	2	6	—	2	11	—	3	4	—	3	9	—	4	2
[28]	—	3	6	—	4	1	—	4	8	—	5	3	—	5	10
30	—	3	9	—	4	4½	—	5	0	—	5	7½	—	6	3
40	—	5	0	—	5	10	—	6	8	—	7	6	—	8	4
50	—	6	3	—	7	3½	—	8	4	—	9	4½	—	10	5
[56]	—	7	0	—	8	2	—	9	4	—	10	6	—	11	8
60	—	7	6	—	8	9	—	10	0	—	11	3	—	12	6
70	—	8	9	—	10	2½	—	11	8	—	13	1½	—	14	7
80	—	10	0	—	11	8	—	13	4	—	15	0	—	16	8
[84]	—	10	6	—	12	3	—	14	0	—	15	9	—	17	6
90	—	11	3	—	13	1½	—	15	0	—	16	10½	—	18	9
100	—	12	6	—	14	7	—	16	8	—	18	9	1	0	10
[112]	—	14	0	—	16	4	—	18	4	1	1	0	1	3	4
200	1	5	0	1	9	2	1	13	4	1	17	6	2	1	8
300	1	17	6	2	3	9	2	10	0	2	16	3	3	2	6
[365]	2	5	7	2	13	2¾	3	0	10	3	8	5¼	3	16	0½
400	2	10	0	2	18	4	3	6	8	3	15	0	4	3	4
500	3	2	6	3	12	11	4	3	4	4	13	9	5	4	2
600	3	15	0	4	7	6	5	0	0	5	12	6	6	5	0
700	4	7	6	5	2	1	5	16	8	6	11	3	7	5	10
800	5	0	0	5	16	8	6	13	4	7	10	0	8	6	8
900	5	12	6	6	11	3	7	10	0	8	8	9	9	7	6
1000	6	5	0	7	5	10	8	6	8	9	7	6	10	8	4
2000	12	10	0	14	11	8	16	13	4	18	15	0	20	16	8
3000	18	15	0	21	17	6	25	0	0	28	2	6	31	5	0
4000	25	0	0	29	3	4	33	6	8	37	10	0	41	13	4
5000	31	5	0	36	9	2	41	13	4	46	17	6	52	1	8
6000	37	10	0	43	15	0	50	0	0	56	5	0	62	10	0
7000	43	15	0	51	0	10	58	6	8	65	12	6	72	18	4
8000	50	0	0	58	6	8	66	13	4	75	0	0	83	6	8
9000	56	5	0	65	12	6	75	0	0	84	7	6	93	15	0
10000	62	10	0	72	18	4	83	6	8	93	15	0	104	3	4

	2¾ Pence.			3 Pence.			3¼ Pence.			3½ Pence.			3¾ Pence.		
Value	L.	s.	d. f.	L.	s.	d.	L.	s.	d. f.	L.	s.	d. f.	L.	s.	d. f.
of 2	0	0	5½	0	0	6	0	0	6½	0	0	7	0	0	7½
3	—	—	8¼	—	—	9	—	—	9¾	—	—	10½	—	—	11¼
4	—	—	11	—	1	0	—	1	1	—	1	2	—	1	3
5	—	1	1¾	—	1	3	—	1	4¼	—	1	5½	—	1	6¾
6	—	1	4½	—	1	6	—	1	7½	—	1	9	—	1	10½
7	—	1	7¼	—	1	9	—	1	10¼	—	2	0½	—	2	2¼
8	—	1	10	—	2	0	—	2	2	—	2	4	—	2	6
9	—	2	0¾	—	2	3	—	2	5¼	—	2	7½	—	2	9¾
10	—	2	3½	—	2	6	—	2	8½	—	2	11	—	3	1½
11	—	2	6¼	—	2	9	—	2	11¾	—	3	2½	—	3	5¼
12	—	2	9	—	3	0	—	3	3	—	3	6	—	3	9
13	—	2	11¾	—	3	3	—	3	6¼	—	3	9½	—	4	0¾
14	—	3	2½	—	3	6	—	3	9½	—	4	1	—	4	4½
15	—	3	5¼	—	3	9	—	4	0¾	—	4	4½	—	4	8¼
16	—	3	8	—	4	0	—	4	4	—	4	8	—	5	0
17	—	3	10¾	—	4	3	—	4	7¼	—	4	11½	—	5	3¾
18	—	4	1½	—	4	6	—	4	10½	—	5	3	—	5	7½
19	—	4	4¼	—	4	9	—	5	1¾	—	5	6½	—	5	11¼
20	—	4	7	—	5	0	—	5	5	—	5	10	—	6	3
[28]	—	6	5	—	7	0	—	7	7	—	8	2	—	8	9
30	—	6	10½	—	7	6	—	8	1½	—	8	9	—	9	4½
40	—	9	2	—	10	0	—	10	10	—	11	8	—	12	6
50	—	11	5½	—	12	6	—	13	6½	—	14	7	—	15	7½
[56]	—	12	10	—	14	0	—	15	2	—	16	4	—	17	6
60	—	13	9	—	15	0	—	16	3	—	17	6	—	18	9
70	—	16	0½	—	17	6	—	18	11½	1	0	5	1	1	10½
80	—	18	4	1	0	0	1	1	8	1	3	4	1	5	0
[84]	—	19	3	1	1	0	1	2	9	1	4	6	1	6	3
90	1	0	7½	1	2	6	1	4	4½	1	6	3	1	8	1½
100	1	2	11	1	5	0	1	7	1	1	9	2	1	11	3
[112]	1	5	8	1	8	0	1	10	4	1	12	8	1	15	0
200	2	5	10	2	10	0	2	14	2	2	18	4	3	2	6
300	3	8	9	3	15	0	4	1	3	4	7	6	4	13	9
[365]	4	3	7¼	4	11	3	4	18	10¼	5	6	5½	5	14	0¾
400	4	11	8	5	0	0	5	8	4	5	16	8	6	5	0
500	5	14	7	6	5	0	6	15	5	7	5	10	7	16	3
600	6	17	6	7	10	0	8	2	6	8	15	0	9	7	6
700	8	0	5	8	15	0	9	9	7	10	4	2	10	18	9
800	9	3	4	10	0	0	10	16	8	11	13	4	12	10	0
900	10	6	3	11	5	0	12	3	9	13	2	6	14	1	3
1000	11	9	2	12	10	0	13	10	10	14	11	8	15	12	6
2000	22	18	4	25	0	0	27	1	8	29	3	4	31	5	0
3000	34	7	6	37	10	0	40	12	6	43	15	0	46	17	6
4000	45	16	8	50	0	0	54	3	4	58	6	8	62	10	0
5000	57	5	10	62	10	0	67	14	2	72	18	4	78	2	6
6000	68	15	0	75	0	0	81	5	0	87	10	0	93	15	0
7000	80	4	2	87	10	0	94	15	10	102	1	8	109	7	6
8000	91	13	4	100	0	0	108	6	8	116	13	4	125	0	0
9000	103	2	6	112	10	0	121	17	6	131	5	0	140	12	6
10000	114	11	8	125	0	0	135	8	4	145	16	8	156	5	0

	4 Pence.			4¼ Pence.			4½ Pence.			4¾ Pence.			5 Pence.		
Value	L.	s.	d.	L.	s.	d.f.	L.	s.	d.f.	L.	s.	d.f.	L.	s.	d.
of 2	0	0	8	0	0	8½	0	0	9	0	0	9½	0	0	10
3	——	1	0	——	1	0¾	——	1	1½	——	1	2¼	——	1	3
4	——	1	4	——	1	5	——	1	6	——	1	7	——	1	8
5	——	1	8	——	1	9¼	——	1	10½	——	1	11¾	——	2	1
6	——	2	0	——	2	1½	——	2	3	——	2	4½	——	2	6
7	——	2	4	——	2	5¾	——	2	7½	——	2	9¼	——	2	11
8	——	2	8	——	2	10	——	3	0	——	3	2	——	3	4
9	——	3	0	——	3	2¼	——	3	4½	——	3	6¾	——	3	9
10	——	3	4	——	3	6½	——	3	9	——	3	11½	——	4	2
11	——	3	8	——	3	10¾	——	4	1½	——	4	4¼	——	4	7
12	——	4	0	——	4	3	——	4	6	——	4	9	——	5	0
13	——	4	4	——	4	7¼	——	4	10½	——	5	1¾	——	5	5
14	——	4	8	——	4	11½	——	5	3	——	5	6½	——	5	10
15	——	5	0	——	5	3¾	——	5	7½	——	5	11¼	——	6	3
16	——	5	4	——	5	8	——	6	0	——	6	4	——	6	8
17	——	5	8	——	6	0¼	——	6	4½	——	6	8¾	——	7	1
18	——	6	0	——	6	4½	——	6	9	——	7	1½	——	7	6
19	——	6	4	——	6	8¾	——	7	1½	——	7	6¼	——	7	11
20	——	6	8	——	7	1	——	7	6	——	7	11	——	8	4
[28]	——	9	4	——	9	11	——	10	6	——	11	1	——	11	8
30	——	10	0	——	10	7½	——	11	3	——	11	10½	——	12	6
40	——	13	4	——	14	2	——	15	0	——	15	10	——	16	8
50	——	16	8	——	17	8½	——	18	9	——	19	9½	1	0	10
[56]	——	18	8	——	19	10	1	1	0	1	2	2	1	3	4
60	1	0	0	1	1	3	1	2	6	1	3	9	1	5	0
70	1	3	4	1	4	9½	1	6	3	1	7	8½	1	9	2
80	1	6	8	1	8	4	1	10	0	1	11	8	1	13	4
[84]	1	8	0	1	9	9	1	11	6	1	13	3	1	15	0
90	1	10	0	1	11	10½	1	13	9	1	15	7½	1	17	6
100	1	13	4	1	15	5	1	17	6	1	19	7	2	1	8
[112]	1	17	4	1	19	8	2	2	0	2	4	4	2	6	8
200	3	6	8	3	10	10	3	15	0	3	19	2	4	3	4
300	5	0	0	5	6	3	5	12	6	5	18	9	6	5	0
[365]	6	1	8	6	9	3¼	6	16	10½	7	4	5¾	7	12	1
400	6	13	4	7	1	8	7	10	0	7	18	4	8	6	8
500	8	6	8	8	17	1	9	7	6	9	17	11	10	8	4
600	10	0	0	10	12	6	11	5	0	11	17	6	12	10	0
700	11	13	4	12	7	11	13	2	6	13	17	1	14	11	8
800	13	6	8	14	3	4	15	0	0	15	16	8	16	13	4
900	15	0	0	15	18	9	16	17	6	17	16	3	18	15	0
1000	16	13	4	17	14	2	18	15	0	19	15	10	20	16	8
2000	33	6	8	35	8	4	37	10	0	39	11	8	41	13	4
3000	50	0	0	53	2	6	56	5	0	59	7	6	62	10	0
4000	66	13	4	70	16	8	75	0	0	79	3	4	83	6	8
5000	83	6	8	88	10	10	93	15	0	98	19	2	104	3	4
6000	100	0	0	106	5	0	112	10	0	118	15	0	125	0	0
7000	116	13	4	123	19	2	131	5	0	138	10	10	145	16	8
8000	133	6	8	141	13	4	150	0	0	158	6	8	166	13	4
9000	150	0	0	159	7	6	168	15	0	178	2	6	187	10	0
10000	166	13	4	177	1	8	187	10	0	197	18	4	208	6	8

	5¼ Pence.			5½ Pence.			5¾ Pence.			6 Pence.			6¼ Pence.		
Value	L.	s.	d.f.	L.	s.	d.f.	L.	s.	d.f.	L.	s.	d.	L.	s.	d.f.
of 2	0	0	10½	0	0	11	0	0	11¼	0	1	0	0	1	0½
3	——	1	3¾	——	1	4½	——	1	5¼	——	1	6	——	1	6¾
4	——	1	9	——	1	10	——	1	11	——	2	0	——	2	1
5	——	2	2¼	——	2	3½	——	2	4¾	——	2	6	——	2	7¼
6	——	2	7½	——	2	9	——	2	10½	——	3	0	——	3	1½
7	——	3	0¾	——	3	2½	——	3	4¼	——	3	6	——	3	7¾
8	——	3	6	——	3	8	——	3	10	——	4	0	——	4	2
9	——	3	11¼	——	4	1½	——	4	3¾	——	4	6	——	4	8¼
10	——	4	4½	——	4	7	——	4	9½	——	5	0	——	5	2½
11	——	4	9¾	——	5	0½	——	5	3¼	——	5	6	——	5	8¾
12	——	5	3	——	5	6	——	5	9	——	6	0	——	6	3
13	——	5	8¼	——	5	11½	——	6	2¾	——	6	6	——	6	9¼
14	——	6	1½	——	6	5	——	6	8½	——	7	0	——	7	3½
15	——	6	6¾	——	6	10½	——	7	2¼	——	7	6	——	7	9¾
16	——	7	0	——	7	4	——	7	8	——	8	0	——	8	4
17	——	7	5¼	——	7	9½	——	8	1¾	——	8	6	——	8	10¼
18	——	7	10½	——	8	3	——	8	7½	——	9	0	——	9	4½
19	——	8	3¾	——	8	8½	——	9	1¼	——	9	6	——	9	10¾
20	——	8	9	——	9	2	——	9	7	——	10	0	——	10	5
[28]	——	12	3	——	12	10	——	13	5	——	14	0	——	14	7
30	——	13	1½	——	13	9	——	14	4½	——	15	0	——	15	7½
40	——	17	6	——	18	4	——	19	2	1	0	0	1	0	10
50	1	1	10½	1	2	11	1	3	11½	1	5	0	1	6	0½
[56]	1	4	6	1	5	8	1	6	10	1	8	0	1	9	2
60	1	6	3	1	7	6	1	8	9	1	10	0	1	11	3
70	1	10	7½	1	12	1	1	13	6½	1	15	0	1	16	5½
80	1	15	0	1	16	8	1	18	4	2	0	0	2	1	8
[84]	1	16	0	1	18	6	2	0	3	2	2	0	2	3	9
90	1	19	4½	2	1	3	2	3	1½	2	5	0	2	6	10½
100	2	3	9	2	5	10	2	7	11	2	10	0	2	12	1
[112]	2	9	0	2	11	4	2	13	8	2	16	0	2	18	4
200	4	7	6	4	11	8	4	15	10	5	0	0	5	4	2
300	6	11	3	6	17	6	7	3	9	7	10	0	7	16	3
[365]	7	19	8¼	8	7	3½	8	14	10¾	9	2	6	9	10	1¼
400	8	15	0	9	3	4	9	11	8	10	0	0	10	8	4
500	10	18	9	11	9	2	11	19	7	12	10	0	13	0	5
600	13	2	6	13	15	0	14	7	6	15	0	0	15	12	0
700	15	6	3	16	0	10	16	15	5	17	10	0	18	4	7
800	17	10	0	18	6	8	19	3	4	20	0	0	20	16	8
900	19	13	9	20	12	6	21	11	3	22	10	0	23	8	9
1000	21	17	6	22	18	4	23	19	2	25	0	0	26	0	10
2000	43	15	0	45	16	8	47	18	4	50	0	0	52	1	8
3000	65	12	6	68	15	0	71	17	6	75	0	0	78	2	6
4000	87	10	0	91	13	4	95	16	8	100	0	0	104	3	4
5000	109	7	6	114	11	8	119	15	10	125	0	0	130	4	2
6000	131	5	0	137	10	0	143	15	0	150	0	0	156	5	0
7000	153	2	6	160	8	4	167	14	2	175	0	0	182	5	10
8000	175	0	0	183	6	8	191	13	4	200	0	0	208	6	8
9000	196	17	6	205	5	0	215	12	6	225	0	0	234	7	6
10000	218	15	0	229	3	4	239	11	8	250	0		260	8	4

	6½ Pence.			6¾ Pence.			7 Pence.			7¼ Pence.			7½ Pence.		
Value of	£.	s.	d.f.	£.	s.	d.f.	£.	s.	d	£.	s.	d.f.	£.	s.	d.f
2	0	1	1	0	1	1½	0	1	2	0	1	2½	0	1	3
3	—	1	7½	—	1	8¼	—	1	9	—	1	9¾	—	1	10½
4	—	2	2	—	2	3	—	2	4	—	2	5	—	2	6
5	—	2	8½	—	2	9¾	—	2	11	—	3	0¼	—	3	1½
6	—	3	3	—	3	4½	—	3	6	—	3	7½	—	3	9
7	—	3	9½	—	3	11¼	—	4	1	—	4	2¾	—	4	4½
8	—	4	4	—	4	6	—	4	8	—	4	10	—	5	0
9	—	4	10½	—	5	0¾	—	5	3	—	5	5¼	—	5	7½
10	—	5	5	—	5	7½	—	5	10	—	6	0½	—	6	3
11	—	5	11½	—	6	2¼	—	6	5	—	6	7¾	—	6	10½
12	—	6	6	—	6	9	—	7	0	—	7	3	—	7	6
13	—	7	0½	—	7	3¾	—	7	7	—	7	10¼	—	8	1½
14	—	7	7	—	7	10½	—	8	2	—	8	5½	—	8	9
15	—	8	1½	—	8	5¼	—	8	9	—	9	0¾	—	9	4½
16	—	8	8	—	9	0	—	9	4	—	9	8	—	10	0
17	—	9	2½	—	9	6¾	—	9	11	—	10	3¼	—	10	7½
18	—	9	9	—	10	1½	—	10	6	—	10	10½	—	11	3
19	—	10	3½	—	10	8¼	—	11	1	—	11	5¾	—	11	10½
20	—	10	10	—	11	3	—	11	8	—	12	1	—	12	6
[28]	—	15	2	—	15	9	—	16	4	—	16	11	—	17	6
30	—	16	3	—	16	10½	—	17	6	—	18	1½	—	18	9
40	1	1	8	1	2	6	1	3	4	1	4	2	1	5	0
50	1	7	1	1	8	1½	1	9	2	1	10	2½	1	11	3
[56]	1	10	4	1	11	6	1	12	8	1	13	10	1	15	0
60	1	12	6	1	13	9	1	15	0	1	16	3	1	17	6
70	1	17	11	1	19	4½	2	0	10	2	2	3½	2	3	9
80	2	3	4	2	5	0	2	6	8	2	8	4	2	10	0
[84]	2	5	6	2	7	3	2	9	0	2	10	9	2	12	6
90	2	8	9	2	10	7½	2	12	6	2	14	4½	2	16	3
100	2	14	2	2	16	3	2	18	4	3	0	5	3	2	6
[112]	3	0	8	3	3	0	3	5	4	3	7	8	3	10	0
200	5	8	4	5	12	6	5	16	8	6	0	10	6	5	0
300	8	2	6	8	8	9	8	15	0	9	1	3	9	7	6
[365]	9	17	8½	10	5	3¾	10	12	11	11	0	6¼	11	8	1½
400	10	16	8	11	5	0	11	13	4	12	1	8	12	10	0
500	13	10	10	14	1	3	14	11	8	15	2	1	15	12	6
600	16	5	0	16	17	6	17	10	0	18	2	6	18	15	0
700	18	19	2	19	13	9	20	8	4	21	2	11	21	17	6
800	21	13	4	22	10	0	23	6	8	24	3	4	25	0	0
900	24	7	6	25	6	3	26	5	0	27	3	9	28	2	6
1000	27	1	8	28	2	6	29	3	4	30	4	2	31	5	0
2000	54	3	4	56	5	0	58	6	8	60	8	4	62	10	0
3000	81	5	0	84	7	6	87	10	0	90	12	6	93	15	0
4000	108	6	8	112	10	0	116	13	4	120	16	8	125	0	0
5000	135	8	4	140	12	6	145	16	8	151	0	10	156	5	0
6000	162	10	0	168	15	0	175	0	0	181	5	0	187	10	0
7000	189	11	8	196	17	6	204	3	4	211	9	2	218	15	0
8000	216	13	4	225	0	0	233	6	8	241	13	4	250	0	0
9000	243	15	0	253	2	6	262	10	0	271	17	6	281	5	0
10000	270	16	8	281	5	0	291	13	4	302	1	8	312	10	0

	7¾ Pence.			8 Pence.			8¼ Pence.			8½ Pence.			8¾ Pence.		
Value	L.	s.	d.f.	L.	s.	d.	L.	s.	d.f.	L.	s.	d.f.	L.	s.	d.f.
of 2	0	1	3½	0	1	4	0	1	4½	0	1	5	0	1	5½
3	—	1	11¼	—	2	0	—	2	0¾	—	2	1½	—	2	2¼
4	—	2	7	—	2	8	—	2	9	—	2	10	—	2	11
5	—	3	2¾	—	3	4	—	3	5¼	—	3	6½	—	3	7¾
6	—	3	10½	—	4	0	—	4	1½	—	4	3	—	4	4½
7	—	4	6¼	—	4	8	—	4	9¾	—	4	11½	—	5	1¼
8	—	5	2	—	5	4	—	5	6	—	5	8	—	5	10
9	—	5	9¾	—	6	0	—	6	2¼	—	6	4½	—	6	6¾
10	—	6	5½	—	6	8	—	6	10½	—	7	1	—	7	3½
11	—	7	1¼	—	7	4	—	7	6¾	—	7	9½	—	8	0¼
12	—	7	9	—	8	0	—	8	3	—	8	6	—	8	9
13	—	8	4¾	—	8	8	—	8	11¼	—	9	2½	—	9	5¾
14	—	9	0½	—	9	4	—	9	7½	—	9	11	—	10	2½
15	—	9	8¼	—	10	0	—	10	3¾	—	10	7½	—	10	11¼
16	—	10	4	—	10	8	—	11	0	—	11	4	—	11	8
17	—	10	11¾	—	11	4	—	11	8¼	—	12	0½	—	12	4¾
18	—	11	7½	—	12	0	—	12	4½	—	12	9	—	13	1½
19	—	12	3¼	—	12	8	—	13	0¾	—	13	5½	—	13	10¼
20	—	12	11	—	13	4	—	13	9	—	14	2	—	14	7
[28]	—	18	1	—	18	8	—	19	3	—	19	10	1	0	5
30	—	19	4½	1	0	0	1	0	7½	1	1	3	1	1	10½
40	1	5	10	1	6	8	1	7	6	1	8	4	1	9	2
50	1	12	3½	1	13	4	1	14	4½	1	15	5	1	16	5½
[56]	1	16	2	1	17	4	1	18	6	1	19	8	2	0	10
60	1	18	9	2	0	0	2	1	3	2	2	6	2	3	9
70	2	5	2½	2	6	8	2	8	1½	2	9	7	2	11	0½
80	2	11	8	2	13	4	2	15	0	2	16	8	2	18	4
[84]	2	14	3	2	16	0	2	17	9	2	19	6	3	1	3
90	2	18	1½	3	0	0	3	1	10½	3	3	9	3	5	7½
100	3	4	7	3	6	8	3	8	9	3	10	10	3	12	11
[112]	3	12	4	3	14	8	3	17	0	3	19	4	4	1	8
200	6	9	2	6	13	4	6	17	6	7	1	8	7	5	10
300	9	13	9	10	0	0	10	6	3	10	12	6	10	18	9
[365]	11	15	8¼	12	3	4	12	10	11¼	12	18	6½	13	6	1¾
400	12	18	4	13	6	8	13	15	0	14	3	4	14	11	8
500	16	2	11	16	13	4	17	3	9	17	14	2	18	4	7
600	19	7	6	20	0	0	20	12	6	21	5	0	21	17	6
700	22	12	1	23	6	8	24	1	3	24	15	10	25	10	5
800	25	16	8	26	13	4	27	10	0	28	6	8	29	3	4
900	29	1	3	30	0	0	30	18	9	31	17	6	32	16	3
1000	32	5	10	33	6	8	34	7	6	35	8	4	36	9	2
2000	64	11	8	66	13	4	68	15	0	70	16	8	72	18	4
3000	96	17	6	100	0	0	103	2	6	106	5	0	109	7	6
4000	129	3	4	133	6	8	137	10	0	141	13	4	145	16	8
5000	161	9	2	166	13	4	171	17	6	177	1	8	182	5	10
6000	193	15	0	200	0	0	206	5	0	212	10	0	218	15	0
7000	226	0	10	233	6	8	240	12	6	247	18	4	255	4	2
8000	258	6	8	266	13	4	275	0	0	283	6	8	291	13	4
9000	290	12	6	300	0	0	309	7	6	318	15	0	328	2	6
10000	322	18	4	333	6	8	343	15	0	354	3	4	364	11	8

	9 Pence.			9¼ Pence.			9½ Pence.			9¾ Pence.			10 Pence.		
Value	L.	s.	d.	L.	s.	d.f.	L.	s.	d.f.	L.	s.	d.f.	L.	s.	d.
of 2	0	1	6	0	1	6½	0	1	7	0	1	7½	0	1	8
3	—	2	3	—	2	3¾	—	2	4½	—	2	5¼	—	2	6
4	—	3	0	—	3	1	—	3	2	—	3	3	—	3	4
5	—	3	9	—	3	10¼	—	3	11½	—	4	0¾	—	4	2
6	—	4	6	—	4	7½	—	4	9	—	4	10½	—	5	0
7	—	5	3	—	5	4¾	—	5	6½	—	5	8¼	—	5	10
8	—	6	0	—	6	2	—	6	4	—	6	6	—	6	8
9	—	6	9	—	6	11¼	—	7	1½	—	7	3¾	—	7	6
10	—	7	6	—	7	8½	—	7	11	—	8	1½	—	8	4
11	—	8	3	—	8	5¾	—	8	8½	—	8	11¼	—	9	2
12	—	9	0	—	9	3	—	9	6	—	9	9	—	10	0
13	—	9	9	—	10	0¼	—	10	3½	—	10	6¾	—	10	10
14	—	10	6	—	10	9½	—	11	1	—	11	4½	—	11	8
15	—	11	3	—	11	6¾	—	11	10½	—	12	2¼	—	12	6
16	—	12	0	—	12	4	—	12	8	—	13	0	—	13	4
17	—	12	9	—	13	1¼	—	13	5½	—	13	9¾	—	14	2
18	—	13	6	—	13	10½	—	14	3	—	14	7½	—	15	0
19	—	14	3	—	14	7¾	—	15	0½	—	15	5¼	—	15	10
20	—	15	0	—	15	5	—	15	10	—	16	3	—	16	8
[28]	1	1	0	1	1	7	1	2	2	1	2	9	1	3	4
30	1	2	6	1	3	1½	1	3	9	1	4	4½	1	5	0
40	1	10	0	1	10	10	1	11	8	1	12	6	1	13	4
50	1	17	6	1	18	6½	1	19	7	2	0	7½	2	1	8
[56]	2	2	0	2	3	2	2	4	4	2	5	6	2	6	8
60	2	5	0	2	6	3	2	7	6	2	8	9	2	10	0
70	2	12	6	2	13	11½	2	15	5	2	16	10½	2	18	4
80	3	0	0	3	1	8	3	3	4	3	5	0	3	6	8
[84]	3	3	0	3	4	9	3	6	6	3	8	3	3	10	0
90	3	7	6	3	9	4½	3	11	3	3	13	1½	3	15	0
100	3	15	0	3	17	1	3	19	2	4	1	3	4	3	4
[112]	4	4	0	4	6	4	4	8	8	4	11	0	4	13	4
200	7	10	0	7	14	2	7	18	4	8	2	6	8	6	8
300	11	5	0	11	11	3	11	17	6	12	3	9	12	10	0
[365]	13	13	9	14	1	4½	14	8	11½	14	16	6¾	15	4	2
400	15	0	0	15	8	4	15	16	8	16	5	0	16	13	4
500	18	15	0	19	5	5	19	15	10	20	6	3	20	16	8
600	22	10	0	23	2	6	23	15	0	24	7	6	25	0	0
700	26	5	0	25	19	7	27	14	2	28	8	9	29	3	4
800	30	0	0	30	16	8	31	13	4	32	10	0	33	6	8
900	33	15	0	34	13	9	35	12	6	36	11	3	37	10	0
1000	37	10	0	38	10	10	39	11	8	40	12	6	41	13	4
2000	75	0	0	77	1	8	79	3	4	81	5	0	83	6	8
3000	112	10	0	115	12	6	118	15	0	121	17	6	125	0	0
4000	150	0	0	154	3	4	158	6	8	162	10	0	166	13	4
5000	187	10	0	192	14	2	197	18	4	203	2	6	208	6	8
6000	225	0	0	231	5	0	237	10	0	243	15	0	250	0	0
7000	262	10	0	269	15	10	277	1	8	284	7	6	291	13	4
8000	300	0	0	308	6	8	316	13	4	325	0	0	333	6	8
9000	337	10	0	346	17	6	356	5	0	365	12	6	375	0	0
10000	375	0	0	385	8	4	395	16	8	406	5	0	416	13	4

	10¼ Pence.			10½ Pence.			10¾ Pence.			11 Pence.			11¼ Pence.		
Value of	£.	s.	d.f.	£.	s.	d.f.	£.	s.	d.f.	£.	s.	d.	£.	s.	d.f.
2	0	1	8½	0	1	9	0	1	9½	0	1	10	0	1	10½
3	—	2	6¾	—	2	7½	—	2	8¼	—	2	9	—	2	9¾
4	—	3	5	—	3	6	—	3	7	—	3	8	—	3	9
5	—	4	3¼	—	4	4½	—	4	5¾	—	4	7	—	4	8¼
6	—	5	1½	—	5	3	—	5	4½	—	5	6	—	5	7½
7	—	5	11¾	—	6	1½	—	6	3¼	—	6	5	—	6	6¾
8	—	6	10	—	7	0	—	7	2	—	7	4	—	7	6
9	—	7	8¼	—	7	10½	—	8	0¾	—	8	3	—	8	5¼
10	—	8	6½	—	8	9	—	8	11½	—	9	2	—	9	4½
11	—	9	4¾	—	9	7½	—	9	10¼	—	10	1	—	10	3¾
12	—	10	3	—	10	6	—	10	9	—	11	0	—	11	3
13	—	11	1¼	—	11	4½	—	11	7¾	—	11	11	—	12	2¼
14	—	11	11½	—	12	3	—	12	6½	—	12	10	—	13	1½
15	—	12	9¾	—	13	1½	—	13	5¼	—	13	9	—	14	0¾
16	—	13	8	—	14	0	—	14	4	—	14	8	—	15	0
17	—	14	6¼	—	14	10½	—	15	2¾	—	15	7	—	15	11¼
18	—	15	4½	—	15	9	—	16	1½	—	16	6	—	16	10½
19	—	16	2¾	—	16	7½	—	17	0¼	—	17	5	—	17	9¾
20	—	17	1	—	17	6	—	17	11	—	18	4	—	18	9
[28]	1	3	11	1	4	6	1	5	1	1	5	8	1	6	3
30	1	5	7½	1	6	3	1	6	10½	1	7	6	1	8	1½
40	1	14	2	1	15	0	1	15	10	1	16	8	1	17	6
50	2	2	8½	2	3	9	2	4	9½	2	5	10	2	6	10½
[56]	2	7	10	2	9	0	2	10	2	2	11	4	2	12	6
60	2	11	3	2	12	6	2	13	9	2	15	0	2	16	3
70	2	19	9½	3	1	3	3	2	8½	3	4	2	3	5	7½
80	3	8	4	3	10	0	3	11	8	3	13	4	3	15	0
[84]	3	11	9	3	13	6	3	15	3	3	17	0	3	18	9
90	3	16	10½	3	18	9	4	0	7½	4	2	6	4	4	4½
100	4	5	5	4	7	6	4	9	7	4	11	8	4	13	9
[112]	4	15	8	4	18	0	5	0	4	5	2	8	5	5	0
200	8	10	10	8	15	0	8	19	2	9	3	4	9	7	6
300	12	16	3	13	2	6	13	8	9	13	15	0	14	1	3
[365]	15	11	9¼	15	19	4½	16	6	11¾	16	14	7	17	2	2¼
400	17	1	8	17	10	0	17	18	4	18	6	8	18	15	0
500	21	7	1	21	17	6	22	7	11	22	18	4	23	8	9
600	25	12	6	26	5	0	26	17	6	27	10	0	28	2	6
700	29	17	11	30	12	6	31	7	1	32	1	8	32	16	3
800	34	3	4	35	0	0	35	16	8	36	13	4	37	10	0
900	38	8	9	39	7	6	40	6	3	41	5	0	42	3	9
1000	42	14	2	43	15	0	44	15	10	45	16	8	46	17	6
2000	85	8	4	87	10	0	89	11	8	91	13	4	93	15	0
3000	128	2	6	131	5	0	134	7	6	137	10	0	140	12	6
4000	170	16	8	175	0	0	179	3	4	183	6	8	187	10	0
5000	213	10	10	218	15	0	223	19	2	229	3	4	234	7	6
6000	256	5	0	262	10	0	268	15	0	275	0	0	281	5	0
7000	298	19	2	306	5	0	313	10	10	320	16	8	328	2	6
8000	341	13	4	350	0	0	358	6	8	366	13	4	375	0	0
9000	384	7	6	393	15	0	403	2	6	412	10	0	421	17	6
10000	427	1	8	437	10	0	447	18	4	458	6	8	468	15	0

Value of	11½ Pence. £.	s.	d. f.	11¾ Pence. £.	s.	d. f.	12 Pence. £.	s.	d.	12¼ Pence. £.	s.	d. f.	12½ Pence. £.	s.	d. f.
2	0	1	11	0	1	11½	0	2	—	0	2	0½	0	2	
3	—	2	10½	—	2	11¼	—	3	—	—	3	0¾	—	3	1½
4	—	3	10	—	3	11	—	4	—	—	4	1	—	4	2
5	—	4	9½	—	4	10¾	—	5	—	—	5	1¼	—	5	2½
6	—	5	9	—	5	10½	—	6	—	—	6	1½	—	6	3
7	—	6	8½	—	6	10¼	—	7	—	—	7	1¾	—	7	3½
8	—	7	8	—	7	10	—	8	—	—	8	2	—	8	4
9	—	8	7½	—	8	9¾	—	9	—	—	9	2¼	—	9	4½
10	—	9	7	—	9	9½	—	10	—	—	10	2½	—	10	5
11	—	10	6½	—	10	9¼	—	11	—	—	11	2¾	—	11	5½
12	—	11	6	—	11	9	—	12	—	—	12	3	—	12	6
13	—	12	5½	—	12	8¾	—	13	—	—	13	3¼	—	13	6½
14	—	13	5	—	13	8½	—	14	—	—	14	3½	—	14	7
15	—	14	4½	—	14	8¼	—	15	—	—	15	3¾	—	15	7½
16	—	15	4	—	15	8	—	16	—	—	16	4	—	16	8
17	—	16	3½	—	16	7¾	—	17	—	—	17	4¼	—	17	8½
18	—	17	3	—	17	7½	—	18	—	—	18	4½	—	18	9
19	—	18	2½	—	18	7¼	—	19	—	—	19	4¾	—	19	9½
20	—	19	2	—	19	7	1	0	—	1	0	5	1	0	10
[28]	1	6	10	1	7	5	1	8	—	1	8	7	1	9	2
30	1	8	9	1	9	4½	1	10	—	1	10	7½	1	11	3
40	1	18	4	1	19	2	2	0	—	2	0	10	2	1	8
50	2	7	11	2	8	11½	2	10	—	2	11	0½	2	12	1
[56]	2	13	8	2	14	10	2	16	—	2	17	2	2	18	4
60	2	17	6	2	18	9	3	0	—	3	1	3	3	2	6
70	3	7	1	3	8	6½	3	10	—	3	11	5½	3	12	11
80	3	16	8	3	18	4	4	0	—	4	1	8	4	3	4
[84]	4	0	6	4	2	3	4	4	—	4	5	9	4	7	6
90	4	6	3	4	8	1½	4	10	—	4	11	10½	4	13	9
100	4	15	10	4	17	11	5	0	—	5	2	1	5	4	2
[112]	5	7	4	5	9	8	5	12	—	5	14	4	5	16	8
200	9	11	8	9	15	10	10	0	—	10	4	2	10	8	4
300	14	7	6	14	13	9	15	0	—	15	6	3	15	12	6
[365]	17	9	9½	17	17	4¾	18	5	—	18	12	7¼	19	0	2½
400	19	3	4	19	11	8	20	—	—	20	8	4	20	16	8
500	23	19	2	24	9	7	25	—	—	25	10	5	26	0	10
600	28	15	0	29	7	6	30	—	—	30	12	6	31	5	0
700	33	10	10	34	5	5	35	—	—	35	14	7	36	9	2
800	38	6	8	39	3	4	40	—	—	40	16	8	41	13	4
900	43	2	6	44	1	3	45	—	—	45	18	9	46	17	6
1000	47	18	4	48	19	2	50	—	—	51	0	10	52	1	8
2000	95	16	8	97	18	4	100	—	—	102	1	8	104	3	4
3000	143	15	0	146	17	6	150	—	—	153	2	6	156	5	0
4000	191	13	4	195	16	8	200	—	—	204	3	4	208	6	8
5000	239	11	8	244	15	10	250	—	—	255	4	2	260	8	4
6000	287	10	0	293	15	0	300	—	—	306	5	0	312	10	0
7000	335	8	4	342	14	2	350	—	—	357	5	10	364	11	8
8000	383	6	8	391	13	4	400	—	—	408	6	8	416	13	4
9000	431	5	0	440	12	6	450	—	—	459	7	6	468	15	0
10000	479	3	4	489	11	8	500	—	—	510	8	4	520	16	8

	12¾ Pence.			13 Pence.			13¼ Pence.			13½ Pence.			13¾ Pence.		
Value of	£.	s.	d.f.	£.	s.	d.	£.	s.	d.f.	£.	s.	d.f.	£.	s.	d.f.
2	0	2	1½	0	2	2	0	2	2½	0	2	3	0	2	3½
3	—	3	2¼	—	3	3	—	3	3¾	—	3	4½	—	3	5¼
4	—	4	3	—	4	4	—	4	5	—	4	6	—	4	7
5	—	5	3¾	—	5	5	—	5	6¼	—	5	7½	—	5	8¾
6	—	6	4½	—	6	6	—	6	7½	—	6	9	—	6	10½
7	—	7	5¼	—	7	7	—	7	8¾	—	7	10½	—	8	0¼
8	—	8	6	—	8	8	—	8	10	—	9	0	—	9	2
9	—	9	6¾	—	9	9	—	9	11¼	—	10	1½	—	10	3¾
10	—	10	7½	—	10	10	—	11	0½	—	11	3	—	11	5½
11	—	11	8¼	—	11	11	—	12	1¾	—	12	4½	—	12	7¼
12	—	12	9	—	13	0	—	13	3	—	13	6	—	13	9
13	—	13	9¾	—	14	1	—	14	4¼	—	14	7½	—	14	10¾
14	—	14	10½	—	15	2	—	15	5½	—	15	9	—	16	0½
15	—	15	11¼	—	16	3	—	16	6¾	—	16	10½	—	17	2¼
16	—	17	0	—	17	4	—	17	8	—	18	0	—	18	4
17	—	18	0¾	—	18	5	—	18	9¼	—	19	1½	—	19	5¾
18	—	19	1½	—	19	6	—	19	10½	1	0	3	1	0	7½
19	1	0	2¼	1	0	7	1	0	11¾	1	1	4½	1	1	9¼
20	1	1	3	1	1	8	1	2	1	1	2	6	1	2	11
[28]	1	9	9	1	10	4	1	10	11	1	11	6	1	12	1
30	1	11	10½	1	12	6	1	13	1½	1	13	9	1	14	4½
40	2	2	6	2	3	4	2	4	2	2	5	0	2	5	10
50	2	13	1½	2	14	2	2	15	2	2	16	3	2	17	3½
[56]	2	19	6	3	0	8	3	1	10	3	3	0	3	4	2
60	2	3	9	3	5	0	3	6	3	3	7	6	3	8	9
70	3	14	4½	3	15	10	3	17	3½	3	18	9	4	0	2¼
80	4	5	0	4	6	8	4	8	4	4	10	0	4	11	8
[84]	4	9	3	4	11	0	4	12	9	4	14	6	4	16	3
90	4	15	7½	4	17	6	4	19	4½	5	1	3	5	3	1½
100	5	6	3	5	8	4	5	10	5	5	12	6	5	14	7
[112]	5	19	0	6	1	4	6	3	8	6	6	0	6	8	4
200	10	12	6	10	16	8	11	0	10	11	5	0	11	9	2
300	15	18	9	16	5	0	16	11	3	16	17	6	17	3	9
[365]	19	7	9¾	19	15	5	20	3	0¼	20	10	7½	20	18	2¾
400	21	5	0	21	13	4	22	1	8	22	10	0	22	18	4
500	26	11	3	27	1	8	27	12	1	28	2	6	28	12	11
600	31	17	6	32	10	0	33	2	6	33	15	0	34	7	6
700	37	3	9	37	18	4	38	12	11	39	7	6	40	2	1
800	42	10	0	43	6	8	44	3	4	45	0	0	45	16	8
900	47	16	3	48	15	0	49	13	9	50	12	6	51	11	3
1000	53	2	6	54	3	4	55	4	2	56	5	0	57	5	10
2000	106	5	0	108	6	8	110	8	4	112	10	0	114	11	8
3000	159	7	6	162	10	0	165	12	6	168	15	0	171	17	6
4000	212	10	0	216	13	4	220	16	8	225	0	0	229	3	4
5000	265	12	6	270	16	8	276	0	10	281	5	0	286	9	2
6000	318	15	0	325	0	0	331	5	0	[illegible]	10	0	343	15	0
7000	371	17	6	379	3	4	386	9	2	393	15	0	401	0	10
8000	425	0	0	433	6	8	441	13	4	450	0	0	458	6	8
9000	478	2	6	487	10	0	496	17	6	506	5	0	515	12	6
10000	531	5	0	541	13	4	552	1	8	562	10	0	572	18	4

	14 Pence.			14¼ Pence.			14½ Pence			14¾ Pence.			15 Pence		
Value	£.	s.	d.	£.	s.	d.f	L.	s.	d.f.	£.	s.	d.f	£.	s.	d.
of 2	0	2	4	0	2	4½	0	2	5	0	2	5½	0	2	6
3	—	3	6	—	3	6¾	—	3	7½	—	3	8¼	—	3	9
4	—	4	8	—	4	9	—	4	10	—	4	11	—	5	0
5	—	5	10	—	5	11¼	—	6	0½	—	6	1¾	—	6	3
6	—	7	0	—	7	1½	—	7	3	—	7	4½	—	7	6
7	—	8	2	—	8	3¾	—	8	5	—	8	7¼	—	8	9
8	—	9	4	—	9	6	—	9	8	—	9	10	—	10	0
9	—	10	6	—	10	8¼	—	10	10½	—	11	0¾	—	11	3
10	—	11	8	—	11	10½	—	12	1	—	12	3½	—	12	6
11	—	12	10	—	13	0¾	—	13	3½	—	13	6¼	—	13	9
12	—	14	0	—	14	3	—	14	6	—	14	9	—	15	0
13	—	15	2	—	15	5¼	—	15	8½	—	15	11¾	—	16	3
14	—	16	4	—	16	7½	—	16	11	—	17	2½	—	17	6
15	—	17	6	—	17	9¾	—	18	1½	—	18	5¼	—	18	9
16	—	18	8	—	19	0	—	19	4	—	19	8	1	0	0
17	—	19	10	1	0	2¼	1	0	6½	1	0	10¾	1	1	3
18	1	1	0	1	1	4½	1	1	9	1	2	1½	1	2	6
19	1	2	2	1	2	6¾	1	2	11½	1	3	4¼	1	3	9
20	1	3	4	1	3	9	1	4	2	1	4	7	1	5	0
[28]	1	12	8	1	13	3	1	13	10	1	14	5	1	15	0
30	1	15	0	1	15	7½	1	16	3	1	16	10½	1	17	6
40	2	6	8	2	7	6	2	8	4	2	9	2	2	10	0
50	2	18	4	2	19	4½	3	0	5	3	1	5½	3	2	6
[56]	3	5	4	3	6	6	3	7	8	3	8	10	3	10	0
60	3	10	0	3	11	3	3	12	6	3	13	9	3	15	0
70	4	1	8	4	3	1½	4	4	7	4	6	0½	4	7	6
80	4	13	4	4	15	0	4	16	8	4	18	4	5	0	0
[84]	4	18	0	4	19	9	5	1	6	5	3	3	5	5	0
90	5	5	0	5	6	10½	5	8	9	5	10	7½	5	12	6
100	5	16	8	5	18	9	6	0	10	6	2	11	6	5	0
[112]	6	10	8	6	13	0	6	15	4	6	17	8	7	0	0
200	11	13	4	11	17	6	12	1	8	12	5	10	12	10	0
300	17	10	0	17	16	3	18	2	6	18	8	9	18	15	0
[365]	21	5	10	21	13	5¼	22	1	0½	22	8	7½	22	16	[illegible]
400	23	6	8	23	15	0	24	3	4	24	11	8	25	0	0
500	29	3	4	29	13	9	30	4	2	30	14	7	31	5	0
600	35	0	0	35	12	6	36	5	0	36	17	6	37	10	0
700	40	16	8	41	11	3	42	5	10	43	0	5	43	15	0
800	46	13	4	47	10	0	48	6	8	49	3	4	50	0	0
900	52	10	0	53	8	9	54	7	6	55	6	3	56	5	0
1000	58	6	8	59	7	6	60	8	4	61	9	2	62	10	0
2000	116	13	4	118	15	0	120	16	8	122	18	4	125	0	0
3000	175	0	0	178	2	6	181	5	0	184	7	6	187	10	0
4000	233	6	8	237	10	0	241	13	4	245	16	8	250	0	0
5000	291	13	4	296	13	6	302	1	8	307	5	10	312	10	0
6000	350	0	0	356	5	[illegible]	362	10	0	368	15	0	375	0	0
7000	408	6	8	415	12	6	422	18	4	430	4	2	437	10	0
8000	466	13	4	475	0	0	483	6	8	491	13	4	500	0	0
9000	525	0	0	534	7	6	543	15	0	553	2	6	562	10	0
10000	583	6	8	593	15	0	604	3	4	614	11	8	625	0	0

Value of	15¼ Pence. L.	s.	d.f.	15½ Pence. L.	s.	d.f.	15¾ Pence. L.	s.	d.f.	16 Pence. L.	s.	d.	16¼ Pence. L.	s.	d.f.
2	0	2	6½	0	2	7	0	2	7½	0	2	8	0	2	8½
3	——	3	9¾	——	3	10½	——	3	11¼	——	4	0	——	4	0¾
4	——	5	1	——	5	2	——	5	3	——	5	4	——	5	5
5	——	6	4¼	——	6	5½	——	6	6¾	——	6	8	——	6	9¼
6	——	7	7½	——	7	9	——	7	10½	——	8	0	——	8	1½
7	——	8	10¾	——	9	0½	——	9	2¼	——	9	4	——	9	5¾
8	——	10	2	——	10	4	——	10	6	——	10	8	——	10	10
9	——	11	5¼	——	11	7½	——	11	9¾	——	12	0	——	12	2¼
10	——	12	8½	——	12	11	——	13	1½	——	13	4	——	13	6½
11	——	13	11¾	——	14	2½	——	14	5¼	——	14	8	——	14	10¾
12	——	15	3	——	15	6	——	15	9	——	16	0	——	16	3
13	——	16	6¼	——	16	9½	——	17	0¾	——	17	4	——	17	7¼
14	——	17	9½	——	13	1	——	18	4½	——	18	8	——	18	11½
15	——	19	0¾	——	19	4½	——	19	8¼	1	0	0	1	0	3¾
16	1	0	4	1	0	8	1	1	0	1	1	4	1	1	8
17	1	1	7¼	1	1	11½	1	2	3¾	1	2	8	1	3	0¼
18	1	2	10½	1	3	3	1	3	7½	1	4	0	1	4	4½
19	1	4	1¾	1	4	6½	1	4	11¼	1	5	4	1	5	8¾
20	1	5	5	1	5	10	1	6	3	1	6	8	1	7	1
[28]	1	15	7	1	16	2	1	16	9	1	17	4	1	17	11
30	1	18	1½	1	18	9	1	19	4½	2	0	0	2	0	7½
40	2	2	10	2	11	8	2	12	6	2	13	4	2	14	2
50	3	3	6½	3	4	7	3	5	7½	3	6	8	3	7	8½
[56]	3	11	2	3	12	4	3	13	6	3	14	8	3	15	10
60	3	16	3	3	17	6	3	18	9	4	0	0	4	1	3
70	4	8	11½	4	10	5	4	11	10½	4	13	4	4	14	9½
80	5	1	8	5	3	4	5	5	0	5	6	8	5	8	4
[84]	5	6	9	5	8	6	5	10	3	5	12	0	5	13	9
90	5	14	4½	5	16	3	5	18	1½	6	0	0	6	1	10½
100	6	7	1	6	9	2	6	11	3	6	13	4	6	15	5
[112]	7	2	4	7	4	8	7	7	0	7	9	4	7	11	8
200	12	14	2	12	18	4	13	2	6	13	6	8	13	10	10
300	19	1	3	19	7	6	19	13	9	20	0	0	20	6	3
[365]	23	3	10¼	23	11	5½	23	19	0	24	6	8	24	14	3¼
400	25	8	4	25	16	8	26	5	0	26	13	4	27	1	8
500	31	15	5	32	5	10	32	16	3	33	6	8	33	27	1
600	38	2	6	38	15	0	39	7	6	40	0	0	40	12	6
700	44	9	7	45	4	2	45	18	9	46	13	4	47	7	11
800	50	16	8	51	13	4	52	10	0	53	6	8	54	3	4
900	57	3	9	58	2	6	59	1	3	60	0	0	60	18	9
1000	63	10	10	64	11	8	65	12	6	66	13	4	67	14	2
2000	127	1	8	129	3	4	131	5	0	133	6	8	135	8	4
3000	190	12	6	193	15	0	196	17	6	200	0	0	203	2	6
4000	254	3	4	258	6	8	262	10	0	266	13	4	270	16	8
5000	317	14	2	322	18	4	328	2	6	333	6	8	338	10	10
6000	381	5	0	387	10	0	393	15	0	400	0	0	406	5	0
7000	444	15	10	452	1	8	459	7	6	466	13	4	473	19	2
8000	508	6	8	516	13	4	525	0	0	533	6	8	541	13	4
9000	571	17	6	581	5	0	590	12	6	600	0	0	609	7	6
10000	635	8	4	645	16	8	656	5	0	666	13	4	6[illegible]7	1	8

	16½ Pence.			16¾ Pence.			17 Pence.			17¼ Pence.			17½ Pence.		
Value	L.	s.	d.f.	L.	s.	d.f.	L.	s.	d.	L.	s.	d.f.	L.	s.	d.f.
of 2	0	2	9	0	2	9½	0	2	10	0	2	10½	0	2	11
3	—	4	1½	—	4	2¼	—	4	3	—	4	3¾	—	4	4½
4	—	5	6	—	5	7	—	5	8	—	5	9	—	5	10
5	—	6	10½	—	6	11¾	—	7	1	—	7	2¼	—	7	3½
6	—	8	3	—	8	4½	—	8	6	—	8	7½	—	8	9
7	—	9	7½	—	9	9¼	—	9	11	—	10	0¾	—	10	2½
8	—	11	0	—	11	2	—	11	4	—	11	6	—	11	8
9	—	12	4½	—	12	6¾	—	12	9	—	12	11¼	—	13	1½
10	—	13	9	—	13	11½	—	14	2	—	14	4½	—	14	7
11	—	15	1½	—	15	4¼	—	15	7	—	15	9¾	—	16	0½
12	—	16	6	—	16	9	—	17	0	—	17	3	—	17	6
13	—	17	10½	—	18	1¾	—	18	5	—	18	8¼	—	18	11½
14	—	19	3	—	19	6½	—	19	10	1	0	1½	1	0	5
15	1	0	7½	1	0	11¼	1	1	3	1	1	6¾	1	1	10½
16	1	2	0	1	2	4	1	2	8	1	3	0	1	3	4
17	1	3	4½	1	3	8¾	1	4	1	1	4	5¼	1	4	9½
18	1	4	9	1	5	1½	1	5	6	1	5	10½	1	6	3
19	1	6	1½	1	6	6¼	1	6	11	1	7	3¾	1	7	8½
20	1	7	6	1	7	11	1	8	4	1	8	9	1	9	2
[28]	1	18	6	1	19	1	1	19	8	2	0	3	2	0	10
30	2	1	3	2	1	10½	2	2	6	2	3	1½	2	3	9
40	2	15	0	2	15	10	2	16	8	2	17	6	2	18	4
50	3	8	9	3	9	9½	3	10	10	3	11	10½	3	12	11
[56]	3	17	0	3	18	2	3	19	4	4	0	6	4	1	8
60	4	2	6	4	3	9	4	5	0	4	6	3	4	7	6
70	4	16	3	4	17	8½	4	19	2	5	0	7½	5	2	1
80	5	10	0	5	11	8	5	13	4	5	15	0	5	16	8
[84]	5	15	6	5	17	3	5	19	0	6	0	9	6	2	6
90	6	3	9	6	5	7½	6	7	6	6	9	4½	6	11	3
100	6	17	6	6	19	7	7	1	8	7	3	9	7	5	10
[112]	7	14	0	7	16	4	7	18	8	8	1	0	8	3	4
200	13	15	0	13	19	2	14	3	4	14	7	6	14	11	8
300	20	12	6	20	18	9	21	5	0	21	11	3	21	17	6
[365]	25	1	10½	25	9	5¾	25	17	1	26	4	8¼	26	12	3½
400	27	10	0	27	18	4	28	6	8	28	15	0	29	3	4
500	34	7	6	34	17	11	35	8	4	35	18	9	36	9	2
600	41	5	0	41	17	6	42	10	0	43	2	6	43	15	0
700	48	2	6	48	17	1	49	11	8	50	6	3	51	0	10
800	55	0	0	55	16	8	56	13	4	57	10	0	58	6	8
900	61	17	6	62	16	3	63	15	0	64	13	9	65	12	6
1000	68	15	0	69	15	10	70	16	8	71	17	6	72	18	4
2000	137	10	0	139	11	8	141	13	4	143	15	0	145	16	8
3000	206	5	0	209	7	6	212	10	0	215	12	6	218	15	0
4000	275	0	0	279	3	4	283	6	8	287	10	0	291	13	4
5000	343	15	0	348	19	2	354	3	4	359	7	6	364	11	8
6000	412	10	0	418	15	0	425	0	0	431	5	0	437	10	0
7000	481	5	0	488	10	10	495	16	8	503	2	6	510	8	4
8000	550	0	0	558	6	8	566	13	4	575	0	0	583	6	8
9000	618	15	0	628	2	6	637	10	0	646	17	6	656	5	0
10000	687	10	0	697	18	4	708	6	8	718	15	0	729	3	4

	17¾ Pence.			18 Pence.			18½ Pence.			19 Pence.			19½ Pence.		
Value of	£.	s.	d.f.	£.	s.	d.	£.	s.	d.f.	£.	s.	d.	£.	s.	d.f.
2	0	2	11½	0	3	0	0	3	1	0	3	2	0	3	3
3	—	4	5¼	—	4	6	—	4	7½	—	4	9	—	4	10½
4	—	5	11	—	6	0	—	6	2	—	6	4	—	6	6
5	—	7	4¾	—	7	6	—	7	8½	—	7	11	—	8	1½
6	—	8	10½	—	9	0	—	9	3	—	9	6	—	9	9
7	—	10	4¼	—	10	6	—	10	9½	—	11	1	—	11	4½
8	—	11	10	—	12	0	—	12	4	—	12	8	—	13	0
9	—	13	3¾	—	13	6	—	13	10½	—	14	3	—	14	7½
10	—	14	9½	—	15	0	—	15	5	—	15	10	—	16	3
11	—	16	3¼	—	16	6	—	16	11½	—	17	5	—	17	10½
12	—	17	9	—	18	0	—	18	6	—	19	0	—	19	6
13	—	19	2¾	—	19	6	1	0	0½	1	0	7	1	1	1½
14	1	0	8½	1	1	0	1	1	7	1	2	2	1	2	9
15	1	2	2¼	1	2	6	1	3	1½	1	3	9	1	4	4½
16	1	3	8	1	4	0	1	4	8	1	5	4	1	6	0
17	1	5	1¾	1	5	6	1	6	2½	1	6	11	1	7	7½
18	1	6	7½	1	7	0	1	7	9	1	8	6	1	9	3
19	1	8	1¼	1	8	6	1	9	3½	1	10	1	1	10	10½
20	1	9	7	1	10	0	1	10	10	1	11	8	1	12	6
[28]	2	1	5	2	2	0	2	3	2	2	4	4	2	5	6
30	2	4	4½	2	5	0	2	6	3	2	7	6	2	8	9
40	2	19	2	3	0	0	3	1	8	3	3	4	3	5	0
50	3	13	11½	3	15	0	3	17	1	3	19	2	4	1	3
[56]	4	2	10	4	4	0	4	6	4	4	8	8	4	11	0
60	4	8	9	4	10	0	4	12	6	4	15	0	4	17	6
70	5	3	6½	5	5	0	5	7	11	5	10	10	5	13	9
80	5	18	4	6	0	0	6	3	4	6	6	8	6	10	0
[84]	6	4	3	6	6	0	6	9	6	6	13	0	6	16	6
90	6	13	1½	6	15	0	6	18	9	7	2	6	7	6	3
100	7	7	11	7	10	0	7	14	2	7	18	4	8	2	6
[112]	8	5	8	8	8	0	8	12	8	8	17	4	9	2	0
200	14	15	10	15	0	0	15	8	4	15	16	8	16	5	0
300	22	3	9	22	10	0	23	2	6	23	15	0	24	7	6
[364]	26	19	10¾	27	7	6	28	2	8½	28	17	11	29	13	1½
400	29	11	8	30	0	0	30	16	8	31	13	4	32	10	0
500	36	19	7	37	10	0	38	10	10	39	11	8	40	12	6
600	44	7	6	45	0	0	46	5	0	47	10	0	48	15	0
700	51	15	5	52	10	0	53	19	2	55	8	4	56	17	6
800	59	3	4	60	0	0	61	13	4	63	6	8	65	0	0
900	66	11	3	67	10	0	69	7	6	71	5	0	73	2	6
1000	73	19	2	75	0	0	77	1	8	79	3	4	81	5	0
2000	147	18	4	150	0	0	154	3	4	158	6	8	162	10	0
3000	221	17	6	225	0	0	231	5	0	237	10	0	243	15	0
4000	295	16	8	300	0	0	308	6	8	316	13	4	325	0	0
5000	369	15	10	375	0	0	385	8	4	395	16	8	406	5	0
6000	443	15	0	450	0	0	462	10	0	475	0	0	487	10	0
7000	517	14	2	525	0	0	539	11	8	554	3	4	568	15	0
8000	591	13	4	600	0	0	616	13	4	633	6	8	650	0	0
9000	665	12	6	675	0	0	693	15	0	712	10	0	731	5	0
10000	739	11	8	750	0	0	770	16	8	791	13	4	812	10	0

	20 Pence.			20½ Pence.			21 Pence.			21½ Pence.			22 Pence.		
Value	£.	s.	d.	£.	s.	d. f.	£.	s.	d.	£.	s.	d. f.	£.	s.	d.
of 2	0	3	4	0	3	5	0	3	6	0	3	7	0	3	8
3	—	5	0	—	5	1½	—	5	3	—	5	4½	—	5	6
4	—	6	8	—	6	10	—	7	0	—	7	2	—	7	4
5	—	8	4	—	8	6½	—	8	9	—	8	11½	—	9	2
6	—	10	0	—	10	3	—	10	6	—	10	9	—	11	0
7	—	11	8	—	11	11½	—	12	3	—	12	6½	—	12	10
8	—	13	4	—	13	8	—	14	0	—	14	4	—	14	8
9	—	15	0	—	15	4½	—	15	9	—	16	1½	—	16	6
10	—	16	8	—	17	1	—	17	6	—	17	11	—	18	4
11	—	18	4	—	18	9½	—	19	3	—	19	8½	1	0	2
12	1	0	0	1	0	6	1	1	0	1	1	6	1	2	0
13	1	1	8	1	2	2½	1	2	9	1	3	3½	1	3	10
14	1	3	4	1	3	11	1	4	6	1	5	1	1	5	8
15	1	5	0	1	5	7½	1	6	3	1	6	10½	1	7	6
16	1	6	8	1	7	4	1	8	0	1	8	8	1	9	4
17	1	8	4	1	9	0½	1	9	9	1	10	5½	1	11	2
18	1	10	0	1	10	9	1	11	6	1	12	3	1	13	0
19	1	11	8	1	12	5½	1	13	3	1	14	0½	1	14	10
20	1	13	4	1	14	2	1	15	0	1	15	10	1	16	8
[28]	2	6	8	2	7	10	2	9	0	2	10	2	2	11	4
30	2	10	0	2	11	3	2	12	6	2	13	9	2	15	0
40	3	6	8	3	8	4	3	10	0	3	11	8	3	13	4
50	4	3	4	4	5	5	4	7	6	4	9	7	4	11	8
[56]	4	13	4	4	15	8	4	18	0	5	0	4	5	2	8
60	5	0	0	5	2	6	5	5	0	5	7	6	5	10	0
70	5	16	8	5	19	7	6	2	6	6	5	5	6	8	4
80	6	13	4	6	16	8	7	0	0	7	3	4	7	6	8
[84]	7	0	0	7	3	6	7	7	0	7	10	6	7	14	0
90	7	10	0	7	13	9	7	17	6	8	1	3	8	5	0
100	8	6	8	8	10	10	8	15	—	8	19	2	9	3	4
[112]	9	6	8	9	11	4	9	16	—	10	0	8	10	5	4
200	16	13	4	17	1	8	17	10	—	17	18	4	18	6	8
300	25	0	0	25	12	6	26	5	—	26	17	6	27	10	0
[365]	30	8	4	31	3	6½	31	18	9	32	13	11½	33	9	2
400	33	6	8	34	3	4	35	0	—	35	16	8	36	13	4
500	41	13	4	42	14	2	43	15	—	44	15	10	45	16	8
600	50	0	0	51	5	0	52	10	—	53	15	0	55	0	0
700	58	6	8	59	15	10	61	5	—	62	14	2	64	3	4
800	66	13	4	68	6	8	70	0	—	71	13	4	73	6	8
900	75	0	0	76	17	6	78	15	—	80	12	6	82	10	0
1000	83	6	8	85	8	4	87	10	—	89	11	8	91	13	4
2000	166	13	4	170	16	8	175	0	—	179	3	4	183	6	8
3000	250	0	0	256	5	0	262	10	—	268	15	0	275	0	0
4000	333	6	8	341	13	4	350	0	—	358	6	8	366	13	4
5000	416	13	4	427	1	8	437	10	—	447	18	4	458	6	8
6000	500	0	0	512	10	0	525	0	—	537	10	0	550	0	0
7000	583	6	8	597	18	4	612	10	—	627	1	8	641	13	4
8000	666	13	4	683	6	8	700	0	—	716	13	4	733	6	8
9000	750	0	0	768	15	0	787	10	—	805	5	0	825	0	0
10000	833	6	8	854	3	4	895	0	—	895	16	8	916	13	4

	22½ Pence.			23 Pence.			23½ Pence.			2 Shillings			2s. 1d.		
Value of	£.	s.	d.f.	£.	s.	d	£.	s.	d.f.	£.	s.	d.	L.	s.	d.
2	0	3	9	0	3	10	0	3	11	0	4	0	0	4	2
3	—	5	7½	—	5	9	—	5	10½	—	6	0	—	6	3
4	—	7	6	—	7	8	—	7	10	—	8	0	—	8	4
5	—	9	4½	—	9	7	—	9	9½	—	10	0	—	10	5
6	—	11	3	—	11	6	—	11	9	—	12	0	—	12	6
7	—	13	1½	—	13	5	—	13	8½	—	14	0	—	14	7
8	—	15	0	—	15	4	—	15	8	—	16	0	—	16	8
9	—	16	10½	—	17	3	—	17	7½	—	18	0	—	18	9
10	—	18	9	—	19	2	—	19	7	1	0	0	1	0	10
11	1	0	7½	1	1	1	1	1	6½	1	2	0	1	2	11
12	1	2	6	1	3	0	1	3	6	1	4	0	1	5	0
13	1	4	4½	1	4	11	1	5	5½	1	6	0	1	7	1
14	1	6	3	1	6	10	1	7	5	1	8	0	1	9	2
15	1	8	1½	1	8	9	1	9	4½	1	10	0	1	11	3
16	1	10	0	1	10	8	1	11	4	1	12	0	1	13	4
17	1	11	10½	1	12	7	1	13	3½	1	14	0	1	15	5
18	1	13	9	1	14	6	1	15	3	1	16	0	1	17	6
19	1	15	7½	1	16	5	1	17	2½	1	18	0	1	19	7
20	1	17	6	1	18	4	1	19	2	2	0	0	2	1	8
[28]	2	12	6	2	13	8	2	14	10	2	16	0	2	18	4
30	2	16	3	2	17	6	2	18	9	3	0	0	3	2	6
40	3	15	0	3	16	8	3	18	4	4	0	0	4	3	4
50	4	13	9	4	15	10	4	17	11	5	0	0	5	4	2
[56]	5	5	0	5	7	4	5	9	8	5	12	0	5	16	8
60	5	12	6	5	15	0	5	17	6	6	0	0	6	5	0
70	6	11	3	6	14	2	6	17	1	7	0	0	7	5	10
80	7	10	0	7	13	4	7	16	8	8	0	0	8	6	8
[84]	7	17	6	8	1	0	8	4	6	8	8	0	8	15	0
90	8	8	9	8	12	6	8	16	3	9	0	0	9	7	6
100	9	7	6	6	11	8	9	15	10	10	0	0	10	8	4
[112]	10	10	0	10	14	8	10	19	4	11	0	0	11	13	4
200	18	15	0	19	3	4	19	11	8	20	0	0	20	16	8
300	28	2	6	28	15	0	29	7	6	30	0	0	31	5	0
[365]	34	4	4½	34	19	7	35	14	9½	36	10	0	38	0	5
400	37	10	0	38	6	8	39	3	4	40	0	0	41	13	4
500	46	17	6	47	18	4	48	19	2	50	0	0	52	1	8
600	56	5	0	57	10	0	58	15	0	60	0	0	62	10	0
700	65	12	6	67	1	8	68	10	10	70	0	0	72	18	4
800	75	0	0	76	13	4	78	6	8	80	0	0	83	6	8
900	84	7	6	86	5	0	88	2	6	90	0	0	93	15	0
1000	93	15	0	95	16	8	97	18	4	100	0	0	104	3	4
2000	187	10	0	191	13	4	195	16	8	200	0	0	208	6	8
3000	281	5	0	287	10	0	293	15	0	300	0	0	312	10	0
4000	375	0	0	383	6	8	391	13	4	400	0	0	416	13	4
5000	468	15	0	479	3	4	489	11	8	500	0	0	520	16	8
6000	562	10	0	575	0	0	587	10	0	600	0	0	625	0	0
7000	656	5	0	670	16	8	685	8	4	700	0	0	729	3	4
8000	750	0	0	766	13	4	783	6	8	800	0	0	833	6	8
9000	843	15	0	862	10	0	881	5	0	900	0	0	937	10	0
10000	937	10	0	958	6	8	979	3	4	1000	0	0	1041	13	4

	2s. 2d.			2s. 3d.			2s. 4d.			2s. 5d.			2s. 6d.		
Value	L.	s.	d.	L.	s.	d.	L.	s.	d.	L.	s.	d.	£.	s.	d.
of 2	0	4	4	0	4	6	0	4	8	0	4	10	0	5	0
3	——	6	6	——	6	9	——	7	0	——	7	3	——	7	6
4	——	8	8	——	9	0	——	9	4	——	9	8	——	10	0
5	——	10	10	——	11	3	——	11	8	——	12	1	——	12	6
6	——	13	0	——	13	6	——	14	0	——	14	6	——	15	0
7	——	15	2	——	15	9	——	16	4	——	16	11	——	17	6
8	——	17	4	——	18	0	——	18	8	——	19	4	1	0	0
9	——	19	6	1	0	3	1	1	0	1	1	9	1	2	6
10	1	1	8	1	2	6	1	3	4	1	4	2	1	5	0
11	1	3	10	1	4	9	1	5	8	1	6	7	1	7	6
12	1	6	0	1	7	0	1	8	0	1	9	0	1	10	0
13	1	8	2	1	9	3	1	10	4	1	11	5	1	12	6
14	1	10	4	1	11	6	1	12	8	1	13	10	1	15	0
15	1	12	6	1	13	9	1	15	0	1	16	3	1	17	6
16	1	14	8	1	16	0	1	17	4	1	18	8	2	0	0
17	1	16	10	1	18	3	1	19	8	2	1	1	2	2	6
18	1	19	0	2	0	6	2	2	0	2	3	6	2	5	0
19	2	1	2	2	2	9	2	4	4	2	5	11	2	7	6
20	2	3	4	2	5	0	2	6	8	2	8	4	2	10	0
[28]	3	0	8	3	3	0	3	5	4	3	7	8	3	10	0
30	3	5	0	3	7	6	3	10	0	3	12	6	3	15	0
40	4	6	8	4	10	0	4	13	4	4	16	8	5	0	0
50	5	8	4	5	12	6	5	16	8	6	0	10	6	5	0
[56]	6	1	4	6	6	0	6	10	8	6	15	4	7	0	0
60	6	10	0	6	15	0	7	0	0	7	5	0	7	10	0
70	7	11	8	7	17	6	8	3	4	8	9	2	8	15	0
80	8	13	4	9	0	0	9	6	8	9	13	4	10	0	0
[84]	9	2	0	9	9	0	9	16	0	10	3	0	10	10	0
90	9	15	0	10	2	6	10	10	0	10	17	6	11	5	0
100	10	16	8	11	5	0	11	13	4	12	1	8	12	10	0
[112]	12	2	8	12	12	0	13	1	4	13	10	8	14	0	0
200	21	13	4	22	10	0	23	6	8	24	3	4	25	0	0
300	32	10	0	33	15	0	35	0	0	36	5	0	37	10	0
[365]	39	10	10	41	1	3	42	11	8	44	2	1	45	12	6
400	43	6	8	45	0	0	46	13	4	48	6	8	50	0	0
500	54	3	4	56	5	0	58	6	8	60	8	4	62	10	0
600	65	0	0	67	10	0	70	0	0	72	10	0	75	0	0
700	75	16	8	78	15	0	81	13	4	84	11	8	87	10	0
800	86	13	4	90	0	0	93	6	8	96	13	4	100	0	0
900	97	10	0	101	5	0	105	0	0	108	15	0	112	10	0
1000	108	6	8	112	10	0	116	13	4	120	16	8	125	0	0
2000	216	13	4	225	0	0	233	6	8	241	13	4	250	0	0
3000	325	0	0	337	10	0	350	0	0	362	10	0	375	0	0
4000	433	6	8	450	0	0	466	13	4	483	6	8	500	0	0
5000	541	13	4	562	10	0	583	6	8	604	3	4	625	0	0
6000	650	0	0	675	0	0	700	0	0	725	0	0	750	0	0
7000	758	6	8	787	10	0	816	13	4	845	16	8	875	0	0
8000	866	13	4	900	0	0	933	6	8	966	13	4	1000	0	0
9000	975	0	0	1012	10	0	1050	0	0	1087	10	0	1125	0	0
10000	1083	6	8	1125	0	0	1166	13	4	1208	6	8	1250	0	0

	2s. 8 Pence			2s. 9 Pence			3 Shillings.			3s. 3 Pence			3s. 4 Pence		
Value	L.	s.	d.	L.	s.	d.	L.	s.	d.	L.	s.	d.	L.	s.	d.
of 2	0	5	4	0	5	6	0	6	0	0	6	6	0	6	8
3	—	8	0	—	8	3	—	9	—	—	9	9	—	10	0
4	—	10	8	—	11	0	—	12	—	—	13	0	—	13	4
5	—	13	4	—	13	9	—	15	—	—	16	3	—	16	8
6	—	16	0	—	16	6	—	18	—	—	19	6	1	0	0
7	—	18	8	—	19	3	1	1	—	1	2	9	1	3	4
8	1	1	4	1	2	0	1	4	—	1	6	0	1	6	8
9	1	4	0	1	4	9	1	7	—	1	9	3	1	10	0
10	1	6	8	1	7	6	1	10	—	1	12	6	1	13	4
11	1	9	4	1	10	3	1	13	—	1	15	9	1	16	8
12	1	12	0	1	13	0	1	16	—	1	19	0	2	0	0
13	1	14	8	1	15	9	1	19	—	2	2	3	2	3	4
14	1	17	4	1	18	6	2	2	—	2	5	6	2	6	8
15	2	0	0	2	1	3	2	5	—	2	8	9	2	10	0
16	2	2	8	2	4	0	2	8	—	2	12	0	2	13	4
17	2	5	4	2	6	9	2	11	—	2	15	3	2	16	8
18	2	8	0	2	9	6	2	14	—	2	18	6	3	0	0
19	2	10	8	2	12	3	2	17	—	3	1	9	3	3	4
20	2	13	4	2	15	0	3	0	—	3	5	0	3	6	8
[28]	3	14	8	3	17	0	4	4	—	4	11	0	4	13	4
30	4	0	0	4	2	6	4	10	—	4	17	6	5	0	0
40	5	6	8	5	10	0	6	0	—	6	10	0	6	13	4
50	6	13	4	6	17	6	7	10	—	8	2	6	8	6	8
[56]	7	9	4	7	14	0	8	8	—	9	2	0	9	6	8
60	8	0	0	8	5	0	9	0	—	9	15	0	10	0	0
70	9	6	8	9	12	6	10	10	—	11	7	6	11	13	4
80	10	13	4	11	0	0	12	0	—	13	0	0	13	6	8
[84]	11	4	0	11	11	0	12	12	—	13	13	0	14	0	0
90	12	0	0	12	7	6	13	10	—	14	12	6	15	0	0
100	13	6	8	13	15	0	15	0	—	16	5	0	16	13	4
[112]	14	18	8	15	8	0	16	16	—	18	4	0	18	13	4
200	26	13	4	27	10	0	30	0	—	32	10	0	33	6	8
300	40	0	0	41	5	0	45	0	—	48	15	0	50	0	0
[365]	48	13	4	50	3	9	54	15	—	59	6	3	60	16	8
400	53	6	8	55	0	0	60	—	—	65	0	—	66	13	4
500	66	13	4	68	15	0	75	—	—	81	5	—	83	6	8
600	80	0	0	82	10	0	90	—	—	97	10	—	100	0	0
700	93	6	8	96	5	0	105	—	—	113	15	—	116	13	4
800	106	13	4	110	0	0	120	—	—	130	0	—	133	6	8
900	120	0	0	123	15	0	135	—	—	146	5	—	150	0	0
1000	133	6	8	137	10	0	150	—	—	162	10	—	166	13	4
2000	266	13	4	275	0	0	300	—	—	325	0	—	333	6	8
3000	400	0	0	412	10	0	450	—	—	487	10	—	500	0	0
4000	533	6	8	550	0	0	600	—	—	650	0	—	666	13	4
5000	666	13	4	687	10	0	750	—	—	812	10	—	833	6	8
6000	800	0	0	825	0	0	900	—	—	975	0	—	1000	0	0
7000	933	6	8	962	10	0	1050	—	—	1137	10	—	1166	13	4
8000	1066	13	4	1100	0	0	1200	—	—	1300	0	—	1333	6	8
9000	1200	0	0	1237	10	0	1350	—	—	1462	10	—	1500	0	0
10000	1333	6	8	1375	0	0	1500	—	—	1625	0	—	1666	13	4

	3s. 6 Pence			3s. 8 Pence			3s. 9 Pence			4 Shillings.			4s. 3 Pence		
Value	L.	s.	d.	L.	s.	d.	L.	s.	d.	L.	s.	d.	L.	s.	d.
of 2	0	7	0	0	7	4	0	7	6	0	8	0	0	8	6
3	—	10	6	—	11	0	—	11	3	—	12	-	—	12	9
4	—	14	0	—	14	8	—	15	0	—	16	-	—	17	0
5	—	17	6	—	18	4	—	18	9	1	0	-	1	1	3
6	1	1	0	1	2	0	1	2	6	1	4	-	1	5	6
7	1	4	6	1	5	8	1	6	3	1	8	-	1	9	9
8	1	8	0	1	9	4	1	10	0	1	12	-	1	14	0
9	1	11	6	1	13	0	1	13	9	1	16	-	1	18	3
10	1	15	0	1	16	8	1	17	6	2	0	-	2	2	6
11	1	18	6	2	0	4	2	1	3	2	4	-	2	6	9
12	2	2	0	2	4	0	2	5	0	2	8	-	2	11	0
13	2	5	6	2	7	8	2	8	9	2	12	-	2	15	3
14	2	9	0	2	11	4	2	12	6	2	16	-	2	19	6
15	2	12	6	2	15	0	2	16	3	3	0	-	3	3	9
16	2	16	0	2	18	8	3	0	0	3	4	-	3	8	0
17	2	19	6	3	2	4	3	3	9	3	8	-	3	12	3
18	3	3	0	3	6	0	3	7	6	3	12	-	3	16	6
19	3	6	6	3	9	8	3	11	3	3	16	-	4	0	9
20	3	10	0	3	13	4	3	15	0	4	0	-	4	5	0
[28]	4	18	-	5	2	8	5	5	0	5	12	-	5	19	0
30	5	5	-	5	10	0	5	12	6	6	0	-	6	7	6
40	7	0	-	7	6	8	7	10	0	8	0	-	8	10	0
50	8	15	-	9	3	4	9	7	6	10	0	-	10	12	6
[56]	9	16	-	10	5	4	10	10	0	11	4	-	11	18	0
60	10	10	-	11	0	0	11	5	0	12	-	-	12	15	0
70	12	5	-	12	16	8	13	2	6	14	-	-	14	17	6
80	14	0	-	14	13	4	15	0	0	16	-	-	17	0	0
[84]	14	14	-	15	8	0	15	15	0	16	16	-	17	17	0
90	15	15	-	16	10	0	16	17	6	18	-	-	19	2	6
100	17	10	-	18	6	8	18	15	0	20	-	-	21	5	0
[112]	19	12	-	20	10	8	21	0	0	22	8	-	23	16	0
200	35	0	-	36	13	4	37	10	0	40	-	-	42	10	0
300	52	10	-	55	0	0	56	5	0	60	-	-	63	15	0
[365]	63	17	6	66	18	4	68	8	9	75	-	-	77	11	3
400	70	0	-	73	6	8	75	0	-	80	-	-	85	0	0
500	87	10	-	91	13	4	93	15	-	100	-	-	106	5	-
600	105	0	-	110	0	0	112	10	-	120	-	-	127	10	-
700	122	10	-	128	6	8	131	5	-	140	-	-	148	15	-
800	140	0	-	146	13	4	150	0	-	160	-	-	170	0	-
900	157	10	-	165	0	0	168	15	-	180	-	-	191	5	-
1000	175	-	-	183	6	8	187	10	-	200	-	-	212	10	-
2000	350	-	-	366	13	4	375	0	-	400	-	-	425	0	-
3000	525	-	-	550	0	0	562	10	-	600	-	-	637	10	-
4000	700	-	-	733	6	8	750	0	-	800	-	-	850	0	-
5000	875	-	-	916	13	4	397	10	-	1000	-	-	1062	10	-
6000	1050	-	-	1100	0	0	1125	0	-	1200	-	-	1275	0	-
7000	1225	-	-	1283	6	8	1312	10	-	1400	-	-	1487	10	-
8000	1400	-	-	1466	13	4	1500	0	-	1600	-	-	1699	0	-
9000	1575	-	-	1650	0	0	1687	10	-	1800	-	-	1911	10	-
10000	1750	-	-	1833	6	8	1875	0	-	2000	-	-	2124	0	-

Value of	4s. 4d. £.	s.	d.	4s. 6d. £.	s.	d.	4s. 8d. £.	s.	d.	4s. 9d. £.	s.	d.	5s. £.	s.	d.
2	0	8	8	0	9	0	0	9	4	0	9	6	0	10	0
3	—	13	0	—	13	6	—	14	0	—	14	3	—	15	0
4	—	17	4	—	18	0	—	18	8	—	19	0	1	0	0
5	1	1	8	1	2	6	1	3	4	1	3	9	1	5	0
6	1	6	0	1	7	0	1	8	0	1	8	6	1	10	0
7	1	10	4	1	11	6	1	12	8	1	13	3	1	15	0
8	1	14	8	1	16	0	1	17	4	1	18	0	2	0	0
9	1	19	0	2	0	6	2	2	0	2	2	9	2	5	0
10	2	3	4	2	5	0	2	6	8	2	7	6	2	10	0
11	2	7	8	2	9	6	2	11	4	2	12	3	2	15	0
12	2	12	0	2	14	0	2	16	0	2	17	0	3	0	0
13	2	16	4	2	18	6	3	0	8	3	1	9	3	5	0
14	3	0	8	3	3	0	3	5	4	3	6	6	3	10	0
15	3	5	0	3	7	6	3	10	0	3	11	3	3	15	0
16	3	9	4	3	12	0	3	14	8	3	16	0	4	0	0
17	3	13	8	3	16	6	3	19	4	4	0	9	4	5	0
18	3	18	0	4	1	0	4	4	0	4	5	6	4	10	0
19	4	2	4	4	5	6	4	8	8	4	10	3	4	15	0
20	4	6	8	4	10	0	4	13	4	4	15	0	5	0	0
[28]	6	1	4	6	6	0	6	10	8	6	13	0	7	0	0
30	6	10	0	6	15	0	7	0	0	7	2	6	7	10	0
40	8	13	4	9	0	0	9	6	8	9	10	0	10	0	0
50	10	16	8	11	5	0	11	13	4	11	17	6	12	10	0
[56]	12	2	8	12	12	0	13	1	4	13	6	0	14	0	0
60	13	0	0	13	10	0	14	0	0	14	5	0	15	0	0
70	15	3	4	15	15	0	16	6	8	16	12	6	17	10	0
80	17	6	8	18	0	0	18	13	4	19	0	0	20	0	0
[84]	18	4	0	18	18	0	19	12	0	19	19	0	21	0	0
90	19	10	0	20	5	0	21	0	0	21	7	6	22	10	0
100	21	13	4	22	10	0	23	6	8	23	15	0	25	0	0
[112]	24	5	4	25	4	0	26	2	8	26	12	0	28	0	0
200	43	6	8	45	0	0	46	13	4	47	10	0	50	0	0
300	65	0	0	67	10	0	70	0	0	71	5	0	75	0	0
[365]	79	1	8	82	2	6	85	3	4	86	13	9	91	5	0
400	86	13	4	90	0	0	93	6	8	95	0	0	100	0	0
500	108	6	8	112	10	0	116	13	4	118	15	0	125	0	0
600	130	0	0	135	0	0	140	0	0	142	10	0	150	0	0
700	151	13	4	157	10	0	163	6	8	166	5	0	175	0	0
800	173	6	8	180	0	0	186	13	4	190	0	0	200	0	0
900	195	0	0	202	10	0	210	0	0	213	15	0	225	0	0
1000	216	13	4	225	0	0	233	6	8	237	10	0	250	0	0
2000	433	6	8	450	0	0	466	13	4	475	0	0	500	0	0
3000	650	0	0	675	0	0	700	0	0	712	10	0	750	0	0
4000	866	13	4	900	0	0	933	6	8	950	0	0	1000	0	0
5000	1083	6	8	1125	0	0	1166	13	4	1187	10	0	1250	0	0
6000	1300	0	0	1350	0	0	1400	0	0	1425	0	0	1500	0	0
7000	1516	13	4	1575	0	0	1633	6	8	1662	10	0	1750	0	0
8000	1733	6	8	1800	0	0	1866	13	4	1900	0	0	2000	0	0
9000	1950	0	0	2025	0	0	2100	0	0	2137	10	0	2250	0	0
10000	2166	13	4	2250	0	0	2333	6	8	2375	0	0	2500	0	0

	5s. 3d.			5s. 4d.			5s. 6d.			5s. 8d.			5s. 9d.		
Value	L.	s.	d.	L.	s.	d.	L.	s.	d.	L.	s.	d.	L.	s.	d.
of 2	0	10	6	0	10	8	0	11	0	0	11	4	0	11	6
3	—	15	9	—	16	0	—	16	6	—	17	0	—	17	3
4	1	1	0	1	1	4	1	2	0	1	2	8	1	3	0
5	1	6	3	1	6	8	1	7	6	1	8	4	1	8	9
6	1	11	6	1	12	0	1	13	0	1	14	0	1	14	6
7	1	16	9	1	17	4	1	18	6	1	19	8	2	0	3
8	2	2	0	2	2	8	2	4	0	2	5	4	2	6	0
9	2	7	3	2	8	0	2	9	6	2	11	0	2	11	9
10	2	12	6	2	13	4	2	15	0	2	16	8	2	17	6
11	2	17	9	2	18	8	3	0	6	3	2	4	3	3	3
12	3	3	0	3	4	0	3	6	0	3	8	0	3	9	0
13	3	8	3	3	9	4	3	11	6	3	13	8	3	14	9
14	3	13	6	3	14	8	3	17	0	3	19	4	4	0	6
15	3	18	9	4	0	0	4	2	6	4	5	0	4	6	3
16	4	4	0	4	5	4	4	8	0	4	10	8	4	12	0
17	4	9	3	4	10	8	4	13	6	4	16	4	4	17	9
18	4	14	6	4	16	0	4	19	0	5	2	0	5	3	6
19	4	19	9	5	1	4	5	4	6	5	7	8	5	9	3
20	5	5	0	5	6	8	5	10	0	5	13	4	5	15	0
[28]	7	7	0	7	9	4	7	14	0	7	18	8	8	1	0
30	7	17	6	8	0	0	8	5	0	8	10	0	8	12	6
40	10	10	0	10	13	4	11	0	0	11	6	8	11	10	0
50	13	2	6	13	6	8	13	15	0	14	3	4	14	7	6
[56]	14	14	0	14	18	8	15	8	0	15	17	4	16	2	0
60	15	15	0	16	0	0	16	10	0	17	0	0	17	5	0
70	18	7	6	18	13	4	19	5	0	19	16	8	20	2	6
80	21	0	0	21	6	8	22	0	0	22	13	4	23	0	0
[84]	22	1	0	22	8	0	23	2	0	23	16	0	24	3	0
90	23	12	6	24	0	0	24	15	0	25	10	0	25	17	6
100	26	5	0	26	13	4	27	10	0	28	6	8	28	15	0
[112]	29	8	0	29	17	4	30	16	0	31	14	8	32	4	0
200	52	10	0	53	6	8	55	0	0	56	13	4	57	10	0
300	78	15	0	80	0	0	82	10	0	85	0	0	86	5	0
[365]	95	16	3	97	6	8	100	7	6	103	8	4	104	18	9
400	105	0	0	106	13	4	110	0	0	113	6	8	115	0	0
500	131	5	0	133	6	8	137	10	0	141	13	4	143	15	0
600	157	10	0	160	0	0	165	0	0	170	0	0	172	10	0
700	183	15	0	186	13	4	192	10	0	198	6	8	201	5	0
800	210	0	0	213	6	8	220	0	0	220	13	4	230	0	0
900	236	5	0	240	0	0	247	10	0	255	0	0	258	15	0
1000	262	10	0	166	13	4	275	0	0	283	6	8	287	10	0
2000	525	0	0	533	6	8	550	0	0	566	13	4	575	0	0
3000	787	10	0	800	0	0	825	0	0	850	0	0	862	10	0
4000	1050	0	0	1066	13	4	1100	0	0	1133	6	8	1150		0
5000	1312	10	0	1333	6	8	1375	0	0	1416	13	4	1437	10	0
6000	1575	0	0	1600	0	0	1650	0	0	1700	0	0	1725	0	0
7000	1837	10	0	1866	13	4	1925	0	0	1983	6	8	2012	10	0
8000	2100	0	0	2133	6	8	2200	0	0	2266	13	4	2300	0	0
9000	2362	10	0	2400	0	0	2475	0	0	2550	0	0	2587	10	0
10000	2625	0		2666	13	4	2750	0	0	2833	0	0	2875	0	0

	6 Shillings.			6s. 3 Pence.			6s. 4 Pence.			6s. 6 Pence.			6s. 8 Pence.		
Value	£.	s.	d.	£.	s.	d.	£.	s.	d.	£.	s.	d.	£.	s.	d.
of 2	0	12	0	0	12	6	0	12	8	0	13	0	0	13	4
3	—	18	–	—	18	9	—	19	0	—	19	6	1	0	0
4	1	4	–	1	5	0	1	5	4	1	6	0	1	6	8
5	1	10	–	1	11	3	1	11	8	1	12	6	1	13	4
6	1	16	–	1	17	6	1	18	0	1	19	0	2	0	0
7	2	2	–	2	3	9	2	4	4	2	5	6	2	6	8
8	2	8	–	2	10	0	2	10	8	2	12	0	2	13	4
9	2	14	–	2	16	3	2	17	0	2	18	6	3	0	0
10	3	0	–	3	2	6	3	3	4	3	5	0	3	6	8
11	3	6	–	3	8	9	3	9	8	3	11	6	3	13	4
12	3	12	–	3	15	0	3	16	0	3	18	0	4	0	0
13	3	18	–	4	1	3	4	2	4	4	4	6	4	6	8
14	4	4	–	4	7	6	4	8	8	4	11	0	4	13	4
15	4	10	–	4	13	9	4	15	0	4	17	6	5	0	0
16	4	16	–	5	0	0	5	1	4	5	4	0	5	6	8
17	5	2	–	5	6	3	5	7	8	5	10	6	5	13	4
18	5	8	–	5	12	6	5	14	0	5	17	0	6	0	0
19	5	14	–	5	18	9	6	0	4	6	3	6	6	6	8
20	6	0	–	6	5	0	6	6	8	6	10	0	6	13	4
[28]	8	8	–	8	15	0	8	17	4	9	2	–	9	6	8
30	9	0	–	9	7	6	9	10	0	9	15	–	10	0	0
40	12	0	–	12	10	0	12	13	4	13	0	–	13	6	8
50	15	0	–	15	12	6	15	16	8	16	5	–	16	13	4
[56]	16	16	–	17	10	0	17	14	8	18	4	–	18	13	4
60	18	–	–	18	15	0	19	0	0	19	10	–	20	0	0
70	21	–	–	21	17	6	22	3	4	22	15	–	23	6	8
80	24	–	–	25	0	0	25	6	8	26	0	–	26	13	4
[84]	25	4	–	26	5	0	26	12	0	27	6	–	28	0	0
90	27	–	–	28	2	6	28	10	0	29	5	–	30	0	0
100	30	–	–	31	5	0	31	13	4	32	10	–	33	6	8
[112]	33	12	–	35	0	–	35	9	4	36	8	–	37	6	8
200	60	–	–	62	10	–	63	6	8	65	0	–	66	13	4
300	90	–	–	93	15	–	95	0	0	97	10	–	100	0	0
[365]	109	10	–	114	1	3	115	11	8	118	12	6	121	13	4
400	120	–	–	125	0	0	126	13	4	130	0	–	133	6	8
500	150	–	–	156	5	–	158	6	8	162	10	–	166	13	4
600	180	–	–	187	10	–	190	0	0	195	0	–	200	0	0
700	210	–	–	218	15	–	221	13	4	227	10	–	233	6	8
800	240	–	–	250	0	–	253	6	8	260	0	–	266	13	4
900	270	–	–	281	5	–	285	0	0	292	10	–	300	0	0
1000	300	–	–	312	10	–	316	13	4	325	–	–	333	6	8
2000	600	–	–	625	0	–	633	6	8	650	–	–	666	13	4
3000	900	–	–	937	10	–	950	0	0	975	–	–	1000	0	0
4000	1200	–	–	1250	0	–	1266	13	4	1300	–	–	1333	6	8
5000	1500	–	–	1562	10	–	1583	6	8	1625	–	–	1666	13	4
6000	1800	–	–	1875	0	–	1900	0	0	1950	–	–	2000	0	0
7000	2100	–	–	2187	10	–	2216	13	4	2275	–	–	2333	6	8
8000	2400	–	–	2500	0	–	2533	6	8	2600	–	–	2666	13	4
9000	2700	–	–	2812	10	–	2850	0	0	2925	–	–	3000	0	0
10000	3000	–	–	3125	0	–	3166	13	4	3250	–	–	3333	6	8

	6s. 9 Pence.			7 Shillings.			7s. 3 Pence.			7s. 4 Pence.			7s. 6 Pence		
Value	L.	s.	d.	L.	s.	d.	L.	s.	d.	L.	s.	d.	L.	s.	d.
of 2	0	13	6	0	14	—	0	14	6	0	14	8	0	15	0
3	1	0	3	1	1	—	1	1	9	1	2	0	1	2	6
4	1	7	0	1	8	—	1	9	0	1	9	4	1	10	0
5	1	13	0	1	15	—	1	16	3	1	16	8	1	17	6
6	2	0	6	2	2	—	2	3	6	2	4	0	2	5	0
7	2	7	3	2	9	—	2	10	9	2	11	4	2	12	6
8	2	14	0	2	16	—	2	18	0	2	18	8	3	0	0
9	3	0	9	3	3	—	3	5	3	3	6	0	3	7	6
10	3	7	6	3	10	—	3	12	6	3	13	4	3	15	0
11	3	14	3	3	17	—	3	19	9	4	0	8	4	2	6
12	4	1	0	4	4	—	4	7	0	4	8	0	4	10	0
13	4	7	9	4	11	—	4	14	3	4	15	4	4	17	6
14	4	14	6	4	18	—	5	1	6	5	2	8	5	5	0
15	5	1	3	5	5	—	5	8	9	5	10	0	5	12	6
16	5	8	0	5	12	—	5	16	0	5	17	4	6	0	0
17	5	14	0	5	19	—	6	3	3	6	4	8	6	7	6
18	6	1	6	6	6	—	6	10	6	6	12	0	6	15	0
19	6	8	3	6	13	—	6	17	9	6	19	4	7	2	6
20	6	15	0	7	0	—	7	5	0	7	6	8	7	10	—
[28]	9	9	0	9	16	—	10	3	0	10	5	4	10	10	—
30	10	2	6	10	10	—	10	17	6	11	0	0	11	5	—
40	13	10	0	14	0	—	14	10	0	14	13	4	15	0	—
50	16	17	6	17	10	—	18	2	6	18	6	8	18	15	—
[56]	18	18	0	19	12	—	20	6	0	20	10	8	21	0	—
60	20	5	0	21	0	—	21	15	0	22	0	0	22	10	—
70	23	12	6	24	10	—	25	7	6	25	13	4	26	5	—
80	27	0	0	28	0	—	29	0	0	29	6	8	30	0	—
[84]	28	7	0	29	8	—	30	9	0	30	16	0	31	10	—
90	30	7	6	31	10	—	32	12	6	33	0	0	33	15	—
100	33	15	0	35	0	—	36	5	0	36	13	4	37	10	—
[112]	37	16	0	39	4	—	40	12	0	41	1	4	42	0	—
200	67	10	0	70	0	—	72	10	0	73	6	8	75	0	—
300	101	5	0	105	0	—	108	15	0	110	0	0	112	10	—
[365]	123	3	9	127	15	—	132	6	3	133	16	8	136	17	6
400	135	0	—	140	0	—	145	0	—	146	13	4	150	0	—
500	168	15	—	175	0	—	181	5	—	183	6	8	187	10	—
600	202	10	—	210	—	—	217	10	—	220	0	0	225	0	—
700	236	5	—	245	—	—	253	15	—	256	13	4	262	10	—
800	270	0	—	280	—	—	290	0	—	293	6	8	300	0	—
900	303	15	—	315	—	—	326	5	—	330	0	0	337	10	—
1000	337	10	—	350	—	—	362	10	—	366	13	4	375	—	—
2000	675	0	—	700	—	—	725	0	—	733	6	8	750	—	—
3000	1012	10	—	1050	—	—	1087	10	—	1100	0	0	1125	—	—
4000	1350	0	—	1400	—	—	1450	0	—	1466	13	4	1500	—	—
5000	1687	10	—	1750	—	—	1812	10	—	1833	6	8	1875	—	—
6000	2025	0	—	2100	—	—	2175	0	—	2200	0	0	2250	—	—
7000	2362	10	—	2450	—	—	2537	10	—	2566	13	4	2625	—	—
8000	2700	0	—	2800	—	—	2900	0	—	2933	6	8	3000	—	—
9000	3037	10	—	3150	—	—	3262	10	—	3300	0	0	3375	—	—
10000	3375	0	—	3500	—	—	3625	0	—	3666	13	4	3750	—	—

	7s. 8d.			7s. 9d.			8s.			8s. 3d.			8s. 4d.		
Value	£.	s.	d.	£.	s.	d.	£.	s.	d.	£.	s.	d.	£.	s.	d.
of 2	0	15	4	0	15	6	0	16	—	0	16	6	0	16	8
3	1	3	0	1	3	3	1	4	—	1	4	9	1	5	0
4	1	10	8	1	11	0	1	12	—	1	13	0	1	13	4
5	1	18	4	1	18	9	2	0	—	2	1	3	2	1	8
6	2	6	0	2	6	6	2	8	—	2	9	6	2	10	0
7	2	13	8	2	14	3	2	16	—	2	17	9	2	18	4
8	3	1	4	3	2	0	3	4	—	3	6	0	3	6	8
9	3	9	0	3	9	9	3	12	—	3	14	3	3	15	0
10	3	16	8	3	17	6	4	0	—	4	2	6	4	3	4
11	4	4	4	4	5	3	4	8	—	4	10	9	4	11	8
12	4	12	0	4	13	0	4	16	—	4	19	0	5	0	0
13	4	19	8	5	0	9	5	4	—	5	7	3	5	8	4
14	5	7	4	5	8	6	5	12	—	5	15	6	5	16	8
15	5	15	0	5	16	3	6	0	—	6	3	9	6	5	0
16	6	2	8	6	4	0	6	8	—	6	12	0	6	13	4
17	6	10	4	6	11	9	6	16	—	7	0	3	7	1	8
18	6	18	0	6	19	6	7	4	—	7	8	6	7	10	0
19	7	5	8	7	7	3	7	12	—	7	16	9	7	18	4
20	7	13	4	7	15	0	8	0	—	8	5	0	8	6	8
[28]	10	14	8	10	17	0	11	4	—	11	11	0	11	13	4
30	11	10	0	11	12	6	12	0	—	12	7	6	12	10	0
40	15	6	8	15	10	0	16	0	—	16	10	0	16	13	4
50	19	2	4	19	7	6	20	0	—	20	12	6	20	16	8
[56]	21	9	4	21	14	0	22	8	—	23	2	0	23	6	8
60	23	0	0	23	5	0	24	0	—	24	15	0	25	0	0
70	26	16	8	27	2	6	38	0	—	28	17	6	29	3	4
80	30	13	4	31	0	0	32	0	—	33	0	0	33	6	8
[84]	32	4	0	32	11	0	33	12	—	34	13	0	35	0	0
90	34	10	0	34	17	6	30	0	—	37	2	6	37	10	0
100	38	6	8	38	15	0	40	0	—	41	5	0	41	13	4
[112]	42	18	8	43	8	0	44	16	—	46	4	0	46	13	4
200	76	13	4	77	10	0	80	—	—	82	10	0	83	6	8
300	115	0	0	116	5	0	120	—	—	123	15	0	125	0	0
[365]	139	18	4	141	8	9	146	—	—	150	11	3	152	1	8
400	153	6	8	155	0	—	160	—	—	165	0	—	166	13	4
500	191	13	4	193	15	—	200	—	—	206	5	—	208	6	8
600	230	0	0	232	10	—	240	—	—	247	10	—	250	0	0
700	268	6	8	271	5	—	280	—	—	288	15	—	291	13	4
800	306	13	4	310	0	—	320	—	—	330	0	—	333	6	8
900	345	0	0	348	15	—	360	—	—	371	5	—	375	0	0
1000	383	6	8	387	10	—	400	—	—	412	10	—	416	13	4
2000	766	13	4	775	0	—	800	—	—	825	0	—	833	6	8
3000	1150	0	0	1162	10	—	1200	—	—	1237	10	—	1250	0	0
4000	1533	6	8	1550	0	—	1600	—	—	1650	0	—	1666	13	4
5000	1916	13	4	1937	10	—	2000	—	—	2062	10	—	2083	6	8
6000	2300	0	0	2325	0	—	2400	—	—	2475	0	—	2500	0	0
7000	2683	6	8	2712	10	—	2800	—	—	2887	10	—	2916	13	4
8000	3066	13	4	3100	0	—	3200	—	—	3300	0	—	3333	6	8
900	3450	0	0	3487	10	—	3600	—	—	3712	10	—	3750	0	0
10000	3833	6	8	3875	0	—	4000	—	—	4125	0	—	4166	13	4

	8s. 6d.			8s. 8d.			8s. 9d.			8s. 10d.			9s.		
Value	£.	s.	d.	£.	s.	d.	£.	s.	d.	£.	s.	d.	£.	s.	d.
of 2	0	17	0	0	17	4	0	17	6	0	17	8	0	18	–
3	1	5	6	1	6	–	1	6	3	1	6	6	1	7	–
4	1	14	–	1	14	8	1	15	–	1	15	4	1	16	–
5	2	2	6	2	3	4	2	3	9	2	4	2	2	5	–
6	2	11	–	2	12	–	2	12	6	2	13	–	2	14	–
7	2	19	6	3	0	8	3	1	3	3	1	10	3	3	–
8	3	8	–	3	9	4	3	10	–	3	10	8	3	12	–
9	3	16	6	3	18	–	3	18	9	3	19	6	4	1	–
10	4	5	–	4	6	8	4	7	6	4	8	4	4	10	–
11	4	13	6	4	15	4	4	16	3	4	17	2	4	19	–
12	5	2	–	5	4	–	5	5	–	5	6	–	5	8	–
13	5	10	6	5	12	8	5	13	9	5	14	10	5	17	–
14	5	19	–	6	1	4	6	2	6	6	3	8	6	6	–
15	6	7	6	6	10	–	6	11	3	6	12	6	6	15	–
16	6	16	–	6	18	8	7	0	–	7	1	4	7	4	–
17	7	4	6	7	7	4	7	8	9	7	10	2	7	13	–
18	7	13	–	7	16	–	7	17	6	7	19	–	8	2	–
19	8	1	6	8	4	8	8	6	3	8	7	10	8	11	–
20	8	10	–	8	13	4	8	15	–	8	16	8	9	0	–
21	8	18	6	9	2	–	9	3	9	9	5	6	9	9	–
22	9	7	–	9	10	8	9	12	6	9	14	4	9	18	–
23	9	15	6	9	19	4	10	1	3	10	3	2	10	7	–
24	10	4	–	10	8	–	10	10	–	10	12	–	10	16	–
25	10	12	6	10	16	8	10	18	9	11	0	10	11	5	–
26	11	1	–	11	5	4	11	7	6	11	9	8	11	14	–
27	11	9	6	11	14	–	11	16	3	11	18	6	12	3	–
[28]	11	18	–	12	2	8	12	5	–	12	7	4	12	12	–
29	12	6	6	12	11	4	12	13	9	12	16	2	13	1	–
30	12	15	–	13	0	–	13	2	6	13	5	–	13	10	–
40	17	0	–	17	6	8	17	10	–	17	13	4	18	0	–
50	21	5	–	21	13	4	21	17	6	22	1	8	22	10	–
[56]	23	16	–	24	5	4	24	10	–	24	14	8	25	4	–
60	25	10	–	26	0	–	26	5	–	26	10	–	27	0	–
70	29	15	–	30	6	8	30	12	6	30	18	4	31	10	–
80	34	0	–	34	13	4	35	0	–	35	6	8	36	0	–
[84]	35	14	–	36	8	–	36	15	–	37	2	–	37	16	–
90	38	5	–	39	0	–	39	7	6	39	15	–	40	10	–
100	42	10	–	43	6	8	43	15	–	44	3	4	45	0	–
[112]	47	12	–	48	10	8	49	0	–	49	9	4	50	8	–
200	85	0	–	86	13	4	87	10	–	88	6	8	90	0	–
300	127	10	–	130	0	–	131	5	–	132	10	–	135	0	–
[365]	155	2	6	158	3	4	159	13	9	161	4	2	164	5	–
400	170	0	–	173	6	8	175	0	–	176	13	4	180	0	–
500	212	10	–	216	13	4	218	15	–	220	16	8	225	0	–
600	255	0	–	260	0	–	262	10	–	265	0	–	270	0	–
700	297	10	–	303	6	8	306	5	–	309	3	4	315	0	–
800	340	0	–	346	13	4	350	0	–	353	6	8	360	0	–
900	382	10	–	390	0	–	393	15	–	397	10	–	405	0	–
1000	425	0	–	433	6	8	437	10	–	441	13	4	450	0	–
2000	850	0	–	866	13	4	875	0	–	883	6	8	900	0	–

	9s. 3 Pence.			9s. 4 Pence.			9s. 6 Pence.			9s. 8 Pence.			9s. 9 Pence.		
Value of	£.	s.	d.	£.	s.	d.	£.	s.	d.	£.	s.	d.	£.	s.	d.
2	0	18	6	0	18	8	0	19	0	0	19	4	0	19	6
3	1	7	9	1	8	0	1	8	6	1	9	0	1	9	3
4	1	17	0	1	17	4	1	18	0	1	18	8	1	19	0
5	2	6	3	2	6	8	2	7	6	2	8	4	2	8	9
6	2	15	6	2	16	0	2	17	0	2	18	0	2	18	6
7	3	4	9	3	5	4	3	6	6	3	7	8	3	8	3
8	3	14	0	3	14	8	3	16	0	3	17	4	3	18	0
9	4	3	3	4	4	0	4	5	6	4	7	0	4	7	9
10	4	12	6	4	13	4	4	15	0	4	16	8	4	17	6
11	5	1	9	5	2	8	5	4	6	5	6	4	5	7	3
12	5	11	0	5	12	0	5	14	0	5	16	0	5	17	0
13	6	0	3	6	1	4	6	3	6	6	5	8	6	6	9
14	6	9	6	6	10	8	6	13	0	6	15	4	6	16	6
15	6	18	9	7	0	0	7	2	6	7	5	0	7	6	3
16	7	8	0	7	9	4	7	12	0	7	14	8	7	16	0
17	7	17	3	7	18	8	8	4	6	8	4	4	8	5	9
18	8	6	6	8	8	0	8	11	0	8	14	0	8	15	6
19	8	15	9	8	17	4	9	0	6	9	3	8	9	5	3
20	9	5	0	9	6	8	9	10	0	9	13	4	9	15	0
21	9	14	3	9	16	0	9	19	6	10	3	0	10	4	9
22	10	3	6	10	5	4	10	9	0	10	12	8	10	14	6
23	10	12	9	10	14	8	10	18	6	11	2	4	11	4	3
24	11	2	0	11	4	0	11	8	0	11	12	0	11	14	0
25	11	11	3	11	13	4	11	17	6	12	1	8	12	3	9
26	12	0	6	12	2	8	12	7	0	12	11	4	12	13	6
27	12	9	9	12	12	0	12	16	6	13	1	0	13	3	3
[28]	12	19	0	13	1	4	13	6	0	13	10	8	13	13	0
29	13	8	3	13	10	8	13	15	6	14	0	4	14	2	9
30	13	17	6	14	0	0	14	5	0	14	10	0	14	12	6
40	18	10	0	18	13	4	19	0	0	19	6	8	19	10	0
50	23	2	6	23	6	8	23	15	0	24	3	4	24	7	6
[56]	25	18	0	26	2	8	26	12	0	27	1	4	27	6	0
60	27	15	0	28	0	0	28	10	0	29	0	0	29	5	0
70	32	7	6	32	13	4	33	5	0	33	16	8	34	2	6
80	37	0	0	37	6	8	38	0	0	38	13	4	39	0	0
[84]	38	17	0	39	4	0	39	18	0	40	12	0	40	19	0
90	41	12	6	42	0	0	42	15	0	43	10	0	43	17	6
100	46	5	0	46	13	4	47	10	0	48	6	8	48	15	0
[112]	51	16	0	52	5	4	53	4	0	54	2	8	54	12	0
200	92	10	0	93	6	8	95	0	0	96	13	4	97	10	0
300	138	15	0	140	0	0	142	10	0	145	0	0	146	5	0
[365]	168	16	3	170	6	8	173	7	6	176	8	4	177	18	9
400	185	0	0	186	13	4	190	0	0	193	6	8	195	0	0
500	231	5	0	233	6	8	237	10	0	241	13	4	243	15	0
600	277	10	0	280	0	0	285	0	0	290	0	0	292	10	0
700	323	15	0	326	13	4	332	10	0	338	6	8	341	5	0
800	370	0	0	373	6	8	380	0	0	386	13	4	390	0	0
900	416	5	0	420	0	0	427	10	0	435	0	0	438	15	0
1000	462	10	0	466	13	4	475	0	0	483	6	8	487	10	0
2000	925	0	0	933	6	8	950	0	0	966	13	4	975	0	0

	10 Shillings			10s. 3 Pence			10s. 6 Pence			10s. 9 pence			11 Shillings.		
Value	L.	s.	d.	L.	s.	d.	L.	s.	d.	L.	s.	d.	L.	s.	d
of 2	1	0	0	1	0	6	1	1	0	1	1	6	1	2	—
3	1	10	—	1	10	9	1	11	6	1	12	3	1	13	—
4	2	—	—	2	1	0	2	2	0	2	3	0	2	4	—
5	2	10	—	2	11	3	2	12	6	2	13	9	2	15	—
6	3	—	—	3	1	6	3	3	0	3	4	6	3	6	—
7	3	10	—	3	11	9	3	13	6	3	15	3	3	17	—
8	4	—	—	4	2	0	4	4	0	4	6	0	4	8	—
9	4	10	—	4	12	3	4	14	6	4	16	9	4	19	—
10	5	—	—	5	2	6	5	5	0	5	7	6	5	10	—
11	5	10	—	5	12	9	5	15	6	5	18	3	6	1	—
12	6	—	—	6	3	0	6	6	0	6	9	0	6	12	—
13	6	10	—	6	13	3	6	16	6	6	19	9	7	3	—
14	7	—	—	7	3	6	7	7	0	7	10	6	7	14	—
15	7	10	—	7	13	9	7	17	6	8	1	3	8	5	—
16	8	—	—	8	4	0	8	8	0	8	12	0	8	16	—
17	8	10	—	8	14	3	8	18	6	9	2	9	9	7	—
18	9	—	—	9	4	6	9	9	0	9	13	6	9	18	—
19	9	10	—	9	14	9	9	19	6	10	4	3	10	9	—
20	10	—	—	10	5	0	10	10	0	10	15	0	11	—	—
21	10	10	—	10	15	3	11	0	6	11	5	9	11	11	—
22	11	—	—	11	5	6	11	11	0	11	16	6	12	2	—
23	11	10	—	11	15	0	12	1	6	12	7	3	12	13	—
24	12	—	—	12	6	0	12	12	0	12	18	0	13	4	—
25	12	10	—	12	16	3	13	2	6	13	8	9	13	15	—
26	13	—	—	13	6	6	13	13	0	13	19	6	14	6	—
27	13	10	—	13	16	9	14	3	6	14	10	3	14	17	—
[28]	14	—	—	14	7	0	14	14	0	15	1	0	15	8	—
29	14	10	—	14	17	3	15	4	6	15	11	9	15	19	—
30	15	—	—	15	7	6	15	15	0	16	2	6	16	10	—
40	20	—	—	20	10	0	21	0	0	21	10	0	22	—	—
50	25	—	—	25	12	6	26	5	0	26	17	6	27	10	—
[56]	28	—	—	28	11	0	29	8	0	30	2	0	30	16	—
60	30	—	—	30	15	0	31	10	0	32	5	0	33	—	—
70	35	—	—	35	17	6	36	15	0	37	12	6	38	10	—
80	40	—	—	41	0	0	42	0	0	43	0	0	44	—	—
[84]	42	—	—	43	1	0	44	2	0	45	3	0	46	4	—
90	45	—	—	46	2	6	47	5	0	48	7	6	49	10	—
100	50	—	—	51	5	0	52	10	0	53	15	0	55	—	—
[112]	56	—	—	57	8	0	58	16	0	60	4	0	61	12	—
200	100	—	—	102	10	0	105	0	0	107	10	0	110	—	—
300	150	—	—	153	15	0	157	10	0	161	5	0	165	—	—
[365]	182	10	—	187	1	3	191	12	6	196	3	9	200	15	—
400	200	—	—	205	0	0	210	0	0	215	0	0	220	—	—
500	250	—	—	256	5	0	262	10	0	268	15	0	275	—	—
600	300	—	—	307	10	0	315	0	0	322	10	0	330	—	—
700	350	—	—	358	15	0	367	10	0	376	5	0	385	—	—
800	400	—	—	410	0	0	420	0	0	430	0	0	440	—	—
900	450	—	—	461	5	0	472	10	0	483	15	0	495	—	—
1000	500	—	—	512	10	0	525	0	0	537	5	0	550	—	—
2000	1000	—	—	1025	0	0	1050	0	0	1074	10	0	1100	—	—

	11s. 3d.			* 11s. 4½d.			11s. 6d.			11s 9d.			12s.		
Value of	£.	s.	d.	£.	s.	d.f.	£.	s.	d.	£.	s.	d.	£.	s.	d.
2	1	2	6	1	2	9	1	3	0	1	3	6	1	4	0
3	1	13	9	1	14	1½	1	14	6	1	15	3	1	16	—
4	2	5	-	2	5	6	2	6	—	2	7	—	2	8	—
5	2	16	3	2	16	10½	2	17	6	2	18	9	3	0	—
6	3	7	6	3	8	3	3	9	—	3	10	6	3	12	—
7	3	18	9	3	19	7½	4	0	6	4	2	3	4	4	—
8	4	10	-	4	11	0	4	12	—	4	14	—	4	16	—
9	5	1	3	5	2	4½	5	3	6	5	5	9	5	8	—
10	5	12	6	5	13	9	5	15	—	5	17	6	6	0	—
11	6	3	9	6	5	1½	6	6	6	6	9	3	6	12	—
12	6	15	-	6	16	6	6	18	—	7	1	—	7	4	—
13	7	6	3	7	7	10½	7	9	6	7	12	9	7	16	—
14	7	17	6	7	19	3	8	1	—	8	4	6	8	8	—
15	8	8	9	8	10	7½	8	12	6	8	16	3	9	0	—
16	9	0	-	9	2	0	9	4	—	9	8	—	9	12	—
17	9	11	3	9	13	4½	9	15	6	9	19	9	10	4	—
18	10	2	6	10	4	9	10	7	—	10	11	6	10	16	—
19	10	13	9	10	16	1½	10	18	6	11	3	3	11	8	—
20	11	5	-	11	7	6	11	10	—	11	15	—	12	0	—
21	11	16	3	11	18	10½	12	1	6	12	6	9	12	12	—
22	12	7	6	12	10	3	12	13	—	12	18	6	13	4	—
23	12	18	9	13	1	7½	13	4	6	13	10	3	13	16	—
24	13	10	-	13	13	0	13	16	—	14	2	—	14	8	—
25	14	1	3	14	4	4½	14	7	6	14	13	9	15	0	—
26	14	12	6	14	15	9	14	19	—	15	5	6	15	12	—
27	15	3	9	15	7	1½	15	10	6	15	17	3	16	4	—
[28]	15	15	-	15	18	6	16	2	—	16	9	—	16	16	—
29	16	6	3	16	9	10½	16	13	6	17	0	9	17	8	—
30	16	17	6	17	1	3	17	5	—	17	12	6	18	0	—
40	22	10	-	22	15	0	23	0	—	23	10	—	24	0	—
50	28	2	6	28	8	9	28	15	—	29	7	6	30	0	—
[56]	31	10	-	31	17	0	32	4	—	32	18	—	33	12	—
60	33	15	-	34	2	6	34	10	—	35	5	—	36	0	—
70	39	7	6	39	16	3	40	5	—	41	2	6	42	0	—
80	45	0	-	45	10	0	46	0	—	47	0	—	48	0	—
[84]	47	5	-	47	15	6	48	6	—	49	7	—	50	8	—
90	50	12	6	51	3	9	51	15	—	52	17	6	54	0	—
100	56	5	-	56	17	6	57	10	—	58	15	—	60	0	—
[112]	63	0	-	63	14	0	64	8	—	65	16	—	67	4	—
200	112	10	-	113	15	0	115	0	—	117	10	—	120	0	—
300	168	15	-	170	12	6	172	10	—	176	5	—	180	0	—
[365]	205	6	3	207	11	10½	209	17	6	214	8	9	219	0	—
400	225	0	-	227	10	0	230	0	—	235	0	—	240	0	—
500	281	5	-	284	7	6	287	10	—	293	15	—	300	0	—
600	337	10	-	341	5	0	345	0	—	352	10	—	360	0	—
700	393	15	-	398	2	6	402	10	—	411	5	—	420	0	—
800	450	0	-	455	0	0	460	0	—	470	0	—	480	0	—
900	506	5	-	511	17	6	517	10	—	528	15	—	540	0	—
1000	562	10	-	568	15	0	575	0	—	587	10	—	600	0	—
2000	1125	0	-	1137	10	0	1150	0	—	1175	0	—	1200	0	—

* *This Column will answer for a Half Guinea Table.*

	12s. 3d.			12s. 6d.			12s. 9d.			13s.			13s 3d.		
Value of	L.	s.	d.	L.	s.	d.	L.	s.	d.	L.	s.	d.	L.	s.	d.
2	1	4	6	1	5	0	1	5	6	1	6	0	1	6	6
3	1	16	9	1	17	6	1	18	3	1	19	—	1	19	9
4	2	9	0	2	10	—	2	11	0	2	12	—	2	13	0
5	3	1	3	3	2	6	3	3	9	3	5	—	3	6	3
6	3	13	6	3	15	—	3	16	6	3	18	—	3	19	6
7	4	5	9	4	7	6	4	9	3	4	11	—	4	12	9
8	4	18	0	5	0	—	5	2	0	5	4	—	5	6	0
9	5	10	3	5	12	6	5	14	9	5	17	—	5	19	3
10	6	2	6	6	5	—	6	7	6	6	10	—	6	12	6
11	6	14	9	6	17	6	7	0	3	7	3	—	7	5	9
12	7	7	0	7	10	—	7	13	0	7	16	—	7	19	0
13	7	19	3	8	2	6	8	5	9	8	9	—	8	12	3
14	8	11	6	8	15	—	8	18	6	9	2	—	9	5	6
15	9	3	9	9	7	6	9	11	3	9	15	—	9	18	9
16	9	16	0	10	0	—	10	4	0	10	8	—	10	12	0
17	10	8	3	10	12	6	10	16	9	11	1	—	11	5	3
18	11	0	6	11	5	—	11	9	6	11	14	—	11	18	6
19	11	12	9	11	17	6	12	2	3	12	7	—	12	11	9
20	12	5	0	12	10	—	12	15	0	13	0	—	13	5	0
21	12	17	3	13	2	6	13	7	9	13	13	—	13	18	3
22	13	9	6	13	15	—	14	0	6	14	6	—	14	11	6
23	14	1	9	14	7	6	14	13	3	14	19	—	15	4	9
24	14	14	0	15	0	—	15	6	0	15	12	—	15	18	0
25	15	6	3	15	12	6	15	18	9	16	5	—	16	11	3
26	15	18	6	16	5	—	16	11	6	16	18	—	17	4	6
27	16	10	9	16	17	6	17	4	3	17	11	—	17	17	9
[28]	17	3	0	17	10	—	17	17	0	18	4	—	18	11	0
29	17	15	3	18	2	6	18	9	9	18	17	—	19	4	3
30	18	7	6	18	15	—	19	2	6	19	10	—	19	17	6
40	24	10	0	25	0	—	25	10	0	26	0	—	26	10	0
50	30	12	6	31	5	—	31	17	6	32	10	—	33	2	6
[56]	34	6	0	35	0	—	35	14	0	36	8	—	37	2	0
60	36	15	0	37	10	—	38	5	0	39	0	—	39	15	0
70	42	17	6	43	15	—	44	12	6	45	10	—	46	7	6
80	49	0	0	50	0	—	51	0	0	52	0	—	53	0	0
[84]	51	9	0	52	10	—	53	11	0	54	12	—	55	13	0
90	55	2	6	56	5	—	57	7	6	58	10	—	59	12	6
100	61	5	0	62	10	—	63	15	0	65	0	—	66	5	0
[112]	68	12	0	70	0	—	71	8	0	72	16	—	74	4	0
200	122	10	0	125	0	—	127	10	0	130	0	—	132	10	0
300	183	15	0	187	10	—	191	5	0	195	0	—	198	15	0
[365]	223	11	3	228	2	6	232	13	9	237	5	—	241	16	3
400	245	0	0	250	0	—	255	0	0	260	0	—	265	0	0
500	306	5	0	312	10	—	318	15	0	325	0	—	331	5	0
600	367	10	0	375	0	—	382	10	0	390	0	—	397	10	0
700	428	15	0	437	10	—	446	5	0	455	0	—	463	15	0
800	490	0	0	500	0	—	510	0	0	520	0	—	530	0	0
900	551	5	0	562	10	—	573	15	0	585	0	—	596	5	0
1000	612	10	0	625	0	—	637	10	0	650	0	—	662	10	0
2000	1225	0	0	1250	0	—	1275	0	0	1300	0	—	1325	0	0

	13s. 6 Pence			13s. 9 Pence			14 Shillings			14s. 3 Pence			14s. 6 Pence		
Value	L.	s.	d.	L.	s.	d.	L.	s.	d.	L.	s.	d.	L.	s.	d.
of 2	1	7	–	1	7	6	1	8	—	1	8	6	1	9	–
3	2	0	6	2	1	3	2	2	—	2	2	9	2	3	6
4	2	14	–	2	15	–	2	16	—	2	17	–	2	18	–
5	3	7	6	3	8	9	3	10	—	3	11	3	3	12	6
6	4	1	–	4	2	6	4	4	—	4	5	6	4	7	–
7	4	14	6	4	16	3	4	18	—	4	19	9	5	1	6
8	5	8	–	5	10	–	5	12	—	5	14	–	5	16	–
9	6	1	6	6	3	9	6	6	—	6	8	3	6	10	6
10	6	15	–	6	17	6	7	0	—	7	2	6	7	5	–
11	7	8	6	7	11	3	7	14	—	7	16	9	7	19	6
12	8	2	–	8	5	–	8	8	—	8	11	–	8	14	–
13	8	15	6	8	18	9	9	2	—	9	5	3	9	8	6
14	9	9	–	9	12	6	9	16	—	9	19	6	10	3	–
15	10	2	6	10	6	3	10	10	—	10	13	9	10	17	6
16	10	16	–	11	0	–	11	4	—	11	8	0	11	12	–
17	11	9	6	11	13	9	11	18	—	12	2	3	12	6	6
18	12	3	–	12	7	6	12	12	—	12	16	6	13	1	–
19	12	16	6	13	1	3	13	6	—	13	10	9	13	15	6
20	13	10	–	13	15	–	14	0	—	14	5	–	14	10	–
21	14	3	6	14	8	9	14	14	—	14	19	3	15	4	6
22	14	17	–	15	2	6	15	8	—	15	13	6	15	19	–
23	15	10	6	15	16	3	16	2	—	16	7	9	16	13	6
24	16	4	–	16	10	–	16	16	—	17	2	–	17	8	–
25	16	17	6	17	3	9	17	10	–	17	16	3	18	2	6
26	17	11	–	17	17	6	18	4	—	18	10	6	18	17	–
27	18	4	6	18	11	3	18	18	—	19	4	9	19	11	6
[28]	18	18	–	19	5	–	19	12	—	19	19	–	20	6	–
29	19	11	6	19	18	9	20	6	—	20	13	3	21	0	6
30	20	5	–	20	12	6	21	–	—	21	7	6	21	15	–
40	27	0	–	27	10	–	28	–	—	28	10	–	29	0	–
50	33	15	–	34	7	6	35	–	—	35	12	6	36	5	–
[56]	37	16	–	38	10	–	39	4	—	39	18	–	40	12	–
60	40	10	–	41	5	–	42	–	—	42	15	–	43	10	–
70	47	5	–	48	2	6	49	–	—	49	17	6	50	15	–
80	54	0	–	55	0	–	56	–	—	57	0	–	58	0	–
[84]	56	14	–	57	15	–	58	16	—	59	17	–	60	18	–
90	60	15	–	61	17	6	63	–	—	64	2	6	65	5	–
100	67	10	–	68	15	–	70	–	—	71	5	–	72	10	–
[112]	75	12	–	77	0	–	78	8	—	79	16	–	81	4	–
200	135	0	–	137	10	–	140	–	—	142	10	–	145	–	–
300	202	10	–	206	5	–	210	–	—	213	15	–	217	10	–
[365]	246	7	6	250	18	9	255	10	—	260	1	3	264	12	6
400	270	0	–	275	0	–	280	–	—	285	–	–	290	–	–
500	337	10	–	343	15	–	350	–	—	356	5	–	362	10	–
600	405	0	–	412	10	–	420	–	—	427	10	–	435	–	–
700	472	10	–	481	5	–	490	–	—	498	15	–	507	10	–
800	540	0	–	550	0	–	560	–	—	570	0	–	580	–	–
900	607	10	–	618	15	–	630	–	—	641	5	–	652	10	–
1000	675	0	–	687	10	–	700	–	—	712	10	–	725	–	–
2000	1350	0	–	1375	0	–	1400	–	—	1425	–	–	1450	–	–

	14s. 9 Pence			15 Shillings			15s. 3 Pence			15s. 6 Pence			15s. 9 Pence		
Value	£.	s.	d.	L.	s.	d.	L.	s.	d.	L.	s.	d.	L.	s.	d.
of 2	1	9	6	1	10	—	1	10	6	1	11	0	1	11	6
3	2	4	3	2	5	—	2	5	9	2	6	6	2	7	3
4	2	19	0	3	0	—	3	1	0	3	2	0	3	3	0
5	3	13	9	3	15	—	3	16	3	3	17	6	3	18	9
6	4	8	6	4	10	—	4	11	6	4	13	0	4	14	6
7	5	3	3	5	5	—	5	6	9	5	8	6	5	10	3
8	5	18	0	6	0	—	6	2	0	6	4	0	6	6	0
9	6	12	9	6	15	—	6	17	3	6	19	6	7	1	9
10	7	7	6	7	10	—	7	12	6	7	15	0	7	17	6
11	8	2	3	8	5	—	8	7	9	8	10	6	8	13	3
12	8	17	0	9	0	—	9	3	0	9	6	0	9	9	0
13	9	11	9	9	15	—	9	18	3	10	1	6	10	4	9
14	10	6	6	10	10	—	10	13	6	10	17	0	11	0	6
15	11	1	3	11	5	—	11	8	9	11	12	6	11	16	3
16	11	16	0	12	0	—	12	4	0	12	8	0	12	12	0
17	12	10	9	12	15	—	12	19	3	13	3	6	13	7	9
18	13	5	6	13	10	—	13	14	6	13	19	0	14	3	6
19	14	0	3	14	5	—	14	9	9	14	14	6	14	19	3
20	14	15	0	15	0	—	15	5	0	15	10	0	15	15	0
21	15	9	9	15	15	—	16	0	3	16	5	6	16	10	9
22	16	4	6	16	10	—	16	15	6	17	1	0	17	6	6
23	16	19	3	17	5	—	17	10	9	17	16	6	18	2	3
24	17	14	0	18	0	—	18	6	0	18	12	0	18	18	0
25	18	8	9	18	15	—	19	1	3	19	7	6	19	13	9
26	19	3	6	19	10	—	19	16	6	20	3	0	20	9	6
27	19	18	3	20	5	—	20	11	9	20	18	6	21	5	3
[28]	20	13	0	21	0	—	21	7	0	21	14	0	22	1	0
29	21	7	9	21	15	—	22	2	3	22	9	6	22	16	9
30	22	2	6	22	10	—	22	17	6	23	5	0	23	12	6
40	29	10	0	30	0	—	30	10	0	31	0	—	31	10	0
50	36	17	6	37	10	—	38	2	6	38	15	—	39	7	6
[56]	41	6	0	42	0	—	42	14	0	43	8	—	44	2	0
60	44	5	0	45	0	—	45	15	0	46	10	—	47	5	0
70	51	12	6	52	10	—	53	7	6	54	5	—	55	2	6
80	59	0	0	60	0	—	61	0	0	62	0	—	63	0	0
[84]	61	19	0	63	0	—	64	1	0	65	2	—	67	3	0
90	66	7	6	67	10	—	68	12	6	69	15	—	70	17	6
100	73	15	0	75	0	—	76	5	0	77	10	—	78	15	0
[112]	82	12	0	84	0	—	85	8	0	86	16	—	88	4	0
200	147	10	0	150	0	-	152	10	0	155	0	—	157	10	0
300	221	5	0	225	0	—	228	15	0	232	10	—	236	5	0
[365]	269	3	9	273	15	—	278	6	3	282	17	—	287	8	9
400	295	0	0	300	—	—	305	0	0	310	0	—	315	0	0
500	368	15	0	375	—	—	381	5	0	387	10	—	393	15	0
600	442	10	0	450	—	—	457	10	0	465	0	—	472	10	0
700	516	5	0	525	—	—	533	15	0	542	10	—	551	5	0
800	590	0	0	600	—	—	610	0	0	620	0	—	630	0	0
900	663	15	0	675	—	—	686	5	0	697	10	—	708	15	0
1000	737	10	0	750	—	—	762	10	0	775	0	—	787	10	0
2000	1475	0	0	1500	—	—	1525	0	0	1550	0	—	1575	0	0

	16s.			16s. 3d.			16s. 6d.			16s. 9d.			17s.		
Value	L.	s.	d.	£.	s.	d.	£.	s.	d.	£.	s.	d.	£.	s.	d.
of 2	1	12	0	1	12	6	1	13	0	1	13	6	1	14	0
3	2	8	—	2	8	9	2	9	6	2	10	3	2	11	—
4	3	4	—	3	5	0	3	6	—	3	7	0	3	8	—
5	4	0	—	4	1	3	4	2	6	4	3	9	4	5	—
6	4	16	—	4	17	6	4	19	—	5	0	6	5	2	—
7	5	12	—	5	13	9	5	15	6	5	17	3	5	19	—
8	6	8	—	6	10	0	6	12	—	6	14	0	6	16	—
9	7	4	—	7	6	3	7	8	6	7	10	9	7	13	—
10	8	0	—	8	2	6	8	5	—	8	7	6	8	10	—
11	8	16	—	8	18	9	9	1	6	9	4	3	9	7	—
12	9	12	—	9	15	0	9	18	—	10	1	0	10	4	—
13	10	8	—	10	11	3	10	14	6	10	17	9	11	1	—
14	11	4	—	11	7	6	11	11	—	11	14	6	11	18	—
15	12	0	—	12	3	9	12	7	6	12	11	3	12	15	—
16	12	16	—	13	0	0	13	4	—	13	8	0	13	12	—
17	13	12	—	13	16	3	14	0	6	14	4	9	14	6	—
18	14	8	—	14	12	6	14	17	—	15	1	6	15	6	—
19	15	4	—	15	8	9	15	13	6	15	18	3	16	3	—
20	16	0	—	16	5	0	16	10	—	16	15	0	17	0	—
21	16	16	—	17	1	3	17	6	6	17	11	9	17	17	—
22	17	12	—	17	17	6	18	3	—	18	8	6	18	14	—
23	18	8	—	18	13	9	18	19	6	19	5	3	19	11	—
24	19	4	—	19	10	0	19	16	—	20	2	0	20	8	—
25	20	0	—	20	6	3	20	12	6	20	18	9	21	5	—
26	20	16	—	21	2	6	21	9	—	21	15	6	22	2	—
27	21	12	—	21	18	9	22	5	6	22	12	3	22	19	—
[28]	22	8	—	22	15	0	23	2	—	23	9	0	23	16	—
29	23	4	—	23	11	3	23	18	6	24	5	9	24	13	—
30	24	0	—	24	7	6	24	15	—	25	2	6	25	10	—
40	32	0	—	32	10	0	33	0	—	33	10	—	34	0	—
50	40	0	—	40	12	6	41	5	—	41	17	6	42	10	—
[56]	44	16	—	45	10	0	46	4	—	46	18	—	47	12	—
60	48	0	—	48	15	0	49	10	—	50	5	—	51	0	—
70	56	0	—	56	17	6	57	15	—	58	12	6	59	10	—
80	64	0	—	65	0	0	66	0	—	67	0	—	68	0	—
[84]	67	4	—	68	5	0	69	6	—	70	7	—	71	8	—
90	72	0	—	73	2	6	74	5	—	75	7	6	76	10	—
100	80	0	—	81	5	—	82	10	—	83	15	—	85	0	—
[112]	89	12	—	91	0	—	92	8	—	93	16	—	95	4	—
200	160	—	—	162	10	—	165	0	—	167	10	—	170	0	—
300	240	—	—	243	15	—	247	10	—	251	5	—	255	0	—
[365]	292	—	—	296	11	3	301	2	6	305	13	9	310	5	—
400	320	—	—	325	0	—	330	0	—	335	0	—	340	—	—
500	400	—	—	406	5	—	412	10	—	418	15	—	425	—	—
600	480	—	—	487	10	—	495	0	—	502	10	—	510	—	—
700	560	—	—	568	15	—	577	10	—	586	5	—	595	—	—
800	640	—	—	650	0	—	660	0	—	670	0	—	680	—	—
900	720	—	—	731	5	—	742	10	—	753	15	—	765	—	—
1000	800	—	—	812	10	—	825	0	—	837	10	—	850	—	—
2000	1600	—	—	1625	0	—	1650	0	—	1675	0	—	1700	—	—

	17s. 3d.			17s. 6d.			17s. 9d.			18s.			18s. 3d.		
Value	L.	s.	d.	L.	s.	d.	L.	s.	d.	L.	s.	d.	£.	s.	d.
of 2	1	14	6	1	15	0	1	15	6	1	16	0	1	16	6
3	2	11	9	2	12	6	2	13	3	2	14	—	2	14	9
4	3	9	0	3	10	—	3	11	0	3	12	—	3	13	0
5	4	6	3	4	7	6	4	8	9	4	10	—	4	11	3
6	5	3	6	5	5	—	5	6	6	5	8	—	5	9	6
7	6	0	9	6	2	6	6	4	3	6	6	—	6	7	9
8	6	18	0	7	0	—	7	2	0	7	4	—	7	6	0
9	7	15	3	7	17	6	7	19	9	8	2	—	8	4	3
10	8	12	6	8	15	—	8	17	6	9	0	—	9	2	6
11	9	9	9	9	12	6	9	15	3	9	18	—	10	0	9
12	10	7	0	10	10	—	10	13	0	10	16	—	10	19	0
13	11	4	3	11	7	6	11	10	9	11	14	—	11	17	3
14	12	1	6	12	5	—	12	8	6	12	12	—	12	15	6
15	12	18	9	13	2	6	13	6	3	13	10	—	13	13	9
16	13	16	0	14	0	—	14	4	0	14	8	—	14	12	0
17	14	13	3	14	17	6	15	1	9	15	6	—	15	10	3
18	15	10	6	15	15	—	15	19	6	16	4	—	16	8	6
19	16	7	9	16	12	6	16	17	3	17	2	—	17	6	9
20	17	5	0	17	10	—	17	15	0	18	0	—	18	5	0
21	18	2	3	18	7	6	18	12	9	18	18	—	19	3	3
22	18	19	6	19	5	—	19	10	6	19	16	—	20	1	6
23	19	16	9	20	2	6	20	8	3	20	14	—	20	19	9
24	20	14	0	21	0	—	21	6	0	21	12	—	21	18	0
25	21	11	3	21	17	6	22	3	9	22	10	—	22	16	3
26	22	8	6	22	15	—	23	1	6	23	8	—	23	14	6
27	23	5	9	23	12	6	23	19	3	24	6	—	24	12	9
[28]	24	3	0	24	10	—	24	17	0	25	4	—	25	11	0
29	25	0	3	25	7	6	25	14	9	26	2	—	26	9	3
30	25	17	6	26	5	—	26	12	6	27	—	—	27	7	6
40	34	10	0	35	0	—	35	10	0	36	—	—	36	10	0
50	43	2	6	43	15	—	44	7	6	45	—	—	45	12	6
[56]	48	6	—	49	0	—	49	14	—	50	8	—	51	2	—
60	51	15	—	52	10	—	53	5	—	54	—	—	54	15	—
70	60	7	6	61	5	—	62	2	6	63	—	—	63	17	6
80	69	0	—	70	0	—	71	0	—	72	—	—	73	0	—
[84]	72	9	—	73	10	—	74	11	—	75	12	—	76	13	—
90	77	12	6	78	15	—	79	17	6	81	—	—	82	2	6
100	86	5	—	87	10	—	88	15	—	90	—	—	91	5	—
[112]	96	12	—	98	0	—	99	8	—	100	16	—	101	4	—
200	172	10	—	175	0	—	177	10	—	180	0	—	182	10	—
300	258	15	—	262	10	—	266	5	—	270	0	—	273	15	—
[365]	314	16	3	319	7	6	323	18	9	328	10	—	333	1	3
400	345	0	—	350	0	—	355	0	—	360	—	—	365	0	—
500	431	5	—	437	10	—	443	15	—	450	—	—	456	5	—
600	517	10	—	525	0	—	532	10	—	540	—	—	547	10	—
700	603	15	—	612	10	—	621	5	—	630	—	—	638	15	—
800	690	0	—	700	0	—	710	0	—	720	—	—	730	0	—
900	776	5	—	787	10	—	798	15	—	810	—	—	821	5	—
1000	862	10	—	875	0	—	887	10	—	900	—	—	912	0	—
2000	1725	0	—	1750	0	—	1775	0	—	1800	—	—	1825	10	—

	18s. 6 Pence			18s. 9 Pence			19 Shillings			19s. 3 Pence			19s. 6 Pence		
Value	£.	s.	d.	£.	s.	d.	£.	s.	d.	£.	s.	d.	L.	s.	d.
of 2	1	17	0	1	17	6	1	18	—	1	18	6	1	19	0
3	2	15	6	2	16	3	2	17	—	2	17	9	2	18	6
4	3	14	0	3	15	0	3	16	—	3	17	0	3	18	0
5	4	12	6	4	13	9	4	15	—	4	16	3	4	17	6
6	5	11	0	5	12	6	5	14	—	5	15	6	5	17	0
7	6	9	6	6	11	3	6	13	—	6	14	9	6	16	6
8	7	8	0	7	10	0	7	12	—	7	14	0	7	16	0
9	8	6	6	8	8	9	8	11	—	8	13	3	8	15	6
10	9	5	0	9	7	6	9	10	—	9	12	6	9	15	0
11	10	3	6	10	6	3	10	9	—	10	11	9	10	14	6
12	11	2	0	11	5	0	11	8	—	11	11	0	11	14	0
13	12	0	6	12	3	9	12	7	—	12	10	3	12	13	6
14	12	19	0	13	2	6	13	6	—	13	9	6	13	13	0
15	13	17	6	14	1	3	14	5	—	14	8	9	14	12	6
16	14	16	0	15	0	0	15	4	—	15	8	0	15	12	0
17	15	14	6	15	18	9	16	3	—	16	7	3	16	11	6
18	16	13	0	16	17	6	17	2	—	17	6	6	17	11	0
19	17	11	6	17	16	3	18	1	—	18	5	9	18	10	6
20	18	10	0	18	15	0	19	0	—	19	5	0	19	10	0
21	19	8	6	19	13	9	19	19	—	20	4	3	20	9	6
22	20	7	0	20	12	6	20	18	—	21	3	6	21	9	0
23	21	5	6	21	11	3	51	17	—	22	2	9	22	8	6
24	22	4	0	22	10	0	22	16	—	23	2	0	23	8	0
25	23	2	6	23	8	9	23	15	—	24	1	3	24	7	6
26	24	1	0	24	7	6	24	14	—	25	0	6	25	7	0
27	24	19	6	25	6	3	25	13	—	25	19	9	26	6	6
[28]	25	18	0	26	5	0	26	12	—	26	19	0	27	6	0
19	26	16	6	27	3	9	27	11	—	27	18	3	28	5	6
30	27	15	0	28	2	6	28	10	—	28	17	6	29	5	0
40	37	0	0	37	10	0	38	0	—	38	10	0	39	0	0
50	46	5	0	46	17	6	47	10	—	48	2	6	48	15	0
[56]	51	16	0	52	10	0	53	4	—	53	18	0	54	12	0
60	55	10	0	56	5	0	57	0	—	57	15	0	58	10	0
70	64	15	0	65	12	6	66	10	—	67	7	6	68	5	0
80	74	0	0	75	0	0	76	0	—	77	0	0	78	0	0
[84]	77	14	0	78	15	0	79	16	—	80	17	0	81	18	0
90	83	5	0	84	7	6	85	10	—	86	12	6	87	15	0
100	92	10	0	93	15	0	95	0	—	96	5	0	97	10	0
[112]	103	12	0	105	0	0	106	8	—	107	16	0	109	4	0
200	185	0	0	187	10	0	190	0	—	192	10	0	195	0	0
300	277	10	0	281	5	0	285	0	—	288	15	0	292	10	0
[365]	337	12	6	342	3	9	346	15	—	351	6	3	355	17	6
400	370	0	0	375	0	0	380	0	—	385	0	0	390	0	0
500	462	10	0	468	15	0	475	0	—	481	5	0	487	10	0
600	555	0	0	562	10	0	570	0	—	577	10	0	585	0	0
700	647	10	0	656	5	0	665	0	—	673	15	0	682	10	0
800	740	0	0	740	0	0	760	0	—	770	0	0	780	0	0
900	832	10	0	833	15	0	855	0	—	866	5	0	877	10	0
1000	925	0	0	937	10	0	950	0	—	962	10	0	975	0	0
2000	1850	0	0	1875	0	0	1900	0	—	1925	0	0	1950	0	0

	19s. 9 Pence			20 Shillings			l. 1 0s. 3d.			l. 1 0s. 6d.			l. 1 0s. 9d.		
Value of	£.	s.	d.	£.	s.	d.	£.	s.	d.	£.	s.	d.	£.	s.	d.
2	1	19	6	2	—	—	2	0	6	2	1	0	2	1	6
3	2	19	3	3	—	—	3	0	9	3	1	6	3	2	3
4	3	19	0	4	—	—	4	1	0	4	2	0	4	3	0
5	4	18	9	5	—	—	5	1	3	5	2	6	5	3	9
6	5	18	6	6	—	—	6	1	6	6	3	0	6	4	6
7	6	18	3	7	—	—	7	1	9	7	3	6	7	5	3
8	7	18	0	8	—	—	8	2	0	8	4	0	8	6	0
9	8	17	9	9	—	—	9	2	3	9	4	6	9	6	9
10	9	17	6	10	—	—	10	2	6	10	5	0	10	7	6
11	10	17	3	11	—	—	11	2	9	11	5	6	11	8	3
12	11	17	0	12	—	—	12	3	0	12	6	0	12	9	0
13	12	16	9	13	—	—	13	3	3	13	6	6	13	9	9
14	13	16	6	14	—	—	14	3	6	14	7	0	14	10	6
15	14	16	3	15	—	—	15	3	9	15	7	6	15	11	3
16	15	16	0	16	—	—	16	4	0	16	8	0	16	12	0
17	16	15	9	17	—	—	17	4	3	17	8	6	17	12	9
18	17	15	6	18	—	—	18	4	6	18	9	0	18	13	6
19	18	15	3	19	—	—	19	4	9	19	9	6	19	14	3
20	19	15	0	20	—	—	20	5	0	20	10	0	20	15	0
21	20	14	9	21	—	—	21	5	3	21	10	6	21	15	9
22	21	14	6	22	—	—	22	5	6	22	11	0	22	16	6
23	22	14	3	23	—	—	23	5	9	23	11	6	23	17	3
24	23	14	0	24	—	—	24	6	0	24	12	0	24	18	0
25	24	13	9	25	—	—	25	6	3	25	12	6	25	18	9
26	25	13	6	26	—	—	26	6	6	26	13	0	26	19	6
27	26	13	3	27	—	—	27	6	9	27	13	6	28	0	3
[28]	27	13	0	28	—	—	28	7	0	28	14	0	29	1	0
29	28	12	9	29	—	—	29	7	3	29	14	6	30	1	9
30	29	12	6	30	—	—	30	7	6	30	15	0	31	2	6
40	39	10	0	40	—	—	40	10	0	41	0	0	41	10	0
50	49	4	6	50	—	—	50	12	6	51	5	0	51	17	6
[56]	55	6	0	56	—	—	56	14	0	57	8	0	58	2	0
60	59	5	0	60	—	—	60	15	0	61	10	0	62	5	0
70	69	2	6	70	—	—	70	17	6	71	15	0	72	12	6
80	79	0	0	80	—	—	81	0	0	82	0	0	83	0	0
[84]	82	19	0	84	—	—	85	1	0	86	2	0	87	3	0
90	88	17	6	90	—	—	91	2	6	92	5	0	93	7	6
100	98	15	0	100	—	—	101	5	0	102	10	0	103	15	0
[112]	110	12	0	112	—	—	113	8	0	114	16	0	116	4	0
200	197	10	0	200	—	—	202	10	0	205	0	0	207	10	0
300	296	5	0	300	—	—	303	15	0	307	10	0	311	5	0
[365]	360	18	9	365	—	—	369	11	3	374	2	6	378	13	9
400	395	0	0	400	—	—	405	0	0	410	0	0	415	0	0
500	493	15	0	500	—	—	506	5	0	512	10	0	518	15	0
600	592	10	0	600	—	—	607	10	0	615	0	0	622	10	0
700	691	5	0	700	—	—	708	15	0	717	10	0	726	5	0
800	790	0	0	800	—	—	810	0	0	820	0	0	830	0	0
900	888	15	0	900	—	—	911	5	0	922	10	0	933	15	0
1000	987	10	0	1000	—	—	1012	10	0	1025	0	0	1037	10	0
2000	1975	0	0	2000	—	—	2025	0	0	2050	0	0	2075	0	0

Value of	1*l.* 1*s.* £.	s.	d.	1*l.* 1*s.* 6*d.* L.	s.	d.	1*l.* 2*s.* L.	s.	d.	1*l.* 2*s.* 6*d.* £.	s.	d.	* 1 Guinea. L.	s.	d.
2	2	2	—	2	3	0	2	4	0	2	5	0	2	5	6
3	3	3	—	3	4	6	3	6	—	3	7	6	3	8	3
4	4	4	—	4	6	—	4	8	—	4	10	0	4	11	0
5	5	5	—	5	7	6	5	10	—	5	12	6	5	13	9
6	6	6	—	6	9	—	6	12	—	6	15	0	6	16	6
7	7	7	—	7	10	6	7	14	—	7	17	6	7	19	3
8	8	8	—	8	12	—	8	16	—	9	0	0	9	2	0
9	9	9	—	9	13	6	9	18	—	10	2	6	10	4	9
10	10	10	—	10	15	—	11	0	—	11	5	0	11	7	6
11	11	11	—	11	16	6	12	2	—	12	7	6	12	10	3
12	12	12	—	12	18	—	13	4	—	13	10	0	13	13	0
13	13	13	—	13	19	6	14	6	—	14	12	6	14	15	9
14	14	14	—	15	1	—	15	8	—	15	15	0	15	18	6
15	15	15	—	16	2	6	16	10	—	16	17	6	17	1	3
16	16	16	—	17	4	—	17	12	—	18	0	0	18	4	0
17	17	17	—	18	5	6	18	14	—	19	2	6	19	6	9
18	18	18	—	19	7	—	19	16	—	20	5	0	20	9	6
19	19	19	—	20	8	6	20	18	—	21	7	6	21	12	3
20	21	0	—	21	10	—	22	0	—	22	19	0	22	15	0
21	22	1	—	22	11	6	23	2	—	23	12	6	23	17	9
22	23	2	—	23	13	—	24	4	—	24	15	0	25	0	6
23	24	3	—	24	14	6	25	6	—	25	17	6	26	3	3
24	25	4	—	25	16	—	26	8	—	27	0	0	27	6	0
25	26	5	—	26	17	6	27	10	—	28	2	6	28	8	9
26	27	6	—	27	19	—	28	12	—	29	5	0	29	11	6
27	28	7	—	29	0	6	29	14	—	30	7	6	30	14	3
[28]	29	8	—	30	2	—	30	16	—	31	10	0	31	17	0
29	30	9	—	31	3	6	31	18	—	32	12	6	32	19	9
30	31	10	—	32	5	—	33	0	—	33	15	0	34	2	6
40	42	0	—	43	0	—	44	0	—	45	0	0	45	10	0
50	52	10	—	53	15	—	55	0	—	56	5	0	56	17	6
[56]	58	16	—	60	4	—	61	12	—	63	0	0	63	14	0
60	63	0	—	64	10	—	66	0	—	67	10	0	68	5	0
70	73	10	—	75	5	—	77	0	—	78	15	0	79	12	6
80	84	0	—	86	0	—	88	0	—	90	0	0	91	0	0
[84]	88	4	—	90	6	—	92	8	—	94	10	0	91	11	0
90	94	10	—	96	15	—	99	0	—	101	5	0	102	7	6
100	105	0	—	107	10	—	110	0	—	112	10	0	113	15	0
[112]	117	12	—	120	8	—	123	4	—	126	0	0	127	8	0
200	210	0	—	215	0	—	220	0	—	225	0	0	227	10	0
300	315	0	—	322	10	—	330	0	—	337	10	0	341	5	0
[365]	383	5	—	392	7	6	401	10	—	410	12	6	415	3	9
400	420	—	—	430	0	—	440	0	—	450	0	0	455	0	0
500	525	—	—	537	10	—	550	0	—	502	10	0	568	15	0
600	630	—	—	645	0	—	660	0	—	675	0	0	682	10	0
700	735	—	—	752	00	—	770	0	—	787	10	0	790	5	0
800	840	—	—	860	0	—	880	0	—	900	0	0	910	0	0
900	945	—	—	967	10	—	990	0	—	1012	10	0	1023	15	0
1000	1050	—	—	1075	0	—	1100	0	—	1125	0	0	1137	10	0
2000	2100	—	—	2150	0	—	2200	0	—	2250	0	0	2275	0	0

* *This Column will answer for a Guinea Table.*

CONCLUSION.

As Books of this nature are calculated ſolely for Men of buſineſs, to ſecure preciſion, and promote diſpatch; I don't know that theſe purpoſes can be better anſwer'd, than by preſenting my Readers (by way of Concluſion) with the Maxims of a Grand-Duke of Tuſcany; by adhering to which, it is ſaid, he acquired an immenſe property.

They are theſe.———*Never to defer 'till to-morrow what can be done to-day.*

Never to do any thing by proxy, that is, never to requeſt another to do that for us, which we can do ourſelves.

And not to deſpiſe the ſmalleſt profit, or be inattentive to the moſt trifling expence.

The natural tendency of a conſtant and inviolable adherence to theſe Maxims, muſt be *proſperity;* becauſe they are founded in nature, and confirmed and enforced by *reaſon* and *revelation.*

If we conſider the nature of *time,* be it extended to ever ſo many *ages,* it is all meaſured out by ſingle *moments;* the laſt is irrecoverably gone; it is in the paſt eternity:—the next is in the eternity to come; over which we have not any power, and of which we cannot make any uſe. The *preſent moment,* the infinitely important NOW, only is ours. To mourn or to be dejected for the miſcarriages or misfortunes of the *paſt;* to be anxious or fearful of the conſequences of the *future,* (which may never happen) only renders us unable to improve the *preſent:* — And if thro' any indolence or dejection of ſpirit, we put off what may be done now, to the next moment, there is ſome danger that it may be put off for ever; for who can tell what hindrances may intervene: ſo that there is not any one axiom in geometry, more ſelf-evident than this, that be our lives ever ſo long, we only live the preſent moment; and there is ſcarcely a human being on earth, ſo ignorant as not to know, what (in that ſhort period) ought either to be done or avoided.

It is alſo as evident, that we ought to exerciſe the abilities which GOD hath given us, not only in our own ſervice, but alſo in that of others; not aſking any one to do that for us, which we can do ourſelves: becauſe thereby we pre-

ſerve

ſerve our independance, and become imitators of HIM, *who came not to be miniſtered unto, but to miniſter*; and who has ſaid, *he that will be the chief among you, let him be the ſervant of all.*

With reſpect to our attention to ſmall profits, and ſmall expences———Who is there that does not know, that as the longeſt duration of time, is only the aggregate of ſingle moments; ſo the greateſt quantity of matter, even this terraqueous globe on which we live, is only an accumulation of particles, much ſmaller than can be diſcovered by the microſcope; and we ſee daily, however minute and contemptible a ſingle grain of ſand may be, yet collectively it ſets bounds to the tempeſtuous ocean, and *ſays to its proud waves, hitherto ſhalt thou come, and no further*. Let us then conſtantly bear in mind this divine admonition, *He that regardeth not little things, ſhall periſh by little and little.*

If theſe conſiderations were duly attended to, they would produce in us an uniform regularity of conduct, in ſome degree imitative of GOD; the beauty and regularity of whoſe works, evince to us his eternal power and Godhead; for when *we conſider the Heavens, the work of his Fingers, the Moon and Stars which he has made*, we ſhall find that their motions are ſo regular and conſtant, that their tranſits and eclipſes may be calculated to a ſecond of a minute, and are never interrupted by any delay or diſappointment: ſo wiſe and regular is GOD, *who hath appointed the Moon for ſeaſons, and the Sun knoweth his going down.*

It only remains that we conſtantly and earneſtly endeavour ſo to paſs thro' things temporal, that we may not loſe things eternal, but that in all our words and works, begun, continued and ended in HIM, we may glorify his holy name; and finally, by his mercy, obtain everlaſting life, through JESUS CHRIST, our LORD. *Amen.*

FINIS

www.ingramcontent.com/pod-product-compliance
Lightning Source LLC
Chambersburg PA
CBHW020925120726
47905CB00008B/2378